W9-AKT-357

The Mammoth Book of

SCOTTISH ROMANCE

Edited and with an Introduction by

TRISHA TELEP

ROBINSON

RUNNING PRESS
PHILADELPHIA · LONDON

Constable & Robinson Ltd
3 The Lanchesters
162 Fulham Palace Road
London W6 9ER
www.constablerobinson.com

First published in the UK by Robinson,
an imprint of Constable & Robinson, 2011

A copy of the British Library Cataloguing in Publication
Data is available from the British Library

UK ISBN 978-1-84901-452-6

1 3 5 7 9 10 8 6 4 2

First published in the United States in 2011 by Running Press Book Publishers.

US Library of Congress Control number: 2009943395
US ISBN 978-0-7624-4403-0

Running Press Book Publishers
2300 Chestnut Street
Philadelphia, PA 19103-4371

Visit us on the web!
www.runningpress.com

Printed and bound in the EU

Contents

Acknowledgments

"Highland Heart" © by Heather McCollum. First publication, original to this anthology. Printed by permission of the author.

"The Pagan Bride" © by Patricia Grasso. First publication, original to this anthology. Printed by permission of the author.

"Wolfish in Sheep's Clothing" © by Marta Acosta. First publication, original to this anthology. Printed by permission of the author.

"Forever Knight" © by Jackie Ivie. First publication, original to this anthology. Printed by permission of the author.

"Curse Me Wicked" © by Elle Jasper. First publication, original to this anthology. Printed by permission of the author.

"At Last" © by Jacquie D'Alessandro. First publication, original to this anthology. Printed by permission of the author.

"Magick in the Mist" © by Debbie Mazzuca. First publication, original to this anthology. Printed by permission of the author.

"The Rebel" © by Julianne MacLean. First publication, original to this anthology. Printed by permission of the author.

"The Curse of Wolf Crag" © by Susan Sizemore. First publication, original to this anthology. Printed by permission of the author.

Introduction

William Wallace, Robert the Bruce, Rob Roy (not to mention the Loch Ness Monster): Sir Walter Scott certainly knew a country that bred brave, bigger-than-life heroes when he saw it. It's no wonder that the lush mountain scenery of the Scottish Highlands, and the majestic sweep of 790 islands (!), is the perfect backdrop for epic romance. And although the highlands are no longer peopled by the fabled, chivalrous, unruly Highlander clans of old – those fierce Scottish outlaws, martyrs, traitors and deadly warriors who seemed to get under the skin of the bloodless English with increasing regularity – their fame lives on in the accounts of their deeds (and even in the discredited, but no less brilliant, Ossian poems of James MacPherson).

Any self-respecting Scot knows that a good tartan is the solution to everything: it tells you what you are, where you belong, who your friends and family are. Forget the Vikings: those guys just can't hold a candle to a delicious battle-weary warrior whose fighting skills and wicked sex appeal have spawned a thousand Scottish heartthrobs. From the gothic castles and over the windswept moors, with the broadsword, the claymore, the dirk, the flai, and the Lochaber axe, one of the most time-tested, evocative and romantic superheroes known the world over in video games, comic books and romance novels hails from nowhere other than Scotland.

And from the fierce battle-torn highlands we move to the magic steeped lowlands, where the ley lines meet and the most powerful witches lie in wait, mystical energy flowing as swiftly as the River Tweed. Where *glaistigs* snatch unfortunate souls straight from their beds, and carry them into the night on headless horses, and *bean shìth* moan and wail in dark woods. Make sure to leave an empty place at the dinner table for the dead on Samhain for you just might find yourself breaking bread with a ghostly lady in white, or a horseman with no head, or a demon, a dark fairy, a bristling loch monster, or a haunting phantom from the other side of the grave. The Scottish hills are alive with the sound of supernatural slithering.

So, although the ell, the stone, the boll and the firlot are no more, and I have been many times a witness to the sorry sight of café owners in London refusing Scottish pound notes as if they were monopoly money, do not despair. The stories in this collection are rowdy, wild, irresistible examples of the kind of history, magic and sex you're sure to encounter if you ever find yourself on a dark, lonely road in the middle of the Scottish wilderness, face to face with a half-naked man in a tartan. It's always best to be prepared.

Trisha Telep

Highland Heart

Heather McCollum

One

Edge of Loch Tuinn, Highlands of Scotland, August 1512

Rachel Brindle sat her mare with ease, just like any well-bred Englishwoman. She twisted an escaped curl of dark brown hair and poked it under her velvet cap. The wagons of provisions rambled behind Rachel and her sister, Isabelle, as they skirted the large lake that glittered with a million diamond-like bits of sunlight. The water looked so cool, but their father hadn't allowed them to wade in it. She and Isabelle had been commanded to sip water and pray while everyone else refreshed.

Rachel huffed at the rebellious curl. She looked askance to her sister. "Do you think we're almost there?"

Isabelle shielded her eyes against the sun. "Father said it would be after noon. I'd say we're close."

They travelled to Munro Keep to meet with the elderly Hamish Munro, great Highland chieftain and her father's business partner. William Brindle brought shillings and provisions in exchange for the fine wool that the Munros grew on their herds.

"I'm melting." A trail of perspiration tickled between Rachel's breasts under her gown. Perhaps she shouldn't have begged their father to bring them along to escape the boredom of country life. Even with the summer heat, her father had insisted she wear long sleeves to hide her strange dragonfly-shaped birthmark. She dabbed at her forehead and chest with a lacy handkerchief.

"If I succumb to the vapours will you revive me?" Rachel teased. As usual, Isabelle frowned at any mention of their special healing abilities.

"I'll pour water on your face," her sister threatened.

Rachel laughed, the sound cutting off as her glance strayed through the copse of thick pines on their left. Her lips dropped open on an unuttered gasp as her gaze locked with the intense stare of a man. He sat statue-like on his horse, a hundred yards back in the thick growth. His massive chest was bare like that of a barbarian. Red-brown hair nearly reached his broad, tanned shoulders, giving him a wild look. Though the forest shadows dappled along his skin, Rachel could see sculpted muscles protecting his ribs. He held a sword in one arm, and his biceps looked accustomed to holding its weight for long periods of time.

Narrowed eyes assessed her, judging, waiting perhaps for her outcry. But Rachel kept silent, her thudding heart the only warning. Her chin rose as she met his defiance.

"Did you see that plant?" Isabelle pointed into the high grass of the small meadow they crossed. "I think it's shepherd's purse."

Rachel forced her eyes from the man, even though the effort seemed ridiculously difficult. "Nay, Isabelle, I missed it," she murmured. Should she alert her father? Who was the barbarian? Rachel didn't even know whose land they rode across. She knew that the Munros warred with a neighbouring clan, but surely her father would have kept their route along friendly territory.

"Isabelle," Rachel asked casually. "Do you have your bow near you?"

"Yes, but I don't think father wants me hunting this close to the Munros."

"Keep it close," Rachel looked at her sister, her eyes severe. "Just in case."

Rachel pulled her dagger out and set it amongst the folds of her green muslin. Granted it was only one small weapon, but with a single flick of her wrist she could lodge it into a man's skull. Theoretically, of course, since she only practised on turnips at home.

Isabelle nocked an arrow into the bow lying across her lap. She glanced around. "You saw something," she whispered.

Rachel tipped a brief nod. "Just keep alert."

"You should tell—"

"Munros! *Batail*!" The roar sliced through her sister's words. It echoed off the trees and boulders flanking them. Rachel whirled around in her saddle, dagger poised. Men ran and jumped through the trees, not towards them but back the way they had come.

"Ride girls!" their father yelled from up ahead.

Rachel kicked her mount's flanks and leaned low as it lurched forward. Isabelle raced next to her. The meadow ended and they fled into the dappled light of the thick woods. Their father waved his arm overhead to urge them to follow as he wove through the trees.

The guttural sounds and clang of steel mixed with Gaelic curses. Did the barbarian pursue them? Rachel glanced at Isabelle, her sweet, dutiful younger sister. Would she be murdered by marauders because Rachel had failed to warn everyone? She swallowed against the dry panic in her throat as she thought of the man, his piercing eyes, his proud stare. What if he was in jeopardy? Or what if he was to be their killer?

"Watch out!" Isabelle shouted as they galloped towards a thick uprooted tree. Rachel veered and yanked the reins to the right, steering the horse in a tight circle. Her gaze wove through the dense trees as she tried to discern the sound of the battle over her thumping heart. She continued to circle, hoping to find a clear-cut path through the thickets.

"Blast!" she cursed low and looked up at the giant trees. She had absolutely no sense of direction. She shifted in her seat, breathing the moist earthy air while the halted horse quivered beneath her. "Which way?"

She scanned the woods looking for any familiar path. And stopped. The barbarian stood amongst the leaves. Blood streaked down the sword he held ready, his legs braced apart as if waiting for another target to strike. In a fluid motion he pivoted, sharp eyes connecting once again with Rachel's as if they were magnets. He took a step towards her.

The *whoosh* of an arrow made Rachel drop against her horse's neck, but her wide eyes watched in horror as the arrow slammed into the man's shoulder.

"No!" Rachel screamed and pushed her horse through the undergrowth to him. She slid down into the ferns. Her little slippers found no purchase and she tripped and slipped towards him where he lay surrounded by green fronds. He wore a kilt draped loosely around narrow hips. His eyes were closed but he swallowed. The tip of the arrow protruded from his chest, its shaft buried in his back.

Rachel ignored her shaking and placed her hands on his hot skin. She closed her eyes and released the bubble of power that churned behind her ribs, funnelling it through him. His blood surged with energy. His stomach and bladder were empty. His heart beat hard against the strain of the injury. The whisper of a leak caught Rachel's breath – a nick in the artery, blood pooling in his chest cavity.

"Holy Lord," she whispered and opened her eyes. In the distance she could hear shouting, guttural and fierce. Rachel's eyes dropped. "Yes," she breathed, and dug a fist-sized rock from beside the wet ferns, hefting it into her hand. "Holy Lord help me." She slammed it into his chest, against the protruding arrowhead. The man gasped but didn't wake. "I'm so sorry," she whispered and yanked his arm. Holy Lord, he was heavy! She braced her muddied feet against the side of a large pine and used her legs to turn him on to his side. When she'd first laid eyes on him, in the shadows, she hadn't seen the criss-crossing of scars marring his smooth skin. This man had seen battle, a lot of battle. Guilt took hold of her, lending her strength. He'd survived all this time only to be shot when she stole his attention.

The shouts crept closer. Were they looking for him? Rachel sunk lower into the ferns as she wedged her feet against his bloodied back. With a great yank the shaft slid free and the man gave a deep groan. She straddled him, kicking her skirts out of the way. He was so broad that her knees didn't reach the ground and she balanced on his hip while slamming one hand on to each of his wounds, front and back.

She breathed in the tang of blood, the sweat and mud, his masculine scent, as she released her magic, directing it through her splayed hands into his body. The nick first. She cringed as she felt the larger tear along the thin artery, a consequence of removing the splintery shaft. Her eyes flickered closed as she imagined the smooth lines of healthy tissue. Moving outwards, she pushed her power into the torn muscles, repairing, smoothing. She knitted the splintered edges of a rib and healed the broken and seeping capillaries feeding the muscles. Finally, the torn skin. Rachel breathed deep, feeling her energy feeding into the man. Would she have enough strength to escape? Her head swam and she slumped forwards, draping him in blood-stained green muslin.

"Lass." The whisper tickled at her ear and she felt her body lowered gently to the soft earth. Warm fingers brushed the hair from her cheeks and her eyes fluttered open. "What are ye?" Dark blue eyes stared down into her own, questioning, stunning her.

"There! A horse! I know I shot him. Over there!" The barbarian glanced over his shoulder and then back at her. His sensuous lips thinned into a line of frustration.

"I'll come for ye."

Come for her? Where was she going? Rachel felt her consciousness slip over the edge into comfortable darkness.

Two

Rachel became aware of the sway of the horse under her and stirred. *Where am I?* As her memory crashed into place, her eyes snapped open. *The barbarian?*

Grey clouds pushed against blue overhead. Horses clipped along at a quick gait around her, the slight jostling of armaments and bridles indicating a large number. Cold fingers touched her cheek, drawing her to the eyes of a stranger. She struggled to pull away.

"Whoa there, lass," the young man said. "I'm not going to hurt ye." He grasped her arms so she wouldn't tumble from the horse. Rachel's gaze circled the small army marching across the moor. Curious stares from rough dirty faces met her. "Ye're English?" She nodded but didn't say anything. "Now what was a bonny thing like ye doing all muddy and bloody amongst the ferns on the border of Munro land?"

Her gaze returned to his. Genuine confusion wrinkled his dirty forehead, but a twinkle livened his kind eyes.

"I . . ." What should she say? "I . . . was travelling with my father. He has business up in the Highlands. He's a wool merchant." She glanced past the man's shoulder back towards the thick forest beyond. "I need to go back." Had Isabelle escaped?

The man didn't say anything for a few long moments. "If yer da has dealings with the Munros, we aren't likely to take ye back."

Rachel's heart sped and she turned to study the landscape. The man leaned closer. "I'm Angus Riley, friend and warrior to The Macbain of Druim. And ye are?"

Rachel kept her chin high and her lips tight.

"Now if I'm to introduce ye as a . . . guest at Druim, I must know yer name, lass. Prisoners doona fair well in the dungeons. It be dark, cold and skittery down there."

A threat or a fair warning? "Rachel Brindle. And you will return me to my father, William Brindle, please."

"Ah, now Miss Brindle, how is it that ye have so much blood on ye?"

Rachel glanced down at her hands. They were streaked red. So they hadn't found the man she'd saved. "I . . . I must have cut myself," she murmured.

"I see no gash upon yer lovely skin, lass. Not even a bump from falling off yer mount."

Rachel's mind whirled. "I don't remember." She shook her head and noticed that the torturous velvet cap at least was gone. Would her father find it amongst the ferns and know she'd been taken? Or would she be lost forever at Druim?

I'll come for ye. The barbarian's words came back to her. Would he? Rachel let out a long sigh. She wouldn't count on it.

The cost of her name was so incredibly worth the warm water enveloping Rachel in the deep bathing bucket in the room she'd been given at Druim. "Guest" was *certainly* better than "prisoner". Angus Riley had kept his word and introduced her to the tall, grim-faced leader of their clan as a damsel in distress. She'd been given food and drink and a small room above the main hall.

What would happen to her tomorrow was unknown, but for the night, she was told she could bathe, sleep and recover from her obvious ordeal. Bathing and eating played a part in Rachel's plan, but not sleeping. She intended to escape. For despite their gentility, she knew her current protectors would turn captors once they confirmed her connection to their enemy.

Rachel rubbed the floral soap along her limbs but resisted the urge to relax. Escape was a priority, before Druim realized just how capable she was. Her bedraggled and exhausted appearance upon arrival had lowered their defences. There wasn't even a guard outside her door.

Rachel dried and dressed in her stained green gown. It was

still damp from her attempt to wash away the blood. Rachel fingered her clean hair. It was dark outside the window slit. She cracked open her door to an empty corridor dimly lit. She walked with purposeful stealth. The main stairway would lead to a great hall filled with warriors. Her eyes studied the shadows. This was a huge fortress. They needed at least one other exit. Rachel nearly fell into a rectangular hole cut into the floor at the end of the corridor. Her heart thudded as she gathered her long kirtle.

The ladder within the hole led down into a low-ceilinged hallway. The earthy smell of roots and grain indicated that it was a storage area. Perfect. Rachel crept along the dark, rough wall into a kitchen. Several cloaks hung from pegs. She threw one over her dress and pulled the hood up. Could she disguise herself as a servant and sneak out the gates past the guards?

Rachel whirled around at a muffled gasp. A woman stood in the doorway, a bit older than she. *Evelyn*, if Rachel remembered the woman's name from her earlier introductions – the maid who watched the chief's young children. Evelyn's eyes were wide in her round face. Rachel grabbed her stiff hand. She poured just enough power into it to warm the servant. A blue glow surrounded their clasped hands.

"Holy Lord our Father," Evelyn murmured and passed the sign of the cross over her chest with her free hand. Rachel stared into her frantic eyes.

"I have powers. They are good powers, but if you don't help me I will turn them against you." The woman didn't say anything. Did she not care what happened to her? "I can turn them against your young charges." Evelyn's eyes nearly popped at the lie. She bobbed her head nervously. Rachel smiled. "Good. I think you want me gone as much as I want me gone now. So you're going to walk me out of here, past the guards, past the gate to where I can find a horse."

The night was cool as they left the building and it felt good against Rachel's flushed face. As much as she dreamed about adventure, the actual participation in it was stressful. Perhaps she would agree to settle down with a docile Englishman like her father wished. She and Evelyn walked arm in arm, like two young maids heading home for the evening.

"Wave with me," Rachel whispered, and Evelyn lifted her hand to the watchman. He tipped his head at the girls and walked the

other way along the wall. "You're good at this, Evelyn," Rachel
murmured and patted the girl's rigid arm. Evelyn passed another
sign of the cross before her chest. Rachel frowned. She didn't like
scaring the woman.

Evelyn hurried with her through the streets towards a corral.
"You know, I fibbed back there," Rachel said in the dark. "My
powers only heal. I can't hurt you or your wards. And I wouldn't
anyway."

Evelyn stopped before a low barn. "There are horses. Now go."
She turned a fierce expression on Rachel. Evelyn certainly wouldn't
be inviting her over for supper anytime soon.

"Not a word, Evelyn." Rachel held a finger against her lips then
lowered it quickly. Could the girl see her finger tremble? "You'll
look guilty if you admit helping me get away."

Evelyn fled. Rachel entered the barn and went to work. She
selected a horse and worked a bridle between its teeth. It wasn't her
horse, but it was a fair swap. She led the beast through the darkness,
keeping to the rear of all the houses. She knew exactly where she
was headed. The moor that stretched wide and bare in front of
Druim would allow no hiding and a single rider out at night would
arouse suspicion. No, the mountains behind the castle were the best
way to go. "Holy God, please guide my way to safety," she whispered into the hazy mist floating down along the ledges of granite.

Rachel led the horse along a narrow path between the castle wall
and the rock face. Thunder rumbled and Rachel tipped her head
upwards with a soft groan. The horse nickered. "Shh," Rachel
whispered. Rain began to tap the summer leaves overhead just as
she spotted a fairly large ascending path. She tramped up it, under
the trees. Lightning sparked across the moor behind followed by a
deafening clap of thunder. She jumped at the noise and the horse
easily yanked the reins from her grip.

"Bloody horse," she hissed after its retreating tail. "Please. Come
back here," she called weakly. She spent a full minute trying to
decide what to do. Go after the horse or continue on foot? In the
end the rain decided it for her. Under the thick canopy, Rachel was
dry. She gathered her skirts and started to climb.

She walked blindly, her thin slippers barely protecting her feet
from sharp rocks. She wanted to put some distance between her
and Druim before finding a safe place to sleep for the night. Rachel
wondered what type of animals roamed these woods. She glanced
up nervously as God lit up the forest with another flash of

lightning. The deafening crack of thunder barely registered in Rachel's shocked mind for, standing on a boulder just above her, was the barbarian. He *had* come for her.

The light retreated, leaving her blind until her blinking eyes adjusted again to the shadows. He stood staring down at her as if cut from the rugged granite around them, a fortress like the mighty castle behind her. Curiosity and shock mixed on his face. As distant lightning lit up the trees again, she watched his eyebrows rise and the corner of his lush mouth crook upward into a lopsided grin. Rachel's heart danced, flushing her with heat that, luckily, he couldn't see in the dark. He'd come for her. A man who kept his promise.

Rachel wasn't sure what to do. Should she walk to him or wait in the dark? What was the protocol for a rescue? She huffed. Some rescue. She'd done most of it herself. And for all she knew she was being rescued by someone much more dangerous than those at Druim.

The man's shadow moved in the darkness and Rachel jumped, frowning at herself. Even if she could barely see, she definitely could hear.

"Who are you?" she asked, her voice sharp in the stillness.

"Alec Munro." His deep voice, drawn rough and strong, reflected his Highland heritage. Rachel released her breath and nodded in relief. He was a Munro. Thank the Holy Lord. "And ye are?"

"Rachel Brindle. I was travelling with my father and sister to Munro Keep when the Macbains attacked."

"And ye circled around into the fight to . . ."

Rachel felt guilt bubble up inside. She certainly hadn't meant to ride back and distract him. "My sense of direction is quite poor," she murmured. "I did not intend to disturb you."

"Yer father travels to meet with The Munro?"

A flash of lightning showed him much closer than she'd thought, his gaze assessing. She refused to back away even though her foot lifted involuntarily. "My father trades with Hamish Munro."

"Hamish Munro is dead."

"Oh . . . I am sorry. My father did not know. I suppose he will want to discuss trade with your new chief." The man remained silent and still. Rain dripped on Rachel's head and she wiped at it. "Do you have a horse?"

She took two stumbling steps past Alec before he placed his hands on her shoulders and gently turned her in another direction, laughing softly. Rachel ignored the thrill that shot down her arms at the solid hold.

She sniffed, irritated at his amusement. "If you plan to help in my rescue at all, please lead the way." Her words were terse and her frustration was growing to the point she just might choke on it. She'd done the hard work of escaping a fortified castle without alerting the guard. The least the Highlander could do was lead her to Munro Keep.

Alec's hand slid down her sleeved arm, his strong fingers wrapping around her wrist. He stepped close as they walked along a twining path upwards into the forest. Rachel nearly screamed when she felt his warm breath against her chilled ear. His words were quiet but as firm as his hold. "I am not rescuing ye, Rachel Brindle." Rachel's breath caught in her chest as she stared out into the dark shadows flickering sporadically with brilliant lightning. She shivered as his lip grazed her skin. "I am capturing ye."

Three

The cave was cool and the lass even cooler, in body and in mood. Alec Munro draped a wool blanket around the girl's wet shoulders where she sat against the rough, curved wall. She ignored him. He bent to the small pile of brush and scraped flint into it. Sparks caught and soon a flame snapped upward. He blew gently, feeding the fire.

He glanced at Rachel. Even in her exhaustion she was bonny, her soft brown hair curling wildly as it dried around a heart-shaped face. A lovely English lass, smooth skin, long lashes, small and delicate. He smiled – "delicate", but also able to escape Druim single-handedly. His smile faltered. Able to heal the mortal wound he'd taken earlier in the woods.

When Alec had spotted the small group winding their way through Munro territory, he'd been surprised to see the two lasses riding with the English bastard who had been swindling his father for years. Hamish Munro had fallen to a Macbain sword during a bloody battle at Loch Tuinn three months ago, leaving Alec, his remaining son to lead the huge Munro clan.

His father had never allowed anyone to view the family accounts, and now Alec knew why. His father had been a mighty warrior, but he had no accounting education. The books were a mess. Alec doubted that Hamish even realized that William

Brindle had been giving him far less than promised for Munro wool over the years.

Rachel took a crumbly oat cake he offered. For a moment, Alec thought she'd refuse or even throw it at him. "Thank you," she gritted out and took a bite. His eyebrows rose in silent astonishment. Manners, even to one's captor. He shook his head. He'd never understand the English.

Alec spitted a skinned hare over the fire. Wind and rain thrashed outside. Thunder rumbled and shook. There was no journeying to Munro Keep tonight. His horse was safe enough, tied farther down the mountainside in the shelter of another cave he'd found. These three mountains running behind Druim all the way to Munro Keep held numerous caves and conduits. He'd explored them as a child and still didn't know where they all led.

"We'll wait out the storm here," Alec commented, though Rachel didn't look his way. Alec ran a finger over the puckered skin across his heart. "So . . ." he watched Rachel closely. "I had a hole through my chest this noon." Rachel's bannock dropped into her lap. "Yet it is healed and I'm alive." He paused, but she didn't answer. "Not what I expected when that arrow took me down."

"You hit your head." Rachel met his eyes. "That is just one of many scars you seem to have received in the past."

Alec shook his head. "A warrior knows each one of his marks." He extended a leg and turned it so that his flexed calf showed. He ran a finger down a six-inch scar. "The winter of 1501, raid on the moor before Druim." He ran a palm along the jagged line down his side. "Summer of 1503, Loch Tuinn." Alec pushed his hair back from his forehead revealing a small divot. "A rock from a Macbain slingshot, fall of 1508." There were others, but he'd made his point. Rachel stared. He reached over his shoulder to touch the matching hole on his back. "Macbain arrow, Munro woods, noon today."

Alec rubbed the back of his neck. "It would have been my last mark if ye hadn't . . ." he gestured to her hands clenched in the folds of her green gown. "What exactly did ye do?"

Rachel looked at her hands. "I prayed," she whispered. "It's a gift from God." She looked up, her eyes fiery. "I am no witch. I only do good."

Alec nodded. He wasn't superstitious but understood her concern. Witch hunters revelled in finding anyone who was different – especially weak, unprotected lasses who they could brutalize and eventually kill. "Praying is good," he commented and watched her inhale slowly. "So this 'praying' . . . it can heal injuries. Can it do anything else?"

Rachel shook her head, but then stopped. "Well I can tell if someone is ailing," her voice lowered. "By touching them. So I know what to fix." Her head was bent, but she watched him from under long lashes.

"A blessing." She smiled just a bit. Alec's breath hitched in his throat at the gentle curve of her lips. She was stunning. He cleared his throat and turned the hare. "I mean, that's beneficial. Ye could save a lot of lives."

She nodded. "That's what I do. I try not to let anyone see, but I must help people when they are sick. It would be cruel not to." The words tumbled out of her as if she'd held them back for a long time.

"Does anyone know about yer . . . praying?" Alec asked and then wished he hadn't because her eager smile faded.

"My sister knows and cautions me. My father knows and commands me not to help people."

"Yer mother?"

"She had the power, but she died. An accident. She fell from a horse and hit her head. She died before I could reach her."

"I'm sorry," he said. The shine of unacknowledged tears glistened in her eyes. There was a long pause. "Thank ye for your aid today."

"I . . . I didn't mean to distract you. It was my fault you were hit."

Alec snorted. Her fault? "It was my own bloody fault for letting a bonny lass pull my attention from battle."

She looked confused. "Why then am I your prisoner?"

Alec poked at the fire. "Because yer father has been cheating my clan for the last ten years, making the Brindles enemies to the Munros."

Rachel's forehead furrowed. "The wool?"

"Aye, William Brindle has promised a fair price, but then not delivered."

Rachel's eyes moved back to the fire. "Mother was always Father's conscience. When she died . . ."

A low moan saturated the dark tunnel. Rachel's head snapped around to stare into the darkness. Lightning splashed white light into the cave for a long moment, illuminating what looked like the long, ridged throat of a beast. Alec heard her gasp as the thunder ebbed.

"'Tis just the wind, let in through a hole to the outside some-where down the tunnel." Rachel nodded but edged closer to him. "Although some say," he began and her wide eyes swung his way. "That it's the wretched sobbing of Lady Elspet as she weeps over the deaths of her two suitors, Jamie Macbain and Morgan Munro."

"Macbain and Munro?"

"Aye, 'twas the start of our feud nearly a hundred years ago."

Rachel looked incredulous. "You are battling over . . . a woman . . . dead a hundred years?"

Alec's anger simmered, narrowing his eyes. What did this English woman know of loyalty and justice? "I battle to avenge my father, my brothers, my grandfather, my great-grandfather, all the way to Morgan Munro who died because he loved a little Englishwoman. We've fought ever since, and one day we will be victorious."

Her lips were still tight. She shook her lovely head. "I'll never understand men." She snorted. "You create a tradition based on hate and death."

"Of course ye doona understand," he said. "Ye are a woman, an Englishwoman, and a healer. My ways are foreign to ye." He shrugged as if he didn't care about the condemnation in the set of her lips. Did he care? *Bloody hell – no.* He frowned and rose. The lightning had moved farther off but the rain continued to pelt in slants.

Alec was tired of smelling like blood and death. He grabbed a thin slice of soap from his satchel and headed out to the mouth of the cave. "Doona try to escape through the caves. They are danger-ous," he spoke without looking back.

He pulled his kilt from his hips, dropping it at the edge of the dry cave, and walked out into the storm. The cool rain felt good against his heated body. The air refreshed him after sitting in the stuffy cave. Alec rubbed the soap over himself and through his hair, scrubbing his own blood from his chest and limbs.

His own blood. If he'd died today, would the Macbains have considered it a final victory since he was the last of his father's sons? He grimaced. A distraction had nearly cost him everything. He could easily blame the girl as she seemed ready to take it on. But the truth was that she'd captured his usually unwavering attention simply with her presence.

She'd stared at him through the trees without a sound, without a hint of fear. He'd looked wild, yet she sounded no alarm. Rachel Brindle may be English, she may be the daughter of a swindler, she might even be a witch, but she was no coward. Cunning and courage delivered her from Druim. Alec rinsed the soap from his body and shook the heavy rainwater from his hair. He turned just as Rachel's scream shot out of the cave and straight into his heart.

Four

Rachel dangled. The toes of her torn slippers dug into any foothold she could find. Her fingers wrapped around a large rock. She'd merely been trying to find a private spot to see to her needs when she'd walked over the edge of this crater.

She panted. "Help!"

"Rachel!" Alec's pounding footfalls washed relief through her trembling body.

"Stop!" she huffed. "You'll fall."

His footsteps stopped not too far from her in the absolute darkness. "Where are ye?" His feet shuffled, loose pebbles rolling along the jagged floor.

"Over a ledge."

"Bloody hell," he cursed. "Can ye light yerself? I canna see."

"I think so." Her words were breathless and she tried to keep the panic from weakening her hold. Rachel funnelled magic towards the faint cut on her leg. A blue glow flooded out of her hands, displaying the horn-shaped rock sticking out of the cliff wall less than a foot down.

"Bloody damn hell! Hold on!"

"That was the plan," she panted.

His head appeared over the side. "Just look at me."

Rachel stared at his perfect face. High cheekbones, a slender nose with just a small bump like it had been broken once. He probably knew the date, place and person who had broken it. His jaw was square and strong. His perfectly formed lips pinched tight with thought. Wet hair framed his face as he leaned over. A clean soap scent mixed with the smell of the dank earth before her face.

Alec's chin nearly touched the rock to which she clung. His hands encircled her wrists and he began to pull. But before she could even let go of the rock, the ties holding her long sleeves ripped. A small scream flew out of her as she felt herself begin to slip out of her sleeves. She dug her toes in and stilled, her nose smashed into the dirt covered rock.

A string of curses, most in Gaelic, echoed. "I need to pull these bloody sleeves off so I can grab yer arms. Who bloody wears long sleeves in the summer?" She didn't answer. "Are yer feet on a rock?"

"My toes."

"One hand at a time." He tugged gently on her right sleeve and Rachel released her fingers. The sleeve ripped out of the bodice, and Alec was able to slide his hand around her bare wrist. "Now the other." Rachel felt the tug but couldn't seem to let go. It was as if fear had captured her muscles and they no longer obeyed her will. She shook.

"Rachel."

Rachel blinked, her gaze moving back up to Alec's face. "I have yer wrist now." He squeezed her right wrist gently. "Ye're not going to fall, but to get ye up easier, I need both of yer arms."

Rachel blinked. "I'm scared," she whispered.

A lopsided grin broke along Alec's face. "Ye jumped into battle, yanked an arrow from my bloody chest, rode with a horde of hostile Macbains, and escaped Druim on yer own, lass. And now ye're afraid to give me yer sleeve."

Rachel's pinched lips relaxed as she breathed. "I'm ready." He nodded. As soon as she released her grasp, the sleeve whooshed from her arm and Alec's other hand caught her wrist. He dragged her up. Rachel's toes dug at the side of the cliff. "Ahh!"

"What?" He froze.

"My dress, it's caught." Rachel felt the snag. She tried to kick a foot at it and began to slip. She gasped and Alec pulled hard.

Rrrrrip!

Rachel's feet churned up the vertical granite and dirt wall until her knees found the edge. She let her light go out as she scrambled up, climbing into Alec's lap.

Rachel wrapped trembling arms around his warm, hard chest. She burrowed her face into his skin, and inhaled his fresh scent. Alec gently moved her arms up over his shoulders. Some part of her realized that she straddled his lap. Her thin chemise seemed to be the only material between them and it rode up high around her thighs. But at the moment she didn't care, didn't care about anything except that she wasn't falling into an unmarked grave on a remote Highland mountain.

Alec's arms remained strong and unmoving around her waist. He neither pulled her closer nor let her go. Rachel sat in the dark listening to their shallow breaths. She rested her cheek on his chest and filtered her senses through his body. She glowed softly, piercing the shadows with her magic.

"Your blood is flowing so fast," she whispered, her lips brushing the skin over the scar he'd earned that day. "Your heart is racing like you're in battle. Your muscles hold so much excess energy you could probably lift a horse right now." Rachel pulled back enough to look at him – and forgot to breathe.

Alec's eyes were black in the deep shadows of the cave; only the light from her body illuminated them. They were piercing, smouldering as he stared at her. Rachel swallowed hard, her own heart fluttering like a bird. So slowly that she couldn't be sure which one of them moved first, Alec's face was before her own. And then he kissed her.

Rachel let her light fade, giving into the rush of sensation flooding her body. Heat – a giddy churning, a burning pool of desire – poured through her blood, her muscles. Alec tilted her face to slant against his lips. When she felt the tip of his tongue touch her lip, she groaned and opened her mouth to taste him fully. Alec drew her into his lap and her legs hiked up around his waist as the two of them sat on the cave floor. He pushed intimately against the scrap of material separating them. Rachel's flush burned across her skin. She should be shocked, repelled at the carnal exposure, but instead her thrumming body gripped him tighter, her own blood begging for more. He shifted her against him and a deep growl climbed up through his chest. He pulled back.

The cool air pressed against Rachel's scorching cheeks. She took deep breaths to clear her head. Alec's body was throbbing as fast and hot as her own.

He cleared his voice. "Ye're welcome."

"What?" Rachel gasped as Alec cupped her backside and rose, her legs still around his waist. He walked to the front of the cave.

"If that indeed was ye thanking me."

Rachel's blush intensified to a point near pain. Did he think this was how she thanked a man? As they stepped into the firelight, she struggled to get him to put her down. He lowered her slowly, letting her slide down his nude body. Rachel kept her eyes centred on the small scar on his forehead.

"Do you usually kiss your prisoners? Because there is a word for accosting young maids," she snapped.

His grin hardened as his eyes turned to ice. "It seemed a mutual response."

Rachel glanced down at her white cotton shift, careful to keep her gaze away from Alec's body. He didn't seem to mind being totally naked in front of her. Was he used to parading around women naked? The thought twisted her stomach. Alec snatched up the wool blanket and tossed it to her as he strode to the mouth of the cave. He came back tucking his kilt into place around his narrow hips.

Rachel draped the blanket around her shoulders, pulling the ends together in front of her barely concealed breasts. She collapsed into a sitting position before the fire. Her body still trembled from the near fatal fall. And the kiss. Rachel kept her eyes on the fire. Alec removed the hare from the spit, cut off some of the warm, delicious-smelling meat and handed it to her. She barely stifled her automatic response of "thank you" as she took it. Anger and embarrassment made the meal tasteless, but it stopped her stomach from growling.

"I have no sweets to finish the meal," he said with a half grin. Was he trying to dispel the thick unease between them?

"Raspberries sweetened with honey," Rachel murmured.

"Raspberries?"

"'Tis my favourite," she mumbled but her mortification wouldn't allow her to look him in the eye. He walked around her to place another blanket out on the ground furthest from the rain misting into the cave. Rachel stiffened as he neared.

Alec squatted down, his eyes level with hers. "I doona rape, Rachel. So ye can sleep soundly knowing that I willna kiss ye again." A small grin played at the corners of his mouth. "At least not until ye ask me to."

Munro Keep surged out of the cliffs as Alec's horse loped through the tall pines. Relief relaxed his face. He inhaled, craving the fresh heather-scented air off the moor that stretched before the village encircling his home. The flowery scent that flowed into him, tangling his thoughts, though, was not of the field before him, but of the silky, dark tresses feathering against his face.

Alec frowned and purposely opened his mouth to breathe without being tempted by the lass's sweetly edible scent. He'd been riding since dawn with her lovely, barely-concealed backside pressed against him. Her warmth melted into him each time his mount surged forward. And her damnable curls teased him ceaselessly. He'd stopped counting the times he almost buried his face in her hair. What the hell had he been thinking, telling her he wouldn't kiss her again? Every inch of his body rebelled against his oath.

His captain of the guard saw him coming and raised the thick iron-toothed gate. Alec clopped into the bailey, dismounting before the horse completely stopped. He lifted Rachel from her seat. She followed him with downcast eyes like a dutiful prisoner.

"Phillip."

His friend and second-in-command leapt from the table in the great hall. "Bloody hell, am I glad to see ye," he greeted and grabbed Alec in a thumping hug. Alec smiled at the obvious worry in his friend. "We found Macbain bodies and ye were gone."

"Someone was praying for me," Alec quipped, his glance catching Rachel's wide eyes.

Phillip's gaze turned to her, his smile becoming predatory. Alec frowned. "I take it, William Brindle and his other daughter made it here?" Phillip nodded without taking his eyes off Rachel. Alec walked over to stand in front of her.

Phillip's eyebrow rose at the show of protection. "Aye. They are in the dungeon."

Rachel gasped.

"Ye placed a woman in the dungeon?" Alec shouted.

Phillip shrugged. "I meant to put her in Dugger's room, but she wouldn't leave her father and *he* deserves the dungeon."

Alec rolled his eyes at Phillip. "What?" Phillip asked, eyes innocent. "I made sure the lass had plenty of blankets, food and water."

Alec caught Rachel's wrist and towed her behind him. He grabbed a torch from the wall as they descended to the cells. Phillip followed. The smell of rotting food and animal waste permeated the air. Alec shook his head. This wasn't endearing Rachel to him.

"Isabelle! Father!" Rachel called when she spotted them in the dim cell. Alec released her and unlocked the bars. Rachel flew inside, her blue light glowing faintly. If he hadn't been looking for it, he'd barely notice.

"Good God," William Brindle rebuked. "Where are the rest of your clothes? Your mark is visible! Cover yourself." He threw his blanket over the birthmark Alec had noticed on Rachel's wrist. "And stop that . . ." he swatted at her and Rachel dutifully let her light go out. She hugged her sister.

"We're fine, really," Isabelle said. "What happened to you?"

"I got lost."

"And ended up nearly naked, out in the night with . . ." he indicated Alec.

Alec crossed his large arms over his bare chest. "Alec Munro, the chief of Clan Munro and yer captor." Alec glanced at Rachel. Her eyes seemed large in the darkness. Was she surprised at his title?

William's lips pressed tight. "You cannot hold an English subject," but the force had left his voice.

"Ye are charged with thievery and trickery for deceiving my father over the last decade." Alec watched guilt flash in the man's watery, weak eyes before Brindle turned them towards the filthy straw floor. "We will discuss this matter after ye've had a chance to think." He motioned to Rachel where she clung to her sister. "Come, we'll give ye a room above stairs."

Rachel shook her head. "We stay with our father."

Alec waited for Brindle to insist they go above, but the coward kept his mouth clamped. The man gave no comfort to his daughter, who could have died or been attacked during their night apart, yet he let her protect him. Alec stalked past Phillip, almost out of the hearing of the prisoners.

"Place William Brindle in Dugger's old room. See that his daughters are given my sister's quarters. Have Maddie bring them some of Catherine's dresses." Phillip nodded to each instruction. "Warm baths for the ladies, and Phillip . . ." Alec paused without turning.

"Aye?"

"Doona touch her," he said in Gaelic. He switched back to English. "She is mine."

"Which one?" Phillip asked, but Alec just stalked away.

Five

She was *his*? What did that mean?

Rachel mulled over the three simple words that had captured her more firmly than the iron bars she'd stood behind just an hour ago.

Now bathed and dressed in a blue gown, Rachel waited with

Isabelle for an escort to the evening meal. She and her sister were now guests. Their father was housed in one of the cramped servant's quarters, but he probably deserved worse. Rachel sighed. Her father's morals had turned dark ever since their mother had died. His whole life now centred around material wealth and finding a higher placement in the hierarchical ladder at court.

"So he's the chief," Isabelle commented, her raised eyebrows adding unspoken questions. The edges of her mouth turned up subtly. Rachel nodded with a meek shrug. "And he captured you outside the Macbain's castle." Isabelle already knew this from her sisterly inquisition earlier so Rachel didn't feel the need to respond. "And you spent . . . a whole night together in a cave wearing only your shift." Rachel ran her fingertip absently along the beaded pattern embellishing her snug velvet bodice. A long pause stretched. "Did you kiss him?" Isabelle whispered. Rachel snapped a look at her sister.

Isabelle laid her hand on Rachel's wrist where the bruise from her rescue in the cave shone. A faint light gave Rachel's skin a bluish tint as Isabelle dissolved the pools of blood beneath her skin. Rachel was certain that her sister could also detect her deep blush and the way her heart raced. Isabelle smiled broadly at the unspoken admission. "He's quite handsome in a robust, wild type of way," Isabelle commented.

"It wasn't like that," Rachel defended. "Thank you," she whispered as Isabelle smoothed her now healthy-looking skin.

"So, how was it then?"

"He'd just saved me from certain death. I was panicky, grateful, overwhelmed."

"Hmm . . . 'overwhelmed'," Isabelle said, as if understanding, even though Rachel knew her sister had never been overwhelmed in that way before.

A sharp rapping on the door made them both jump off the bed. A smiling face peeked around the frame. "Time to sup." A little grey-haired lady with more wrinkles than last year's apples beckoned them.

Rachel and Isabelle grasped hands as they followed the maid down the winding steps. They walked on silent slippers under an archway into the great hall. A churning tide of deep, guttural voices ebbed, slowly fading to silence as all eyes turned towards them. Isabelle nearly squeezed the blood from Rachel's hand. The only other women in the room whisked around with platters of meat and baskets of bread. Two long tables with short benches held tankards and bread trenchers along their polished surfaces. Their father was absent.

Rachel spotted Alec easily by the hearth. His height and breadth set him apart. Even with the loose linen shirt covering his chest, the broad strength of his form could not be concealed. Rachel swallowed as she recalled the smooth, hot skin of his stomach, the soft sprinkling of hair across his chest, the thin lines of scars giving evidence of his continued survival in this harsh land. Her inhale cut off when she met his smouldering gaze. She couldn't look away. It was as if an invisible tether tied her. Isabelle tugged her to a table and Rachel had to break the connection, else trip over her own skirts.

Dinner dragged as Rachel endeavoured to make pleasant talk in broken Gaelic. Only a few of the Munros spoke English. Rachel had expected hostility from them because of the fact that she and her sister were English and that their father was imprisoned above stairs. But the Munros only smiled and patiently corrected her pronunciation.

Alec remained on the far side of the room throughout the meal. Towards the end, he walked over. "Chief Munro," Rachel began formally and lowered her eyes.

"Alec," he corrected with the hint of a grin in his voice. He waited until she looked up. "Aye?"

"We would know what you have planned for our father," Rachel said.

Alec's grin turned to a wry frown. "He's admitted his guilt." Alec looked only at Rachel. "He's willing to trade one of ye for his freedom." Rachel swallowed hard and felt Isabelle grasp at her arm, but she nodded. It didn't surprise her. She was certain which one he'd likely give up. Alec looked away as he spoke. "I told him that I doona take slaves as payment, and a person given away without their consent is a slave."

Rachel wet her dry lips. Her heart beat hard, the edge of alarm making it hard to speak. "If," she squeaked, "you have my consent, will you release my sister and father?"

Alec's gaze swung back. Anger muted the shock cut into his features. "Ye would surrender yerself to save that man?"

"And my sister," Rachel added.

"No, Rachel," Isabelle whispered.

"Yer sister is not in jeopardy," Alec said.

"She will be if you send her back to England without a protector, a father to see her supported and married well." Determination straightened Rachel's spine. "And regardless of his crimes, I am loyal to my family." Alec must understand clan loyalty. The silence was uncomfortable. "I could stay on as a servant." Her gaze trailed one woman carrying two tankards to the far table.

"Ye are no servant, slave, or prisoner. Ye are free to do as would make ye happy," Alec murmured. "This I promise." Rachel's pulse fluttered and her stomach tightened at the kindness in his vow. Before she could respond with more than wide-eyed surprise, the door banged open and a man strode across the rushes towards Alec.

"A message from The Macbain." He handed over a sealed missive. Phillip flanked Alec as he broke the seal. The room hushed, waiting. Alec thumped his fist down on the table making the wooden bowls wobble and Rachel and Isabelle flinch.

Alec looked up with a mischievous grin. "It seems that the great Macbain has misplaced the daughter of a wool merchant visiting our Highlands." Rachel felt the eyes in the room turn from Alec to her. "Seems he's willing to give over quite a reward for her safe return to Druim." Phillip translated in Gaelic and soon the whole room was laughing, deep guffaws. Rachel and Isabelle looked at one another. Rachel watched Alec as he read the rest of the missive. His smile turned stony. He eyed the messenger.

"Tell The Macbain and this Angus Riley that Rachel Brindle is a guest of Munro Keep and will soon be a permanent member of Clan Munro. I doona trade women for cattle." He snorted as if offended.

Rachel's fingers curled in her lap at the word "permanent". Hadn't Alec just sworn that she could do anything that made her happy? Happy as long as she remained with the Munros. Isabelle placed a comforting hand on her shoulder. She leaned her head against Rachel's neck. "I will stay with you," Isabelle whispered. Rachel just shook her head. She rose from her bench, Isabelle next to her. Linked arm-in-arm, they turned to the steps.

"Where are ye going?" Alec's question boomed across the murmurs in the room.

Rachel paused but didn't turn around. The room quieted. "It would make me happy to retire to my pen." She glanced back at Alec, her eyes piercing. "It's on Munro land so I assume it's within my allowed territory." He looked confused for a moment at the cattle reference, but then his face hardened. Rachel didn't wait for a nod but walked out of the room with Isabelle.

Rachel curled on her side next to her soundly slumbering sister. *Sleep, sleep,* she repeated, to dam the swirl of thoughts flooding her mind. But they tumbled over. It was even difficult to close her eyes, because every time she did she felt Alec's hard, warm chest under her cheek, his hips clenched between her thighs, his strong hands holding her face as he kissed her in that black cave. *Sleep!* She shouted in her head and squeezed her eyes shut, replacing the carnal picture with one of fluffy sheep roaming the green fields before Munro Castle.

Rachel's ears caught the thud of footsteps up the narrow stairway. The tread slowed, grew softer as it neared her door. It stopped. Rachel pushed up in the bedcovers, glaring. "He posts a guard on us," she whispered. So she wasn't a slave, wasn't a prisoner anymore? Ha!

Anger, fuelled by irritation at her own rampant musings, propelled her from bed. She yanked a blanket around her shoulders and threw the door open. Her lips parted to insist to the guard there that she wasn't going anywhere in the middle of the night. She froze.

Alec stood in the low light of the lighted sconce along the stone wall. His gaze slid from her bare toes, up her form, to her bewildered expression. "Alec?"

"Ye left before the final course. I'm also partial to sweets." Rachel realized he held a wooden bowl.

He placed it in her hand. "Raspberries?"

"Sweetened." His voice was soft in the dark. "I saved ye some." He indicated the door. "I thought to leave it."

He remembered her favourite sweet. "I . . . I," she tripped over her words. "Thank you." Rachel tipped her head to the side and studied the tall, brawny warrior. He'd been demanding, booming, boastful down in the great hall, but then he brought her this wonderful surprise. "Alec Munro," she spoke softly in the small space between them as she met his eyes. "You are by far the most thoughtful barbarian I've ever met." She allowed the grin she felt growing to relax along her face and popped one of the delectable berries in between her lips.

Alec leaned forward, his stare intent on her mouth as if following the path of the sweet fruit. He splayed one hand against the wall on either side of Rachel, trapping her close enough that she could feel the heat from his body. She inhaled and was assaulted by his clean, masculine scent. His dark eyes watched her savour the berries. She swallowed the sweet treat. His face moved closer and Rachel felt her heart beat a rapid song. She held her breath as the rough pad of his thumb traced her full bottom lip.

"Ye're welcome," he murmured. The silence stretched as if he waited for her to reply, but all the clever quips flew from her head as she memorized the pressure of his thumb that moved against her cheek. "Good eve." Alec pulled away and clipped down the hall, leaving Rachel breathing heavily, clutching the wooden bowl of sweetened raspberries.

"Why the hell is he riding here?" Alec grumbled in frustration. The last thing he needed was the priest's suspicions and hell-burning sermons.

"Father Daughtry rides with Colin Macleod of Lewis," Phillip supplied with a shrug. "I think he was visiting The Macbains for a baptism."

"Let him know we are without any bairns to bless," Alec said as he watched the stairs. It was well past dawn and Rachel still hadn't emerged from her chamber. Would the lass hide away from him all day? "Phillip, have Fiona check on our lady guests and encourage them to come break their fast."

"Ask her yerself. I've a priest to thwart." Phillip slapped Alec on his shoulder and trudged out the door.

"I'll run up," Fiona called from a corridor near the stairwell.

"Thank ye," Alec called and drank some clear spring water as he contemplated exactly what to demand from William Brindle. The man had seemed more eager to leave behind a daughter than to pay the shillings he owed. Alec frowned over his tankard until the sound of slippers on the stairs pulled his gaze.

Rachel wore a pale blue dress that sculpted against her lush figure, displaying all the ripe curves just perfect for a man's hand. The dress stood in lovely contrast to the dark curls shrouding her slim shoulders. She was petite but her stance was strong, making her seem taller, sturdy. Her long lashes were as dark as her hair and lay against her moonlight pale skin. She smiled in greeting.

He stood, inhaling fully. "Good morn." His gaze flicked to Isabelle and he bowed his head to her as well.

"And good morn to ye, old friend," came a booming voice from the doorway. Alec's smile froze and tightened. He pivoted on one heel to face Colin Macleod. Tall and considered handsome by the lasses of Lewis and beyond, the man exuded a gentle strength that he usually held in reserve. Father Daughtry stood beside him glancing around the hall. The ordained man was not much more than a score and ten years but had already started to develop the paunch of a well-fed clergyman. He'd recently fled the manic climate of England.

Someone clomped in from another corridor. "Good morning, father," Rachel called.

"And to you," William Brindle replied as he sat down at the table and began to devour a small loaf of oat bread.

"And good morning to you, Father," Isabelle called to the priest.

Two fathers, neither of them wanted. Alec's forced smile soured. Phillip came in behind Colin and Daughtry, and Alec threw a stoic glare his way. Phillip shrugged and indicated the letter that Colin held.

"Which one is Rachel?" Father Daughtry asked, his gaze perusing the rolls on the table.

Rachel stepped closer, but Alec held up his hand. She actually stopped. He almost smiled. "What do ye want with Rachel Brindle?"

Colin passed him the missive with the Macbain seal. "The Macbain is looking for her."

"I know that. He sent a man last night and I replied." Alec unfolded the paper.

The priest frowned. "Your reply is the problem." His gaze fastened on Rachel. "You need to give her back."

"And why would I do that?" Alec's scowl intensified.

"Because," Father Daughtry reprimanded, "she's handfasted to Angus Riley."

"What?" Rachel exploded.

Colin looked from Isabelle to Rachel. "Ye're married to Angus, lass, at least for a year and a day."

Six

"But I barely spoke to the man," Rachel fumed where she paced by the empty hearth.

"You spent the night on Macbain land," Father Daughtry replied and took a sip of ale.

"In a cave on the mountain," Rachel nearly yelled, but reined in her hysteria when Isabelle touched her arm. "*Without* Angus Riley," Rachel added in a firm but softer tone.

"You are but a woman," the priest continued and Rachel clamped her teeth shut. "A man must have been with you. How else did you escape Druim?"

"I escaped by using my brain," she responded evenly to the insult.

"Rachel was with me." Alec's granite-edged words filled the room. It was a simple statement but easily misinterpreted. Phillip smiled roguishly. Colin merely glanced at her from where he sat staring at Isabelle who tried to pretend she wasn't staring back at him. Confirmation of Rachel's wickedness flared in the eyes of Father Daughtry and her own father.

"Whore," her father hissed low, condemnation in his wild eyes.

The twang of steel sliding free broke through William's sputtering. "Shut yer thieving, lying mouth else I cut yer tongue from it," Alec growled, his sword a natural extension of his arm as he moved into a battle stance. Rachel stood rooted to the stone floor. Concern for her father's life warred with fury that he'd judged her without any evidence or defence.

"Rachel Brindle is as intact as when I found her on the mountain outside Druim," Alec gritted out, his stare taking in the witnesses to her humiliation. "And if she says she was untouched at Druim, she was untouched. Angus Riley lies." Alec held his sword until Father Daughtry finally nodded.

"He comes here to claim her from ye," Colin said. "Noon, Elspet's meadow."

"That's the best news I've heard today," Alec said and sheathed his sword. "We'll finish this."

"No," Rachel exhaled. "I will not have blood spilled over me."

Alec's eyes turned to her. They still held fury, but their blue depths softened. "It's our way, lass." He indicated the large tapestry hanging on the wall depicting the death scene that had started the feud a hundred years ago. "I willna have ye slandered, and I willna give ye up to those lying bastards."

She stepped closer to him, her eyes and face as hard as his own. "Then I'm coming." Her voice dropped. "To clean up whatever mess you all make." If she couldn't stop them from fighting, she could stop them from dying.

*   *   *

Rachel inhaled the light fragrance of heather and gorse on the summer breeze. The sun beat hard against the low clouds, breaking through to touch the bright green field. Elspet's meadow – the place where Macbain and Munro had battled for a woman. *Blasted dramatic Highlanders*. Rachel frowned at the powerful man who slid from his horse. Angus's eyes sought hers and his easy smile faltered at her fury. Did the man honestly think she welcomed his slander?

"Are ye well?" Angus called across the space where wildflowers danced in a swirling frenzy.

Rachel tucked an errant curl behind her ear. "I did not handfast with you, Angus Riley. I don't even know you. Withdraw your ridiculous claim and walk away from this cursed field."

Another man, taller and broader, dismounted. He had the conceited look of authority.

The Macbain.

"Whether ye are aware or not, Angus Riley claimed ye when he brought ye to my castle. He took ye without force. Ye went along willingly."

"I was unconscious," Rachel snorted.

"When ye woke, ye did not ask to turn around."

She threw up her hands. "I did!" Isabelle placed a comforting arm around her shoulders. It was his word against hers.

Alec stepped before her, sword in hand. Angus's sword sang out as he strode forward. A ray of sun broke through the clouds to shine down between the enemies as if Elspet herself tried to bar them from making the same mistake they did a century ago. Rachel's fingers dug into the back of Alec's shirt. When he turned towards her and lowered his sword, Angus lunged.

"No!" Rachel screamed and twisted to defend Alec. But Angus's momentum was too great. The point of his sword lowered from his strike but he couldn't stop the thrust in time. Rachel gasped as hot pain ripped through her middle, piercing her intestines, slicing arteries, veins and muscles. The solid blade tore back out of her as he withdrew.

Alec roared and caught her wilting body, cushioning it as she crumpled to the sunlit wildflowers. "Rachel! Nay!" His exhales were fierce pants. "Doona not leave me."

Alec's words swam in her head, mixed with the clenching pain and spreading numbness. The tang of blood and bile obliterated the subtle aroma of summer. Rachel gasped, straining for air, and shivered.

On the next ragged inhale she felt warmth. Heat wrapped around her middle and she blinked her eyes open. Alec stared down at her. Deep emotion turned his blue eyes darker, more intense. A brilliant array of lighter blues shot out from his pupils. She reached a blood-streaked hand to his face. "Beautiful," she whispered.

"Hold on, Rachel," he pleaded and rubbed her hand along his warm cheek.

Pain ebbed as warmth woke Rachel's senses.

A startled gasp came from Father Daughtry and several others gathered around. "She's glowing."

Rachel glanced down her body where Isabelle rested her hands near the wound. Her sister's eyes were closed in concentration as she fed her magic into her.

"Isabelle?" William choked.

Rachel reached for Isabelle's hands, at the same time feeding her own magic, now revived, throughout her body to knit the worst of her wounds.

"No, father. It is me." Rachel met Isabelle's eyes and she nodded, a smile touching her lips. Isabelle removed her hands but the glow continued. "I am the one who glows, not sweet Isabelle." Rachel continued.

"Witchery!" Father Daughtry clutched his heavy crucifix.

Rachel heard murmurs around them, but Alec's face blocked the men's view. "I'm sorry I distracted you again," Rachel whispered to Alec.

He rolled his eyes and exhaled in a gust. After a full breath, his worry relaxed into a broad smile. "Bloody hell, thank ye Lord for magic." Rachel smiled at his blasphemous prayer. His eyes closed for a brief moment as he shook his head, his smile turning grim. "I swear, Rachel, I'll never let ye near danger again." With that oath, Alec lifted her into his arms. She let him carry her, her strength depleted. Rachel glanced at Isabelle where she leaned against Colin. Colin nodded to Rachel, subtle appreciation and respect in his gaze.

"We shall not suffer a witch to live," Father Daughtry recited and clenched his rosary.

"I would keep yer name calling to yerself," Colin advised when Alec's hard stare shot across the distance to pierce the cleric. Rachel glanced over Alec's shoulder at the flabbergasted Macbains. Angus's sword sagged, its blade dark with her blood, the tip lost in the green grass.

"Go home Macbains," Alec growled without turning. "No one believes yer lies." He paused, turning to stare hard at Angus. "Rachel Brindle is mine."

Rachel's healed stomach fluttered with Alec's words and she found it difficult to inhale fully. She could easily read the energy surging through Alec, muscles contracting with power, heart thudding in time with his footfalls. Rachel's pulse surged as she replayed his words.

Rachel Brindle is mine. Did that make Alec Munro hers? Her hands slid to his well-muscled biceps.

"Ye are well?" he spoke low. She nodded. They rode back to the keep in silence. Rachel leaned her head against his chest, listening to the steady thrum. Alec's essence enveloped her – his clean masculine smell, his heat, his corded arms pulling her into the shelter of his chest. Even his legs braced around her, supporting her easily without complaint.

Rachel insisted on returning to the great hall after changing yet another ruined gown. Between Father Daughtry's condemnation and her father's spluttering, she wasn't about to sit above in her room while they slandered her.

"Never seen anything like it," Father Daughtry shook his head. "Must be from the Devil."

"She prays." Alec's voice sounded annoyed. "'Tis a blessing from God. She saved my own life that day Angus stole her."

Rachel and Isabelle stepped into the great hall. Father Daughtry stared directly at Rachel, his cross held tightly. "Have you fornicated with the Devil?"

"I am a maid," she replied, eyes wide.

"With healing magic you could remake yourself a maid every day," her father said and Rachel gasped at his crudeness.

Alec's sword rang with promise as he levelled it at William's throat. "The only reason yer heart does not bleed itself dry on the end of this blade is because it would distress yer daughter." William's eyes bulged and he backed away. Alec brought his sword around to point at Father Daughtry. "She is not a witch and the only devil she will be consorting with is me." Rachel opened her mouth and shut it. At least he hadn't said *fornicating.*

"The church may want to investigate this further," Father Daughtry mumbled.

"The church will need to go through me," Alec said, his scowl so murderous it made the priest cross himself.

Phillip stepped beside Alec in front of Rachel. "And every warrior belonging to Clan Munro."

Colin left Isabelle's side to stand on the other side of Alec. "And Clan Macleod."

Rachel blinked several times. Never before had anyone defended her besides her sister. And now it seemed she had the protection of two whole Highland clans.

After a battle of stares, Father Daughtry nodded and kissed his cross. "What then would you have me do? It is my duty to fight for your souls up here in this heathen land."

"Then bless us," Alec said. "Our union." Rachel turned to stone.

"What?" Her father's face flushed.

Alec sheathed his sword and pointed at him. "Ye, William Brindle will give yer daughter, Rachel, to me." He pointed to Phillip and Colin. "Ye two will witness." He swivelled back around to Father Daughtry. "And ye will sanctify our marriage with yer bloody blessing." For another long moment it seemed everyone had been frozen, until Phillip slapped Alec on the back, a smile on his roguish face.

"And what would you have me do?" Rachel's voice seemed small compared to Alec's mighty roar – small but strong. She held her gaze steady as he turned to her.

His face was chiselled, jaw tight, eyes sparking. But his voice was gentle. "Ye will say 'I do'."

Rachel met him with her own spark. "I haven't heard a question." With that she walked away through the maze of statues to the doors and stepped into the summer breeze.

Indignation warred with hope. Marriage? She barely knew Alec Munro. All the reasons she should be furious and appalled tumbled through her head. But . . . the thought of Alec, his warmth, his strength, his easy acceptance of her powers, fluttered within Rachel's stomach and squeezed her heart.

Rachel's feet brought her to the stables and she entered, breathing in the pungent smell of fresh hay. The large lashed eyes of several mares turned her way as they munched, tails swishing. Rachel leaned against the wooden wall. She barely had time to think before she heard Alec's footfalls grinding into the pebbles of the bailey. They paused outside the stable doors and she closed her eyes. The man could obviously track.

The light crunching paused before her and she smelled the clean male scent that was all Alec. "Rachel." His voice started a shiver that catapulted through her body. She slowly opened her eyes and stared up at the massive Highland warrior. "Life flashes by too fast up here to waste time courting."

Rachel's eyebrows rose. "Too fast for a simple question?" She propped hands on hips. "Let me teach you a little something about women, Alec Munro," she leaned forward to stare up into his face. "You men may dream about your first battle, mentally preparing for it from the moment you can walk. Well, women dream about . . ." she suddenly felt foolish. Her hands slipped from her hips.

Alec caught her chin. "What, Rachel, what have ye dreamed about since ye were a wee lass?"

She pursed her lips and ignored the sting of moisture in her eyes. "The bloody question! Delivered reverently by a gallant knight."

Alec ran his thumb over her cheekbone and grinned. "I'll never be a gallant knight, Rachel."

"Agreed," she sniffed, her eyes looking to the ceiling before meeting his again. She huffed, "Delivered, then, by a stubborn, domineering, overbearing mountain of a man."

His grin increased. "And here I was afraid ye would say ye didn't even know me."

She glanced down. "I don't."

His voice softened. "But I know a lot about ye." He ran fingers through her curls, encouraging that shiver to the tips of her toes. She braced her trembling legs against the wall. Alec's dark blue eyes focused on hers. "I know ye are the bravest woman I have ever met."

He closed the scant distance between them. Rachel tried to breathe evenly. "I know ye trust me." She frowned at his arrogance. "In the woods ye didn't sound an alarm." When she didn't refute he continued. "Ye possess magic and it's a blessing, but it should only be used when necessary because it tires ye." He raised her wrist and traced the wings of the brown dragonfly mark.

Alec's nose skimmed the pulse of her neck, his lips hovering up to her jaw. Rachel's heart pounded. "I know yer scent." He inhaled and goose bumps rippled along her arms.

His hand moved to her chest, palm against her heart, fingers stretched up along her collarbone. "I know the sound of yer heart racing and how yer sky blue eyes turn darker when I am close." She would have denied it but guessed it was true.

"Ye like sweetened raspberries and are exceedingly clever." His palms cupped her cheeks and Rachel's lips opened on their own accord but he held himself apart. She almost groaned in frustration. "And I know ye meddle and get into trouble when ye think 'tis the right thing to do. We're certain to yell a bit at each other. For ye have spirit, lass, to match my own."

His nose touched hers and she hardly breathed. Several heartbeats passed. His heat scorched her. His scent filled her every breath. His strength radiated outward, encompassing her, making her weak and mighty at the same time.

Rachel cleared her throat. "But there's more to me."

"And we have decades to learn the particulars," he whispered so close to her lips she felt the breeze of his words. She nodded, brushing his forehead. He lowered his hands and straightened, a look of mild disappointment tightening his face.

"And what do ye know of me, besides the fact that I'm stubborn and a mountain of a man?" He flexed his thick biceps as if proving her physical description.

She smirked. "You forgot domineering and overbearing." He tipped his head in acceptance and a small laugh broke from her grin. "Well . . . you are kind to let my father live." He nodded vehemently. "You have a good sense of direction and know how to cook a rabbit."

"And find raspberries," he added.

"Charming" – she could add that. Charming when he wanted to be. "A leader of a great clan." He nodded. "And I think . . . honourable."

"I *always* keep my promises, lass."

"You are good with a sword and you smell clean and wholesome," she added quickly.

He flashed white teeth. "Because I *am* clean and wholesome." He stepped close again. "But ye forgot a most important part of me, something that I've recently stumbled upon." His face grew serious, almost pained for a moment, as he caught a curl and tucked it behind her ear with a caress. "When that bastard Macbain stabbed ye –"

"Because I was meddling."

"Aye," his quick grin faded just as fast as it was born. His gaze moved to the ceiling. "Let me back up." He paused until he looked

her in the eye again. "I hate the Macbains." Pure loathing shook his
voice. "They killed my father, my two brothers, and would have
killed me." He took a large breath of air. "But when Angus Riley,"
he nearly spit the name, "stabbed ye, all I could think about was
saving ye, holding yer warm body against mine again, kissing ye."
Rachel felt her blush but couldn't look away. "I could have turned
and killed him there, possibly killed The Macbain himself, but," he
shook his head, "they meant nothing." His eyebrows rose as if
surprised. Alec's fingers brushed her cheek and she suddenly realized a tear had trailed down it. "All I could think about was Rachel
Brindle and how much . . ." his lips tightened as if he were about to
say something foreign. "How much . . . I love ye."

Rachel's breath caught. Alec took her hand in his and his voice
deepened with his oath. "*Tha gaol agam ort*, Rachel. *Gu bràth*,
forever." He leaned in so close, his bottom lip brushed hers. He
waited. "I doona break my promises."

Rachel moved her lips against his but he held still. The memory
of his oath in the cave surfaced. He'd kept his promise not to kiss
her until she asked. This wild, headstrong barbarian was her gallant
knight. "I love you too." She took his face in her hands. "Kiss me,
Alec Munro."

As if her words broke through a dam, Alec's entire being swamped
her. His lips, hot and urgent, melded with her own. His arms caught
her up, fitting her into the shelter of his body, pressing her tightly to
his muscled form. The physical difference between them sent a giddy
rapture spiralling through Rachel. She let him hold her up as sensation after sensation washed away everything but his taste, his scent,
his touch. The rough board at Rachel's back that Alec pressed her
against faded from her consciousness, as did everything but their
hearts racing together. Alec's kisses trailed down Rachel's neck and
she moaned softly. Only then did she hear the polite cough.

She stiffened and Alec growled. "Be gone, Phillip." Alec's hot
lips feathered back up to Rachel's and she relaxed as his hands ran
caresses down her arms.

A deep chuckle. "It's customary for the bride to say 'I do'
before . . ."

"I do," Rachel breathed against Alec's lips. He paused and she
blinked open to see his broad smile. His blue eyes shone bright and
he threw back his head and laughed. She couldn't help but join
him. Alec picked her up. Rachel gasped on a giggle and clung hard
to his neck as he carried her towards the altar.

"I do, too," Alec said against her ear. The heat in his words scorched her. "Let us tell the good father quickly then. I have a desire to learn everything about ye. From the curls of yer lovely head to the tips of yer wee toes, and *everything* in between." He paused to seal his oath.

Rachel's blood surged with the promise in Alec's kiss, a promise of adventures and passion, a promise of a lifetime of love.

The Pagan Bride

Patricia Grasso

Aberdeenshire, Scotland, 1565

Hot as a hare, blind as a bat, dry as a bone, red as a beet, mad as a hatter.

Standing beside the boy's pallet, Avril Gordon recalled her late mother's instructions and placed her palm against his burning forehead. His lips looked parched, his face crimson. She snapped her fingers in front of his unseeing eyes, and he mumbled nonsense as if caught in a nightmare.

"Gavin has eaten nightshade berries." Avril turned to the earl's farrier, the man's ashen-faced wife, and his oldest son.

"I dared him to eat the berries," ten-year-old Duncan admitted, his misery apparent. "I promised to do his chores for a week."

Avril slid her gaze to Duncan. "You may be doing his chores forever."

The farrier slapped the ten-year-old. "You've killed your brother."

"Fergus, beating this son will not cure the other." Avril looked at Duncan, "Fetch me a cup of water."

Avril set her mortar and pestle on the table and removed two packets of herbs from her satchel. Placing both herbs into the mortar, she ground them into a powder and stirred the powder into the water.

"Carry Gavin outside," she ordered the farrier. "Hold him in a kneeling position."

Outside, Avril crouched beside the eight-year-old and pressed the cup to his lips. "Drink, Gavin. Small sips will cure what ails you."

I hope. Murmuring soothing words of encouragement, Avril managed to get the boy to down the water.

"What now?" Fergus asked.

"We wait."

Several minutes later, the eight-year-old vomited and vomited and vomited. Avril placed her palm against his forehead and gazed into eyes that seemed more focused. His babbling had ceased, his high colour was beginning to recede.

"Gavin will sleep," Avril said, standing, "and all will be well."

"Lady Avril, you are a credit to your mother's memory." The farrier carried his youngest inside.

"I owe you my son's life," the wife said. "Whatever will we do when you marry and leave us?"

"That day lives in the future." Avril patted the woman's shoulder and then rounded on the ten-year-old. "You will do your brother's chores for a month, and you will never dare anyone again."

"I promise, my lady."

Avril walked away, her relief making her legs weak. Once out of sight, she used her sleeve to wipe the sweat from her temples and brushed a damp wisp of red hair from her face. She owed the Goddess thanks for saving the boy. Many thanks. Profuse thanks.

Slipping out through Huntly Castle's postern gate, Avril followed the path through the woodland to her favourite clearing. She felt protected there, surrounded by trees – especially the oaks – the kings and queens of the forest.

Reaching the clearing, Avril gathered nine stones at random and began making a circle. She placed the first stone in the northwest and, moving clockwise, set the rest of the stones down to represent each earthly direction. Avril entered the circle from the west and moved to close it behind her with a stone.

"*Sister,*" The Earl of Huntly stood at the clearing's edge, his arms folded across his chest. "Step out of the circle."

With an inward groan, Avril wished her parents weren't dead. Her brother was tougher than her father.

Avril sent the Goddess a silent prayer of thanks and then collected the stones in reverse direction. She walked towards her brother.

The Earl of Huntly tugged her fiery braid and, throwing his arm around her shoulders, ushered her down the path. "The Old Ways endanger you."

Avril gave him a sidelong glance. "What do you want, George?"

"We leave for Edinburgh in the morning," he answered. "Your Campbell husband requires your presence."

That surprised Avril. "I thought he'd forgotten about me."

"Campbell was waiting until you ripened."

"Does he consider me fruit to ripen?" Avril countered, insulted. "Vows spoken between a five-year-old girl and a fifteen-year-old boy scarcely signify a marriage."

"Your husband needs his wife with him at court," her brother told her. "Darnley has bewitched Queen Mary. You can gain the queen's confidence and hear the women's gossip."

"What if the queen dislikes me?" Avril said. "Besides, I wouldn't know my own husband if I passed him on the road."

"Trust me, sister. Once you see Campbell, you will never forget him.

Edinburgh

Nervous anticipation and simmering anger coiled inside her. How she began would signal how she continued. Avril stood in her bedchamber at Campbell Mansion. For the first time in her life, she suffered the urge to throttle someone.

Her husband hadn't been home to welcome her when she and her brother arrived. George had instructed the majordomo to send for him at court.

Magnus Campbell did not seem like quality husband material. Avril would know for certain whether to stay or to go once she'd met him. Like her mother before her, Avril had been blessed with special, unworldly gifts. Her sixth sense allowed her to see beneath the masks people wore.

Humiliated by her husband's disrespect, Avril had retreated to her bedchamber to freshen herself. Now Magnus Campbell and her brother waited in the great hall.

Her husband needed a lesson in the proper treatment of a wife. She was no biddable child and would not be ruled in this marriage, nor would she rule him. Waiting was a humbling experience, and humility would be good for his soul.

Avril inspected herself in the pier glass. She wanted to look perfect without seeming to exert any effort.

Her gown was the current fashion. Thankfully, the paleness of the yellow did not declare war on her hair as most colours did.

Her hair was too red, her height too short – Avril turned sideways – her breasts too small. She yearned for dark hair, several inches in height, and bigger breasts. Much bigger breasts.

Avril could not postpone the inevitable. Lifting her skirt, she strapped the leather garter to her leg. She never ventured outside without her last resort dagger and felt the need for protection more in Edinburgh than in the Highlands.

Downstairs, Avril stepped into the great hall. Her legs weakened at the first sight of her husband. She felt as if she'd been struck with the blunt end of a claymore.

Magnus Campbell stepped out of every maiden's dream. He cut an imposing figure, his well-honed physique shown to best advantage in perfectly tailored, conservative midnight blue. His features were pleasing, his smile irresistible, his silvery-grey eyes the colour of mist.

She loved mist, which shrouded the tangible, allowing one to see beyond the horizon to the spirit realm – or so her mother had taught her.

"Magnus, I present your wife Avril," George Gordon introduced them. Her brother looked at her fascinated expression, adding, "Sister, I told you so." He left them without another word.

Magnus Campbell, the Marquis of Argyll, stared at her.

Avril Gordon, his wife of fifteen years, returned his stare.

"You have grown into a beautiful woman," Magnus said, breaking the awkward silence. "I have never forgotten your unusual eyes."

"Many people have blue eyes and green eyes," Avril said. "There's nothing unusual about it."

"Most people are born with one colour or the other, not one of each," Magnus said, bowing over her hand. "Are you ready to begin your life as my mate?"

Avril felt disoriented. She could not sense anything from his touch. She'd never met anyone she couldn't judge by touch.

"I must speak with you first." Ignoring his guarded look, Avril gave him an ambiguous smile.

Magnus motioned her to sit and, when she did, dropped into the chair beside hers. He managed to keep his expression bland, but his piercing gaze made her blush.

Damn. She'd inadvertently drawn his attention to her major flaw. Redheads were notorious blushers. On the other hand, only a blind man would miss her brazen red hair.

"What do you want to discuss?"

"We must clarify a couple of issues before we begin married life," Avril told her hands, folded in her lap.

Her husband chuckled. "Issues?"

She snapped her gaze to his. "Don't you have concerns?"

"Do you usually answer questions with questions?"

"Do you?" When he laughed at her impertinence, Avril answered his smile with her own. She liked his sense of humour and even temper.

"Tell me what troubles you," Magnus said, "and we will settle these concerns."

"I–I . . ." Avril felt her face heating with another blush.

"My lord?" Donald, the majordomo, served the marquis a glass of whisky and offered her a glass of lemon barley water.

"I prefer whisky," Avril told him. She peeked at her husband who was watching her, the hint of a smile flirting with his lips.

When the majordomo returned, Avril tasted the whisky and handed him the glass saying, "I prefer Highland whisky, not this Lowland drink."

"My wife is a Highlander," Magnus told his man. "She can taste the difference between full-bodied Highland and floral Lowland."

After the majordomo had served them two glasses of Highland whisky, Magnus turned to her. "Please continue."

"I don't want sex," Avril blurted, watching his placid expression register surprise. "I mean, I feel uncomfortable sharing intimacy before we reacquaint ourselves."

"Are you afraid?"

Avril looked into his silvery-grey eyes. "I fear nothing."

Her husband studied her for a long moment, his face expressionless. "I will give you a week," he said, "but we will share a bed for appearances.

Avril inclined her head and gulped the whisky in one swig, relieved that was settled. "Tell me about court and the queen."

"Storm clouds are gathering over the court," Magnus said. "Keep your lips shut, your ears open, and do not discuss religion. Anything you say will be used against you at a later date."

"By whom?" His sharing important information impressed Avril. She doubted her own brother would confide in her.

"Friends come and go at court," Magnus answered, "but

enemies accumulate. Trouble is brewing between the old and new kirks. Mary is Catholic, but the new kirk has won the support of many nobles and commoners."

"Do you mean John Knox's new kirk?"

"Some on the privy council are Catholic," Magnus said, nodding, "and the others – including the queen's half-brothers – follow the new kirk."

"New kirk or old, God hears everyone's prayers," Avril said, shaking her head. "Which kirk do you support?'

"I support whatever is politically expedient for Clan Campbell," Magnus answered. "Travelling through life is easier with the wind on our backs."

Our backs. Avril liked the sound of that, implying they were equal partners. Perhaps a marriage between them would work.

"I understand." And Avril *did* understand. She understood politics jeopardized her husband's soul, and she intended to save him.

"Queen Mary is beautiful, vivacious and intelligent," Magnus was saying, "but her political inexperience makes her dangerous to herself and others. Darnley, her petulant suitor, lacks subtlety and possesses more ambition than intelligence."

"What a charming place to visit," Avril drawled.

Magnus smiled at that. "Mary loves golfing, hawking and hunting as well as gentler pursuits."

"I do not kill God's creatures," Avril told him. "I do golf, though."

"You eat creatures others kill in order to survive," her husband reminded her.

"I do *not* eat God's creatures," she corrected him. "The thought nauseates me."

"God's balls," he muttered. "Unusual eating habits will draw attention."

"Then I will pretend to eat whatever is served."

"Pretending is good," Magnus said, "but what will you do if served haggis?"

Avril winked at him. "I'll swoon."

"Swooning is good," Magnus said. "You know, lass, the first time I saw you, I knew you'd grow into a great beauty."

A great beauty? Avril couldn't credit what he'd said. Red hair, small stature and less than generous breasts did not make for a great beauty.

"What did you think of me?"

"I thought you were elderly."

★   ★   ★

Her husband abandoned her.

After enjoying a companionable supper, Magnus announced that the privy council required his presence at court, but he would soon return.

Apparently, "soon" was a relative time. The hour grew late. Avril sought her bed, but sleep eluded her.

Her husband should have stayed home and courted her. Not only did the prospect of sleeping beside a man – albeit, her husband – make her nervous, but his inattention humiliated her.

Hearing the door open, Avril snapped her eyes shut in feigned sleep. She heard him moving around. The bed creaked, and the mattress dipped when he climbed in beside her.

Was he naked? Avril felt a heated blush. Thankfully, the chamber was dark.

"Good night, wife."

Avril opened her eyes. Her husband was leaning over her.

"I was sleeping."

"No one sleeps with a death grip on the coverlet." She heard the smile in his voice.

Magnus dipped his head to kiss her. His lips were warm, firm, and oh-so-inviting.

"You taste like whisky."

"I've been celebrating my marriage," Magnus told her, and then hiccupped. "Oops, pardon me."

"You should have celebrated with your wife."

"You missed me."

"A woman cannot miss what she never had."

Magnus smiled. "You can have me now."

"You're drunk." Avril rolled on to her side, showing him her back.

"You wound me, lass," he mumbled.

Lying there in silence, Avril listened to her husband's even breathing. A long, long time passed before she fell into a less than peaceful sleep.

Avril awakened during those hushed, magical moments before dawn. Beside her, Magnus still slept.

Bare-chested, her husband lay on his back with the coverlet pulled up to his waist. His face appeared boyish in sleep yet exuded an aura of power.

Avril studied his handsome features. His jaw was strongly

chiselled, his lips sensuously formed, inviting sweet surrender to his kiss.

She slid her gaze lower. There was strength in his well-muscled chest with its mat of brown hair. She struggled against the urge to touch him, feel his muscles rippling beneath her fingertips.

Her gaze reached the boundary of body and coverlet. She wondered if the coverlet was the only barrier between his nakedness and her. That thought frightened and excited her.

Taking herself out of temptation's path, Avril rose from the bed to complete her morning ritual of greeting the new day. She padded on bare feet around the bed but paused to lift her husband's discarded doublet off the floor. The garment reeked of rose perfume.

Mixing a shrivelling potion appealed to her, but she knew she'd be spiting herself. Madame Rose would never again get close enough to leave her scent.

Avril tossed the offending doublet aside and walked to the window. Down the road on her left stood Holyrood Palace, and a mile down the Esplanade on her right rose Edinburgh Castle. On the opposite side of Holyrood Road stood a copse of trees, shrouding Holyrood Park from view.

June had coloured the world green. Wild and cultivated flowers supplied shades of red, yellow and blue. The early morning air smelled crisp and clean, and the chirping from the trees signalled birds awakening.

Avril lifted her gaze to the sky. The eastern horizon glowed with light. The rising sun, different each day of the year, seemed especially inspiring this morning.

Pressing her palm on the window pane, Avril whispered, "Father Sun kisses Mother Earth . . . Father Sun kisses— "

Movement across the road caught her attention. A tall gentleman stepped from the trees and hurried in the direction of Holyrood Palace. A moment later, a blond boy appeared and, walking at a slower pace, headed in the same direction.

What was happening behind the trees at this early hour? Had the gentleman and the boy been together? If so, why had they left separately?

"What is the hour?" her husband asked, his voice drowsy.

"Early."

"What are you doing?"

Avril glanced over her shoulder at him. "I'm greeting the dawn."

"Agh, my head is pounding," he groaned, his eyes closed, "and my stomach is protesting the whisky and food."

Avril faced him, noting his greenish pallor. "Those who indulge must suffer the consequence."

"Spare me the sermon."

"I can cure your hangover."

Magnus opened one eye to look at her. "Then cure me, wife."

Avril crossed the chamber to the cabinet to retrieve her mortar, pestle and herb satchel. She dropped a pinch of two herbs into the mortar and ground them into powder. Then she stirred them into a cup of water.

Magnus eyed the offered cup. "What is it?"

"The cure," she answered. "You must drink it all."

"Does it taste bad?"

"I promise there is no taste."

Magnus drank the mixture and passed her the empty cup. Then he lay back on the bed. "When will I feel better?"

"Soon." Avril gave him an ambiguous smile and walked away, busying herself picking his discarded garments off the floor.

"How long—?" Magnus bolted from the bed and dashed for the chamber pot behind the privacy screen.

Avril whirled away, his nakedness startling her. The sound of his retching nauseated her, and she placed a hand on her throat quelling the urge to gag.

"You fed me poison," Magnus accused her.

"Cover yourself." Hearing the bed protest his weight, Avril rounded on him. "How do you feel?"

"I do feel better," Magnus said, after a long pause. "Bring me food."

"Do I look like your maid?"

"You look like my wife. Please?"

Avril shrugged into her bedrobe and tied the sash. "I'll bring you oatmeal porridge and old man's milk."

"Leave the egg from the milk," Magnus said, "and add an extra shot of whisky."

Avril opened the bedchamber door.

"I want sausage, too."

"If you want sausage," she told him, "get it yourself."

"Why?"

"I disapprove of eating animals." Avril stepped into the corridor.

"God's balls," she heard her husband groaning, "I married a lunatic."

"You look beautiful."

At the sound of her husband's voice, Avril turned away from the pier glass. Created in midnight blue silk, her gown sported a squared neckline and long, fitted sleeves with puffed shoulders.

Her husband wore midnight blue, too. She hoped that proved a good omen.

"I lack sophistication," Avril said. "The other courtiers will laugh at me."

"You possess something more valuable than sophistication," Magnus said, sauntering across the chamber. "You, my dear wife, personify natural beauty and unaffected youth."

"Thank you for trying to bolster my confidence."

With one finger, Magnus tilted her chin up and gazed into her blue and green eyes. "I brought you a gift." He reached inside his doublet and produced two boxes. "Open this one first."

Avril opened its lid. On a bed of black velvet lay a necklace, its long golden length punctuated with diamonds, emeralds, rubies and sapphires.

"I will cherish it always."

Avril slipped the necklace over her head.

Magnus opened the smaller box, which contained a ring, its gold setting holding a rare, six-point star ruby. He slipped the ring on to the third finger of her right hand.

"Legend says a guardian spirit lives inside the ruby," Magnus told her. "If danger approaches, the stone grows darker than pigeon's blood."

The ring and its magical legend appealed to Avril. She planted a chaste kiss on his lips.

"I love the necklace and ring and legend," Avril said, "but I love the thought behind the gifts even more."

"If the ruby ever darkens, scream for me." Magnus offered her his arm. "Shall we go?"

Hand in hand, Magnus and Avril entered Holyrood Palace. Thankfully, her husband knew where they were going.

Walking down the corridor towards the reception hall, Avril felt like a woman going to the gallows. She disliked the disorienting feeling of entering an unfamiliar situation, but her husband's hand on hers bolstered her courage.

Magnus and Avril stepped into a crowded reception hall. Ladies and gentleman loitered in small groups, conversing in hushed voices. The gentlemen's dark clothing provided the women's gowns and jewels with a perfect background.

Mingling perfumes clashed. Avril wished someone would open a window.

"The Queen hasn't arrived." Magnus ushered her across the hall towards her brother. He greeted friends and acquaintances but never paused to introduce her.

"I feel conspicuous," she whispered.

"Everyone is curious about my Gordon bride."

"Sister, how goes the married life?" George Gordon asked when they reached him.

"My delayed return last night annoyed my bride," Magnus answered for her.

Avril looked at him, "My brother was speaking to me, husband."

"Duly noted, wife."

George Gordon smiled. "I can already hear the sound of crockery crashing."

"Campbell and Gordon, I bid you good day."

Avril turned towards the deep voice and felt dwarfed. The gentleman was well over six feet and as handsome as he was tall. He seemed vaguely familiar though she'd never met him.

"Lord Darnley, I present my bride, Avril Gordon," Magnus introduced them.

"A pleasure, my lady." Charles, Lord Darnley, bowed over her hand. "Best wishes on your marriage."

His touch on her hand sent Avril reeling. She suffered an uncanny awareness.

Swirling fog in her mind's eye dissipated, revealing . . . Darnley and a boy hidden within the copse of trees . . . And then the fog rolled in again.

"Lady Campbell?"

"I apologise, my lord." Avril blushed, mortified being caught off-guard. She should have prepared for this eventuality. "My mind wandered,"

"I understand." Darnley's uncomfortable expression told her the opposite. "Excuse me, please."

"Is there a problem?" Magnus asked her. "You looked vacant."

"I sensed something sinister about Darnley."

"Do *not* start mouthing your hocus-pocus," George warned, his voice an urgent whisper.

Magnus looked confused. "What is her 'hocus-pocus'?"

"My sister believes she has the Sight."

Avril could have throttled her brother. She did not want a husband who considered her peculiar.

Magnus smiled. "You must be joking."

"There is nothing amusing about the Sight," Avril said. "My gift feels like a curse."

Magnus leaned close to whisper in her ear, appearing like a love-struck husband. "Forget about the Sight, wife, or we burn as witches."

"Good evening, Lords Gordon and Campbell."

Avril lifted her gaze to James Stewart, the Earl of Moray, the Queen's illegitimate half-brother. Dressed in black, the earl was almost as tall as Darnley. Stewart was a handsome man in spite of his pinched expression.

"I present my wife Avril," Magnus introduced them.

The Earl of Moray bowed over her hand before she could hide it behind her back. Again Avril suffered an uncanny awareness.

Fog swirled in her mind's eye and then dissipated . . . Outlined in black, Moray held an infant and the crown of Scotland in his hand . . . The fog rolled in again, blocking her view.

"Are you enjoying Edinburgh, Lady Campbell?"

"Actually, I prefer a simpler life in the Highlands."

James Stewart smiled at her. "Most young ladies would enjoy the excitement."

"I am not most young ladies." Avril gave him her sweetest smile. "Too much excitement can kill almost as easily as a dagger."

The earl inclined his head. "Campbell, you are the most fortunate of men to have wed a woman without ambition." And then he moved on.

Avril watched the Earl of Moray walk away. Then she blessed herself by making the sign of the cross.

Her brother smiled. He was accustomed to her eccentricities.

"What are you doing?" Magnus demanded.

"Keeping Old Clootie at bay." Avril glanced around. "Moray begrudges Mary her crown."

"Heed my sister's opinions of people," George advised her husband. "She inherited the knack of seeing into people's hearts."

"Too bad she can't see into their minds," Magnus said, and then looked at her. "I urge discretion, wife. The survival of the Campbells and the Gordons depend on that."

"I don't want anyone else touching me." Avril doubted she could remain sane if all the courtiers hid sinister hearts.

An older gentleman approached them. With him walked a voluptuous, dark-haired woman.

"Avril, meet William and Fiona Seton, the Earl and Countess of Melrose," Magnus said.

Melrose started to bow over her hand but couldn't find it. Avril had hidden her hands within the folds of her gown.

"I mean no offence, my lord, but—"

"My wife dislikes being touched," Magnus finished.

The Earl of Melrose raised his brows. "I hope you can handle that, Campbell."

The Countess of Melrose gave Avril a feline smile. "Your wife is a lovely child, Magnus. We wish you well."

Avril narrowed her gaze on the woman. Fiona Seton had been her husband's lover, and she didn't need the Sight to tell her so. The woman reeked of rose perfume.

And then Queen Mary walked into the reception room, capturing Avril's attention. With the queen were her ladies, including her life-long friends, the four Marys.

Regal and graceful, Queen Mary was unusually tall, auburn-haired and beautiful. She was everything Avril had ever imagined and then some.

With her ladies at her sides, Queen Mary sat in a chair on a raised dais. The queen motioned Magnus and George forward.

"Your Majesty, I present my wife, Avril Gordon," Magnus said.

Avril executed a deep curtsey, her head bowed but her gaze on the queen.

"Arise, Lady Campbell," Queen Mary bade her, "My dearest George, your sister looks nothing like you."

"Alas, Your Majesty, this woman is an imposter," George joked, his smile infectious. "The fairies stole my true sister and left this changeling in her place."

Queen Mary giggled, and Avril blushed. The other courtiers laughed at her brother's success entertaining the queen.

"What say you to that, Lady Campbell?"

"His teasing tormented my entire life," Avril answered. "Unfortunately for my brother, my husband is duty bound to protect me and will surely give George a thrashing later."

The queen laughed and clapped her hands, enjoying the brother's and sister's barbs. Everyone laughed when the queen laughed.

"Your name means April in French," Mary told her.

"I was born on the first day of April," Avril said, "and my mother named me Avril Mairi in Your Majesty's honour."

"How nauseatingly sweet," murmured a female voice.

"Fiona," she heard the Earl of Melrose caution.

Avril felt interested gazes on her back. Some wished her well, others emanated unspoken hostility.

"What an exquisite necklace," Mary complimented her.

"Thank you, Your Majesty." Avril raised a hand to touch her necklace. "My husband is a generous man, but this ring" – she held her hand out – "comes with a marvellous legend."

The queen beckoned her forward. "I would hear this story."

"A guardian spirit lives inside this six-pointed star ruby," Avril said, stepping closer. "If danger approaches, the ruby warns me by darkening to pigeon's blood red."

"I could use one of those," Mary murmured.

"No one could ever wish you harm, Your Majesty." Avril told her. "Your devoted subjects waited years for your return and rejoiced at your homecoming."

Avril hoped her words proved true, but Darnley's smile hid deceit. Even worse, the queen's own half-brother coveted the crown.

"Do you golf, Lady Campbell?"

"Yes, I do golf."

"You must golf with me and my ladies tomorrow."

"Your invitation honours me."

"The gentlemen will serve as caddys," Lord Darnley said, advancing on the dais. "I would be honoured to carry your golf bag, Your Majesty."

Queen Mary dismissed Avril at Darnley's approach. Magnus was there to escort her away.

"Well done, wife."

"We must speak privately," Avril whispered.

Magnus ushered into the corridor. "We can speak outside."

Leaving the palace, they strolled away as if taking the air. "Enemies surround the queen," Avril said. "Those whom she loves and trusts will prove disloyal."

"Do *not* repeat that."

The topic was treason, endangering their queen. That required action, not discretion.

"We must warn her."

"Would you endanger the Campbells and the Gordons?" Magnus countered. "I will send you to Argyll if you persist."

Avril arched a copper brow at him. "Then you can resume your affair with Fiona Seton. Do not bother denying it. Your doublet reeked of rose perfume."

Magnus held his open hands out. "I danced with the lady, nothing more."

"Fiona Seton is no lady."

"True."

"Mary must not marry Darnley." Avril said, her tone urgent. "Someone must discourage that romance."

"You will do or say nothing," Magnus ordered her. "Darnley is short on brains and long on ambition but a harmless, affable blockhead."

"Darnley is *not* harmless and will bring Mary toppling down."

"You met the man *once*," Magnus argued. "How do you know?"

"I know because . . ." Avril lifted her small nose into the air. "Sometimes I know what others do not."

"Hocus-pocus?" Magnus planted a kiss on her lips. "What does the future hold for our clans?"

"The Campbells and the Gordons will survive the storm," Avril answered, "but Mary will not survive the Darnley problem."

Her husband ran a hand down his face and sighed in obvious frustration. "What is the Darnley problem?"

"Only God knows everything, husband."

"How well do you golf?"

Inspecting herself in the pier glass, Avril adjusted the forest green hat that matched her gown and jacket. Then she faced her husband.

"I know what I'm doing."

"Mary excels at golf," Magnus said. "She wants to win against a good golfer."

"Trust me husband." Avril stepped closer, so close their bodies touched, and inhaled his clean scent. "You smell like mountain heather."

"I love your lilac scent."

"More than rose perfume?"

"Rose perfume stinks like the English." Magnus lifted her golf bag and slung it over his shoulder. "We cannot keep Mary waiting."

Magnus and Avril arrived at Holyrood Park ahead of the queen. A golf course had been landscaped in the park. Tin cups sat in small holes placed strategically at measured distances, and flags marked the cups.

Closing her eyes, Avril inhaled deeply. The world smelled green. Singing birds provided nature's music accompanied by the sensuous swish of wind caressing trees. Overhead, the sun shone in a clear blue sky. Nary a cloud marred its oceanic perfection.

Queen Mary and her entourage arrived, including both players and spectators. The Countesses of Melrose and Moray planned to golf while the four Marys, never far from their royal namesake, would watch the game.

Darnley carried the queen's golf bag, and James Stewart carried his wife's. Surprisingly, George Gordon carried Fiona Seton's.

"What are you doing here, brother?"

George rolled his eyes. "Melrose enlisted me to caddy for his wife."

Queen Mary teed off first. The ball landed on the green, not far from the first hole. All the spectators clapped for the queen.

"Good shot, Your Majesty." Avril knew the queen's height gave her a strength advantage.

The Countess of Moray set the leather-covered ball on the tee. She swung her driver but missed the ball.

"I hate this game," she complained. "I apologise, Mary, and will watch today."

"Practise keeping your eyes on the ball," Avril advised the countess, "and follow through when you swing."

"Lady Campbell knows golfing," Lord Darnley said.

"What else can she do in the Highlands except count sheep and hit golf balls?" Fiona Seton quipped.

Avril rounded on her. "Do you want to golf, Lady Seton, or discuss the Highlands?"

That earned her a deadly look from the woman. The spectators' smothered laughter did not help.

Taking a driver from her golf bag, Fiona gave George Gordon an arch look. He placed the ball on the tee for her.

Fiona hit the ball but twisted her leg. "Ouch, my ankle hurts." She limped back and forth on it. "I don't think I can play."

"Perhaps you should return to the palace and keep your leg raised," Queen Mary suggested, her concern apparent.

"I would prefer to watch the game," Fiona said.

"You Majesty, our numbers are dwindling," Avril said, "but I would like us to continue the game."

"I do love golfing," the queen said.

"Shall we spice our game with a friendly wager?" Avril asked. "The woman who holes the ball first wins a gold piece."

Mary flicked a glance at her brother, the Earl of Moray, whose face remained expressionless. Avril suffered the feeling that Mary feared making a misstep.

"I see no problem with wagering," Lord Darnley said.

"Neither do I." Avril ignored her husband's unspoken warning and looked at Moray. "Both the old and new kirks frown on gambling but" – she smiled – "forgiveness for this small sin requires a prayer of contrition, not the purchasing of an indulgence."

When the Earl of Moray laughed, Queen Mary leaned close to Avril. "I've scarcely seen James laugh before you arrived yesterday."

"Alas, many people laugh at me," Avril whispered.

"Are you ladies golfing or sharing confidences?" Moray asked.

Avril approached Magnus, who was holding her golf bag. She donned her fingerless leather gloves and grabbed her ash driving club, balls and tee.

"I know what I'm doing," she whispered.

"That scares me."

Avril sidled up to the tee. Gently but firmly, she gripped the driver and, without taking her eyes off the ball, swung in an arc.

Wham. The ball flew high in the air and landed close to the queen's. The surprised spectators remained silent.

"Great shot, Lady Campbell." Queen Mary applauded her. "I have found a worthy opponent."

"Call me Avril."

The queen slipped her hand through Avril's arm. "Let's walk together."

"Did you hear the story about Reverend John Knoxious?"

Mary smiled at her wit. "Tell me."

"Knox sneaked away for an illicit solo round one Sunday afternoon," Avril said, "but God saw the hypocrite golfing and punished him with a hole in one. Saint Peter protested that a hole in one was no punishment. God cocked an eyebrow at the saint and said, "Oh, no? Who can the righteous reformer tell?""

Queen Mary laughed. "I love it."

"Do not tell your brother," Avril whispered.

"I will tell Lord Darnley," Mary said. "What is your opinion of him?"

"Lord Darnley is an exceedingly handsome gentleman."

"We look good dancing together, don't you think? Most gentlemen are shorter than I."

Avril managed a smile. "Height does not make the man, Your Majesty."

"You are correct," Queen Mary agreed. "What counts most is honour and integrity which Lord Darnley has in abundance."

Avril glanced over her shoulder. Her husband was watching her like a hawk on the hunt. Beside him, Fiona Seton had looped her hand through his arm.

That friendship would die. Soon. Permanently. One way or another.

At the green, Queen Mary took her putter and skillfully dropped the ball into the cup. "You'll need to equal my shot or forfeit a gold piece. Lord Campbell might regret your bold wager."

"Campbell can afford it," Avril said, smiling in his direction. "My husband tells me I married a wealthy man."

Avril stood beside the tee, measuring the distance between the ball and the cup. Then she made a show of walking to the cup and judging the distance from that angle. On her return to the tee, she paused to remove a tiny twig from her intended path.

With putter poised, Avril stood at the tee, her head down and eyes on the ball. Then she tapped it.

The golf ball rolled towards the tee, heading straight for the cup. At the last moment, the ball veered to the right and missed its target.

"Great shot," Mary said, "but you owe me a gold coin."

Avril glanced at her husband. Magnus looked relieved.

And so it went. Avril needed one or two extra shots at each hole, and Queen Mary won the game.

"I would love to play again," Queen Mary said.

"You honour me, Your Majesty." Avril looked in her husband's direction, calling, "Can we afford any more games, my lord?"

All the spectators, including the queen, laughed. Lord Darnley stepped forward to escort the victorious queen to Holyrood Palace.

George Gordon, golf bag slung over his shoulder, escorted Fiona Seton to the Palace. Avril struggled against the urge to draw her *sgian dubh* – the deadly little dagger strapped to her leg – and threaten the Countess of Melrose. The woman wasn't worth the scandal.

Magnus and James Stewart were speaking. Avril approached the two men.

"What were my sister and you discussing?" Moray asked her.

"Nothing important, my lord." Avril noted the earl's gaze narrow on her. "I told her a silly joke about John Knox golfing on Sunday."

"You must share this joke with me," Stewart said, "but I can see you are weary from the game." With that, the earl walked away.

"You do look tired."

"Losing by one or two shots at each hole is more tiring than trying to win."

Magnus looked surprised. "You were purposely losing?"

Avril nodded. "Mary wanted a challenge, not a better golfer to beat her."

"I have underestimated you, wife. How did you become so skilled a golfer?"

"Counting sheep and hitting golf balls provide the only entertainment in the Highlands," Avril answered, echoing Fiona Seton's words.

Magnus laughed and, grasping her upper arms, drew her against the muscular planes of his body. His smile was the last thing Avril saw before his mouth captured hers in a demanding kiss, stealing her breath, sending her senses reeling. His tongue persuaded her lips apart to ravish the sweetness of her mouth.

Avril moaned, her body on fire with her first passionate kiss. Entwining her arms around his neck, Avril moulded her body to his and returned his smouldering kiss in kind.

"Shall we lock ourselves in our bedchamber tonight?" Magnus asked, his voice husky.

Avril answered with a soft smile and pressed her lips against the side of his neck.

"I will consider that a *yes*."

She liked making love.

Avril awakened early the next morning, a drowsy smile on her face, her naked husband beside her. If she had known what awaited her, she would have demanded her conjugal rights three days ago.

The chamber's dimness told her the hour was early, much too early to rise but . . .

She needed to thank the Goddess for sending her this special man for her mate.

She needed to ask the Goddess to protect the queen and allow her to see the true man beneath Darnley's smiling mask.

She needed to worship outside in the open air, where she felt closer to the Goddess.

Avril slipped out of bed without waking her husband. She donned yesterday's gown and jacket, and grabbed her pouch of magic stones. She glanced at her sleeping husband and left the chamber.

Stepping outside the mansion, Avril paused to verify no one would see her and then sprinted across Holyrood Road to the safety the trees provided. She emerged on the other side of the copse. Discretion demanded she cast the circle near the trees instead of at the park's centre.

Avril faced the north and emptied the contents of the pouch into her hand. There were five stones: emerald, aventurine, ruby, amethyst and black obsidian.

Using these stones, Avril made a makeshift circle. She placed the emerald in the north, the aventurine in the east, and the ruby in the south.

"All disturbing thoughts remain outside," she whispered, closing the circle with the amethyst in the west.

Walking to the circle's centre, Avril set the black obsidian down. Then she drew her *sgian dubh* and, starting in the east, fused the circle's invisible periphery shut.

Avril returned to the circle's centre and paused, gathering the proper emotion. "Great Mother Goddess, hear my prayer," she whispered, closing her eyes. "I beseech you to keep Mary Stuart safe. Open my queen's eyes that she may see true hearts, not the disguises people wear. And, I give thanks for sending me a magnificent mate in Magnus Campbell."

Bending to retrieve the black obsidian, Avril noticed her ring. The star ruby had darkened to pigeon's blood red.

Surprised, Avril looked around. Lord Darnley was leaning back against a tree approximately twenty-five yards away. Kneeling in front of him was a boy with pale blond hair. Avril wished she'd worn a hooded cloak; her red hair was impossible to miss.

Refusing to panic, Avril gathered her stones and pretended not to see the men. She felt Darnley's gaze on her. Ignoring his presence, she escaped into the copse and sprinted across Holyrood Road to Campbell Mansion.

Her thoughts twisted in turmoil. Would Darnley accuse her of witchcraft? Would he risk explaining what he'd been doing there at such an early hour?

Should she tell Magnus what happened? She didn't need the Sight to know her husband would be angry. Very angry. Frothing-at-the-mouth angry.

Avril looked at her ring. The dark red was fading, the danger had passed.

Magnus was still sleeping when she returned to their chamber. She disrobed, climbed into bed, and snuggled against his back.

Magnus rolled over, his voice drowsy. "You're shivering."

Avril wrapped her arms around his neck and pressed her body against his. "Warm me, husband."

"With pleasure, wife."

Avril dreaded seeing Darnley at court.

Remaining at Campbell Mansion was not an option, though. Not only would she consider herself a coward, but Darnley would believe she was frightened.

Avril had trouble choosing a gown to wear. She needed to look conservative in case Darnley had been whispering in the queen's ear about what he'd seen that morning. Black seemed too sinister so she opted for grey, the same silvery shade of her husband's eyes.

Walking beside her husband, Avril felt secure. Could he save her if Darnley accused her of witchcraft?

Entering the queen's reception hall, Magnus and Avril saw George Gordon and the Earl of Moray in conversation on the opposite side of the chamber. They walked in that direction, but a voice stopped their progress.

"Lady Campbell?" The Countess of Moray stood there.

"I'll meet you later." Magnus left her.

Avril smiled at the other woman. "Good evening, my lady."

"Walk with me," the countess said, looping her hand through Avril's arm. "I commend your golfing ability and—"

"How else can a woman entertain herself in the Highlands?" Avril quipped.

"Do not let Fiona Seton bother you," the Countess of Moray said.

"The only woman who escapes that witch's sharp tongue is the queen."

"If we could trick Fiona into sniping at the queen" – Avril slashed a finger across her throat – "we need never listen to Fiona Seton again."

The Countess of Moray smiled. "One simple action solves a nagging annoyance."

"Lady Campbell?" Avril recognized Darnley's voice before she turned around. "May I have a word?"

"Which word would you like, my lord?"

The Countess of Moray nodded at Darnley. "I will leave you to your conversation."

Darnley watched the countess walk away and then asked, "Are you practising witchcraft?"

"Do not speak nonsense," Avril said, her tone contemptuous. "Witches exist only in small minds like yours."

"You should speak with respect to the man who may marry the queen," Darnley warned her.

The man was an idiot. A snivelling idiot. A dangerous snivelling idiot.

"My husband will be wondering where I've gone," Avril said. "What do you want?"

"I want to know what you were doing this morning."

Avril looked him straight in the eye. "What were *you* doing this morning?"

Her question caught him off-guard, colouring his face crimson. A smidgen of respect entered his eyes when he realized bullying her would not work.

"Mary likes you," Darnley said. "Singing my praises to the queen would help me forget what I saw."

The man had lost his wits if he expected her to believe that. In the unlucky event he did marry the queen, Darnley would silence Avril by using fair means or foul.

"What do you say, Lady Campbell?"

"I'm sorry," Avril answered, "but I never lie or make deals with the devil." She showed him her back and walked away.

Lost in thought, Avril bumped into the queen's half-brother. The Earl of Moray grasped her arms to prevent her falling.

"I apologise, my lord."

"The fault belongs to me."

His touch disturbed her, but she sensed something else.

Moray's machinations would fail if the queen did not marry Darnley.

"Do you adhere to the new kirk?" she asked him.

The Earl of Moray's smile did not reach his eyes. "From where did this question come?"

Avril gave him an ambiguous smile. "Mere curiosity."

"Walk with me, Lady Campbell." James Stewart smiled and offered his arm.

Avril inclined her head. She was silent for a long moment, the wolves at court worrying her. She needed to save the queen from an unwise decision, and she needed to do that without condemning herself, the Campbells, and the Gordons.

"You have unusual eyes," the earl remarked.

"I inherited my father's blue and my mother's green," Avril said, "Do my eyes trouble you?"

"Disturbing me takes more than blue and green eyes," Moray answered. "Which kirk do you prefer?"

"I prefer whatever my husband prefers," Avril answered, "and my husband places his faith in political expediency."

"If Queen Mary joined the new kirk," Moray asked, "would Campbell follow?"

"I cannot speak for my husband," Avril answered. "Personally, I don't give a fig about churches. God hears everyone's prayers and knows what lies in our secret hearts."

"Well said, Lady Campbell, but do not let Reverend John Knox hear that."

"The reverend fears women," Avril said, "which is the reason he dislikes them. I pray that man burns in hell."

"How indiscreet to say so," Moray remarked, the hint of a smile on his lips. "Have you met Reverend Knox?'

"I never met Old Clootie," Avril answered, "but I know the devil is evil."

His lips twitched. "You believe Reverend Knox is evil?"

Avril slid her gaze across the hall and caught her husband's pointed look. "Campbell is warning me to discretion, but do not allow Queen Mary to marry Darnley."

Moray gave her an interested stare. "Why do you say that?"

Avril wished she'd kept her mouth shut. On the other hand, preventing marriage to Darnley would keep both the queen and her safe.

"My woman's intuition tells me Darnley is not what he appears,"

Avril glanced towards the dais. "The queen will regret marrying him. Darnley's brain is no bigger than a rooster's testicle."

"I like you, Lady Campbell," Moray said, smiling, "and I admire your loyalty to my sister. Take my advice. Return to Argyll and give your husband a dozen children."

"Is that a warning or threat?"

"I would never wish you harm," Moray assured her. "Politics is dangerous business, and you are too kind-hearted."

"What about the queen?"

The Earl of Moray slid his gaze to the dais. "My sister cannot escape her destiny." He offered his arm. "Shall we join the others?"

Magnus and George were conversing with Queen Mary and Darnley. With them were the Earl and Countess of Melrose.

"I hope your ankle has recovered," Avril said to the countess.

"I feel much better today," Fiona said. "I dare say, I won't be dancing for a few days, and I do adore partnering your husband."

Avril slid her gaze to her husband and then her brother. George looked as if he'd sucked a lemon. She knew he was waiting for her to strike back.

"My husband does move incredibly well," Avril said, her expression pleasant.

"I can vouch for that." Fiona gave her a decidedly feline smile. "Your eye colour is quite unusual. Have you ever been accused of witchcraft?"

Everyone, including the queen, laughed at such a ridiculous notion. Avril wondered if Darnley had begun spreading rumours.

"Have *you* been accused of witchcraft?" Avril countered. "Your tongue cuts like an evil old crone's."

Fiona paled at the insult. An awkward cloud of silence hovered over the group.

Avril refused to look at her husband or her brother. She had no wish to see their expressions of disapproval.

A footman, his hair the palest blond, arrived at that moment to serve them wine. Avril stared at the young man's hair and then looked at Darnley, who was smirking at her.

"If you were my wife," Darnley said, "I would poison your wine."

Avril gave him an insincere smile. "If I was your wife, I would drink it."

The Earl of Moray shouted with laughter. "Lady Campbell, you will never bore your husband."

"Your Majesty, please excuse my wife's lapse in manners."

Avril rounded on Magnus, ready for battle. But she remained silent, heeding the warning in his gaze.

"I apologise for my sister," George Gordon added.

"Charles provoked Avril," Mary said. "It was a poor joke but no harm intended."

The danger had merely been delayed. Protecting herself from Darnley, Avril placed her palm against her midsection. "The babe rules my tongue."

"You should not have golfed in your condition," Queen Mary said. "I had no idea."

Magnus put his arm around her. "We decided to wait before sharing our good news."

"It's early days yet," Avril said, leaning against her husband.

"Too early, if you ask me."

"Nobody asked you, Darnley," the Earl of Moray said. "I know from personal experience that babes upset their mothers from the moment of conception."

"With your permission, I will take my wife home," Magnus said, "before the babe insults someone else."

"I understand." Queen Mary looked at Avril, saying, "I envy your good news."

"Your day will come, Your Majesty. Until then, I will name my daughter in your honour."

And they left the reception hall.

Avril cast a sidelong glance at her husband, who stared straight ahead. Only a blind woman could miss his tight-lipped anger.

"Magnus?"

"Do not speak."

Magnus marched her like a recalcitrant child into Campbell Mansion and up the stairs to their bedchamber. "Sit in front of the hearth," he ordered, pausing to lock the door.

Avril felt a momentary panic. "Why are you doing that?"

"Do not play the henwit," Magnus said, walking towards her. "I'm not planning to beat common sense into you." He dropped into the chair beside hers. "Tell me everything."

"What do you mean?"

"Damn it, wife." Magnus banged his fist on the arm of the chair. "Darnley is sniping at you, Moray is defending you, and you are announcing a non-existent pregnancy."

"I know the situation looks bad," Avril said, "but enemies surround the queen."

"I want facts, not hocus-pocus."

"Do not play the unconscious brick," Avril said. "Even you should feel the negative undercurrents swirling around court."

"Begin at the beginning," Magnus said, reaching for her hand. "Include facts along with your intuition."

"Darnley is morally corrupt," Avril said, "and Moray's soul is darker than the inside of a grave."

"You mentioned that Moray covets the crown," Magnus said, "but he can never claim it because of his birth."

"Even bastards harbour ambitions, more than properly-born men."

"I agree. Please continue."

"Marriage to Darnley will ruin Mary," Avril said, "and marriage to another gentleman will neutralize Moray."

Avril did not want to tell her husband that she'd jeopardized them by worshipping outside but if he was going to handle the situation, he needed to know the whole truth.

"When I awakened early this morning, I was happy about marrying a magnificent man but worried about the queen's future," Avril told him. "I decided to consult the Goddess."

Magnus looked flabbergasted. "Whom did you consult?"

"The Great Mother Goddess protects her children," Avril answered.

Her husband was staring at her as if she'd grown another head. "What are you?"

"Like my mother before me, I follow the Old Ways."

"Sweet Jesus, you're a pagan?"

His attitude did not sit well with Avril. "Pagans do not slaughter each other," she defended herself. "Only squabbling kirks encourage murder."

"Stifle the sermon."

"An irresistible impulse grabbed me this morning," Avril said. "I sneaked out of the house and dashed across the road to Holyrood Park. I cast the magic circle and worshipped the Goddess. It was then I noticed the star ruby had darkened into pigeon's blood red. Nearby I saw Darnley and a blond boy. They were lovers."

Her husband's expression registered shock. "You saw this?"

"Darnley tried to blackmail me tonight," Avril added. "He asked if I practised witchcraft. We must warn Mary so she won't marry him."

"What matters to me is your safety," Magnus said. "You've made an enemy in Darnley. Your enemies are my enemies and your brother's."

"I insulated myself from his venom by claiming pregnancy," Avril said, "and Moray defended me because he dislikes Darnley."

"Argyll offers the best refuge," her husband said. "We'll need to leave Edinburgh."

"I do not fear Darnley," she argued. "Our queen needs us,"

"Kings and queens come and go," Magnus said, standing, "but the clans must survive. I'll need to return to court and ask the queen's permission to leave for Argyll."

"I want to bid Mary a personal farewell before we leave."

Magnus stared at her for a long moment. "I'll see what I can do."

"How long will you be gone?"

"I do not answer to you." Magnus unlocked the door and quit the chamber. "I will return when I return."

Avril waited hours. She paced the chamber, peered out the window, and then sat in the chair. Again and again and again.

Still, Magnus did not return. Where was he? Was he dancing with Fiona Seton? Or worse? What would she do if he left her in Argyll and returned to Edinburgh?

The door opened, drawing her attention. His expression weary, Magnus crossed the chamber to sit in the chair beside hers. "Queen Mary will receive you late morning."

"Thank you, husband."

Magnus gave her a tired smile. "I never imagined a wife could create this much trouble, but I agree with your assessment of Darnley and Moray." He took her hand in his. "Mary likes George, and your brother will do whatever he can without endangering the Campbells and Gordons."

Avril felt a weight lifted from her heart. "Then you aren't dumping me in Argyll or divorcing me?"

Magnus gave her hand a gentle squeeze. "Why would a man divorce the woman he loves?"

Love? Avril couldn't credit what she'd heard, and her expression mirrored confusion.

Without another word, Magnus rose from the chair and opened

his cabinet. After rummaging through his belongings, he returned with three miniature portraits.

Magnus handed her the first miniature, a portrait of her at age eight. The second miniature showed her at age twelve, and the third at sixteen years.

"I asked your father to send me your portraits as you aged." Magnus offered her his hand as if requesting a dance. "Can we go to bed now?"

Avril looked from his hand to his eyes. She placed her smaller hand in his and rose from the chair. Entwining her arms around his neck, she pressed her body to his and rested her head against his chest.

Magnus and Avril stood wrapped in embrace for a long, long time.

At noon the next day, Magnus guided Avril through Holyrood Palace's winding corridors and up narrow staircases. Mary had invited Avril to visit the royal apartment instead of the reception hall.

"You will go inside alone," Magnus said, tapping on the sitting room door. "Mary and I said our good-byes last night."

"How do I look?" Avril asked him.

Magnus inspected her from the top of her fiery mane down her body – clad in a blue riding outfit – to her boots. "Your beauty could entice John Knox to sin."

"You are an incorrigible flatterer."

One of the four Marys opened the door. She smiled at Avril and beckoned her into the room. Queen Mary was alone except for her four ladies-in-waiting.

"I do apologise if I've done or said anything to upset you," Avril said, curtseying to the queen. "I will think of you often and always remain your devoted subject."

Queen Mary smiled at that. "You will return to court after the babe is born."

"I fear we will never meet again in this lifetime." With tears welling in her eyes, Avril knelt in front of the queen. She removed the ruby ring from her finger and offered it to the queen. "Please accept this token of my loyalty."

Unexpectedly, Queen Mary placed her palm against Avril's cheek. Then the queen slipped the ring on to the third finger of her right hand.

"Danger lurks when the stone darkens," Avril reminded her. She lowered her voice to an urgent whisper. "No matter what happens in Scotland, do not set foot in England unless Elizabeth Tudor is dead."

Queen Mary seemed bewildered by the warning. "I will remember your words."

What else could she have expected from the queen? Mary Stuart had been loved, protected and pampered – deservedly so – since the hour of her birth. Perhaps she would never understand the evil ambitions and hatreds simmering below the surface of the court and Scotland.

On impulse, Avril kissed the queen's hand and stood. Then she backed her way to the door and left the royal sitting room.

Waiting in the hallway, Magnus wiped the tears rolling down her cheeks. Avril gave him a sad smile. Even her husband would never believe the rising storm headed for Scotland.

Knowing what others did not would forever prove a curse.

Avril kissed her husband's cheek and murmured, "When Mary Stuart goes, we will never see such a bonny queen again, and Scotland will be the poorer for it."

Inverary Castle, 1568

Avril rested in a chair in front of the hearth in the great hall. Gordon, her one-year-old son, sat on her lap and gave her a two-toothed smile.

"Some day I will teach you to golf with King James," Avril told him. "You must learn to lose without seeming to do so. Understand?"

Gordon pointed a chubby finger at the centre of her face. "Nose."

"Very good, my son." Avril pointed at his face. "What's that, Gordy?"

"Nose."

"And what is this?" She pointed to his mouth.

"Kiss, kiss, kiss." Gordon pressed his drooling mouth on hers.

Avril laughed. Gordon laughed when she did.

"Ah, there are my two favourite people in the world." Looking travel weary, Magnus stood in the doorway.

"Da."

Avril rose from the chair and set her son down on his feet. "Stay there. Gordy has a surprise for you." She whispered to her son, "Walk to Da."

Holding his arms out for balance, Gordon tottered towards his father. Behind him hovered his mother, ready to catch his fall.

Magnus grabbed his son and lifted him high, making the boy laugh. Then he planted a kiss on Avril's mouth. "I missed you."

They sat together in front of the hearth, the baby resting his head against his father's shoulder. Magnus reached inside his leather jerkin and passed her a letter.

Avril looked at the letter from Queen Mary, currently imprisoned in England. She broke the seal, asking, "Why didn't you read it?"

"The queen addressed the letter to you, not me."

"Mary wishes us well and sends best wishes to our son," Avril told him, tears welling in her eyes. "Mary yearns to see her own son and should have listened to my warning. She thinks of me often and would love to play another round of golf. Only this time—"

Raw emotion caught in her throat, making swallowing difficult. "Only this time she would prefer I do not purposely lose. Oh, Magnus, I have so much and the queen so little."

Her son reached to touch her cheek. "Wet, Mama."

Avril kissed her son's fingers. "Is there any possible way to free Mary?"

Magnus shook his head. "I doubt it."

"I curse Elizabeth Tudor," Avril said, "and I curse the Earl of Moray.

"Moray does not wear the crown," Magnus reminded her.

"Moray rules Scotland for his nephew. Where lies the difference?" Avril fell silent for a long moment. "How much does an assassin cost?"

"What?" Her husband had paled by several shades.

"You heard me," Avril said. "The Hamiltons have long been loyal to Mary and share a connection to France. Do you think—?"

"I think," Magnus interrupted, "I will not discuss murder in my hall." He lifted his son into the air and kissed his belly, making the boy laugh. "Always obey your mother, Gordy, because she is a bloodthirsty wench."

"Seeking justice is not bloodthirsty."

"You are hitting justice over the head, darling, not seeking it."

"Admit it," Avril said with a smile. "You love me the way I am."

"I do love your big heart" – Magnus dropped his gaze to her body – "as well as several interesting body parts."

Magnus shifted his son in his arms. Then he leaned close to her, his mouth capturing hers.

"Kiss," Gordon chirped. "Kiss, kiss, kiss."

Wolfish in Sheep's Clothing

Marta Acosta

As Katherine Samuelson trudged up Princes Street, she cursed her best friend, Emma MacNeil, and she cursed the sleet that slanted down, making every step a chore. Kathy tucked her chin to hold the handle of her umbrella, and balanced bags on each shoulder while dragging a wheeled suitcase behind her. Edinburgh was supposed to be a high point of this vacation. "It will be a life-changing experience," Emma had said. "I can see it perfectly."

"Not one of your *visions*," Kathy had answered, trying to toss back her hair – but her dark reddish curls only bounced.

"I am a seer, you know that." Emma's own head toss had been much more successful, since her sandy blond hair was a long straight fall. "I have the famous MacNeil sight, and I see a man . . ."

"Emma, the way you look, I'm surprised you don't see a whole army of men."

"A man in a kilt."

At that point, Kathy had laughed so hard that Emma had sulked until she apologised. They'd met when Kathy had answered an ad for a roommate, but since then Emma had gone through a dozen boyfriends and was now engaged.

Most of Emma's predictions were easy to ignore. Occasionally, however, Emma was unnervingly right, like the time that she'd begged Kathy not to go to a Christmas party that ended in tragedy when the holiday decorations caught fire. So Kathy considered this outlandish vision. Besides, she wanted to go on a trip with her friend. She scrimped and saved for over a year. She sublet the space in her tiny knitting shop – Stitch in Time – to a quilter to hold classes.

When Emma cancelled at the last minute, Kathy was furious. Emma had said, "I'm sorry, but everything's gone all on the wonk with Tommy and if I leave I'm afraid it will be over."

"*We'll* be over if you don't come."

"You don't mean that. You want me to be happy."

"You'll be happy when you find your man in a kilt."

"I didn't see Tommy's horrible knobby knees in my vision. Then I had the vision again and this time you were there in a sapphire blue coat. Don't be mad, Kitty Kat."

"Don't call me that. In fact, don't call me at all."

What was supposed to be a grand adventure had turned into a lonely journey getting lost and fending off predatory men who were attracted to the solitary woman with gleaming mahogany curls. Kathy had downgraded all her hotel reservations to save money because she lived by her parents' credo: waste not, want not. Now, she was exhausted, cold, and lost again as she approached a lavish hotel she had already passed twice. At least she had a warm coat.

The ultramarine lambswool coat had been her one extravagance. When she'd seen it in the window of a boutique on the Avenue de l'Opéra, she'd stopped to stare. The A-line style was so classic that the coat would always be chic. Emma had said that she'd seen a sapphire blue coat in her vision. It was a crazy thing to do, but Kathy bought it.

She had just paused to adjust her bags, when a sleek black Citroen sedan pulled up to the curb in front of the hotel ahead.

A doorman with an enormous umbrella escorted a couple out of the hotel as a parking valet jumped out of the car and opened the passenger door for a beautiful blonde woman. Then the parking valet rushed to hold the other door for a tall dark-haired man in a black trench coat.

When the tall man glanced at the valet, Kathy saw that he had high cheekbones, a long strong nose, dark eyes and a firm jaw. He was the sort of man who drove expensive new cars, dated beautiful blondes, and stayed in luxury hotels.

Kathy yearned for that confident, gorgeous, successful kind of man, that kind of life, one of elegance and luxury. She forgot about her exhaustion as she watched him get into the car. Then the car drove off and suddenly swerved into a puddle, splashing up a wave of filthy gutter water as it passed her.

Kathy looked down and saw the huge muddy splotches covering one side of her exquisite coat. She released the umbrella from under her chin, dropped her tote and said, "No, no, no!" Then she gathered her things up, her bags banging against her sides, and splashed up to the hotel.

A doorman tipped his hat to her. "Morning, madam."

"That man splashed my coat when he drove by! You saw him. Who is he?"

The doorman looked at her with sympathy and his shoulders went up a little. "Apologies, but I don't know."

Before Kathy had been too embarrassed to ask at the hotel for directions, but now she stormed inside, her wheeled case rattling behind her. She saw a concierge at a side desk and went directly to the woman, who smiled pleasantly, noticed the dirty coat, and said, "Good day. May I help you?"

"Hello. One of your guests just ruined my coat. It's brand new and . . . and he just left without even looking. Your doorman saw it all."

"I apologise for your misfortune," the concierge said in a calm, quiet voice.

"Thanks. If you could give me his name and contact info. He just left here with a blond woman and he was wearing a black trench."

"I'm sorry, but we're not at liberty to discuss guests' private information."

Kathy blinked back tears. "It's a very expensive coat, the best thing I own . . ."

The manager dropped her voice and said, "We cannot discuss our guests, but if someone was *not* a guest . . . I think I recall the gentleman you mean. I believe he came for a meeting in one of the conference rooms, but I'm afraid I don't know who he is."

Kathy finally noticed her opulent surroundings and realized that her bags, her coat and even her hair were dripping on the fine carpet. "Maybe it can be dry-cleaned," she said sadly.

"I'm sure it can." A few minutes later, Kathy had a cleaner's business card as well as a map with directions to her economy hotel.

The hotel was a narrow building on a narrow street. The manager led her to a tiny, but clean room on the third floor with a cramped bathroom and a shallow armoire. Kathy noticed the effort that had been made to make the room comfortable: an electric kettle and assortment of teas on a side table, a mixed bouquet of bright flowers in a vase, and pretty prints of the city.

The manager said, "Pity you're visiting in this *draich*. You look like you've got the worst of it."

"Someone splashed my coat when he drove by."

"I'm sorry to hear that." She made a *tching* sound.

As soon as she was alone, Kathy took off her coat and examined the muddy splotches. She spread it out on the bed and used a wet facecloth and a bar of soap to dab at the marks. It didn't take long for Kathy to realize that the muddy water had contained motor oil and no amount of effort would remove the stains.

She sat on the thin mattress and wept. She could feel sorry for herself, or she could enjoy her holiday. Kathy wiped her eyes and decided to make the very best of today.

After all, it was her twenty-ninth birthday.

She unpacked and put all her things away neatly, because her mother had taught her, "A place for everything and every thing in its place." Then Kathy made a cup of tea and drank it while studying a guidebook and a map.

When she felt revived, she put on her stained coat and went out to explore the city on foot. The rain had let up to a steady drizzle, and Kathy did what she enjoyed, stopping in the knitting shops and examining the marvellous goods. Even though she was still mad at Emma, she bought a robin's-egg blue cashmere cardigan for her. She saw a pair of chocolate brown lambskin gloves and she thought of how her mother would have liked them.

Kathy's lunch was a packaged salad that she bought in a grocery store and quickly ate outside under an overhang. It wasn't something she normally did, but the trip wasn't normal for her either, and she felt unfettered and a bit reckless, like a well-behaved pet that discovers an open gate.

Then Kathy strolled to the National Museum and spent an hour viewing the fossils and artefacts. She kept returning to a richly textured painting of three sheep on a hilly landscape in a place called Orkney. She felt a sense of peace and happiness when she gazed at the rugged hills and stormy sky.

Darkness came early and Kathy returned to her hotel and rested. Because of the occasion, she'd kept her reservation for dinner at one of the city's best restaurants. Emma had promised to treat her, and now Kathy missed her lunatic friend and thought of how Emma would have made her laugh about the careless jerk.

Kathy felt better after a shower. Her everyday clothes were cotton, so it was a treat to dress up. She began with her undergarments, wearing a black silk bra and panties. She hated the feel of nylon on her skin so now she carefully pulled on black silk thigh-high stockings with stretchy lace tops.

Then she put on a teal silk-knit jersey wrap-around dress with a deep v-neckline that accentuated her full breasts, made her waistline smaller, and flowed smoothly over the generous curve of her hips. To counteract her winter pallor, she used dramatic dark shadow and kohl around her golden-hazel eyes, layers of mascara, and deep rosy lipgloss.

She slid her feet into black pumps with teetering narrow heels and added a lustrous gold cuff bracelet and earrings. Her ex-boyfriend had given them to her as a birthday present when she was twenty-three. It seemed like a long time ago.

When she looked in the mirror, she saw a sophisticated and sexy woman, not the pretty, but rather ordinary girl-next-door she really was. She grabbed her ruined coat and went downstairs.

The hotel manager said, "Why aren't ye bonny! Special occasion, is it?"

"Yes, it's my birthday. Can you tell me if there's an internet café nearby?"

"Happy birthday! You can use the computer in our business centre, sweetie."

The business centre was a closet with a narrow desk under the staircase. When she checked her email, there were several birthday greetings, including a dozen from Emma. All but one of them read "Happy birthday!"

The last message was odd, even for Emma, who'd written "*Carpe diem*. Dare to be someone different today . . . let your wicked side out. I saw it in a dream. Also, I have arranged a special birthday treat for you! A visit to my mother's cousin's cousin's historic castle. Will send details tomorrow. Cancel all other plans. Am I forgiven?"

Kathy smiled and wrote, "Weather is dreadful and so are you. Wish you were here. I'll reserve the date." After thinking for a second, she added, "Forgiven for what? Love, K" and sent it off.

Kathy asked the manager to call a cab, and the woman said,

"You cannae go out in that coat." She went to the office closet and brought back an old-fashioned moss-green mohair coat. "It's warm and the colour suits. It's been left here for years, so keep it."

Kathy took the unexpected birthday present and said, "Thank you! You're too kind." A few minutes later, she was in the back seat of a small warm car, dashing up the hill towards Edinburgh Castle. The wet surfaces reflected shop lights and street lights, making the city look magical.

The restaurant was set beside theatres and bustling with Friday evening excitement. Kathy inhaled marvellous aromas as she took off her coat and left it in the cloakroom. As Kathy was escorted to her seat, men turned to watch, while women gave her more subtle once-overs.

The maitre d' showed her to a table in a corner. It was too dark to study her guidebook here, but at least she could observe others. A waiter soon glided over with a menu. The prices were awfully high, though, and she was mentally converting pounds to dollars when the maitre d' returned with a concerned smile.

"Yes?" Kathy said, looking up.

"I apologise for disturbing you, but we inadvertently doubled-booked a table and I thought you might not mind, considering the circumstances . . ." He spoke with the precise accent of a BBC Scotland announcer.

"Mind what?" She hoped that he wasn't going to ask her to move outside to the covered terrace, where latecomers huddled by patio heaters, because she wasn't going to move, not on her birthday.

"I thought you might not mind sharing your table with another guest."

Kathy wondered how she would have felt if her table had been given away. "Of course not," she said, hoping that the other guest wasn't talkative or rude.

"Thank you! You've saved me. Allow me to offer you a complimentary drink?"

"I think a glass of champagne would be nice."

"Only a glass?" said a deep voice with a warm soft brogue. "Why nae a bottle?"

Kathy turned her head and saw a gorgeous man – the careless man who had ruined her coat. He looked at the maitre d' and said,

"The '99 Ayala," and the maitre d' replied, "Excellent choice, sir," and left.

The man seemed bigger up close – about six foot three – and those dark eyes were blue as they caught her own glance and then travelled down the neckline of her dress to the curves of her breasts. One corner of his wide, well-shaped mouth lifted in appreciation.

Kathy felt her cheeks grow hot in anger and self-consciousness and watched him seat himself across the small table. His hair was deep chestnut, a little long and brushed back from a widow's peak, and his shoulders were wide in an inky black-blue suit. He wore a pale blue shirt that was open at the collar.

A waiter came over quickly, handed the man a menu, and left. The man smiled at Kathy and said, "Thenk ye for sharing yer table." His voice was as beguiling as a fresh breeze.

"It's no problem." Kathy picked up her menu and tried to focus on the descriptions.

"A'm Calder, an ye . . . ?"

She looked up and right into the dazzling eyes of the man who had ruined her beautiful coat. Then she remembered Emma's advice: dare to be someone different today, be wicked. "I'm Kat."

"A pleasure to meet ye, Kat," he said, and the name sounded right to her, the sort of name a sophisticated world-traveller would have. "Please allow me to buy dinner in exchange for depriving you of yer tranquillity." He rolled his r's luxuriously, as if he had all the time in the world to talk to her.

Kathy was going to decline, and then thought – *be wicked!* "I do enjoy my solitude, so I'll accept your offer."

"You're an American?" he asked, clearly pronouncing "you're".

"Yes, but I'll try not to hold it over you." She glanced at his hand and saw that he wasn't wearing a wedding band – but some men didn't.

He grinned. "You have that American look of self-sufficiency. I'll try to speak so you can understand me."

The waiter came by with their champagne and an ice bucket on a stand. Kathy kept her eyes on the menu as the waiter went about opening the bottle and Calder tasted it. She was now looking at the most expensive items on the menu so that she could at least eat part of her loss back.

"Would you like to order now?" the waiter asked.

Kathy – no, Kat, said, "Yes, I'll start with the smoked salmon.

Then I'll have the halibut with mussel sauce. For dessert, I'd like the chocolate mousse with sorbet."

Calder snapped the menu shut and said to the waiter, "I'll have the same."

"Sir?" asked the waiter, puzzled.

"Also a bottle of still water," Calder said. "We'll finish with the Highland Park. Thanks."

When the waiter left, she let herself gaze boldly at her host, but she couldn't help smiling.

He lifted his glass and said, "Guid health." She lifted hers, too, and said, "Cheers."

"It's unusual to see a woman confident enough to dine alone."

"Is it?" She had been about to tell him about her coat, but she didn't want to ruin his image of her now with a vague recollection of someone trudging in the rain with an umbrella under her chin. She took a sip of her champagne and looked at him over the top of the flute.

"Certainly. Women always seem to travel in herds, or with some girlfriend. If they go to a café, they hide in a book," he said. "I'm glad you're not hiding your lovely face."

It had been a very long time since a man had flirted with her, and no man this handsome had flirted with her since before . . . before she made the mistake of wasting five years of her life with mundane Will Sloat, who decided that he needed "space" and actually told her, "It's not you. It's me," before moving out.

Kat just nodded her head slightly, accepting Calder's compliment.

"Are you on holiday or do you live here?" he asked.

"I'm travelling. I started in Paris, went to London, and now I'm here in Scotland."

"Travelling by yourself, Kat?"

"Yes, unless you're going to tell me that most women vacation in pairs, or on guided tours."

Their first course arrived and the waiter refilled their champagne, even though Kat didn't remember finishing her glass.

"I must seem terribly old-fashioned to you," Calder said. "Actually I admire independence in a woman."

"I'm ecstatic to have earned your approval," she said, and he laughed. "What about you? Do you usually intrude on strangers' tables and order whatever it is they order?"

"Never before, Kat, but the experience is proving so delightful that I believe I'll make a habit of it."

Now she was the one who laughed. As they began sampling the delicious and duplicated dishes, she said, "Do you live here, or are you visiting?"

"I'm here on business for a few days."

She noticed that he didn't say where he lived, and she could guess what kind of business he'd have with a beautiful woman in an expensive hotel.

Kat took a bite of the silky smooth smoked salmon. "What's your business?"

"I'd rather not blether about it now, because it's nothing but trouble. How about you? Do you have a business, or does your husband want to keep you at home for himself?"

Kathy's knitting business was in a corner of a shared artspace and she was constantly anxious that the rent would be increased. She loved her store, but it was far from her dream business, so she replaced the reality with the dream. "I live in the Northern California countryside and raise sheep and goats. It's very beautiful and I have week-long retreats there for women . . . and the occasional man . . . to learn knitting techniques and needlecrafts. My next step is a course in hand-dying wool and I'm ordering looms."

Calder's eyes twinkled. "Are you now? And I thought *I* was old-fashioned."

"The old is new again, Calder. Teens are excited to carry on traditions."

"Do you do this all on your own?"

She did everything on her own, including repairing the plumbing and installing the light fixtures. "Heavens, no, I have staff. Things are going so well that I'm going to expand my retreats. I'll have chefs to teach cooking sessions, authors to lead writing workshops, and vintners and cheesemakers to have lectures and tastings."

His eyebrows knitted together and, maybe it was the champagne, but Kat thought she'd never seen such a charming expression. He said, "What an interesting occupation. Do you have classes year-round?"

"Oh, yes! In summer, we sit under the trees and work for hours before all cooking a meal together. We make jams and jellies from the fruits grown on the property. In the winter, we gather in the great room, with a fire in the hearth keeping us warm, and bake bread and make stews. We drink local wines, play the piano, and sing." Kat could describe it because she'd envisioned the scenes hundreds of times. "People come back year after year."

"Are there other retreats like this in the States?"

"There are weekend retreats and even cruises, but I think my place is special," she said. "But I don't want to bore you."

"You aren't boring me in the least, Kat. I think your country estate must be quite civilized, because I can't imagine you chasing goats out of the lounge."

Kat ran her fingers up and down the stem of the champagne flute. "We're talking about me again."

"It's become my favourite subject."

They ate quietly for several minutes and finally the waiter brought their second courses, trying to find room for them on the small tabletop. When he had gone, Calder said, "You can ask me anything you like."

"You can tell me whatever you choose."

He considered and then said, "My mother and aunts knit beautifully. Although when I was a boy, I didn't appreciate wearing handmade jumpers and long scarves. I wanted to wear what the other lads were wearing, track jackets and anything with sports logos."

"You were a heathen."

"To be sure. I would purposely fall from my bike or skateboard hoping to destroy things, but then my mother would mend them, which made things worse. My mates would all laugh at me."

So Calder was a poor boy who'd made good in the big city, she thought. A boy who didn't understand thriftiness and gifts made with love. A careless boy who had become a careless man.

"School?" she asked.

"Hated it, but I did exceedingly well, because when I do anything, I do it exceedingly well. *Anything*."

Calder's upper body didn't move, but Kat felt his leg against her own, making her every nerve jump. It was only the lightest, possibly *accidental* touch, but Kat didn't think so when she saw the smile playing on his lips. She was suddenly thinking of what else he did quite well.

"Calder, if you need more room for your legs, you can set your chair back."

"My legs are comfortable where they are. I thought yours might be cold," he said, pressing his leg more boldly against hers.

His flattery and confidence excited and confused her, because he was so very beautiful, and she was just . . . "If you think you're entitled to anything because you're picking up the bill, you're wrong. I came here expecting to pay for my own meal, not to trade favours for it."

"I wasn't implying . . ."

She took a bite of the delicious fresh halibut and enjoyed his chagrined expression. "It's all right," she said.

"You'll forgive me?"

"I'm forgiving a lot of people today. Yes."

"Who else needs forgiveness?"

"A friend who told me I should come on this trip. She claims to have 'the sight', and said I'd meet a man in a kilt."

"Don't mock 'the sight'. Many women in my family have it." He grinned roguishly. "*I* have a kilt."

"So does every man in every tourist shop here."

Sighing dramatically, he said, "You're making me feel very unappreciated."

"I'm sure your ego will recover."

"It will if you'll still allow me to pay for the meal."

"Yes, but only because I feel sorry for you, Calder," she said, and they laughed together.

Dessert came and their conversation became lighter, although Kat was always aware of his long legs under the table, his blue eyes, and the tension between the two of them. Between Calder and confident, sexy Kat.

She'd wondered what he'd ordered last and, as it turned out, the Highland Park was a single-malt scotch. Calder lifted his glass to her and said, "Most welcome sunshine on a chilly day. Hold it in your mouth and let it bloom inside."

Even though he hadn't said anything improper, Kat thought it sounded dirty. Maybe it was her imagination, which kept thinking of what those large hands would feel like on her skin. She took a sip of the drink and tasted an almost honeyed sweet note, faint smoke and peat, orange blossoms, unlike anything she'd had before. "It's delicious."

"The distillery is in Orkney. The islands are said to be inhabited by *trows*."

Orkney sounded familiar, and she remembered the marvellous painting she'd seen. "What are trows?"

"Like leprechauns, though not as nice. Evil hideous little buggers that cause naught but mischief in the night."

"Have you ever seen one?" she teased.

"My mother says that I *am* one," he answered. "A giant trow baby, so big that they feared what I would become, so the trows stole away her own *buey bain* and placed me in his crib, which is why I've a passion for music and song, like my true wicked kin. They say that at the weetin' of my heid," and here Calder tapped his head to show her what he meant, "I toasted my father and asked him for a proper tipple."

She laughed in a way she hadn't since she was young. "Your suit is camouflage then, like your brogue, which comes and goes. You're trying to pass as a civilized human being, but there's still some wildness in you."

"Perhaps you can domesticate me, Kat."

"I'm sure other women have tried and failed."

He winked and said, "There's always the first time." He held his glass so that it caught the light from the candle on their table. "This is the same amber as your eyes, Kat."

"Does your wife know you flirt like this?"

"If I had a wife, she'd know. Would you like to marry me?"

"Not now. Ask me later." She took another sip of the scotch and felt tingly and sexy.

"Then would you like to hear some music? Or if you prefer some place posh . . ."

"I'd like to go where the locals go."

She was aware of the maitre d's satisfied glance as they left together. Calder helped her into her coat and stared at her oddly when she had it on.

A valet brought Calder's car, and Kat had a moment of trepidation as Calder held the door open for her. "You won't kidnap me, will you?"

If he had answered, "You can trust me," the catch phrase of every sleazy man she'd ever met, Kathy would have said goodnight and caught a taxi. But Calder said, "Nae, lassie, because I think you've a taste for the finer things, and I'm still a bit of a heathen."

Calder drove to an outlying neighbourhood and turned into a car park. "If you don't like it I'll take you back to your hotel, or wherever you wish to go." He got out and opened the car door for Kat, and then led her down a lively street of shops, cafés and restaurants. Music *thump-thumped* outside the pub, and Calder paid for their entrance, took her arm, as he guided her inside the packed room.

A rollicking bar band blasted out a brash folky-rock song, and they found space standing against a wall. Calder leaned down to speak into her ear and she could smell his faint woody aftershave. He said, "Is this acceptable?"

Kat looked up into his dark eyes, smiled and nodded. "Yes."

He shrugged out of his jacket and helped her off with her coat, and then he got drinks for them. Kat quickly drank a bottle of water, hoping to clear her head because she felt dizzy from the music, Calder beside her, the heat of the room, the loud voices. He said, "Will ye dance wi me?" and drew her into the melee. She felt the thrill of dancing wildly on a Friday night in an exciting city with a sexy man.

One song led to another and another and then there was a slow number, and Calder pulled her close. When he looked into her eyes, her breath caught. She felt the muscles in his back and the slight dampness of the shirt clinging to his skin; his hand on her lower back, his fingers extending down to her hip.

When the song was over, he kept his arm around her waist and said, "It's hot in here." He grabbed their coats and led her out a side door and into a narrow dark alley. The drizzle and chill night air were delicious on her hot skin, and Calder pulled her tightly to him and bent down to kiss her.

It wasn't a tentative, gentle, first-date kind of kiss. It was firm and hungry, an uncivilized, dangerous kiss, and she opened her mouth and felt his tongue slide in against hers. He tasted of scotch and his hands dropped lower on her hips, clutching her to his own.

She'd reached into his shirt, feeling the hot skin beneath, and his hands were moving now, too. She had the giddy sense that someone would catch them like this, kissing as madly as teenagers.

His mouth went to her ear, her neck, the curve of her breast, and he said huskily, "Kat . . . do you want to go to your hotel?"

She thought of the tiny room, the thin mattress, and said, "Where are you staying?"

"Close by. No one is there."

"Let's go," she said, which was crazy because she *never* did things like this. Or Kathy never did. Kat was laughing with Calder as he took her hand and they rushed to a nearby residential block off the main road.

The townhouse looked very expensive and old, with steps leading to two glossy black doors. Calder unlocked one and he held Kat's hand as they went upstairs. He flicked on a lamp when they reached the landing. She saw a wide dining room that opened to a living room with polished hardwood floors, creamy walls, modern furniture and abstract oil paintings.

Calder turned to her and ran the back of his fingers over her cheek. She leaned into his caress, and he said, "You're quite beautiful, you know, like this, your hair every which way and your makeup smudged and looking like a wild creature. A very beautiful wild Kat."

He kissed her as they went down the hall. She saw the door to the bathroom, and said, "I'll just be a moment." When she was alone and the door closed, she took a minute to wonder if this was what she wanted to do, and the answer was yes, yes, yes. She freshened up, but left her hair as it was, a mass of corkscrews and frizz.

When she came out, she saw light from an open doorway and went to it, saying, "Calder?" Fragrant beeswax candles in pewter candlesticks cast a soft glow on a stylish room in ivory and sea-green with black minimalist furniture. Calder smiled at Kat she went to him. He took her hand and lifted it to his lips, kissing it gently.

Then he said, "Kat, I think you're a woman who always gets *what* you want, *when* you want it, but we'll take things at my pace now."

She could feel her heart pounding in her chest and felt a flush of annoyance. "Why the rush?"

"On the contrary, I'm going to show you the value of patience." He ran his forefinger over her lips softly and she opened them and took his finger into her mouth, sucking and biting down. She saw the rise and fall of his chest and reached out, but he stepped back and said, "Patience, Kat."

She was so surprised – and very intrigued.

Calder just stared at her for a moment, up and down, his eyes resting longest on her breasts, then moving downward in a way that made her body tense and excited. He leaned down and began kissing above the deep v-neck of her dress. His fingers would lightly graze the curve of her breasts and then move to stroke her hip.

Hers was an ordinary body, with practical hips and practical breasts, and a practical small curve of tummy, and legs that could stand or walk all day long. But Calder's touch made her feel the wonder of it, the loveliness of being a woman.

She let out a small sound of pleasure when he pulled the fabric of her dress up to caress her thigh. His fingers explored the lace tops of her thigh highs and his eyes widened. He let her hem fall again, and began running his fingers beneath her neckline into the cups of her bra. When she'd press towards him, he'd stop and nuzzle her neck.

Thrilled and frustrated, she stood still. Finally, he tugged at the tie that held her dress closed, slowly unwrapping the dress and letting it fall to the white sheepskin rug. He gazed at her in her black bra, panties, thigh-highs and heels, and he inhaled deeply.

"Silk stockings," he said, pleased. "You're full of surprises, Kat."

She watched as Calder pulled off his shirt. The hair on his chest was dark and his shoulders were muscled. She thought of his story about being a trow.

He was leisurely as he removed his belt, his shoes and socks, and finally his trousers and briefs, and stood facing her, just out of her reach. He was even more beautiful now, naked and primal and fully excited. She wanted to drop to her knees and take him in her mouth, and she shivered with anticipation.

He picked her up and laid her on the bed, standing beside it and gazing at her for long seconds. Then he leaned over and began kissing her belly, circling his tongue on the sensitive nerves of her navel, and she raked her fingers through his thick dark hair.

His tongue moved to her panties. He nipped the fabric and pulled it up, and slid his finger beneath, but only at the edge. Then he moved towards her stockings, running his fingertips along the lace tops, brushing his fingers ever so lightly down the silk on her legs.

He took off one of her heels and kissed the top of her foot, and then did the same with the other, and used his thumbs to press into her arch. He stroked upwards along her legs now, and she was trembling with anticipation when he put his mouth on her silk panties, his warm breaths coming through the thin material.

When she arched her hips, wanting him, he said, "Not yet." He flipped her over on to her stomach and then got on the bed and straddled her. Slowly, but firmly, he kneaded the muscles that ran along her spine, from her shoulders down. She felt his hardness pressing against her. She didn't want him to draw away again, so she gripped the pillow to keep from reacting, but she couldn't help making small noises of mingled pleasure and desire.

Every inch of her body tingled with sexual awareness in a way she'd never experienced before.

Kat felt Calder unclasp her bra and then his warm mouth kissed her back, all the way down. He turned her over again and pulled the bra straps off her arms. He threw the delicate garment across the room, and his breathing was rough and fast.

When Calder took her nipple in his mouth, sucking and flicking his tongue, the sensation electrified her. He reached to her other nipple, teasing it, until she was saying, "Please, please, please!" and reaching down for him and raising her hips upward, trying to urge him to hurry.

He sat back on his heels and said, "Good things come to those who wait, Kat."

She swallowed and forced herself to lay back. When she was still, he pulled down her panties and spread her legs. "Oh, Kat," he said before sliding down and tenderly kissing the insides of her thighs. When he did more, she could no longer stay motionless. He pushed her thighs up and did impossibly marvellous things with his fingers, lips, tongue.

Every time she felt the pleasure in her rising to its cusp, he'd pull back, until she thought she couldn't bear it anymore. "Please, Calder, please!" she cried out, and he finally moved up on the bed. He reached to the nightstand, opened a drawer and took out a condom. He tore open the package, and she reached for the condom and rolled it over him with trembling hands.

Then Calder finally entered her, filling her, and taking her up and over the edge until all she felt was wave after wave of pleasure. She thought the feeling couldn't continue, but he didn't stop until the sensation increased more intensely and she was crying out and sinking her fingernails into his hips, urging him on harder and faster.

Then they shuddered together and her arms went limp. They were breathing heavily, damp with sweat, and she felt in a daze with the sheer joy of it all.

He brushed a curl from her forehead and said, "My beautiful wild Kat," then kissed her tenderly before slowly slipping away and moving to lie beside her.

She admired the width of his shoulders and the way his dark hair curled at his neck. Kat rolled to her side to face him. She kissed his mouth and his chest and then put her arms around him.

He stroked her head and said, "You were very patient."

"It was worth it."

"Good, because it nearly killed me," he said, and she felt his chest shake with laughter. "I wanted you the moment I saw you sitting so self-assured by yourself."

She remembered watching Calder on the street, and how she yearned for him then. "Calder, you're beautiful," she said and ran her hand over his back and his firm hip.

"You're indulging yourself on holiday, darlin'. You'll go back to your husband or lover . . . which is it?"

"I'll go home. Who will you go home to?"

"To my work. To remembering the beautiful American woman with hair that gleamed like the autumn fields at sunset, and amber eyes, and the patience of a saint. A very provocative, lusty saint in silk stockings."

"How did you know they're silk?"

"I'm a man who knows quality, Kat. You're quality."

They slumbered for an hour and then woke up touching each other. This time she was the one who reached over to the night table and opened the drawer. It was filled with dozens of condom packets.

Calder saw her expression and said, "My friend's idea of a joke for the guest room."

"Funny friend," she said, taking a packet and handing it to Calder. She climbed atop him and said, "My turn to be in charge." She moved against him slowly at first, then hurrying as he held her hips and guided her up and down. The pleasure in her built again, and she was crying out as sensation flooded through her.

When Kat collapsed atop him, she laughed and said, "Next time, I'll do it at a glacier's pace, I'll kiss and lick and nip and suck you until you're begging me, *please, please, please*, but this time was still good."

"It was bloody brilliant." His breathing became slow and even, and he murmured, "Sorry, I was up very early. Tomorrow we'll have all day and all night. Tomorrow you'll make me beg. Sweet dreams, wild Kat."

In a few minutes, he was asleep. Kat got up and went to the bathroom to wash up. She put toothpaste on her finger to brush her teeth. Seeing herself naked, with her crazy tumbled hair, her lips red from kissing, and pale violet love bites, her bare full breasts, Kat had never felt more beautiful or womanly.

She went to the kitchen and got a glass of water. She drank it as she walked back to the bedroom. A door off the entryway was ajar and she pushed it open out of curiosity. It was a small office with spare Scandinavian furniture. She flicked on the light and saw a desktop with a large monitor, neat files, and a silver cup filled with pens.

She looked at the framed photo beside the monitor and saw Calder and the blonde woman, his arm over her shoulder, smiling to the camera. Calder was heartbreakingly handsome in his evening jacket and kilt, and the woman was radiantly beautiful in an ivory wedding dress.

Calder was Emma's man in the kilt.

Suddenly responsible Kathy returned. What had she just done, and whom had she done it with?

She was quiet as she gathered her clothes from the bedroom. She took one last look at gorgeous, lying, cheating Calder. Then she blew out the candles, quickly dressed in the hallway, picked up her purse, and left the flat.

It was late, but she remembered the direction of the main street and walked there. A few people chatted in groups on the street, and Kathy stood shivering until a taxi approached.

When she returned to her hotel, she thought the night clerk was leering at her. She went to her room and showered under the hottest water she could endure. She got in bed, pulled the blankets up to her neck, and began crying.

It was both the best and the worst birthday she'd ever had and she wished she'd never left home.

When the grey light of morning came, Kathy opened her eyes and remembered where she was and what had happened. Her thighs ached from the night before and her head was heavy from guilt and alcohol. She listened to the rain outside and the city noises: delivery trucks, raised voices, horns, construction sounds from a renovation nearby. She didn't want to go downstairs to the usual complimentary English breakfast so she drank tea while staring out the window.

Kathy alone was responsible for going with a strange man to his "friend's" place. She wondered if Calder was awake yet, or if he wondered where she'd gone.

Kathy dressed in jeans, one of her knitted sweaters, and tennis shoes, and went downstairs to the business centre. She checked her email and saw that Emma had, as promised, sent an invitation to stay at a "magnificent castle": "I've made all the arrangements with the housekeeper, Jemma. The laird, Humphrey MacNeil, is some kind of workaholic, obsessed with saving his village from becoming more lost than Atlantis. Supposedly, there are sheep, so at least you can talk about wool if you can comprehend his brogue. Have you found your man in a kilt yet? Did you buy a blue coat?"

Emma said that Kathy could show up anytime in the next week and suggested she take an afternoon train that went north before proceeding on to the small atoll in Orkney.

Kathy remembered the painting she'd loved and wanted to be in that landscape right now. She sent back a note to Emma saying, "Thank you! Can't wait to get home!"

Packing took only a few minutes, and she was glad the manager wasn't at the front desk when she checked out. She left the stained blue coat there. Maybe someone could salvage the fabric.

Before walking outside, she put on a long scarf and tucked all her hair into a brown hat, because she didn't want to be recognized in case . . . But he wouldn't be looking for her. When she saw her reflection in a mirror, she looked like her old ordinary self.

Before she went to the train station, she stopped at a small knitting shop and bought fine merino yarn and needles. Her mother had always said that idle hands were the devil's plaything, and her hands had never been idler than when she lay still while Calder stroked and kissed her.

When the train left, Kathy began making a scarf for Humphrey. She hoped he wouldn't be like young Calder, disdaining handmade things, things made with care.

Her yarn was wrapped in an orderly sphere, but her thoughts were a tangle of regrets, anger, and the memories of Calder's touch, his taste, that smile, the scent of him, the sound of his voice and his laughter. The way he gazed at her and murmured, "Kat".

Although it was raining and cold when she finally arrived in St Margaret's Hope, her spirits lifted as she looked with wonder at the peaceful cove and the brick buildings of the old town.

The housekeeper's husband met Kathy at the ferry landing. Mike was a taciturn raw-boned and middle-aged man, but gave her a thermos of hot tea and a thick wool blanket once she was in his motorboat.

He had ignored her initial pleasantries about the weather and the scenery, and after several minutes of silence, Kathy said, "My friend, Emma MacNeil, says you have sheep."

He barked out a laugh and when he spoke she worked to interpret what he was saying, the gist being, "Aye, sheep and cows are all we have, though Humphrey – that's Mr MacNeil – is chuffed with some 'brilliant' new scheme for a business. He's got us clearing rooms as if anyone would want to come and stay. No use telling him, because he's so *contermashious*."

"It's a castle, right? Everyone wants to stay in castles."

Mike turned his grey eyes on her and said, "It isn't Balfour, lass, if that's what you're thinking."

"Oh, no, I didn't expect Balfour." She didn't.

He docked the boat at a small weathered pier. Gulls cawed overhead and the cold wind whipped at Kathy's clothes, but she didn't mind because she was staring at the green island. Mike handed her up, and she could see the tiny village ahead; buildings made of pale stone lined a street. Beyond were fields and hills with outcroppings of stone.

The briny air was invigorating and Kathy felt an unexpected thrill. "It's so beautiful."

"Aye, Miss, it may be a rock, but it's a gem."

He carried her bags to a car parked nearby, rusty from the salty air. "I'll take you up to the castle and then you can meet the missus."

He put her bags in the back of the car and then drove over a hill and on a gently curving road leading to a cliff. He parked on a gravel circle and said, "It's here."

Kathy didn't see any buildings and had a sudden fear that Mike was going to push her over the edge in some barbaric ancient folk sacrifice. She walked very cautiously after him on the path that led to the precipice. She could see the deep blue-green water below, crashing into white foam against the layered sandstone face of the cliff.

"There's Old Humphrey's Castle," Mike said as he pointed to a tall column of rock that rose perilously from the water's surface.

"Where?"

"That sea stack, that's Old Humphrey. It's one of the best around. Let's get you to the house, so ye can get settled. How long is it you're staying?"

"Two days," she said as they went to the car. Then she would return to London.

Mike said, "You can see the whole place in ten minutes. Will you want to have a look about the town? Not that there's much to see but the women knitting, especially since most of us got made redundant when the management company consolidated in Glasgow."

"I'd love to see women knitting, Mike."

She got back in the car and said, "I feel rather foolish. I thought I was going to stay *in* a castle."

He grinned. "Local joke, miss. Your Emma said you were a good sport."

Kathy burst out laughing. "Emma! She's been the cause of all my troubles. She says she has the gift of second sight."

"Some do, you know. What else has she seen?"

"Mostly lotto numbers that are wrong. She swore that I would meet a man in a kilt, but all I met was a wicked trow."

Mike grinned. "We've got both of those here."

He steered the car around a bend and she looked down the hill to a grand building built in a cove. It was three storeys high of pale stone, with a slate roof and many chimneys. It faced a serene inlet and was surrounded by an emerald lawn.

Kathy felt a strange sense of déjà vu, as if she knew this place. Maybe Emma had shown her a photo, or she'd seen it in a guide-book, because it was so very familiar. On a hillock beyond she spotted sheep grazing against the grey sky, just like the painting.

Mike drove down to the house and parked around the side. An old yellow lab ambled up to greet him, and then a middle-aged woman in corduroys and a sweater came out. "Welcome, welcome!"

"Hi, I'm Kathy."

"I'm Janna. Hope your trip was good."

"It was, and Mike showed me the castle."

She looked at her husband and they both laughed. Janna said, "There was a castle here once, but we like this place fine. Come in out of the cold."

Mike excused himself, saying, "The boss gave me a list of tasks. He's coming in this evening."

Janna took Kathy into the house through the front entrance, which led to a marbled entry and huge room with pale grey walls, a mix of modern and antique furniture and paintings that made it seem both timeless and contemporary. "The Great Hall," she said.

"Mr MacNeil keeps saying that he's to sell off all the valuables, so enjoy them now."

"Why would he do that? It's perfect."

"It is, but he thinks he can save all of us from going hungry. I keep telling him to look out for himself, and the rest of us will manage. It's no wonder he doesn't have time for a wife."

Janna led Kathy up a wide staircase with carved wood banisters. "Your friend said you have a knitting business."

"Yes, a small one. Trying to meet my bills is always a challenge. Your sweater is lovely. Is the pale green a natural dye?"

"You've an eye. The wool is from our own herd and I made the dye from kelp, which is also what the sheep eat."

"I've never heard of that!"

"Even our local sheep are odd," Janna said, leading Kathy down a panelled hallway with a faded carpet. "Them that eat the kelp are an old breed, and the laird's parents raised other old breeds. As if anyone wants to see a sheep museum." Janna opened a door at the end of the hallway. "The furnace here works, so you'll be warm, and you've got the afternoon sun."

The large comfortably furnished room had pretty chintz wallpaper and a fireplace. "Thank you. It's very nice."

"If you come to the morning room, we'll have tea and then I'll give you a tour of the house and grounds."

Kathy put away her things and then looked out the tall narrow window. The rain had let up and golden rays of sun beamed out between the slate clouds. This place might not be a castle, but it was fantastic.

She washed up in the adjoining bathroom and thought that she'd enjoy a leisurely soak tonight in the deep tub. The image of Calder's long body in the bath came to her unbidden and she felt a throb of something between lust and loss. Her mind kept returning to him, not just what they'd done, but what she wanted to do with him, to him.

However, another woman, the blonde woman, had exclusive rights to those pleasures.

Kathy washed her hands, smoothed on tinted lip-gloss and followed Janna's directions to the morning room. Tea was set up, but Janna was nowhere around. Kathy sat and waited. After a few minutes, she poured a cup and drank it. Then she went to find Janna.

She searched the ground level and discovered a dining room, a wing of empty bedrooms, and a snooker room. There was a long library with french windows looking out to a stone terrace . . . but no kitchen. Then she found a staircase leading down and went to the basement. She followed the scent of cooking food to an expansive, out of date kitchen.

Janna was talking on an old wall phone and cursing a blue streak. Her source of aggravation was the sink. When she saw Kathy, she tempered her voice and continued her conversation: "I would appreciate it if you could fix it as soon as possible. Thank you." She hung up and looked at Kathy. "Everything goes wrong in an old house."

"Maybe I can help. I know a little about plumbing."

"You're a guest."

"Guests can help. I like to feel useful."

"The main sink won't drain and it's a bother using the others." Janna waved towards a deep sink that was filled with murky water.

"Do the other sinks drain? Because if it's only the one, then it's a local clog. Do you have any tools and a bucket?"

Ten minutes later, Kathy was under the sink removing the U-trap. When she finished and turned on the water, it swirled quickly down the drain. "There," she said, smiling at Janna. "If you pour a kettle of boiling water down the drain monthly, it helps prevent buildups."

"You're a very practical young lady. I hate to have you work on your vacation."

"My parents always taught me to take care of things myself so I wouldn't have to pay others to do them for me." Kathy washed her hands and dried them on a kitchen towel. "Being on vacation is exhausting. I like *doing* things, being useful."

Janna laughed. "You may regret saying that." She made a new pot of tea and told Kathy about the local sights, and said, "You'll be bored by this evening. This is why we can't get tourists, although Humphrey's concocted a grand plan to lure them here. Bless that man, but . . ."

"But?"

"He should have left when he was young and he could have had a real life." Janna smiled a little sadly. "But we love him for staying." She glanced out the window and said, "There's a break in the rain. Would you like to borrow wellies for a tramp?"

Kathy bundled up and walked across to the inlet, then up a hill to enjoy the views. She snapped photos of sheep, trees, storm clouds, rocks. When she returned to the house, Janna had prepared lunch: a salad made from homegrown greens and locally made feta with warm bread. It was eerily like the setting Kathy had imagined for her fantasy business.

Janna sighed and said, "Well, I've got to sort out the furniture in storage, because Humphrey wants the bedrooms set up for guests.

"Can I help?"

Janna didn't take much convincing and Kathy spent the rest of the afternoon helping pull old furniture out of piles in the basement storage rooms. She fixed wobbly legs and polished the pieces with Janna's homemade beeswax paste.

In the evening, Janna went home, leaving Kathy alone with the old dog and her knitting. The next day Kathy went into the tiny village. Everyone was friendly and asked if she'd met Humphrey MacNeil.

"Not yet. He's very kind to let me stay."

The owner of the cheese shop winked and said, "He must have heard how pretty you are. He's not married, you know, and quite a catch – as smart and kind as he is handsome."

Kathy didn't believe for a second that anyone named Humphrey was handsome. He must be very peculiar if everyone was so desperate to find a wife for him. "I'm sure some girl will snatch him up."

"He'd have no problem if he was willing to leave us. He's too loyal, Humphrey is."

Kathy smiled, but she wasn't interested in some ancient workaholic. She returned to the house and helped Janna sweep, polish and wash linens for the guest rooms. They chattered away and shared tips and recipes.

Jenna said, "You sound very close to your parents. Do you live near them?"

"I used to, but my mother passed away several years ago and my father remarried and moved, because he kept remembering how difficult it was for her at the end. Now it's just me."

"You're always welcome here, Kathy."

"Thank you. I really like it here." Kathy paused and then said, "Janna, I was going to return to London tomorrow. Would it be all right if I stayed until the end of the week?"

Janna grinned. "Of course, you can! You're a dream, Kathy, and if Humphrey could see what a hard working lass you are . . . well, he complains about those who are only interested in being coddled and spoilt."

Kathy didn't say anything, but she thought that Humphrey was probably more interested in a servant than a wife.

Her last full day at the island came too quickly and Kathy already felt a pang of nostalgia for this lovely place and the friendly locals.

Before she took her last visit to the sights, Kathy wanted to finish putting up drapes in one of the bedrooms. She was standing on a ladder, facing the window with its views of verdant hills, while she tried to balance a long rod with heavy brocade drapes. At the sound of footsteps behind her, she said, "I've almost got this."

As a rule, Kathy was careful. But she was caught up in her sadness about leaving this place and she stretched farther than she should. When the ladder rocked, she shifted her weight . . . but the rod was too long and heavy.

She let it drop and as it clattered on the floor, there was that awful moment when Kathy realized that she couldn't save herself. She was falling and the next instant strong arms were around her, catching her.

She grabbed on to the person and found herself looking right into Calder's blue eyes. Seeing him again made her speechless.

Calder's astonished expression swiftly changed into delight. "I've been looking all over Edinburgh for you and I've finally caught my wild golden-eyed Kat."

"Goddamn you! Put me down."

"Not even a welcome home kiss? Or more? I recall a promise . . ."

She brought her arms forwards and shoved at his chest. She could feel his firm flesh under a fine dove-grey cashmere sweater. When he let her down, he said, "Why did you leave and how did you find me?"

Kathy stepped away from him, catching her foot in the fallen valance, then kicking it away. "I left because you're married, and I *didn't* find you. I'm staying with my friend's relative, Humphrey MacNeil."

"*You're* Kathy?"

"Yes, I'm Kathy. Does Janna know you're here?"

"I suppose so." He looked towards the doorway and called out, "Isobel, did you tell Janna I'm here?"

Kathy followed his glance and saw the beautiful blonde woman come in. She was dressed in an elegant shell pink sweater and tight jeans tucked into boots. The woman, Isobel, said to Calder, "Of course, I told her," while gazing at Kathy. Then the woman shrieked and cried to Calder, "That's her! That's the woman!"

Kathy felt sick with guilt and anger. She wanted to push Calder out the window. She wanted to scream. She wanted to disappear.

Calder looked confused. "Calm yourself, Isobel. This is Kat. I *told* you about her. Kat, or Kathy, is it?, Isobel."

"You *told* her?" Kathy said with horror. To Isobel, she said, "I'm so sorry. I didn't know, or I never would have . . ."

"Kat is the woman I saw!" Isobel cried, looking at Calder.

He looked at the blonde as if she was mad. "Isobel, not now, please." He turned to Kathy and said, "Ignore her. She's crazy."

"I am not!" Isobel pointed at Kathy and said to Calder, "She's the one you slept with? The one in the blue coat?"

"Her coat is green, Isobel."

Kathy thought that Isobel must have remembered her from the street. "I *had* a blue coat. He splattered it with mud when you were driving on Princes Street."

Calder tilted his head and said, "You saw me before we met at dinner?"

Isobel glared at Calder and said, "I was right, you fool! I knew you wouldn't be able to stay away from her."

Kathy took a breath and said, "He said he wasn't married."

Isobel's expression softened. "Of course, he's not married. He's *supposed* to marry you. I've been telling him to find the girl in the blue coat, and when I saw you with the umbrella, I screamed at him to stop the car, but he never takes the MacNeil sight seriously."

"But the wedding photo of you two . . ."

Calder laughed. "Isobel is my sister!"

"That was *my* wedding," Isobel said. "It didn't last and that's the only photo from it I can bear to look at." She smiled at her brother. "Humphrey, *next* time you'll believe in my sight."

Kathy said to her, "My friend Emma has the sight, too. She told me to get a blue coat."

"I think you both have something to discuss," Isobel said, and left the room.

Calder looked Kathy up and down, and she became self-conscious about her grimy jeans, dusty sweater, and the kerchief tied over her head. "You said your name was Calder."

"So it is. Humphrey Calder MacNeil. When my father was alive, they all called me Calder, but since he passed, they insist on Humphrey."

"Like the castle."

"Aye, lass," he said, with a sheepish grin. His expression became serious and he said, "I didn't know why you left me."

"I thought you were a wicked trow, deceiving me, with your drawer full of condoms and a wife." She glanced down at her clothes and said, "I was the one deceiving you. I'm not a woman who dines alone in expensive restaurants. This is how I look most days. This is who I am really."

"Who you are *really* is a lass who can tease me, a lass who can laugh while she dances in a crowded pub, a lass who can take as good as she can give, a lass who wears silk stockings." He reached for her hands and held them. "I knew these weren't pampered hands, darlin'." He lifted them to his lips and kissed them.

"So you're Humphrey, a loyal workaholic, who spends all of his time here."

"The very one. When you talked about your retreat, I thought, that's it. That's what I need to do to create jobs here and to share the beauty."

"But I lied," she said. "All I have is a puny business. I love it, but it's just me and a few classes."

"Then I wouldn't be asking you to give up everything if I asked you to stay, Kat. Would you stay here with me? Help me set up your retreat here?" He pulled the kerchief off her head and kissed her temple.

"Well, I don't think I should leave before you replace my blue coat."

His arms went around her, bringing her tight against his large firm body, and she sighed at the touch of him, the scent of him, and slipped her arms around his waist. He said, "The lambs won't be born until next spring. It will take some time before their wool is ready to sheer. Then there's the cleaning, dying, spinning and looming. It will be best if you settle in for a long stay. Since you're a visitor, there may be problems, unless . . ."

"Unless what?"

"Would you consider marrying a Scotsman, Kat? You said I could ask you later."

"I did say that, and it was a very special coat, Calder. Besides, would it do us any good to fight the MacNeil vision?"

"I think not, darlin'. We may as well give in to fate, to long days of work and longer nights of making love. The trow in me especially enjoys the nights. If that's what you want."

"What I want, Calder, is to hear you beg me *please, please, please.*"

He lifted her up until they were face to face. "That's what I hoped you'd say, my beautiful wild Kat."

Forever Knight

Jackie Ivie

One

"Heave, lads! A bairn wouldn't feel that gentle touch!" Grunts followed Gavynn's cry, but little else. "Put your backs and arms into it!"

"Perhaps you could put your mouth into it as well?"

One of the lumps of straining men muttered it. Gavynn ignored him. He had to. Iain's freedom depended on it. And the man wasn't accurate. Gavynn had been right in the struggle with them until he'd stepped away to assess their progress. And lack, thereof, from what could be seen.

Rainfall washed them, making it difficult to see. That was just and right and necessary. Rain helped hide perfidy such as pulling down a castle wall, cloaking the thirty-four men anchored to its base with a series of thickly woven ropes.

"Courage, lads! You're acting as if 'tis constructed with more than sand and piss!"

"'Tis solid cursed stone!"

One of the lumps quit straining in order to yell the answer. Gavynn shouted louder. "Verra well. I'll admit they may have tossed in a bit of dung. But only on occasion. You'll need to pull harder! Find the weakness! Move in rhythm! We just need a bit of luck."

"We've na' much luck tonight. What with the rain and nae light."

"The night does its work. As does my cousin, Arran, with his pipes. You ever hear such loud disjointed playing?"

Gavynn used the same volume with each yell. He'd be hoarse if he didn't cease, but that didn't stop him. He had to keep men straining against the wall. Those that flagged needed constant needling and exhortation from a loud voice, regardless of how the words felt sucked away the moment they'd been uttered. Very little made it through to men aware only of the thump of heartbeat in their ears. Not even the loud sound of pipes playing discordantly somewhere in the castle.

"Arran and his men have vast amounts of . . . hot air tonight." One of them put Gavynn's thought into words.

"Aye. And na'much brawn." Another man agreed, although it came with an insult directed at Gavynn. "Appears he's na' the lone one. Just listen to the laird!"

The slur galvanized Gavynn. "That's it! Move your worthless hides. I'll show you how 'tis done!"

Gavynn pushed his way to the front of a line of men, slipping more than once in brine-soaked earth. Such was the result of constructing a castle encircled by a trickle of sea-fed moat. They'd drained what they could just before dusk as they waited. Planning. Worrying. There were other things he'd rather be doing, lots of other things. But he didn't have a choice. He had to rescue his little brother, Iain.

The rope was slickest near the wall, due to the water level. Gavynn looped an arm about hemp, scraping flesh as he pulled, feeling the strain against solid stone. He'd been denigrating the rock walls without proof. Lord Dillbin had built his castle well, funded by Sassenach silver. There was little give to it. Despite the rain, the mud they'd shovelled out of the way, the hours spent chiselling about the cornerstones, nothing moved. Gavynn yanked until tendons in his jaw hurt with the effort.

And then the rope slackened, going limp. There was the gravest rush of noise, accompanied by a thud of something large landing in the muck, sloshing brine-mixture all over him. He launched backwards, landing flat on his back in the mess, putting his hands out instinctively to catch whatever heaven sent at him.

He didn't know he'd been successful until they lifted a chunk of masonry from atop him.

"We're . . . through?" He sounded like a girl-bairn. Every word felt ground against bone. He suspected bruised ribs. If he was in luck. What was he thinking? Luck had deserted them.

"Help me lads! Quick! Get this off him!"

His clansman Rory said it. Gavynn groaned as little lights danced through his vision. It was joined by the chore of breathing. And then he was freed, hauled to his feet, to stand gaping at the size of rock they'd lifted from him. If he hadn't been in soaked soft earth, he'd have been flattened. Fully.

He swayed, pulling in small chunks of air while the others stood about, indecisive. That got Gavynn angered, and that covered over any pain.

"Have we just . . . taken down a wall . . . to mill about?" The words were broken with each inhalation of air. His volume was missing, as well. He'd worry over that later.

"We have na' reached Iain, my Laird."

"'Tis truth. Look for yourself." Rory spoke again, level-headed and efficient-sounding. As usual.

"We took down . . . his dungeon?" Gavynn asked.

"Aye. But we got the wrong one."

"The man has but one dungeon!" Gavynn's voice was coming back. As was his purpose. Strength couldn't be far behind. He hoped. "And if fate played us so ill, then move your arses! Get out of . . . my way!"

It would've had more effect if he hadn't gone down to a knee. Gavynn covered his weakness with a slap at the boulder that had pinned him, and forced his legs to support his weight.

"Is there a leader . . . out here?"

A voice filtered through the fog of rainfall and failure filling Gavynn's ears. Someone answered, pointing at him. He couldn't tell who. Muck covered the men, making anonymous lumps in the torchlight from inside the dungeon walls. Gavynn looked at the gaping hole in Dillbin's English-built castle, blinked on rain that wouldn't cease, and then his mouth dropped open.

A woman picked her way towards him, lifting her skirts with one hand, while the other slid along rubble. That manoeuvre kept her upright, although clumsy-looking. She was bare-headed, lengthy locks of an indeterminate shade clinging to her, mostly due to the night and amount of rainfall. It didn't seem to bother her that a contingency of muck-covered men silently watched with their mouths open.

Gavynn straightened, breathing in small snippets of air that kept the ache tolerable. He swept a hand across his forehead to clear the water. Only he knew his hand trembled.

"Are you leading . . . this—?"

She'd reached him and looked up, motioning with her hand to the broken wall behind her.

"Rescue," Gavynn supplied.

"Rescue?"

"Over here!"

Gavynn ignored her sarcasm and looked over her towards Iain's voice. The squealed words betrayed weakness. Frailty. Youth. Gavynn could see an arm waving at them through a myriad of bars. "They . . . moved him?"

"He wouldn't cease his whining and—"

He had her throat in his hand, his eyes narrowed to look her over in the dim light and he tightened his grip on her. "Whining?"

"The outer cell is most . . . damp."

She whispered it but nothing on her looked cowed. She met his look unblinkingly. That was odd. Having a band of thirty-five men pull down a segment of prison wall should've put fear into those dark eyes. Gavynn loosened his grip on her throat slowly, keeping his hand where it was. There was a huge groan happening in the air about them, filtering through the rain sounds.

"That wall is coming down!"

"Greggor's right! Better to banter words from a distance!"

"What of him?" Gavynn motioned with a head toss at his brother. And then other sounds added to the night. Defence sounds: a thrum of drums, blare of pipes, shouts of men. He got splashed beneath his kilt as something landed beside him.

"We need to move, my Laird! Now!"

"What of . . . my brother?" Gavynn asked again.

"We canna' fetch him from the grave!"

Gavynn hid the failure. "Go then. I'll bring the lass. She has . . . use." He moved his attention back to the woman.

"Use?"

She asked it with sarcasm touching the words. He tightened his fingers. Another deep groan came from the wall.

"Gavynn . . . *please*! Doona' leave me!"

His brother was at full-out screaming, although it was mostly muted. Gavynn didn't look. There wasn't any way to change it. The night was sending blocks of stone to pepper the sodden ground about them. It was due to luck that only more mud-tainted water hit Gavynn. He pulled at the woman, transferring his hand to a slender wrist, squeezing with intent. It wasn't neces-sary. She wasn't fighting. She was helping.

Once they reached the hill at the back of Castle Dillbin, she was the one pulling at him, forcing him up the steep sides and on to the moor; leading him to the largest horse . . . and then heralding his weakness by standing docilely at his side.

Everyone felt like they were watching for him to somehow get astride his stallion, Crusader, force the wench up there with him, and do it without succumbing to the chasm of faintness opening in front of him.

"He needs assist?"

One of the hired men asked it. There was a thump as someone silenced him. The remark was ill-advised. Gavynn slit his eyes. Concentrated. Willed away the effects of a night of work, getting hit by a chunk of masonry, and then forced to run uphill with little ability to gain breath. He refused to submit to anything as defence-less as a swoon. He was laird of Clan MacEuann. He hadn't gained that through weakness. Gavynn pulled in short huffs of air and watched the wash of blur turn into horsehair again.

"Well, that horse is a handful to mount. And hell to ride."

"I've got it in hand, lads." Gavynn still held to the saddle.

"What of the woman?"

"Her, too," Gavynn answered.

"How do you ken she's hell to ride?"

One of the mercenaries joshed it. The woman at Gavynn's side stiffened. "I'll answer that slur on . . . the morrow. With fists. Now mount!"

Hurt thumped through his chest, but nothing felt broken. Bruised. Pained. But not broken. As was just and right. He'd be hell-bound before he let a Sassenach castle kill him. He turned to the wench. She was watching him with an unblinking gaze. As if she knew he was staying upright by willpower. That was disconcerting.

"Can you ride?" He lowered his voice to ask it.

She tilted her head back a bit, allowing night-cast light to caress and mould her features. Showing off beauty. There was worse than eyes that seemed to look deep into a man. Even in a rain-filled night he knew how much worse. This wench was bonny enough to cause argument and dissent. If Gavynn was too weak to stop it.

He set his jaw. Looked her over dispassionately. She had use: Iain's release. For that she had to remain unmolested and safe. And he had to guarantee it.

"Well?"

*   *   *

Brielle nodded. Something about him clogged her throat, taking air she needed to speak. That was strange. Unfamiliar. Unfair. And unacceptable.

It wasn't lack of knowledge. She'd been around men. Lots of men. Sometimes dressed in costly fabrics, smelling of lye soap and spirits. Sometimes covered in armour and leather and reeking of sweat and other odours she'd rather not decipher. And other times she'd administered to men who'd been clothed in nothing but fear, pain and blood while they trembled, groaned and sometimes died.

But she'd never been near a man like this.

She started with his size. He was immense. The top of her head reached mid-chest. She added in his strength. He was fit. Brawny. Seemingly immune to pain. He should be suffering. She'd seen the boulder lifted off him. No man could've endured that and be standing barking orders and glaring at her. He'd be dead.

For the first time she tasted uncertainty and fear. This was a real Highlander. Not a spineless youth like Iain. This was a man fitting the tales. She'd heard them. Everyone had. From the moment she'd left civilization to reside in Scotland, she'd been regaled with tales of prowess, strength, endurance, regardless of the odds. She'd shivered when she was younger, and then disbelieved. And grown cynical. She'd thought them fables. Lore dreamt in fertile minds, conjured to frighten. Demons. Barbarians. Brielle couldn't stop the goose flesh running her body. She didn't even try.

"Well? Can you or canna' you?"

"What?" she mouthed.

"Mount."

Low snickers came from the horde about them. Brielle didn't move her gaze from his. "Cup your hand," she requested.

"Why?"

"Have you never mounted a woman before?"

She had her cool tone back. The one that usually meant immediate obedience. This time it got jeers and laughter. Her face went hot as she assigned meaning. Then she had large hands gripped around her waist as he tossed her on to the span of horse. On her belly.

Brielle hadn't time to gasp before he was mounted, an arm about her midsection, plastering her to him with an iron grasp. He wasn't even breathing hard while her heart felt lodged in her throat, choking off the scream.

He clicked his tongue and the horse moved. That gave her another bit of information about Highlanders. They knew horses. That could put leagues between her and safety. A flicker of worry started. Brielle swallowed before she got more impressions to deal with. The feel of him made her head spin. This much proximity to any man was alien. Odd. Foreign.

They hadn't ridden long before something changed. It might've been the slight groan attached to each breath he made. It might've been the feather touch of air across her forehead and on to her nose. It could've been the heavy thud of heartbeat emanating from where her ear pressed, creating sensations she'd never felt before. And wouldn't have believed.

The totality of it got worse as they reached treeline and started ducking and dodging. He seemed to possess a second sense, swaying, bending and dipping to avoid rain-blurred obstacles before they were seen. Brielle tried ignoring the arms about her, muscle flexing everywhere, even in the hard thighs that pinned her legs together. She felt sensitive. Alert. Aware. Alive with a tingle that just kept coming. She had to change it. Brielle moved her head slightly, the only range of movement he left her, to put whispered words against his neck.

"You shouldn't be riding," she whispered. "You're injured."

He grunted but didn't deny it.

"Loose me. I won't escape," she added.

"Doona' fash. 'Tis . . . little."

His words gapped with a catch of breath. Brielle stirred and the hand at her cheek pushed, smashing her to him.

"I . . . I'm versed in nursing." She tried again, biting her lower lip this time. She only did that when beset. Worried. "The longer you wait . . . the worse it may get. Loose me, and I'll see to it."

She got a grunt. This wasn't easy. The man was dense. Immune.

"Why not?" She said it louder, with a cross tone.

"I canna' protect you"

"Protect me? From . . . what?"

"A man does na' claim what he canna' hold, Lass. We reach Feegan's Roost . . . you can nurse me there. Or kill me off. Until then, cease . . . this argue."

"I'm not—" Brielle stopped. Anything she said could be perceived as arguing.

A slight sniff that could be his amusement touched her eyelashes. It was instantly followed by a tremor all through him.

"You'll never make this Feegan's place," she informed him.

"I need rest, Lass. Less . . . woman-words."

"*Men.*" The word held her disgust. And got a few snorts of laughter from about them.

He settled somehow, forming a cocoon about her that contained a steady, thick heartbeat at the core. Brielle shifted, but little moved. She debated struggling. Kicking. Twisting. If only he didn't make such a comfortable berth; kilt-covered thighs about hers; a chest formed for snuggling into; a rocking motion of the horse beneath them. All of it combined to close her eyes and relax into him . . . and sleep.

Two

The woman smelt clean. Fresh. Wondrous. Her form felt good in his arms, too. Almost like she belonged; swaying slightly with every step from Crusader . . . taking them further from Iain. Gavynn stopped the thought. It heightened the dull ache pumping through his chest.

"You're in pain?"

Her quick breath cursed him, brushing at his chin with sweetness.

"You should be dead. I saw the stone that hit you."

He grunted slightly; tightened the arm about her chest, crushing full breasts against his arm. He thoroughly enjoyed it, before the lass pestered him with words again.

"You needn't hide it. I told you. I've . . . nursing skill."

Gavynn looked heavenwards, gaining a raindrop for his trouble. She didn't obey the slightest thing. Her presence caused trouble. Hired men weren't easy to control when filled with bloodlust. They obeyed a strong leader. One who could keep and protect a captive he claimed. The lass might be versed in nursing, but she knew nothing about warring men.

"I doona' need *nursing.*"

He heard sounds of amusement from about them. Somewhere in the rain-filled night, men rode pillion, listening, evaluating. Gavynn frowned. He'd hired the strongest, stoutest men silver could purchase. He needed them to pull down a wall. He hadn't worried over trust.

"But—"

"If you doona' hush, I'll gag you."

"What? Why?"

Gavynn pulled the rein into his mouth, lowered his freed hand to his kilt hem, and started ripping.

"What . . . are you doing?"

"Getting your gag," he replied through his teeth.

The lass went stiff and then she went silent. All about could be heard movement, murmurs, jangling of harness. Gavynn waited, while the lass hardly seemed to breathe.

"You'll hush?"

He whispered it and got a nod along his throat. It came with another tremor from her body. He didn't like that. And wondered why.

Feegan's Roost turned out to be a portion of ancient monastery, frozen in jagged chunks of disembodied stone that reached heavenwards. It was shrouded in a thick layer of mist, lit by the glow of a new day. Brielle opened an eye, caught her breath at such beauty and then yawned. Her eyelids felt heavier than usual, her limbs stiff.

The moment Brielle moved to stretch, memory returned, awakening her fully and rapidly. She yanked both eyes open, to a span of male chest glossed by air that sparkled. Blinking didn't change it. Then her vision got peopled with shaggy-looking horses, worse-looking hulks of men, and everywhere they had weaponry. Sharpened spear-tips, arrows, hand-axes and large swords honed to edges that caught light, were speckling the area with glint.

Brielle felt completely out-of-sorts. Damp. Sweaty-warm. Cramped. Her captor was a brute, too. She wriggled, trying to ease the numbing of both legs. She got tighter arms and legs about her. She'd never slept atop a horse before . . . nor locked in a man's embrace. She knew why now: misery.

"Let . . . me . . . go!" Her hiss of voice halted as one of his men spoke up.

"You need assist with that, MacEuann?"

One of the hulks lifted a mud-covered head to grin, his teeth brown against a full beard.

Her captor grunted, and then yelled a name. "Pells?"

"Aye?"

"Get to Reeb. As planned. Rory?"

"My Laird?"

"Send a message to the earl. Tell him I demand my brother's freedom."

Sounds of what could be hilarity and might be argument, filtered through the throng. Brielle subconsciously leaned back into the mass of man holding her, much to her own dismay.

"Tell him I offer a trade! This woman . . . for Iain."

"Her?"

"Aye. And a-fore her presence wearies me further. You write that?"

Brielle's eyes went wide as they all looked, grins splitting more beards. She swallowed on the moisture in her mouth, and then again as it got replenished. She didn't know fear had a taste. Bitter. Metallic.

"How do you ken he'll trade? He kept her in his dungeons."

"I would house her there, as well. As punishment for a displeasing tongue. Go. Deliver my message. Use Greggor. He's the best aim. And you! Get a fire going. Set a kettle to boiling. You! See to the horses. And Gleason?"

"My laird?"

"Hunt a stag for roasting. At the verra least, a hare or two. Take as many men as you need. We've a long day ahead. And I, for one, am na' waiting with an empty gullet."

He was trembling by the end of his speech, moving Brielle with his tremors. None of the others noted. She watched as men scurried to do his bidding until there were none left. Brielle wriggled again, fully expecting tighter bands about her.

"You want me to loosen my hold?"

She hunched her shoulder against the puff of whisper; nodded.

"You promise you'll na' run?"

Where was she going to run? She didn't have a weapon, a horse, knowledge of the land, and she was thoroughly exhausted; cramped into immobility. Then there was the threat of so many men . . . all looking like they wanted to devour her. This Gavynn was dense.

Brielle tipped her head and suffered the most annoying spate of sensation when she connected with his gaze. He had light green eyes, totally at odds with his hair and brows. He hadn't grown a beard, leaving lips and jaw uncovered. Brielle gulped, her heart dropped to pound heavily from her depths and there was something wrong with her breathing as well.

"I . . . need . . . a moment." She replied with such a shaky whisper she knew he felt it. And then he frowned.

"As do I. But first . . . your promise."

"I'm no fool," she told him.

He lifted an ebony-shaded eyebrow.

"You're injured, you can't control your men, and you're all I have for protection. Why would I run?"

He lifted his head away, clicked his tongue and that moved the horse around a far wall and into a small cleared area framed by ruined walls and a fringe of trees. Once there, he loosened his hold and slid her to the grass. He motioned her towards the greenery, shadowed and private. She was pushing her way back through to him when she heard the thud as he fell off his horse.

Brielle was on her knees beside him quickly. She shook her head. "I was right. You're injured."

"Jesu'!"

The hunch of man cursed it, while the naked back he displayed flexed and moved. Brielle looked over four scars scoring his flesh.

"Can you move?" She waited long moments before he answered. And then she had to lean to hear it.

"Aye."

"Then do so. Before someone spots you." She stood.

"Is this . . . what you call nursing?"

"No. This is called survival."

He sighed, shuddered, and started unfolding from the pile of limbs until he became a seated male with long legs before him, bare from thigh to socks.

"How bad is it?" she asked.

"I'm bruised a bit and numbed to deadness."

"Then recover quickly, Gavynn MacEuann."

He looked up at her through his lashes. "You ken my name?"

"Your brother never ceased talking. Or whining."

The jibe hardened his face, as well as everything else he'd put on display. She stepped back as he went to a crouch, using his arms for stability. And then he went to a stand, stretched, yawned, and then growled. And then he walked past her to the shrubs.

Brielle whirled, giving him privacy. But that was stupid. One kept their eyes on the enemy. Then they wouldn't have to rely on sound to locate them.

"Verra well, Lass. I'm up. Relieved. What would you have of me now?"

Brielle kept her back to him while shivers rippled all over her. She crossed her arms and glared at the wall. She refused to let him unsettle her. It made her reply harsh. "You're not injured."

"I dinna' say I was. 'Twas your summation."

A yell came from somewhere. Something about breakfast. Gruel. Griddle cakes fried in fat. Brielle's belly answered. It'd been two full days since she'd been put on bread and water. The single crust she'd saved was long gone. She studied the ruined wall and tried ignoring the man behind her.

"You thinking to run?" he asked.

Of course she wasn't running. The only thing that changed was his health. Brielle sighed, turned, and hadn't realized how close he stood. Her spin knocked her into him. Hands grabbed each arm; not to catch, but imprison. He lifted until her feet dangled and even if she had more than slippers on her feet, it wouldn't have done much as she kicked and twisted.

"You're fair . . . vexing. You ken?"

He grunted several times until Brielle conceded. If he was injured it didn't affect his strength. She could only hope her father answered the message . . . and soon.

Gavynn felt her give up, but that didn't loosen anything about his hold. He'd been right earlier. She was a beauty. Lengthy locks of russet-coloured hair covered her back messily, obviously needing a brushing. Nothing marred the perfection of her skin, either. Not one pock, freckle, or even a bump. He was alarmed even before he factored in her smell. He stood, breathing her scent, while his body reacted. She was definitely affecting him. His senses told him even as his mind ordered against it. She was his bargaining wedge. Nothing more. Touching her was foolhardy, holding her like this pure insanity. He almost wished for an injury vast enough to stay his body from the priming that happened. Hardening him. Gavynn pulled his hips back, hoping the sporran hid him well enough. He watched her catch at her bottom lip, tip her chin, and move her gaze to him, and then endured a roar that went right through his ears.

"You can unhand me now. Truly. I won't run."

Sarcasm filled the words. They still sounded of honey. Gavynn lowered his head and caught her inhalation of breath with his mouth. As he did the strangled cry that followed. If she hadn't turned it into a moan before flicking her tongue at his, he'd have been better able to stop the kiss and leave her be.

Maybe.

A hand snaked around his neck, fingers twined about the ends of his hair, taking him closer, and that's when Gavynn ceased anything resembling thought. All he could do was feel; firm breasts against his chest, the heft of her buttocks once he slid a hand to lift her, clenching and moulding her exactly to him, and the solid tremor matching her frame exactly to his. It wasn't just her moan riding through his senses as he sucked his way about her mouth, deepening the kiss into something tangible, raw . . . urgent.

A hiss of air at his cheek stopped him. Gavynn went to a crouched spin, pulling his claymore while one arm pinned the lass to him. But it was only his man, James MacPherson, nodding at them before walking past to pull his arrow from a far tree. Gavynn was standing, his sword tip at the ground when James returned. The woman had moulded fully to him, her face hidden against his shoulder. Gavynn watched James note it.

"I'll be for paying that back," Gavynn informed him.

The man grinned. "I had nae other choice. You dinna' hear my call."

Gavynn shrugged. The woman moved with it. "Now that you've interrupted, what do you want?"

"Rory sent me. He averred you might need . . . assist. I doona' ken with what."

Gavynn grunted.

"I'll fetch your repast. For the woman, as well. Try na' to miss me."

She jerked then started to shiver. Gavynn held her through it. He was still in a fog of want. He tried tamping it. She smelt of womanly delight and warmth. She felt better. She sent small snippets of air feathering across his upper arm. She was in a cling of provocation. None of it helpful. James nodded as if he realized all of it, before he turned and left, whistling the entire time.

Three

Purgatory wasn't deep enough to hold the embarrassment and shock. It was enough that the combination sapped at her strength. Brielle hadn't any experience with passion and desire . . . and with a Highlander? It wasn't fair!

She kept her head averted, pulling in gasp after gasp of his smell. Her skin rippled with shivers, her frame trembled, and it was difficult to breathe. She felt as tightly strung as a lyre, with every sense heightened and alert and tensed. She'd been kissed once, by a drunken lord who'd over-stepped his boundaries and received a slap for his effort. It was nothing like this. She'd never felt a whoosh of warmth so vast her entire being throbbed. Such a thing was immoral. Illicit. Unbridled. Wanton. And it just kept radiating outward, sending tremors with it. Why was it this man to do this to her? Within moments of time? Using little more than his mouth?

Brielle trembled and endured and worked at squashing a reaction she hadn't known existed. It was so mortifying, tears drilled at her eyes. She didn't know if she could face him again. Or his man.

"Lass?"

She shook her head slightly at the rumble of voice. The motion rubbed her forehead against his skin.

"You need to unhinge from me. A-fore James returns."

Brielle shook her head again. He sighed.

"Doona' take offence. I'm na' against tupping with you."

"Tupping?" The word was choked.

"Aye. With great force and passion. That sort of tupping."

Her eyes went wide.

"I'd na' thought a Sassenach wench would be so . . . ardent. Or free. It . . . makes me hard and readied for you. I vow, I've rarely felt such need. Canna' you face me? 'Tis difficult to speak to the top of your head."

"Don't say . . . one more word. Not one." Brielle enunciated carefully and then stepped back. Nothing about the morn felt warm. It was cold. Harsh. Brielle wrapped her arms about her, looked up to face him, and ignored the lurch her body made. He'd lowered his chin, favouring her with a look she had no trouble deciphering. He hadn't been speaking of his condition idly, either. He was definitely readied for her. His plaid was distorted with size and hardness. All of which was shocking and frightening. And yet enticing at the same time. Brielle forced her eyes to stay focused on his face.

"Doona' look at me that way, Lass. You ken I canna' take you. Na' now. And for certain, na' here."

"No." The word sounded strangled but he ploughed right over it anyway.

"Cease looking at me that way. You doona' ken how 'tis."

"Nor do I wish to," she replied.

"What?"

His confusion was real. A line etched across his forehead with his frown.

"I don't wish . . . *anything* to do . . . with you," she clarified.

He crossed his arms about his chest, thrusting defined muscles into her line of sight. And then he pushed his upper body forward in an aggressive-looking stance.

"That is a lie," he stated.

"It is not." She tossed her hair for emphasis.

"You deny what your frame displays?"

His glance flicked to her completely covered breasts as if he'd find validation. Brielle moved her crossed arms higher and gritted her teeth so hard she heard the sound through her skull.

"I suffer . . . morning chill," she told him.

"Morning chill?"

"If . . . a lady is denied a bed . . . and then forced to endure the elements . . . she gets chilled." Her teeth were chattering. Her voice warbled with it.

"What's your name?" He surprised her with the change of topic as well as his gentle tone.

"Why?"

"So I have a name other than wench and lass."

"Either will do . . . at present."

He grinned. "Verra well. I'll state it. You're the lady Brielle, heiress of Dillbin."

"No." The word warbled.

"Another lie? No wonder he placed you in his dungeon."

"How do you know I wasn't there . . . visiting prisoners? Bringing broth . . . a-a-and thick blankets to the poor souls?"

"Because you escaped with me. And only prisoners do that."

Brielle clamped her lips shut and fiddled with the bit of lace at her elbow.

"What does your father want with my brother?"

"I don't know." She bit her tongue the moment she answered, but it was too late. She didn't need his chuckle to verify it.

"That . . . was too easy, my Lady."

Brielle lifted her chin and watched him for long heart-pounding moments. She didn't say a word.

"I'm hungry. James had best return soon. And with a full platter."

With that, Gavynn MacEuann sat down with the wall at his back and tanned bare legs before him.

The wench unsettled, annoyed, and totally frustrated him . . . yet still he was hard for her. Despite everything he kept telling himself. Gavynn was contemplating the toes of his boots when James walked back around a section of vine-draped stone, carrying a wooden slab that sent steam into the air.

"Lover's spat?" The man asked it as he set his burden down, winking as he did so.

Gavynn regarded him without expression until the humour faded. "You'd be of more use checking on Rory."

"Nae need. They'll be back a-fore long."

"They could na' have reached the castle already."

"Dinna' have to. His lordship has men out. Armed and mounted. Spanning the demesne. Searching."

"Go then. Await word."

"I'd best stay here."

"Why? I'm na' much injured. Just a mite sore."

"You still need a guard."

Gavynn tore into an oatcake; blew at steam before pushing it into his mouth. He chewed silently, and had the bite swallowed before he replied.

"I've na' turned into a spineless sapling." Gavynn tore off another bite. Shoved it in. Chewed.

"You canna' protect much . . . if you're occupied."

Gavynn swallowed. Winced. "You saw wrong, James. The wench means naught to me."

"You offering her up?"

Gavynn felt her tense. Evaluated it. Lady Brielle feared his answer. Standing beyond reach and pretending, he could still sense it radiating from her.

"Nae," he finally replied. "She has value. Just as I suspicioned last eve."

Gavynn folded the last bit of the cake, shoved it into his mouth, and spent his time chewing. He lifted the sporran and twisted the stopper cork from it. He caught her glance while he gulped at whiskey that burned and revived, and then returned his attention to James.

"How so?"

"She wears costly clothing and possesses an educated, albeit sharp, tongue. All signs of value."

"Why was she housed in his dungeon?"

"She does na' say. Yet. A bit more time in my presence with naught else for company, and that may change."

James grunted, and left them. Gavynn picked up another cake, motioned for her to join him, and found her amusing when she turned her back on him, preferring hunger and a view of trees.

The wait was the worst part. It was interminable and broken only by the presence of her captor. Brielle practiced ignoring him as morn lengthened into mid-day, and then further. This Gavynn rarely rested. If it was weakness causing him to groan, drop his burden, or take a knee with his head bowed and everything taut on him, it didn't slow him much. Sweat covered him before long, darkening his kilt and putting sheen to his skin, totally exposing her idiocy in worrying over nursing him.

Brielle surreptitiously watched him about his regimen, even the times he rested, panting for breath while apparently deciding another bit of work. He acted as if he was alone the entire time. And he was rarely still.

It began right after finishing the entire platter of breakfast, once she'd turned her back on it. He'd started with hand-sized stones before graduating to larger and larger boulders; hefting them above his head, squatting with them, toting them about the area, setting them down, re-lifting them, and occasionally pitching one into the trees, making leaves and deadfall rustle. Sunlight invaded the area, cursing her with the weight and heft of her velvet over-dress. It was thickly-woven. Warm. But what had seemed practical in a castle two nights ago was a curse now. Brielle lifted hair from her neck to cool and dry her skin throughout the day while her belly rumbled and pained with emptiness.

His activities wearied her. Beneath it was the worry of what

Father would do. Or not do. The heat added to it. If she dozed, it was to jerk awake, focusing on the stained skirt, the grasses beneath her, or the ruin of stone wall and forest fringe.

The aroma of roasting venison filled the air near dusk, making her mouth water and her belly ache. Then into her misery came Gavynn, going to his knees to look across at where she slouched against a bit of rock. He had a bag slung across one shoulder, hooked on his sword. Everything on him looked sweaty or dirty. Or both.

"Come."

He held out a hand. Brielle shook her head.

"I'll force you."

She shoved his hand aside, went to a crouch before collapsing, her legs spiked with pain of inaction. Brielle held the cry before getting pulled across his free shoulder. As if she was another boulder he'd decided to heft. He stood then, tossing her slightly for balance.

She could kick. Struggle. Beat at his back where her hands kept slipping on sweat-covered skin. She could also easily lose consciousness from lack of food, two days incarceration, and now being dangled upside down. Brielle endured until he tipped forward, set her on her feet, then waited for her wobbling to cease.

"What . . . do you want?"

If she'd eaten when he offered and slept when possible, she wouldn't be stammering and stuttering, and having to blink through a stupid film of tears. All of which was caused by her own obstinate nature.

"Take off your dress. And whatever else you can spare."

Brielle's eyes went wide. "No."

"You'll take it off, or I'll force you. And I tire of the threat."

He was working at the clasp of his belt as he spoke. Brielle backed a step, then another, before he reached out, snagged an arm, and yanked her back.

"Don't do this!"

Fright made her voice shrill. He had her twirled into him, bound by an arm while the other hand covered her mouth. And then he was whispering harsh words.

"I'm doing little! You reek. I've my fill of the stench. You'll bathe in yon burn with me or I'll toss you in. Fully clothed. You ken?"

She nodded. He moved his hand.

"I do not reek."

He had his hand back. She heard a hissed curse, followed by

more words. "Do you ken naught, lass? I want you. 'Tis massive. Hard to staunch. I've spent a full day trying and I've na' much left."

Shock iced her. Staying her tongue and catching at her breath.

"You're verra bonny . . . and I'm nae saint!"

She was trembling. With that came even more weak feeling.

"I'm for a swim. In cold water. I canna' do it and protect you at the same time. So you're coming with me. To help . . . or curse us both. You ken what I speak of yet?"

She nodded. At least the limp woman in his arms did. This time when he removed his hand, she didn't make a sound. She wasn't capable of it as he simply tugged his belt, bent forward slightly, and let his attire fall off. That left nothing but a strap across his chest holding his sword at his back. Brielle spun but the movement upset her balance, gaining her the feel of him against her again. Naked. Taut. Large. She held her breath and watched odd-shaped dots dance before her eyes.

"You doona' listen to anything! I'm begging here. I need a dunking and I need you to cease fighting. Get that velvet off. Keep the kirtle and what-all else. I doona' care. They'll dry. Now move!"

He released her and if she hadn't felt so faint, her fingers would've worked better.

Four

She'd be the death of him yet.

Gavynn ducked his head under the water, then slid his hands though his hair, ignoring where the lass stood, arms wrapped about her while she shivered in place. The burn was hip-deep on him. Cold. Clean. Fast moving. Difficult to hear over. Gavynn amended that. He couldn't hear much over his own heartbeat. All of it made him vulnerable. This wasn't a good idea, but he hadn't had one since meeting her. His chest and belly were tender with bruising, his muscles throbbed with the work he'd forced on them, and the woman's linen under-dress was as useless as a film of white mist would be.

She was true beauty . . . in form as well as face. Well-formed. Lush. Curved in all the proper places. Possessing heavy, hand-filling breasts, a narrow waist, and hips well-rounded to greet and satisfy a man. When she'd bent forward to wash her face, his groan almost made it through clenched lips. Gavynn grabbed hand-scoops of water, angrily splashing cold and wet all over. Then he bent his knees, dipping to his armpits in chill. All in an effort to divert the pressure building in his groin as blood filled the area, engorging and hardening, and angering him with how little his mind controlled anything.

Nothing worked. He couldn't keep his eyes and thoughts off her. Gavynn lifted his head to the twilit sky, close to howling his frustration. And when he brought his head back down he got a full dose of his utter stupidity. He hadn't even heard them. Gavynn sent the curses soundlessly before rising to face a solid wall of armour-clad men atop horses. They carried torches. Full weaponry. And all he claimed was the sword at his back.

Gavynn had it drawn and the woman to his front, ignoring her gasp as their wet, chilled linen-covered flesh contacted. She'd probably be fighting him, if the steel across her throat didn't silence her as much as the men they faced. Nobody said anything as the horses parted. Gavynn blinked water out of his vision at the sight of a friar picking his way through the knights. The man shoved the cowl from his shaved head and then he started yelling, sending words into the air at a volume impossible to overlook.

"Greetings, your Grace!"

Gavynn flexed, pushing the edge of steel against her throat in reply.

"Are you Gavynn MacEuann? Duke of Ethelstone, Earl of Euann, Laird and Chieftain of Clans Ethel and MacEuann?"

Brielle sagged, gaining him dead-weight. Gavynn was forced to move his sword away as helms were removed and weapons lowered. None of them looked angry. They were mostly smiling. Amused. Entertained. At Gavynn's predicament. He'd faced death before but never against such odds and at such a disadvantage.

"You are the duke . . . are you not?" The man pestered again.

Gavynn nodded slowly. Once.

"Good. 'Tis for your ears that I address these words."

"Address them, then." Gavynn had to be satisfied with the threat his voice carried. He had nothing save his sword. And Lady Brielle's life.

"I bring words from the earl!"

"Where's my brother then?"

"At the castle. Awaiting."

"I'll na' give her over unless I have Iain."

"The earl is aware of it. 'Tis why he sent me. You doona' care if

I join you?" The man squatted at the bank, pulled off his boots, and stepped into the stream. "'Tis powerful cold, your Grace."

"'Tis deadly, as well." Gavynn slashed at the air before returning the blade to her throat.

"I am a man of God."

"You'll still bleed."

"Ah. Therein lies a truth." The friar raised a hand and pointed a finger in the air. "You dare na' kill me. Or her. Because of your brother."

The man took a step closer. It didn't look easy. Gavynn noted how the water darkened and weighed down the cassock he wore.

"Have you na' wondered why there was no ransom demand for Iain?"

Gavynn twisted the sword hilt, sending glints on to the water from the torches they carried, letting the steel speak for him.

"The earl decided it served little purpose. He's tired of ceaseless wars and killing with you and your kind."

"My kind? You're Scot, too, Father."

The friar smiled. "'Tis true enough. I've also seen too much of war and killing a-tween the Sassenach and us. The earl has decided to change it. Using her. The woman you hold."

"Call it true, old man. She's his daughter," Gavynn answered.

"You ken that?"

"'Tis known the earl's daughter has beauty, alongside a tongue of spikes."

"And you dinna' wonder at why she was there? Easy to reach? Ripe for the kidnap?"

"She has a mouth of spikes. As I just spoke."

The friar chuckled. The others might have, as well. Brielle wasn't breathing. Or it was so slight he couldn't feel it.

"The earl tired of her refusals to wed. So . . . he selected a bride-groom for her. And sent her to the dungeons to consider her refusal."

Gavynn inclined his head to one side. "My brother, Iain?"

The friar stepped closer, moving his arms against the water for the movement. "Perhaps. I'm not privy to the workings of the earl's mind. All I ken is that he's verra satisfied with events. Verra."

The man was smacking his lips and rubbing his hands as if to demonstrate. Gavynn swallowed and lowered his chin, touching minutely on Brielle's head before moving away.

"The earl believes a much more suitable union is with you."

"I canna' marry her. I'm wed." Gavynn tried a bluff.

"Nae longer. You're widowed. A season past."

Gavynn felt his shoulders twitch slightly.

"You need forgive me, Laird MacEuann, but you doona' have the choice. Look."

The friar motioned again with his finger. Gavynn twisted, taking Brielle with him and swishing water. Now he knew where his Honour Guard had gone. As well as the men he'd hired. They were bundled into a group encircled by countless archers, all poised with bows pulled taut, arrows readied. Gavynn felt an emotion close to fear. And then defeat. The combination weakened a man. He'd thought them long vanquished. He could feel it happening now, though, sapping strength. He'd been hooked, reeled in, and netted like a salmon. The worst was that he'd done it to himself.

All of it.

"You do see? You'll marry the Lady Brielle . . . right now. And in exchange your brother will be freed. And wouldn't we all be better off moving from this water first? Although I'm na' averse to wedding you both right here . . . but 'tis powerful cold for the consummation. All of that aside . . . your roasting sup is making my mouth water."

Gavynn lowered his sword, hefted Brielle up against him, and worked at controlling the rage making his heart thump, his muscles tense, and smearing his vision with red. He knew he wasn't successful.

"Verra well, Father. I'll wed with her. But from shore. Attired in my *feile-breacan*. As is proper."

"And the consummation afterwards?"

"Doona' force it, Father. I'm warning you. I'll wed her, and then I'll bed her. But there'll be nae witness. Or you'll be responsible for what ensues."

Gavynn didn't care if the friar agreed or not. He was beyond it.

If Brielle could've halted her hearing, she would have. Long before the acid-toned vows Gavynn spoke during the ceremony that included her father's Man-At-Arm to speak for her, and well before the words pronouncing them wed. Deafness would be a blessing. Or oblivion. Despite everything she'd fought against, she was being wed against her will. Exactly as Father had ordered, and to the man he'd aimed for.

Brielle realized the extent of their treachery while standing motionless and silent at the Highlander's side, suffering shivers caused by more than a wet under-dress, covered over with a plaid blanket. It was as clear as the night sky above them. She'd been naïve and blind. She'd known the king needed Highlanders at his court. The most powerful clans. The fiercest warriors.

That was why she'd been sent to the dungeons for arguing; the true reason she'd been put in that particular cell; the purpose behind the marks weakening the stone. They'd planned this. All of it. The cunning amazed her even as the success of it stunned.

She should feel anger and shock. Hatred. Disgust. Embarrassment. Humiliation. Brielle tried to find even one of those. And failed. It would be easier if the man they'd forced to her side wasn't this particular one. Gavynn MacEuann was more male than she knew existed. He affected her more in the one day she'd known him than anyone else had managed. Just standing beside him, she felt him. Everything seemed to spark a reaction; an unbidden glimmer of desire and passion; a stir of longing. Yearning. She was at a full tremble when he turned, watching the friar bind their hands together, blessing their union. Her fingers were cold. She wondered if he noticed. Brielle dared the tiniest glance up before getting held. An ocean wave of noise went through her ears, her heart fluttered about like a caged bird, and his fingers tightened on hers. She heard the words pronouncing their union. Until death.

And then she heard all kinds of things. Intruding. Frightening. Extolling. Shouting.

Something was yelled about requirements being fulfilled. Sending word. Gaining Iain MacEuann. Above that, Brielle heard calls for a bedding ceremony, sending her heart to the bottom of her belly, pounding weakness through her from there. Jeering happened. Angered voices got louder. Arguing. Challenging. Blending into a cacophony of noise. And then without warning, laughter erupted. Like a bubble bursting. Someone started singing, the thump of a keg getting opened sounded. Ale got dipped out, mugs tippled.

And then all of it got obliterated by the sight, feel and smell of her new husband pulling at her, using the bond of their hand. Brielle seemed rooted in place. Unmoving. His visage grew larger. His frame more immense. The feel of ground beneath her bare feet faded, changing to a cloud substance.

Someone yelled about consequences. Proof. It got answered with a man's word being his bond, and the laird had already given it. She heard more angered voices about blood proof . . . and then someone said to hush and watch what was happening and they'd not need witness. Nor further argue.

Her humanity was replaced with a reality that was Gavynn. His chest felt chiselled from stone, his belly cut from rock-hard ropes of muscle, and his shoulders might be blocks of flesh-covered iron. Brielle was crushed to all of it, breathing every inhalation with him as the din about them grew and then ebbed. And then grew again.

Brielle felt stewed, as if she'd drunk a tankard of their strongest ale; heated, as if she knelt before an open flame; adrift, as if the berth in his arms were a cradle. Alive. Tingly aware. She'd been lifted; her knees arched over his forearm, while the other supported her back; mesmerized in place by light green eyes that glowed whenever torchlight touched them.

Laughter came in spurts about them; ribald and lewd, loud and full. More murmurs of voices. Speaking of lust being a grand thing. It excelled through the most acrimonious of unions. Covered hate. Tempted angels from their perches. It was a panacea for all ills. Hatred. Dislike. Marriage to an enemy. Toasts were spoken, heralding great things of progeny . . . especially given the virility of the husband. That remark got more swells of laughter.

Music started; first as a melodic strain from a lute, leading men to sing in off-key voices. A horn joined; drums. The addition of bagpipes only added to the melee encircling them, making a whorl of noise with Gavynn at the centre of it.

Brielle barely heard anything. Her entire sphere was Gavynn, his breathing harsh and quick against her forehead, his eyes intent. Dangerous. He ducked slightly, swivelled, and passed through a tent flap, without releasing her gaze and without blinking. She'd never felt so odd. Tense. Primed. Needful. Brielle licked at her bottom lip before pulling it into her mouth. His eyes dropped there for the briefest moment before he bent forward, releasing her to an unsteady stand on the fabric of a pallet.

"Can you ride?"

He was sideways to her, adjusting clothing and grabbing at weaponry slung in pegs on the walls. Tucking wicked-looking knives along his belt, slinging a bow across his back where it joined his scabbard, ignoring her.

"R-r-ride?"

"Can you sit a horse or na'?"

"Now?"

"Aye. Now."

His words were curt. Angered. Causing a flurry of emotion all over. Sending tears if she didn't get them staunched quickly enough. Brielle locked every limb in the fight against them. And hid it with a nod.

"Good. Here."

He flung a pouch at her. Brielle missed it and got a snorted sound from his lips as she reached for it.

"You need to hurry, Wife. We've na' much time."

Wife? Brielle blinked tears into existence on her cheeks, then wiped at them as quickly as she could. It was bad enough he didn't wish intimacy with her, without feeling how it rankled. It would be immeasurably worse if he saw . . . and guessed. Yet despite her efforts, more stupid moisture cursed her eyes, and that got more wiping.

"We may yet catch them!"

"Catch . . . them?" She should've kept the question unsaid. The sound of his movements halted momentarily. She knew why. He had heard her fighting tears.

"Reeb. My brother. Going about the war I ordered."

Brielle blinked more tears down her cheeks. Used the woven material of the pouch to absorb them. Nodded again. Swallowed. Barely kept from sobbing.

"Do you need an assist?"

She shook her head. He went to a knee, one of their short thin knives in his hand. The blade paused. And then a hand came into her vision, cupping her chin and raising her face. Brielle shut her eyes.

"You . . . cry?"

She shook her head again. She didn't trust her voice not to howl with horridness. It had to be the effects of incarceration; going without food, water, or rest; being kidnapped; forced to wed a barbarian . . . anything but this rejection. Anything.

He dropped her chin. She watched him slice his forearm, opening a cut that immediately welled blood. He swiped it in large swooping motions on to the pallet; ripped a strip of plaid from his hem; bound it tightly on to the wound; tied it with his free hand, all the while punctuating his movements with vicious-toned words.

"You cry without reason. I'm na' a bad choice to husband. There are many families wishful of my hand, should I offer. And look. I am full cursed. Again. There. We've consummated this. Now, come. A-fore we're stopped."

Fresh tears obliterated the reddish streaks on the pallet. She blinked but more came. Filling and refilling her eyes to the point of madness.

He sighed. Heavily. The next moment she was lifted, being jostled about as he slipped through a back opening of the tent. The jog to his horse was worse, as was the feel of him behind her, pulling her close, and clicking his tongue.

Her tears slowed when they reached open moors, before dissolving to hiccups of effort. Brielle had never been so exhausted. Limp. Drained. She felt his legs tightening on the horse's sides, the long strides that rocked her in place, Gavynn's heavy breath touching her nose with precise rhythm. All combined to total security.

And then she felt absolutely nothing.

Five

He heard Reeb before he saw him. It wasn't difficult. Clansmen were about the chores of feeding a group of battle-hardened men, pushing a wheeled siege tower towards their objective, while an onager gave them trouble in the sodden fields, carving at a downed tree in rhythm that would ram the gates. He whistled the alert at his presence. The activity grew slack and then died away as Gavynn rode up, to where Reeb was atop the catapult, hammering lines into place so they could send missiles against Dillbin Castle walls.

Gavynn spurred the horse, held his wife closer, and galloped into the centre of camp, looking across and up at his brother.

"Reeb! Halt!"

Gavynn's brother was an older image of Iain; immense, sturdily built, awe-inspiring . . . unless one saw him standing beside his older sibling. There any resemblance ended. Reeb had a head of red-blond hair and a beard to match. He was wearing little more than paint beneath his battle-scarred, faded *feile-breacan,* as were the others milling about. He stopped pounding at the onager bolt and turned.

"Good. You're here. Right in time. Help me with this!"

"Call off the siege."

Reeb's jaw split, parting his beard. And then the shock

transferred to his voice, proving he possessed the MacEuann power of speech. "What?"

The word roared through the early morn camp, stopping anyone still working. It didn't affect the woman in Gavynn's arms in the slightest. He knew why: exhaustion. He'd faced it often enough.

"You heard me. Call it off."

"The man will na' release Iain!"

"He will now. I have his daughter." Gavynn tilted his head towards the unconscious woman in his arms.

"What wizardry is this?" Reeb jumped down, sinking into ground that was full saturated, and then stepping towards Gavynn's horse. He looked from the bundle in Gavynn's arms back to him. "Where's your Honour Guard?"

"Last seen, they were splitting a keg with Dillbin's troops."

"Good news! The castle will be unguarded. You hear that, lads?"

"I ordered it called off, Reeb. I meant it."

His brother gave a huge sigh. "I already sent word of what he'll face once we break through."

"Nae need."

"The man has na' even answered! He's the basest coward. You expect me to accept that? And back off my demands?"

Gavynn shook his head, getting a whiff of her hair. "The man possesses cunning, Reeb. Mount your men and ride with me. He'll open the gate willingly. You'll see."

Reeb sucked in his belly, puffed out his chest, and looked angered. "'Twill na' matter which MacEuann he faces, brother. The man is Sassanach. Overly boastful, and full-bold. He does na' ken what it means to face us. He'll na' open those gates."

"He will. I'm his new son-by-law."

This time Reeb's jaw completely dropped. Gavynn couldn't help his smile.

"Up, my Lady! Up. You can't sleep much longer . . . although heaven knows, you have need." The cheerful words accompanied movement about the room, pulling drapes and opening shutters. "Now Elspeth. Mary. Direct the freemen about the bath. Before the fireplace. And be quick on it!"

Brielle opened her eyes to a coverlet, embroidered all over with stitches she'd designed and executed, using thread of a pristine white against the ecru-shaded linen. She lifted her head, groaned at the ache that happened, and dropped back to her pillow. It smelled fresh. Clean. And she'd slept on her belly. Face-down. That was totally foreign and made her neck hurt, too.

"You needn't rush it, my Lady. There's plenty of time a-fore the banquet."

"Banquet?" Brielle addressed the word to her pillow, moving numbed arms in position for a roll to her side. Or something. Her mind was in denial of what her senses told her. She was in her own chamber, her own maid in attendance. All of it impossible.

"Aye. A grand affair. I vow, there's not been such goings-on since your dear mother passed on, God rest her soul. Why . . . the preparations alone are mind-spinning. They've got more game meats roasting than we had spits for. They had to construct more out on the list, where the smell rouses more than one appetite. And for certain the cook staff is flustered, what with orders to prepare all sorts of tempting breads and puddings. The aleswoman is beside herself. She's had to break into the stock for enough brew. Even her mead. And you know that woman brews a stout mead." There was the sound of smacking lips. "'Twill be quite the affair. His Lordship even hired real musicians this time. Not like that horrid Arran fellow from the other night. That man can't play a pipe to save his arse!"

The maid chuckled at her own jibe, and then sent a scraping sound through the chamber. Brielle rotated her head and watched her privacy screen get set up. Just like normal. As if she hadn't left this room four days ago with a cowl about her for warmth and an escort of guards on her way to the dungeon. Brielle groaned.

"Here, Lady Brielle. I've brought you a bit of that mead. Warmed. Just as you like it. It'll be just the thing. You'll see. We'll have you up and dressed in your finery for presentation in no time." Brielle was on her side, and then she was working at sitting up, all of it accompanied by massive ache that had no centre. She scooted back into layers of pillows fronting her headboard, accepted the mug of steamed liquid and sipped. And then she looked over at her maid.

"Presentation?" The word was low-toned and harsh. It was a good thing she'd swallowed the mead, otherwise she'd possess no voice at all. Brielle frowned. Sipped.

"Your new husband ordered it so."

Her throat revolted and Brielle choked, coughed and then had to wipe the moisture from her cheeks. Through it all, she could feel ache spreading. She knew where it originated now and hated everything about it. She didn't dare feel anything for him. She couldn't. And nothing that could be labelled as love. It wasn't warranted. It wasn't feasible. It wasn't possible.

And she knew she lied.

"The MacEuann is a prime catch. Your father is announcing it to all. Has sent word to the king! He's proud of you, My Lady. You've gone and captured the MacEuann laird!'"

"'Tis a shame he doesn't want me. Is Father announcing that?"

"What nonsense is this? You're an heiress! MacEuann's been assessing your dowry all afternoon. What man wouldn't want that?"

"I said he doesn't want *me*. Not the riches that come with my hand."

The maid stopped her fussing, put her hands on her hips and regarded Brielle. "He looked full pleased to me."

"When?" Brielle lifted the mug and took a sip.

"I was here when he carried you in, held real close. He placed you with extra care. Stood looking at you, and I'm telling you. He sure had the look of wanting his bride. Now come. Drink up. We've got to bathe and dress, and that water is na' getting any warmer while you tarry."

Brielle sipped at her mead and regarded her maid. And hoped.

No afternoon had seemed longer or more tedious; filled with looking over the castle, examining the treasury, listening to everything that came with Brielle's hand. As if they hadn't already wed, satisfying both families' honour. Gavynn was bored before reaching the armoury, long before a tour of the battlements, looking at the land claimed as a demesne, and nothing kept him from swaying from foot to foot when they examined the stables. It was Brielle's hand that mattered, not what came with it.

Gavynn followed the steward's words, hiding the sense of anticipation just beneath the surface. It had been there when he'd awakened, and it just kept growing. Preparing. Readying. Going to a dizzying increase of pulse-beat whenever he thought of seeing her again. He had no choice but to temper it. And then hide it.

And now, here he was, at the time when the meats would be removed from the Great Hall, and his new wife had yet to even show herself. Gavynn put another tasteless bite in his mouth, chewed it and glanced at Iain, looking pale and thin in a position beside Reeb. Gavynn knew the lad expected and dreaded punishment for being the catalyst behind this marriage. Iain didn't know there wouldn't be any. And Gavynn wasn't saying. Yet.

He smiled slightly at his brother's discomfiture. Such a thing was punishment enough for being caught reaving without taking a clansman for assist.

The slightest change alerted Gavynn of Brielle's entrance. A ripple went along the crowded tables below him, lifting man after man to his feet. Silently. In homage. Gavynn half-stood as well, despite being on an elevated dais. Then he settled back into an indolent position, as if she meant little. He couldn't do anything about the increase of heart-beat as Lady Brielle neared, wearing a silver-cast satin that shimmered in the torch-light, while the same shade of veil trailed from the point of her headdress. It framed and highlighted her beauty. Needlessly.

Despite the hold he exerted, Gavynn couldn't prevent a lurch towards her . . . as if beckoned. As if she actually wanted him. It also evidenced how little he'd managed to temper his own desire. The anticipation was humming through him, sending frustration with it. Gavynn shook in place. This was much worse than his first wedding. He'd been eighteen then, and forced as well. His bride had turned her nose up at him, too, but it hadn't felt like this. He'd had to force his feet to her bedchamber. This time, he'd be doing the opposite: running away.

Gavynn rubbed his palms along his thighs, moving wool plaid with the motion. He missed her approach due to it, but he knew it was happening. Silence seemed to fill the area about her, a reverent kind of sound. And then she was there. At his side. Being seated with a swish of satin, the slightest scent hovering about, sending his senses into alarm and fright, and kicking his heart into sporadic, heavy thumps that had nothing rhythmic to them. He turned his head to watch as she put a morsel to her mouth. Chewed it. Swallowed. His throat made an answering gulp. And then she spoke.

"My Laird?"

Her whisper carried even more sweetness! Gavynn tightened his fingers about each knee before turning fully to her and forced his gaze to hers. The moment their eyes touched, she jerked hers away, putting dark lashes against her cheeks.

He reached for his tankard. "Aye?"

"I need to ask you . . . something."

Her voice was hesitant and light. It was going to haunt his every waking moment! It already was, he decided.

"Ask it," he replied curtly.

"I need you to keep silent . . . a bit . . . longer. Please?"

Gavynn wasn't pretending the confusion over her words. His entire body suffered it. He grunted what went for an answer.

"He m-may not . . . release your b-brother . . . if he . . . knows."

Her stammered words tied him in a thousand knots and then pulled at each of them. Gavynn lifted the drinking vessel to his lips to disguise the shake. "Kens what?"

"That I . . . displease you."

Displease him? Gavynn choked, felt the sear, and forced the cough away by sheer will. It made his eyes water and his throat burn, but it was done.

"What?"

The croak of voice carried his surprise. He put the tankard back down with a slam, blinked moisture out of his eyes, and watched her look out over the assemblage, the slightest pout to her lips.

"You were forced to – to . . . wed me."

"What of it?" *And God curse the effect she has on me!* Gavynn held his sporran in place with both hands before it alerted any who looked of his inability to control his own desire for his new wife. He waited two full heartbeats. Then she moved, tipping her chin to meet his gaze full on, stopping every other sound in the room.

"I . . . don't understand, then."

"What?"

"Last eve . . . when you – you—"

Her voice trailed off. His pulse ramped up, sending rushing water noise through each ear. "When I . . . what?" he prompted.

"You forged proof of . . . the consummation."

He guessed from her lips what the words were. It wasn't possible to hear them. "I will na' take an unwilling woman to my bed, Lass. Ever." His answer was cold. Curt.

"You . . . thought me . . . unwilling?"

Gavynn went still. Coiled both hands into fists about his sporran. Gulped.

"Aye."

"Oh, no. I mean . . . I—" She lifted dark eyes to his, and blushed. He watched the pink suffuse her cheeks. "I don't know . . . what to say," she offered.

Gavynn cleared his throat. "Here is what you say. 'I am na' averse to wedding with you, Gavynn MacEuann. And I am willing to tupp with you as well.'"

She gasped. He watched her silver-satin-encased bosom rise with it. "I can't say that!"

"Infer it, then." He was stirring. Growing heavy and hard for her right then. And right there. He couldn't help it.

She twisted her fingers together. Looked away. Flitted back to look at him. Away again.

"Perhaps you could just nod, Wife. That would suffice for the same."

She nodded and went even redder. The rush overtaking his body was severe enough he shook with it. She lifted her gaze to his. Stilled. He watched her eyes widen at what she saw.

"I've a great need of privacy. And little need of food. Or drink. You agree?"

She nodded.

"Good."

"But . . . the guests." She waved a hand out towards the faceless crowd.

"Can finish without us. Rory! Greggor! Reeb!" Gavynn yelled the names as he stood.

"My Laird?"

There was reaction happening about him. Laughter. Jibing. Hilarity. Gavynn wasn't facing it. Maybe tomorrow, when tales of his eagerness would probably get written into love-imbued sonnets. Maybe then. But not now.

"See us to my chamber. Now!"

She was walking at first, taking steps so small they irritated with delay. Gavynn had her in his arms before they reached the archway leading to the towers. Much to everyone's further amusement.

Six

They'd given him the largest tower room, where a fireplace warmed the interior. Brielle kept her face firmly into his neck the entire time it took to reach there. She knew the sounds of entertainment filling the great room they'd left, felt the firm grasp holding her for a jog up the stairs, heard the slam of the door, felt the instability of shaky legs on a wooden floor, and then watched as he dropped the bolt, sealing them in.

Alone.

Her legs were trembling, threatening a drop as he approached, moving with steady silent strides towards her, before stopping within reach, his chest expanding with huge gulps of breath.

"I . . . uh . . ." Her voice was missing. Brielle swallowed.

"Doona' say anything. Please?"

"But, I—"

"You doona' obey the slightest thing! I warn you, Wife." He moved a step closer, taking up her entire vision, while both hands reached, stopping just shy of clasping her about the waist.

"You've a voice to melt ice, breath that torments, and words that steal wits. I've little left to fight it. Verra little."

"Fight . . . what?"

"This!"

He had her yanked into an embrace, her feet off the floor, and his lips at her forehead. Heavy heartbeats pumped from his chest into hers, while each breath cooled heated cheeks. Brielle's heart met each and every beat. Her breaths mingled with his, and then he trailed his mouth to hers, taking her lips in a kiss unlike any before. If she could have, Brielle would've swooned. She knew it would feel like the disembodied sensation of him carrying her to his enclosed bed, tossing her without thought on to the coverlet and following the motion with his body.

She felt her shoulder strap slide, warmth following as his fingers trailed her arm, pushing fabric. He went to a bow shape to press his kiss to her throat. His hands shoving and sliding fabric, until the naked awareness of her nipples met the linen of his shirt. Brielle gasped, moved her hands to his shoulders, rubbing and massaging and gaining vast reservoirs of wet and want that started at her core and spread from there. And then he was sending the torment to higher levels, using his tongue to trace a trail of ice and fire right to where her nipples were hard darts of ache. And then he lapped at a nipple, sending her body into an arch of sensation and wonder.

Brielle melted. Throbbed. Pulsed. Careened. And sent a cry until her breath ran out and she had to gain another. His chuckle made the sensation worse. So much worse, Brielle grabbed at his arms to hold him in place. Was still there as he lifted, brought his kiss back to hers, and lapped where she couldn't gain enough.

His belt fell, landing momentarily at where the satin pooled at her waist, before he shoved it aside. His kilt followed, as a sail of fabric she barely saw. Brielle was beyond it. Her arms were wrapped about his chest, glued there to keep the sensations of both nipples to a livable level. Panted with him. And then accepted his weight.

Her skirts tore. She heard it as well as felt the release of material separating their loins, and then she felt the strangeness of him. Hard. Thick. Hot. Huge.

"Open for me, Love. Open . . ."

The whisper trembled through her ear, sent in gasps of breath that slithered over where he'd lifted in a push-up from her. His hair had come untied as well, leaving strands to brush and tickle her cheeks, her nose . . . her lips. Brielle held on.

"Wrap your legs about me."

He lowered his head, into the space beside her shoulder, using it as a fulcrum to release his hands. Brielle felt them at her hips, lifting her. Holding her in place so he could slide against her innermost area, toying. Exciting. Stimulating. Inciting and agitating and creating a whorl of pleasure unlike anything she'd ever known.

Brielle went wild.

Surges of absolute bliss flew into her, and she shoved back, accepting and expanding, and then learning absolute agony.

"Easy, lass."

"It . . . hurts, Gavynn. It—"

"I ken, Love. 'Tis only the first time. Truly, and – Lord! Doona' do that again!"

Brielle's eyes went wide as red suffused every bit of his flesh. His entire body went tense, taut, and statue-still, trembling with a vast-ness that moved her with it. A long groan fled his lips, pushed with his exhalation. Gavynn dropped his head, found her mouth, and sucked every breath she gave.

Brielle's moan matched his, her tongue as well, rinsing the pain into a memory with every lunge he made. Every pull from the embrace of her flesh. Return. Over and over, with increasing need and energy fuelling each thrust.

Brielle clung harder, holding to every bit of the wild thing that was Gavynn as he bucked and heaved. Her arms and legs strained, filled with the ache of holding, her mouth moved, sucking on the delicate skin just below his ear, while her entire experience filled with tension. Building. Rising. Sending flickers of excitement with every touch of his body into hers. Creating tendrils of sensation that kept coming. And just when she didn't think she could catch another breath, everything erupted.

Brielle cried aloud, her eyes clenched tight as waves of wonder flowed over her, taking her higher than the room could contain and wider than the sky could manage. And keeping her there for entire heartbeats of time while he continued pumping into her, sending waves atop the others. And just when she thought she might die of the ecstasy, he ceased all movement.

Brielle held on as Gavynn's entire body tightened as he groaned, long and low, his body heaving and pulsing against hers. And then he stopped, opened his eyes to look down at her, and then collapsed; rolling at he did so, and taking her with him.

His heartbeat was at thunder level, hurtful to her ear, while each breath was heavy, matching hers and sending his muscled belly into hers. He was covered in a thin film of wet, making a godlike creature that glowed with each flare from the fire. Brielle had never seen or experienced anything so beautiful. She reached with a finger and trailed it alongside his face, and then traced his lips. He kissed it.

"Gavynn?"

"Aye?"

One eye slit open, catching her rapt gaze, and then his body pulsed alongside hers, moving her with it.

"That was . . ." Brielle stopped. She didn't know how to describe the ecstatic feeling still filling her.

"I dinna' hurt you overmuch?" He asked.

Brielle's eyes widened. "You meant to hurt?"

He smiled, showing every bit of handsomeness and making her heart lurch. She was frightened for what that could mean. And with a man she barely knew. She watched him lift a lock of her hair and take it to his lips. And place a kiss reverently on the hair strands, his eyes never leaving hers.

"Nae. Never. The first time always pains, love. 'Tis na' much a man can do to prevent such. 'Twill na' pain the next time."

"Next . . . time?"

His smile widened. "I'm verra certain there'll be a next time. And a time after that. And then more. That is how a man shows his wife he's verra much in love with her."

"In love?" Her voice was missing. It got lost in tears that obliterated him until she blinked them out of the way.

The smile spread to his eyes. "Damn my tongue for admitting it, but aye. I'm in love with you, Wife, or I'm ill. Either frightens me."

It wasn't the best time to cry, but that didn't stop her. Brielle would tell him later why. For now he had to guess it from her happy embrace.

Curse Me Wicked

Elle Jasper

Village of Dunmorag, North West Highlands, Scotland, October

"So you think you can handle this one, huh, newbie?"

I glanced at Paxton Terragon, the arrogant, senior field agent I'd been training with for the past three months. He was in his mid-thirties, wore white spiked hair and looked like Billy Idol. I narrowed my gaze, sick to death of being called *newbie*. "Hell yeah."

Pax laughed, grabbed the keys from the ignition, jumped out and slammed the door. I did the same and Pax peered at me over the top of the car. "Fearless Ginger Slater, WUP's most notorious risk-taking newbie field agent is ready for a little action, huh?"

The agency we worked for, WUP – Worldwide Unexplained Phenomena – had partnered me with an idiot. A biting wind whipped across the car park and sank clear to my bones, and I pulled the edges of my leather jacket closer. I frowned at Pax. "I was a shape-shifters/curses specialist for two years prior to joining WUP so lay off and let's go." As I rounded the back of the Rover, my eyes searched the grey, bleak village of Dunmorag.

Pax chuckled. "So you have a couple of years behind you and what?" He cocked his head and stared at me. "Think you're ready?" He shook his head and popped the hatch. "I've been at this for ten years, newbie, and trust me – you're never ready."

I met Pax's stare for a few seconds, told him to *eff-off* in my head, grabbed my pack and shouldered it. Then I *really* took a good look around at the secluded Highland village. Desolate was the first word that came to mind. Half-dozen grey stone and white-washed buildings hugged the pebbled crescent shore of a small lake – rather, loch. Beyond the village were the Rannoch Moors, which were even more desolate than Dunmorag. Tufts of dead grass, brown heather and rock stretched for miles. Far in the distance, dark, craggy mountains threw long shadows and loomed ominously. The skies were grey. The moors were grey. Even the water in the loch was grey. Well, black.

Foreboding. That was the second word that came to mind.

"You gonna stand here all day and take in the scenery or what?" Pax asked.

I gave him a hard look, which he ignored and instead inclined his head to the pub behind us. "I'm ready," I said, shifted my pack, shrugged my leather jacket collar closer to my neck, and together we crossed the small car park. The wind bit straight through my clothes and I shivered as I stepped on to the single paved walk that ran in front of the stores. I glanced down the row of buildings. A baker. A fishmonger. The post office. A grocer. An inn and a pub. *And absolutely no people around.* Weird. Very, very weird. Good thing weird was our speciality.

A black sign with a sliver of a red moon painted on it swung above the pub on rusted hinges, and the creaking noise echoed off the building. In silver letters the sign read *The Blood Moon.* Pax pushed in through the double red doors – quite befitting, the red – and I followed. Inside, it took my eyes several seconds to adjust to the dimmer light. A hush fell over the handful of people gathered in the single-room dwelling. "Guess we found the villagers," I whispered to Pax. Everyone stopped what they were doing, or saying, to stare at us. No one uttered a word.

I glanced at Pax, then all around, until my eyes lighted on the man behind the bar. He had dark, expressionless eyes, reminding me of a shark's, and they bore straight into me. His head, shaved bald, shone beneath the pub's overhead light. He said nothing. I walked up to him and met his gaze. "We're looking for Lucian MacLeod," I said. "Know where we can find him?"

The bartender shot a quick glance to someone behind us – I don't know who – before returning his heavy gaze to me. "He's no' here," he said, his brogue so thick I barely caught all the words. "Best you and your friend just go." He stared. "Lucian willna be back anytime soon."

I smiled. "Could you just point us in the right direction? We came a long way."

The bartender looked first at Pax, then back at me. "From

America, aye?" he said, regarding both of us. Then he leaned across the bar, his hard gaze settled on me. "You know the moors, do you girl?"

I shrugged. "Not really but we can find them. Why, is that where he's at?"

"Callum, dunna do it," an older woman said in a hushed voice from a table near the window. She looked at the bartender, but not me. "'Tis wrong."

Callum shot the woman a hard look.

"Look, Callum," I said. "Lucian contacted us for our services, so," I leaned forward, "why don't you just tell us where to find him and we'll be on our way."

The bartender studied me for several seconds before answering. "He's on the far north of the Rannoch Moors, in a little stone bothy," he said. "'Tis the only one out there. But I'm givin' you fair warning, lass," his voice dropped. "Get your business done and off the moors by nightfall. If you canna find MacLeod, leave."

I held his gaze. It took a lot more to frighten me than a *moor warning*. Besides – ole Callum had *no* idea what we were used to. "Thanks." I glanced at Pax and inclined my head towards the door. "Let's go."

Outside, I swear the wind felt ten degrees colder. And it had started to rain. Freaking great.

"Food." Pax wasn't asking, he was telling. His gaze wandered up the walk.

I glanced first at my watch, then gauged the darkening sky. "There's no time."

Pax swore, then headed towards the car, muttering something about fish and chips and beer.

I followed, and as my stomach growled – yeah, I was hungry too – I looked up the one-track lane of Dunmorag, at the bleak buildings, the grey skies, at The Blood Moon pub. A sharp gust of wind whipped by and I squinted against its harshness. An uneasy feeling crept over me. Something wasn't right; something about this whole case didn't sit well with me and I couldn't put a finger on it. And something about Dunmorag wasn't right, either. *Creepy.* It was just so freaking creepy.

It made me wonder just who Lucian MacLeod truly was. To say he'd been vague when he'd called the agency was an understatement; he'd simply asked a few questions, requested a specialist in curses and paid a hefty fee up-front just to procure that specialist. But it was his final plea that had stuck with me when we'd spoken on the phone; *you're my last hope.* I don't know if it'd been the desperation in his voice, or the words themselves; either way, I found I was fascinated. Even if it meant suffering a trans-Atlantic flight and three hours in the car with Pax Terragon, I was still enthralled and interested to sit down and find out the full scoop on Lucian's problem – whatever it was.

We left the dreary Highland village behind, with only four and a half hours left of daylight – if that's what you called it – and headed for the even drearier moors.

"Crisp?" Pax asked, shaking his chip bag at me.

"Let me get this straight," I said, turning sideways in the seat to look at my partner. "You stick your hand in the bag. You pull out a chip; put it in your mouth. Lick your fingers. Then back in the bag they go." I shook my head. "I'll pass."

Pax laughed and crammed several more chips into his mouth. "Whatever, newbie." He jerked a thumb towards the window. "Doesn't look like we'll find anywhere out here to eat."

I glanced around the barren moors and decided Pax was right. There wasn't anything in sight, in any direction, except dead heather, grass and rock. Several brown bunnies had shot across the one-track lane but that was it. No other signs of life existed. Heavy grey and black clouds had claimed the waning afternoon light, throwing the moors into a weird sort of eerie, shadowy hue. The rain had continued, a light drizzle, but constant. I pressed my palm to the window's glass and shivered at its coldness. The temperature outside was dropping. By nightfall, with the rain? Almost unbearable. I preferred the warmth, sunshine, sandy beaches and crystal-clear waters. Neither cold nor gloom ranked as one of my top five faves but both seemed to go hand-in-hand with WUP assignments. Go figure.

"There it is," Pax said, pulling me out of my thoughts. I glanced in the direction he pointed, across the moors, to a small, single-storey stone cottage. A mist had drifted in and settled like a sheet of wispy fog over the dead clumps of grass and heather. Smoke puffed out of the chimney. "MacLeod's here."

"Looks like it," I answered. What the bartender call it? A bothy? It was the only dwelling around, so it had to be it. "Turn there," I said suddenly, noticing a narrow lane veering off towards the cottage. "Has to be the only way over there."

"Right." Pax followed the dirt and rock lane as it wound across the moors, straight towards the bothy. Several minutes later we pulled in front of the cottage, parked, and jumped out. I reached the door to the cottage first, so I knocked.

No answer.

I glanced at Pax, then knocked again – louder. "Mr MacLeod?" I said, close to the door. "It's Ginger Slater from WUP. We spoke on the phone?" I put my hand on the door knob and Pax stopped me.

"Never enter a situation without your gear, newbie," he said, and shoved my pack at me, and I was surprised to see he had his stunner – a ten-inch stainless steel electric probe that packed enough voltage to bring down a horse, or a madman – palmed. Pushing ahead, he opened the door and stepped inside. Feeling like an idiot, I followed. The interior was dim, save the fireplace which had something – not wood – smouldering in the hearth. It smelled earthy. One lamp burned in the corner, next to a recliner and side table; a book lay open, pages face down, spine creased outward. A beer bottle sat beside it.

"MacLeod?" Pax said, his voice stern, throaty, a little threatening. "You in here?" He glanced at me, pointed across the room, then inclined his head towards a hallway, and I nodded. As I pulled my own stunner from my pack, he disappeared down the hall, and I eased towards the only other room visible. I stopped at the side table and grasped the beer bottle; it was still cool and half-full. My fingers tightly gripped the hilt of the stunner, I held my breath, and pushed open the kitchen door.

I never saw inside the room.

A figure lunged at me, knocking me backward several feet where I landed hard on my back. My stunner flew from my hand and skidded somewhere across the floor. I couldn't scream – the air whooshed from my lungs in one gush, my eyes widened, but I saw nothing but . . . mass. Bulk. Shadow. Eyes. It hovered over me, blocking my view, crowding my body, my senses. I couldn't breathe as it was but fear paralyzed me even more. What the *hell*? Then, in the next instant, the figure leapt and was out the door. Rolling to my stomach, I turned, coughing and sputtering as I tried to call out but the air wouldn't come. Whoever had just knocked me over was strong as hell – and gone.

Pax emerged, his stunner raised. He glanced at me. "You okay?"

I nodded and waved, still a little in shock, and Pax nodded once before he disappeared out the front door.

It was no more than three minutes before I finally caught my breath enough to stand. Then, I got up, found my stunner against the wall, and ran after Pax.

As I stood outside the cottage, peering through the now-soupy Highland mist and darkening skies, my mind raced wildly, and I recalled Lucian MacLeod's phone call. *How experienced are you with curses? Creatures? How strong is your stomach, girl? You're my last hope* . . . It hadn't made much sense then – I'd had cases with curses before, and a few involving shape-shifting. Both were handled similarly by binding the victim and searching for the correct curse-reversal – or shape-shifter cure. I'd had one victim shift into a hawk right before my eyes—

A long, deep sound of an animal baying broke through the twilight and mist; it raised the hairs on the back of my neck and quickened my pulse. As my gaze raked slowly over the ground, I fished inside my pack, felt the cool steel beneath my palm, and withdrew my crossbow. I saw nothing out of the ordinary as I assembled the bow and loaded the clip with blades. But a sense of foreboding filled me, choked me, and my insides shook as I eased away from the cottage. I couldn't see a damn thing through the mist; barely my own hand in front of my face. The constant drizzle and heavy mist weighed my hair down, soaked through my jeans, and although twilight was nearly at its end, I eased on to the moors. No way was I hanging out at the cottage alone.

"Pax?" I called out, picking my footing carefully, straining my eyes as I tried to make out my partner's form. "Hey? Where are you?" Dammit, he couldn't have gone too far. We were in the middle of nowhere.

Within minutes my slow movements had carried me far enough away into the mist that I could no longer make out the cottage. Thick white surrounded me, and at once I caught the distinct sound of breathing – heavy breathing – not far from me.

"Pax?" I called again. "Come on, you're freaking me out."

The breathing drew closer.

And became an angry snarl.

I was being stalked. My heart leapt, and I turned and changed direction. That noise hadn't come from my partner – that much I knew. Pax was an ass but he wasn't stupid. I began to hurry, my pace quickening, and just when I thought I was making some ground, it came again.

Closer.

My grip tightened on my bow as I raised it; while I wanted to run like hell, I knew it'd do no good. Something was on the moors, in the mist, *with me.* I swallowed – hard. It didn't help. My heart beat so hard and so fast I could hear it out loud. I waited.

"Gin, run!"

I whipped around and saw the hazy shape of someone moving towards me; Pax's voice spilled over the foggy white, commanding me to run, but I couldn't. I stood frozen in place, confused, scared. I looked up, and only then did I notice the moon above me; it was crescent in shape, and – I blinked my eyes – red. The damn thing looked red.

"Ginger, goddamit, get the hell outta here!" Pax yelled, panic making his voice shake.

I watched as he grew closer, his features clearer, and finally, I turned. I had no idea what direction to run in. I glanced back. "Pax, I—"

Something large, something dark, fast, leapt from below the mist and pulled Pax down. He screamed, so shrill and so terrifying that it made my blood feel cold. An awful crunching sound echoed through the fog.

One last, horrifying, gurgling sound emerged from my partner before the silence hit. Silence, save the heavy breathing that definitely didn't belong to Pax.

Whatever had been shut down in me now flickered to life; I turned and ran. Blindly, as darkness now sifted through the mist and red hue from the moon. My boots scuffed clumps of heather and grass as I hurried, but it didn't mask the sound of footsteps behind me. Footsteps and that damned breathing. Finally, with my heart in my throat, I stopped, dropped to one knee and lifted my crossbow. I stared down the site and waited.

I didn't have to wait long.

With a deep growl and heavy breath, a massive figure lunged from the mist at me; I didn't wait to see who or what it was. I fired three rounds before it landed on me, and the pain of two sharp blades piercing straight through my leather jacket and into my shoulder made me cry out. The blades sank clear to the bone, and the intenseness of it made me nearly pass out. Suddenly, the mass was shoved off, another figure appeared above me, and a pair of angry, lethal amber eyes glared down. Then, my vision fogged. Fiery pain ripped through my body just before a wave of suffocating blackness swept me into nothingness.

Heat. Fire. Skin burning. I sat up with a harsh breath, confusion taking over my brain and making me dizzy. I put a hand to my temple to stop the swirling, but it didn't help. I opened my eyes but everything looked blurred, fuzzy, out of focus. My skin – Jesus, it felt like it would burst into flames – burned sickly hot. I tried kicking out of whatever covered me and I quickly found I hadn't a stitch of clothes on. Not even panties. Totally naked and I couldn't care less. I was smouldering.

"Lay back."

I turned my head towards the voice, but could see nothing more than a hazy figure in shadows. "Where am I?" I asked, struggling to stay up. I dug the heels of both hands hard into the mattress; my arms still shook. "Hot," I said, trying to move. "Burning up."

A firm hand pressed against my chest and with the slightest of pressure, eased me back. "'Tis your DNA altering," the voice said, deep, raspy, and heavily brogued. "It will get worse."

What the hell was he talking about? DNA? I didn't care – I just wanted relief. "Water," I said, my throat dry. I wanted my body extinguished. "Bath. Shower. Ice." My eyes drifted shut.

Strong fingers pushed the hair from my face. "It willna help."

Agony washed over me, and blessed shadows dragged me back under.

A crackling and snapping noise awakened me and when I opened my eyes, I instantly noticed the pain had subsided. I blinked several times to clear my vision; foggy and disoriented at first, then slowly, the room came into focus. I stared hard at my surroundings. In the hearth, a low fire glowed, and again I noticed the earthy scent it released. The flames gave the room a tawny hue, and shadows played against the bare stone walls. A single lamp burned in the corner, on a side table next to a leather recliner.

I sat straight up and gasped, breathless, as recognition and memories assailed me. WUP. Assignment. Scotland. Moors. I glanced around once more.

I was inside Lucian MacLeod's cottage.

Worse memories – recent ones – assaulted me and my body

jerked as they crowded my mind. Pax. Baying. Creature. Pain. Bones crunching.

"Pax!" I shouted, although it came out gravel, hoarse, broken. I struggled to untangle myself from the bed covers, anger and fear causing a sob to escape. "Pax—"

"You're partner isna here," a deep, brogued voice came from the shadows. "'Tis only you."

I pulled up the sheet to cover my nakedness. "Who the hell are you?" I asked, scanning the room for the speaker. "Where's my partner?"

Then, a slight movement from a darkened corner caught my eye; a figure rose and moved into the firelight. Dark, wavy hair brushed his shoulders; a white, long-sleeved shirt, loosely buttoned, hung casually untucked against a pair of worn jeans. A pair of silvery-blue eyes stared down at me. A small scar, just below his left eye, marred otherwise flawless pale skin.

"I'm Lucian MacLeod. Your partner is dead," he said, matter-of-fact and seemingly without remorse. His uncanny gaze bore angrily into mine. "You were no' to come here."

I stared, disbelieving, yet . . . I knew. Those sounds hadn't come from a surviving victim. I still questioned it. "Dead?" I asked, and suddenly I was afraid – of Lucian. I wanted to run, get away. Panic gripped my insides. "What do you mean?" I slid slowly to the edge of the bed and swung my legs over. I briefly wondered where my gear bag was and I gave the room a quick scan but didn't see it.

"You're no' the same, Ms Slater," he said. He didn't move. "Not the same person you were when you arrived. And you're no' leavin' here."

I leapt from the bed and hit the floor running, sheet pulled tightly around me. I didn't know where I thought I was going, barefoot and naked, but I *was going*.

I was caught and slammed against the wall before I ever got close to the door. Lucian's large frame towered over me, crowded my body with his and sufficiently trapped me; he placed a hand on either side of my head then lowered his head to look me in the eye. I breathed hard, my heart slammed, and I stared furiously back.

"You're no' listening, Ms Slater," he began slowly. "You're no' leaving."

"The hell I am," I ground out, and pushed against him. It was like trying to move a rock. It only made him draw closer.

"What do you remember about that eve on the moors?" he asked, his eyes lowering to my mouth. "Tell me."

My mind spun and suddenly, the memory returned. I immediately lifted a hand to my shoulder. "We came here looking for you, but you were no where. There was a lot of thick mist, and Pax – he chased someone out of here. He was attacked. By a big dog maybe. I couldn't tell what it was." I lifted my chin and met Lucian's gaze straight-on. "It turned on me and I shot it."

Lucian's hand moved from the side of my head to my bare shoulder. Calluses raked over my skin, and I couldn't help it – I shivered. "You were bitten." He grazed the flesh again. "By a wolf."

My gaze left Lucian's and I glanced down, at my shoulder. His fingers brushed over two puncture marks; the skin puckered but healed. I looked back at him. I couldn't have heard him right. "What?"

"You've been here nearly three weeks," he said.

My knees gave out and Lucian caught me. I sagged against his body, felt the warmth – *intense warmth* – of his arms around me as he lifted me. He carried me to the bed and settled me down. He leaned over me, and his hair brushed my collar bone.

"You were never supposed to be here," he said, his raspy voice sounding regretful. "Only Agent Terragon." He shook his head. "I requested just him. No' you."

I didn't understand; nothing made sense. A freaking *wolf*? The flames from the hearth flickered and caused shadows to play against Lucian's face, making his already-forceful stare even weightier. I was mesmerized by it. His face, I mean. He was . . . beautiful. It bothered me that I even noticed. I quickly looked away, cleared my throat, and pulled the sheet taut across my breasts.

"Why?" I asked, needing to know more. Needing to know what was so important that Pax had to die. "Why did you call WUP? And why didn't you tell us what we were walking into?"

Lucian turned his face from me and shoved a hand through his hair. "How well versed are you on ancient curses, Ms Slater?" he said, facing the wall.

I sighed and looked at his back, watched the material pull across his shoulders. "I'm a new agent. I've only studied curses for a couple of years, and have been training with Pax for just a few months."

He turned then, his face all sharp planes and shadows. All except his eyes. They literally *glowed*. I gasped.

"I didna mean for you to get involved," Lucian said, his voice grave. "We only wanted help." Grasping his shirt tail, he lifted it, exposing a long, lean abdomen ripped with muscle – and a fresh, healing wound in the shape of a ragged star, just at his ribcage. His head raised, his gaze met mine. "You shot *me*, Ms Slater."

I blinked, stunned. My mind reeled, thoughts pounding the inside of my skull until it ached. "That thing was not you," I said, almost a whisper.

"Aye," Lucian said. "It most certainly was." He stared down at me. "And within the week, 'twill be you, as well."

My body went numb with shock; it was too much to take in and I wasn't positive I believed any of it. Inside, I began to shake. I'd not been ready to take on an assignment. I was too new – a newbie. Pax had been right all along. I was treading in unfamiliar territory now and doing it totally alone.

"Here," Lucian said, tossing a bag onto the bed. "Get dressed. We've things to talk about and time's runnin' out."

We sat at a well-used oak table in the kitchen, across from each other, and I was on my third – yes, third – hamburger steak. No bread, nothing else but the meat. I was ravenous and could have eaten the whole cow, if given it. I felt guilty for eating, yet I couldn't make myself stop.

A single bulb hung over the table, leaving the tiny kitchen barely illuminated. Lucian regarded me closely while I ate, watching every move I made. More than once he followed my fork to my mouth and let it linger. It caused my insides to grow uncomfortably hot. Outside, the rain continued, the wind picked up and slashed at the cottage's window panes. Every so often a lightening bolt would flash and light up a darkened corner. I don't know why but I kept thinking I'd see something horrifying. I didn't. Finally, I'd had enough and I pushed my plate away.

"Thanks," I said. I looked at Lucian. "Why can't I remember the past three weeks?"

"You've been transitioning," he replied, lacing his fingers together on the table. "Your DNA is altering at a high rate. Your core temperature rises and it exhausts your body. You mostly slept."

I nodded, liking the way his r's rolled, then looked at him. Hard. "Did you kill my partner?"

"No."

My gaze never left his. I didn't believe him. "You tried to kill me."

He leaned forward, his voice dropping low. "You dunna know what was behind you when I leapt at you."

My blood ran cold; a new memory hit me. "I remember you falling on top of me, and someone else shoved you off." I thought hard. "I remember angry, amber eyes."

"'Twas Tristan. My kinsman," he answered.

My eyes stretched. "There are more of you?" I shook my head, scrubbed my eyes, then met his gaze. "Who *are* you?"

Lucian sat back and crossed his arms over his chest. "Let's just say I was born this way," he said. "A verra long time ago. 'Tis my MacLeod bloodline, no' a curse. We have honour. A code. Rules we abide by." He shoved a hand through his hair. "But there are others. Dangerous rogues. Lawless, with no regard to human life. At first, there were very few." He looked at me. "But they've bred. They've bitten. And they're out o' control." His eyes smouldered. "They kill for nothin' more than reckless pleasure." He shook his head. "I'm sorry I couldna save your partner. But there were more than one and it was either him, or you." His gaze pinned me. "I chose you."

I felt glad, and that made me feel guilty. "What happened to Pax's body?" I asked. "What about WUP? Didn't they come looking for us?"

"Aye," he answered. He rose and walked to the window and peered out. "Another agent came, after I called. He looked about, asked a few questions, and left." He glanced at me over his shoulder. "The others – they took your partner."

"Took?" I asked incredulously, rose and set my dishes in the sink. I crossed the room and leaned against the wall – a safe distance away from Lucian. "What do you mean?"

Lucian stepped towards me. "They did no' kill him. He'll become *one of them*."

I stared, and then, strange as it sounds, I laughed. "You're kidding me, right? We have *both* become *monsters*?"

"You're not a monster," he said, his voice almost a growl, his brows furrowing into an angry frown. "We come from an ancient noble bloodline of Pict warriors. We've vowed to protect humans at all costs – even with our own lives. 'Twas the price our ancestors paid for our lineage."

I pinched the bridge of my nose, closed my eyes for a few seconds, then opened them again. I stared hard at Lucian. "You keep saying *we*. Who's *we*?"

"My clansman. There are six of us. You, despite being a mistake, make the seventh."

Once again, shock froze me. "So that's it? Like it or not I'm a MacLeod wolf by association?"

He moved so fast my eyes barely kept up. One second Lucian was standing several feet away, in the next less than three inches separated us. He lifted his hand to my shoulder and pressed the pads of his fingers against my wound. "'Tis by much more than association, girl. You've got my blood rushing through your veins now and there's no' a WUP agent alive who can cast it out of you."

I could feel my heart race at his touch; my skin heated several degrees and I tried to move past him. He wouldn't let me. I felt his eyes on me, studying me with such intensity I had no other choice but to look at him.

"What do you want from me?" I asked. I found myself breathless in his close proximity. I felt hysterical tears push behind my eyelids. "What am I supposed to do?"

Lucian's silvery-blue gaze regarded me for a long time before answering. "For now, you rest. You're goin' to need it." He moved away. "Then, we train."

For the longest time that night, my eyes remained wide open. Hours maybe. Lucian had left the bothy, but I knew he was close by – maybe just outside the door, probably waiting for me to go to sleep. I got the sense that he knew me way better than I knew him; almost as though he could read my thoughts, knew my fears, and strangely enough, consider them.

I stared at the dark wooden beams of the ceiling and let my thoughts ramble. Had Pax known about the ancient rogue curse, and about Lucian's clan, would things have turned out differently? Would he be now transitioning into the very thing he hunted? I shivered at the thought of Pax's fate; I hated it. It was weird, though. Part of me felt like WUP had abandoned us. The other part, though, knew they'd done exactly what they had to do. Pax and I had both been well aware of the risks involved in being a WUP agent and part of that risk was maintaining the agency. I suppose I'd never considered being bitten by a wolf.

"Do you have family?"

I hadn't even heard Lucian enter the bothy, but he had; he now stood just in the recesses of the shadows of the room. I'd not noticed the storm that had begun raging outside; it was there, scratching and clawing the windows of the cottage. "No," I answered, sitting up. "Not really."

"What do you mean?" he asked, his voice strangely seductive, raspy, deep.

I strained to see him. "Foster kid. You know, in the system? A ward of the state. I was shuffled around from one foster home to another until I was eighteen. Then, I was on my own."

Lucian was quiet for some time before answering. "It's better if you've no family, no one to miss you," he said, and moved closer. I could see nothing more of him than an outline; yet I felt his gaze hard on me. "No previous life ties."

"What's it like?" I asked out of nowhere, intensely curious about what my body was going through.

Again, Lucian was quiet. "As your body changes, your senses will heighten. Your hearing mostly and sense of smell. You'll gain mortal strength – which you'll have to learn control over – as well as your wolf self."

I considered that; it was hard to take in. A myriad of random thoughts hit me at once. "Where am I supposed to live?" I asked. "How the hell will I earn money? Support myself?" Those along with a million other thoughts crowded my brain. "This is insane," I muttered under my breath. "Not happening." I rose and walked to the single window facing the moors; a red hue illuminated the night sky.

Then, Lucian was there, behind me, not touching but so close I could feel the heat radiating off his skin. "Aye, 'tis happening," he said, his voice low, and his breath brushed the side of my neck and made me shiver. "You will say goodbye to your old life, Ms Slater, mourn its loss, and get over it." His hands grasped my shoulders and turned me around. His eyes flashed silver in the filtered light. "This is your life now."

The way Lucian's illuminated gaze bore into mine mesmerized me. I know it sounds crazy, but I felt as though I'd known him my whole life. And, as strange as it sounds, even *before* then. We stood in the shadows of the bothy – I had no idea what time it was – and stared. I'm not sure if he waited for my acceptance, or a reaction, or if we were simply trapped in a powerful moment. I didn't care. There was a palpable, physical attraction – so strong it felt feral and unlike anything I'd ever experienced. He hadn't released my shoulders, but his grip loosened and now, it felt intimate and hesitant at once. I wasn't sure if my new senses had kicked in, or if it was because we stood so close, but I could hear Lucian's heart beat. It was a strong, steady sound that reverberated inside my head and overpowered every other sound in the room. His hands slid from my shoulders to the column of my throat, then cradled my face. My heart beat quickened.

"You weren't supposed to be here," he said again, his brogued, raspy voice low and strained. "But once you were, I knew I could never let you leave."

"What do you mean?" I asked, my voice barely above a whisper. I wanted to touch him, but I kept my hands balled into fists, hanging at my sides.

His thumbs grazed my jaw. "MacLeod wolves mate for life," he said, his head lowering. "We're marked from birth, as are our mates. Sometimes, the pair never encounters, and they spend eternity at a loss," he nuzzled my neck with his chin, whispering in my ear. "The mark at your left shoulder blade," his lips brushed the shell. "I've an identical one. Destiny brought you here, Gin, to *me*, and I'm verra sorry – I couldna let you go."

I stared up at him, entranced, excited, completely drawn to him. "You bit me on purpose," I said softly, and I knew the answer before it came.

"Aye," he said against my ear. "I did." He nuzzled me again, his cheek to mine. "'Twas the only way to make you mine."

Timidly, I lifted my hands to rest against his chest, and then slipped them higher, to encircle his neck. Gently I tugged him closer.

I didn't have to ask for anything else.

Lucian's mouth found mine, settled there and lingered; he breathed deeply, and his heart's pace quickened. With a gentle nudge, he pushed my lips open with his, our tongues touched, and a low groan escaped his throat as he pulled me hard against him and kissed me. Desperation laced every taste; agonizing, intense sexual attraction raged within him – I could *feel* it. It raged within me, as well, and I fell against him, dying to be closer, feeling as though we were already one, needing more.

Lucian, as though he could read my thoughts, walked me backward, our mouths never parting and together we fell to the bed. My clothes burned me, I wanted them off, and Lucian obliged. I felt out of control, and I grasped his shirt and yanked hard; buttons flew, and I pushed the material off. He managed his jeans, and barely fast enough. Finally, nothing separated us and Lucian moved on top of me, his weight pressing into my body; I revelled in the feel of it.

He looked down at me, his face sharp planes and shadows. Bracing his weight with his elbow, his other hand lifted to my face. With his fingers, he traced my lips, my chin, my throat. "You're mine, Ginger Slater," he said. He lowered his head and brushed my lips. "Mine," he whispered hoarsely against them, and my heart raced, my breath quickened, and I shoved my hands into his hair and kissed him hungrily. Lucian groaned and kissed me back, starving, his touch desperate and everywhere, and I wrapped my legs around his waist and opened for him; he took me, pushed deep inside of me, filled me.

"Lucian," I whispered against his mouth. "*You're mine.*"

He sighed, whispered – a language I did not know, words unfamiliar to my ears, then kissed me and began to move; slow at first, then becoming frantic, as though he couldn't get enough, and I matched his rhythm with my own frenzied moves. The orgasm started deep within my core, slowly built through every sensitive nerve-ending in my body, and then shattered within me; a thousand shafts of light splintering into tiny specks behind my eyes. I held on to Lucian as he followed. I felt his orgasm grow, explode, and he wrapped both arms around my body and held me as our releases calmed, our heartbeats slowed. He rolled on to his back and dragged me atop him, my breasts resting against his chest, our skin melding into one. He lifted a hand to my cheek; his thumb grazed the line of my jaw, then he slid his hand around my neck and pulled my mouth to his and kissed me long, slow, erotic. His other hand slipped over my buttocks, my back, and settled in the lower curve there, holding me firmly in place. Then, he broke the kiss and looked at me for several moments.

"I couldna just let you go," he said quietly.

I traced his full lips with my index finger. "I wouldn't have wanted you to."

We needed no more words; just our bodies melding, our hands exploring, our mouths tasting. We joined again, slower this time, so much slower, seductive, both of us silently claiming the other. Finally, we slept.

It was the only night I slumbered without nightmares of Pax.

*   *   *

Over the course of the next week, Lucian slowly introduced me to my new world, my new body, my new senses. I'd not be able to master them all for some time; my hearing was exaggerated and sometimes hurt my ears and insides. My sense of smell was so good, it overwhelmed me and I couldn't determine one smell from the other – except for Lucian's scent. His was unique and solely Lucian's and I could detect it a mile away. My strength and speed was immature but growing fast; almost too fast. I tripped, I fell, I hurled myself to speeds which my old body couldn't handle yet. I busted my ass more times than I could count. But Lucian was right there to help me up.

Each night, we made love and fell asleep wrapped in each other's arms. Each night, I dreamt. Pax pursued me in his human form, always in a heavy mist, always through a dense wood. The white fog slipped through the trees and brush like long reaching fingers, and I ran hard, stumbling and not in control of my new speed and strength. Pax, for some reason, was. His white spiked hair appeared behind every tree, every rock, as though he toyed with me. And every time, he'd catch me, back me against the base of a tree. *This is your fault, newbie. I'm here, trapped as an abomination, all because of you. I don't know whether to thank you or rip your throat out.* I'd awaken, shaking violently, breathless, just before Pax shifted into his wolf form and lunged at me, teeth bared. I kept the dreams from Lucian. I thought I could handle them, or that they'd just go away. I was so very wrong.

It was weird, mine and Lucian's relationship. I felt completely at ease with him, as though we'd known each other forever. He'd had nearly three weeks to come to terms with the fact that I was his marked mate; I'd had about twenty-four hours. Still, I accepted it readily and willingly. It felt . . . natural, as though my life was to turn out no other way other than here, in the Highlands of Scotland, with an ancient Pict warrior-wolf. It felt even more natural to *become* one. I can't explain it without sounding like a lunatic, but there you go.

Lucian and I left the bothy the last day of my transition and travelled north and west to the MacLeod stronghold. Situated on a sea loch, the massive grey stone fortress, complete with four imposing towers, dominated the seascape. It literally robbed my breath.

"You live here?" I asked incredulously. I glanced at him.

Lucian laughed, and reached over and grasped my hand. "Nay. *We* live here."

My heart swelled at his words. We'd not exchanged the L-word yet; somehow, it just didn't seem right. But we'd both claimed one another, and the word *mine* sounded nearly as powerful, if not more so, than the word love. There would be an adjustment period, for both of us. But of one thing I was absolutely positive: we were meant to be together.

Lucian pulled onto a single-track gravel lane that led to the massive front doors of the castle, and before we had the Rover in park, five big guys emptied the entrance and made their way towards us. All dark-haired, with bodies that looked like they swung axes and swords and kicked ass for a living. They made their way towards us.

Lucian glanced at me and laughed. "They won't bite."

I looked at him and raised a brow. "Doubt that."

I climbed out of the Rover, slammed the door, and faced the MacLeods.

"Gin, my brothers. Arron, Raife, Christopher, Jacob, and Tristan."

Arron walked up and embraced me; the others followed. "Welcome," Arron said, his eyes flashing quicksilver.

"About time we had a lass around the place," Jacob said, and the other laughed.

The MacLeods welcomed me, and as it was with Lucian, the same held true with his brothers. It felt like I'd known them my entire life.

The MacLeod fortress entailed no less than 200 acres and the shoreline, and inside the castle, a modernized habitat befitting of an ancient wolf clan of Pict warriors. Primeval mixed perfectly with contemporary. It was mind-numbing to think how long ago Lucian and his brothers were born; how long they'd lived.

They prepared me for my transition that night; in all honesty, there wasn't much they could do except stand by and wait; help out if needed. Lucian warned me the first time was painful, and he apologised more times than I could count. He held me in his arms, kissed me, smoothed my hair from my face, and promised to not leave my side until it was over.

By nightfall, as the moon began to rise, Lucian and his brothers walked me to the shore line, encircled me, and waited. I immediately knew it had begun when my skin began to itch. I felt as though I wanted to crawl right out of it, and I clawed and scratched at my arms, my neck, my abdomen. My temperature rose, higher and higher until I thought I would self-combust. My skin was on fire, and I began to pull at my clothes. No matter that it was October in the Highlands; I was *hot*. I didn't have time to yank them off, either. I felt my skeleton give way, the popping and rubbing sounds reverberating inside my head. I cried out in pain, and in my peripheral sight I saw movement and knew it was Lucian. He stopped abruptly, and didn't advance further.

My heels and long bones shifted, elongated, contorted, and just when I thought I couldn't take the pain and heat a second longer, I fell to the ground, let out a low, long, bay, and it was over. I leapt up, shook my body, and met the silver gazes of six other wolves, their shaggy dark coats glistening in the moonlight.

We ran that night, my new brothers, my mate and I. We ran from the west coast of Scotland clear to the east, along the shores of the North Sea, and it was invigorating, mind-freeing. My new body rocked with sensations and I wanted to keep running. I saw everything through my new eyes, and it was as though I saw the world for the very first time. Lucian ran beside me, his silvery blue gaze watching me closely. We spoke to each other in our minds. He never left my side. At some point, exhaustion overtook me, we made it home, and I fell hard asleep.

When next I woke, I was in my human form, tucked closely against Lucian's body. The sun had not yet risen and I felt invigorated. I wanted to explore the shore, so I slipped from our bed, quickly dressed, and headed outside. No one else stirred. I was the only one awake.

The brisk Highland air greeted me, along with a healthy dose of mist. I found it strange not to be cold, but my core stayed at over 100 degrees, so there was no need for a jacket. I breathed in the air, sweet with clover and something else I couldn't name, and I took in my surroundings. On the left side of the gravel lane, a meadow and at its edge, a dense copse of wood filled with towering pines and oaks.

Then, I saw it. Through the slender ribbons of mist I saw something white move into view. I stared, my newly sharpened vision trained on the spot. Before my brain registered what my eyes saw, I knew it. Pax. He waited for me. Without a thought, I took off towards him at a jog and by the time I reached the wood line, I was at a full run. Pax had disappeared.

I eased through the trees, the canopy above keeping out any light that may have filtered in, and I searched for Pax. Deeper into the wood I moved, determined to settle things with my old partner. Surely, no matter his fate or mine, we could come to terms. We'd been partners. We'd sort of been friends. He'd watched out for me. I knew, despite the awful dreams, he wouldn't hurt me.

In the next instant something heavy slammed into my body and I was knocked hard against the base of an aged oak. I was turned abruptly and when I looked, the man who pinned me against the tree was not Pax. I frowned, shoved and cursed. "Get the hell off of me," I growled and shoved my knee into his balls. "Now!"

He sucked in a breath but quickly recovered. "Oh, no, love," he said, his accent thick, his tone full of hatred. He pushed me hard against the tree. "We've been waiting at the chance to get at Lucian MacLeod and his brothers and you're it." Without warning, he punched me – caught me right in the jaw and my head snapped back and slammed into the hard wood of the tree.

I glared at him. "He'll kill you," I said, my pitch lowering.

The man laughed. "Right. We'll see about that."

Four other men emerged from the wood. One of them was Pax. He ambled up to me, his eyes laced with disgust. He pushed the guy away from me and leaned close to my ear. "You did this to me, newbie," he said, just like in my dream. "I can never go home now. I'll never see my wife again, thanks to you." His breath brushed my neck. "I've half a mind to just rip your throat out now instead of letting these assholes use you to bait your mate."

I met Pax's hard glare. "Do it," I said. "Stop talking about it and do it."

A low growl escaped Pax's throat, and in the next second he shifted into his wolf form. His fangs, dripping with saliva, hovered close to my ear and my throat. In my head, I imagined myself in my wolf form; nothing happened.

In the next second, in a flurry of fur and fangs, a pack of nearly-black wolves entered the wood at full speed. The men with Pax shifted and the fight began. I was knocked to a tree where I fell to the ground, crouched and watched.

I couldn't make myself change. I was helpless.

The melee was horrific. Bones crunched. Blood. Cries of pain. No human words met my ears, but I heard them in my head.

Then, a large wolf with a band of white on his chest charged me. It was Pax. I knew it. And I was no match for him. I rose, my back against the tree, and kept my eyes trained on my old partner.

Just before he lunged, a large black wolf leapt from out of

nowhere and slammed Pax to the ground. They fought; fangs gnashed, massive claws raked, bodies smashed into one another. The black wolf was Lucian – of that I had no doubt. With a final agonizing cry, Pax's neck was broken, and Lucian – God, it was awful – tore into his throat.

Then it was over.

Lucian moved towards me, shifted and stood naked before me. He was covered in Pax's blood. Anger radiated off of him. Anger and relief.

"Let's go," he said, and grasped my hand in his, threading his fingers through mine. "This is over," he said, and squeezed my hand. "For now."

Together, we walked back to the hall where Lucian bathed and got dressed. One of Lucian's brothers cleaned up the aftermath while Lucian explained to me what was to come. I can't say that I was shocked.

"I'm verra sorry about your partner," he said, folding me into his embrace. He rubbed my back, a rhythmic motion that calmed me instantly. "He was no longer himself, you understand that?"

I nodded against his chest. "Yes."

He looked at me long, searching my eyes. "There are others from all over the world, no' just Scotia. We go where we're needed. We fight to protect innocents. And you are one of us now, Gin. Your skills will grow and you'll become as fast, as strong as I." He kissed me then. When he pulled back, his gaze all but worshipped me. "But you're not there yet, and I'll no' take any more chances with your life. You're mine," he whispered against my mouth, then brushed his lips across mine. "And I'll no' leave your side until you have full control over all of your new powers." He rested his forehead against mine. "I canna lose you, Gin. You're mine forever."

Lucian MacLeod then completely enveloped me in his arms, pressed his mouth to mine and kissed me long and slow, his tongue brushing mine, causing my heart to race, my breath to catch. I kissed him back. Again, he mouthed the words against my lips that he'd said the first night we'd made love. I pulled back and looked at him.

"What does that mean?" I asked, nipping at his lower lip.

The intense longing in his eyes made my knees weak. "It means I've found you, my love, at long last." He smiled, kissed me and nuzzled my neck. "I've waited centuries for you, Gin Slater," he said softly. "My warrior wolf. My mate."

As he drew me into another long kiss, I knew my life was forever changed. I didn't know what it had in store, but I knew that as long as Lucian MacLeod was there with me, I could handle it. Gladly handle it.

It was the longest, most sensual kiss I'd ever experienced.

And he was all *mine* . . .

At Last

Jacquie D'Alessandro

London, 1820

One

"Dear God, what is *he* doing here?"

The words rushed past Sophia Mallory, Countess Winterbourne's lips in a horrified whisper, her gaze riveted on the tall, raven-haired man who stood framed in the carved archway leading into the elegant ballroom. The sounds of Lord and Lady Benningfield's annual soiree – laughter mixed with the hum of conversation, the lilt of the musician's waltz, the clink of fine crystal – all faded to a dull buzz in Sophia's mind, as did the more than two hundred guests milling about. Everything fell away except him.

Ian Broderick.

His name reverberated through her brain and she blinked, certain he was some figment of her imagination – not a completely farfetched notion as, in spite of her best efforts to forget him, he'd invaded her mind daily since she'd left him six months ago. She blinked again, but his image remained in the doorway, larger than life, striking panic in her heart.

How had he, a man of no social standing, managed to secure an invitation to one of society's premier events of the season? Her stunned gaze flicked over the midnight blue cutaway jacket that exactly matched his eyes and emphasized the breadth of his shoulders. The intricate knot of his snowy cravat, the burgundy and green plaid waistcoat that proclaimed him a Scot. Perhaps his

current elegant attire, freshly shaved face and neatly trimmed hair
– all the complete antithesis of the rough, workmen's clothing, day-
old stubble, and untamed locks he'd sported the last time she'd
seen him – might have rendered him unrecognizable to some, but
Sophia would have known him anywhere, would have sensed his
presence even had the room been completely dark instead of illuminated by dozens of candles. Where on earth had a groundskeeper
from the small Scottish town of Melrose procured such expensive,
perfectly tailored clothes?

The questions flew from her mind and her stomach clenched
when her attention returned to his face and she noted his sharp
gaze intently panning the room. He couldn't possibly be looking for
her – could he? No, she'd been very careful to hide her full identity
from him. Yet, the very fact he was here rippled a fissure of terror
through her that his unexpected appearance somehow had something to do with her.

Escape. She had to escape. Immediately. Before he saw her. For
even if he weren't at this soiree because of her, his discovering her
here would set in motion any number of scenarios, none of which
would end well for her.

He hadn't seen her yet – but based on the way his gaze scanned
the room, those intense eyes would fall upon her within seconds. In
spite of the crowd, her unfashionable height unfortunately made
her easy to spot. With her heart pounding hard enough to bruise
her ribs, she started to turn away, her every instinct intent upon
escape. A gloved hand grasped her upper arm, stilling her.

"Heavens, who is that utterly divine man?"

Sophia tried to shake loose of Christine Archer, Viscountess
Handley's, hold, but her best friend's tenacious grip tightened. As
Christine was staring towards the archway across the room,
Sophia didn't question to which "utterly divine man" Christine
referred.

"I . . . I must go." Sophia pulled her arm free and desperately
looked for the nearest exit. Her gaze lit upon the french windows
leading to the terrace and she quickly stepped in that direction. But
her hopes for a fast escape were thwarted by the seemingly endless
wall of revellers standing between her and freedom.

"Sophia, are you all right?" asked Christine. She stepped directly
in front of Sophia and her expression immediately turned to one of
deep concern. "Darling, you're pale as wax. You look as if you've
seen a ghost."

I have. In the form of a man she'd hoped never to see again. A ghost from her past she'd been trying desperately to forget, lest it cost her everything. And right now that past stood terrifyingly close. If the truth were to come out—

She ruthlessly cut off the thought and, keeping her back towards the man on the opposite side of the room, she offered Christine what she hoped passed for a sheepish expression. "Too much champagne, I'm afraid," she lied, praying her very observant friend wouldn't recall she'd imbibed nothing stronger than lemonade. "I've the most dreadful headache and simply cannot stand the noise and this crush."

Christine's gaze turned sympathetic. "A good night's sleep is what you need. Although I hate that you're leaving, especially since that luscious stranger just appeared in the doorway. I've no idea who he is, but I intend to find out."

Dread rippled down Sophia's spine. "Your husband would surely object to such fascination in another man."

Christine laughed. "Darling, I'm married – not *dead*. There is no sin in merely looking." Her gaze shifted over Sophia's shoulder and a mischievous grin curved her lips. "Although I'd wager that man knows a great deal about sin." She returned her attention to Sophia. "I'm certain my Henry *would* object to my fascination – if that fascination was purely on my behalf. However, it is *you* I'm thinking of, Sophia. You need something – or some*one* – to lift your spirits." Christine reached out and gently squeezed Sophia's hands. "It's been nearly three years since Robert's death. It's time to stop mourning. Time to live again."

An image of her deceased husband's face, his warm brown eyes sparkling with humour flashed through Sophia's mind, a mental picture that was instantly replaced by one of intense dark blue eyes that seemed to burn a hole through her skin.

"I'm fine," she said, her battle to remain calm rapidly slipping away. "I'll start living again tomorrow – after a good night's sleep to rid me of this headache." She slipped her hands from Christine's and with her head down and knees bent to minimize her height, she began weaving her way through the throng towards the french windows.

"I'll hold you to that promise," Christine called after her. "Expect me to call upon you tomorrow afternoon."

Sophia nodded without turning around and focused on fleeing. When she reached the windows, she grasped the curved brass handle and opened the paned glass panel just enough to slip outside. A gust of unseasonably chilly air, heavy with the threat of rain, swirled around her, pebbling her skin, but she barely noticed the discomfort. Heart pounding, she anxiously peered back into the ballroom, her staccato breaths fogging the glass. Dread seized her when she noted Ian no longer stood under the archway leading into the ballroom, but then she spied the back of a dark head standing on the far side of the room, near the punch bowl. The man's height identified him as Ian and Sophia sucked in a quick breath of relief. Thank God. Now she just needed to circle around to the front of the mansion then request her carriage be sent. She cursed the delay that would entail, but intending to ask Christine and Henry to escort her home, she'd dismissed her driver. At least she'd escaped the ballroom undetected. And once ensconced inside her vehicle, with the velvet curtains drawn, she'd be safe.

She turned. And froze at the sight of the snowy cravat mere inches from her nose.

"Going somewhere, Sophia?" Ian's husky voice, rich with the flavour of Scotland, filled the darkness between them.

And with a sinking heart Sophia knew, that with those three simple words, everything she'd tried to escape had found her.

Two

Ian stared at the woman who, for the past six months he'd moved heaven and earth to find and two words pounded through his head, in perfect time to his thundering heart.

At last.

She looked at him through those huge, golden brown eyes that had grabbed him by the throat the first moment he'd seen her. He'd been taking his customary solitary walk through the cool forest that marked the border between the outskirts of Melrose and the secluded, back acreage of Marlington Hall. As he'd neared the forest's end, where the shade melted into a golden blaze of late summer sunshine, he'd been so engrossed in his thoughts, he didn't notice her until a mere twenty feet separated them.

She'd stood in profile to him, framed in sunlight, amidst an explosion of colourful wildflowers, holding a bouquet of pink roses obviously picked from the abundance surrounding her. He'd halted, surprised at the unexpected sight of her, and irritated at the disruption of his solitude. A visitor to the area, he decided, as the locals all knew and respected Marlington Hall's property boundaries.

In no mood for company, he was about to withdraw without making his presence known when she reached up and slowly pulled the pins from her hair. Suddenly transfixed, he watched a curtain of glossy sable curls unfurl down her back. After shaking her head, she closed her eyes and raised her face. A slow smile spread across her sun-gilded features, and with a delighted laugh, she spread her arms wide and spun around in circles, her glorious hair and plain brown gown flying around her.

The sight had enchanted him. When was the last time he'd felt such pure joy? He couldn't recall. Couldn't tear his gaze from her. Couldn't remember why he'd wanted to be alone. Then, with her cheeks flushed and lips still curved in a smile framed by a pair of beguiling dimples, she'd stopped and caught sight of him.

His first look into those warm, golden brown eyes had walloped him right in the heart. Heat that had nothing to do with the bright sunshine raced through him and in the space of a single heartbeat, he'd found himself . . . something. Smitten? Bewitched? Neither word seemed adequate to describe the struck-by-lightning sensation that had rendered him incapable of doing anything more than staring and drinking her in. All he knew was that catching her in that unguarded, carefree moment had touched a place deep inside him, one that had felt dead for so damn long. And that for the first time in a year he'd felt something other than bleak numbness – his constant companion since the accident that had irrevocably changed his life.

She'd raised her hand to shade those Scotch whisky eyes, then moistened her lips, a gesture that riveted his gaze on her lush mouth. For several seconds she stared at him as if she too had been struck, but then her smile faded, and uncertainty, along with a flash of fear flickered in her gaze, rousing him from his stupor. Of course she'd be wary of a stranger in such an isolated spot, and God knows he hadn't wanted to scare her off . . .

*   *   *

"Good afternoon," he said, stepping from the shade into the sunlight. "Ye've chosen a braw day to explore the grounds of Marlington Hall."

Distress joined the wariness in her gaze. "Forgive me," she murmured, her accent immediately identifying her as English. "I'm

visiting this area . . . I just arrived in Melrose this morning, and
didn't realize I'd wandered on to private property. If you'll excuse
me . . ."

She turned to leave and a sense of loss unlike anything Ian had
ever experienced gripped him, propelling him forward. "No
need to worry," he assured her. "I'm well acquainted with the
owner and while some might consider him a bit o' a crabbitt,
he'd have no objection to such a bonny lass enjoying a stroll on
his land."

She pivoted back to him and her gaze flicked over his scuffed,
dusty boots and sturdy nankeen trousers and shirt. Certainly not
clothing that would proclaim him lord of manor, but it was his
preferred attire on his long, solitary walks.

"Crabbitt?" she repeated in a bewildered tone.

"Aye. What an English lass would call a curmudgeon."

Understanding dawned in her eyes. "You're employed here?"

A bark of laughter rose in his throat. Bloody hell, that question
marked her a stranger like no other could have. He knew he should
inform her he'd been teasing and that the reason he was so well
acquainted with Marlington Hall's curmudgeon master was
because he was himself the curmudgeon. Yet the words stuck in his
throat. This stranger knew nothing of him, of his past, of the accident. For the first time in a year someone was looking at him
without a trace of calculation or pity.

And not just any someone. No, this someone was a bloody beautiful woman with the most gorgeous eyes and full, kissable lips he'd
ever seen. Of course if she remained in Melrose any length of time
she'd eventually learn the truth – gossip concerning the reclusive
Earl of Marlington swirled about the village like thick fog. Yet it
was so refreshing for someone to see him simply as himself he
couldn't resist delaying the inevitable. After all, what harm could
possibly come of such an innocent deception?

"Aye, I work here." Not precisely a lie as his title came with a
daunting amount of responsibility. He halted an arm's length from
her and discovered that although she wasn't a lass in her first bloom
of youth – he judged her closer to thirty than twenty, perhaps even
a wee bit on the other side of thirty – she attracted him like no
younger woman, or even one his own age ever had. And those eyes
– bloody hell, he felt as if he could stare into their soulful, expressive depths for hours. They held hints of secrets and sadness,
laughter and happiness, hopes and dreams – an intoxicating

combination that beckoned him to learn more, to discover everything about her.

Her eyes alone branded her a beauty in his mind, rendering her high cheekbones, creamy complexion, bewitching smile and delicate brows all but superfluous. She was tall, unfashionably so, but then so was he, and he liked that she stood up straight and regal instead of slouching to disguise her height. Even her charmingly undone appearance didn't diminish her elegance. Her gown was plain, but of fine quality, marking her as woman of some means.

"I'm in charge of the grounds." He shot the bouquet she held a pointed look. "I see you found the wild roses."

More colour bloomed in her cheeks. "I adore flowers and roses are my favourite. They were so beautiful I couldn't resist picking a few. However, I would have refrained had I known this was private property."

A snippet of his favourite Christopher Marlowe poem drifted into his mind – *And I will make thee beds of roses, and a thousand fragrant posies*. It was all he could do not to reach out and touch her. "Ye should never have to refrain from taking what your heart desires."

"You should if it belongs to another."

"Not if it is freely given, and as I am the keeper of the roses, you are welcome to pick as many as you like."

"Thank you, Mr . . .?"

To prolong the inevitable, he offered his middle name rather than his surname. "Broderick. But you may call me Ian – all my friends do."

Amusement glinted in her eyes. "We've hardly been acquainted long enough to be considered friends, Mr Broderick."

"Perhaps, but the fact that ye picked my roses makes us instant friends. 'Tis a law here in Melrose."

She hoisted a brow. "Indeed?"

"Aye. In fact, there's another law that once you pick a man's roses, you're obliged to stroll through the rest of the gardens with him."

She pinned him with a stern stare, one rendered far less threatening by the twitching of her lips. "I know a Banbury tale when I hear one, Mr Broderick."

"Ian. And I'm certain you do, but 'tis the truth I speak. Lord Marlington himself declared it a law."

"For what reason?"

"Why, so the other flowers wouldn't be jealous of the roses, of course. Ye wouldn't want the other blooms to suffer from neglect, would you, Miss . . . ?"

He swore something flickered in her eyes, but it was gone before he could be certain. "Mallory. Sophia Mallory."

Sophia Mallory. Her name echoed through his mind like a siren's call, and he suddenly knew precisely how Ulysses had felt – inexorably drawn, unable to resist. "'Tis a great pleasure to make your acquaintance, Miss Mallory."

"Thank you, although it's Mrs Mallory."

Disappointment crushed him. Of course she would be married, would belong to someone else. While Ian had done many things he wasn't necessarily proud of, and he'd told her to always take what your heart desired, he wasn't a man to pursue another man's wife – no matter how much he might want her. Still, he couldn't rescind his invitation at this point. "Your husband is welcome to join us—"

"I'm afraid that's impossible. He passed away several years ago."

Ian's conscience kicked him at the wave of relief washing through him. Damn it, he shouldn't feel such joy that any man was dead. Especially as his own loss had left him gutted – until he'd seen Sophia laughing and spinning in his meadow. Before he could stop himself, he reached out and lightly grasped her hand. Their palms met and warmth spread through him. "I'm sorry. I suffered a similar such loss and wouldn't wish it upon anyone."

She stilled and for several seconds he thought she meant to pull away, wouldn't have blamed her for doing so. But instead she gently squeezed his hand. "My sympathies for your loss."

He would have thanked her, but bloody hell, the sensation of her skin against his robbed him of his ability to speak. Instead he brushed his thumb over the silky smooth back of her hand and simply nodded.

Her gaze locked on his and something that looked like heat kindled in her eyes, giving him hope that she felt this . . . whatever it was grabbing him by the throat. Had his very life depended upon it, he couldn't have looked away. And he sure as hell hadn't wanted to release her when she gently withdrew her hand. Indeed it required a Herculean effort not to snatch her hand back and press it against his chest, so she could feel his heart pounding, could know how deeply she affected him.

"You're certain the earl wouldn't object to you showing his private gardens to a stranger?"

He had to swallow twice to locate his voice. "He'd insist upon it – unhappy flowers wilt and if there's one thing that makes the earl even more crabbity than usual, 'tis wilted posies. He'd issue you the invitation himself were he in residence. Indeed, he'll have my head if his blooms are withered when he returns." He heaved a dramatic sigh. "I can only hope ye'll obey the law and save me from his wrath."

Again she hesitated and Ian forced himself to remain quiet, to not give in to the unprecedented and uncharacteristic urge to drop to his knees and beg her join him. To spend the day with him. The day? He nearly laughed. More like a fortnight. A month. A decade. He wasn't certain what had come over him, but whatever it was, there was no denying this fierce, overwhelming desire to spend more time with her.

"Very well, Mr Broderick. I shall save you this once."

As they walked along he pointed out different plants and regaled her with humourous stories of life in Melrose, loving the sound of her laughter, enjoying her tales of England, every moment strengthening his attraction to her. When they paused by a trellis draped with fragrant roses, he paused and looked into her intoxicating eyes. "These are Marlington Hall's finest roses. Would you like to gather some, Mrs Mallory?

She studied him and he tried his damnedest keep his expression blank to hide the want burning inside him, but wasn't certain he succeeded, wasn't certain it was even possible to do so. Wariness flickered in her eyes, followed by curiosity, and then . . . then there was no mistaking the flare of desire that kindled in her gaze, a heat that stole his breath. Stole his heart.

"Are you trying to tempt me with your roses . . . Ian?"

Bloody hell, the mere sound of his name on her lips drove every intelligent thought from his head. He searched his empty mind for something witty, for a clever rejoinder, but the blatant truth simply spilled out. "Yes. Are you tempted, Sophia?"

For an answer she held out her hand . . .

                     ★   ★   ★

He'd wrapped his fingers around hers, a gesture that marked the start of the most incredible, happiest, bloody amazing six weeks of his life. Sophia became his friend. His lover. The axis upon which his world revolved. They'd stayed at the small secluded hunting lodge on his property, a place he'd never shared with anyone. She assumed it was the groundskeeper cottage, and he didn't disabuse her of the notion. She didn't speak of her past, didn't ask about his. Instead they focused solely on each other and the moment. He wanted to tell her the truth, but the time never seemed right, even less so the longer they spent together. But one night, when her time in Scotland was nearing its end, after making love with a passion unlike anything he'd ever known, he watched her sleep and could no longer rationalize his deception. After vowing to tell her the truth the next morning, he'd gone to sleep. And woken up alone. She left behind only a brief note – and a man who was determined to find her. Little had he known how difficult that quest would prove. Because as he soon learned, she'd been equally dishonest with him about who she was.

Looking at her now, the darkness cloaking them, Ian fought to align his conflicting emotions. His profound relief that he'd finally found her. His anger at the way she'd left him. The enervating hurt that she *could* leave him. It didn't help assuage his pain that rather than being pleased by his presence, she looked distressed and desperate to flee.

To ensure that she didn't, he grasped her upper arm, then pulled her away from the arc of light spilling from the windows, behind topiary potted in an enormous stone urn.

"What are you doing here, Ian?" She tried to pull free of his hold, but he didn't let go.

"I'm here to see you, Sophia. Or should I say Lady Winterbourne?" Before she could reply, he continued, "Nay, not Lady Winterbourne – that's far too formal after the intimacies we shared. Do you recall those intimacies, Sophia? Those times when I was so deep inside your body you said it felt as though I touched your heart?"

She closed her eyes and turned her face away from him, and all the hurt and anger, frustration and confusion that had consumed him since that morning he'd woken up alone rushed to the surface and he stepped closer, forcing her back until her shoulders touched the rough stone.

"Look at me, damn it." She complied with obvious reluctance, then regarded him with a dispassionate expression he'd never seen from her before. "Yes, I remember," she said, her voice matching that blank look in her eyes. "You know who I am, my title. That I wasn't honest with you. You're obviously angry—"

"Yes, I bloody well am angry, but not because you're a countess." By God, it was all he could do not to shake her. "I don't give a damn if you're a scullery maid or a royal princess."

A frown puckered her brow. "Then why are you here?"

"*Why am I here?*" An incredulous sound escaped him. "Surely it can't surprise you that I'd come after you, especially after you left with no explanation—"

"I wrote you a note."

"Aye. And a bloody inadequate note it was."

"It said everything that needed to be said."

"Indeed?" He reached into his waistcoat pocket, withdrew the missive she'd left, and held it up to her. He didn't need to look at the words – they felt etched in blood on his heart. "'Dear Ian, please forgive my abrupt departure, but it is for the best. I'll always treasure our time together and wish you every happiness.'" He crumbled the paper in his fist and leaned forwards until mere inches separated their faces. "I want to know how you could possibly think those words were in any way adequate after what we'd shared. Or why you leaving was 'for the best'."

Instead of appearing in any way cowed, she lifted her chin and narrowed her eyes. "I've no intention of answering any of your questions until you answer mine, the first of which is how did you gain entrance to this soiree?"

Reluctant admiration at her courage in the face of his ire washed through him and he leaned back. "I sent Lord Benningfield a note informing him I'd be arriving in London this evening and requested an invitation, which he kindly provided."

She frowned. "Why would he do that?"

"Why wouldn't he? He'd hardly turn away the Earl of Marlington."

"I agree. But surely he'd turn away his groundskeeper . . ." Her words trailed off and realization dawned in her eyes. "Dear God. You're not . . . you can't be—"

"Ah, but I am – the crabbitty curmudgeon himself." He offered her a formal bow. "Lord Marlington, at your service."

Three

Feeling as if the flagstones shifted beneath her feet, Sophia stared in disbelief at the man she'd unsuccessfully tried to forget for the last six months. The man she'd had to force herself to leave. "The Earl's name is William Ferguson," she whispered, shaking her head.

"Aye. And I am he – William Ian Broderick Ferguson."

Her gaze drifted over his perfectly tailored formal attire – garments that clearly cost a fortune, and suddenly things about him that had seemed incongruous with a groundskeeper clicked into place. His love of literature and poetry. His regal bearing. His expertise at riding. The ease with which he conversed on any subject. Why hadn't she seen the clues? No doubt because she was keeping her own secrets and therefore hadn't wanted to too closely examine any discrepancies in his behaviour lest they lead to questions about hers. The fact that she'd been so utterly besotted with him clearly hadn't helped her thought processes. Even as she realized he now spoke the truth, part of her still couldn't quite believe it.

"You lied to me," she said, not certain if she were more angry at him for his deception or at herself for not suspecting the truth.

His brows shot upward. "Now isn't that a wee bit o' the pot calling the kettle black – *Lady Winterbourne*."

Botheration, he had a point, which only served to annoy her further. "I told you my true name. I merely omitted my title."

"As did I."

"I had reasons, *valid* reasons for not telling you I was a countess."

"Just as I had my valid reasons for not telling you I was the earl." He stepped closer and Sophia drew in a quick breath, one she instantly regretted as it filled her head with his scent . . . that intoxicating mixture of warm skin and sandalwood and something elusive that belonged to Ian alone. It required all her will not to throw her arms around him and bury her face against his neck and simply breathe him in. Tell him how much she'd missed him. Explain how it had required her every ounce of her fortitude to leave him. How she hadn't been the same since the day she'd met him. Nor since the day she'd left him.

"I was on the verge of telling ye the truth, but when I awoke, you were gone." He cupped her face between his hands and Sophia's heart nearly stalled at the intensity of his gaze, at the hurt and desire and confusion burning in his eyes. "How, Sophia? How could you leave me like that?"

The question sounded tortured, and panic filled her at how badly she wanted give in to the yearning ambushing her. At how easy it would be to forget all the reasons she'd ended their affair so abruptly. Summoning a cool demeanour she was far from feeling, she said, "We both knew I had to return to England."

"Aye, but not for another fortnight. And earlier that last night we'd discussed you remaining longer."

Yes. Which had precipitated her leaving . . . while she still had the heart to do so.

A muted peal of laughter reached her and she recalled the hundreds of guests just beyond the french windows. If she were found out here, alone with Ian . . . she shuddered at the thought of the scandal that would ensue – the very sort of scandal she'd left him to avoid.

"What we shared was lovely while it lasted, Ian," she whispered in a rush, desperate to end this confrontation and get away before they were discovered – or before she gave in to the overwhelming need to touch him. "But we both knew it was only temporary. I'm truly sorry I hurt you. That was never my intention."

"It may have started as temporary, but that changed very quickly, and you bloody well know it." His eyes narrowed and she locked her knees not to shrink under his sharply assessing gaze. "Or are you trying to tell me that my feelings were one-sided all those weeks?"

"I'm trying tell you – *again* – that our . . . liaison of last summer is over. And now if you'll excuse me—"

Her words chopped off with a gasp when he slapped his large palms against the stones on either side of her head, caging her in. "*Liaison*?" He pinned her in place with a look that simultaneously froze and heated her. "The woman standing in front of me is no' the same woman who shared my bed, my home, my every bloody thought for all those weeks. Which means one of you is a damn liar. I'll give you one chance – *one* chance, Sophia – to tell me which one of you is false before I find out for myself."

"There is nothing to tell. I'm the same woman and—"

His mouth came down on hers, ending her words, the raw passion and naked need in his kiss obliterating her every thought. She tried to remain unresponsive, fought to keep her longing and desire contained, but they ripped through her, a razor sharp sword that sliced through her resolve and shredded her good intentions. He ran his tongue over her bottom lip and the battle was lost. With a groan she was helpless to contain, she wrapped her arms around his neck and parted her lips. And instantly felt as if she'd arrived home after an arduous journey.

He crushed her to him, deepening the kiss. The irresistible heat of his body surrounded her, and she rose up on her toes, desperate to get closer. With a sound that resembled a growl, he curved one large hand around her bottom, pressing her tighter against his hard arousal. Dear God, he felt so good. Tasted so good. And she'd missed him so much. Wanted him so badly.

He lifted his head, ending their kiss, and Sophia barely refrained from moaning in protest. Clinging to his broad shoulders, her head flopped weakly forward. His heartbeat thundered against her forehead, in unison with his rapid breaths beating warm against her temple. She squeezed her eyes shut in a vain attempt to block out the recriminations falling upon her like bricks.

One kiss. That's all it had taken for every one of her fine resolutions and good intentions to crumble to dust. For him to render her breathless. Boneless. Just as he had from that first moment she'd seen him in the meadow, when he'd stepped into a shaft of sunlight and utterly dazzled her. Her momentary fear at finding herself alone with a stranger in such an isolated spot vanished when she'd looked into his eyes.

While those beautiful dark blue depths clearly harboured secrets, they also reflected a vulnerability and sadness that told her without any words that he'd suffered great loss. As she'd suffered the same, she felt an instant kinship with him, one that went far deeper than the physical attraction she'd felt. Between his commanding height, muscular physique, thick, unruly hair, bold features, and mischievous grin, he was nothing short of spectacular.

In spite of the fact that at five and twenty he was twelve years her junior, she'd been unable to resist him – an affliction that given her current breathless, boneless state, clearly hadn't lessened one iota. She'd tried so hard these last six months to forget him, the magic between them, bury her feelings, and she'd thought she'd succeeded. One kiss proved she'd completely failed.

Filled with self-directed reproach, Sophia pulled in an unsteady breath, then opened her eyes and raised her head. And found Ian studying her with grim satisfaction.

"Well, that answered that question," he said in his hoarse Scottish burr. He leaned forwards to nuzzle her neck with his warm lips, rushing a sigh of pleasure into her throat. How such a firm mouth could be so wickedly soft, she didn't know.

"*Caileag bhrèagha*," he murmured in Gaelic against her skin. "My beautiful girl. The girl I met in the meadow." He lightly sucked on her sensitive skin, then with a tortured sound he raised his head. Framed her face between his palms. And regarded her through very serious eyes that burned with suppressed passion. "As much as I'm aching to continue this right here, right now, 'tis not the place."

She flicked a glance towards the windows and gave a tight nod. Dear God, she was fortunate they hadn't already been discovered. "Not the place," she concurred, "and discretion is called for. We cannot return to the ballroom together."

He briefly glanced at her mouth then nodded. "One look at us and even the most casual observer would know we shared more than conversation out here and I've no wish to give rise to any speculation that could harm your reputation. There's no need to return to the ballroom at all. My carriage awaits us in the mews."

Without another word, he took her hand and led her down the terrace steps. Questions bounced through Sophia's mind, begging to be voiced, but she shoved them aside. All that mattered now was escaping the party without being noticed.

Once in the garden, she followed him along the shadows near the high stone wall surrounding the property. His warm, strong fingers remained wrapped firmly around hers, guiding her safely over the uneven ground and shooting pleasurable tingles up her arm. Mental images of his big, sun-browned, calloused hands flashed unbidden through her mind. Removing her clothes. Exploring every inch of her skin. Teasing her feminine folds. Soaping her body as she lounged in his brass bathtub. Feeding her morsels of food he bought in the village. Bringing her more pleasure than she'd ever dreamed possible . . .

They arrived at the wooden gate at the rear of the garden and silently slipped into the mews. After helping her into the waiting carriage, Ian settled himself on the seat opposite her, then tapped on the roof, and the vehicle started with a jerk. Ensconced in the safety of the dark, curtained interior, moving swiftly away from the party, Sophia drew what felt like her first deep breath since she'd seen Ian standing across the ballroom.

As much as she dreaded their upcoming conversation, there was no avoiding it. Best to get it over with as quickly as possible then send him on his way back to Scotland. She'd listen to his explanations, offer her own – making absolutely certain he understood there could be no further relationship between them. Then they'd both return to their lives.

Lives that had briefly intersected, but never would again.

Four

Sophia's pulse jumped when Ian moved from the opposite side of the slow-moving carriage to sit next to her.

He reached out and touched her cheek. "Sophia. God, how I've missed you. You've not left my thoughts for even a moment these past six months."

The anguish in those whispered words flayed her. "I've thought of you, too, Ian, but—"

He pressed a fingertip to her lips. "No 'but'. The fact that you thought of me is enough for this moment."

"Where are we going?"

"Mayfair. I've let a townhouse on Park Lane."

Sophia's brows shot up. "That's the most exclusive part of town."

"Aye." One corner of his mouth lifted. "Ye didn't expect an earl – even a Scottish one – to stay in a hovel, did you?"

Embarrassment heated her face. "Of course not. I'm simply not accustomed to thinking of you as an earl, especially as you seemed very much at home living in the groundskeeper cottage."

A sheepish expression crossed his handsome features. "That was actually my private hunting lodge, and I'm used to being there alone. I enjoy occasionally fending for myself, not being surrounded by servants. It's my . . . sanctuary. No one has ever accompanied me there." He raised her hand and pressed a kiss against her palm. "Until you."

Her common sense screamed at her to pull her hand from his, but her inner voice whispered to take this opportunity and enjoy his touch.

The whisper defeated the scream.

"How long do you intend to remain in London?" she asked.

"Just a few days. I must return to Melrose to attend to estate affairs I've put off."

"Put off because you were looking for me?"

"Aye. They paled in importance to finding you, but now that I have, there are duties I cannot postpone any longer."

Silence swelled between them. Ian looked at Sophia and bludgeoned back the desire threatening to strangle him. He'd inwardly vowed not to pounce on her like a starving mongrel, yet he knew he'd do exactly that if he gave in to the overwhelming temptation to kiss her again.

Determined to keep the promise he'd made to himself, he said, "I'm waiting to hear why you kept your title a secret from me."

"I'd prefer to hear your explanation first."

"Very well." He drew a deep breath, then began, "The day I met you had, until that moment, been very difficult for me, as had the entire preceding year. It was the anniversary of a carriage accident. One that took the lives of both my parents and my sister."

His words seemed to hang in the air between them and Ian braced himself for the onslaught of painful memories bombarding him. Shocked distress filled her eyes and she captured his hands in hers. "Oh, Ian. How awful. I'm so sorry."

He gave a tight nod and gripped her hands. Bloody hell, he hated talking about this. Hated the horrible images flashing through his mind. Determined to get this over with, he continued in a rush, "We were returning to Melrose after an extended visit with father's sister and her family. It had rained hard the night before, and the roads were rutted and slippery. We should have waited to leave . . ."

He looked down and whispered the words that had haunted him since that day, words he'd never spoken aloud. "It was my fault."

"Ian, no—"

"*Yes*." Gut churning, he raised his gaze to hers. "*I'm* the one who wanted to return to Melrose. For a riding party scheduled for the following day." A bitter sound escaped him and he pulled his hands from hers to press the heels of his palms against his throbbing forehead. After drawing a shuddering breath he continued, "The carriage threw a wheel and went over a rocky ledge." The sickening sensation of the carriage rolling over and over tightened his stomach and the sound of his mother's and Fia's screams, mingled with his father's and Ian's shouts echoed through his mind. And then the silence . . . the terrifying silence.

He dragged his hands down his face. "I lost consciousness. I don't know how long for. When I came around, I discovered that my mother, my father, my sister Fia, as well as the driver were dead."

The carriage passed beneath a gas lamp, illuminating Ian's features and Sophia's heart squeezed at the raw anguish in his eyes. "Dear God, Ian." She reached out and once again clasped his hands, noting that they were cold and trembling. "I don't know what to say other than I'm so terribly sorry for your loss. And that you must stop blaming yourself."

"Why? If I hadn't been so intent on returning home, they'd still be alive. They all died, yet I was barely injured. Just a bump on my head, some bruised ribs and a broken arm." He looked at her through bleak eyes. "Why I didn't die as well? God knows I wanted to, and God knows I considered taking my own life."

The pain in his eyes, in his voice pierced Sophia's soul and she clung tighter to his hands. "Thank God you didn't."

A humourless sound escaped him. "The only reason I didn't was because the people of Melrose and the neighbouring villages that had depended on my father and Marlington lands for their livelihood now depended on me and the responsibility wasn't one my conscience would allow me to shirk. Looking back, I'm not certain how I did it when the mere act of drawing a breath seemed an effort."

"I understand that feeling very well," she murmured. "Losing someone you love is like losing part of yourself. I cannot imagine the pain of simultaneously losing three people you loved.

He nodded, then continued, "It wasn't the responsibilities of running the estate that confounded me – my father had taught me well. Indeed, I was grateful to have something to occupy my time. What I couldn't tolerate was people looking at me with pity. And the constant talk of the accident – I didn't want to talk about it. The stream of callers never stopped, and as the months passed the callers came to include mothers toting along their marriage-aged daughters. That's when it dawned on me that I was one of the most sought-after bachelors in Scotland.

"In the months that followed, I felt like a hunted man. I couldn't venture into the village without hearing the whispers. Matchmaking mothers from every level of the peerage sought an audience with me under the guise of sympathy calls, not to mention the women themselves who thought a man in my position required a mistress, or at least a short term liaison. I finally stopped accepting callers and no longer left the estate. I soon was referred to as a crabbitty recluse."

With his gaze steady on hers, he said, "The day I met you, I'd wandered the estate for hours, reflecting on the horror of the past year and all I'd lost. Wondering how, where I'd find the will to face another year. To face another day. And then I saw you. You were like a vision in the sunshine, sent to remind me what happiness looked like, felt like. I'd been numb for so long, and when I realized you didn't know who I was, thought I was the groundskeeper, I couldn't resist allowing you believe it, at least for a little while."

He reached out and Sophia's breath caught when he gently brushed his fingertips over her cheek. "That first magical afternoon with you was the first time in a year I'd felt anything other than pain and misery. You saw only Ian – no title, no wealth. You cannot imagine how refreshing, how liberating that was. Plus, you were clearly no more anxious to speak of the past than I was, a relief to be sure. After you agreed to send for your things at the inn and stay with me in the hunting lodge you believed was the groundskeeper cottage, I decided there was no immediate need to tell you. I knew in my heart I needed to, but as the weeks passed I was not only unsure *how* to tell you, I also feared you'd be so angry I hadn't been honest from the beginning, that you'd leave. And I wanted you to stay. More than I wanted my next breath. But you left anyway. And I had to find you. To tell you the truth. To beg your forgiveness for being less than completely honest. And to let you know how much our time together meant to me." He regarded her through solemn eyes. "Everything, Sophia," he said softly. "It meant everything."

Hot moisture pushed behind Sophia's eyes. Framing his face between her hands, she said, "I knew the moment I saw you that you'd suffered great loss – it was the source of the immediate kinship I experienced with you. I simply didn't know how very great that loss was. I'm sorry for all you've suffered. Sorry you still blame yourself. It was God's will, Ian, and something only He understands. Please don't blame yourself for living. Embrace the gift of life you were given and live it to the fullest. You're a wonderful man. In every way. And you deserve every happiness."

A shudder wracked his large frame. He closed his eyes and turned his head to press a fervent kiss against her palm, a gesture that made the area surrounding her heart go hollow. "Thank you, Sophia. Telling you everything . . . I feel as if a weight has been lifted from my shoulders."

His whispered words blew warm against her palm, and unable to stop herself, she touched her lips to his forehead. "I'm glad. And for that reason alone I wish you'd told me sooner. And now I owe you the same courtesy – the truth."

After pressing another kiss against her palm, he leaned back. "I'm listening."

"I travelled to Scotland because I was desperately unhappy. And lonely . . . so horribly lonely. Even when I was surrounded by people I felt alone. Not even the company of my closest friends brought me comfort. I prayed that a holiday somewhere I'd never been would cure my melancholy. That a complete change of scenery, where I knew no one and no one knew me, would help me regain the part of myself that had died along with my husband."

"You must have loved him very much."

"Yes . . . but not at first. My father, who wasn't titled, inherited a great fortune when I was fifteen, one he was determined to use to marry his only child into the peerage. I was apprehensive, especially as Robert was nearly thirty years my senior, but my fears were allayed when I met him. He was very kind and needed to marry an heiress to fill the empty family coffers. It wasn't a love match, but our affection grew into a mutual love and respect. He was an exceptional man. Intelligent and witty. A loving husband." She hesitated, then added softly, "And father."

Ian went perfectly still. "Father? You . . . you have children?"

"A son. Edward."

"How old is he?"

"Fifteen." As it always did, her heart swelled at the thought of her son. "He's a compassionate and extraordinary young man. After Robert's death, Edward became the only bright spot in my existence, which I learned is a terrible burden to place upon a child. Rather than concentrating on his studies at Eton, Edward spent his time worrying about me. I was bereft last year at the thought of once again being alone when the new school term commenced after his summer holiday. While I never told him, he clearly sensed my distress because he informed me he didn't wish to return to Eton. He wanted to remain in the country with me and be taught by private tutors. He wouldn't admit that my melancholy was the reason, but of course it was. That was the moment I realized I had to fix myself – for my son's benefit as much as my own."

"So you travelled to Scotland."

"Yes. I promised Edward that if he would focus on his studies at Eton, I would return as the mother he'd known before Robert's death. I had no idea how I intended to keep that vow, but I was determined to do so. Pure chance led me to Melrose. For reasons I didn't fully understand, I omitted my title when registering at the inn there. Looking back, I suppose I was trying to recapture the happy, carefree days of my youth, before I became an heiress and was sought after for my fortune."

"Not very pleasant – being wanted primarily because of your wealth."

"No, it's not," she agreed. "So, in Melrose, I was merely Sophia Mallory. Eager to explore, I went for a walk as soon as I arrived. I wandered into a beautiful meadow and picked a handful of roses. Holding those flowers, feeling the warmth of such a lovely day, it suddenly felt as if something inside me shifted – like a dark cloud dissipating so the sun could shine through. A joy I hadn't felt since before Robert's death bubbled up inside me. I spun around in pure delight, feeling free in a way I hadn't since I was a girl. And when I stopped spinning, I saw you. I considered telling you my title, but when you confirmed you were the groundskeeper, I changed my mind. A groundskeeper wouldn't converse so informally with a countess – and I had no desire to end our conversation. By the end of our walk through the garden I knew I wanted us to become lovers."

His lips twitched. "I'm heartbroken it took you that long to real- ize it. I knew the instant I laid eyes on you."

"I still considered telling you, but after a few weeks with you in the cottage, my title simply ceased to matter. I loved the simplicity of our existence. Loved being simply Sophia. I knew I'd have to return to my world, but until that time, I didn't want anything of my life in England to intrude on my happiness. Because Ian, I was truly happy. I never thanked you properly, so I hope you'll accept my gratitude now."

"Then why did you leave? And so abruptly?"

"When you mentioned me staying longer than the two months I'd planned, it burst the bubble surrounding me. I realized I'd inadvertently led you to believe our arrangement could continue for an extended duration. It seemed too late to tell you the truth, yet I couldn't bring myself to lie to you any longer. That last night, it became clear that your feelings for me were stronger than I'd ever anticipated them becoming." She drew a deep breath, then added, "As were my feelings for you."

Fire, and something that looked alarmingly like hope kindled in his eyes. He lifted her hands to his lips and gently kissed the backs of her fingers. "You've no idea how glad I am to hear of these strong feelings for me, Sophia."

Before she could tell him that he shouldn't be glad, that those feelings were impossible, the carriage jerked to halt.

"We have arrived," Ian said softly.

Five

Sophia halted just inside the drawing room. "What's all this?" she asked, sweeping her arm towards the round table set before the hearth where a cheery fire crackled.

Ian assessed the table with a critical eye and was pleased to note his instructions to the staff had been perfectly carried out during his absence. "A surprise. For you."

She walked across the room then slowly circled the table. "Roses, cherries, marzipan, scones and raspberry conserve," she murmured, gently trailing her fingertips around the polished wood edge. "All my—"

"Favourite things. Aye." Ian leaned against the hearth and crossed his arms over his chest – the only way he could keep from yanking her into his arms. Bloody hell, if he'd thought it difficult not to pounce upon her before, it was nearly impossible not to do so now, when no more secrets existed between them. When he'd bared his soul to her, and she'd admitted to having strong feelings for him.

Based on her reaction to their kiss on the terrace, he didn't doubt he could seduce her, but he wanted more than a quick romp. Wanted more than her body. He wanted her heart. And wanted her to know she owned his. Although she'd owned it from the moment he'd seen her, he'd never *told* her so, something he'd castigated himself for every day for the past six months. Surely if he'd told her, she wouldn't have left him. He'd intended to, but hadn't felt the need to rush, especially as he believed she knew, even without the words, how deeply he cared for her. Bloody hell, it had seemed as if his feelings all but glowed from him.

It was a mistake he wouldn't repeat. Before this evening was over, Sophia would know, without a doubt, how much he cared for her – out of the bedchamber as well as in it.

So, instead of sweeping her into his arms and carrying her to the nearest bed, he offered her a smile and teased, "I'd wager you're now sorry you never expressed to me a love for diamonds and emeralds."

She laughed, a magical sound that flowed over him like warm honey. "In truth I'm not overly fond of diamonds or emeralds. I much prefer—"

"Pearls."

"I mentioned that?"

He nodded. "Once."

"And you remembered?"

"You sound surprised."

"I suppose I am."

She returned her attention to the table and picked up one of the sea shells decorating the surface. As he knew she would, she held the shell up to her ear, and his heart turned over at the delighted smile that lifted her lips. "You also remembered how I love the sound of the sea."

"I recall every detail of our time together. Everything about you is . . . unforgettable."

Colour rushed into her cheeks and she quickly set the shell back in the bowl. "Ian, what I said in the carriage regarding my feelings . . . there are things we need to discuss—"

"I agree. And what better way to begin than with your favourite things?" He slid back one of the mahogany chairs from the table in invitation.

Her gaze lingered over the arrangement of pink roses set in a crystal vase in the centre of the table. "I believe you are once again trying to tempt me with your roses."

"I am. And let's not forget the cherries, marzipan, scones and raspberry jam."

She moistened her lips, a gesture that tightened Ian's fingers around chair back. "I *am* a bit hungry," she murmured.

"Excellent. Shall we sit?"

She hesitated, and he prayed the wariness in her eyes was a result of not trusting herself – bloody great news as far as he was concerned – as opposed to not trusting him: a bloody depressing thought. Finally she nodded, then gracefully sat and murmured her thanks. Ian took the seat across from her and popped a piece of marzipan in his mouth. While enjoying the almond-flavoured treat as well as several cherries he watched her spread jam on a scone then take a delicate bite.

"Is it to your liking?"

"Yes. Thank you for going to such trouble on my behalf."

"'Tis no trouble to give you the things you enjoy, Sophia."

His gaze riveted on a speck of jam dotting her bottom lip. Unable to resist, he reached out and brushed a fingertip over the spot. "You missed a bit of jam." With his gaze steady on hers, he sucked the morsel from his fingertip. Her eyes darkened at the gesture – which he might perhaps have been able to resist, but when her gaze dropped to his mouth and she whispered his name, the fire racing through him incinerated his every good intention, and the battle not to touch her was well and truly lost.

Without taking his gaze from her, he stood and strode around the table. Lifted her into his arms. Carried her swiftly to the sofa. Set her on the chintz-covered cushion, then covered her body with his.

"Missed you so bloody much," he murmured in a rough whisper, interspersing kisses along her jaw and neck between words. "Couldn't eat. Couldn't sleep. Couldn't think o' anything but you. Finding you. Touching you. Loving you."

Every thought fled his mind when she tangled her fingers in his hair and urged his mouth to hers for a lush, tongue-dancing kiss. *More.* Needed more. He insinuated his hand beneath her gown's hem and skimmed his palm up her leg.

"Ached for you . . . God, Sophia, I've ached for you every minute of the last six months." They both groaned when he touched her folds. "Wet," he rasped, running his tongue down her throat as he teased her with a light, circular motion then slipped two fingers inside her. "You're so beautifully wet."

She moaned and arched beneath him, spreading her legs wider. "I've ached for you as well, Ian." She stroked his hard length through his breeches, and he gritted his teeth against the intense pleasure.

Helpless to remain still, he thrust into her hand. "I won't last long if you continue doing . . . ahhh . . . that." Long? Bloody hell, he was a heartbeat away from ripping open his breeches and mindlessly sinking into her. Which was precisely what he'd promised himself he wouldn't do. Damn it, he was going to do this properly even if it killed him – which it bloody well might.

With a groan that felt ripped from his soul, he sat up, bowed his head, and fought to control his ragged breathing.

"Ian . . ." She sat up and kissed his neck, dragging another groan from him. "You didn't need to stop. I want us to have this night. One last night to be together."

A frown pulled down his brows and he turned towards her. "One last night? What are you talking about?"

"Us . . . spending the night together. Enjoying each other."

"And then . . . ?"

"And then I'll go home. And you'll return to Scotland."

Bloody hell. He'd not only pounced on her, he'd lost his mind and forgotten all his fine plans for the evening. "Sophia. I stopped because I didn't come here for a quick romp—"

"I understand. Which is why I want you to know we can have the entire night."

"No, you don't understand at all. I didn't come to London to resume our affair or to spend a night with you. I came here to tell you that I love you. So much it hurts to even breathe without you. I don't want you to be just my lover. I want you to be my wife." He withdrew a square velvet box from his waistcoat pocket then lowered himself to one knee. Looking into her eyes, he opened the box to reveal the pearl ring he'd commissioned especially for her. "Sophia, will you marry me?"

Six

The blank shock, followed by dawning dismay, on Sophia's face was definitely not the reaction Ian had hoped for. She rose from the sofa then moved to the fireplace, putting the length of the Axminster rug between them. "*Marry* you? You cannot be serious."

Hurt and – damn it – anger propelled him to his feet. He set the ring aside then reached her in two long strides and grasped her shoulders. "I've never been more serious in my life. I love you, Sophia. I want ye to be my wife. To share my life."

She shook her head and tried to shrug off his hold, but he wouldn't let her. "It's impossible, Ian."

"Why?"

"*Why?* Surely you can see this could never work between us. Your place is in Scotland. Mine is here, in England, being the sort of mother to Edward I promised him I'd be. The sort whose behaviour is above reproach. A scandal would not only cast shame upon me, but Edward as well. Just last year a terrible scandal erupted when a viscountess was discovered having an affair with a footman. Her husband publicly gave her the cut direct, and many in Society, not wishing to incur the viscount's wrath, cut not only the viscountess but her children as well, including her son, whose political aspirations suffered as a result. Edward has political aspirations as well. I cannot, will not subject him to any such possible shame."

"I'm not a footman, Sophia, and I'm asking you to be my wife – not my mistress. We are of the same social class. No scandal would touch you or your son if we married."

"The age difference between us is enough to set tongues wagging. I'll be labelled a cradle snatcher – or worse. My God, Ian, you're not only twelve years younger than me – you're only ten years older than my son!"

"You make it sound as if I'm a child rather than a man of five and twenty. What precisely is it you think I'm too young for?"

"A woman of seven and thirty."

He muttered a Gaelic curse. "There is naught I can do about my unfortunate lack of age, except to reiterate that it doesn't matter to me and to remind you that I *will* get older."

"As will I. I know how difficult an age gap can be in a marriage—"

He cut her off with a dismissive wave. "Twelve years is hardly the same as the thirty-year difference you had with your husband."

"You'll change your mind when you're still a young man and I'm an old hag."

"That's bloody ridiculous. You're the most beautiful woman I've ever met."

"Beauty fades with age."

"Not inner beauty. But using your theory, any good looks you believe I possess will also fade. You'll look at me and see a crabbitty old coot."

She shook her head. "Ian, it was one thing for us to be together in Scotland, where I was unknown and had no one but myself to consider. It was a wonderful, special time and I'll always be grateful to you for showing me how to live again. For making me *want* to live again. But it wasn't real."

"The hell it wasn't. It was the most real thing I've ever known."

"While it lasted. But it had to end."

"Not if we care for each other."

Her eyes begged for understanding. "I must set a good example for Edward, and that good example does not include being with a man twelve years my junior."

"I don't give a damn about the twelve years!"

"You should. What of an heir? It's very unlikely I can bear another child."

"I've male cousins who can inherit the title."

"Every man wants a son of his own."

"I canna speak for every man – only myself. And what I want is a woman to love. A woman who makes me laugh. Who makes me happy. Having a child would be a great blessing, but 'tis not vital to my happiness. Whereas *you*, Sophia, are absolutely vital." He smoothed his hands down her arms and entwined their fingers. "I also want a woman who loves me, as much as I love

her. As far as I'm concerned, that's the *only* reason us marrying
would be impossible – if you don't love me." He searched her
gaze, wishing he could read her thoughts, but her expression was
impossible to decipher. "So the only question left is: do you love
me?"

"I . . . I care for you very much—"

"That is no' what I asked. Do you *love* me? 'Tis a simple question – and requires only a simple yes or no answer."

Tenderness shimmered in her eyes, filling him with relief and
hope. "Yes, Ian. I love you. But—"

He cut her off with a hungry kiss filled with all the pent-up love
and frustration and passion he'd held in check for what felt like an
eternity. She loved him. Nothing else mattered. He deepened the
kiss and the words *at last* thundered through his brain. *At last* she
was back in his arms, where she belonged. *At last* they would be
together. *At last.*

A shudder shook her and he lifted his head. And stilled at the
tears in her eyes . . . golden brown pools that shimmered with
sadness and regret rather than happiness. And suddenly he felt as if
he'd turned to ice.

She stepped back and his arms fell to his sides. "Ian . . . I cannot
marry you. I do love you – so much that it is nearly impossible to
recall that I have responsibilities beyond my own happiness and selfish desires. Which is the biggest reason I had to leave you in Scotland
– because I was so tempted to forget everything but you. To think of
nothing, no one but myself. But I cannot think only of myself. I
cannot risk any sort of scandal. If there was only me to consider . . .
but there's not. Perhaps if Edward were an adult . . . but he's
not. If I were younger or you were older . . . but that isn't the case.
I wish with all my heart our circumstances were different . . . but
they're not."

Ian heard her words, but after she'd said *I cannot marry you*, they
all blurred together. It didn't really matter what she said – in spite
of her regret, her resolute determination was clear to see. His heart
screamed at him to argue, to persuade her, but his mind knew there
was no point. Perhaps she loved him, but it didn't matter. Because
she didn't love him enough. And no amount of arguing or persua-
sion would change that.

He had to clear his throat to locate his voice. "Well, that's that
then." He sounded as gutted as he felt.

She reached out and rested her hand on his chest. Right above the heart she'd just broken. "Yes, but we still could have tonight, Ian. One more night. And then say good-bye."

He briefly closed his eyes and pressed her hand tighter against his chest. Then shook his head. "I can't have you again then let you go. I can't have you again then say good-bye. I want it all, Sophia. All or nothing."

A single tear slid down her cheek and fell on his cuff. "Then I'm afraid it's . . . nothing."

Ian watched the droplet soak into the white linen, until the tear was gone, as if it had never existed. Just like the happiness they'd shared last summer. He gave a tight nod, then without a word he crossed the room and pulled the bell cord. Only several seconds passed until a knock sounded. At Ian's bid to enter, the butler opened the door. "Please have the carriage brought round and see that Lady Winterbourne is escorted safely home."

"Yes, my lord."

The butler withdrew, and Ian turned to Sophia. He almost wished he could take some satisfaction in the fact that she looked as pale and eviscerated as he felt, but it was impossible to feel anything when his entire body was numb. Heavy silence fell between them. He searched his mind for something to say, but he had no words left.

The butler returned a moment later. "The carriage is ready, my lord," he said, then withdrew.

Ian watched Sophia cross the room. Felt her touch his hand. Heard her say softly, "I wish you much happiness, Ian." And then she quit the room. He stared at the empty doorway after she exited then listened for the sound of the front door closing. The click reverberated through his mind like a death knell.

She was gone.

And she'd taken his heart with her.

Seven

The following afternoon, Sophia – exhausted after a sleepless night – reluctantly agreed to receive Christine, but only because Christine had scrawled *it's urgent I see you* on the back of her card. The instant her normally unflappable friend entered the drawing room Sophia knew something was amiss.

"What's wrong?" she asked, taking Christine's proffered hands.

Her concern doubled when she felt her friend's fingers trembling.

Confusion passed over Christine's features, then her eyes widened. "Dear God, you don't know."

"Know what?"

"Let's sit."

Sophia preferred to stand, but given Christine's pallor, she led her friend to the settee. "Tell me what's wrong," Sophia said. "Are you ill?"

"Only in my heart – for you."

"*Me?* Why?"

Christine squeezed Sophia's hands. "You were seen sharing a passionate kiss with the very young Scottish Lord Marlington on the terrace at the Benningfield soiree last evening. You were further observed leaving the party with him, arriving at his townhouse, where you reportedly remained for an 'indecent amount of time', and looked . . . dishevelled when you left."

Dear God. "Who told you this?"

"Lady Chapman. She claims she saw the kiss with her own eyes."

Sophia's heart sank at the mention of the ton's most notorious gossip. "And of course she told everyone."

"Everyone," Christine confirmed. "It will certainly be reported in tomorrow's *Times* society page." Christine's gaze searched hers. "Is it all true?"

Sophia pressed a shaking hand to her mid section. "I'm afraid so."

Christine nodded grimly. "Although I'm burning with curiosity as to how it all came about, explanations will have to wait. Right now we must discuss your best course to weather the tidal wave of gossip and ensuing scandal. Given the lascivious nature of the story, you're in for a rough time. Every man in London will believe you're now available for a dalliance. Henry told me the betting book at White's is already filled with wagers as to who you'll take as your next lover."

The knot in Sophia's stomach cinched tighter and she jumped to her feet. "Edward . . . I must go at once to Eton to speak to him. Prepare him."

"I'll come with you. But Sophia – at the rate this story is spreading, I wouldn't be surprised if he's already heard."

A humourless, bitter sound escaped Sophia at the irony. She and Ian hadn't made love last night, yet still the thing she most dreaded

– a scandal – had come to pass. Filled with trepidation, she hurried to the foyer, Christine on her heels.

An hour later she returned to Christine's waiting carriage on Eton High Street. "Did you see Edward?" Christine asked in an anxious voice.

Sophia fought the panic threatening to overwhelm her. "No."

Sympathy flooded Christine eyes. "He's already heard and refused to see you?"

"He heard. Early this morning. A fellow student confirmed it." Dear God, she could barely speak around the lump of dread clogging her throat. "Edward wasn't there, Christine. He became extremely distraught upon hearing the gossip and left school. No one knows where he is."

When the carriage arrived back at her townhouse, Sophia ran up the brick walkway, praying there would be some word of Edward, that he'd come home or sent a note. If not, she planned to go directly to Bow Street and hire a Runner to locate him. The instant she entered the foyer, she asked Monroe, "Have you received any word from Edward?"

"Young Lord Winterbourne arrived home moments after you left, my lady," the butler said, taking her wrap. "He awaits you in the library."

Relief weakened Sophia's knees and she clutched Christine's arm. "Thank God."

"Do you want me to stay?" Christine asked.

"Thank you, but no." She hugged her friend tightly. "I cannot tell you how grateful I am for your friendship and support."

"You'll always have it."

Sophia blinked back her tears and after Christine departed, she drew a bracing breath and squared her shoulders. She could cry later. Right now she had to see Edward. Before she could take a single step towards the library, however, Monroe cleared his throat.

"Lord Winterbourne is not alone in the library, my lady."

Sophia frowned. "Who is with him?"

"The Earl of Marlington."

Eight

With her heart beating so hard she could hear its echo in her ears, Sophia entered the library. And froze at the sight that greeted her.

She wasn't sure what she'd expected but it certainly wasn't her son and her former lover playing backgammon.

"You've the devil's own luck, my lord," Edward exclaimed. "That's the third double six you've rolled this game."

Ian grinned. "'Tis skill, not luck."

"And that's a Banbury tale if I've ever heard one."

"And precisely what ye deserve after the trouncing I suffered at your hands the last game."

Just then Edward glanced towards the door and saw her. "Mother!" He jumped to his feet and hurried towards her. Swallowing the sob that rose in her throat, she met him halfway and enveloped him in a tight hug. Over his shoulder she saw Ian rise. He regarded her through serious eyes that gave away nothing.

Edward pulled back from their embrace. His dark brown eyes, so like his father's, reflected worry. "Where have you been?"

"Eton. To see you. You've . . . heard."

Colour rushed into his cheeks and he nodded.

"You left school hours ago. Where have *you* been?"

"I went to see Lord Marlington."

Sophia blinked. "Why?"

Edward raised his chin. "I wanted to confront the cad who damaged my mother's good name. Tell him what I thought of him. Show him as well." He flexed his fingers, drawing Sophia's attention to his hand. She gasped at the sight of his reddened knuckles. "Good heavens. You *struck* Lord Marlington?"

"Planted him a facer," Edward confirmed, looking inordinately pleased with himself.

"Bloody well hurt," Ian said, from across the room, rubbing his jaw.

"But according to Lord Marlington I could have done better. He's promised to give me some pugilistic pointers."

Sophia's gaze bounced between her son and Ian. "I'm afraid I'm confused. You two have—"

"Spent the day together," Edward broke in. "After I planted him the facer, we talked. He told me everything."

Sophia's gaze flew to Ian. "*Everything*?"

"Edward demanded to know why I'd dishonoured his mother," Ian said. "I explained that was never my intention. That I love you and want to marry you. And that you said you love me as well."

Edward touched her arm, recalling her attention. "If you love him, why don't you want to marry him, Mum?" he asked softly so only she could hear.

"I . . . it's complicated, Edward."

"Is it because of me? Because if so, I must tell you, I like him. And I can tell he really loves you."

"Adores you, actually," Ian called from across the room. "Sorry – I'm not deaf. And just so you know, I like you as well, Edward – even though you trounced me at backgammon."

Edward grinned at Ian over his shoulder then turned back to Sophia. "Father always said you can tell a great deal about a man by the way he handles himself playing backgammon. Everything I learned about Lord Marlington today showed me he's a fine man." Edward squeezed her hand, then leaned forwards to whisper, "I want you happy, mother. And if Lord Marlington makes you happy . . . you have my blessing." He gently kissed her cheek then said in his normal voice, "If you'll both excuse me . . ." After offering Ian a formal bow, Edward quit the room, closing the door behind him.

In an effort to align her careening thoughts, Sophia closed her eyes, pressed her palms to her trembling mid section and drew several deep breaths.

"He's an exceptional young man, Sophia."

She opened her eyes and found Ian standing before her. The profound love, raw desire and deep admiration glowing in his eyes stole her breath. "Th . . . thank you. You two clearly shared quite a day together."

"Aye. It didn't begin particularly well—" he touched the faint bruise marring his jaw, "but after we talked, things rapidly improved. Just before you arrived he told me I have his blessing to marry you. In the hopes that that will change your mind . . ." He reached into his waistcoat pocket and withdrew the magnificent pearl ring he'd presented to her last night. Then, as he had the previous evening, he lowered himself to one knee before her. "Sophia . . . I've loved you since the first moment I saw you, and I promise I'll love you until the day I die. Will you do me the honour of marrying me?"

Sophia looked into his beautiful eyes and her throat swelled shut at the wave of love swamping her. She'd refused him to avoid scandal, yet the scandal had happened anyway. She'd tried to protect her son, but Edward was clearly capable of taking matters into his own hands. And he'd given her his blessing.

Ian cleared his throat. "In case you need a bit more convincing, I'll point out that a wedding would put a stop to all the gossip. And should anyone be foolish enough to say a word against you or cast aspersions on my unfortunate lack of age, I assure you your son is well prepared to take them to task. Boy packs quite a wallop."

With hot moisture pushing behind her eyes, Sophia took Ian's hands and urged him to his feet. When he stood before her, she said, "I can't marry you to stop gossiping tongues, Ian."

He clearly meant to argue and she pressed her fingers to his lips. "But I *can* marry you because you're wonderful. Because you make me happy. Make me laugh. Because I know you'll be good to my son. And because I love you so much I can barely breathe."

"Is that a 'yes?'"

A half laugh, half sob escaped her. "Yes!"

In the space of single heartbeat he slipped the pearl ring on her finger and yanked her into his arms and kissed her breathless. "I hope you don't want a bloody long engagement," he murmured against her lips.

"I don't," she assured him. "Although I'll have your promise that you'll not mention our age difference."

"What age difference?"

She framed his face between her hands and laughed. "God, I love you."

He held her tighter and whispered something in Gaelic in her ear. "What does that mean?" she asked.

"*At last*, my love. It means at last."

Magick in the Mist

Debbie Mazzuca

Craigievar Castle, November 1598

One

Isobel Forbes waited patiently by the hearth in the sun-filled parlour of her family's tower house in the Grampian Hills. Patience was not a virtue anyone of Isobel's acquaintance would ascribe to her, but it was one she'd had no choice but to develop when it came to Ewan Mackenzie, the man her nana had predicted was Isobel's true love. As she'd been waiting for this day for nine years, Isobel felt she'd developed more patience than was good for a body. It seemed unfair to her that her sisters – all five of them, who were much more suited to the virtue – had within a matter of months married the men their nana had predicted to be their true loves.

Her amused gaze followed her seven exuberant nieces who chased one another through the cluttered room while their harried mothers and handsome fathers tried to rescue the pitchers of flowers and side tables they knocked over in their enthusiasm, and a smile curved her lips. Her time had come. On this day, Isobel would wed Ewan Mackenzie, the man who'd rode through the mist on a moonlit night just as her nana had foreseen. Not once, but twice.

The corners of her mouth turned down ever so slightly as her mind returned to the day she'd learned that the handsome high-lander, who set the hearts of women – both young and old – afluttering, was to be hers. Isobel, at fifteen, had barely been able

to contain her excitement the night her nana sent her to their neighbours' lands with the Forbes heart stone in hand – a heart-shaped
piece of red sandstone that had come from the magickal Stone of
Destiny – and a promise that the first man to ride through the mist
on that moonlit night was destined to be Isobel's true love.

Nothing could have prepared Isobel for the sight of Ewan
Mackenzie that night. She'd been rendered speechless, a rare
occurrence for her. The only thing she'd managed to mumble in
response to his question – asked in a deep voice that had sent
heated shivers through her body – was that she'd been waiting for
him. But when the second anniversary of that day had passed without Ewan coming to claim her, Isobel complained to her sister
Edeen about the long delay. It was then she'd learned what her
sisters had been trying to keep from her. Ewan Mackenzie had been
betrothed to another.

Certain her nana must have misinterpreted her vision, and Ewan
was not her true love after all, Isobel had returned that very night
to the Burnetts' moors in hopes of finding the man who was. Her
body had trembled with anticipation as the horses had thundered
through the fog. Her jaw dropped as, once again, Ewan Mackenzie
rode masterfully through the mist on his great black steed. His
damp honey-gold hair was slicked back from a face she hadn't
thought could become more beautiful, but it had, breath-stealingly
so. Her heart had fluttered in her chest when she'd lifted her gaze
to his. Eyes reputed to be the colour of sapphires locked with hers
and the night went silent. In that moment, there had been nothing
but the two of them. A heated awareness had sizzled from the top
of her head to the tips of her toes. As though he'd felt the same,
he'd jerked back. And then she'd remembered, he was promised to
another.

Her dreams of a happily-ever-after destroyed with that one
thought, she'd turned her mount and fled from the Burnett lands.
Her father had come upon her crying in the stables and had berated
her nana for filling Isobel's head with fanciful nonsense. Nana had
swiftly disabused him of the notion and Isobel of hers. Ewan's
betrothed – Jenny McRae – had married his cousin.

Determined to seek Ewan out at first light and introduce herself,
Isobel went to the Burnett's where the annual gathering was being
held, only to be told Ewan was participating in the hunt. Undeterred,
she'd dressed with care for the festivities planned that eve. While
she wove her way through the heated crush in search of him, the

guests raised their glasses to toast the announcement of Ewan Mackenzie's betrothal to Lorna Sinclair. Isobel forced the memory from her head and a smile to her lips.

Three weeks ago a missive had arrived from Castle Leod with the offer for her hand. Her father, William, furious at the manner in which the offer had been made, had all but denied the match until her sisters and nana intervened. Privately, Isobel thought he'd conceded because he'd begun to despair she'd ever wed. Of late the offers for her hand had slowed to a trickle. Over the years there had been several she'd given serious consideration to, but all she had to do was look to her sisters' happy marriages and think on what had become of her father and Anna when they'd not heeded her nana's visions. It had become easier to refuse when last year she'd learned Ewan was a widower.

Isobel smiled at her sister Edeen, who'd come to stand beside her. Edeen gave a comforting squeeze to Isobel's shoulder. "You had a pensive look aboot you, Izzie. You're no havin' second thoughts, are you?"

"The time for second thoughts is long past. Although da appears to be havin' a few of his own," she said wryly, watching her father pace from one end of the room to the other, a sure sign of his growing temper. William's temper was as fiery as the curly red hair atop his head.

"Och, Willie, would ye sit doon. Ye're makin' me dizzy." Their nana, with her pretty lightly-lined face and silver hair pulled back neatly at the nape of her neck, called from where she sat on the blue settee surrounded by her great granddaughters. She gave Isobel a reassuring wink.

Edeen smiled. "Well, the groom is a touch late."

"Since you ken how long I've been waitin', you'll understand an hour doesna concern me overmuch."

Her sister wrapped her arm around Isobel's shoulder. "Aye, you have, but then you ken what happens when a Forbes doesna wed the one nana has foreseen."

"Aye," Isobel said quietly, thinking of their eldest sister Anna, who'd done just that and paid for it with her life.

"Sorry, love, 'tis no' the time for sad thoughts, no' with you lookin' so bonny on your weddin' day."

Isobel fingered the low-cut décolletage of the yellow gown her sisters had insisted she wear. They said it showed off her long chestnut curls and hazel eyes to best advantage. She'd heeded their advice. She wanted to look her best for Ewan. Although Isobel had been told often enough that she was pretty, Lorna Mackenzie had been stunning, as breathtakingly beautiful as her husband.

A commotion in the entry hall drew her attention from her shortcomings when compared to Ewan's first wife.

"Aboot bloody time," her father muttered.

"Willie," her nana admonished. Setting the bairns aside, Olivia Forbes came to stand by Isobel. "Yer mon has come, my bonny, just as I promised ye he would."

"Be happy, love. We'll miss you." Edeen kissed her cheek then went to stand with their sisters who blew Isobel kisses. Mimicking their mothers, her nieces did the same. Isobel blinked back tears. Overjoyed her wedding day had finally come, she hadn't thought of all she stood to lose. She adored her family and would miss them something fierce. Leod was several days ride from Craigievar and visits would be few and far between. She held on to the thought that one day soon she'd have bairns of her own to spoil as she did her nieces.

An elderly man entered the hall.

"Laird Roderick Mackenzie," the manservant announced.

"Sweet Mother of God, 'tis the wrong one," Isobel gasped.

Beneath a shock of white hair, the man's bright blue eyes twinkled. "Nay, lass, I'm here on my grandson Ewan's behest. I'm to wed ye to him by proxy."

Astride his black steed, Ewan Mackenzie bid farewell to the men who'd fought under his command in France. Their purses now heavy with coin, they were anxious to return to their families – as anxious as Ewan was to return to his own. It had been a year since he'd seen his young sons. Too long for bairns to be without their da, but it couldn't be helped. The Mackenzies were in dire need of coin, and a sword for hire had been the only way for Ewan to raise the much needed funds. He scowled, thinking of his grandda and the missive that had made its way to Ewan across the channel.

"He's scowlin' again, Randall. 'Tis certain he's thinkin' on grandda." His dark-haired cousin Callum observed with a laugh. Both Callum and his twin brother Randall had fought alongside Ewan in France and now accompanied him to Leod.

"Aye, I'm thinkin' if he wishes to see another day he'd best no' have contacted the Forbes," Ewan said irritably.

"Mayhap 'tis no' a bad idea, Ewan. You said yourself you were tired of the fightin' and missin' your wee lads. William Forbes is reputed to be the richest man in Scotland. I'm sure the lass's tocher would allow you to give up the sword," Randall said.

Ewan's fingers tightened on the leather reins. "Aye, I am, but I'll no' be tied to another wench of his choosing so I can do so. The old man canna see past the coin to the viper he saddles me with."

Randall bristled. "Jenny is no' a viper."

"Nay, I was referring to Lorna. But if ye hadna kidnapped Jenny, I'd be wed to her and the three of us would be miserable."

"I wouldna had to kidnap her if you'd stood up to grandda," Randall grumbled.

"Aye, well, I was but a lad of twenty and wanted nothin' more than to please the old man." His grandda had taken the place of Ewan's parents when they'd died of fever, and Ewan would've done anything for Roderick and the clan. It had been the same when he'd wed Lorna Sinclair. Although, he admitted, he'd been as enamoured with her beauty as all the men had been, it hadn't taken long for him to discover she was a cold-hearted, treacherous bitch beneath her angelic facade. If she hadn't died fleeing Scotland with one of her many lovers, Ewan would have found some way to divorce her, no matter the shame it brought his family.

Mayhap if she'd been any kind of mother to his sons, he would have been satisfied to lead separate lives, but she'd spared the bairns not a moment of her time or affection. He shoved aside the thought the lads may not be his. It didn't matter. If they were not sons of his loins, they were sons of his heart.

"I understand how you feel after what you suffered at Lorna's hands, but for all you ken Isobel Forbes is a grand lass and would make you a fine wife. Your lads need a mother, Ewan."

"Callum's right. I've never heard 'aught said against the Forbes lassies. They were always aboot when we attended the gatherin's at the Burnetts'. Are you sure you doona ken them, Ewan?"

"Nay," Ewan grunted. His cousins were wasting their breath. Ewan would not marry again, especially a woman of his grandda's choosing. He'd done his duty – he'd provided heirs. But they were right about one thing – he was determined to remain at Leod with his sons. He just had to find a way to provide for the clan so he could.

"Ewan, you canna tell me you doona recall the gatherin's at

the Burnetts'. Doona you remember the lass you went chasin'
through the woods after, only to end up knockin' yourself out
instead?"

How could he forget? There'd been something about the lass
that had called to him. A charged jolt of awareness when his eyes
met hers, a feeling he'd never experienced before or since. It was as
though his body recognized her and urged him to claim her, make
her his own. Unbeknownst to his cousin, Ewan hadn't taken part in
the hunt that day. He'd scoured the countryside for her, only to
return in time for the festivities to hear his grandda announce his
betrothal to Lorna Sinclair.

Randall chuckled. "Must be somethin' aboot the moonlight and
the Burnetts' moors that calls the lassies to our cousin here. Do you
recall the lass we met up with the summer before grandda
announced your betrothal to Jenny?"

He hadn't, not until his cousin mentioned it. They'd come
through the mist to find a bonny wee lass astride her horse. Ewan
had asked what she was doing on her own. His lips twitched as he
recalled her sweet, innocent smile and her answer. *"I'm waitin' for
you."* He'd laughed and promised to come back for her. He started
at the thought; the two lassies were one and the same. He shook off
his bemusement. He had no time for whimsical fancy of bonny
lassies waiting for him in the moonlight.

In the valley far below from where they sat astride their horses,
Castle Leod shimmered in the midday sun. The sweet scent of
heather filled the warm summer air and Ewan's chest tightened.
Aye, 'twas good to be home.

"Is that grandda?" Callum asked. Shielding his eyes with one
hand while he waved the other, he called out to the old man who
appeared to be chasing a woman through the heather.

"If 'tis, lets hope the woman has coin and grandda can wed her
because he'll no be gettin' me to the altar again."

Two

Isobel blew her flour-dusted hair from her eyes. The kitchens were
sweltering. Her body was slick with sweat beneath the old gown
she'd chosen for the task the bairns had set out for her. Robbie and
Connor watched her closely, their eyes wide as she turned out the
honey cakes they'd asked her to bake in honour of their father's
return. She tried to ignore the nervous flutter in her belly at the

knowledge that the man who was now her husband would arrive on the morrow.

"Nay, Robbie." Connor shook his head of auburn curls and grabbed his brother's hand before he could stick his finger in the cake.

"Can we have a wee taste, mam? Please," Robbie begged, lifting his startling blue eyes to hers.

Isobel's chest tightened as it did every time she looked upon their sweet faces. Roderick hadn't mentioned Ewan's children until they'd arrived at the castle. For Isobel, it had been a welcome surprise. She'd been living at Castle Leod for well over six months now and, recently, Connor and Robbie had taken to calling her mam. The first time they did so she'd been moved to tears. She'd come to love them as if they were her own.

Isobel ruffled Robbie's golden curls – a shade lighter than the colour she remembered his father's to be – about to concede.

"Mam," Connor said sternly. "They're for da, remember?"

Isobel bit back a laugh at the reproachful look in Connor's light blue eyes. Connor, who seemed much older than his six years, thought Isobel spoiled Robbie terribly as he was wont to tell her at least twice a day. Noting the quiver in Robbie's bottom lip, she said, "There's two. Surely your da wouldna mind if I give you both a wee piece?" With her thumb and forefinger, she indicated the size.

"Nay, da is a verra braw man. You canna have any, Robbie," Connor said mulishly.

"I promise, I'll make another one on the morrow, Connor." Isobel prayed the kitchens would not be as hot then. It wouldn't do to meet her husband in the sorry state she now found herself. She doubted Lorna Mackenzie had ever looked anything short of perfect.

Upon her arrival at Leod, Isobel had worried how the Mackenzie clan – and more importantly, Ewan's children – would respond to her. Would they find her lacking? But not once had she'd been made to feel that way. She'd been happy and relieved to be so readily accepted, but couldn't help wonder why not once in all this time had Lorna been mentioned. From what little she could pry from Roderick – who insisted Isobel call him grandda – she'd learned Robbie had been only one when his mother died. Isobel thought Connor, at least, would have some difficulty accepting her in the role of his mother. He hadn't. Far from it.

Roderick had been no more forthcoming in regards to how her betrothal had come about than he'd been about Lorna. She'd mentioned it to her nana, who at her father's insistence had accompanied Isobel to Leod, but Olivia had simply brushed her worries aside with the admonishment that her second sight had yet to fail her.

"Nay," Connor said arms crossed. The sight of his three-year-old brother's tears not bothering him in the least.

They bothered Isobel, and she was about to try and cajole Connor into relenting when the side door opened. Roderick, with his trews and tunic rumpled and his shock of white hair standing on end, rushed past her. He came to an abrupt halt and backtracked. Taking her by the shoulders, he kissed her cheek. "Ye're a grand lass. Ken if I breathe my last this day, I've come to love ye most dearly, henny. Ye, too, my bairns. If anyone asks, I've been on my deathbed this past week," he shouted the last over his shoulder as he rushed from the kitchens.

Barely had Isobel recovered from her surprise when her nana hurried through the door. Olivia's hair hung loose about her shoulders, bits of heather clinging to her silver locks, her grey gown grass-stained. "Nana, you look like you've been rollin' around in the . . ." Isobel's eyes widened as a rosy flush tinted her nana's face. That was exactly what she'd been doing and she'd been doing it with Roderick! Isobel shouldn't be surprised, the two of them had been acting like a pair of lovesick fools of late.

"No time, my bonny, I must see to Roderick."

"It appears that the way you've been seein' to the man has just aboot killed . . ." Isobel rolled her eyes when her nana fled the room.

"Mam, Robbie stole the cakes!" Connor cried, racing from the kitchens.

Sweet Mary Mother of God, the heat must be drivin' them all mad.

Isobel set off after Connor, certain he'd pummel his brother if he got ahold of him. "Connor, Robbie," she called out. Rounding the corner, she came to a shocked standstill. Her husband stood in the entry hall, looking every inch the battle-hardened warrior Roderick proudly proclaimed him to be. His grandson's exploits were the notable exception to Roderick's reticence. Ewan Mackenzie, majestically tall with broad shoulders and rippling muscles, surveyed his home. Two dark-haired men stood at his back, but Isobel barely registered their presence.

Ewan's sapphire gaze came to rest upon her, causing a heart-stopping tremor in her throat. A frisson of heat raced through her and Ewan jerked back, as though he felt the same. He frowned, his eyes roaming her face. She couldn't drag her gaze from his, mesmerized by his beauty. Time had chiselled away the softness of youth. He looked hard, dangerous, with the dark stubble shadowing his strong jaw. Growing uncomfortable under the intensity of his stare, Isobel ran her tongue over her lips.

His gaze dropped to her mouth and a slow, sensual smile curved his. "You must be new to Leod. I doona recall seein' you before and I'd remember if I did." His voice was low, a seductive purr. The intention of his remark was not lost on Isobel. While a part of her acknowledged his attraction pleased her, the fact that as a married man he'd give his attention to another lass tempered her pleasure – even if that lass was herself.

"Doona be shy, angel, give me your name," he cajoled, taking a step towards her.

"Mam!" Connor raced to her side. Tears streaming down his wee face, he wrapped his arms around her legs. "Robbie ate the cakes. There's none left for my da," he sobbed.

Ewan's startled eyes jerked from Isobel to his son then back to her. "Who are you?" His blue eyes darkened to black.

"Isobel—"

He cut her off with a curse. "Where's Roderick?" he grated out, ignoring her shocked gasp.

"His chambers, he's—"

"I'm goin' to kill the meddlin' bastard," he roared as he charged up the stairs. The two men who'd stood with him cursed and gave chase.

Ewan slammed into Roderick's darkened chambers and crossed to where his grandda lay in the massive four-poster bed with his bedcovers drawn to his chin, his eyes squeezed shut. "Is that ye, laddie?" Roderick asked, raising a feeble hand in Ewan's direction. "Tell me I'm no' dreamin' and my favourite grandson has returned home to me."

"I thought *I* was your favourite," Callum quipped with a grin.

Ewan shot his cousin a quelling look then returned his attention to his grandda "Open your damn eyes and you'll see you're no' dreamin'. But when I get through with you, you'll wish you were."

Roderick opened his eyes slowly as if the effort cost him dearly. "Och, laddie, ye have come back to me before I die."

Callum and Randall snorted their amusement from behind Ewan.

"You're no' dyin'. Callum saw you out rollin' aboot in the heather." Ewan reached over and plucked a sprig of the stuff from his grandda's hair and held it up to him. "Now, tell me why Isobel Forbes is here?" And why the hell did his son call her mam? That was something else he wished to know. Christ, he'd been so furious he hadn't even greeted Connor. Beneath the heat of his anger a remnant of his strange reaction to the lass simmered. His response to her had thrown him off balance. The lass had a sweet face, to be sure, and what looked to be an even sweeter body but, as Ewan had known his fair share of women more beautiful, it did not explain the effect she had wrought on him.

"I doona ken where that heather came from. I've been abed—"

Ewan threw back the covers to reveal his grandda lying abed with his boots and trews on beneath his nightshirt. "Explain yourself."

Roderick scowled at him. "What would ye have me do? I thought I was soon to die and fer all I kent, ye had. I couldna leave the bairns without someone to see to them, so I found ye a wife."

"I doona want a wife and, as you can see, I'm no' dead so you'd best go down there and send the lass on her way." Ewan pushed past his cousins, who attempted not to laugh. He had to leave before he throttled the three of them.

"I canna do that. The bairns love Isobel and ye're already wed to the lass," Roderick mumbled the last under his breath.

Nay, he couldna have heard him right. Hand on the latch, Ewan turned. "What did you say?"

His grandda scrambled from the bed and positioned himself behind Randall and Callum. "Ye're wed to the lass. I wed her to ye by proxy more than six months ago." Roderick squealed when Ewan lunged for him.

"Doona do it," Randall said as he and Callum fought to hold Ewan back. He shook free of their hands. His blood boiled and his gut coiled in a painful knot. "You'll no' get away with this. I'll seek an annulment. I'll no' let you tie me to another lass of your choosing." He'd not allow grandda to force his hand. Ewan and his sons had barely survived the hell Lorna had put them through.

Olivia worried the heart stone in her hand, the ancient script worn smooth by generations of Forbes women. Her gift of second sight had never failed her, but nor had a lass waited as long as Isobel for her true love to claim her. Over the last year, no matter how hard her granddaughter had tried to hide it, Olivia had noticed the toll the wait had taken on Isobel's resilient spirit and sunny nature. It was then Olivia had decided to give the Fates a nudge. She'd sent a missive to Roderick Mackenzie proposing the match between their grandchildren. She only hoped by doing so, she hadn't destroyed Isobel's chance for happiness.

Ewan Mackenzie's love for his sons had been obvious, as obvious as his shock at the bond that had developed between the bairns and Isobel. If not for Robbie and Connor, Olivia felt certain she and her granddaughter would already be on their way to Craigievar.

During the evening meal, Ewan's anger at his grandfather had not extended to them. He'd been coolly polite. Since Isobel, along with everyone else in the keep, had heard that Ewan intended to annul the union, Olivia had been proud of how her granddaughter had conducted herself. Beautiful and poised, no one would've known she was heartbroken.

A quiet knock drew Olivia's gaze from her granddaughters sleeping form. For a brief moment she wondered if Ewan had come to his senses and decided to join his wife in their chambers. Considering he'd been well in his cups by the time she and Isobel had left the hall – thanks to his cousin's attempts to get him there – she doubted it. But he was a verra braw lad so one could not be sure and Olivia hadn't missed the furtive looks he'd cast in Isobel's direction when he thought no one was looking. Each time the bairns made Isobel laugh, his gaze would seek her out. Aye, Olivia thought, all they needed was time.

She opened the door to see Roderick pacing the corridor, his shock of white hair dishevelled. "How's our wee bonny, Livie?" he asked, coming to stand beside her.

Olivia was torn between wanting to shake him for wedding Isobel to his grandson without the young man's knowledge or consent, and wanting to kiss him for the love and concern he showed her granddaughter.

"Her husband wants no part of her, Roderick. How do ye think she is?" At his crushed expression, she sighed. "She'll be fine. She's sleepin' now. I slipped a wee somethin' into her mead."

"Good, 'twill make it easier to carry out my plan. Leave it to me, Livie, I'll make it right. The lad judges all women by Lorna's actions. He just needs time to get to ken our Isobel. Randall, Callum, bring him along now," he called down the torch-lit corridor.

His grandsons, carrying an unconscious Ewan between them, staggered down the corridor. "You ken, grandda, if no' for the fact the lass would be shamed by our cousin's actions, we'd have no part in this," Randall growled at his grandfather as they entered the chambers.

Roderick waved a dismissive hand at his grandsons. "Now, Livie, do ye think ye can make it look as if they've had . . ." He flushed, tipping his chin towards the bed where the lads set their cousin beside Isobel.

Realizing what he intended, Olivia grinned. "Aye, 'tis a good plan, Roderick."

Callum shook his head. "One is as bad as the other, Randall. I for one doona wish to be here when Ewan awakens. We'll leave for home at first light."

Three

Ewan inhaled the delicate floral scent, letting it fill his senses. It had been a long time since he'd smelt something so good, so clean and pure. A stark contrast to the smell of sweaty males, horseflesh and battle he'd grown accustomed to as a sword for hire. But it didn't compare to the warm, silken skin his hands caressed – soft, lush, womanly curves.

Sweet Christ. His eyes shot open. It wasn't a dream. He held a woman in his arms, his face buried in a mass of heather-scented chestnut curls. He groaned. It was Isobel. What the hell had possessed him to crawl into her bed? As he wanted the union annulled, it was the last place he should be. But the question had barely entered his mind and he knew the answer already. No matter how angry he'd been at finding himself wed to Isobel, last eve he'd been unable to keep his gaze from her delicate features, the maternal warmth in her gold-flecked eyes as she looked upon his sons – the feminine laugh that had made him smile despite himself. He'd been as enchanted by her as his sons appeared to be, but Ewan knew better than most how adept a woman could be at concealing her true nature.

He carefully eased her away from him. She mumbled a protest and snuggled back into place against his chest with a contented sigh. The door to his chambers creaked open and his grandda stepped inside with a self-satisfied smile. "Och, laddie, 'tis glad I am to see ye came to yer senses."

Isobel stiffened in Ewan's arms. She eased back, her eyes widening as they met his.

With a dismayed gasp, she sat up, the bedcovers pooling at her waist. The door slammed shut. "Doona worry, henny, I didna see a thing."

A mortified cry escaped her parted lips and she grabbed hold of the bedclothes to conceal her full ripe breasts from view. Scrambling from the bed, she dragged the covers with her, exposing Ewan's raging erection and the drops of blood that stained the sheet. He cursed roundly. Between the evidence on the bed and his grandda having witnessed them there, Ewan's hopes for an annulment fled as quickly as Isobel had fled his bed. His curse drew her attention and she looked at him over the delicate slope of her creamy white shoulder. Her innocent stare rounded as she took in his naked body. His erection had been easing as the reality of his situation hit home, but at the sight of her luscious behind – that she didn't realize she exposed to him – it once more shot to life.

"Oh," she gasped, and in an effort to put more distance between them, promptly tripped on the covers to fall on her face.

Ewan leaned over and grabbed his plaid from the floor. "Are you all right, lass?" he asked as he went to her.

"Aye," she muttered, trying to right herself while she held the covers to her chest with one hand, the other holding them to her behind.

"Let me help." He scooped her up and set her on the edge of the bed. Cupping her chin, he tilted her face. Her bottom lip was puffed up and her small, freckle-sprinkled nose was scraped at the tip. He shook his head. "One look at you and they'll all be sayin' I beat my wife."

"'Twill be your fault if they do. Last eve you looked as though you wished to murder me."

He winced. "Mayhap my grandda, but no' you," he conceded, surprised she didn't appear to be intimidated by him. Most women, as well as a fair number of men, were. With their naked bodies covered, she seemed to regain her composure. He sighed at the disbelieving look she gave him and sat beside her. It wasn't her fault the Mackenzies needed coin and his grandda had used the lass as a means to an end. "I apologise for my behaviour last eve, Isobel. It had been a long journey home and I . . ." He didn't know what to say without offending her.

"Didna expect to return home to find yourself wed. Aye, you

made that perfectly clear. If you wish to talk aboot it, I'd prefer to do so dressed. Close your eyes, please."

Ewan was beginning to think it would be best if they had their conversation with her still naked. Not only because he wanted another look at her body, which had been as close to perfection as he'd ever seen, but because it appeared he'd need whatever advantage he could find when dealing with the lass.

He crossed his arms over his chest, his muscles flexing, and gave her a look that had caused many a man to quiver in his boots.

She snorted her disdain. "You can save your fierce looks. You're no' on the battlefield now."

Brow arched, she waited for him to cede to her wishes. If Ewan didn't have the uneasy feeling he *was* in a battle, and one he might not win, he would've laughed at the sight of the adorable wee lass staring him down with her bonny green and gold-flecked eyes.

With a drawn-out sigh, he did as she asked. He heard the whoosh of the covers fall to the floor and his hands clenched on his thighs at the thought she stood within an arms reach of him – naked. The light splash of water in the basin cooled the erotic images that heated his blood as he realized she washed away the evidence of what had taken place between them. He cleared his throat. "Isobel, did I hurt you?" She was innocent of what took place between a man and a woman and last eve he'd been in no condition to be considerate of the fact.

The muscles in his belly clenched when she didn't answer right away. "Isobel?"

"Nay, no' that I remember. For truth, I doona recall anythin' at all. My head is a touch fuzzy this morn. I had more wine than is my custom, mayhap 'tis the reason."

While he was relieved he hadn't caused her pain, he wasn't happy that he'd made love to a lass who'd been in her cups. Nor was he pleased the experience had been so unmemorable she bloody well couldn't remember it. Which went to prove she wasn't the only one with a fuzzy head this morn. What he should be was furious he'd destroyed the one to chance to have their marriage annulled.

He scrubbed his hands over his face. There was nothing for it now. Whether he liked it or not, they were wed. He was honest enough to admit that the thought he would not have to take up his sword to raise coin was a welcome one. Surely he and Isobel could come to an arrangement that suited them both. His sons and grandda were fond of her and 'twas no' as though she'd expect his love. He would keep her at a distance. He couldn't afford to lower his defences, let his emotions become involved. Enamoured as he'd been with Lorna, he'd been blind to her manipulations and many had suffered as a result. He tamped down his annoyance that it meant keeping Isobel from his bed, but, as he'd learned from experience, women tended to equate making love with being in love.

Isobel shrugged into her nightshift while keeping an eye on Ewan to be certain he wasn't keeping one on her. Taking advantage of the opportunity to look upon his masculine beauty, she perused his glorious sun-bronzed, battle-hardened body. The sight of his broad chest lightly dusted with golden hair, the sculpted ridges lining his taut belly, caused a heated clutch in the pit of her stomach. His big hands with their long blunt fingers rested on his thickly muscled thighs and her skin tingled at the memory of the gentle caress of his powerful, calloused palms skimming over her body. She'd thought she'd been dreaming until Roderick so rudely interrupted them.

She wished she remembered more. She didn't think it fair she had no memory of their joining. Her sisters had assured her the few moments of pain she would experience was nothing compared to the pleasure she would receive. Although considering the size of her husband's manhood, she thought perhaps it was a good thing she didn't remember. She lingered on the thick bulge beneath his plaid and her cheeks heated.

"Have you looked your fill, lass?" he asked in his deep, rumbling voice.

Her gaze shot to his and she didn't miss the glint of amusement in his sapphire eyes. It was a welcome change from the anger that had darkened the brilliant blue to black last eve, but since it was at her expense, she took no pleasure in it. She had yet to forgive him for his behaviour upon learning she was his wife. Although she could understand his surprise – his shock – she felt his anger was uncalled for. Since he'd come to her bed, he'd obviously recovered from his fit of pique and she made a mental note not to surprise him in the future.

She shouldn't have let her disappointment get the best of her last eve. Although she'd hid it well at the evening meal, she'd been overwrought by the time she'd come to her bed. She should've trusted her nana's gift despite Ewan's reaction. Her sisters had warned her men could be frustratingly slow to acknowledge that special fated bond.

He sighed. "Isobel?"

She blinked. "Yes."

He stood and adjusted his plaid. She tilted her head to look up at him. "As I am sure you are now aware, our marriage canna be annulled. We shall have to make the best of it. I promise I will do everythin' in my power to ensure you are content with the union."

Isobel frowned. *Make the best of it? Content?* She didn't wish to be content. She didn't wait all this time to simply be *content*. She wanted to be happy. She wished to be loved – like her sisters were loved. He angled his head as though awaiting her answer. "As will I." Taken aback by his statement, she didn't know how else to respond.

"As long as my sons are happy and well cared for, I will be content."

Isobel began to think she disliked the word "content" even more than she disliked the word "patient". Did he not wish his sons to be loved? Did he not wish to be loved? Recalling Edeen's advice, her disquiet eased. Her sister had warned her that men had a difficult time expressing their love, their emotions – battle-hardened high-landers being the most reticent of all. Edeen had implied the best place to break through their defences was in the bedchamber. Isobel might be innocent, but she knew her husband desired her. She felt it in his touch – his swollen manhood pressed to her belly – saw it in the way he looked at her. It made perfect sense that her battle for Ewan's affections would be fought in their bedchambers. She was certain – in a week at most – her victory would be declared.

Four

Three weeks later, sitting in the great hall breaking her fast, Isobel's jaw hurt from gritting her teeth and from smiling when it was the last thing she wanted to do. Her husband was the most infuriat-ingly frustrating man she'd ever met. Her plan to win his heart had failed miserably – he had not visited their chambers once since that first night. If she hadn't seen him with his sons, she'd think him the coldest, most distant man she'd ever known. But with Robbie and Connor, he was gentle and loving. What Isobel wouldn't give to have him look at her the way he did his sons. The bairns followed him everywhere he went and not once had Isobel heard him utter an impatient word.

Oh, aye, she'd felt him watching her, caught the flare of desire in his heavy-lidded blue eyes before he quickly looked away, but it went no further than that. He engaged her in polite conversation and was most considerate of her needs, but other than when they met at mealtimes, he seemed to go out his way to spend as little time in her company as possible.

This morn, after awakening alone once more, Isobel's much-vaunted patience was nowhere to be found. In its place was the temper her nana said Isobel had inherited from her father. She scowled at Nana who sat at the far end of the table breaking her fast beside Roderick, tittering like a lovestruck girl of sixteen. "Foolish old woman," Isobel muttered under her breath.

"Is somethin' amiss, Isobel?" Ewan asked, a frown creasing his brow.

"Nay," she snapped and shoved a spoonful of porridge into her mouth.

Ewan blinked. Robbie and Connor, who sat on either side of their father, looked up.

"What's the matter, mam?" Connor asked.

Upon seeing the concern on Connor's sweet face, Isobel berated herself for allowing her impatience to show. "Nothin' is the matter, dear heart." She forced a smile to her lips. "I'm goin' to work in the garden today, would you and Robbie like to help?" she asked hopefully. She didn't begrudge them the time they spent with their father, but over the last few weeks she'd hardly had any time with Robbie and Connor, and she missed them. She hoped the idea of playing in the dirt would be the incentive she needed to keep them with her this day.

Connor cast a sidelong glance at this father, who studiously avoided his gaze. "Da's goin' to take us ridin'. Mayhap—"

"Aye, mam, da says I can ride a horsie all by myself," Robbie broke in excitedly.

Isobel's incredulous gaze shot to Ewan. "You canna seriously be thinkin' to allow Robbie to ride on is own? He's no' yet four."

Ewan raised a brow. "Aye, I am. 'Tis best to—"

She gave a disproving shake of her head. "Nay, I'll no' allow it." From the end of the table, Roderick and her Nana looked at her in open-mouthed astonishment.

"*You*, willna' allow it?" Ewan's tone was cold, a muscle twitching in the hard set of his jaw.

"Mam, I want to go." Robbie pouted, his bottom lip quivering.

"Nay, I won't," she said firmly to Ewan, then reached over to pat Robbie's hand. "I'll make you a honey cake and—"

Ewan's chair scraped across the stone floor as he pushed back from the table. "Isobel, I would speak to you alone. Now." The tension bracketing his full mouth left no doubt he expected her to obey. Since she wanted to tell him exactly how foolish she thought he was being, she followed him from the hall.

He strode to the study and held the door open for her. She flounced past him. Unimpressed with his dictatorial manner, she turned on him as soon as he closed the door behind them. "Three," she said, holding up her fingers. "He's three years old, Ewan. He's a bairn and I'll no' let—"

His gaze hardened. Looming over her, his powerful warrior's body crowded her and she took a step back, bumping into the edge of the desk.

"He's my son and I'll decide what he'll do or no' do," he ground out.

She pressed her palms to his broad chest, refusing to be intimidated by his size and the icy glint in his eyes. "And I'm his mother. I willna let you put him in harm's way."

"You're no' his mother and I'll no' have—" He stopped at her sharp intake of breath.

She turned away so he wouldn't see how much his words hurt her. She'd come to think of Robbie and Connor as her own and now he took that away from her – just as his cold indifference had stolen her hope for a happy marriage. She tried to push away from him but he brought his hands to her shoulders and held her firmly in place. "Let me go," she whispered.

"Nay." He placed his fingers beneath her chin and forced her look at him. His gaze softened. "I'm sorry, Isobel. I ken you love Robbie and Connor. I shouldna have said what I did."

She bit her lip, trying to contain her tears, but one after another they slid down her cheeks.

"Nay, please, doona cry." He pulled her into his arms. "Shh, now," he said, rubbing her back.

The warmth of his embrace, his apology and soothing touch, eased some of the hurt, but not her concern for Robbie. She sniffed into his chest and swiped at her tears. Tipping her head to look up at him, she said, "Truly, Ewan, Robbie is much too young to ride on his own. I only wish to keep him safe."

He eased back and framed her face with his big hands. "As do I. You coddle them, Isobel. You're goin' to turn my . . . our lads into lassies." He smiled at her, a tender smile.

She wrinkled her nose. "I'm doin nothin' of the sort."

He chuckled and kissed the tip of her nose. "Aye, you are. I promise, I'll keep them safe.

Isobel stared after him as he left the study. A warm glow of hopefulness unfurled inside her. Mayhap they had a chance after all. Her happy smile faded when she realized he'd completely disregarded her concerns.

Ewan sighed when, through the teeming rain, he saw Isobel framed in the entrance to the keep as they approached the stables. Robbie shivered in his arms. The bairn had been doing fine until a bolt of lighting had frightened his horse. Ewan managed to grab him before he fell from his mount, but the lad had hit his head on the pommel gaining him a knot the size of an egg. Ewan shook his head as his wife, heedless of the rain, ran towards them.

"Mam looks plenty fashed, da," Connor said as he slid from his horse.

"Aye, she does." Fashed and verra bonny, he thought, with her long chestnut hair curling about her adorable face, the rain dampening her pink gown, moulding it to her voluptuous curves.

These past weeks, Isobel had tried Ewan's restraint to the breaking point. With each passing day it had become harder for him to ignore the lust she aroused in him. After this morn, he knew he fought a losing battle. Harder to admit was that it was not only the memory of what she'd looked like naked, or the silken feel of her skin beneath his hands, that made him desire her. Isobel, unlike Lorna, adored Robbie and Connor. She was everything he could've hoped for in a mother for his sons. He'd not meant to hurt her earlier, but she'd roused his temper when she challenged him, and his growing attraction to her had already cast a pall over his good humour.

"What were you thinkin' keepin' them out in this weather?" Scowling at him, she reached for Robbie, her eyes widening when she caught sight of the bump on the lad's forehead. "Oh, my poor bairn," she cried, taking him into her arms.

His son, who'd been laughing only minutes earlier, thrust out his bottom lip and appeared ready to cry. "Doona baby him, Isobel, he's fine. I didna plan for the storm, it blew up of a sudden, catchin' me unawares." He felt the need to add more after the condescending look she shot him. Bloody hell, she had a way of makin' him feel like an irresponsible lad.

"Hhmph," she said and hurried off in the direction of the keep.

Robbie, his legs wrapped around her waist, was smiling over her shoulder.

"What is the wee imp up to?"

"He likes the kisses and cuddles mam gives when she thinks you're hurt."

"Smart lad," Ewan murmured. Watching the sway of her bonny arse, the thought of kissing and cuddling with his wife had him rethinking his plan to keep his distance.

"I like them, too," Connor added and took off after his brother and Isobel. Reaching them at the door to the keep, Connor held up his hand. "Oh, my poor bairn. Mam will make it all better." He heard her say. From the look she sent Ewan over her shoulder, he doubted she'd be giving *him* a kiss or a cuddle anytime soon.

Ewan got the horses settled before heading to his chambers. His grandda waylaid him on his way up the stairs. "Yer wife is no verra happy with ye. She was goin' to round up the men and send out a search party."

"With her no doubt leadin' the way," Ewan said dryly.

His grandda grinned. "Aye, she's a determined lass." Roderick's smile faded as he handed a missive to Ewan. "The McRaes are in need of yer sword arm against the Gunns. The bastards made off with three of the McRaes' lassies."

Ewan ran a frustrated hand through his damp hair. He'd all but made up his mind that this night he'd return to his wife's bed. He'd been a fool keepin' his distance from Isobel. The lass was nothin' like Lorna and it was about time he let go of the past.

Once he'd changed into dry clothes and prepared for his journey, Ewan followed the sound of laughter to Robbie's chambers. A smile tugged at the corner of his mouth as he leaned against the doorframe. His sons, tucked beneath a mound of blankets, lay snuggled in Isobel's embrace. Their wee faces alight with happiness as her melodious voice wove a tale of a handsome warrior riding through the mist to claim his one true love.

He frowned, not sure filling the impressionable heads of his young sons with notions they would find a lass destined for them – and them alone – was a good idea. He thought back to that moonlit night of long ago when he'd been tempted to believe just that, but he'd never found the lass. And his marriage to Lorna had quickly vanquished any thoughts of a life filled with love and laughter. Such notions were fine for lassies, but no for lads.

His brow furrowed, wondering if Isobel believed in a love such as that. Since she was the one telling the tale, he thought mayhap she did. If that were so, she must be sorely disappointed to be wed to him. He didn't like to think she was unhappy, but there was not much they could do about the situation. They'd just have to make the best of it.

"Da, come listen to mam's story." Connor waved him over.

Isobel's startled gaze leapt to his and her cheeks pinked. He blinked, shaking off the thought that, in that one instant, she had the look of the lass he'd met all those years ago. "I wish I could, son, but I have to leave now for Eilean Donan." At the concern in Connor's gaze, he added, "I'll no' be gone long, a fortnight at most."

"Nay, Robbie, doona cry," Isobel said, "We'll make honey cakes for your da's return, and if the weather improves, I'll take you to the loch and teach you to swim." As she rattled off a long list of what she and the bairns would do while he was away, Ewan had the feeling she'd be glad to be rid of him so she could have Robbie and Connor to herself. He felt a moment of regret that he hadn't included her over the last weeks. She'd obviously missed spending time with the lads. He'd be more considerate of her feelings on his return.

She searched his face, worrying her full bottom lip between her small white teeth. "You willna be in danger, will you?"

"Nay." He grinned. She might as well have told him. "*I want you gone, but not dead.*" He leaned over and kissed his sons goodbye. "What aboot mam?" Robbie asked when Ewan straightened.

Isobel lowered her eyes, about to protest when Ewan bent down and kissed her. He'd only meant to brush her lips with his, but her mouth had tempted him for too long and he couldn't resist deepening the kiss, if only for a moment. Feeling her soft pliant lips beneath his, he vowed that once he returned, his wife would no longer be sleeping alone.

"You lads be good for your mother and mind what she tells you." At her grateful smile and the shimmer in her topaz eyes, Ewan cursed the Gunns.

Five

At the sight of Leod in the valley below, Ewan urged his steed to a gallop. He was as anxious to return home as he'd been a month ago, maybe more so. He'd missed Isobel as much as he'd missed his sons. Missed the sound of her warm laugh, the sight of her smile and the way she looked at him when she didn't think he'd notice.

Covered in sweat and dust, he turned down the path to the loch. He grinned at his sons' shouts of laughter above the raucous splashing and Isobel's feminine shriek. He supposed he should have warned her that the bairns could swim like fish when she spoke of teaching them. With the loch so close at hand, for the bairns' safety he'd ensured they'd learned at an early age.

Ewan tied off his horse and stripped to his braies. He came to a halt at the edge of the clearing, swallowing hard at the sight of Isobel standing knee deep in the water. Her heavy linen chemise clung damply to her luscious curves. Robbie and Connor were splashing her, her full breasts jiggling as she tried to get away from them. Ewan crept unseen around the rocks lining the loch. It wasn't as though he could walk up and greet them, not in the aroused state he was in after seeing Isobel.

He picked a spot he was familiar with and dived beneath the cool azure waters. Robbie and Connor squealed when he came up behind them.

"Da!" They cried and flung their arms around his neck. "You're home!"

"Aye." He laughed as their slippery bodies attempted to climb up his. "Just in time to save your mother from bein' drowned by the two of you." He met Isobel's gaze and smiled.

She pushed her wet curls from her face, her breasts straining beneath the chemise with the movement of her hands. He couldn't draw his gaze from her delectable feminine form, so close all he had to do was reach out and pull her to him.

"Da, throw us in the deep part," Connor pleaded.

"Yeah, da, throw us," Robbie chimed in.

"Aye," he rasped. Reluctantly dragging his gaze from his smiling wife, he tossed first Connor then Robbie into the water.

"Ewan, 'tis too deep. Where—" Her frightened cries faded when Connor and Robbie's heads popped up from beneath the water, laughing as they swam back to him.

Ewan raised a brow in Isobel's direction. She rolled her eyes and cupped her hand to shoot a spray of water at him. "You coulda told me they swim as well as the fishes."

"Throw mam, da, throw her in."

Isobel's eyes widened and she held up her hands, shaking her head. "Nay, Ewan Mackenzie, doona even think aboot it."

He prowled towards her and she took several quick steps back. "You *did* splash me, my wee wife, 'tis only fair." The bairns cheered him on.

She gasped. Stumbling to get away from him, her feet slipped out from under her and she fell backwards. She pulled herself from beneath the water, sputtering as she did. Glaring up at him as he tried to contain his laughter, she grumbled, "'Tis no' funny."

He helped her to her feet. "Aye, 'twas." He pushed the wet curls from her face and kissed her, swallowing her startled gasp. "I missed you, Isobel," he murmured against her lips.

"I missed you, too," she said shyly, looking up at him through the cover of her water-spiked lashes.

"Come." He tugged on her hand. "I promise, I'll no' throw you in."

"Nay, play with Robbie and Connor. I'll set out the food I brought. Are you hungry?"

"Aye, verra hungry." If he could go by the flush staining her cheeks, his wife knew he didn't refer to food.

After an hour of cavorting with his sons, Ewan carried an exhausted Robbie under one arm and an equally tired Connor under the other. Depositing them on the blanket Isobel had spread out beneath the chestnut tree, he was disappointed to find her chemise had dried and no longer clung to her curves. Isobel watched in wide-eyed wonder as he and the lads polished off the food. While they ate, she filled Ewan in on what had taken place at Leod in his absence. He laughed at her disgruntled retelling of her nana and his grandda's burgeoning romance. She smoothed Robbie's hair from his face where he lay curled up beside her sound asleep. "It looks like we've bored the bairns with our chatter." She smiled, tipping her chin at Connor who'd fallen asleep beside Ewan.

"More like I wore them out," Ewan said, stroking Connor's silky curls from his cheek.

"They're happy to have you home safe. They were worried aboot you."

"Were—" Ewan stopped, his attention drawn to the shaking leaves of the branches just down from where they sat. A woman giggled and Isobel leaned forward, her brow furrowed.

From behind the bush, his grandda ran naked for the loch – tugging Isobel's equally naked nana along with him.

Ewan cursed and his grandda turned around.

"Sweet Mary Mother of God." Isobel groaned and lay back on the blanket, covering her eyes.

"Bloody hell, grandda, get in the water. Both of you," Ewan

yelled. "That's it, I'm havin' the banns read and the two of you will be wed in a fortnight."

The bairns sat up, rubbing their eyes. Connor looked out over the loch. "Can I go swimmin' with grandda and nana?"

"Nay!" Ewan said at the same time as his wife.

Settling both lads on his steed, Ewan took the reins in one hand, his wife's hand in the other. He leaned towards her. "You ken, Isobel, our grandparents spend more time alone than we do and they appear to be havin' a grand time doin' so. Mayhap 'tis time we did the same."

Her cheeks pinked and she nodded. "I'd like that."

Ewan brought her slender hand to his mouth and pressed a kiss to her soft palm. He winked at her. "Your da is tired, lads. I think we'll have an early night," he said, yawning.

"We had a nap, da. Mam says when we have a nap we can stay up late," Connor told him earnestly.

"Did you say that?"

"Aye, I'm afraid I did," she said, laughing at his frustrated groan.

Isobel sat on the edge of the bed then lay down to stare up at the canopy. Five minutes later, she sighed and rolled off the bed to pace the stone floor. She didn't understand why Ewan had yet to come to their chambers; he'd seemed as anxious to be alone with her as she was to be with him. She smiled at the memory of his warm, teasing manner during the evening meal. It was a smile that hadn't left her face since returning from the loch. For the first time since Ewan had returned from France, it appeared she would finally have a husband who would love her as much as she loved him. Her worries that her nana's second sight had failed after being expended on Isobel's sisters had been for naught.

At the sound of heavy footfalls coming down the corridor, she hurried to the bed and slid beneath the covers. She calmed the nervous excitement in her belly with the knowledge this was not the first time she and her husband had made love. The thought would have been somewhat more comforting if she could recall the event. The door opened and the candle on the table beside the bed flickered. At the sight of the sensual smile creasing her husband's beautiful face as he strode into the room, her nervousness was replaced with heated anticipation.

"Grandda needed help wordin' his missive to your father," he said as he pulled his tunic over his head, the muscles in his arms flexing with the movement. "For certain he has a harder time arrangin' his own marriage than he does mine."

Isobel's eyes looked from his sun-bronzed arms to his face, searching for some sign he retained any anger at the way their marriage had come about.

He raised a brow. "What's wrong?"

"Nothin'."

His gaze softened and he sat beside her, the feather-stuffed mattress dipping under his weight. He took her hand in his, stroking her knuckles with his thumb. "Are you nervous?"

She shook her head. "Nay."

"That's good to hear," he said, kissing her hand before he released it. He bent over and removed his boots. When his hand went to his trews, Isobel quickly leaned over and blew out the candle.

Ewan's deep laugh filled their chambers. "I thought you said you were no' nervous?"

"Mayhap a wee bit," she admitted, scooting over when he climbed in beside her.

"Next time doona blow the candle out, angel. I want to see your beautiful body," he said as he drew her sheer nightgown over her head. His low growl of appreciation drew an aroused shiver from her and he folded her into his powerful embrace. She snuggled against him, his long, hard length jerking against her belly. He nudged her face from his chest with his chin. "I hope you were no' plannin' on goin' to sleep just yet," he said, his strong white teeth flashing in the darkened room.

"Nay," she said a little breathlessly.

"Good," he murmured against her lips before he claimed her mouth in a demanding kiss.

She wrapped her arms around his neck, bringing them closer still. He angled his head, slanting his lips over hers, deepening the kiss. His calloused palms smoothed over her back to her bottom and he pressed her tight against him, rocking his hips. Isobel moaned at the heated sensation building between her thighs. Ewan took advantage and swept his tongue past her parted lips to delve deep inside her mouth. Tentatively, she touched her tongue to his and he groaned, kneading her bottom. His exploring tongue grew more insistent and his manhood swelled, growing harder and longer. Her eyes rounded, intimidated by his size.

As though he sensed her dismay, he broke the kiss and held her away from him to look down at her. His eyes glinted with amusement. "Doona worry, you'll no' have pain this time, only pleasure."

"I suppose 'tis a good thing I canna remember the first time," she said as she trailed her fingers through the crisp hairs on his chest, fascinated by his feel of his hard muscles flexing beneath her palm.

He brushed his knuckles over her cheek. "Aye, mayhap 'tis. I wouldna wish to cause you pain, Isobel." He gently nudged her to her back.

She frowned. "Are you sure it will . . . fit?"

He choked on a laugh. "Aye, verra sure, my bonny wife." Watching her, he slid his palm over her belly to the damp curls covering her mound. "Your skin is soft, so smooth," he murmured. His warm breath caressed her cheek as he skimmed his hand over her inner thighs, nudging her legs apart. She inhaled sharply as he touched her slick folds, spreading her wide.

"So hot, so wet," he said as his thick finger probed her inner passage. She gasped, wreathing against his hand. His lips burned a heated path down her neck to her chest. His tongue rasped then laved her breasts before he drew her straining nipple into the heat of his mouth. The hard suction of his lips caused her belly to clench in response and she moaned, growing frantic with desire. She clutched the bedcovers, arching her back to press her breast to his demanding mouth. "Ewan, please," she cried out, not sure what she wanted him to do but needing him to do something. It was as though she was caught in a whirlpool of sensation that only he could release.

"Christ, Isobel, I was a fool no' to come to you sooner."

"Aye, aye you were," she groaned.

His laugh came out a harsh rasp. "I should make you suffer for that but I ken I canna last much longer."

"I am sufferin', Ewan. Please," she begged, "do somethin'."

He kissed her and she could feel him smile against her lips. His tongue delved inside her mouth as his powerful fingers probed inside her moist heat. She closed her lips over his tongue and sucked him deep. He groaned, thrusting his hot, hard erection against her thigh, mimicking the movement of his fingers inside her with his tongue.

He eased his fingers from her and, without breaking their kiss, pulled his body over her, holding his weight above her with his hands. She wrapped her fingers around the rippling muscles in his arms. The thick head of his manhood nudged her opening and she stiffened. He broke the kiss. "Easy, love," he said and slid his hand between them. He stroked her tight nub with practiced fingers, driving her over the edge. She bucked against him and then he thrust inside her. Isobel cried out. Her nails dug into his arms and he froze above her, his shocked gaze jerking to hers. She bit her lip and blinked hard to keep the tears from flooding her eyes.

Ewan cursed and carefully eased from her body. His breathing ragged, he rolled to his back and placed his forearm over his eyes.

"I'm sorry. I didna think it was supposed to hurt. You said . . ."

He lifted his arm from his face and got up from the bed, his movements awkward as he pulled on his trews. "You have nothin' to apologise for, Isobel. It hurt because you were still innocent."

She wiped her eyes. "I doona understand, I thought—"

"Aye, we both did because that's what he wanted us to think. I'm goin' to kill the meddlin' old bastard." Ewan flung open the door and slammed out of the room.

Isobel scrambled off the bed and grabbed her nightshift, afraid this time Ewan truly meant to kill Roderick. She didn't think she'd ever seen him so angry. As she tugged the chemise over her hips, she heard Ewan yelling at his grandda. "Admit it, you set it up to stop me from gainin' the annulment I wanted. You knew . . ."

The last of Ewan's condemning words faded as Isobel darted out of the room and ran down the corridor in the opposite direction. She didn't know where she was going only that she had to get away from him. As soon as he discovered she was still innocent, he'd realized what his grandda had done and he'd been furious – furious at the deception that had stolen his chance to be rid of her. She'd been a fool to think he'd come to love her. He'd simply decided to make the best of a situation he couldn't change.

Isobel entered her nana's chambers, certain Roderick had not acted alone. She choked out a bitter laugh at finding the room empty. Mayhap her nana had seen the wrong Mackenzie with the wrong Forbes. Mayhap it was Roderick who was Olivia's true love. A moonbeam cut across the room, the Forbes heart stone glowing in the bright swath of light. Isobel strode to the table and angrily closed her fingers around the rock, knowing instantly what she had to do. She would not let another Forbes lass suffer her fate. Waste years pining for a man she thought was her true love, only to discover he would never love her in return.

She stifled a broken sob with her hand and ran blindly from the room, down the staircase to the entryway. Opening the door to the keep, she stepped outside into the mist. She ran across the courtyard.

"Isobel, what the bloody hell do you think you're doin'?" Ewan's voice cut through the dense fog.

"Doona you come one step closer, Ewan Mackenzie." She groaned when he stepped through the mist into the moonlit courtyard.

His gaze searched hers and he released a shocked breath. "'Tis you. 'Twas you all along."

"Nay, I had nothin' to do with it. 'Twas your grandda and my nana's fault you—"

He shook his head, looking bemused. "'Twas no' what I meant. You're the lass from the Burnetts' moors."

"Aye, 'twas me," she said with a brittle laugh. "The foolish lass waitin' for her true love to ride through the mist, only it was you and you didna want me then and you doona want me now."

He took a step towards her. "I did want you, Isobel. You were too young that first time. I told you I would come back for you."

"But you never did."

"The second time I tried. I went after you and managed to knock myself out on a branch." He smiled a crooked boyish grin. "I searched for you all the next day and—"

"Your betrothal to Lorna Sinclair was announced that night. I was there." She barely managed to get the words out, her throat painfully tight as she remembered her devastation upon hearing the announcement.

"Aye, it was," he said quietly. "But I've found you now, Isobel, and you're my wife."

"You doona want me. I heard you yellin' at Roderick. You would have had our marriage annulled if he hadna tricked you."

"Aye, and in truth I should have thanked him for doin' so, but I was angry I'd hurt you. I would have taken my time had I kent you were still innocent." He brought his hand to her face. "So are you tellin' me that you've been waitin' for me all this time, that I'm your true love?"

She snorted her disgust. "Aye and I'm goin' to throw this heart stone in the loch on the morrow so no other lass has to suffer."

He frowned. "Why? We're together now."

"Aye, but you doona love me."

His look softened and he stroked her cheek with his thumb. "I do, Isobel. I doona ken how much you've heard aboot my marriage to Lorna, but 'twas no' a happy one. She made my life and that of my sons miserable, 'tis why it took me a little longer to trust you with my heart than it should have. But I do trust you, Isobel," He said, smiling down at her as he swept her into his arms. "Now, why doona I take you inside and show you just how verra much I love you."

Isobel's breath caught in her throat. Ewan's love for her was reflected in his eyes. She fought back tears of joy and wrapped her arms tightly around his neck. "I've waited a verra long time for you, Ewan Mackenzie. You have a lot of years to make up for." Her voice was husky, overwhelmed with the emotion that clogged her throat.

Laughter rumbled in Ewan's chest. "I'll spend my life makin' it up to you, my bonny wife."

Isobel released a contented sigh, certain she'd never been happier than at this moment. "And you, my bonny highlander, were well worth waitin' for. I love you, Ewan and I love Robbie and Connor, too." A thought occurred to her and she frowned.

Ewan looked down at her. "What is it?"

"I'm thinkin' mayhap things worked out as they were meant to. Even though it wasna easy to wait so long for you, if you hadna married Lorna, we wouldna have Robbie and Connor."

He touched his forehead to hers. "Do you ken, Isobel, I doona think I could love you more than I do at this moment."

She kissed him and he tightened his arms around her, deepening the kiss until he had her breathless with desire. "Mayhap we should go inside now," she panted against his lips.

"Aye," he said gruffly, pushing open the door to the keep. Her nana hurried towards them. "Isobel, do ye have the heart stone?"

Isobel's brow furrowed. "Aye," she said, opening her palm. Olivia plucked the stone from her hand and marched out the door. Roderick, wearing only his plaid, came to stand beside them, scratching his head. "Do ye ken why Livie wants me to go lookin' for her in the mist, henny?"

"I suggest you get out there, grandda. If you doona, someone else may claim her before you do," Ewan said with a grin.

"I'm comin', Livie, my henny," Roderick called out.

As Ewan walked up the stairs with Isobel in his arms, he said, "You ken they'll be livin' with us, doona you?"

"Aye, doona worry, I'll no leave you because of it. Besides, we can always send them to visit my da." Isobel laughed. Her patience was finally at an end.

The Rebel

Julianne MacLean

On the field of Sherrifmuir, six miles northeast of Stirling Castle,
November 13, 1715

At the sound of the bagpipes and the roaring command of his chief,
Alex MacLean drew his sword and broke into a run, charging up
the north face of the hill.

A wild frenzy of bloodlust exploded in his veins and fuelled his
body with savage strength and determination, as he and his fellow
Jacobite clansmen advanced upon Argyll's left flank. Their lines
collided in a heavy clash of bodies and weaponry, and suddenly he
was thrashing about in a red sea of chaos. Men shouted and lunged,
shot each other at close range, they severed limbs and hacked each
other to pieces. Blood splattered on to his face as he spun around
and swung his sword at one soldier, then another. Adrenaline fired
his instincts. The fury was blinding. His muscles strained with
every controlled thrust and strike.

Keenly aware of all that was happening around him, he raised his
targe to encumber the piercing point of a bayonet. Dropping to one
knee, he dirked the offending redcoat in the belly.

Eventually, in the distance, beyond the delirium of combat, the
Government dragoons began to fall back, retreating through their
own infantry. The fury was too much for them. Alex raised his
sword.

"*Charge!*" he shouted, in a deep thunderous brogue. "*For the
Scottish Crown!*"

He and his fellow clansmen cried out in triumphant resolve and
rushed headlong at the breaking enemy ranks, while the Jacobite

cavalry thundered past, galloping hard to pursue the Hanoverians into the steep-sided Glen of Pendreich.

Moments flashed by like brilliant bursts of lightning. The battle was nearly won. The redcoats were fleeing . . .

Before long, Alex slowed to a jog and looked about to get a better sense of his bearings. He and dozens of other clansmen were now spread out across the glen with precious space between them, and clean air to breathe.

It was over. Argyll's opposing left flank was crushed. They were retreating to Dunblane.

Stabbing the point of his weapon into the frosty ground, Alex dropped to his knees in exhaustion and rested his forehead on the hilt. He'd fought hard, and with honour. His father would be proud.

Just then, a fresh-looking young redcoat leapt out from behind a granite boulder and charged at him. *"Ahh!"*

He was naught but a boy, but his bayonet was as sharp any other.

Rolling across the ground, Alex shifted his targe to the other hand to deflect the thrust of the blade. The weapon flew from the soldier's hands and landed on the grass, but before Alex could regain his footing, a sabre was scraping out of its scabbard, and he suddenly found himself backing away defensively, evaluating his opponent's potential skill and intentions.

Blue eyes locked on his, and the courage he saw in those depths sharpened his wits.

Carefully, meticulously, they stepped around each other.

"Are ye sure ye want to do this, lad?" Alex asked, giving the boy one last chance to retreat with the others in his regiment. "I've done enough killing this morning. I doona need more blood on my hands. Just go."

But why was he hesitating? The dark fury of battle still smouldered within him. What difference would it make if he killed one more? All he had to do was take one step forward and swing. The boy was no match for him. He could slay him in an instant.

"I'm sure," the lad replied, but his sabre began to tremble in his hands.

Alex wet his lips. "Just drop your weapon and run, boy."

"No."

Alex paused. "You're a brave one, aren't ye? Or maybe you're just stupid."

All at once, the young soldier let out a vicious battle cry and attacked with a left-handed manoeuvre that cut Alex swiftly across the thigh.

He gaped down at the wound in bewilderment.

Musket fire rang out in the distance. The morning chill penetrated his senses, steeled his warrior instincts.

The next thing he knew, he had used his targe to strike the lad in the head, and whirled around with a fierce cry of aggression. The young redcoat stumbled backwards. His sabre dropped from his grasp.

Then, as if it were all happening in a dream, the soldier's tricorne hat flew through the air, and long black tresses unfurled and swung about. The boy hit the ground and rolled unconscious on to his back.

Alex's eyes fell immediately upon a soft complexion and lips like ripe red cherries. All thoughts of war and the Jacobite triumph fled from his mind, as he realized with dismay that he had just struck a woman.

Twelve hours later . . .

Elizabeth's eyes slowly fluttered open. Groggy and disoriented, she blinked up at the thatched ceiling above her, while an explosion of pain erupted inside her skull and drummed against the side of her face.

Laying a hand on her swollen cheek, she attempted to wiggle her jaw back and forth. It did not appear to be broken, but her cheekbone was surely cracked.

Moaning with agony, she sat up on the cot and looked around the small room. Where the devil was she? A single candle blazed on a table by the bed. A grey woollen curtain covered the door to the rest of the cottage – if this was in fact someone's home. She had no idea. The floors were made of dirt, the walls built of stone. It could as easily be a stable or prison.

Again, she cupped her cheek with her hand and winced at the pain, but she would endure it, for she must leave this place immediately and return to Argyll's camp. She could not remain here in Scotland. She'd rather die than linger here.

Rising awkwardly to her feet, she inhaled deeply. She limped towards the curtain and dug deep for the strength and fortitude she would require to walk out of here and travel God knows how far on foot.

Oh, sweet Lord! Her entire body felt bruised and beaten. What had happened on the battlefield? The last thing she remembered was slicing that Highlander's leg open with her sabre. What had happened since then? How in the world did she get here?

Sweeping the curtain aside, doubting if she would ever know the answers to those questions, she suddenly found herself staring up at him directly.

"Goin somewhere, lassie?"

Elizabeth sucked in a breath. Heaven help her, it was him. The golden-haired warrior Scotsman, standing before her like a monstrous guardian.

He was taller than she remembered. Bigger and broader through the chest, and his eyes burned with savage, dangerous intensity.

"That I am, sir," she firmly replied. "Step aside. I mean to leave here and return to my countrymen."

She glanced down at the heavy claymore belted around his waist, and made a mental note of the dagger in his boot, as well as the pistol and powder horn he carried, which was strapped across his chest.

His green eyes flashed with a strange mixture of amusement and irritation, while he took in her soldier's uniform from head to foot. "If ye are referring to the pathetic flock of red-coated sheep that follows a German king – a king who can barely speak a word of English – then I'm afraid I canna let ye go anywhere, lass."

Her heart began to pound, and her mouth went dry. Quickly she looked down at his leg, curious to know how much damage she had inflicted with her sword, but his kilt cloaked any sign of injury. As far as she could ascertain, he was in perfect fighting condition, while she was ready to drop to the floor in a dead faint, on account of the pain in her head and the sheer fright induced by his intimidating presence.

"What is it that you plan to do with me, then?" she boldly asked. "Do you mean to keep me as your prisoner?"

He chuckled at that. She glared at him with bitter rancour, but the passion of her grimace caused her great pain. She groaned and covered the side of her face with a hand. "God in heaven, what did you do me? My face feels like it's been smashed up against a rock."

The Highlander glanced over his shoulder, as if to check the door for prying eyes and ears, then ducked under the top of the curtain to enter the small room. Elizabeth had no choice but to back out of his way.

She suddenly found herself trapped up against the wall, while he blocked the only exit. The curtain fell closed behind him.

"I apologise for that," he said. "I dinna know ye were a woman."

She raised her chin. "What difference should that have made? I was trying to kill you."

His arresting green eyes narrowed slightly, as if he were intrigued by her reply, and it was not until that moment that she realized he was impossibly handsome. He had a face that could only be shaped by an artist, with finely carved cheekbones and a rugged, square jaw. The lips were moist and full – she would almost call them beautiful – and those long lashed green eyes . . . They possessed a mysterious gleaming power that rendered her speechless. She couldn't think. All she could do was stand before him like a bumbling fool and attempt to contemplate the origins of such divine physical perfection. Bestowed upon a Highlander, no less. Was there no justice in the world?

"Aye, and ye fought bravely," he said. "But what were ye doing on the battlefield, lass? It's no place for a woman. And I doona know why you're in such a hurry to return. I know of no British officer who would take kindly to the fact that you're wearing a stolen uniform."

Elizabeth frowned. "First you bash me in the side of the head, and now you call me a thief?"

He inclined his head at her. "Aye, and a damned foolhardy one at that."

Moving further away from him, along the wall, she crossed to the bed and sat down. "All right, so I stole it, but I was fighting for my country."

He palmed the hilt of his sword. "I think ye were fighting for more than that, unless ye know King George personally."

"Of course I do not."

"Then I reckon it's something else that got prickly under your corset, because I doona believe it's as simple as that. Yer regiment was ordered to retreat, but there ye were, leaping out from behind a rock, coming at me with vengeance in your eyes."

Her gaze lifted. "Is that how it looked to you?"

"Aye."

Nodding her head, feeling almost sick from the violent impulses that had plagued her on that battlefield, she curled her hands around the edge of the mattress. "I don't suppose you have anything to numb this pain?"

He was quiet for a moment, then disappeared through the curtain and returned with a bottle of something, which he uncorked with his teeth. "Moncrieffe Whisky, the best in the Highlands." He held it out to her.

"Do you not have a glass to offer a lady?"

He chuckled softly. "Is that what ye are now?"

Their gazes locked, and all the blood in her body seemed to rush to her head.

She swiped the bottle from his grasp, tipped it up and guzzled a few deep swigs. The spirit sizzled and burned down her throat, left her gasping for air.

"That ought to numb at least *something*," the Highlander said under his breath, as he took the bottle away from her.

Elizabeth waited a moment for the spirit to flow through her body, then worked hard to relax her mind. "Thank you."

The Highlander gave no reply. For the longest time, he simply stood patiently before her.

"Feelin' any better?" he asked.

"Yes." Cautiously, Elizabeth lifted her eyes again and took in the finer details of his clothing – the colours and woven textures of his kilt, his brown leather sporran, the loose-fitting linen shirt and the plaid that was draped across his shoulder and pinned with a pewter brooch.

"Where am I, exactly?" she asked. "And what time of day is it?"

There was no window in the room, so she had no idea if it was morning or night.

"Doona worry," he replied. "You're safe here. This house belongs to a friend. And it's nearly ten."

"Ten at night?" Her heart began to race. "I've been unconscious all day?"

"Aye. To be honest, I wasna sure ye were going to survive."

"No thanks to you." She laid her hand on her cheek again.

"Ye had it coming, lass. Ye said so yourself."

Massaging her neck to squeeze out some tension, she had no choice but to surrender to the truth in his words. "I suppose I did."

She was keenly aware of the Highlander's movements as he approached the bed and sat down beside her. His nearness caused her senses to quiver and hum.

"Are ye going to tell me what you were doing out there on the battlefield," he asked, "and how ye came into possession of that uniform?"

Elizabeth set both hands on the edge of the mattress, and sighed heavily. "It belonged to my brother."

"Yer brother . . ." he replied with some scepticism.

"Yes."

"Where is he now?"

She shot an angry look at him. "Where do you *think*?"

The Highlander regarded her intently, and when he spoke, his voice was quiet and low. "I'm very sorry, lass."

She scoffed. "Well! There it is at last – exactly what I was looking for. An apology from a Scotsman."

"I dinna know your brother, so I canna apologise for anything. I was merely offering my condolences. And I doona think an apology was what you were looking for when ye tried to stick me with your bayonet."

She looked down at his lips and could not escape a heavy sense of defeat. "No, I suppose not."

"Vengeance comes with a price, ye know."

Elizabeth's heart began to ache. She wasn't sure how she would have felt if she had actually killed a man – Scottish or otherwise. "No, I *don't* know," she replied. "Until these past few months, I didn't know anything about war and violence and killing, but now I've seen more of those things than I ever wished to see."

He took his time before responding. "When did your brother die?"

"Three weeks ago."

"Did ye witness it?"

Her eyebrows pulled together in a frown. "Yes. I was a nurse, doing what I could for this war. Is this some sort of interrogation?"

"Aye."

She recognized the steady purpose in his eyes and felt all the tiny hairs on her arms and legs stand on end. "What do you want from me?"

"I need to know your connections, lass."

Elizabeth swallowed uncomfortably. "Why?"

"Just tell me."

"Fine. Our father was an infantryman, but he died a year ago. My brother wanted to make him proud, and seek his own vengeance I suppose, so he signed up to follow in his footsteps and help crush this foolish rebellion."

"Foolish. Ye think the people of Scotland fight for no good

reason?" The Highlander stared into her eyes for the longest time, then he tipped the bottle back and took a drink.

Elizabeth accepted it when he held it out to her, and took another drink.

"Ye should get some rest," he said, rising to his feet. "Ye canna go anywhere tonight. It's too dangerous, especially in that uniform, and if anyone finds out what you're hiding under it, you'll be no better off."

She arched a brow. "My shapely figure, you mean?"

His gaze flicked over the curve of her hip, then he turned to go. "Goodnight, lass."

Elizabeth quickly stood. "Wait. Are we alone here, or are there others? Am I being held prisoner?"

He kept his back to her. "Aye, there are others, but for now, it's just us. Get some sleep."

"But I've been sleeping all day," she argued, "and I'm hungry."

He halted at the curtain, while she waited uneasily for his response, wishing she knew what he meant to do with her.

At last, he glanced over his shoulder. "Follow me, then. Ye may sit at the table for a while and have some supper."

With that, he passed through the curtain and held it aloft, his eyes never leaving hers as he waited for her to join him.

"What's your name, Highlander?" Elizabeth asked, wincing with pain as she used her teeth to tear meat off a chicken bone. She had to chew slowly and with great care, otherwise she might end up rolling in agony on the floor.

"Are ye all right, lass?" he asked from the opposite side of the table. "Ye look uncomfortable. Here. Take some more of this."

He handed her the bottle of whisky again, and she welcomed the opportunity to wash down her supper. A moment later, however, she had to wrestle with an unbidden wave of giddiness and laughter. It was a potent spirit indeed.

"Are you trying to get me drunk?" she asked, setting the bottle down.

"Will it make ye reveal your secrets?"

Elizabeth wiped her lips with the back of her hand. "I assure you, I have none. I've already told you everything."

"I doubt that."

She tore off another morsel of the tender, succulent meat. "And you still haven't told me your name."

He eyed her warily. "Nor have ye told me yours."

A log shifted in the grate, and bright sparks of firelight flew up the chimney while they regarded each other with challenge from opposite sides of the table.

"I am Alexander MacLean," he said at last. "I hail from the Isle of Mull."

"Duart Castle?"

"Aye," he replied. "Now tell me yours."

She sat back in the chair. "I am Elizabeth Curtis, and I hail from Portsmouth."

His green eyes narrowed. "You're a long way from home, lassie."

"I have no home. What remained of my family came north to fight in this rebellion, but they're all dead now – all except for one. So here I am. Alone and . . . seeking vengeance, I suppose."

"Who is this *one* you speak of?"

"My uncle. He is a book merchant in Edinburgh, but I have not seen him since I was a child."

The Highlander shifted lower in a lazy sprawl, and glanced down at the knife he had given her to use with her supper. "Have ye always been so bold?" he asked. "So full of daring?"

"Yes."

The corner of his mouth curled up in a small grin of seductive allure. "I find ye very intriguing, Elizabeth Curtis. No woman has ever attacked me with such . . . *passion* before."

She couldn't help but laugh at him. "Be very careful, sir. I told you I was seeking vengeance, and if I grow weary of your questions or insinuations, I may decide to attack you again."

He spoke with a heated grin, holding his hands out to the side. "Be my guest, but doona forget – I saved your life on that battle-field. I carried ye into the woods and stole one of your King's horses for ye, then I held ye across my lap for mile after mile while we plodded through rivers and glades together. If anything, ye owe me a great debt."

Elizabeth slanted a look at him. "Are you flirting with me?"

Just then, something very pleasant and unfamiliar warmed the flow of blood through her veins.

Alex leaned forward. "What if I were? Would it be enough to make ye promise not to use that supper knife on me? Or heaven forbid, that razor-sharp bayonet of yours?"

"I don't have my bayonet," she replied, looking around for it. "I have nothing."

"Nay, lass, that's not true. Ye have yer wits, and y're moderately pleasant to look at."

"Moderately pleasant?" She laughed again. Perhaps it was the whisky. "What a charmer you are."

The firelight reflected in the deep green of his eyes, and she ran the tip of her tongue across her lips, wondering how she could be carrying on in such a way with a man who was her enemy and captor.

"A Highlander killed my brother," she quickly said, her tone growing serious. "So please do not look at me like that."

"Like what?"

"Like you want to carry me back to that bed and do something savage with me."

He chuckled. "Clearly you've been entertaining some wayward thoughts this evening, lassie – but I must ask ye to treat me with some respect. I have no intention of becoming a slave to your lusty urges. I simply won't have it."

Yet again, she laughed. "You bashed me over the head today! So I quite assure you, I have no lusty urges whatsoever. Not a single one."

"Then why do ye keep bringing it up?"

She should have been offended. She should have stood up, slapped his face, and retired to the other room, but something held her rather spellbound. Even dressed in the tartan uniform of her enemy – the weapons a grim reminder of this Highlander's potential ferocity and the death of her brother – he aroused her senses and sent a fever into her blood. It was the sheer might of his brawn, she supposed, and the bewildering fact that he had saved her life today, even after she tried to kill him.

"Why did you help me?" she asked. "You could have just left me there to die."

For a moment he regarded her in the quiet hush of the night, while the flames danced wildly in the hearth. Then at last he spoke. "Because ye were the most beautiful creature I ever laid eyes on."

Excitement pooled deliciously in her belly, just as the door flew open and two bearded Highlanders burst into the room with muskets cocked and aimed at her head. Elizabeth leapt to her feet. She knocked over her chair as she backed up against the far wall.

Slowly and calmly, Alex rose to his feet and turned to face them.

"Lower yer weapons," he said, holding his hands out to ease the sudden tension in the room. "She's not armed. She's just hungry, that's all."

"She can starve, for all I care," the taller one said.

"Aye," the other added. "It's worse than we thought, Alex. The battle was not a triumph."

"What do ye mean, it was not a triumph?" he replied. "I saw the English officers order the retreat. We chased them all the way back to Dunblane."

"Aye, we crushed them with our right flank, but our left flank broke. Argyll's cavalry drove hundreds into the River Allen. Many drowned, and he is calling it a victory for King George."

Without lowering his weapon, the taller one flicked his hair out of his face. "Mar is withdrawing to Perth, and in the morning, despite our victory, Argyll will find himself master of the field."

Alex bowed his head and pinched the bridge of his nose. "All this killing, all these weeks of marching through bogs and icy pellets of rain . . . What was it for? We are still without a king, without a parliament. Without freedom."

Elizabeth dared not speak – not while the other two Scots were fuming with ire, and still held loaded muskets aimed at her nose.

"Did she tell ye anything?" the tall one asked, eyeing her dangerously down the long barrel of his weapon.

Alex looked at her. "She told me enough, and I've determined she's not a threat to us."

"I doona believe that. Did ye ask her about the dispatch?"

Hot flames of panic burst through Elizabeth's core. "Explain yourself, sir," she demanded. "What dispatch? I know nothing of what you speak."

Alex regarded her with a look of regret. "I was going to ask ye about it, lass, as soon as yer belly was full. Come here."

He waved a hand for her to approach the table, then signalled for the other Scotsman to hand over a small, flat parchment.

"We found this in a secret compartment in the pocket of your coat," he explained in a low voice. "Do ye know of it?"

She took it from him and read the contents. "This is a note to Argyll, explaining that a detachment of rebels are on their way to Dumferline. It recommends that he send his cavalry to trounce it."

Alex nodded. "Did your brother deliver this information?"

She glanced up. "How should I know?"

"So you are telling me that you knew nothing of it." He slid her a look, encouraging her to nod in agreement.

"Of course I knew nothing. I stole this uniform off his back after he was killed."

"But why did ye do that, lass?" the tall one asked. "Did ye mean to do some spying on yer own?"

"Of course not," she retorted. "I only wanted to fight."

He scowled at her. "That's a strange hankerin' for a woman. How can we be sure ye are telling the truth?"

"She is," Alex insisted. "I told ye I interrogated her already, and I am willing to stake my life on it. She's not a spy."

Elizabeth's eyes locked with his, and though she did not understand why he was defending her, she was grateful for it.

He turned his attention back to the other clansmen. "Lower yer guns now lads, and fill yer bellies. Tomorrow you'll ride to Perth and find out what Mar intends to do next."

Reluctantly, they released the hammers on their weapons and moved closer to the fire.

"What about the woman?" the shorter one quietly asked. "What will ye do with her tonight?"

Alex locked gazes with her again. His green eyes roamed over her figure, and her heart hammered wildly against her ribcage.

"I have not decided yet," he replied.

The flickering light from a single candle infused the room with a warm, golden glow, while Elizabeth pulled the covers up to her chin.

"Sleep well, lass," Alex said, as he came to stand over the bed. "I'll not let any harm come to ye on this night."

She could hear the others on the opposite side of the curtain, speaking in low tones while they ate their supper.

"Why are you being so kind to me?" she whispered. "After what happened between us this morning . . ."

He sat down on the edge of the bed. "We met on a battlefield, on opposite sides of a war. I cannot fault ye for fighting against me. I fought hard against ye in return."

She laid her hand on her bruised cheek. "You certainly did."

He regarded her for a long, quiet moment while her thoughts grew heavy in her mind. "I'm sorry that I hurt ye," he said. "I would take it back if I could."

"Because I'm a woman?"

"Among other things."

"Such as?"

The candlelight reflected in his eyes like tiny sparks of fire. "I believe ye have suffered enough, lass."

She thought of her brother suddenly, and how she had tried to talk him out of signing up to fight in this war, but she had not been able to persuade him. And so, she had followed instead.

"Ye are remembering yer brother," Alex whispered.

Her gaze flew up. "Yes. How did you know?"

"I can see it in yer eyes."

A strange, beguiling comfort seemed to settle over her, thanks to this Highlander's reassuring presence. Perhaps it was his intuition, and his clear insight into her grief. Or perhaps it was his strength as a warrior, for she believed, with every breath in her body, that he would protect her tonight.

"Sometimes I feel as if the world has come to an end." She studied the strong contours of his face, and the line of his shoulders beneath the tartan. "Do you understand? Have you ever lost someone?"

"Aye, I have. A brother, like yours. He was too young to fight, but he was stubborn and insisted on following me, so I let him. I thought I could protect him, but since then, I have come to realize that God has his own plans. All we can do is keep living the life we are meant to live, and push through the pain."

Elizabeth considered the wisdom in his words. "It takes courage to do that."

"Aye, and ye are very brave. Ye proved that this morning, so I am confident ye will survive this."

Elizabeth shifted on the bed. "But I have no family except for my uncle, and he is a stranger to me. I am alone."

"I predict that will soon change," he said. "One day, ye will meet a good man, marry him, make lots of babies, and all of this will be nothing but a distant memory." He tugged at the coverlet and arranged it snugly over her shoulders. "Go to sleep now, lass. I will wake ye in the morning."

With that, he rose from the bed and exited the room, leaving Elizabeth alone to contemplate the unexpected sense of calm she felt, and her amazing good fortune at having chosen this particular Highlander to attack on the battlefield that morning.

*   *   *

Elizabeth woke to the sound of panicked, angry voices, and a door swinging open, banging against the outside wall.

Heart racing with alarm, she tossed the covers aside, leapt out of bed, and swept through the curtain to the front room. Alex was standing outside with his pistol trained on yet another clansman, mounted high in a saddle. The gargantuan grey warhorse stomped around skittishly.

"Is that her?" the stranger asked, pointing his knife at Elizabeth, who skidded to a halt just behind Alex.

"Aye," he replied, "but it's no concern of yours, Angus MacDonald. I'll thank ye to be on yer way."

The rider wore his tartan up over his head like a hood. She could see his breath in the frosty chill of the morning.

"I heard ye were keeping a spy here," he growled, "and that she charmed ye into letting her live. Give her to me, Alex, and I'll take her to Perth. They'll know what to do with her."

"I'll do no such thing, Angus. The lady is under my protection. Go home now, and forget about her."

The hooded Highlander eyed her with sinister intent. "She's no lady if she's carrying dispatches to Argyll."

"She had nothing to do with that," Alex told him. "It's a stolen uniform she wears."

The Highlander scowled down at Alex, then turned his menacing blue eyes to Elizabeth. He studied her thoughtfully for a moment. "I can see why ye were so enchanted. She's a beauty to be sure, even in that uniform. Why don't ye let me come inside where we can talk about this. I'd like to see for myself how amiable she can be."

Alex cocked his pistol and took a persuasive step forward. "Ride out of here now, Angus, or I'll shoot ye through the heart."

The mounted Highlander raised both hands in the air. "Calm yourself, friend. I'll not intrude upon yer territory. If ye've already claimed her for yourself . . ."

"I've claimed nothing, nor will you, not as long as I live and breathe. Be on your way now."

Angus studied him with cool eyes. "Yer too much like yer father," he said in a low, gruff voice. "Swiftly conquered by a pretty face."

He clicked his tongue and walked his horse away from the cottage. A moment later, he disappeared into the forest like a phantom, and Elizabeth let out a tight breath.

"I take it he was a friend of yours?"

"No' a friend," Alex replied. "He's a ruthless warrior with a heart made of ice." He swung around and eyed her with intensity. "Put your coat on, lass, and gather up yer weapons. We need to leave here. *Now*."

"Why? Will he return?"

"I can't be sure, but if he knows of your presence here, others might have learned of it, too. I canna promise you'll be safe. I must take ye to Edinburgh and deliver ye to your uncle."

Elizabeth needed no further bidding. She hurried to don her brother's red coat.

For the whole of the morning, they rode together on horseback through deep forests and steep-sided glens, making their way steadily south towards Edinburgh. At noon, they stopped to rest in a private glade and eat a small lunch of oatcakes and cheese, while the horse nibbled on sweet green grasses and drank from a shallow burn.

While they sat side-by-side on a fallen log, they spoke of many things – the politics of the rebellion, their families, the death of Elizabeth's parents. She was pleased to learn that Alex's mother and father still lived, and were as passionately in love as they had been on their wedding day. Alex was the eldest of nine children, and he adored all his siblings. He had lost only one – the younger brother who had followed him into danger.

It seemed impossible to imagine that a person could be so blessed during this time of war and rebellion. There was an abundance of love in Alex's life. He was very lucky, for there was no such abundance in hers.

That night, under the light of the full moon, Alex and Elizabeth reached a crofter's cottage on the edge of a fast flowing river, a few miles southeast of Falkirk. A black-and-white sheepdog barked at them as they emerged from the wood and crossed the meadow, but his tail began to wag when they were greeted a few moments later by their hosts in the stable yard – trusted friends from Alexander's youth, a couple recently married and expecting their first child in the spring. Their names were Mary and Scott MacGregor.

Alex embraced them fondly and introduced Elizabeth, assuring them that her soldier's uniform was not a reason for concern. They seemed to trust him completely, and invited Elizabeth, without hesitation, into their home.

A short time later, they were all gathered around the table before the fire, enjoying a hearty supper of rabbit stew and dumplings. Alex arranged for a trade with the MacEwens: Elizabeth's uniform for a plain homespun skirt, a light shift, and stays. By the end of the evening, she could have passed for any typical Scottish lassie, born and bred in the Highlands. As long as she kept her mouth shut, no one would ever have guessed that she was born in England, and had crossed the Scottish border a few short weeks ago as a nurse with the British army – carrying a dark cloud of vengeance in her heart.

"Will we reach Edinburgh tomorrow?" Elizabeth asked in a quiet whisper, as Alex approached to say goodnight. He would sleep in the stable, while she would enjoy a soft pallet by the fire.

"Aye, he replied. "We will reach your uncle's shop by late afternoon."

"But I don't know where it is, exactly."

He chuckled. "How many book shops can there be in Edinburgh, lassie? I would guess only one or two."

In the glow of the firelight, his eyes shone with vitality, and his hair fell in thick, shimmering waves on to his broad muscular shoulders. She felt rather intoxicated by his chivalry. How remarkable, that they had met on a battlefield only two days before and had tried to cut each other in half. It seemed impossible to imagine – for in all the unforgettable moments since, Alexander MacLean had revealed himself to be a gentleman in every way. She had never felt more safe and protected.

Suddenly she realized that everything she'd ever believed about Scotland and its savage breed of Highland warriors meant nothing to her now. All she saw before her was a courageous and decent man who loved his family and wished to live honourably.

A man who sent a heady rush of desire and yearning into her blood.

She gazed wondrously at the beautiful pewter brooch that was pinned to the tartan at his shoulder, and reached out to touch it. How would she ever say goodbye to him tomorrow? She was not ready for that.

"Sleep well," he said, then leaned forwards to kiss her lightly on the lips.

The startling sensation of his mouth upon hers compelled her forwards, and what began as a tender kiss goodnight exploded into a powerful rush of unexpected passion. Her lips parted, and he responded by sweeping his tongue into her mouth, sending ripples of pleasure straight down to her toes. His hand slid around to the small of her back and he tugged her closer, roughly, crushing her breasts up against the solid wall of his chest as he groaned deeply and devoured her mouth with his own.

Gripping the fabric of his shirt in both fists, she held tight, fearing that her knees might buckle under the dizzying onslaught of her emotions. She had never been kissed like this before, and she had no idea how to manage it.

Quickly, he brought the kiss to an exquisite finish and took a step away from her. They stared at each other in dazed bewilderment. Heaven help her. She did not know what to say. There were no words.

"That was . . . unexpected," he whispered.

Her heart began to race. What was happening between them? She was losing sight of all propriety, and wanted to pull him closer and drag him down to the floor. She wanted him to feel the weight of him on top of her. She wanted it with a primal madness she could not begin to comprehend.

Swallowing uneasily, she loosened her grip on his shirt, and dropped her hands to her sides. "I'm sorry," she murmured.

He chuckled. "No need to apologise, lass. Yer lips were sweeter than anything I've tasted in years."

She blushed and dropped her gaze to the floor.

"I've never met a woman quite like you before," he said, "and for that reason, I must leave ye now, because ye look too pretty in that frock, and ye smell good, too. I fear that if I doona back away now, I may do something far worse than just kiss ye goodnight."

Elizabeth shivered with excitement and longing. "Would that be so terrible?"

His eyes smiled at her, then he toyed with the hair over her ear, sending delightful shivers of desire across her flesh. She turned her cheek into the warmth of his wrist and let her eyes fall closed. All the hardships of the world seemed to float away like dust on a summer breeze, as she breathed in the musky scent of his skin . . .

"I really must go now," he whispered in his deep Scottish brogue.

She did not try to stop him, for what she loved most about him was his integrity, and she did not wish to tempt him into doing something he might later regret.

"Goodnight," she said.

He paused at the door and spoke in a quiet, husky rumble. "Good night, Elizabeth."

She let out a soft sigh of besotted rapture, and then, to her hazy disappointment, he was gone.

A moment later, while still greatly aroused from their intimate encounter, Elizabeth settled down on the soft pallet by the fire, pulled the woollen blanket up to her shoulders, and watched the flames dance in the grate for quite some time before she finally managed to fall asleep.

That night, she dreamed only of Alexander MacLean's handsome face in the firelight, and the irresistible magic of his touch.

It had been almost ten years since Elizabeth saw her Uncle Charles, and she was not entirely sure he would recognize her when she walked into his shop. In the years since her mother's passing, they had exchanged very few letters, for he and her father did not agree on much of anything. Her uncle had the "unmitigated gall" to marry a woman from the Scottish Lowlands, and for that reason, they never shared the same political opinions. Hence, Elizabeth's connection to her uncle slowly dwindled away to nothing over the years. To be honest, she was not completely certain he still lived.

It was late afternoon by the time they rode into the crowded streets of Edinburgh. As they trotted through the tight congestion, past the street vendors who were shouting to sell their wares, the stench of stale rubbish assaulted Elizabeth's nostrils. Alex enquired about the bookshop, and they had to ask four people before an older man in spectacles and a tricorne hat was able to point them in the right direction.

Exhausted and hesitant about her future, Elizabeth locked her arms around Alex's waist and rested her cheek on his shoulder. With silent assurance, he steered them through narrow, winding streets.

At last, they came to a tiny bookshop on a busy lane, with a sign out front that said *Morrison's Books*. She knew they must be in the right place, for that was her mother's maiden name.

"I believe this is it." Elizabeth dismounted and stood on the walk for a moment, glancing over all the books in the paned window.

Alex tethered the horse to a post, then came to stand beside her. "I give ye my word that I will not leave ye," he said, "until I am satisfied that ye are in good hands."

A young boy ran by in a panic, cradling a chicken in his arms.

Elizabeth jumped, and realized she felt rather panicked herself. She turned her eyes to Alex, and felt a terrible pang of dread in her belly, for she was not yet ready to leave him.

While the cold November wind lifted his long dark hair off his tartan-clad shoulders, he did not speak a word. Elizabeth shivered in the chill.

"It's time to go inside," he finally said, then took a step forward and opened the door.

"Elizabeth! My word, is it really you?" Her Uncle Charles came bounding down a creaky set of stairs with an open book in his hand. "What in God's name are you doing here?"

He was still as tall and slim as she remembered, but he had aged since she last saw him. His hair was bone white and pulled back in a braid, his skin had grown wrinkled, and he wore spectacles on his nose.

Carefully he navigated his way around tables piled high with dusty books and approached her. He removed his spectacles. "You look so much like your mother."

Elizabeth's heart swelled with both sorrow and joy, as her uncle pulled her into his arms and lovingly embraced her.

"I am so happy to see you," he said.

"And I, you," she replied, weeping and laughing at the same time.

Eventually he stepped back and fixed his spectacles on his nose. "I learned of your father's death," he said, "fighting for King George. I am sorry, Elizabeth."

She dropped her gaze. "Thank you, but I am afraid there is more bad news. James was killed as well, three weeks ago. I am the only one left of our family."

Charles laid a hand on her shoulder and shook his head. "No, Elizabeth. You are not alone. You have family here."

She clung to her uncle's steady gaze. He tapped her nose with the tip of his finger, as he used to do when she was a child, then glanced away, towards the door, where Alex was waiting.

"Who is this man?" her uncle asked. "And why does he carry such a big sword into my bookshop?"

Alex strode forwards. "My apologies, sir. I am Alexander MacLean of Duart Castle, and I fought in the battle at Sherrifmuir. That is where I met your niece."

"He has been my protector, Uncle," she quickly explained. "I was lost and alone after James was killed. Alex found me on the battlefield and saved my life. He has delivered me here safely, so I owe him a great debt."

"As do I, it seems." Charles reached out to shake Alex's hand. "Thank you for bringing my niece home. I should like to repay you somehow."

Alex shook his head. "There is no debt, sir."

"My wife is upstairs tending to our children," Charles replied. "Will you at least stay for supper?"

Elizabeth's heart began to pound, for she knew what Alex's answer would be. The time had come. He was going to leave her now, and she would have to say goodbye.

But she was not ready. She did not want to see him go . . .

Alex paused. "I'm afraid I must return to Perth as soon as possible."

Every breath in her body came short. Her knees went weak under the weight of her anguish.

His eyes locked with hers, and neither of them spoke for what seemed an eternity. He palmed the hilt of his sword, and she wet her lips, feeling as if someone was slowly ripping her heart out of her body. She should say something. She should beg him to stay, just one more night . . .

"I wish good fortune to you both." Alex bowed slightly, then turned and headed for the door. It opened and closed with the tinkle of a bell, and before she could work out what to do, he was gone.

The whole world fell silent, except for the beating of her heart in her ears, like thunder over her head.

No . . .

Picking up her skirts, she dashed around the tables piled high with books, and ripped the door open on its hinges. She hastened out into the street. Her eyes darted left and right. His horse was already gone. Crowds of people and carriages obstructed her view in both directions. Where was he? And why hadn't she told him how she felt? How could she have let him go?

"Alex!" She rushed down the street, shouldering her way past hordes of people who blocked her way. Reaching the corner, she stood up on her toes. "*Alex!*"

But he was nowhere. He had left her to return to his home in the Highlands, and it was not likely she would ever see him again.

She laid her hand on the corner of a building, rested her forehead against it, and closed her eyes. A flash memory of the first moment she saw him on the battlefield came hurling back at her, and she remembered the frightening sound of their steel blades clashing against each other, and the fury in his eyes before he struck her down with his targe . . .

Never in her wildest dreams had she imagined the battle would turn out quite like this. She had not expected to surrender so completely to her enemy – in heart, body and soul.

It was a particularly wet spring in the Highlands, and by the end of April, Edinburgh was an utter sea of muck. Elizabeth had spent the winter mourning the death of her brother, while helping her uncle in his bookshop, assisting customers and organizing his inventory. Her cousins – two boys and one girl, all under the age of ten – lifted her spirits with laughter and games, but each night, after she read them their stories, she retired to her own chamber and whispered a quiet prayer for the safety and happiness of the Highlander who had rescued her from her vengeance. He never ventured far from her thoughts, and she often wondered what he was doing at any given moment during the day. While she was gazing out her window at the moon and the stars, was he, too, admiring the night sky from somewhere on the Isle of Mull?

She liked to imagine him riding his horse through a lush green glen, his dark hair blowing in the wind, his tartan pinned at his shoulder with that exquisite brooch she had once touched and admired. Eventually she began to think she was idealizing his memory, turning him into some sort of god-like, mythical hero, and she tried very hard to push him from her mind.

Then one day, on a clear afternoon at the end of April, while she stood on a stool dusting the books on the highest shelves – the door of the bookshop opened and closed. The hanging bells chimed with their familiar hollow sound, and she heard light footsteps across the plank floor as she so often did, but she did not look away from her task, for her uncle was out front.

Something, however – something she could not begin to explain – caused her heart to beat a little faster. All the tiny hairs on her arms stood on end.

Lowering the dust cloth to her side, she stepped down from the stool and peered around the tall bookshelf. A dark-haired Highlander stood with his back to her while he spoke to her uncle. He wore a kilt, with a sword sheathed at his side.

Was it Alex? A hot fireball of excitement dropped into her belly, and she sucked in a breath to steady herself.

Do not be foolish, Elizabeth. You're dreaming again. Surely it couldn't possibly be . . .

Then he turned around and met her gaze, and her heart exploded with a burst of radiant bliss. It *was* him! Her handsome, heroic Highlander!

What was he doing here? What did he want?

Struggling to contain the juddering thrills that were dancing up and down her spine, she swallowed hard and smoothed out her skirt, before taking a few tentative steps forward to say hello. They met in the centre of the shop, where sunlight streamed in through the windowpanes, creating a sparkling beam of hazy, dreamlike rapture.

"Alex."

She could think of nothing else to say.

His eyes filled with joy. "Ah, lassie. I'm pleased to see that ye did not forget me."

Elizabeth laughed out loud. "*Forget* you? Are you mad?"

They regarded each other with affection and a familiar sense of calm.

Out of the corner of her eye, she noticed her uncle quietly disappearing up the stairs.

"What are you doing here?" she asked, careful not to get her hopes up. Perhaps he had simply walked into the shop to purchase a book.

"Can ye not take one look at me and answer that for yerself?"

There was such hope in his expression. It was contagious, and she experienced a wild, kicking desire to throw her arms around his neck and dance a reel around the room.

"You came to see *me*?"

Oh, how ridiculous it was to speak with such casual curiosity, when her heart was practically beating out of her chest!

He flashed a smile that dazzled her witless, then laid a hand on the side of her neck, his thumb brushing lightly over the sensitive flesh behind her ear. The touch of his huge warrior hand sent a flood of desire through her entire body.

"Of course I came to see ye, lass," he replied. "I've thought of nothing else all winter long but yer bonnie face and feisty nature. I could not live another day apart from ye. I had to see ye again."

"Is that all?" she asked. "You just came to see me? To say hello again? And then goodbye?"

He ran the pad of his thumb over her parted lips, and shook his head. "So stubborn, as always. Can ye not accept that I am in love with ye, and that I mean to ask ye to be my wife?"

All the thoughts in her brain toppled over each other. It was a terrible calamity of epic proportions. "I . . . What are you saying?" She was completely breathless.

He laughed. "Doona play innocent with me, lass. Ye know very well what I am saying. This is a proposal. But if it's too quick for ye, I'll settle for courtin' ye for a short time, at least until ye can make up yer mind whether or not ye wish to love me."

Her need for him erupted out of the joy in her heart. "Of course I wish to love you. I've loved you since the first moment I came charging after you on that battlefield."

"Is that a yes?" he asked.

With a cry of euphoric laughter, she threw herself into his arms and knocked him backwards into a stack of books that toppled off a table on to the floor. A thick cloud of dust puffed into the air.

"Or course it's a yes," she said with a smile, pressing her lips to his and tasting a glistening slice of heaven in his kiss. "I am so happy."

He held her close, and buried his face in the crook of her neck. "As am I, lass. My heart is yours, and I promise to love ye and make ye happy for the rest of my days. I will protect ye and give ye everything that is mine to give."

She hugged him tight, she knew without doubt that he would keep his word. "And I make the same pledge to you."

Then at last his mouth covered hers, and the world was suddenly, miraculously, peaceful and perfect.

The Curse of Wolf Crag

Susan Sizemore

Glasgow can be a bit dicey after dark, but possible danger is hardly any excuse to miss out on the excellent night life. Tara had gone out to celebrate the installation of two tapestries in a Trongate shop and a brand new commission. A night out on the town was certainly justified.

It's a university town, an artsy town, an international town. Tara Thomas loved the place to pieces. But she thought she'd love anywhere that wasn't the isolated, cold, windswept, raining when it wasn't snowing, postage-stamp rocky island where she'd grown up.

Oh, and sheep-infested. Had she mentioned that?

Not that she didn't love wool, she was a weaver, after all. She was an artist with wool as well as every other natural fibre, but she was happy to be away from her family's sheep farm on Wolf Crag.

Never mind the weather, living there was just too – complicated. Most of the younger generation left, even those from the most ancient families. Even though the Crag was as wired to the Internet, mobile phones and the rest of modern technology – weather permitting – as anywhere, the Old Ways lingered, traditions stifled change. You could believe things on Wolf Crag you wouldn't anywhere else. Not that they weren't true everywhere else, it was just that in the misty, rugged isolation of the island you were forced to believe harder, stronger, fiercer. The Crag demanded a lot of your soul.

In Glasgow, Tara could believe in herself, and in the rational, normal human world. She didn't imagine fairies lurking around corners in the whirling hubbub of the city even when fog lent mystery to its streets. No one told her to be 'ware of water horses in puddles, and pixies in the tiny front gardens. None of the wild things of Glasgow required any imagination to believe in. Real thugs with real steel knives didn't need the energy of belief. They needed to be avoided.

Which Tara feared she hadn't done tonight.

A justified celebration or not, she wished she hadn't stayed for one more drink, leaving the pub alone and tipsy at closing time. She wished the streetlights didn't seem so far apart. She wished that the sound of her heels didn't click so loudly in her ears. It was not that she expected trouble, but—

Mostly she wished she hadn't let the woman at the bar read her palm. She didn't mind hearing that the lines in her hand showed she was destined for fame. She did mind being told that she was in great danger – that the love of her life would save her from it.

But the thing she wished most, was that the knowledge deep in her gut that she was being followed wasn't true.

Tara began to run through the shadows, towards lights and the sound of traffic. But the way was very dark, and the heavy footsteps behind came on faster.

"Fang, lad? Are you listening to me?"

"Yes, Gran."

What was the old lady doing up so late? He wouldn't be out right now if he didn't have to walk back a half mile to the car park after a meeting that ran far too long.

"Well, Fang, what are you going to do about it?"

Alistair Douglas winced at the nickname. He knew the old woman had used it just for the purpose of annoying him, reminding him of his place. He almost wished he'd never given the old lady back on the island the mobile phone. He was hundreds of miles away, and yet, here she was howling and whining into his ear as he prowled the late night city streets.

"Listen, I'm sorry about the water rising over your back garden," he told her. "But if you're going to live so close to the sea—"

"Rising sea levels have nothing to do with it, as you know full well. The Crag's disappearing, Fang! It's the curse!"

"Which curse, Gran? The island's under a dozen curses and plagued by even more prophecies. Some of them even cancel each other out."

"It's the Secret Curse, and you know it. You have to stop it!"

"Why me, Gran? How can I—?"

"You're the laird, the alpha and the summer king rolled in to one, that's why! What are you doing in Glasgow when your place is here?"

He didn't think his being on the island would in any way solve the problem. One more Black Douglas wasn't the sort of resident Wolf Crag needed. He was working on solving the Human Curse. "I think I may have the manor house rented to a Yank couple."

"How can you give up your own house?"

"It's not like I'm home that often, Gran. What I'm doing here in Glasgow is necessary. I'm working on attracting tourism to the island," he told his grandmother. "I'm trying to get estate developers interested in building a resort, summer homes, maybe a golf course."

"Your sacred ancestral land is fading into the mists and you're talking about golf courses?! What will the Wild Hunt think about that?"

Gran didn't think in twenty-first-century concepts – or twentieth. She'd barely come to terms with the nineteenth, for that matter. "I'm in talks with Oberon about keeping his folk away from the resort."

"Oh, really? As if the fae will go along with anything for very long."

"They will when there's more than fairy gold involved. The king of fairy has some concept of surviving in the modern world. Besides, I'll do anything to get people to the island," he answered.

He tilted his head, excellent hearing catching a faint noise in the distance. People running, maybe.

"The children of the old families need to return," Gran insisted. "Why don't you find them, persuade them? What about that nice girl you used to be with, Tara Thomas?" Since there was a great deal of complex history between the Douglas and Thomas families, Gran's effort at sounding casual was an utter failure.

"I don't want to talk about Tara any more than you want to talk about her grandfather."

"Oh, I'm happy to talk about that lying, foresworn son of Adam."

"Just not right now, all right, Gran?"

Not that Alistair's plea did any good. He held the mobile away from his ear to let her curse out the old man without having to listen. Andrew Thomas had always been a crusty but kindly neighbour as far as Alistair was concerned, but he knew Gran had good reasons for her loathing of the old man. The loathing was returned by Thomas. The couple had brought grudges and bickering to such an art form over the last sixty years that their feud had become the main source of entertainment for the inhabitants of Wolf Crag.

But his granddaughter Tara wasn't part of their battle. No one had tried to destroy his relationship with her but Alistair himself. Tara's absence from his life still ripped at Alistair's heart.

Tara was—

He heard the scream the same moment he caught the scent – the unmistakeable, undeniable fragrance that was her. The hair on the back of Alistair's neck stood up. He ran. The transformation proceeded with every step. Even if darkness and shadow hadn't shielded him, he wouldn't have bothered checking for witnesses. Within moments he was running on four legs instead of two. His eyes glowed red in the night. His teeth were sharp, white razors. His claws were steel-hard daggers.

Someone was attacking Tara, and that someone was going to die.

There were two of them, Alistair discovered. He found them at the end of a nearby dark alley. A broken streetlight didn't give them the protection of darkness from his red night vision. He saw them bending over a prone figure on the ground. They didn't notice him, not until two hundred pounds of hard muscle and deadly natural weapons barrelled into them.

Their hot blood was delicious on Alistair's tongue. Tearing flesh from bone was a delightful exercise. He didn't toy or play with his prey – he was a werewolf, not a werecat, after all. But the pleasure of the kill was intoxicating after so much time spent living a human life.

Once the attackers were dead he rushed to Tara. She sat up at his approach. He was aware of the scent of her blood, and the shift in body heat that indicated bruising. She looked shaken. But she didn't look surprised to see a large wolf with blood on his mouth leaning his muzzle close to breathe her in.

She put her hand on his head, fingers sinking deep into thick fur. "You are not the love of my life," she said firmly.

Just before she fainted.

Tara woke knowing she was naked, which didn't surprise her – because she recalled who'd come to her rescue in the filthy, stinking alley.

"You had better be laundering my clothes, Alistair Douglas," she said, from beneath the cover of a duvet on a lovely, soft bed.

"You could use a shower," his deep voice rumbled from nearby.

Tara's toes curled in response to that voice. It always sent a thrill through her. She remembered when it had cracked when they were growing up, then changed, deepened. Suddenly, she'd felt closer to being a woman every time he spoke to her.

"I have been rolling around in muck."

"Nonsense, you haven't been to bed with me in years."

She laughed. She couldn't help it. But she bit her tongue on saying anything. The past was very far away when she found herself lying naked in a bed that held Alistair's scent, faint and spicy, in the bedclothes.

She reminded herself that one of her first projects had been spinning his werewolf fur, then weaving it into a lovely, soft scarf. She'd worn it to a fibre arts show on a rainy day and ended up smelling like a wet dog among people she was trying to impress. Black Fang Douglas had always brought her trouble.

Of course, this time, he'd saved her life.

Shouldn't have got herself in trouble to begin with.

She knew she was still a bit tipsy as she sat up, duvet pulled around her. Or maybe the rush of dizziness came from getting her first good look at him in several long years. Since he wasn't wearing anything but a pair of tight black briefs, it was indeed a good look. Was it possible that he was even handsomer than she remembered? Maybe it was that maturity suited him. His was a hard-muscled man's body now, with none of the lankiness of the boy she'd loved. He'd grown into his strong jaw and thrusting beak of a nose. He was as scruffy and fuzzy as ever, with an artfully stubbly jaw and dark hair a bit too long for fashion. Of course he still had a thickly furred chest that trailed into a line that arrowed sexily down his abdomen and disappeared into his underwear.

"You're looking at my crotch, woman."

"Don't sound so pleased about it. You could use a waxing," she added sarcastically.

"And you a shower, as I've already pointed out. And you owe me a new suit. I didn't bother stripping when I came at your call. It was my best suit, now it's a rag."

"I'll get started on making you some tweed, right away."

"Still weaving?" he asked.

"Still practising law?"

Every word out of both of them had grown tight and tense. Tara drew back from the hot anger that suddenly seethed through her. It was far too easy to argue with Alistair rather than talk to him. The anger was longstanding and had nothing to do with the here and now. Here and now, he'd saved her life. Damn! How she hated owing him!

She still made herself say, "Thank you."

"You're welcome." He handed her a black terry robe that was soft as velvet. He turned his back as if he were a gentleman and pointed towards a hallway. "Off with you."

Tara was more beautiful than Alistair remembered. He'd forced himself not to look at her as a woman as he undressed her and checked her for serious wounds. Once he'd stripped away the muddy, bloody clothing and determined she'd be fine he'd covered her and not taken a single peep while she'd been out. He put her clothes in the wash, cleaned himself up, and was drawn back to her side despite the effort to keep busy with other things. He had watched her, studying every line of her fine-featured face. Her features might be described as elfin by anyone not born on Wolf Crag. Tara's features weren't knife blade sharp enough to belong to an elf, nor were her teeth. Though she did well enough biting and nipping with what she had during love-play, as he remembered so well.

He'd stroked her silky dark hair and regretted that she'd cut it short. He'd breathed her in. She was more delicious than ever, the ripe, calling scent of a woman that curled deep into him. It overrode the old wanting and brought out a newer, deeper hunger.

And he didn't have to fear that she'd react with horror when she woke up. She'd accept that her attackers had paid the price they deserved. She understood his nature, and she had always accepted that. He'd missed being around a woman so in tune with his world. It was her world, too, after all.

It was fate. Had to be. Why else would Gran have reminded him of Tara just as Tara cried out for help? It was meant to be. He may have left Wolf's Crag, but he wasn't fool enough to deny when the magic of the place was at work around him. He was trying to save the island. And the island was telling him it needed Tara to come back home.

With him.

Perhaps the island wasn't going that far, but he chose to interpret it that way. Maybe Wolf Crag just wanted its people back, but Alistair Douglas had always known he and Tara were meant to be. Maybe he'd forgotten it, a little, but seeing her drove the knowledge hard back into his blood and brains and bone again. She was his fated mate, alpha to his alpha, no matter how hard he'd run from her once he discovered the world and the women outside the island.

By the time she came back from the bathroom, he had a plan.

Tara lingered in the bathroom as long as she could, taking full advantage of being alone, and the ultra-modern plumbing in Alastair's flat. Hot water helped a lot. It helped the aches, the street stench, it helped to clear her head of the last of the alcohol. It didn't help Tara's physical, visceral reaction to Alistair, but cleaning up the physical mess helped strengthen her wits and willpower. All she had to do was get dressed and get out, get away from him. Of course, she'd have to get her clothes back from him first.

She steeled her nerves, wrapped herself up as tightly as she could in the oversized robe, and returned to the large room that contained a sleeping area, kitchen, office and lounge. The walls were old, exposed brick, the ceiling was high, the wooden floors polished to a glossy sheen.

"Quite the bachelor pad," she said. "You are still a bachelor?" She didn't mean to sound bitter, or hopeful, but heard both mixed in her tone.

He turned from the computer on his desk. "Yes."

His grin made her blush, but she deserved to be embarrassed. At least he'd put on some clothing. Black, of course – tight jeans and T-shirt. Douglas men always wore black. It wasn't an affectation, really, it was that they were colour-blind in human form and their women folk trained them away from fashion mistakes from a young age.

"Is there a man in your life?" he asked.

"I have a boyfriend."

"Aye, but do you have a man?"

She snorted. "Go chase your tail."

His answering laugh sent the familiar dark shiver deep inside her. As it always had and always would, she supposed. It was best that she leave now.

"Where are my clothes?"

"I made tea." He waved towards the lounge area as he stood. "Have a seat. Let's get caught up."

That was not what she should do, but Tara gave in to what she wanted to do. She settled into a comfortable chair, with her legs tucked under her.

"How's your granda?" Alistair asked when he brought her a big mug of tea. "Must be lonely for him with you gone, him being old and frail for a mortal."

Alistair's comments stirred niggles of worry and guilt in her, but Tara said, "Theo Simmones moved in with him a while back."

"What? That old goat? He can't be much company for old Randall Thomas."

"He was talking about making up a couple of the spare bedrooms and hanging out a B&B sign. Not that tourists make their way over to the Crag that often."

Alistair leaned back in the chair opposite and looked at her over the steam rising from his tea. His blue eyes were suddenly bright with enthusiasm. "That's going to change soon. I'm working on opening a resort on the south side of the Crag."

"I'm appalled."

"You look it. Even the folk on Wolf Crag change with the times – and we could certainly use the revenue summer people would bring."

"Yes, but – what if some nosey mortal found out about—"

"I've already got faefolk lined up to run security for the resort. If anything got out of hand, a glamour would be thrown over the mortal's memory."

Tara sipped tea. And thought. And missed her grandfather and the ancient Thomas farmhouse, and summer on Wolf Crag. The place was always trying to pull you back if you let it. Maybe it was seeing Alistair again that was putting a travel plan into her head.

"I don't see how you can attract tourists, Fang, when the ferry only makes the trip once a week, and only holds two cars," she pointed out.

"We're adding an airline service," he answered proudly. "Three trips a week via Phoenix Air."

"The Phoenix brothers have an airplane?" She was horrified. They weren't exactly phoenixes, and their name was actually McCabe.

"And pilots' licences. And thousands of hours of flying in the air force. They aren't the reckless kids you remember. None of us are reckless kids anymore, Tara."

She heard his sincerity, and the meaning behind what he said. Maybe it would be best if she went back to Wolf Crag for a while, now that she'd finally encountered her old nemesis here in Glasgow. He is not the love of my life, she thought resolutely, and stood up. She thrust the half-full mug into his hands when he rose from his seat.

"Lovely seeing you," she said. "Thanks for saving my life. Where're my clothes? Never mind." She saw neatly folded clothing, along with her shoes and purse, resting on the kitchen counter. She snatched everything up.

"I put out a T-shirt for you," he said. "There was no saving the blouse."

At least he didn't try to stop her. He didn't offer to give her a lift home. She couldn't help but be a bit miffed at his easy dismissal of her as hurried out to flag down a cab in the light of dawn.

The ferry ride was a long nine hours north from the Isle of Skye, and the sea wasn't exactly calm and cooperative along the way. Tara didn't mind the rough sea, and relished being the only passenger. It gave her time and privacy to adjust to the change from the normal world to the strange place where she was returning.

She didn't mind that no one met her on the dock. She checked her watch and decided it was long enough before sunset to safely make the three-mile walk home. And after sunset? Well, she wore silver bracelets, there was a small amount of cold iron in her backpack, and her walking stick was made of hawthorne. That would be enough to keep the fae folk away, and she had pepper spray for anything else.

She heard some siren singing along the way, and a ghost or two lingered in shadows. They beckoned, but listlessly, not really trying to draw her into shadowland. She had to stop to chat with a lonely dryad that wanted to complain about land taxes and dogs pissing on her tree, but none of Tara's magical protections proved necessary. The walk in the fresh air was invigorating, even if the rocky terrain was more rugged than she remembered. The path she took was officially a road, but it was a courtesy term rather than the truth. Legend said it was a fair folk road, and one was careful to never insult anything to do with them.

The path on to the Thomas property was marked by an ancient stone arch that was said to be Roman, though no Romans had ever made it to the Crag as far as history was aware. Family legend had it otherwise, though it was a sordid and tragic tale spoken of in whispers around the children. The actual story didn't seem so sordid to modern sensibilities, so all the anticipation of finding out about the founding of the clan had been anticlimactic when Tara finally did.

The path up to the huge house was lined with low drystone walls, through fields dotted with sheep. Sheepdogs kept watch over them, and ignored her as she made her way to the house.

Tara found a large goat munching on a rose bush near the back door and they exchanged a nod as she opened the heavy old door. The goat followed her inside.

"Hello, Theo," she said.

Air swirled and dimmed around the goat and it turned into a paunchy old satyr. Tara looked away to give him a moment of privacy to cover his huge genitalia with a tea towel.

"Where's Granda?" she asked once Theo was presentable.

"Here," Granda said, coming into the kitchen.

There were still a few ginger strands in his thick silver hair and beard. But perhaps there were a few more wrinkles, and a bit of a droop to his broad shoulders she hadn't noticed during their latest webcam chat.

He held out his arms.

Tara dropped her stick and bag and rushed into his embrace. His hold was strong and tight and she leaned into it with gratitude. "I was worried about you," she whispered as she hugged him back hard.

He gave her shoulders a squeeze. "Can't think why. I always worry about you," he added. "That's my job."

Her parents had fled the Crag with her younger siblings for a quiet life in New Zealand when she was in her late teens. She'd had no intention of leaving home, her textile apprenticeship with her grandmother – or Alistair – back then. Granda had convinced her parents to let him finish raising her. Maybe if she'd gone with them Alistair wouldn't have broken her heart, but other than that she was glad she'd stayed then, and glad for the life she had now. Except, now that she was back on Wolf Crag where the air was clear and the natives were strange, she was happier than she'd been in years.

"I don't know why I didn't come back to the Crag sooner," she said.

"Good thing you came back while it's still here," Theo said darkly. "I've got rose bushes to trim before they're swallowed by mist."

She turned to the satyr, but he morphed back to his goat form and wandered out to the garden before she could ask what he meant. "Uh – Granda?"

The old man gave a satisfied, evil cackle – which told her that whatever followed involved bad news for dear old Gran Douglas. The two of them were never going to forgive each other for as long as they lived. Maybe Thomas and Douglas blood was never meant to mix, no matter what legends, prophecies and curses said about their undying true love through the generations. As far as Tara knew, no Douglas and Thomas had ever made a successful love match, no matter how often passion burned between them. Of course she'd thought she and Alistair would be different – before he decided to sleep with every woman he met when he left the island.

In Gran and Granda's case, the Second World War had got in the way. He'd been reported dead when, in fact, he was a POW, and Gran had married one of her Douglas cousins for the sake of keeping the werewolf bloodline strong. When Granda came home to find his love married and a mother, he'd never forgiven her. She'd taken the attitude that he should never have left her or the Crag in the first place. Their war continued to this day.

"A landslide took away half of the old bitch's property last week," Granda said. "Serves her right for living so close to the sea now that the ice caps are melting." He sounded as if Gran Douglas was personally responsible for global warming.

"The Crag's a small island," Tara said. "All of it's close to the sea."

"Small, and getting smaller all the time." He picked up her backpack. "Your old room's ready for you. And your packages arrived yesterday."

Tara had brought her work with her. "I'm dying to set up Grandma's workroom. Thanks for letting me use her looms."

"They're your looms, now. She left them to you when she died. She was so proud of your talent with weaving." He sighed. "I was never as good to that woman as I should have been."

He'd married late, and they'd only had one child, her father. As far as Tara could tell it had been a happy marriage but, of course, there'd always been the shadow of his youthful fling with Gran Douglas hanging over whatever relationship he'd had. She was determined that her ruined romance with Alistair wasn't going to throw the same dark shadows over her love life – though so far she hadn't formed any attachments serious enough to matter.

She was not going to consider that her feelings for Alistair might have anything to do with her current lack of intense interest in any other male. She did consider just how tired she was as she followed her grandfather up two flights of stairs to the loft under the roof.

She loved the view of Tor Rock and the wild coast beyond from the high loft windows. She hurried over to take a look before the last of the light of the long summer day faded. She was oddly disappointed. The Tor didn't seem as high and grand as she remembered. And was the sea somehow encroaching?

She looked back at her grandfather. He was watching her pensively. "Is the ocean eating away the coastline?"

"Things are changing around here, lass."

Tara's heart jumped with worry. "Things never change on the Crag."

Saying it could make it so, couldn't it? Magic worked on Wolf Crag, after all.

He snorted. "They're building a golf course."

Which was all he'd say on the matter. He kissed her on the forehead and bid her good night.

She did not have a good night. She dreamed of curses and prophecies – and there was an incubus dream where her body twined and tangled with Alistair's that woke her up panting and sweating and filled with carnal aching.

"Damn the man!" she muttered as she got out of bed. And she didn't care that she was blaming Fang Douglas for something that wasn't his fault.

She flung open the window and took deep, bracing breaths of the cool morning air. Unsurprisingly, it was rainy, with mist obscuring the distance between the house and the Tor. The smell of frying eggs drew her attention away from the landscape.

Once she'd dressed and headed down to the kitchen, she'd also got her mind and libido off of Alistair Douglas.

Who was standing by the stove.

"What the devil are you doing here, Fang Douglas?" she demanded as she marched up to him.

He turned to her with a grin. "Making breakfast."

"I told you I was turning the place into a B&B," Granda said from a seat at the kitchen table. "I rent Fang a bed, but he insists on providing the breakfast."

"But—" She gestured, vaguely in the direction of the Douglas property. "What about the manor house?"

"I'm renovating and renting it out." Alistair stepped closer to her, making her very aware of his masculine presence. "The place is too big to live in alone. Now, if I had a wife and some bairns to fill the house up—"

"Oh, leave off!" she complained.

Annoyance didn't stop a hot thrill going through her. A domestic picture of them together, as man, wife and parents filled her head. Combining that with last night's dream—

"Bother," she grumbled. Tara put her hands on her hips, facing Alistair belligerently.

"How do you like your eggs?" he asked. The look in his eyes told her he knew exactly what she'd been thinking – wishing.

"You weren't on the ferry. How did you get here? And you know very well how I like my eggs."

"Over easy, it is. I flew in with Andy McCabe last night."

"Oh. Right."

He had told her about the new island air service. He hadn't done anything wrong. He'd saved her life, and started her thinking about an overdue visit home. Alistair wasn't being trouble – but her nerves screamed a danger warning that grew stronger with every moment near him. He wasn't up to anything, had no reason to be, but . . .

"I'm going for a walk," Tara said, and escaped out the back door before another word was spoken. She could feel Fang looking after her as she went.

Theo was in the garden, in satyr form and wearing boxer underwear. He was sitting on a low, moss-dotted wall, sipping a mug of tea. She joined him when he gestured her over. When she took a seat he looked around furtively.

This was her cue. "All right. What's really going on?"

"We're doomed," he said. "The curse is coming to pass."

Tara folded her hands in her lap, not in the least disconcerted. "Which one this time?"

"The one about Adam's children leaving the border of faerie."

"I don't think I've heard of that one."

"We keep it quiet around humans. Knowledge of some things is forbidden to those it would give power to. But when the time comes—"

"Right. The curse has something to do with humans leaving Wolf Crag, is that it?"

The satyr nodded solemnly. "There's a balance necessary between the mortal lands and the lands of the fae. You are of the rock, we are of the mist. For those of the mist to dwell in the land of rock, there must be a strong presence of the people of rock to believe in the place where we dwell. Once the balance shifts to more of us than Adam's children in a place, the place begins to retreat into the world of fae." He put his mug down on the wall and gave her a disgusted look. "Frankly, we like it right here in the mortal world." Theo heaved a great sigh and walked away, shaking his shaggy grey, horned head.

Tara sat on the wall looking at the garden for a while. She was perfectly calm on the outside, seething on the inside. After a while she got up and began walking towards Tor Rock.

"We'll see about this," she murmured.

"Tara! Tara, where are you off to?"

She'd gone quite a distance across the sheep pastures when Alistair called to her, but his deep voiced was pitched to carry. She ignored him and kept going. She'd reached the base of the steep hill when the wolf loped up beside her.

"Put on some pants," she told Alistair when the wolf transformed into a gloriously gorgeous naked man.

She walked on.

He must have had them tied around his neck, because when he caught up with her in a few seconds he was wearing black sweatpants.

He grabbed her arm, and pulled her to face him. "What's wrong, love?"

"Love? Don't you use that word to me, Fang Douglas!"

Her shout was so angry and adamant that he took a shocked step back. But in an instant his own temper flared to match hers. A faint red glow lit deep in his blue eyes. "How many times do I have to apologise to you?"

"Since you haven't apologised even once yet, I don't know!"

Shock returned. "What are you talking about? Of course I've—" His gaze went unfocused, his expression thoughtful. "Maybe I never said anything, but you have to know—"

"No, I don't!"

Tara's heart was breaking all over again, and she wasn't going to stand here and let it happen in front of Alistair Douglas. She wasn't going to let him know how bad it still was – she hadn't known herself until just now. Now – her heart was being flayed to pieces by shards of broken glass.

She began climbing the crooked path up from the base of Tor Rock. If he followed she couldn't hear over the rumble of landslides and roar of the wind. Besides, werewolves moved quietly, even in human form. Also, Tara was cursing loudly inside her own head.

When she stopped abruptly to avoid a boulder rolling across the path, Alistair bumped hard into her back. She was knocked forwards, but his hands came around her waist to keep her from falling. He didn't let go, but turned her to face him.

"We need to talk, Tara."

There was nothing but sadness and sincerity in his deep voice and blue eyes. She didn't believe a bit of it, though her heart wanted to.

"Plus, we should get away from Tor Rock," he added. "It's not safe here."

Safer than having his arms around her. "Please let go of me," she said.

He didn't. Instead, he pulled her back down the path and into a stand of trees surrounding a bubbling spring at the base of the hill. A stream threaded away from the spring across Thomas land. Locally, it was known as the Roman Spring, and there were complaints about filmmakers stealing the name for movie titles from older generations of the family.

He swung her up on the huge worn boulder which had always been used as a bench and moved in very close. He stood between her legs, with his hands on her shoulders. The warmth of his skin permeated her. His closeness tried to overwhelm her.

"We are now going to have the talk we should have had a decade ago," he told her.

"A talk you seem to think we'd already had," she snapped back. "It's too late now."

"I'm sorry," he said. "I've been sorry I hurt you every day for the last dozen years. I ran away from you, I did you wrong—"

"You slept with every woman you met off the island."

He nodded. "Aye. I did. For a while. I didn't try to hide it from you. I didn't sneak around and pretend I wasn't a complete bastard. I am so sorry about the time you walked in on my flat in Glasgow."

"Two women!" she shouted. "You were in bed with two women! And you laughed when you saw me standing there. You didn't try to explain. You didn't come after me when I ran out."

"I was in no condition to run after you!" he shouted back. "There was no reason to try to make excuses for what was obvious! I'm sorry if I laughed – I don't remember laughing."

"I've heard that laugh in my nightmares for years!"

He winced. "Damn it, Tara, I'm sorry!" He stroked her cheek. "I've missed you. Missed you and wanted you . . . but I did what I did and all I can do is ask you for a chance to start over. We're fated to be together, love, don't you remember that?"

She caught herself leaning into his cupped hand and jerked away. "Fated? Then why did you—?"

"Because we were fated to be together! I fought fate," he told her. "When I left the island all I wanted to do for a while was run away from everything – and everyone – Wolf Crag represented. I wanted my freedom. I wanted to find out who I was. I wanted to make my own choices and decisions and to hell with magic and fate and all the nonsense that I'd had fed to me from birth."

"Our love was nonsense?"

He gave a tight nod. "Yes, it was. For a while. I went looking for something better – because I was a young idiot. I never found anyone I cared for more than you. I stopped looking soon enough. By the time I knew you were the only love of my life the damage had been done. I accepted that the curse of a Douglas and Thomas had taken over my life."

"Oh, I see. You didn't believe in fate, but you believe in the curse?"

He stroked his hands down her arms. "What I believe now is that we can start again. When we met again in Glasgow, I knew that if we both went home, I'd have a chance to make everything up to you – here, where we belong."

She wanted to believe it – especially when he was so close to her, especially with his hands touching her so sensually, so gently. Need raced through her, but Tara wasn't going to fall for it just because she'd never stopped wanting him.

"Liar!" she said at last. "The Crag's dying without people. You tricked me into coming back!"

"The devil with Wolf Crag! I need you!"

"Don't talk of the devil, you fool!"

"I need you," he repeated. "I love you. I want you. I tricked you, all right. I admit I exaggerated about your granda. I teased you to come and see the changes in the place. I reminded you of home. But I wanted you here to be with me."

His sincerity touched her deep in her soul. His hands stirred her other senses. She couldn't stop her fingers from touching his stubbled cheek, tracing his lips. She wanted to believe him. She fought not to believe him.

Then it didn't matter, because the earth started shaking so hard it knocked her off the boulder, and Alistair came down with her. They tangled together as the world bucked and rolled beneath them. Daylight turned to twilight, and a thick blue mist began to boil through the trees. The spring began to hiss and steam.

The world was coming to an end. Tara didn't doubt that for a moment.

Funny thing though – she wasn't scared.

She pulled Alistair's mouth to hers and kissed him. Desire roared through them. Her hands tugged at the waist of his sweatpants. Then cupped his bare ass. He growled in response. She arched against him as his hands found her breasts.

There was no way the world was ending before she'd had her way with her werewolf love one last time. One new time – as a woman, not a girl. She needed him now in ways her mind fogged with teenage lust could never have imagined. But, this being the end of the world, she'd settle for a quick, hard shag.

Alistair came up from a deep, hard kiss. "No! Wait!"

"What?" she shouted back.

The earth was still bouncing them around with bruising force. A freight train roar filled the air. The mist drew closer, grew darker. This was no time to talk!

He held her face in his hands, made her look him in the eye. "Say it!" he demanded. "Tell me!"

"Of course I love you!" she told him. She'd never spoken words more intensely in her life. Or more truthful. "I've always loved you. Always will. You're my fate. Now kiss me."

He did.

Tara forgot the chaos around them completely. She lost herself in every kiss, caress and thrust. He moved inside her and she moved to meet him. They reached the shattering point together and she didn't care one bit if the world ended then and there.

Only, it didn't.

Once she came down from the soaring pleasure she became aware that they were surrounded by stillness. By silence except for their ragged breaths. All she could feel was Alistair's racing heart-beat against her chest.

All she heard was his rough whisper in her ear, "Did the world just stop moving for you, too?"

Tara couldn't stop the laugh, and he laughed with her. They held each other, hugged and kissed for a while. It was wonderful – to be alive, to be together, to be naked and entwined and holding on to each other. The past didn't fade away, but the pain of it was over-ridden by hope for the future.

"The world didn't end," she said eventually. "At least, the Crag's still here." She looked over Alistair's naked shoulder. "Does Tor Rock look normal to you?"

He rolled off her and helped her to stand before glancing up at the sheer cliff behind them. "It looks as obviously phallic as ever," he judged.

"The mist is gone," Tara said.

Alistair rubbed his jaw. "I'm thinking the curse has been lifted." He hugged her tightly, then lifted her in the air and swung her around. "Tara, we did it!"

"So we did," she said with a sex-drunk grin when he put her down. "Let's do it again." She tried to drag him back to the ground.

But Alistair wouldn't budge, and he was serious. Damn.

"What are you talking about?" she asked.

"We broke the curse! You and I making love, broke the curse."

He'd tried not to believe in fate, now he was believing in curses. "Which curse? The one about the island disappearing?"

"Of course."

"But, I thought that had to do with humans leaving the Crag. What's that got to do with a Douglas and a Thomas having sex?"

"Being in love," he corrected.

"That too."

He ran a hand through his shaggy hair. "Don't you recall the prophecy, the one about the Weaver and the Wolf? We learned it in school."

The curriculum on Wolf Crag was a bit different than what students learned on the mainland. "Weaver and Wolf does sound familiar. How did it go? When the Weaver and the Wolf hearts be at peace and as one something something vanishing something banished something the Crag as solid as love will be. You think that prophecy is about us?"

"You're a weaver. I'm a werewolf. The world didn't end. Let's not try to analyze it any more than that, shall we?"

She took his point.

He took her hands in his. "My world's solid as long as you love me."

She pulled his head down for a kiss. "Then I believe Wolf Crag is going to be here for a good long time."

Beloved Beast

Lois Greiman

Swift Torree smiled as she swung her beaded reticule in time to her lively stride. It was a braw day in New Town. The bluebells were just beginning to bloom, the apple blossoms smelled like a wee bit of heaven, and the sun had made a rare spring appearance, sparkling on Edinburgh like firelight on brilliants. Stilling her tiny purse so as to avoid striking any oncoming pedestrians, she tucked it tight between her arm and her well-dressed ribcage. Today she wore a walking gown of pink muslin decorated with intricate embroidered flowers she had stitched herself. It was, after all, the details that separated the middling pickpocket from the truly gifted. And *she* was gifted.

Her pert little sleeves were capped at her shoulders, then hugged her arms all the way to her knuckles, making it frightfully simple to slip recently purloined items from her hand into hiding. Her straw chapeau was wide-brimmed enough to conceal her face, and her undergarments were nonexistent; she was all for keeping up appearances, but why bother with frills no mark would ever have a chance to appreciate.

Besides it was a warm April day and . . .

Ho there. A likely looking couple had just turned the corner on to Princes Street and was strolling towards her. The woman was small, plump and cute as a kitten. The man was tall and fit, which was rather a disappointment, for though Swift's name was aptly given, it spoke more of her dexterity than fleetness of foot. Just then, however, the gentleman glanced into the lady's upturned face, and in that instant Swift recognized his expression: adoration. Fascination. And maybe . . . if her luck held . . . maybe a smidgen of obsession.

Swift smiled to herself. Fifteen feet separated her from them, and there was no easier mark in the world than a man in love. It addled his thinking, slowed his reflexes, lightened his mood.

And this one . . . this one kept his wallet in his breast pocket. How very kind of him. Oh, and the lady, paragon of generosity that she was, seemed to be wearing a diamond bracelet. What a big-hearted lass. That little bauble would go a far ways towards Tavis's education.

Unfortunately the cobbled walkways were all but empty, making it impossible to appear to have been jostled from behind. Another tactic, then, Swift thought, and gripped the little reticule in her right hand. Inside, the initials SVT were embroidered, but that didn't bother her. For all she knew her own name had contained just those letters. She'd pilfered the bonny bag from a manor house on Brunswick. Perhaps she should have taken the snuffbox she'd seen there, too, but 'twas wrong to be greedy. Blind Pete had instilled that thought into her consciousness from her earliest memory.

The couple was closing the gap between them. Just enough time to glance into the reticule's empty interior. Just a second to bobble inattentively on the uneven stone. Just an instant to gasp and teeter and grapple for stability. But too late. Oh dear, she was already falling, hands splayed, skirts flying, and eyes wide with dismay as she lifted them towards the gentleman.

With the grace of a diving swallow, she collapsed five inches in front of him.

"Gracious!"

"Careful there!"

The pair took a guarded step to the rear. Swift knew that without glancing up, knew and realized she must do something quick. A little moan might turn the trick.

She emitted a soft sigh of misery, remained absolutely still and hoped to God her feet were tucked firmly beneath her beribboned skirt. Her gown may be Parisian in design, but her shoes were better suited for the mines . . . or a lively chase. Despite her eye for detail, she was no slave to fashion. Or anything else come to that.

"My dear?" The lady lisped a little as she crouched. "My dear, are you quite all right?"

"Yes. Yes," Swift said and lifted her head as if disoriented.

"Here then, you've taken a nasty spill. Let me help you sit up."

"Oh." She looked into the woman's eyes, catching her full attention as they clasped fingers. "I fear I am a dreadful clod. Murdoch always says as much."

"You're no such thing," said the lady. "Is she, Henry?"

The man seemed late to the party, but rallied when he realized *he* was about to look the clod should he fail to show some sympathy post-haste. "Certainly not," he said. "'Tis these damnable cobbles. Rough as the sea at midday. You didn't twist your ankle did you?"

"No."

"Better let me take a look. I'm a physician, you know, and—"

"No!" she repeated and jerked her feet more firmly beneath the lacy hem of her stolen skirt. If the damned thing had any more frippery, she'd be tripping for real and earnest. "I'm quite well. Not to worry."

"Ah, well, can I give you a hand up at the least?"

She caught his gaze with her own lavender eyes. He had a long, hooked nose, a narrow face, and sallow skin. While Swift was . . . well . . . today she had chosen to be almost plain. She'd made certain of that in the small shard of mirror she kept stowed beneath her bed.

"That's ever so kind of you," she said, and carefully keeping her homely footwear well hidden, shifted her feet beneath her. She was the best dipper in all of Edinburgh, but it was entirely possible that she'd have to be hot-footing it down Hanover Street in another few seconds. Reaching for his hands, she held his gaze as they rose in unison.

"My thanks, good sir," she said and smiled tremulously into his eyes.

"'Twas nothing at all. Are you certain you're quite all right?"

"Of course," she said, then let her eyes drift closed and bobbled as if about to faint.

He caught her about the waist. "Here now," he crooned and drew her close to his chest . . . and his wallet.

"Oh my," she said and lifted her hand to her heart as if to still its palpitations. It was just a matter of inches and nerve to his inside pocket. Inches, nerve, and the innate ability to appear to be what you are not. "Oh, my most abject apologies." She stood with her back to the lady and steadied herself on the gentleman's chest for a fraction of a second. If what Terrible Tull said was true, most things involving men took no longer than that.

"You'd best sit."

"No, no," she said and straightened resolutely. Her cheeks felt flushed. It was one of her most notable abilities. "I've inconvenienced you and your beautiful lady far too long already." She stepped back, goods firmly stowed away. "Please, do be about your day," she said, and, happy with her morning's work, stepped carefully past them.

She hadn't taken five full strides before a voice from her right startled her. "Nicely done, luv." A man stepped out of an alleyway, lips twisted with derision. "Quite impressive."

Her heart stopped dead in her chest. Indeed, she no longer cared if the couple behind her realized she'd robbed them or not. Knobby Hooks had seen her poaching birds in Cryton's territory. And that was enough to strike terror in any dipper's heart had she half a brain in her noggin. But she forced a cocky smile, curtsied prettily, and matched his harsh Glasgow accent. "My thanks, good sir. Praps you'll give us a bob for the performance."

"A bob is it?" He stepped forward. There was something in his eyes, uncertainty maybe. Could it be that he thought she actually hadn't recognized him? She would remember Knobby Hooks till the day she died twitching on the gallows and probably long after.

"A bob ain't nothing for a gent like you," she said, edging her voice with just a sparkle of flirtation.

"And what would I get for my coin?" he asked and stepped up close.

"You want a wee sample, do ya?" she asked.

He shrugged, mouth tilted up, smug as hell.

She smiled as she reached for his shoulders, tilted her head prettily, then slammed her knee into his crotch. But her aim was a little off. He jerked back. Her knee skimmed his thigh, just injuring him, but that was enough for her. Grabbing her skirts in both hands, she pivoted like a charger and bolted across the street. She could hear him rally before she'd reached the opposite side. He straightened with a growl. The feral sound raised the hair on the back of her neck, but it did nothing to slow her flight. She glanced over her shoulder. He was already giving chase. And he was fast, devouring the distance between them.

She dashed down Castle Street and careened on to Rose. One glance over her shoulder assured her she was not alone. Knobby was behind her and gaining. Up ahead, the market would be bustling with people. Maybe she could get lost in the crowd. Or maybe she'd get snatched by a constable. But there was little choice. Knobby was behind, crowds were ahead.

She turned the corner like a courser digging for the home stretch . . . and ran smack into a tall gentleman's back.

She staggered, momentarily stunned. He bobbed forward a few steps, then turned slowly. "I say, what goes on here?" His expression was stern, his tone the same, suggesting London roots. But she realized those truths in only a vague sort of way, for he was wealthy.

He was wearing a fob watch on his waistcoat, a black billycock on his head, and a sharp-cut ruby on his right ring finger. For a moment the entirety of Swift's attention was riveted on those facts, but a squeal from behind brought her abruptly to her senses.

"My apologies, sir." Her London accent was a bit rusty, but she pushed ahead. "I fear I'm in a terrible rush. I was to meet my dearest father at the . . ." Behind her, a man growled a warning. Feet scuffled. She imagined Knobby careening towards her. Her mind stalled, frozen in terror, but she kicked it impatiently back into gear, raised her gaze past the gentleman's left ear and found inspiration in the small stone church at the end of the street. "At the chapel," she finished breathlessly, "And I must away."

It was all she could do to remain steady as she strode past the venders and hawkers that lined the boulevard. Behind her in the growing crush, a woman gasped and a man cursed. Reaching up with stiff fingers, she slipped the straw chapeau from her head. Every fibre in her ached to glance over her shoulder, but she resisted. Instead, she pulled the copper pins from her hair and dropped them into her reticule. Chestnut curls fell around her face and down her back as she shifted her eyes side to side, searching for relief. And then she saw it.

Two young men were watching the crowds from a dark alcove. One was tall and gawky, one near her own height. And now she did chance a glance over her shoulder. Knobby was not yet in sight.

"I've a proposition." She joined them in the shadows. They straightened abruptly. Perhaps their cocky, devil-may-kill expressions should have scared her, but she knew nothing of these boys, and far too much of Knobby Hooks.

"A proposition?" said the gawky one and shifted his weight restlessly. "Might it involve you flat on your back with me—"

"It involves this hat," she said, and kept herself from wasting precious time by listening to him jabber.

"Methinks I'm more interested in you."

"How about in this?" she asked and held up a fob watch. She hadn't really meant to take it from the gentleman she'd last bumped into, but if he didn't want it filched why did he wear it right out in the open like that?

"You giving us a watch, Strawberry?" asked the shorter of the two.

"I shall," she said, "if you'll wear the hat and run through the crowds until you reach the square."

They stared at her for a second, then snorted in derision.

"Tell me this then, Strawberry, why don't we just grab you and the watch all together?"

She took time to give them her most comely smile. She'd left plain behind some minutes ago. "Because I'll knee you in the forbiddens and scream bloody murder. How long do you think you'll last when that swell mob finds you molesting one of their own?"

"I think—"

From some yards away a man's affronted voice rang out. "Hey there, watch what you're about."

"Time's up!" she said. "Do it or don't."

"I'll do it," said the shorter of the two, and snatching the hat from her hand, slammed it on to his head. She handed over the watch with barely a shiver of regret, and then he was gone, leaping from the alcove towards Charlotte's Square.

Swift hid in the deepest shadows, but even from there she could see Knobby dodge past, skirting skirts and careening after her straw chapeau.

She almost smiled as she watched him go, but just then she noticed a baby-faced constable scowling in the direction of the rapidly retreating Knobby. Chances were good the authorities would never connect her with the criminal element dressed as she was, but there seemed little reason to take chances. She'd had a fine, relaxing morning thus far and had no wish to ruin it now. So, dodging her eyes right and left, she stepped from the alcove and strode to the end of the street. Ducking her head in silent reverence, she opened the arched, iron-bound door of a small, stone kirk. Inside, it was cool and dim. A dozen stout candles flickered near the chancel.

She paused momentarily, admiring the stain glass windows, the vaulted ceiling, the trio of wooden confessionals.

She'd always appreciated churches. They were fine places to hide. Quiet and dark, they more often than not had a mite box set out to collect alms for the poor.

She was poor.

Bowing her head, she made the sign of the cross against her chest as she'd seen others do. Kneeling on a padded plank, she glanced surreptitiously from side to side. No one seemed to be minding the store. And, thank the good and gracious Lord, there was the collection box. Iron bound, it was cylindrical in shape and crafted of dark wood. A small slit had been cut into the top and it was kept by a rusty metal hasp.

God was with her.

Opening her reticule, she rose to her feet and stepped forward. To an observer, it may well have seemed as if she was fetching a coin. Instead, a small copper pin came away in her hand.

Head bowed again, she sheltered the wooden box with her body while fiddling soundlessly with the lock. In less than ten full seconds it made a rusty creak as it popped open. One more glance to the rear assured her she was alone. The top rose almost soundlessly.

Her fingers were as quick as minnows as she fished out the coins and dropped them into her reticule. One more. Just one more and—

"Might I help ye, child?"

Her breath froze in her throat. The voice came from behind her, cutting off her exit. But surely there was another door. Without moving her head, she glanced right and left. No hope on either side. Easing the mite box closed, she prayed the man behind her was short, ponderously fat and older than black pepper. The lock clicked quietly as it sank home. She gritted her teeth, then fixed a humble expression on her bonny face and turned slowly, eyes lowered.

"Father." She said the word reverently and raised her gaze to meet his. Her eyes travelled up a goodly distance, but they did not encounter the woollen robes she'd expected. Instead, he was dressed in a simple tunic and dark tartan. Belted at his lean waist with a broad strap of leather, the plaid was pinned at his brawny shoulder with a brooch the size of her fist. Beneath the plaid, his thighs bunched with strength. Every shifting muscle spoke of power. His hair, however, was laced with grey. A small indication, perhaps, that the Lord did, indeed, have a rare sense of irony.

"Oh . . ." She smiled shyly. "I assumed you were a priest."

He remained absolutely silent, neither confirming nor denying. If intimidation was his intent, he had a fine start; muscles roiled like mooring lines beneath the turned-up sleeves of his tunic. She swallowed but refused to fidget. "Well, I'd best be off. I but came to leave a wee contribution for the city's poor," she said, and making sure her little purse was well hidden in the folds of her voluminous skirt, glided towards the door.

He said nothing. She could feel the tension build in the soles of her feet and creep up the back of her legs, but she held steady. Many had fallen from weak nerves. She would not be amongst them. Not Swift Torree of Canongate. Instead, she let her reticule fall gently against the slope of her gown and tumble noiselessly behind the solid leg of a pew meant for a parishioner not important enough to obtain one of the private boxes. Though she was loathe to leave it, 'twas far better to be parted from it for a time than to be caught red-handed with the alms in her possession.

"'Tis very generous of ye lass," he said finally. His Highlander's burr seemed to rumble from the very earth beneath them, but she managed to inhale and lowered her gaze modestly. Even staring at the floor, however, she could tell he was already stepping forward, stealing the air from her lungs. And though she told herself to remain calm, she couldn't help but snap her attention to his stern countenance.

Their gazes met and melded, his as grey as a winter storm.

"Is something unright, lass?" he asked.

Unright how? Did he suspect her of thievery? Or—

"Mayhap there be somemat ye wish to tell me?"

"No!" she blurted, but caught herself and lowered her lashes carefully. Who the hell was he? A priest in plain clothing? A parishioner? A guard? A braw Highlander meant to test the fortitude of frail maids? The last seemed most likely, for though his face was stern and unyielding, it spoke volumes of strength and self-control. If a body needed protecting, he'd be just the sort for the task. Luckily for Swift, she was not the needy kind. Nor was she the type to dwell on girlish dreams, though there was that about him that prompted them. "Well, yes. Yes, there is something," she admitted. "I fear I have sinned."

"Have ye now?"

"Might I . . ." She glanced at the narrow trio of rooms set aside for sinners. Had her luck held, the damned boxes would have been adjacent to the door, but anywhere was better than near the alms box. "Might I make an admittance?"

He studied her. He was close now, within four strides. If she bolted would he catch her? He was not a young man, probably past five and thirty years, but judging by the size of his thighs she rather doubted another fifty would make him slow enough to best.

"Might ye mean a confession?" he asked.

"Yes. Of course." She felt herself blush. How the devil had she forgotten that word? "Might I make a confession?"

"Aye," he said and remained absolutely unmoving.

She scowled a little. "I meant . . . in the . . ." She glanced towards the boxes, but when she turned back, he was just lifting his gaze from the floor. Had he noticed her shoes? Tipped on to the edge of panic, she stood very still, not deigning to draw her feet beneath her skirts. Surely that would do nothing but signify guilt. And who was *he* to judge her attire? He was garbed in a wee skirt, for God's sake. Though, in truth, he wore it well. And the tiny, leather-wrapped braid beside his left ear did even less to decrease his manhood. "I meant in one of them confessional . . ." She caught herself just before spinning into her native tongue. The inhabitants of Old Town's Canongate were not known for their elegant speech. She cleared her throat and lifted her chin a little. "I was hoping to be seated in one of the confessional boxes."

"But the confessionals are to hide one's identity," he said and for an instant something flickered in his eyes. She couldn't quite make out what it was. "And I've already seen your face, lass."

"Well . . ." Was there interest in his expression? Was he attracted to her? Because she sure as hell could work with that. "Perhaps you could forget," she said and glanced coyly through her lashes.

His lips twitched with humour. "I fear the Lord has blessed me with a long and faithful memory, lassie. I shan't forget features such as yours."

So he *was* attracted. Praise God! "You've a distinctive visage yourself, Father." She was desperately digging for information regarding his reason for being there. Did priests go about in Highlander garb now and again? She had no way of knowing. It wasn't as if she spent her days in the company of clergy, but her words concerning his features were true nevertheless. Although he was by no means a pretty man, his jaw was chiseled and broad, his chin well nicked by a scar that ran out of sight towards his throat.

"Distinctive," he said and chuckled a little.

The sound was deep and soothing. She smiled, allowing herself a moment of pleasure at the sound. "Did I use the wrong term?"

He shrugged his shoulders. Even through the voluminous tunic they looked heavy with muscle. "I suspect distinctive is well suited," he said. "'Tis the word 'father' that failed the test."

"You're not . . ." She raised her brows, searching for words that wouldn't make her sound like an uneducated guttersnipe, though the description would be apt. "Not ordained?"

"Nay. I am but a postulant hopeful."

So he could copulate without guilt. Or at least he could *hope* to copulate with *less* guilt. God was gracious. "Well," she said, and took a step forward. She wasn't above using the heady aura of attraction that lay like opium smoke between them. "Humility looks good on you. But surely postulant hopefuls can hear confessions as well as any."

They were very close now, forcing him to bend his broad neck to look down at her. Just a few more inches and she would be within striking distance.

"And what grievous sins has such a wee lass as ye committed?"

The question caught her off-guard, for there was no flirtation in his tone. Indeed there seemed to be earnest concern. Concern she wanted no part of. "I thought all sins equal in the eyes of the Lord."

His brows rose slightly. "You know the scriptures, lass?"

She shrugged modestly. Blind Pete had taught her to read even before he'd trained her to lift a brooch. Thievery had proven to be the more valuable of the two, but quoting biblical passages had come in handy at times. She hadn't foreseen a use for it on this particular occasion, but she had learned long ago to roll with the punches, literally and otherwise.

He took a seemingly unconscious step closer. Perhaps she would be wise to leap for the door, but she doubted her ability to best him in a footrace. Surely it was not his masculine allure that kept her there. Nay, she stayed only to incapacitate him. And for that she needed proximity, which she now had. They were inches apart, their bodies all but touching.

She gazed up at him. He looked down at her. Neither breathed.

"I know scriptures well enough to realize I'll sin again," she said, and gripping the belt that encircled his waist, rose on her toes as if to kiss him. His eyes seemed to darken as she drew nearer.

Their lips almost met. His parted.

"By kneeing a postulant hopeful in the stones?" he asked.

"What?" Startled, she tried to step back, but he had already caught her wrist.

"Or were you about to confess for stealing the alms, lass?"

She tugged at her arm. "I've no idea what you're talking about."

"Alms that are meant to aid the city's impoverished youth."

"You're mistaken. I put coins in the box just for that reason."

"Ah, so you're concerned with the wee ones that land in the gutters and brothels of this dark city?"

"Of course."

He watched her, eyes as steady as stone. "Then we'd best check to make certain your donation got safe to its destination," he said and began tugging her towards the mite box.

"Release me!" she insisted, but the air had all but abandoned her lungs, leaving her voice weak. She drew a deep breath, remembering the image she had so carefully erected. She would play it till the end, professing her innocence. 'Twas the only way to win the day. "Loose me this instant!" she demanded. "Or I shall scream for the constable."

He turned towards her, one brow raised over stormy eyes. "That I doubt," he said.

There was challenge in his face. And try as she might, she had not yet learned to resist a challenge.

"Help. Help me!" she shrieked.

She expected him to release her, or at the least, to jerk in surprise, perhaps allowing her a chance to escape, but he barely shifted a muscle.

She caught his gaze with hers, meeting the challenge full on. "Rape!"

The iron-bound door at the end of the ancient kirk thudded open. A constable raced into the sanctuary.

"You there, unhand . . . Mr Mackay?" He slowed to a walk, his tone uncertain. "I thought I heard someone scream."

"Aye," said the Highlander, his gaze never shifting from hers. "'Twas the wee lass here."

"Oh?" He lowered his gaze to hers. 'Twas the baby-faced constable she'd seen but minutes earlier by the alcove where she'd handed off her chapeau. Her heart was beating like a hammer in her chest. Had he seen her pass her bonnet off to the gawky lad? Had he guessed her intent? "Is something amiss, lass?"

"Yes. This man . . ." Her mind spun. She hadn't a leg to stand on. She'd gambled and lost, but surely it was better to deal with a man of the church, no matter how damnably unflappable, than a constable paid to bring in her sort. "This man startled me."

"Startled you?"

"I shouldn't be so fidgety. Everett tells me so time out of count. But my mind had wandered. You see, my poor father is so dreadfully ill, and I've been caring for him endlessly. I don't think he's going to last much . . ." she began, and sniffling softly, buried her face in her free hand.

"Oh." The constable shuffled his feet uncomfortably, suddenly eager to be off. "Is that what happened, Mr Mackay?"

The Highlander was silent for several tense seconds. She prayed for divine intervention.

"'Twas sommat like that," he rumbled.

There was a moment of silence. "Well then, I'll leave you to comfort her," said the constable, and hurried away.

When the door closed, Swift lifted her head and scowled. Mackay raised one brow and stared a question.

"I had no wish to find trouble for you," she said.

"Is it me that should be worried?" he rumbled.

"What would the good constable think if he found you accosting a perfectly innocent woman?"

"Innocent are ye, lass? And here I thought ye had sinned."

"In the past," she said. "Minor offences. I certainly did not take the church's money. I would do no such thing."

"Me own mistake then, lass. Let us fetch your wee bag. I believe ye dropped it beneath the front pew," he said and began dragging her in that direction.

"I don't have a . . ." she began, but he was already bending to retrieve her little purse. Frantic, she kicked at his face, but he twisted abruptly. The blow struck his shoulder. He grunted slightly but didn't loosen his grip on her arm.

"Sir?"

Swift jerked her gaze to the right. A boy of nine or so stood twenty feet away. A red stain marred his cheek, but his eyes were bright.

"Is something amiss, sir."

"Nay, Rye, all is well."

The boy's brows rose above mischievous eyes. "I thought fisticuffs were forbidden, sir."

The Highlander's brows lower slightly. "We're not fighting, lad."

The boy's lips twitched in uncertainty.

"We're not fighting are we, lassie?" the Highlander rumbled.

Although Swift would never be certain why, she straightened her back and shook her head. "Certainly not. That would be wrong."

"There now, go back to your bread and jam," Mackay ordered.

The boy skimmed his quick gaze from him to her. "And you'll join me?"

"As soon as I'm able," he vowed, and the lad disappeared.

Mackay sighed, straightened, and tugged Swift back to the front of the sanctuary. Their gazes met, and then, with one callused hand, he opened the draw string top of her reticule and dropped the contents on to the baptismal font. A wallet, a diamond bracelet, a ruby ring and a mixed handful of coins clattered on to the stone font, spraying against the solid, ceramic pitcher that stood in the exact centre.

She made her eyes go wide. "How dare you rummage through my private possessions like a wild boar on a rampage?"

"*Your* possessions, lass?"

She almost winced as she noticed the name stamped into the wallet's fine leather.

"So you're . . . Sir Edgar Templeton?"

A string of curse words stormed through her head. But she had set her course, thus she held them at bay as a dozen possibilities presented themselves. All of them were flawed. Thus, she cried. It was as simple as that. Her eyes teared up on command. Her nose began to sting, and one hot droplet rolled down her unhappy cheek. She sobbed gently, prettily.

He watched her. "It won't work, lass."

She hiccupped, as pathetic as a lost babe. "What . . . what won't work?"

"Half the young ones in Edinburgh be going to bed hungry most nights of the week. The other half is beaten or raped. Consider yourself fortunate I'm letting you go free," he said and loosed her arm.

She staggered a little. "What?"

"I'm setting you free," he said. "If you'll vow not to steal . . ." He paused, seemed to read her face and toned down his conditions. "If you'll vow not to steal from this wee small kirk again."

She narrowed her eyes and watched him. "What do you want?"

"What's that, lass?"

"I won't prostitute myself."

"But you'll steal for Cryton."

She felt herself tense at the sound of his name. Cryton was the personification of evil. "Not so long as I draw breath," she said.

He nodded. "'Tis good to know ye draw the line somewhere, then."

She watched him in silence for a moment. "You're setting me free with no strings attached?"

He nodded once.

"Why?"

He straightened his back, broad and intimidating. "What's that?"

"I asked you why you're doing it."

"Surely a scholar such as yerself kens that the scriptures has a good deal to say concerning forgiveness."

"So you're . . ." She shook her head. "So you're just going to let me walk out of here."

"Aye."

"Even though the constable is just outside the door."

He shrugged as if weary. "Ye made a fair play of it for a bit, lass. I was beginning to doubt meself."

"What the devil gave me away then?" she asked and tilted her head at him, curious.

"Naught but the evidence. I fear I saw ye drop your wee bag."

"And what of my shoes? Surely you noticed them ugly buggers," she said, lifting her right foot for inspection.

He glanced at her homely footwear, unsurprised. "You don't command the Black Em . . ." He paused. "I'm fair observant."

She remained silent for a moment, thinking. "You were military." She'd heard of the Black Embers. The ensuing tales of heroism and bravery were rarely considered true, but there was something about this man that made the ridiculous seem plausible. She watched him. He had the bearing of a general. The build of a god. "You look the part."

He said nothing.

"A brawny bloke like you must have made a fair bit of coin at it."

Still he remained silent.

"More than you can come by here," she said. "Even if you claim the mite box yourself on a fair regular basis."

He made a quiet sound of derision. "You'd best be off now before the constable—"

"Why?" she asked.

"Because he might not believe you're the blushing innocent the second time around, and Father Thomas takes theft rather—"

"Why are you here?" she asked.

He watched her, face solemn. For a full ten seconds he failed to answer. But she waited.

"Have you ever caused a man's death, lass?"

She shook her head.

"'Tis a hideous thing. A horrible soul-wrenching thing. But it cannot compare to the death of a child."

She said nothing.

"War . . ." He shook his head. The tiny braid brushed his left ear. "'Tis the children what suffer most. The wee—" He stopped, drew a heavy breath and forced a laugh. "Truth be told, I quit when I became weary of the scars. The church is more staid. Less violent," he said and rolled the shoulder she had kicked only moments earlier. "Usually."

"So that's why you joined the kirk here."

"Aye."

She nodded. It was a lie, and not a particularly good one. "I don't suppose you'd be a sweetmeat and let me take the bracelet."

He shook his head once. "It'll fetch a fair bit for the lads."

"So you'll not try to find its owner?"

He shrugged a heavy shoulder. "The Lord works in mysterious ways. I dare not question his methods."

She chuckled, charmed by the spark in his eyes. He'd seen pain. That much was clear. But he was not beyond seeing happiness. 'Twas a rare gift these days. "I don't think you and I are so very different, Mackay."

"Your fingers be a good deal smaller. Better for sleight of hand."

She smiled and turned away. "Would you believe me if I said I, too, was trying to free a young lad from poverty?"

"I fear our brief acquaintance has made me a wee bit of the sceptic."

She stopped at the baptismal font and glanced over her shoulder at him. "I promised old Pete I'd see to Tav's care."

"Blind Pete?"

"My mother," she said, then laughed at his expression. "Or as close to one as I've known. He took me in when I had nowhere else."

"And this Tav?"

"Just another urchin he fostered. Too big for the chimneys, too small for the mines," she said and didn't admit that the lad's happy smile had stolen her heart years ago, long before old Pete's death. "I hope to see him educated. Find him a trade."

"There are better ways to go about it than this, lass."

She heard him approach from behind, felt his hand on her shoulder, and knew he was not immune to her charms.

"Like I says, I'm not one for whoring."

"'Twas not exactly what I had in me mind," he said.

She turned her head slightly. The chemistry was back, that sharp twang of interest sparked by his strength and an unexpected sense of humour. But she had no need for chemistry. "Ah, shall we call it love then?"

He paused a second. "If you like," he said and turned her towards him. But in that instant she lifted the solid pitcher and swung for his head with all her might. It struck the side of his pate like a hammer. He staggered back. It wasn't until that moment that she noticed the bracelet dangling from his fingers.

He stared at her, then dropped to his knees, big body slumping. "I but meant ye could keep the brilliants," he said.

"Oh," she breathed, but a commotion outside caught her attention. No time for regrets or apologies or second guesses. Snatching up her purloined possessions, she fled.

"So you insist on continuing on this foolhardy path?" Father Thomas's tone was disapproving, his face pinched as he leaned heavily on a hewn oak cane.

"*I was a stranger and you took me in.*" Brenan Mackay enjoyed quoting scripture to Father. It made him livid. "*When I was hungry—*"

"I know the gospel of Matthew far better than a bloody mercenary." The old man oft reminded Mackay that he did not belong behind hallowed walls.

"Then you'll know 'tis our duty to help those in need."

"They're thieves and cutthroats, born of thieves and cutthroats," Father said. "You truly believe you can set them right?"

"I believe we can but try."

"As you tried with that girl?"

Mackay stifled a wince, remembering the feel of the pitcher against his head. Not a single dent had appeared in the pitcher. He couldn't say the same of his head. "As I said at the outset, I am sorry to have lost the coins."

"As well you should be. It is not as though we took you in for your spiritual gifts, Mackay."

They had taken him in in the hope that his massive presence

would discourage just the sort of thing that had happened with the girl. Well, for that and the coin he had to offer the coffers. She had been right, after all; killing people had paid considerably better than saving them. Thus, they had struck a deal; he would guard the sanctuary in exchange for the right to collect money in an effort to free a child from poverty now and again. "I believe I have guarded the church well enough these past nine months," he said.

"Had I known you've a weakness for women I would not have accepted you at the start."

"We all fall short of the glory of God."

"Don't quote scripture to me, you hulking Highlander."

Mackay almost laughed. He shouldn't enjoy seeing his superior riled. He was sure of that, but the girl . . . Swift Torree . . . he had learned her name some days after first hearing her melodious voice, would turn the head of any man who still breathed. Except perhaps Father Thomas. His fondness for ale made all other weaknesses dim by comparison.

"As you are sure aware, I replaced the coin that was taken with me own. Added to that what's been collected in the past, I believe I have enough to free a wee lad from the streets."

"You've replaced the coin."

"Aye."

"That makes me wonder from whence a postulant of this humble church secured those funds."

So he was a postulant now. Earlier, he had been informed that he would not be accepted to that lofty position until he had proven himself worthy.

"No answer to that, Mackay?"

He brought his attention back to the aging clergy. *"Be not curious in unnecessary matters; for more things are shewed on to thee than—"*

"Cease—" cried the priest and raised his cane as if to strike, but Mackay caught it easily.

"I shall be going to Cryton's hovel," he said, "and I shall take the coin with me."

Turning, he dropped the money pouch into the horsehair sporran that hung from his belt and left the ancient kirk. It was only a middling walk to Old Town. Less than a full mile. The city disintegrated with every stride.

Near Gregor Wynd, an old woman sat hunched and immobile on a stump fashioned into a stool. Outside a tilted pub, a dog leaned against its leash and snarled a slavering warning.

At the corner of two crooked, unmarked streets, a tall, narrow house slumped towards an alley. Its foundation was sagging, its mortar crumbling. Two men lounged beside the listing door. One was tall and scrawny. The other was short and scrawny.

They rose warily to their feet as he stopped nearby.

"Sod off," said the smaller of the two.

"Good day to you, too, lad," Mackay rumbled.

The pair glanced narrowly at him then each other.

"Who the devil are you and what do you want?"

"I am naught but a man of peace," Mackay said and gave them his best smile, but some had likened his best to a snarling glower.

"Gaw, them men of peace be awful big buggers these days ain't they?" the tall one said and his companion guffawed.

Mackay made certain his own expression never changed. To this sort fear was like the scent of blood to a starving hound. "I've come to see Cryton."

The short, scrawny lad shifted restlessly. "I don't know no one by that name."

"Nay?" He held his smile with stout resolve. "Then I've come to see whoever you're beholden to."

"I ain't beholden to no man," said the tall one, but just then the door opened. A round-faced fellow with a top hat set at a jaunty angle sauntered through, his right arm thrown over the bare shoulders of a woman one could only call a trollop.

"Ho there, what goes on here?" he asked, voice jovial and a little too loud.

"This bloke here says he wants to talk to Cryton. I says I don't know no one by that name."

The man in the top hat shifted his gaze to Mackay and smiled. "Brother Brenan," he said. "You have to forgive Kerry here. He don't have no good memory. 'Tis a pleasure to see you again."

Mackay remained as he was. He was a man of peace, but at times such as these it was difficult to remember why. "I've come for a boy," he said.

The man called Cryton stared at him for a moment, then threw back his head and guffawed at the murky sky. "Ah, you wouldn't know it to look at him would you, luv?" he said, addressing the girl at his side. "But the big beast of a Highlander here has a weakness for the lads."

The girl turned her eyes towards Mackay, but they were all but dead to the world. Too far gone to save. He had seen it a hundred times.

"I heard you have a child called Burch."

"Burch?" Cryton grinned again. His teeth were straight and unstained. His soul was not. "I don't know what you're talking about, Brother. We're good-hearted people here. But we ain't running no foundry."

"Nay, you're—" Mackay began, but stopped himself carefully. "I've coin for his release, same as the last time."

"Release! You make it sound as if we've got children chained to the walls. That's not the case atall, is it, Sil?"

The tall fellow shook his head.

"Sure we stumble across the odd orphan now and again, but we do the godly thing. Give them a place to sleep, maybe a loaf of bread to keep 'em from death's yawning door."

Anger rumbled ominously in Mackay's innards. "You make them steal and beat them senseless if they fail to produce—" He stopped himself again. "As I said at the outset, I'm a man of peace and willing to pay for the child."

Cryton canted his head. "Wear out the last lad so soon, did you?"

Mackay felt his hands grind into fists. "There are brothels and rum houses on half the streets in this burg. Bring the boy out now or I'll take me coin elsewhere."

"I'm telling you, I don't have no spare lads lying about."

Mackay stared at him a long moment, then nodded once and turned away, but Cryton caught his arm. Mackay stared at the hand on his biceps, kept his emotions in careful check, then slowly glanced over his shoulder at the offender.

The younger man dropped his hand and took a cautious step back. "All the lads are out earning their keep." He grinned, but his cockiness had frayed a bit. "Delivering milk and whatnot. Ain't that right, Annie, luv?" he asked. She nodded vaguely, eyes bruised and ancient.

"Why don't you come in and sit for a bit?" Cryton invited. "They're certain to be back soon."

"Aye." The shorter of the two guards pushed the door wide. It moaned like a tortured ghost. "Aye, come on in. We'll fetch you some tea and crumpets."

Mackay knew better than to comply. Knew a serpent when he heard its hiss, but according to his sources the boy named Burch had just arrived there two days before. Not too long to bring him back from the brink. Not too long to find his soul.

He took a long step across the broken threshold.

Inside, it was dark and musty. Debris was scattered across the bare wood floor. He scanned it briefly. No children were in sight, but a slim woman stood against the far wall with her back to them. She was dressed in a ragged, grey frock facing a window that had long ago lost its panes.

"Here we are. Home sweet home. It looks a bit rough now, but . . . Swift!" His tone took on a bright menace. "I believe I told you to clean up this mess."

Mackay's heart thumped at the sound of the name, stopped as she turned towards them.

It was her in flesh and blood. The lass who had struck him unconscious. The lass who had stolen the kirk's alms. But what had they done to her? There was a welt on her temple and purple bruises stretched like long fingers across her throat. Chains encircled her ankles, chafing the skin of her bare feet, but her eyes were the same, sparking with intellect, snapping with life.

Their gazes met with a clash. For a second there was something there. Hope or regret or fear. He wasn't sure which, but in a moment she turned to Cryton and smiled. "Go to hell." Her voice was as softly melodious as he remembered.

The villain's lips curved into a snarl. Then he leapt across the floor and struck her across the face. She staggered back, hitting the wall with a sickening thud.

The sheer violence of it stole Mackay's breath away, but Cryton was moving again, grabbing her by the hair, drawing back his fist for another strike.

Without being entirely aware he had moved, Mackay crossed the distance and caught the villain's wrist, twisting hard, then turning to watch the room at large.

"Hey!" Sil yelled. "Let him go 'less you want your brains spattered clear to Holyrood."

Mackay stood perfectly still, eyes steady on the man with the pistol. "I'm a man of peace." The words were more for himself than anyone. A mild reminder not to snap the other's arm like a dry chicken bone. "Don't make me do something for which I must pay penance."

"Get your fookin' hands off me!" Cryton snarled.

Mackay smiled. The expression felt predatory and tight. *"That which cometh out of the mouth, this defileth the man."*

"What the devil are you talking about?" Cryton hissed, bent away at the waist.

"I'm talking about you telling the tall scrawny lad there to put the gun down."

"Go to—"

Mackay cranked up his arm a little, refusing to enjoy the other's whimper of pain.

"Sil!" he shrieked. "God dammit, drop the pistol."

"But—"

"Drop it!"

Mackay watched it hit the floor and drew a careful breath through his nose. "Now tell the other scrawny lad to drop the knife."

"He ain't got no—"

A little more pressure on his arm. "Tell him."

"Kerry!"

An eight-inch blade struck the hardwood.

"Much better."

"You're dead, you're worse than dead," Cryton snarled, but Mackay ignored him.

"I've changed me mind," he announced to the room, looking at no one in particular. "I want the lass there instead of the boy."

A slow smile spread across Cryton's pale complexion. "Titties like that could make a saint randy, aye?"

Mackay refrained from shattering the bone, though it was a close thing. "You'll let her go," he said.

"The fook I will. She was poaching goods on my turf."

"Leave her to me. She'll poach no more."

"Going to keep her too busy on her back to—" he began, then grunted in pain.

"Unchain her and I'll give you the coin intended for the lad."

Cryton sniggered. "You're bad cooked, old—"

"What lad?" Swift asked.

Mackay didn't turn towards her, though he heard her chains clatter as she moved. "Release her," he ordered.

"What lad?" she asked again and strode towards him, links jangling. He glanced at her against his will. Anger burned like acid at the sight of her bruises.

"Good Brother Brenan here comes to our side of town to buy a fair-haired lad now and again," Cryton said.

"Why?" Her eyes were steady.

"Why do you think, girl?" Cryton asked and made a rude gesture with the arm that wasn't trapped behind his back.

Her face paled as she turned towards Mackay. "Is that true?"

He said nothing in his defence.

"The boy in the kirk . . ." She paused as if remembering back. "The one eating bread and jam . . ." She cleared her throat. "The one you called Rye. He was one of them?"

"I did not bring him from here," Mackay said.

"But you took him in. Fed him."

"Maybe he likes his slaves fat when he foo—" Cryton began, then shrieked in pain.

Swift jerked her gaze from Cryton to Mackay. "Tavis . . . you'll find him in Newberry House on Wendy Close. Take him. He's a good lad. Kind-hearted. Take him before stench like this get their hands on him.

"Stench am I?" Cryton snarled.

"Go *now!*" Swift pleaded. "Before . . ."

But just then there was a sliver of noise from behind, a momentary warning. Mackay twisted about. A pistol appeared against the mouldering window frame. Fire exploded from its muzzle. Pain seared the side of his head. Swift screamed He stumbled backwards. Something struck him from behind, and then he fell, dropping into darkness.

"Are you alive?" a voice hissed.

Mackay opened his eyes, but it did little good. The world was as black as old sins. His head pounded with pain, his body throbbed with feverish heat.

"Wake up." The voice again, whispered from deep shadows. But he recognized it as Swift's. It was still melodious though it had lost the polished sheen he'd first heard from her lips.

"Where am I?" His own voice was barely human, guttural with pain, rusty with disuse.

"The cellar."

Thoughts swirled murkily in his head. Memories streamed past. "Beneath Cryton's hovel?"

"Aye."

"And the lads he keeps?"

"Upstairs."

He nodded. She exhaled quietly as if she'd been holding her breath.

"For such a brawny big bloke, you go down terrible easy, Highlander." Her words may have been sardonic, but her voice trembled, cranking up a little guilt for the worry he had caused her. "Do you oft let others knock you unconscious?"

He raised a hand, testing the wound. Pain shot through him, but the bullet seemed to have just grazed his skull. As luck went, that was as good as his was likely to get. "'Tis a poor habit of mine. That I see now."

"And little else in this damnable hole. Why the devil—"

"*This defileth the man.*" he quoted numbly. His head rocked with pain.

She was silent for a moment. "You don't approve of cursing?"

"Nay, but this seems the proper place for it if there be such a thing."

"Can you sit?"

He shifted, trying. It took all his effort, but finally he was slumped against the rocky wall. She sat beside him, leaning her head against the damp stone. He saw now for the first time that she was chained again and realized that he was too.

"Are you well?" he asked.

"Well?" There may have been humour in her voice, which did not seem quite right considering the circumstances. "They've taken my hard-won baubles. I'm chained to a wall, and . . . oh, Cryton plans to kill me upon his return, but otherwise, aye, I'm fair to middling."

"Why would he wish you dead?"

"You heard him, Highlander," she said. "I was picking pockets in his territory. And doing a rather handsome job of it."

"If you're good at the task, wouldn't he be wiser to use your skills than kill you?"

"Wiser?" she said and laughed a little. "Aye, I'll mention that to him. He's sure to see sense."

Mackay exhaled wearily. "Me apologies," he said.

"Apologies?" Her voice was soft.

"For this . . ." He motioned towards the darkness. "I did not mean to cause you trouble."

She was silent for a long moment. "What *did* you mean, Highlander?"

He remained silent.

"Why did you come? Truly."

A fine question. He glanced to his right, perhaps looking for a way out, but there was little to see. "To make amends, mayhap."

"I believe I struck *you.*"

So she had, clever little nymph. Truth to tell, he didn't oft allow that to happen. He must be getting old. "Amends to God," he corrected. "Or mayhap . . ." He shook his head. It hurt. "Mayhap to the world at large if there be no god."

She didn't seem to wish to argue religion. "So you truly do take in lads."

"I've no wish to see them end up to be the likes of me."

She was silent for a moment. "Foolish enough to let themselves be bested twice in one week?"

He snorted softly. That hurt too. "Without skills," he said. "Good for naught but killing."

"Is that what you are then?"

"'Tis what they wished me to be. 'Tis why they sent me to battle. To war. And war *is* killing," he said. "Little matter how you dress it in pageantry and honour. 'Tis naught but murder made legal. But the murderers are allowed to walk free. Nay, are honoured as if they were heroes and not beasts sent to slaughter the—" His voice failed him. He pressed his eyes closed.

"You are no beast," she whispered.

When he opened his eyes, he saw that she sat a little closer.

"You know not what I've done, lass. I have—" he began, but she reached up and cupped his cheek with her palm. Her touch was warm and tender.

"I know you came to save a boy you've not met," she whispered.

"'Tis only—" he began again, but she trailed a finger across his lips.

"I know you would have saved me."

For a moment he was lost in her eyes, but he would not allow himself to be soothed. He shook his head.

"Do not make me out to be sommat I am not."

"Very well. But I insist you do the same. You are not a beast," she whispered and he wished to believe.

"What am I then, lass?"

She smiled a little. "You are a man," she said. "The good and the bad of it. But in you . . ." She splayed her fingers gently across his cheek. "I think there is more good."

"Then ye are mistaken."

She was silent for a moment. "And here I was thinking the scriptures mentioned something of forgiveness."

"As it turns out, I am not well suited for that sort of thing. For myself or others," he said and she laughed.

"Something amuses ye, lass?'

"Tell your stories to someone who didn't see you spare Cryton. Or me, come to that."

He ignored the latter part of her statement. "Mayhap you forgot his minions were armed."

"They were not armed like you," she said and slipping her hand from his cheek, ran it down his biceps. "No," she said. "You are good. Better than this world deserves."

Their gazes met. A thousand hopeless wishes soared momentarily between them. Each was more foolish than the last, and yet he could not resist kissing her.

Their lips met with careful warmth, pressed, held, healed.

She drew back, breathless. "You're rather good at that for a priest, Highlander."

"Postulant hopeful," he corrected.

She smiled, then sobered and slipped her hand across his chest and on to his throat. Her fingers seemed to burn there. "I've a favour to ask."

He nodded once. It was all he could manage. How long had it been since he'd felt a kind woman's touch?

"Will you take Tav to the kirk where you reside?"

He drew a careful breath through his nostrils. "The boy on Wendy Close."

"Aye."

He lifted an arm. A chain drooped from it. "I fear I've no means to do so, lass."

She nodded stiffly, lavender eyes painfully solemn in the darkness. "If I can free you, will you care for him?"

"If we are free why not care for him your—"

A scrape of noise from above stopped his words.

"Shh!" She jerked towards the sound, then scooted closer, lips all but touching his ear. "Cryton will return in a minute." He could feel her shiver. "To gloat and to . . ." She paused. "He likes untried girls. He'll not kill me before he takes me."

Mackay sat very still, absorbing her words and trying to remain calm. But the beast in him was already rearing its vengeful head.

"He'll have the keys to our chains on his person. I can filch them and toss them to you."

"I cannot kill him, lass," he said, but even in the darkness he could discern the welt on her temple and felt rage flare through him like flame set to pitch. "Though I ache to avenge the marks he put on . . ." He drew a deep breath. "I've made a vow."

"That I know," she whispered, pressing closer still. "You're a good man. A kind man. I do not ask you to bloody your hands. In fact, you must not. You must muffle the sound of the keys and wait. Promise me. He's got underlings. More than you know. He'll take me above. He likes an audience and it's too close down here. We'll leave this hole. But you must stay. They'll think you still confined. Wait till the house goes quiet."

He pulled her hand from his lips, feeling the deep tremble in his own body. "So I should wait till you're dead?" he asked, his voice all but lost in the darkness. "Wait till he's taken your innocence and your life before—"

She breathed a laugh. "I'm no innocent, Highlander. You know that as well as any. I'm a thief. A good one. In truth, I'm the best. And for that he'll let me live."

"You lie. He'll—"

" . . . our guests." Cryton's laughing voice rang from upstairs. His footfalls thudded across the floor.

"Lie down," she hissed and shoved him.

He wanted to argue, to resist, to save her. But with the sudden movement, his head spun. He slumped to the floor.

The trap door creaked open.

"Do you need help down there, Cryton?"

"Not from the likes of you, Knobby," he said, and hanging a lantern on a peg on the nearby wall, descended. "Well then . . ." His voice was jovial with success and stale beer. "I see you've waited for me, luv."

Swift rose to her feet, shielding her eyes against the glare of the lantern. Fear made her limbs stiff, hope made her eager. "Let me go."

"Of course." He chuckled. "Of course I will, luv."

"Now. Before he regains his strength," she said and jerked a nod towards the Highlander.

Cryton's brows rose. His perfect teeth gleamed in the lantern light. "So Snake didn't kill him?" he asked and kicked Mackay's heavy leg.

She prayed he would remain still. He didn't disappoint her. "No, he's not dead," she said. "But it's not too late."

"Ho, I didn't realize you were such a bloodthirsty wench."

"I'm not bloodthirsty. Not like him," she said.

"Him?" He laughed. "I think you're lying to me, sweet Swift. He's a man of peace. Said so hisself."

"And I suppose you're daft enough to believe he won't kill me because—"

He struck her across the mouth. For a moment, the world went grey. She stumbled backwards, pressing shaky knuckles to her bleeding lips.

"Does he look like a saint to you, Cryton?" she asked, forcing herself to speak past the panic. "He's a warlord. A mercenary. He's killed more men than you've robbed. Children too. And women. He told me so himself. Bragged about it."

"Truly?" His tone was intrigued. Thrilled even.

"I swear it's true. He plans to have me, to use me up and murder me."

"You don't say. Why you?"

"I stole from him."

"From a man of God?" He crowed with laughter. "Jesus Christ, you're even more of a bitch than I imagined."

"I stole from him in his church. Shamed him. He's obsessed. Said no other man will ever touch me."

"Did he now?" he asked, and kicked the Highlander again. This time he moaned. "Is that true, old man?"

Mackay rose groggily to one elbow. "Leave her be." His voice was little more than a growl.

"I fear I can't do that." Cryton laughed. The sound was hollow and empty in the narrow space. "She's mine," he said, and reaching out, grabbed her by the hair.

Pain thundered through her scalp, skittered down her neck, chasing fear before it. "Get me out of here," she hissed, "I'll do whatever you wish."

"Believe this, lass," he snarled. "You'll take my orders little matter what I do."

Swift braced herself, playing every card she held as she looked up through her lashes at him. "But how much better would it be if I were willing?" she asked and skimmed one chained hand down his chest to his crotch.

"You want it now?"

"Soon," she said and squeezed. The keys were inches away, bulging in his pants' pocket. "When we're alone." There was no better way to convince him to stay than to ask him to leave. That she knew.

He pressed up against her. "I rather like the idea of him watching," he said and reaching up, ripped her ratty gown down the front.

She couldn't stop the gasp of disgust that rattled from her throat as he pushed her against the wall, but covered it with as moan as she pressed her head against the stone behind her and grappled with his trousers.

"Leave her!" the Highlander snarled, but in that instant she nipped the keys from Cryton's pocket. It was a simple thing. A beautiful thing. For a fraction of a moment she dipped inside, then cupped him intimately with her left hand as she flicked the keys towards Mackay with her right. They sailed silently through the dimness, but her chains impeded the throw. The keys soared for an instant too long, sailing past Mackay's outstretched fingertips to clatter like wind-swept hail against the rocky floor.

For a moment the world went absolutely silent. Cryton turned with careful precision to stare at the keys, then, "You bitch!" he snarled and hit her.

She stumbled back, struck the wall and crumpled, but he was already reaching for her, pulling her to her feet, hitting her again.

She saw Mackay lurch away, grappling for the keys, but his chains snatched him up short.

"You conniving cow!" Cryton rasped and kicked her in the ribs. Pain screamed through her.

Mackay strained towards the keys, but Swift could no longer concern herself with his escape. She scrambled along the wall. Cryton came after her. Slavering with rage, he kicked her again. She sprawled forwards, found her hands and knees and lurched on.

Cryton strode after her, cocky, enraged, and in that moment, the Highlander rose to his feet and lunged towards them.

Cryton was still moving forwards as Mackay swung his arm wide. His chains whipped up and out, encircling Cryton's neck like a loop.

His eyes popped wide. "Sil!" His voice was warbled but loud.

Footsteps clattered above.

"They'll kill you," Cryton rasped, grimacing a smile as he grappled to free himself. "They'll kill you, then fook her till—"

Mackay snapped the links tight against the other's throat. Bones cracked. Cryton jerked spasmodically, eyes bulging, then hung still, suspended by the chains.

Mackay let him fall just as a half dozen others dropped to the floor nearby.

One of them fired a shot. Sparks sputtered in every direction as they struck the wall and ricocheted madly.

Swift screamed. Mackay roared in rage, wrapped his arms in his chains and heaved.

The restraining metal rings popped from the walls just as two men leapt at him, knives drawn. Another bullet hissed past his ear. But in less than thirty seconds, the dungeon went silent.

Seven bodies lay motionless on the floor.

The Highlander staggered, starring dazedly at the carnage. "I'm a man of peace," he whispered. Swift unlocked the last of her chains and stumbled towards him.

"Highlander."

He turned towards her, eyes haunted. "Peace," he said again. His voice was broken, his expression shattered, and she cupped his beloved face in her palm.

"They would have tortured me, Highlander. Tortured and killed me as they've done to others."

"There are better ways . . ."

"Yes," she said. "Yes, sometimes. But not this time. This time your strength was necessary."

He shook his head, but she stilled the motion with a trembling hand. "The boys upstairs will live because of you. Tavis will live," she said.

He looked at her as if seeing her for the first time since Cryton's arrival. "How many lads are there?"

"Five at last count."

He winced. "I can't care for—"

"Six counting Tav."

He shook his head, seeming more himself. "I have funds to help them," he said. "But they'll need more than coin. They're damaged. Broken—"

"We'll mend them," she whispered.

He lowered his eyes to hers.

"We'll mend *us*," she whispered and kissed him.

His Magick Touch

Kimberly Killion

One

Scotland, Inner Hebrides,1587

The bastard was finally going to kill her.

Sorcha trembled inside her wool mantle as icy wind thrashed strands of brown hair over her face. The rope binding her wrists stung, and her battered legs ached where Hector had pushed her down the steps of the keep. But none of it compared to the fear clutching her insides. She craned her neck over her shoulder and gawked wide-eyed at the white waves pummelling the base of the cliff.

"Ye destroyed my crops with hail, infested the clan's meat with maggots, and set the outbuildings afire. 'Tis August, yet snow blankets my land." Hector pressed her closer to the pebbled edge with his dark glare and intimidating size. He stood a full head taller and easily outweighed her by ten stone. "And now this." He held up his sword arm covered with lesions of oozing pus. "Ye give me a whore's disease!"

"I did naught, m'lord. I swear it," Sorcha pleaded between chattering teeth. She considered reminding him that he hadn't come to her bed in over two years, but knew 'twas useless to defend herself. Hector had blamed her for every misfortune that befell Clan Ranald since he'd taken her to wife four years past.

"Ye lying bitch!" He struck her hard across the face with the back of his hand.

Sorcha twisted at the waist and landed on her knees and elbows. The pain stinging her cheek was soon forgotten when Hector kicked her in the side. She heard her rib crack just before an unbearable streak of pain shot through her very core. She couldn't fight, couldn't think, couldn't breathe. The coppery tinge of blood spread over her tongue as she rolled on to her stomach. She spit a string of crimson and pulled herself forwards by her bound hands.

"Think ye I dinnae hear ye chant your spells in the old language?" Hector wrenched her back to her feet.

If she were half the witch he accused her of being, then she might possess the power to save herself. She wished da hadn't ousted grandmum from the clan before she taught Sorcha the Pagan ways.

"Ye have cursed me and my clan for the last time," he bellowed over the howling wind.

"If ye kill me," she panted through the pain, trying to draw upright to stare him in the eye, "my kin will avenge me." 'Twas a false threat, but she was desperate.

A deep throaty chortle burst from Hector's pocked face. "Your da died before naming a tanist to reign in his stead. The MacNeils have no chieftain, no bloodline, save for a sixteen-year-old girl. And your sister will be easy to break."

Sorcha's heart lodged in her throat. The horrid images of what Hector would do to her sister erupted in her mind's eye like a nightmare. Peigi would be powerless to defend herself against Hector and his men.

"As soon as I send ye to your Otherworld, I'll be claiming the Isle of Barra as my own."

Sorcha looked to the grey sky and pleaded with the king of her gods. *Thou Christ of the cross, snatch me from the snares of this evil demon so I might protect my kin.*

A bird cawed overhead, circling them. 'Twas a falcon – a white falcon. Mayhap the Goddess Cliodna had come to escort her to the afterlife.

"Fare thee well, Sorcha of Barra. I'll see ye in Hell." Hector raised his foot high and drove the sole of his boot into her stomach, sending her reeling over the edge of the cliff.

Shock numbed her insides. She wanted to hold on to something, to scream, but she could do neither. Her body seemed to fall faster than her soul, and for one breathtakingly frightening moment, she felt as though her physical being separated from her spirit.

Through it all, she kept her eyes fixed on that white falcon following her downward to her death.

"Heave!" Keiran of Barra bellowed the order to his kinsmen pulling on the oars as he cursed Sorcha's grandmum for not sending him sooner. They were close, but were they close enough to save her?

Standing at the bow of a three-masted carrack staring into thick grey mist, Keiran held fast to the magick thread connecting him to his animal spirit. Through his falcon's eyes, he watched Laird Ranald strike Sorcha. When the poxed pig kicked her, Keiran's fingertips dug into the wooden rail. *Get up! Crawl away from him.*

His falcon, Tàiseal, cried a warning above the scene, just before the cur pushed Sorcha over the cliff's edge.

Keiran's heart jumped against his ribs. "*Bluidy-faugh!*" He snapped his chin over his shoulder and ordered the MacNeil warriors again, "Heave! Heave!", louder this time.

Two heartbeats later, the bowsprit broke through the thick mist. He pushed the falcon's aerial view from his head and watched as Sorcha disappeared into the white waves.

Gasps issued overhead from the topmen perched like gulls in the rigging.

"Oh, Brigid, protect her," Keiran begged the High Mother Goddess as he unsheathed his weapons – a broadsword, two daggers, and a *sgian dubh* – tossing them to the deck. His entire body shook as he heeled off his deerskin boots. He couldn't let her die. Aside from being the queen of his clan, she'd held the key to his heart since she was but ten and six.

"Have ye lost your wits, mon?" Sileas stepped on to the prow, pulling a fur cap tighter over his bushy copper hair. "Ye cannot swim faster than they can row. Besides, you'll freeze to death afore ye reach her."

"If they keep rowing, the bow will splinter on the rock. Stop the starboard rowers and turn the *Cerridwen* around." Keiran pulled his plaid over his head. "Send a long boat. I'm going after her." He stepped up on the rail and dived headlong into the frigid water.

His eyes pinched tight. Tiny needles of ice pricked his body, seizing his muscles, but his spirit urged him on. He burst out of the water and spun in circles, searching for her, but could see naught through the mayhem of rolling foam. Tàiseal screeched overhead, and Keiran immediately tapped into the falcon's vision.

Sorcha clung to the edge of a rock nigh ten feet away from him. A swell broke over her, mocking her efforts to survive, but she was alive. Hope gave him the strength he needed to close the space between them. He kicked and pushed the water behind him until he could see her with his own eyes. Keiran reached for her just as another swell crashed over and pulled her beneath the surface.

Sorcha! He dived deep, refusing to return to the surface without her. Salty brine scoured his eyes, but he dared not close them and lose sight of the dark silhouette descending into the abyss. Pressure squeezed his chest. Just as he feared he would fail, a powerful force clutched his back like a sorcerer's claw and pushed him deeper.

Sorcha's hair feathered across his fingers. He kicked his feet and hooked his arm beneath her breasts. His legs burned with the added weight, but having her in his arms gave him the strength he needed to haul her back to the surface.

Air. Sweet, cool air. He gasped for it, choked on it as he wrenched Sorcha out of the water. Holding her lifeless body against his chest, he located the long boat only feet away. Within seconds, the hands of his kinsmen grasped at him and Sorcha, heaving them over the edge of the boat.

She lay still as stone in a bundle of sodden wool. Her dark hair coiled in a web around her face. An ashen tint darkened the skin beneath her eyes, and her lips were quickly turning blue.

"She is dead," Sileas announced as the others rowed them towards the *Cerridwen*.

Keiran cleared the hair from her mouth, refusing to believe Sileas's words. Her memory had kept him alive all those years he'd spent on the battlefield. She'd been his light of hope and he'd be damned if he would let that light be doused forever.

He flattened his hand over her chest and used the healing technique Magda had taught him to move the water out of Sorcha's lungs.

She convulsed – thank the gods – and spewed salt water from her lungs like a geyser. She gasped for air, choking, coughing, gagging. Blood raced through her veins, turning the hue of her skin from pale grey back to creamy white in an instant.

Relief swept through Keiran as did a smidgen of arrogance. He grinned at Sileas. "She is alive."

Sorcha opened her eyes. Her irises were not the bright blue-green he'd remembered. The colour had dulled, become distant. Confusion wrinkled her delicate brow and tore at his heart. Did she not know him?

Shivering, she clung to him with her bound hands, clawed at his undertunic like a frightened kit, then twisted to look up at the cliff where her husband stood watching. "Help me," she whispered, then collapsed in Keiran's arms.

Two

Sorcha decided the Otherworld was blessedly warm and smelled of sweet spices and leather and brine. A gentle to and fro sway rocked her body like she was a babe in arms. She wiggled slightly, searching for injuries, but nothing hurt, save for a faint pinch in her ribs. Aye, she was definitely dead.

She remembered falling, remembered her spirit reaching up towards the white falcon. Mayhap the goddess had taken her spirit before Sorcha's body hit the rock, saving her from the pain of death. Regardless of how it happened, 'twas a relief to be on the other side and free of Hector's abuse.

She snuggled deeper into a cocoon of furs and wrapped her arms around the warm body stretched out alongside her.

Warm body!

Her eyes snapped open. The warm body belonged to a man – a verra naked man. Her breasts smashed against his finely chiselled chest and the hairs on his thighs tickled hers. His clean scent told her he wasn't Hector as she briefly feared, but she knew not who he was. She tried to inch away from him, but he circled her small frame with thick-muscled arms.

"Be still and rest, Sorcha," he murmured in a deep husky voice then kissed the top of her head.

She sucked in an audible breath and looked up into amber eyes flecked with gold. She recognized those eyes. "I know ye."

His smile was familiar as well – crooked with a single dimple set in the right cheek. "Aye. Ye do."

He'd been two years her senior when he crawled over the curtain wall of Kisimul Castle to give her a satchel of eiderdown feathers for her sixteenth birthday. He'd been known by her kin as the Falconer of Barra. They were worlds apart in station: he, the son of a crofter, and she, the eldest daughter of the chieftain. He'd always reminded her he wasn't worthy of her affections, but that didn't stop him from seeking her out in secrecy the summer before he went to war.

"I taught ye how to skip a rock across the loch," he reminded her when she didn't respond. "And showed ye how to gig a frog," He held her chin and traced her bottom lip with the tip of his thumb. "And I gave ye your first kiss when ye were just a wee lass."

The memory of that kiss exploded in full colour in her head. She'd been so young, so naïve to believe they could have a future together. It seemed like a lifetime ago, but had only been seven years.

"Ye do remember me, aye?" He lifted her chin higher so she might study him better. He had a man's face now – a long lean nose, thick black brows, a high forehead. A coarse shadow darkened his strong jaw beneath sharply angled cheekbones.

"Keiran." She touched a bruise colouring the side of his face, not yet believing him real. Then her gaze dropped to his lips, so perfectly thick and lush and kissable. Her belly filled with sensations, like a school of minnows flipping and flopping on dry land. When his privy parts hardened against her thigh, she became very aware of their state of undress. "I remember ye with more clothes on."

He chuckled, but made no attempt to separate himself from the intimacy of their embrace. His hand slid over her hip and cupped her backside. "'Tis good to see ye again, Sorcha."

Mayhap he never returned from war. Mayhap the sea goddess sent him in her stead to collect Sorcha. "Are ye dead?"

"Nay." His chest bounced with laughter.

"Am I?" Her questions sounded foolish, but given the circumstances she felt justified. She couldn't have survived the fall, and if she did, she would have been bruised from head to toe at the very least. Yet, she felt right as rain.

"Ye almost died, but I saved ye." Pomp and pride lined his expression, but his arrogance was of little import at the moment.

She frowned, confused. Why had he been there? How had she known Hector was going to push her off the cliff? And why wasn't she in pain?

"Ye are safe now, Sorcha." He trailed the tips of his fingers up and down her spine, tickling her.

It felt good to be coddled, to be caressed. She'd longed for tenderness the whole of her life and could easily remain in his arms forever. Keiran had been the only person who'd ever made her feel like she was more than a piece of property. He'd vowed to protect her, but those had been the words of a boy who also promised her the moon for a kiss. The undeniable strength of his erection told her his desires were no longer so innocent. "Where are we and why are we naked?"

Keiran's grin was only half as wicked as his roaming hands. "We are on a ship bound for Barra, and we are naked because I had to warm ye, else ye might have froze to death."

"Thank ye for saving me." Sorcha sat up, pulling the furs with her, worried her gratitude wouldn't be enough payment for his heroics.

"'Tis a vow I made long ago." The light pouring into the small cabin showed her his muscular torso. Battle scars crisscrossed his abdomen, but what caught her attention more were the Pagan symbols covering his left arm like a decorative sleeve. The blue-black markings formed a design that wrapped over his shoulder and around a crucifix over his heart. Many of her kin had been raised as Christo-Pagans, but Keiran and she had both been forbidden by their Christian fathers to practice the Pagan ways.

When he reached for his undertunic, she saw a bruise wrapped around his wrist. Blue ovals tinted his forearm much like the ones Hector had given her when he'd dragged her to the cliff. She looked down at her own wrists where Hector had bound her hands. Not a smidgeon of colour tinted the skin. "Why am I not hurt?"

She caught Keiran wincing as he pulled on his undertunic and spun out of the small bed built into the bulkhead. "Because I took your pain."

Her brows popped up. Obviously, Keiran had gone against his father's wishes to practise the Pagan ways, which meant he was most likely dead.

"Dinnae look so surprised. I've spent the past nine months with Magda."

Sorcha eyed him curiously. "My grandmum is dead."

Keiran shook his head as he draped a blue and yellow plaid over his shoulder and began fingering the pleats into a thick leather belt. "Your grandmum is verra much alive and once again living at Kisimul Castle."

"'Tis not possible." Sorcha had been first in line to offer Grandmum a gift to take to the afterlife. "Ye were at her burial. Ye placed a feather on her grave."

"I know not who we buried that day, but 'twas not Magda." He tied the laces of his deerskin boots. "When I was at war on the mainland, I suffered from what should have been a fatal wound to the side. I was left for dead, but awoke some weeks later in your father's solar at Kisimul Castle. I have no memory of how I came to be there, but Magda nursed me back to health and taught me the Pagan ways while I was abed. Three days past, she sent me to collect ye."

Sorcha struggled to believe his tale, but found herself weakened by the hope that Grandmum was alive and protecting Peigi.

He handed Sorcha a dry undertunic. "Magda is waiting for ye to come home and lead the clan."

"I cannot lead the clan." Sorcha shook her head adamantly. The man was a dunderheid if he thought her capable of such a task.

Both Keiran's brows slid up. He set himself in front of her, then ran his fingers up and down the column of her neck. "Then ye will name a tanist to reign in your stead."

His intentions suddenly became very clear. Had he cared for her at all, he wouldn't have waited til Da died to save her from Hector. He'd always been determined to change his stars. An invisible wall of protection wrapped around her heart as she realized he'd saved her now because he wanted her title. No man had ever wanted her for herself. Da had traded her for an alliance. Hector had married her for land. And now Keiran intended to seduce her with gentle caresses for the power of the chieftainship.

She jammed her fists into the sleeves of the tunic. "I suspect ye think I'll name ye tanist."

"'Tis my hope that ye will find me worthy of the position." His smug grin set her teeth on edge.

S'truth, other clans had named tanists outside of their chieftain's heirs. However, Clan MacNeil had remained true to its bloodline for generations. Regardless of her viewpoint on the matter, she intended to refuse him simply because he'd hurt her. "Unless the laws of our clan have changed, there are only two men who can lay claim to the chieftainship: my husband or Peigi's."

Keiran stared at her, head shaking slightly, lips parted to protest, but she didn't give him the opportunity to sway her with words.

"If the chieftainship is what ye desire, then mayhap ye should set your silver tongue loose on Peigi. She's of marriageable age now." Pent-up anger made Sorcha spout such foolishness.

Keiran's amber eyes darkened, his brows pinched tight in the middle. "I dinnae want Peigi. I want ye."

"I already have a husband," she hissed, knowing hurt drove her words now. Hector never loved her, nor had he been kind by any stretch of the word. S'truth, he'd been a wretched husband, but he taught her one thing during their marriage. "If I live long enough to become a widow, I can assure ye, I'll never take another husband."

Keiran stared at her for long moments before he sheathed his weapons and strode towards the door. "Should ye have need for anything, m'lady, I'm here to serve ye."

Everything Keiran had done in the past seven years had been for her. He'd trained to be a warrior, for her. He'd fought and killed for the clan, for her. He'd learned her religion, and the foolish wench couldn't see that he'd done it all for her.

The afternoon air did nothing to ease his frustration as he paced the quarterdeck, all the while cursing the tenderness in his side. He'd taken her pain away. He'd saved her life. And she accused him of doing it all for the chieftainship.

"Ye seem to be frettin' over a'thing." Sileas descended the steps of a companionway, then leaned against the rail. "Has your woman fallen ill?"

"Nay, she is well. But she is not my woman, nor is she keen on naming me tanist."

"She remains faithful to the old laws," Sileas guessed and rolled a slender piece of wood from one side of his mouth to the other.

Keiran nodded.

"Then we go back and make her a widow," Sileas suggested without pause.

Keiran hadn't raised his broadsword since Leckmelm. His sword arm shook just thinking about what he'd done. "She will think I killed her husband for power."

"The cur pushed her off a bluidy cliff. Ye would be avenging her."

As much as Keiran relished the idea of seeing the man dead, his main goal was to get Sorcha to the stronghold where she would be safe. "We need to be patient. Give her time to see how things have changed."

"The clan has been without a chieftain for too long, and the kinsfolk living on Barra support ye." Sileas retrieved a flask out of his plaid and tipped it to his cracked lips. "What ye did in Leckmelm was foolish, but it earned ye the respect of the clan."

"What did he do in Leckmelm?"

Startled, Keiran spun on his heel. "Sorcha."

"M'lady." Sileas bowed as if she were the bluidy queen, which in all manner of speaking, she was. "'Tis good to have ye aboard. We should have ye safe at Kisimul Castle come the morrow."

"Thank ye." Sorcha offered Sileas a small smile, then redirected her gaze at Keiran. The fury that had fired her blue-green eyes earlier that morning seemed to have softened. Mayhap she regretted the heated words that passed between them.

Keiran now realized he'd been overzealous to think she would be the same person he'd known seven years past. She'd been beaten and used and thrown away like rotted meat. 'Twould take time to gain her trust again.

"Might I offer ye my sympathies regarding the loss of your father." Sileas kept his head lowered and his eyes on his boots. "He was an apt leader."

"My father was a pig," she snapped back. "He married my mother because she shared blood with the chieftain, and then he sold me off to further his gain. Ye need not glorify his name on my behalf."

"Forgive me, m'lady." Sileas side-stepped around the woman and gave Keiran a sympathetic look as he took his leave.

"Think ye I am like your father?" Keiran reached for her, but she angled her body away from him.

"Ye want the chieftainship. I suspect it is something ye have craved since we were in our youth." Her matter-of-fact tone scraped over his nerves like screaming gulls.

Keiran blew air out through his nostrils and shook his head in objection. "If ye think my affections for ye are part of some plan to acquire the chieftainship, then ye are wrong."

The irritable woman obviously needed more time to think. He pushed past her and dropped down the afthatch. He stalked across the gunnerdeck, down another two ladderways, and into the storage chamber where he'd left his satchel of spices. By the time he heard the swishing of her skirts, he was grinding coltsfoot, comfrey and garlic cloves with a stone pestle and mortar.

"I wasn't finished speaking to ye."

"Ye always were one to argue a'thing to death." How had he forgotten that annoying trait?

"'Tis not true." Sorcha rounded the barrel where he worked, her eyes wide, innocent.

"Nay?" He stopped crushing the herbs. "Ye once argued with me for a sennight that the puffin stayed with a single mate for life."

"The puffin do stay with a single mate for life." Her small chuckle washed away the tension. "Forgive me. I've not had anyone to toss barbs with in quite some time."

"Nor I." Keiran broke the connection between them. Being with Sorcha was like taming the falcon. It required devotion, finesse and patience. He then reminded himself of the reward. The thrill he'd experienced the day Tàiseal returned from her first hunt was immeasurable. He drew a pentacle atop the barrel with a piece of coal and prayed Sorcha would one day find her way back to him.

"What are ye doing?"

"I'm about to cast a healing spell so I might rid myself of your wounds."

"'Tis something Grandmum taught ye?"

"Aye."

"How does it work?" As she watched him, he remembered that young curious girl who'd once looked at him like he was a king.

"On faith." He placed a silver coin in the northern direction of the five-pointed star, then offered her a mischievous smile just before he yanked out a few strands of her hair.

"Ow!" She rubbed her scalp. "What did ye do that for?"

"'Twill strengthen the spell." He lit the wick of a red candle on the southern tip of the star, then burned the ends of her hair and laid the remains on the eastern point. After adding water to the herbal mixture, he closed his eyes and focused on cleansing his spirit.

"What are ye doing now? Are ye praying?"

Damn distracting woman. He opened one eye momentarily. "I am attempting to free myself of negative energy. 'Twould be helpful if ye did the same."

"How?"

"Close your eyes and visualize the things that are sacred to ye. Use them to eliminate the burdens darkening your heart."

Less than a minute passed before Sorcha once again interrupted his meditation. "What do ye think of?"

He didn't open his eyes, focused as he was on the memory in his head. "I think of a lass with long sable hair racing across a meadow towards me. Her arms are open and her bright blue-green eyes are filled with a trust that brings light into my heart."

"Ye think of me?"

He nodded and hoped she believed him. Sorcha fell silent while he pushed his plaid and undertunic to his waist. He spread the herbal mixture over the bruises circling his wrists then proceeded to do the same for his rib. "I know ye dinnae trust me, but if ye are still in pain, I can help ye."

She lowered her eyes and contemplated his offer for long minutes before she finally admitted, "My side is tender."

'Twas a small victory, but a victory just the same. His hands shook as he pushed her kirtle off her shoulders and hooked the draped wool at her elbows. She turned her head and closed her eyes when he released the ties of her tunic and lowered the garment to her waist.

He swallowed hard, momentarily mesmerized by creamy white skin. Saliva pooled in his mouth as he watched her soft coral-coloured nipples harden into tight little buds. Then her heart began to visibly pound behind her breast.

Bluidy-faugh! He should have bound his cock to his thigh. He ignored the blood rushing to his groin and quickly spread the mixture over her side. Regardless of how desperately he wanted to take her into his mouth, he resisted the temptation, knowing lust would taint the spell.

Keiran flattened his palm over her rib and felt her tremble when he pulled her into his embrace. "I beseech Thee, Brigid, to help heal your kin." Sorcha's fingers curled around his forearm as he called upon the Great Goddess. "Surround us in Your radiant light, magick power pure and white." He began the chant:

"Fire flame and fire burn, make the mill of magick turn.
By all the power of three times three, transfer her pain into me.
Pains and aches and evil things, fly from us on rapid wings."

He repeated the incantation two more times and after the spell had been cast, he held Sorcha for long moments, wanting to bind her heart to his.

"Is it done?" she whispered, but remained firm in his hold.

"It is." He still didn't release her. "'Twill take some time for transfer."

"Keiran." She traced the blue-black designs marking his skin. "Is there a spell ye can cast to earn someone's trust?"

"Aye, but I would rather earn *someone's* trust without the aid of magick."

She looked up at him. The tears filling the rims of her eyes hurt him more than any blade ever had. "I have never been held by a man who didn't want something from me. My father wanted an alliance. Hector wanted my land. 'Tis difficult for me to believe ye are different."

He covered her breasts with her undertunic and pulled her plaid back in place on her shoulders, then he leaned in and pressed a kiss against each of her eyes. "The only thing I ever wanted from ye was your heart."

Three

Fear no longer owned her, and she was grateful to Keiran for setting her free of its binds.

Sitting on hillock surrounded by sweet-smelling orchids, Sorcha leaned back to let the summer sun warm her face. A dozen passing gulls flew overhead to the nearby sea, but the white falcon that had followed her home to Barra remained on guard atop the thatch roof of Keiran's childhood home. For the first time in four years she felt free.

Upon her arrival at Kisimul Castle a sennight past, she'd been greeted by her people with open arms – some she recognized, most she'd never seen before – but none had been more welcoming than her sister. Peigi had grown into her curves over the past four years, but was still very much a child in so many ways. It was upon seeing Peigi that Sorcha gathered the leaders of her clan into the council chamber and informed them of Hector's intention to seize Barra. The elders had respectfully waited for her to advise them, but she knew nothing of warfare. She knew not how to save Barra from the invasion that was coming, nor could she raise a broadsword to protect her land or her people.

But Keiran could.

She'd watched him aboard the *Cerridwen* with the MacNeil kinsmen and known he'd somehow earned their loyalty. They obeyed his commands without question and showed him the respect that was due a born leader. And he'd treated her with equal respect since the day he rescued her from Hector.

None had questioned her when she called Keiran out of the shadows of the council chamber and assigned him the task of protecting Barra. The following days, she watched him take command of his duty with vigour. He summoned tacticians and gathered the leaders of the mesnie in the Great Hall where they spread maps overtop the trestle tables and strategied a plan. Sorcha had kept Keiran's goblet filled and from time to time she nodded her approval for no other reason than to see him smile at her.

He didn't need noble blood to lead the clan, nor did he need her to name him tanist. He was already playing the role of chieftain, and he did it while paying her the respect of a queen. He walked behind her, bowed to her, and referred to her by the epithet deserving of her status. Come eventide, he would escort her to her solar, bid her good night, and leave her to seek her slumber alone.

Last night, she'd wanted him to stay. She wanted him to hold her like he'd done that first night on the ship. She wanted to feel his strong arms around her and know the tenderness of his touch. But she'd been a coward and said naught to draw him into her chamber.

Sorcha lay back in the cool grasses, splayed her arms out, and inhaled the floral scent that was Barra. She must have dreamed of this place a thousand times while living under Hector's thumb. In her mind's eye she saw herself standing in the open doorway of the croft-house with her and Keiran's bairns tugging at her skirt.

The image warmed her heart. She could have been happy here in the valley, tending a family and loving Keiran. She wished her life had been different. She wished she'd been born a peasant and could have chosen her own husband. She would have chosen Keiran and given herself to him willingly.

The memory of her first coupling with Hector forced its way into her head. She'd been too fearful to fight him. She'd laid in her marriage bed like a cold fish the first time and every time thereafter. Fortunately, Hector had turned to the whores to tend his needs very early on in their marriage.

Making love to Keiran would be different, she decided. No doubt he would be a gentle lover, one who would kiss her with passion and touch her with tenderness. She imagined making love to him beneath a canopy of stars. 'Twas an image she wanted to burn into her memory, even if it was a fantasy. She needed something to push Hector out of her head.

"M'lady."

She opened her eyes to find her dream lover peering down at her.

Unfortunately, his pinched expression was far different from the one he'd been wearing behind her closed eyes.

"Keiran." She smiled up at him, excited to have him near, but her good mood didn't smooth the harsh lines carved into his cheeks.

"Ye should be at the stronghold. Ye must remain guarded at all times." He squatted beside her, still scowling.

"My guard is perched atop the croft-house." She continued to grin.

He rolled his eyes and exhaled a heavy breath. "Why did ye come here?"

"I needed to fill my heart with positive energy."

"Are ye ill?" He set the backs of his fingers over her forehead. "Ye are hot. We should seek out Magda."

Sorcha eyed him warily. She had hoped to reunite with Grandmum, but she hadn't been at Sorcha's homecoming, nor had the woman shown herself at the council meeting. Although later Keiran had sworn on his life that she'd been present at both. Sorcha held no desire to argue with him again on the subject of her Grandmum, be she dead or alive.

"I'm not ill." She sat up. "On the ship, when ye were casting the healing spell, ye asked me to visualize the things that are sacred to me. I had none, save for Peigi."

Keiran gave her a sidelong glance. "And ye came here to . . ."

"I came here to remember."

Keiran unsheathed his broadsword and stretched out his long lean legs beside her. He gestured towards the croft-house. "Ye wanted to remember a raw-boned woman who feared her abusive husband so much that she starved herself to death?" He snorted. "These are the things I try to forget."

Sorcha knew Keiran struggled with his upbringing, but it shaped him into the man he was today. His desire to protect made her trust him. "Do ye still live here?"

"Nay. I guard Kisimul now." Keiran curled her hair over her ear. "And my queen."

"I am no queen." Sorcha hugged her knees, her insides swirling.

"Ye are to me."

The energy igniting between their locked eyes was a force she could no longer deny. It made her scalp tingle and her body hum. She wanted him to touch her again, but he lowered his eyes and tore a buttercup from its stem. He leaned back on his elbows and studied a pink and yellow horizon. "We are ready for him. I have ships positioned in the bay and men walking the parapet atop the keep."

"It won't be long now." Hector was coming. She could feel it in her bones. Every day they awaited his arrival was one day less she had with Keiran. "Ye might think yourself prepared, but Hector is conniving."

"I have no fear of him, nor do my kinsmen."

A small smile touched her lips. "The warriors of Barra respect ye as their leader," she pointed out, hoping he would tell her why. Unfortunately, he held tight to his tongue. Curiosity got the better of her. "What did ye do at Leckmelm?"

"I fought." He watched the puffins gathered on the shore.

"Ye did more than fight. I wish to know how ye earned the respect of my clan."

"*Your* clan?" He looked at her then and raised both brows. "I mean no disrespect, m'lady, but upon your return, did ye recognize all the members of *your* clan?"

Though she didn't appreciate his sardonic tone, she shook her head and waited for him to explain.

"Your da decided we needed to offer our support to our neighbouring clans so we sailed to the mainland to fight for the Kingdom of Ross. Battle after battle, we remained unconquered for we were a unit of five clans in all. After we defeated Clan Gunn at Leckmelm, we followed a group of MacLeod warriors into a village to reap the rewards of our victory. We were told to lay claim to anything we wanted and given orders to kill anyone who attempted to stop us."

"And someone did?" Sorcha's pulse kicked up a notch.

Keiran nodded, his eyes became distant. "Our enemy's womenfolk. We murdered their husbands and brothers and sons on the battlefield, and they had naught more to lose. Your da was eager to prove his prowess in front of the MacLeod chieftain and drove the kinsfolk out of their cot-houses with fire." He paused, his head shook slightly. "Their screams wake me at night even still."

Sorcha wanted to console him, but he held himself aloof.

"The bairns huddled in clusters and watched the curs beat their mams into submission. Then they separated the women into two groups: the ones they would kill and the ones comely enough to take with them."

Sorcha's breathing escalated. War was an ugly thing, and her heart wept for these women and their bairns. But her pity was not nearly as intense as the anger pushing her fingernails into her palms. She expected nothing less from her father, but Keiran must have done something to prevent it. "What did ye do?"

"I wanted no part in it, but your da ordered me and the other MacNeil warriors to take the women to the docks. We were expected to distribute the comely women equally on our allies' ships, and the older, less appealing women – whom your da conveniently deemed Pagans – were to be tied to the oars of the ships."

"Oh Christ! Stop. I dinnae wish to hear more." Sorcha felt ill. Shame washed through her. How could she possibly share blood with such a heinous man? She regretted pushing Keiran. There was nothing noble about what had happened in Leckmelm, nothing honourable, nothing worthy of respect.

"Ye wanted to know and will allow me to finish." Keiran grabbed her wrist when she tried to stand and continued without her consent. "We loaded the women aboard the *Cerridwen* – all of them, then Sileas and I went back for their bairns."

Tears rolled down Sorcha's cheeks. Her heart swelled into her throat. Partly because Keiran had proven himself a champion and partly because she feared the words he'd not yet spoken. "Did they all survive?"

Keiran nodded and brushed the tears from her cheeks. "Sileas brought home sixty-seven women and one hundred and twenty-four bairns. Some of their men – the ones that survived – have since joined the clan."

"What happened to ye?"

Keiran only stared at her for long moments, a mixture of panic and resolve lined his worried face. His chest heaved. A muscle tightened in his jaw. The upset in his eyes sent spirals of icy fear coiling around her spine. She held his hand in both of hers and asked again, "Ye said Sileas brought them back to Barra. What happened to ye?"

"Your da and six of his loyal kinsmen caught us on the docks. I held them off until Sileas could escape out the inlet. I cut down my own kinsmen – your kinsmen – to protect my enemy." The tendons in his neck bulged. "Your da called me a traitor and ran me through with his sword."

Sorcha swallowed a gasp. Her unblinking eyes burned as unexpected fury roiled through her stomach.

"I should have died. I was choking on my own blood, when he

spit on me, and proclaimed himself the victor. But he didn't defeat me, Sorcha."

She heard Keiran's next words in her head before he ever spoke them. "I killed him."

The world stopped for a moment. Her pulse pounded like a drum between her ears. She was stunned, but felt no anger towards Keiran. Had Da loved her or treated her with the slightest amount of dignity, she might have given over to rage. Instead, she felt vindicated.

A flash of unexpected lightning startled her and the boom of thunder that immediately followed sent her into Keiran's arms.

"Come quickly." He pulled Sorcha to her feet, and they raced to the croft-house in front of a sheet of rain.

This storm was Magda's doing, Keiran decided as he watched the steady downpour out of a small window of the croft-house. His auld friend had done her best to force him and Sorcha into seclusion since their arrival, but her conjured rainfall couldn't have been more ill-timed.

He'd been patient with Sorcha, resisted the urge to kiss her every night, resisted the need to touch her, but most of all, he'd resisted the desire to tell her he loved her. And now, she had even more reason to think he only wanted her title. What could he possibly say that would convince her otherwise?

"Keiran." He felt the heat of her body before she touched his arm.

"I did not kill your father for his title," he blurted out. "Ye have to believe me."

"I believe ye."

Surprised by her quick response, he spun around to face her. "Ye do?"

"Ye are Clan MacNeil's champion." She rose up on her toes and brushed her lips over his. "And mine."

Her words and her kiss crushed the last of his resistance.

Keiran claimed her mouth with a fierceness he couldn't control. And Sorcha matched his intensity without a morsel of timidity. Tongues and teeth met, hands searching – he revelled in the reality of what had been a fantasy for far too long.

Desperate for air, he pulled away from her lips and slid his mouth down the column of her neck. She smelled like a shower of floral mist and tasted of sweet clover. Everything about her ripened his senses and heated his blood, especially the way she eagerly tugged at his garments.

His cock jerked beneath his plaid. Knowing his need would soon control him, he stilled her hands on his belt. "Are ye certain this is what ye want?"

She nodded, her eyes nigh shimmered with trust. "I want to know what it feels like to be touched by a man who loves me." When she threaded her fingers through his hair and pulled him back to her mouth, a shudder ripped through him.

Her acceptance was the greatest victory he'd ever known. His chest burned. His heart rejoiced. And his body demanded he claim her once and for all . . . and for ever.

His lips never left her mouth as they disrobed and fell atop the bed in a frenzy. He caressed her arms, her breasts, her hips, and kissed her from chin to navel. His body hummed with desire, thrilled at the sound of her whimpers as he stroked her silken flesh, preparing her for what was to come. Then at last, he settled between her thighs. With his manhood poised at her entrance, he asked the gods to bless their union then committed himself to her spiritually.

"Keiran." She cupped his jaw with both hands, her knees tightened against his hips. "Ye do love me, don't ye?"

If it took the rest of his life, he intended to erase the doubt furrowing her brow. He gently pressed his lips to her forehead. "I love ye more than Morrigan loves Her warriors." He kissed her chin. "I love ye more than Cailleach loves the earth." He bent low and nipped the hardened tip of each breast. "I love ye more than Brigid loves Her daughters." He then laced his fingers in hers and entered her.

She squeezed his hands as she cried out like a virgin on her wedding night.

He bore the ache seizing his loins and waited for her to adjust to him. "Like the puffin, I am now your mate for life."

She smiled then and arched her pelvis when he initiated the rhythm. With each thrust, she spread her legs a little wider, accepting him an inch at a time. She was tight and hot and slick and rippling along his length. She felt good, too bluidy good.

Sweat poured down his chest. His seed boiled in his groin, but he refused to seek fulfilment without her. He reached between their bodies and stroked that swollen pebble hidden inside her curls.

She stiffened. "Keiran, please stop. Something's wrong."

"Naught's wrong. In fact, 'tis verra right."

The first wave of her climax gripped him like a silken fist.

"Oh, Keiran!" she cried out her pleasure, dug her fingernails into his hand, and wrapped her legs around his waist. Hot liquid cascaded over him and triggered his own release.

After the last of his seed left him, he rolled to his back, taking her with him, not yet willing to break the connection between their bodies. Skin to sweat-slicked skin, he held her close in his embrace and waited for their hearts to slow. He kissed her hair and tickled her back while he listened to the dwindling patter of raindrops. A grin played at the corner of his lips. He would have to thank Magda for the rain.

Long minutes passed before Sorcha stirred to life. She lifted herself up and the look she wore was not one he'd ever seen on her before. 'Twas a saucy, mischievous expression. "I know not what ye did to me, but that was incredible."

"Aye. That it was." His body still tingled in the aftermath. His muscles were weak and sated, yet he felt invigorated knowing he'd been the first to ever satisfy her.

"I wish to do it again." She flicked his sensitive nipple with the tip of her tongue and rolled her pelvis round his groin.

"Now?" he questioned even as his cock responded to her movements.

"Now. Tonight. On the morrow . . ." The last of her words were drowned out by Tàiseal's cry.

"Wait." He stilled her rocking hips, closed his eyes, and flew with the falcon over the sea where he saw six ships on the horizon.

"What is it?" Sorcha asked, no doubt reading the worry on his face.

His eyes sprung open. "Your husband has arrived."

Four

"Heave!" Sileas ordered the rowers the moment Keiran stepped aboard the *Cerridwen*. "Did ye not hear the alarm, mon? Where the bluidy hell have ye been?"

Not even a war could lessen Keiran's spirits. He felt invincible, like he could rid the world of his enemies with the flick of his finger. He swaggered towards Sileas and assisted him with the rigging while the topmen overhead raised the canvas. "I've been . . . about."

"About? We're on the brink of battle and—" Sileas paused, stood upright, and scratched his thick copper beard. "Ye bedded her."

Keiran's grin was his only response.

"'Tis about bluidy time." Sileas smacked Keiran on the back then tied off the rope dangling from the yardarm. "The way the gods cling to your shoulders, she is likely already with child. And if she's anything like my Maura, then . . ."

With child. Keiran froze. The merriment fled from his person behind a rush of worry. Of course he wanted bairns – hordes of them – but he didn't want a single one born a bastard. He raked his fingers through his hair and surveyed twelve MacNeil ships forming a V on either side of the *Cerridwen*. "Send a signal to the fleet to take down all but the flagship. I've a personal vendetta to settle with Laird Ranald."

"I hope that vendetta involves making our queen a widow?"

Keiran bore his glare into the approaching ships. "Aye. That is does, my friend. That it does."

As the distance closed between the fleets, Keiran prayed to Morrigan to watch over him and his kinsmen and offered a similar prayer up to Brigid to protect Sorcha until his return. He then soared over Kisimul with Tàiseal and watched Sorcha pace the stone walkway behind the parapet. *Be safe, my love.*

"Load the cannons!" Sileas bellowed the order, drawing Keiran out of his thoughts.

Fully armed for combat, Keiran prepared himself mentally for hand-to-hand warfare. For the first time in his life he anticipated the battle with enthusiasm. He welcomed the moment he would slide his sword between Hector's ribs.

A dark cloud settled over them. Lightning ripped through the sky like clashing swords of gods in battle. He should have known Magda would play her part. Knowing she was with him empowered him all the more.

The first cannon fired with an announcing boom, and the battle began.

Hector's ships stood no chance against the MacNeil fleet. Soon, five of his six vessels were afire. The sea bawled with the oaths of dying men, but Keiran blocked out their pleas and prepared to invade the flagship. The air filled with clouds of acrid stench, scorching Keiran's eyes and lungs. Grey smoke enveloped everywhere, making it difficult to see when he tossed a four-hooked grappling iron over the wooden rail of the enemy ship. Keiran wrestled the ropes alongside his kinsmen until the two vessels sat abreast– bow to bow, stern to stern.

Planks dropped on to the rails of the two ships and the MacNeil kinsmen swarmed the flagship, but there were no men aboard to greet them. No clash of swords. No enemy hanging from the halyards or hiding below deck. And no Hector. The flagship was abandoned save for a terrified boy squeezing the tiller that guided the ship.

"'Tis a ruse," Sileas announced what Keiran already knew.

Trembling, he climbed a companionway at the stern of the ship and gawked at Kisimul sitting unguarded in the bay. "Sorcha," he whispered as fear clutched his entire being.

Paralysed with worry, Sorcha hugged herself around the middle and watched the battle through the crenellated stone work atop the stronghold. The explosions had dwindled, leaving behind an infernal sea of smoke and belching fire. The waiting had soured her stomach hours before, but questions now left a metallic taste on her tongue.

Was Keiran safe? Was he suffocating, drowning, burning? The worst possible scenarios escalated in her head. Had he faced off with Hector? Had he won?

She hated this helpless feeling shredding her insides. She hated the regret eating a hole in her chest. She should have told him how she felt about him before he boarded the ship. Her emotions seemed to attack her all at once as she watched the burning vessels sink. Tears burned her eyes and convulsions rolled through her gut, but she quickly collected herself. She would not show weakness in front of her kinsmen.

"M'lady, ye are needed at once in the Great Hall." The woman who'd been Peigi's wet nurse since her infancy stepped up behind Sorcha.

"What is it, Edina?"

"I cannot say more." Edina clutched the sides of her soiled kirtle and lowered her eyes. "Please, come quickly. 'Tis Peigi."

Sorcha didn't wait for further explanation before she raced down the spiral stairwell of the north tower. She might not be able to raise a broadsword in battle, but she could protect her sister. Her confidence fell to her toes when she entered the Great Hall.

Warriors lined the perimeter the room, weapons drawn. For a fleeting moment she felt guarded until she realized they were not *her* warriors. Icy terror froze her feet to the floor when she laid eyes on Hector sitting at the high table shouting at Peigi to refill his drink.

The scene was surreal, shocking, familiar. His dark soulless eyes found Sorcha's from across the hall, then his lips curled into a threatening snarl. "Good den, *wife*."

A mixture of fury and fear numbed Sorcha's limbs as she watched Peigi pour ale into his goblet. Peigi shook, she cried, she lifted her red swollen eyes to Sorcha in a silent plea to help her. Sorcha bit back the urge to scream at Peigi to run, knowing Hector wouldn't hesitate to give the order to kill her. She was his captive, as was every wide-eyed woman in the hall filling his warrior's troughs.

"Have ye no greeting words for your husband?" Hector emptied the contents of his goblet in a single swallow. His arms were wrapped in soiled bandages, no doubt hiding his disease. Unfortunately, it hadn't killed him yet.

"Ye are unwelcome in my home." She wanted to lunge at him and choke him and watch him die while she strangled the last breath from his lungs.

He held his chest in a mock display of hurt. "I expected a grand celebration to honour my new position."

"Ye have no position here," she snapped back. "I am chieftain over Clan MacNeil."

"Ye are my wife. Everything in your possession is mine – the stronghold, the land, the chieftainship." As fast as a whiplash, Hector threw a dagger that pinned Sileas's wife to a trestle table by her skirt.

Maura screamed and dropped the pitcher she'd been carrying.

The crash of ceramic ripped through Sorcha's ears like a hot blade. She lurched forwards to aid Maura, but caught herself when Hector rose from the table. His dominant stance bound her in invisible shackles. For four years she'd tiptoed around him. She knew his moods, his warning looks, his gestures, and felt defeated to be submitting to him again.

He stalked towards Maura, retrieved his blade, and threatened her with the tip. "Go to the docks and await the arrival of your kinsmen. Tell them I have their chieftain, and if they wish to keep her alive, they will abide by my instructions."

"What are your instructions, m'lord?" Maura choked out.

"Have them board a single ship – all of them. Tell them to toss their shot into the water and return to sea."

Maura's fair skin turned ashen against her flame-red hair. She glanced at Sorcha, awaiting approval, which Sorcha gave without pause. Sorcha knew what Hector was capable of and she had no intention of defying him. For now.

The instant Maura was out of earshot, Hector summoned a dozen of his warriors. "Gather the men off the western side of the isle and board their ships. Go after them, surround them. When the sun breaks the horizon at dawn, load the cannons and blast them to kingdom come."

The kinswomen's sharp gasps hissed through the hall.

Horror gripped Sorcha with sharp claws. She had to do something to save them. To save Keiran. Pleading with Hector was futile. Cursing him would gain naught. Her surrender was what he wanted and exactly what she would give him if it meant protecting her people.

"More ale!" Hector shouted at a serving maid.

Sorcha grabbed a nearby pitcher and hoped her kinswomen followed her lead. They were hesitant at first, but once she informed them of her plan, word travelled quickly. Getting Hector and his kinsmen blootered was the only way the women would ever be able to fight them.

"We will slit their throats in their sleep. Every last one o' them," one woman whispered to another in the cellar as she popped the lid open on another barrel of mead.

"Nay. There are some I want unharmed." Sorcha had spoken very little to Hector's men in the four years she'd been married to him, but she'd known all their wives. "I'll tell you exactly which ones we shall save."

The next few hours proved to be excruciating, but soon Hector's men succumbed to the drink. One by one, they fell upon the floor rushes to seek their slumber. But not Hector.

"Stay with the girl." He issued the order to his seneschal standing beside Peigi, then latched his thick fingers around Sorcha's wrist and dragged her out of the Great Hall. "Your sister will remain untouched as long as ye continue to behave in the manner expected of a wife."

"Where are ye taking me?" Her heels dug into the floor. Her stomach roiled with fear. And her heart beat out of cadence waiting for him to respond. He remained silent as he dragged her up the stairwell and into her father's solar.

"Think ye I am ignorant?" He backhanded her across the face, flinging her into the bedpost. "I know what ye and your kinswomen are doing."

Sorcha clutched the wooden post and readied herself for his next strike, knowing it would come.

"Did ye cast one of your spells on the drink?"

"I am no witch," Sorcha insisted for what seemed the thousandth time.

"Nay?" Hector fisted her hair and wrenched her head back. "Then why was it the moment I pushed ye off that cliff did the sun shine over my head? Green clover blankets my land now."

A screeching caw sounded outside the arrow-slit reminding her of the last time Hector tried to kill her. "Ye are greedy. If all is right on your land, why did ye even come here?"

"Because of this." Hector pushed his plaid and undertunic to his waist, exposing a chest covered with pus-filled boils. "'Tis because of ye my kin fear breathing my air and my mistresses willnae lay with me."

Sorcha stared at him, repulsed. "Think ye I can heal ye?"

"Ye cursed me!" The veins in his neck protruded. His nostrils flared. "My patience for your lies has worn thin. Ye will remove this damned spell or I'll kill your kinswomen one at a time, starting with your sister."

Fury unleashed a strength in her that curled her fingers into her palms. She reared back her fist and threw a punch at him.

He easily caught it. "Ye are a foolish woman."

'Twas as if something snapped inside her. "I hate ye," she screamed at him and reared back her other fist, but before she could follow through, Hector spun a half circle away from her.

He unsheathed his dagger. "What was that?" He jerked as if he'd been pushed from behind. "Who's there?" His stance widened. His eyes frantically searched the empty chamber. He'd gone completely mad.

Sorcha raced out of the solar and was caught mid-flight around the middle by a thick-muscled arm covered with Pagan symbols. Relief washed through her with such intensity she nearly swooned.

"Ye are safe now," Keiran whispered and squeezed her tight, but only long enough for her to inhale the scents of smoke and sulphur and sea.

"The others. Hector is going to—"

Keiran pressed his finger against her lips. "Magda summoned a gale-force wind that is blowing most of the Ranalds back home. But I'm going to need her help to get our ships back."

He pushed Sorcha behind him, then entered the solar, sword drawn. "This is my quarrel, Magda. Ye are needed back at sea."

Confused by his words, Sorcha stepped beneath the doorframe and bore witness to a phenomenon like none she'd ever seen. Smoke curled around a figure standing in front of the window. Long white hair framed a face as familiar to Sorcha as her own.

Hector unsheathed the sword at his hip and circled Keiran. "Who the bluidy hell are ye people?"

"I am the witch who cursed ye and your clan." Grandmum smiled at Hector with glittery blue-green eyes, then pointed at Keiran. "And he is your wife's next husband."

"And the future chieftain of Clan MacNeil," Sorcha added with pride, knowing all would be right.

No doubt stunned by her announcement, Keiran's attention shifted away from Hector. A whirling sound echoed through the chamber, then Hector's blade sank into Keiran's chest clean to the hilt.

Time slowed, nearly stopped along with Sorcha's heart. He sank to his knees, then his strong body fell to the floor.

"Nay!" Sorcha screamed and rushed to him. She held his head as he struggled to draw air through the blood pooling in his mouth. Pain scalded her chest, her throat, her eyes. Tears rolled down her cheeks and dripped on to his. "Dinnae die," she cried and brushed his brow with a shaking hand. "I love ye."

He went still in her arms the same instant Hector's boot tips appeared beside her. "The same fate awaits the rest of your kin, lest—"

"Ye bastard!" Sorcha yanked the blade from Keiran's chest, fully prepared to stand up to Hector once and for all. She reared back, but an invisible force snatched the dagger from her hand.

"Wait!" Grandmum shouted and snapped her arms towards Hector, throwing him against the stone wall. "I need him unharmed." Grandmum raised her arms above her head. "I beseech Thee, Morrigan, and the trinity. Thrust your power upon me." A howling wind erupted inside the chamber. Thunder rolled, vibrating the floorboards. "The pain and grief he is quick to give, must be returned so Your son might live." Mist coated Sorcha's face and bright strikes of lightning blinded her in bursts. "Magick meld love and hate. Reverse the past. Reverse their fate."

A high pierced screech scraped through Sorcha's ears followed by a hoarse wail. Between the flashes of light, she watched with unblinking eyes as the face of the man she loved transformed into the face of the man she most hated.

A steady rain fell inside the chamber, soaking the carpet where Hector now lay dead on the floor. Confusion was one of many emotions spinning inside her head as she looked to Grandmum for explanation.

"Be well, Sorcha. I'll be watching ye," was all Grandmum said before she transformed into the white falcon and flew out the window.

"Mayhap your Grandmum is dead."

Sorcha whirled and watched Keiran pull himself off the floor. The pain of having lost him still clung to her every nerve.

"I was not aware Magda and Tàiseal were one in the same." The man acted as if he'd not been lying dead in her arms only moments earlier. Grandmum's magick might be commonplace to him, but Sorcha didn't trust any of this to be a reality.

"If this is a dream, promise me you'll be beside me when I awaken." She trembled as he approached.

He circled her with his arms. "I promise to always be there to protect ye in this life and the next."

"As my chieftain?" she asked, worried he'd not heard her profess her love for him.

"As your husband." He cradled the nape of her neck. "Your lover." He lowered his head to hers. "And your friend." His lips feathered over hers once, twice, three times. "I fear ye are stuck with me for life." He swallowed her quiet laughter inside a kiss that felt like Heaven, but ended far too quickly.

"Come." He scooped her off her feet and carried her out of her father's solar. "I want to know what it feels like to be touched by the woman who loves me."

The Laird's Vow

Anne Gracie

One

"You're letting the estate run to rack and ruin!" Cameron Fraser thundered.

"Dear boy, I'm bringing civilization to it," his uncle responded. "Thirty years I've lived here," – he shuddered – "and finally it's within my power to make something of the place."

"Make something of it? You're letting it fall to pieces. The great storm was more than two months ago and not one tenant's roof is yet repaired, nor any orders given to begin. Winter's staring us in the face, and what do you do? Order silk hangings from Paris – *silk*!"

His uncle said earnestly, "But dear boy, quality pays. Wait till you see what a difference hangings will make to this gloomy room. Besides, the tenants can fix their own roofs."

Cameron's nails bit into his palms. "Not without money to pay for materials, they can't. Besides, it's our responsibility – *my* responsibility as laird."

His uncle smiled. "Laird? In name, perhaps."

"Aye, I ken well it's in name only. Yet I bear all the shame," Cameron said bitterly. "If Uncle Ian were still alive . . . ."

"I know. Who would have imagined he'd go before me, being so much younger, but there it is," Charles Sinclair said. "So you'll just have to trust me. I have so many plans . . . Nearly five years is it not, before you turn thirty and gain control?"

Cameron clenched his jaw. When both his uncles had been in

charge he'd had paid scant attention to estate finances. Uncle Ian was a Fraser and his love for the estate and its people ran bone deep in him, as it did in Cameron. But now Uncle Ian was dead and the remaining trustee, Uncle Charles, could do as he pleased. And what he pleased was, in Cameron's view, entirely frivolous.

"If those roofs aren't fixed, come winter, people will freeze." Cameron clenched his fists. "Do you *want* the death of women and bairns on your conscience?"

Charles Sinclair returned to the perusal of silk swatches. "Your conscience is too delicate, dear boy. Peasants are hardy folk. Now, look at this design I drew for—"

"You'll not spend a shilling more of my inheritance!"

His uncle glanced up. "Dear boy, how do you propose stopping me?"

"Marriage!" The word burst from Cameron's mouth, shocking himself as well as his uncle. He'd had no intention of marrying, not for years to come, but now he saw it was his only solution. Under the rules of his father's will the trust would conclude on Cameron's thirtieth birthday or his wedding day – whichever came first.

"Marriage? With whom, pray? You've not attended a society event in years."

It was true. Cameron preferred hunting and fishing to dancing and up to now, he'd avoided the marriage mart of Inverness like the plague. As a result he couldn't think of a single likely female. And since half the women on the estate were related to him, officially or unofficially – Grandad had been quite a lad – he had to look further afield.

Cameron's fists clenched in frustration.

His uncle chuckled. "Dear boy, marriages take time to arrange. Your grandfather and mine negotiated for months over my dear sister's marriage to your father, and as your trustee, naturally I will handle any such negotiations on your behalf. And by then you will have a home worthy of a bride." He patted his designs.

"No negotiations will be necessary," Cameron snapped. "I'll marry the first eligible woman I find." He turned on his heel and stormed from the room, nearly cannoning into his two cousins, Jimmy and Donald, waiting outside. Distant cousins, orphaned and raised on the estate, they were like brothers to Cameron.

"What did he—" Donald began.

"Meet you at the stables in fifteen minutes," Cameron snapped. "I'm off to Inverness to find a bride."

Two

They galloped through the village, scattering squawking hens and setting dogs barking. "Marry the first eligible woman you find? You canna be serious!" Donald shouted over the sound of galloping hooves.

"Ye're crazy, mon," Jimmy agreed. "If ye must marry, at least choose the lass wi' care and caution."

"I've no choice," Cameron flung back. "The longer I leave it the more my uncle squanders what little money we have. He's already ordered silk hangings from Paris costing a fortune. The sooner I'm wed, the sooner I can cancel the order. And stop any more."

Rain set in, a thin, relentless drizzle. After half an hour of it Jimmy edged his horse alongside Cameron. "Ach, Cameron this rain is freezin' me to death. Let's go back. We'll find a solution to your woes tomorrow, when we're no' such sodden miseries."

"You go back if you want to, I'm for Inverness. I swore I'd marry this day and so I will." Cameron bent his head against the rain and rode on.

"He swore to his uncle he'd marry," Jimmy told his brother glumly. He pulled out a flask, took a swig of whisky and passed it across.

Donald drank from it. "He'll no go back on his word, then. You know Cameron."

"Aye, pigheaded – a Fraser to the bone." Jimmy drank another dram of whisky and the two brothers rode gloomily on in their cousin's wake.

Cameron took no notice. He was used to his cousin's complaints. They'd stick with him, he knew. He was glad of it. Another few hours to Inverness, and then to find a bride. The whole idea was somewhat . . . daunting.

He'd never given marriage much thought. He liked women well enough, but marriage was a serious business, the sort of thing a man considered in his thirties. But he couldn't let his uncle squander any more of his inheritance.

Cameron's mother and her brother, though of pure Scots blood, had been born and raised in France. Their grandparents were exiles who'd fled with the Prince after the disaster of Culloden. Raised in Parisian luxury, fed on romantic, impossible dreams of Scottish glory, they'd both found Scottish reality, and the poverty that resulted from the effects of war, sorely disappointing.

Cameron's mother had died of an ague when he was a wee lad, but her brother, who'd initially come for the wedding, had stayed on, never marrying, seemingly harmless. Cameron's father had tolerated him, and Cameron was inclined to do that same. Blood was blood, after all.

Though to name him as trustee . . . Who would have expected Uncle Ian to sicken and die of a chill, such a big, hale man.

But if, after nearly thirty years of sponging off the Frasers, Charles Sinclair thought he could now turn a Scottish castle into a mini Versailles, he had another think coming.

They reached the bog at the southern edge of the estate. A narrow raised road had been built across in ages past. At the end of the causeway was the wooden bridge that would take him on to the Inverness road.

In ancient times the bog had proved a useful barrier. The estate lay on a promontory, defended on two sides by water, and on the third by mountains. The narrow, easily defended causeway was the only way to cross the treacherous, muddy land of the promontory, and the bridge over the burn that the bog slowly drained into gave the only access to it. History had lost count of the number of times Frasers had burned the bridge to keep out invaders.

But those times were long past. The current bridge had been built when his grandfather was a boy. It was time to drain the bog and build a sturdy stone bridge, Cameron thought. His father had planned to do it but he'd died.

God grant Cameron would soon have the power to begin the necessary work. All he needed was a wife. It wouldn't take him long, surely, in a town the size of Inverness.

His spirits lifting, he urged his horse along the causeway, galloping into the rain.

A herd of sheep suddenly appeared, ghostly in the misty drizzle, bunched thick along the causeway, blocking the road. Cameron hauled his horse to a standstill. It snorted and moved restlessly, misliking the situation.

The sheep eyed Cameron suspiciously and backed away, but "Get on there!" a voice shouted from behind the herd. "You on the horses, stand still and let the sheep through!"

Cameron squinted into the rain. Dimly he could see a boy in a too-big coat and hat, waving a crook. A dog barked and the sheep bunched and milled and baaaed uncertainly, crowding to the very edge of the causeway.

Behind him Jimmy and Donald's horses plunged to a halt. "Get those beasties out of the way," Jimmy shouted.

"Dinna shout at them, ye fool," the boy snapped. "They're stupid beasts and are like to panic. And if any get into the bog . . ."

Jimmy, being well into the contents of his flask, was inclined to argue – gentlemen on horseback took precedence over sheep – but Cameron held up his hand. "Stay still," he ordered.

The dog barked again and suddenly the first sheep darted past Cameron. The milling herd followed, streaming around and past the men on horseback like a living river, baaing madly, their long sodden woollen skirts swinging frantically as they fled along the causeway. Two little black-faced lambs, however, plunged off the causeway and floundered in the muddy bog. Their mother followed.

"Damn ye tae hell, ye fool beasties!" the boy swore and followed them into the bog with a splash. He grabbed the first lamb and set it back on its feet. It stood, bleating plaintively. The boy then began to heave at the mother, both of them floundering in the mud. Jimmy and Donald watched the show from horseback, grinning.

Cameron barely noticed. The rain had eased and he could see the bridge, a few dozen yards away. Or what remained of the bridge. It was impassable, smashed to pieces, looking more like a scattering of giant toothpicks than a bridge.

It must have happened during the great storm. Rage slowly filled him. His uncle must have known. And he'd done nothing. This was as bad, or worse than the roofs needing repairs. The bridge gave the estate direct access to the Inverness road.

Uncle Charles, however, only cared about access to France, and that was by boat, not road.

Cameron stared at the devastation. He'd have to return the way he'd come, and leave by the westerly border. Hours more travel and they'd still be on the estate.

"Give it up, Cam." His cousin Donald touched his arm. "We've no choice but to turn back now. It'll be dark before we even get home."

"I'll no' go home wi' my tail between my legs," Cameron muttered, though in truth he could see no other alternative. "And I'll not leave the estate in my uncle's hands a day longer than I must."

"There's naught you can do wi' the bridge in that state, though, is there?" Donald said reasonably. "Ye canna cross it, ye must go back."

"Dammit, I can see that!" Thwarted and furious, Cameron glared at the bridge. Hearing laughter behind him, he turned to see his cousin Jimmy swigging whisky and chuckling at the spectacle of the boy still trying to drag his wretched sheep from the bog. The large, ungainly animal was plunging deeper into the bog, struggling desperately, as if the lad were trying to drown it instead of saving it. From where Cameron stood, the sheep was winning. Both lad and beast were black mud to the eyebrows. And on the far side of the struggle the remaining small lamb was sinking fast.

"Make yourself useful, will ye Jimmy? Give the lad a hand."

"And get my new boots filled with black mud?" Jimmy snorted. "Not likely."

Cameron glanced at Donald, who shrugged and made no move. The lad fell for the third time. The tiny lamb struggled to keep its head above the muddy water.

Cameron swore, swung off his horse and waded in. He scooped the lamb out first and set it on its feet beside its twin. Then he hauled the boy out, shoving him close to the bank. "Jimmy! Pull him out."

Jimmy dismounted, gingerly took the boy's dirty hands and dragged him on to the solid causeway. Cameron waded back in and tried to fetch the mother sheep. The stupid thing bucked and fought, and in seconds Cameron himself was black with bog mud.

His cousins watched from the bank, passing the flask back and forth, making bets and roaring with laughter.

But Cameron was strong and big and angry. He wrapped his arms around the sheep's middle and heaved, almost throwing the filthy beast on to the bank, causing his cousins to leap back like ladies to avoid the mud. The sheep shook itself, bleated and trotted indignantly away, followed by the lambs.

Cameron's cousins were laughing fit to burst. He'd fix them. "Help me out." He held out his hands, but they laughed and backed away.

"We're no so far gone we'd fall for that old trick," Jimmy chuckled.

"Canny bastards," Cameron muttered as climbed out of the bog, black mud dripping from him. "And if there's no whisky left in that flask, I swear I'll throw you in anyway."

Laughing, Jimmy tossed him the flask. Cameron was about to

drain it when he saw how the shepherd lad was shivering in the cold. He thrust it towards the boy, saying, "Here, you need this more than me."

The boy accepted it with a surprised expression and took a quick swig. He shuddered violently as the whisky went down, but managed to gasp out his thanks.

"So, boy," Cameron said. "What's your name?"

His cousins guffawed. The shepherd boy gave a quick grin, a cheeky white slash in a muddy face. "Jeannie Macleay, sir, and thank you for getting the sheep out o' the mud, even if you did panic the beasts in the first place. My uncle would've kilt me if I'd lost her." She tried to wipe the mud off her face with her sleeve and only smeared it more.

"Jeannie?" Cameron stared. The coat she wore was a man's coat, too big for her, rolled up at the sleeves and hanging down almost to her ankles, but though it was hard to tell because of the mud, there was a skirt beneath it. The boots she wore were a man's boots, too big, surely for her feet and the hat crammed on her head was a man's hat.

"Are ye married, Jeannie?" Jimmy asked, suddenly intent.

She frowned. "No," she said cautiously.

"And where were ye born?"

"Stop that!" Cameron snapped, realizing what his cousin was up to.

Jimmy gave him an innocent look. "No harm in asking."

"Drop it, Jimmy," Cameron told his cousin. He was not going to marry some ragamuffin he'd just dragged out of a bog.

"She's the first one you've seen," Jimmy insisted.

"The first what?" the girl demanded.

"He couldna take her anyway," Donald argued. "She's just a wee thing, no' a grown woman."

"Take me where? Nobody's taking me anywhere."

"Stow it you two, the whole idea's ridiculous," Cameron said. His cousins took no notice. There was a bet on and the contents of the flask were obviously well absorbed.

"How old are you, Jeannie lass?" Jimmy asked.

"Nineteen," Jeannie Macleay said, eying each man suspiciously. "But I said, nobody's taking me anywhere." She began to edge away.

Jimmy grabbed her by the arm, careless now of any mud, intent only on his wager. "And where were you born, Jeannie, me dear?"

"I'm no' your dear." She yanked her arm from his grip and hurried away, flinging over her shoulder, "And not that it's any of your business, but I was born on the island of Lewis."

At her words, Jimmy let out a whoop of triumph and punched his brother in the shoulder. "Lewis! She's eligible! You owe me a monkey, Donald!"

"The bet's not won until the deed is done," Donald insisted. "Cameron's yet to wed her."

"He will, he will," Jimmy crowed.

Donald snorted. "It's a crazy notion, and Cameron's no the crazy one here."

Jimmy shook his head. "He gave his word, man, and Cameron never goes back on his word."

The girl followed her sheep, putting as much distance between herself and the men as she could, running swiftly despite the clumsy, man-sized boots. Cameron watched her thoughtfully.

When he'd made his rash statement he had no thought of wedding anyone except a lady born. This bog sprite shepherdess was totally unsuitable.

But he'd never broken his word before. Rashness gave way to serious thought; there might be wives to be had in Inverness – ladies – but how long would it take to get one to wed him? And how much would his uncle squander in the meantime?

Jimmy grabbed him by the shoulder. "Well, Cammie, will ye wed her or no? There's a bet on."

Cameron swore softly under his breath. The girl was young, unmarried and born outside the estate. What difference would it make anyway who he wed? Women were for running the house and birthing babes and any female could do that. Getting control of his inheritance was what counted. Besides, the little he knew of ladies born was that they were a lot of trouble. They expected a man to dance attendance on them, whereas a lass like this, country bred and down-to-earth . . . She floundered in the mud. Very down-to-earth.

"Aye, I'll wed her," he declared.

"Aha—" Jimmy began, then let out a yell. "She's getting away. Don't worry, Cam, I'll get her back for ye." And without warning he jumped on his horse and galloped after the girl.

"Och, the mad fool," Donald began. "Whatever will she think—"

Cameron leapt on his horse and set off after Jimmy.

The girl, seeing Jimmy bearing down on her, screamed defiance at him and ran faster. Jimmy let out a whoop, as if he was running down a hind.

"Leave her be, Jimmy," Cameron roared.

But Jimmy was almost on the girl and oblivious. With a blood-curdling yell he scooped her up and tossed her over his saddle. She fought and struggled but Jimmy just laughed and smacked her on the backside as he wheeled his horse around and cantered back to Cameron with a triumphant grin.

"I fetched her for ye – yeeeowww!" He broke off with a yell of pain. He stared down at the girl in shock. "She bit me! The wee vixen bit me!"

The wee vixen moved to bite his leg again and Jimmy hastily shoved her off his horse. She dropped lightly to the ground and glanced warily around, preparing to run again.

"There's no need to be afeared," Cameron said hastily. He dismounted and took a few slow steps towards her, holding his hands up pacifically, saying in a soothing voice, "Nobody here will harm you. My cousin is a wee bit enthusiastic, that's all—"

"He's drunk," the girl said, backing away.

"Maybe, but he meant well," Cameron told her.

She snorted. "Meant well? To kidnap me in broad daylight?"

"Nobody's going to kidnap you," Cameron assured her softly and moved closer. She backed away and glanced at the bog, as if weighing her chances of escaping across it.

"Ye daft wee besom, he wants tae marry you," Jimmy said, still rubbing his leg.

She snorted. "He's drunker than I thought."

It was now or never, Cameron thought. He cleared his throat. "It's true," he said. It came out as a croak.

She made a gesture of disgust. "You're drunk, too."

"I'm not. I'm offering you marriage." There it was out. He was officially crazy. But at least he'd get control of his inheritance.

Away on the moors a curlew called, a mournful, other-wordly cry. The wind blew across the bog, carrying the scent of heather and dank, rotting mud.

The girl scrutinized his face, then turned to look at each of his cousins. "Marriage?" she said eventually. "You're proposing marriage to me? To *me*?"

Cameron nodded. "Aye."

In her dirty, mud-streaked face, her blue eyes gleamed bright with suspicion. "Why?"

Cameron shrugged. "I must marry someone. Why not you?" It was ridiculous when said aloud, but with the eyes of his cousins on him, he wasn't going to back down. He'd never broken his word yet.

But he might not have to. The girl could still refuse. He waited.

Down the road the girl's sheepdog barked. A sheep baaed in response. "You're tetched in the head," she told him. "You canna mean such a thing. Why, you never set eyes on me before today."

"It sounds mad, I know, but it's an honest offer I'm making ye," Cameron told her.

Stunned, Jeannie Macleay chewed on her lip and stared at the solemn young man in front of her. He was asking her to marry him? It couldn't possibly be true. He probably wouldn't even recognize her if he met her again – she was all over mud, anyway. He was drunk, or tetched in the head, but . . . Marriage? The thought gave her pause.

She would have married almost anyone to get away from Uncle Ewen and the sheep. And suddenly, like something out of a dream, here was this tall, beautiful young man, asking her.

Was he one of the fairy folk? She'd never believed in them until now – well, not since she was a little girl – but she'd heard they were invariably beautiful, and this one certainly qualified.

He'd wiped his face clean of mud. His cheekbones and jaw might have been cut with a blade, they were so perfect and sharp. His nose was bold and straight as a sword and his mouth firm and unsmiling. And his chin . . . her mother always used to say a man with a firm chin could be relied on.

Warrior stock, no doubt, like many folk in the highlands, of Viking descent. His hair was brown and sun-streaked yet his eyes weren't Viking blue, but hazel. They watched her steadily, but she sensed an intensity beneath the calm manner.

He was well off, too, going by the quality of his clothes and his horse.

God knew why he'd even looked twice at her, with her in her uncle's old coat and boots and covered in mud, but he had. And try as she might, she could not dismiss it. She pinched herself, hard, to be sure it wasn't a dream.

"I don't know you from Adam," she said to silence the clamour in her head.

"My name is Cameron Fraser."

Fraser. It was a common enough name around here.

Oh Lord. She ought not to even consider his proposal. The poor lad was no doubt a wee bit soft in the head, and his friends were too drunk to realize what he was doing.

But she was only human.

The choices loomed large in her head; life with Uncle Ewen, the stingiest, gloomiest, dourest man in all of Scotland – or life with this tall, solemn young man.

The rest of her life spent on the moors, half the time cold, wet and hungry, looking after Uncle Ewen's sheep – or marriage to this beautiful young man who was probably tetched in the head to be offering marriage to her on so little acquaintance.

No choice at all.

People said better the devil you knew. Not Jeannie.

"Do ye have a house?" she asked.

"I do."

"Would I be its mistress?" It was the summit of her dreams – to have a home of her own, to be beholden to noone. To belong.

He nodded. "My mother died when I was a bairn. You'd be the woman of the house."

The woman of the house. There it was, her dream laid out for her. All she had to do was to say yes. She swallowed. What if he proved to be a madman or violent?

She thought of how he'd plunged into the bog and hauled her and the sheep out. He hadn't given a thought to his fine clothes. And he'd set the lamb on its feet with a gentle hand.

No, he wasn't a violent man, and if she was wrong, well, she was fleet of foot and nimble. She could always run away. She'd been planning to run away from Uncle Ewen anyway, only she hadn't yet worked out how to do it without a bean to her name. A different situation would offer different opportunities.

A home of her own. The woman of the house. Not a servant or an indigent relative, taken in begrudgingly and reminded of it daily. Her own home. And a place of honour in it as his wife.

It was probably a joke. He was making a may game of her, but oh . . . oh, if it were true. Mad or tetched or drunk, he was young and beautiful and the thought of those lithe, powerful limbs wrapping around her made her shiver.

She gazed into his eyes, trying to read his mind. His steady hazel eyes stared back at her, telling her nothing. But they were steady, not wild.

She moistened her lips with her tongue and took the plunge. "Ye truly mean it?"

"I do." He gave a curt nod to emphasize it.

He sounded sincere. He looked sincere. Oh God let him be sincere, she prayed.

She took a deep breath. "Well then, I'll marry you."

The man who'd tried to kidnap her gave a loud whoop, causing his horse to toss its head and plunge restlessly. "She said yes! I win! Pay up, Donald!"

His words punched into Jeannie's gut. All the breath left her lungs. It was a joke after all. A bet. See if you could get the gullible girl to believe a strange man would offer her marriage.

And the fool girl had believed. Had even allowed herself to hope. After all she'd been through in the last few years, had she learned *nothing*?

She tried to look as if she'd known it all along, as if disappointment and humiliation weren't about to choke her. "A bet, was it, lads? A laugh at my expense?" she said with an attempt at breezy unconcern. "Very funny. Enjoy your winnings. I'm awa' then to my sheep." She turned away so they would not see the hot tears prickling at her eyelids.

A firm hand wrapped gently around her elbow, holding her back. "It wasn't a joke," he told her. "There was a bet, yes, but my cousins will bet on anything and everything."

Jeannie stared down at his mud-caked boots, angry and ashamed, hearing the sincerity in his voice and refusing to be caught a second time.

"I meant it," he went on. "And you said you'd wed me."

She jerked her arm away. She wouldn't be made a fool of twice. "As if you'd marry a girl like me, a girl you don't even know. And as if I'd marry a man on an acquaintance of five minutes."

"You said you would."

She made a rude noise. "I was just going along with the joke. Why would I want to marry a man I'd just met?"

"Perhaps because you're desperate—"

She looked up at him then, glaring, ready to spit in his eye.

"—maybe even as desperate as I am," he finished.

His words stopped her cold. "You? Desperate?" she managed after a moment. "Why would you be desperate?"

"I need to gain control of my inheritance. My uncle – my trustee – is spending it like water. I inherit when I turn thirty, or when I wed. If I wait much longer there'll be nothing left."

Jeannie turned his words over in her mind, then shook her head. "You're saying you're to be rich? But there's nobody else you can marry? Just a girl you fished from a bog?"

"There are plenty of other girls," he admitted. "But I swore I'd marry the first woman I met. And that was you."

Marry the first woman he met? Jeannie couldn't believe her ears. She glanced at his cousins who sat on their horses, watching wide-eyed, like great gormless owls, to see what would happen next.

"Is this true?" she demanded. They nodded.

"You'd truly marry a stranger, just to get your hands on your inheritance?"

"I said I would and I never break my word," he said.

"He never breaks his word," the cousins chorused.

"That's the daftest thing I've ever heard," she said.

He shrugged. "Maybe. So, will you marry me?"

Jeannie stared into the steady hazel eyes, trying to read his true intent. She could read nothing, so she looked away into the distance, trying to decide what to do. She could smell the mud on her, feel it tightening on her skin as it dried. She must look a sight.

"I give you my word I'll take good care of you, Jeannie Macleay."

His word. The one he never broke. And he had big, broad, lovely shoulders, even if he was cracked in the head. "When?" she asked.

"Today."

Jeannie closed her eyes, counted to ten, and then counted again, just to make sure. And then she tossed commonsense to the wind. "All right, I'll do it. Were do we go?"

"The nearest kirk. St Andrew's-by-the-burn?"

She nodded. It was the closest church, though her uncle wasn't a believer and she'd never been there.

Cameron Fraser mounted his horse and held out his hand help her up behind him.

She hesitated and glanced back at the sheep waiting in a close huddle at the end of the causeway. Rab, the sheepdog, lay quietly, watching her, watching the sheep, ever vigilant.

Cameron Fraser followed her gaze. "If you want, Jimmy will stay to take care of your sheep."

She looked sceptically at his cousin who swayed on his horse, grinning muzzily. "They'll be safer wi' the dog. Have ye a handkerchief?"

He handed her a clean, folded handkerchief, no doubt thinking she meant to clean herself with it. She was beyond one handkerchief.

She picked up a stone, plucked a sprig of heather growing by the side of the road and knotted them both into the handkerchief. Then she let out a shrill whistle. The dog raced towards her like a dart.

She tied the handkerchief on to his collar. "I'll miss ye, Rab," she whispered, stroking the dog's silky ears. He'd been the only source of love and affection she'd had in four long years. She'd miss him, but Rab would be all right with Uncle Ewen. Her uncle was a lot kinder to animals than he was to people.

"Away home wi' them Rab," she said. "Away home." The dog raced back and began to circle the sheep. A bark here, a nip there and the herd began to move. They'd be home soon.

"Will no one worry when the sheep come home without you?" Cameron Fraser asked her.

"No. My uncle will understand the message in the handkerchief. He won't be troubled, as long as no sheep are missing, and Rab will get them home safe."

It was the exact same message her mother had left when she ran off with her father more than twenty years ago. Mam had left a stone, a sprig of heather and a note. A stone for Grandad's heart and heather for Mam's hopes for the future. Jeannie had no paper for a note, but her uncle would remember.

He frowned. "But he'll want to know where you've gone, surely."

Clearly it didn't reflect well on her that she had no one who cared. Jeannie tried to pass it off with a laugh. "He'll be relieved to have me off his hands."

Cameron Fraser quirked a brow at her. "Trouble, are you?"

"Aye, I eat too much and I'm the worst shepherdess he's ever had."

He smiled for the first time, and it was like the sun reflected off the silvery loch. It set off a flutter deep inside her.

"He never wanted me in the first place. I was dumped on him when my mother died four years ago." Lord, she was babbling. She bit her tongue.

"You can eat what you like and you'll never have to look after sheep again." He held out his hand.

"I'd marry the devil himself for that promise." She took hold of Cameron Fraser's hand, swung up behind him and, heart in her mouth, rode off to meet her fate.

Three

The small stone kirk of St Andrew's-by-the-burn was the last remnant of a hamlet that was slowly dying. The elderly minister and his wife were in the front garden, tending to the rose bushes.

"Good day to ye, Reverend." Cameron dropped lightly to the ground, placed his hands around Jeannie Macleay's waist and lifted her down.

"Cameron Fraser, is it you?" The minister came forward, brushing twigs and leaves from his clothes.

"Aye, Reverend, it is. I hope you and Mrs Potts are well." Cameron was well aware of the minister's shrewd gaze running over them all, noting his cousins' inebriation, his own muddy state and finally coming to rest on the muddy scrap he'd just help dismount.

"And what is it ye want of me, Cameron? This is no' a social call I'll be thinking."

"I need you to perform a marriage." Cameron said it briskly, as if there was nothing at all strange in such a request. He held a hand out to the scrap and drew her to his side. "This is Miss Jeannie Macleay, originally of the Island of Lewis, and we are betrothed."

There was a muffled sound from the minister's wife, but the man himself didn't turn a hair.

Cameron continued, "We wish to be married today. Now, in fact."

The minister frowned. "No banns?"

"If ye can't do it now, just say so and we'll go elsewhere," Cameron said calmly. He'd prefer a church wedding, but Scottish laws ensured he didn't need the minister's cooperation. A declaration before witnesses would do it, and the minister knew it.

He eyed Jeannie dubiously. "Are ye of age, Miss Macleay?"

"I'm nineteen," she said, sounding quite composed for a girl with half a bog on her.

The minister pursed his lips. "Very well, then. I suppose I should be glad you've come to the kirk for it. Better an irregular marriage with God's blessing than a godless arrangement. Come ye in. We'll get the details down. I expect they'll be glad of a cup of tea, Elspeth."

"Indeed, indeed," his wife said, looking curiously at the girl behind Cameron.

Cameron made to lead the scrap into the minister's house, but she didn't budge.

"I'm no' going into the house, not like this." She gestured at her muddy garments. She turned to the minister's wife. "Would it be possible for me to wash around the back of the house, ma'am?"

The minister's wife brightened. "Of course my dear. I can see you've had a nasty encounter with some mud. Come along with me." She held her hand out and gestured to the path around the side of the house.

The minister waited until they'd disappeared from sight and then said, "Now Cameron, you'd better tell me what kind of a mess you've got yourself in this time."

"I'm not in a mess, Reverend Potts," Cameron said stiffly. The man was some kind of distant relation but it didn't excuse his familiarity.

The minister's brows rose sceptically. "Not in a mess? And yet you turn up out of the blue demanding to be wed to a lass who's mud to the eyebrows, here and now, no banns, no witnesses except for those feckless young wastrels—"

The feckless young wastrels made indignant noises, but Rev. Potts swept on, "—and none of the celebrations that one would expect of the wedding of the laird."

"None of that matters," Cameron told him. "Just wed us and be done."

Reverend Potts put a hand on Cameron's arm. "What is it, lad? Has the girl trapped you into this?"

Cameron shook off his hand. "She has not. And I don't propose to discuss it. If you're not willing to marry us, then say so and we'll be off."

The minister took a step back. "Now, now, laddie, no need to be like that. As long as you're happy about it, I'll wed the pair of ye, and gladly." He glanced down at Cameron's muddy breeches and boots. "But you'll not want to be married wi' your boots and breeks in such a state."

"It doesna matter—" Cameron began.

"It's not respectful to your bride to be married in dirt," the minister went on inexorably. "Come ye in and get cleaned up."

She was in an even muddier state, Cameron thought, but he followed the man anyway. He could at least clean up for her, he supposed.

In the large, cosy kitchen at the back of the house, Elspeth Potts and her cook were firmly stripping Jeannie of her muddy clothes. "Och, child, ye canna go to your wedding reeking of the bog, I'd never forgive myself," Elspeth said. "There's plenty of hot water, so just you climb into the tub there and scrub it all off. Your hair, too – Morag, beat up an egg."

"An egg?" Jeannie's stomach rumbled.

"Aye, followed by a vinegar rinse. T'will give your hair a lovely glossy finish. Now hop in, my dear, before you get cold."

With the last of her clothes stripped from her shivering body, Jeannie had no alternative but to climb into the tin bathtub. She'd been prepared to scrub the worst of it off with a bucket of cold water, but Mrs Potts wouldn't hear of it. "Cold water? Nonsense. A bride deserves the best we can give her, isn't that right, Morag?"

So Jeannie luxuriated in a tub of warm water and scrubbed the dirt from her body. The bath water was soon black and the minister's wife ordered a second bath, with hotter water. This time, instead of the strong-smelling soap Jeannie had used the first time, she gave her a small oval cake that smelled of roses.

"It's beautiful," Jeannie said, inhaling the rich scent as she lathered her body for the second time.

"It's French," the older lady admitted. "A terrible indulgence for a minister's wife, but I confess, I cannot resist it. Now, close your eyes and Morag will shampoo your hair with the egg."

It seemed a waste of good food, but Jeannie sat in the deep tin bath with her eyes closed while Mrs Potts and Morag fussed over her. The hot water was blissful. The last four years she'd bathed in lukewarm water: Uncle Ewen's kettle only held a small amount of hot water and he didn't approve of wasting fuel to heat water for baths.

She felt herself relaxing as Morag's strong fingers massaged her scalp. It was so long since anyone had seemed to care if she lived or died, let alone felt clean and smelled good. Four years since Mam had died, but now, with her eyes closed, she could almost believe Mam was here, helping prepare her for her wedding.

She stood while Morag rinsed her down like a child, wrapped her in a large towel and then rinsed her hair carefully, several times, with water, then vinegar, then with a mixture that also smelled of roses.

"There you go, lassie, sit ye down by the fire now and drink this." Morag pushed a cup of hot, sweet tea into her hand. Jeannie drank it gratefully.

She dried her hair by the fire, using her fingers to untangle it. The pile of muddy clothes lay on the stone floor where she'd discarded them and her heart sank. Not much use in being clean and sweet-smelling when the only clothes she had were muddy cast-offs. The dresses she'd brought to Uncle Ewen's four years ago were long outgrown or worn out. The skirt she'd worn today was a patched together creation of what remained of them. But she had no choice. She'd have to dry her clothes by the fire and brush off as much mud as she could.

"Here you are," Mrs Potts swept into the room with an armful of clothes. "We'll find something pretty for you here."

"But—"

"Hush now, I can see you've lost your own clothes, and I'll not let a bride be wed in those." She flapped disdainful fingers towards the muddy pile. "Now, let's see." She pulled out a couple of dresses, held them up, shook her head and tossed them on a chair. "Ah, this one, I think. Matches your bonny blue eyes." She held up a dress in soft blue fabric, glanced at Morag for confirmation, and nodded. "Now, let's get you dressed."

She handed Jeannie a bundle: underclothes of fine, soft lawn, edged with lace, finer than anything Jeannie had worn in her life.

"But I canna accept—" Jeannie began, pride warring with longing for the pretty things.

"Pish tush, they're old things I have no more use for. They don't even fit me now, see?" Mrs Potts patted her rounded shape comfortably. She added in a softer voice, "And it would give me great pleasure, Jeannie Macleay, to know that you go to your wedding dressed as a bride should be, from the skin out. You've a handsome young man there who'll appreciate them later." She winked. "Come now, indulge an old woman."

Blushing and wordless at the unexpected kindness, Jeannie donned the chemise and petticoat. She picked up the stockings and looked up in shock. "These are silk."

Mrs Potts flapped her fingers at her. "Well of course – silk for a bridal. Besides, what use are silk stockings for an old woman like me? Now, no argument. And try these slippers on." She handed Jeannie a pair of soft brown leather slippers.

They were a bit big for Jeannie, but once Morag stuffed the toes with wool, they fitted.

"Now for your hair."

Jeannie began to twist it in a rope around her hand.

"No, no, no! Leave it out. 'Tis your glory, child, and as a married woman you'll be covering it up soon enough. In the meantime leave it out to dazzle that man of yours."

Jeannie wasn't sure she had it in her to dazzle anyone – she was no beauty, she knew – but if Mrs Potts said her hair could dazzle, Jeannie would leave it out.

She had no idea what marriage to Cameron Fraser would be like, but she would do her best to make it work. And Mrs Potts was giving her a head start.

Producing a brush, Mrs Potts brushed out Jeannie's long hair till it shone, then produced a veil of creamy, precious lace, which she placed carefully over Jeannie's head. "'Twas my own bridal veil, and both my daughters wore it at their weddings, too."

She stood back and smiled. "There, a bonny bride you are indeed, is she not Morag? Right now, I'll just—" She broke off, hesitated, then said, "Child, do you have no kith or kin to stand up with you?"

Jeannie shook her head. "There's only Uncle Ewen, and he wouldna come. He doesna like people."

Mrs Potts and Morag exchanged glances. "Would that be Ewen Leith, the one they call 'the hermit'?"

Jeannie nodded. "My mother's brother."

"I never realized he had a young girl living with him. I'm sorry lass, if I'd known you were alone up there in the hills, I would have visited."

Jeannie shrugged awkwardly. "It doesna matter."

The older lady hugged her. "Well, you'll not be lonely any longer with young Cameron Fraser for a husband. I'm amazed you two ever met, let alone had time to court. Right then, I'll away and see if the men are ready. Take her to the church door, Morag, and when you hear the music send her down the aisle." The minister's wife bustled away.

Jeannie and Morag looked at each other. "Could I maybe—" Jeannie began. "Is there a looking glass somewhere, so that I could see . . ."

"Och, of course, lass." Morag looked out into the hallway, then beckoned.

Jeannie stood in front of the looking glass in the hall and stared. Other than in a pool of water, she hadn't seen her reflection in four years. Uncle Ewen didn't believe in wasting money on such things.

She'd changed in four years. Grown up. "I . . . I look like my mother," she whispered. "I look . . ." Pretty, she thought. She couldn't say it aloud. Vanity was a sin. But she thought it and the thought gave her a warm glow. She was still a bit freckled and skinny and her cheeks were red from the cold and her mouth too wide and she still had that crooked tooth but she looked . . . nice. Like a proper bride. A real bride. She adjusted the beautiful lace veil. If not for Mrs Potts's kindness . . .

Emotion surged up in her and her eyes filled with tears.

"Now stop that, lassie, or you'll start me off as well. " Morag said briskly. "Time enough for tears later. Let's get ye to the kirk."

Four

They waited in the vestibule of the small stone kirk until they heard the full chord of an organ sound. Jeannie took a deep breath. One step and she was on her way to wed Cameron Fraser, a man she'd known but a few hours. And once married, there was no going back.

She couldn't move.

"Go on lass," Morag whispered and gave her a hefty shove that sent her stumbling into the aisle.

And there he was, waiting. Cameron Fraser, solemn as a judge and as fine a man as she'd ever seen. To her surprise he wore the kilt, the Fraser dress kilt, a splash of bright colour in the austere little whitewashed kirk.

Jeannie's heart fluttered. She'd always been partial to the sight of a man wearing the kilt. And Cameron Fraser looked as braw and bonny as any man she'd seen. The man had a set of legs on him that fair took her breath away.

The music continued and Jeannie walked slowly down the aisle, drinking in the sight of her groom. He wore a white shirt with a lace jabot at his throat, the foam of the lace in stark contrast at the hard line of his jaw and square, firm chin. Over it he wore a black velvet coat with silver buttons. He looked like a hero out of a painting of old.

His expression hadn't changed. He looked . . . no, she couldn't read his face at all. He ran a finger between his throat and his jabot, as if it was tied too tight.

Was he having second thoughts?

She hoped not because she wanted him, wanted him with a fierceness that burned bright and deep within her. She quickened her step.

Cameron Fraser had made her want him. He'd caused all her long-buried dreams to surface, had tantalized her with possibilities she knew were foolish and impossible, but now she wanted him, wanted the house he'd promised her, the place, the home. Her home. And him. She wanted it all.

He was *not* going to back out now. She hurried the last few steps to where he waited at the altar and when he presented his arm, she grabbed it. And held on tight.

He stared down at her, looking faintly stunned.

Cameron couldn't believe his eyes. This was his muddy little bog sprite? *This*? This lissom young woman walking towards him with shining eyes and a look of hope so transparent it went straight to his heart.

Behind him, one of his cousins said something but Cameron wasn't listening. His attention was entirely on his bride as she made the interminable walk down the aisle, light and graceful in a pretty blue dress.

He straightened, glad now he'd stuffed his kilt and jacket into his saddlebag when he left, glad the minister had insisted it wouldn't do for the laird to be wed in his breeks, even if nobody except a couple of young wastrels were there to witness it. His bride would remember he'd done her honour on this day, the old man said.

Cameron ran a finger around his neck. He hadn't wanted the fussy lace jabot. The minister had pressed it on him at the last moment, completing the full formal dress.

Cameron was glad of it now. His bride was . . . He took a deep breath and faced it: his bride, his little bog sprite was beautiful. Not the perfect, polished beauty in the portraits of his mother, nor the ripe, sensual beauty of Ailine, the widow who'd first taught a brash boy how to please a woman.

Jeannie Macleay's beauty was something quite different.

She was the scent of heather on the wind, the softness of mist in the glen, and the clean, fresh air of the mountains. It was a subtle beauty, like that of his homeland, not delicate and whimsical and demanding as his mother had been, but strong and free and bonny.

She wore a softly draped veil of lace over long, glossy chestnut hair that fell clear to her waist. Where had she hidden that hair? His fingers itched to run through the silken length of it. Her skin was smooth and fresh with a dozen or so small freckles, like brown breadcrumbs sprinkled over cream, her cheeks a wild rose blush echoed in her soft, full lips.

Cameron straightened under his bride's clear gaze. She liked how he looked too, he could tell by the feminine approval in her wide blue eyes. He drew himself up, glad now he'd worn the kilt and even the stupid, fussy jabot.

She gazed up at him, clinging tightly to his arm, and gave him a hesitant, shy, faintly anxious smile that pierced his heart.

His bride.

"Dearly beloved."

They turned and faced the minister. It passed in a blur. Cameron heard himself making his vows. His bride spoke hers in a clear, soft voice.

"Time to sign the register," the minister said. He handed Cameron the pen. Cameron signed it and passed it to his bride.

She took it, but made no move to sign. Her thoughts seemed far away.

Of course, she wouldn't know how to read or write, he realized, and his stomach hollowed as he took in the implications of his rash act.

"Dip the end in the ink and make your mark," Cameron told her in a low voice. "A cross will do. Or a thumbprint if you prefer."

She gave him an odd look, then dipped the quill in the ink and swiftly wrote her name in a stylish copperplate hand.

Cameron blinked. How had a simple shepherdess learned to write like that?

He was still pondering that question while the minister recited some advice about marriage. And then the words, "You may kiss the bride."

Cameron lifted the veil back off her face. To his surprise, his hands were shaking. She turned her face up to him, her eyes shining, trustful, her lips rosy, slightly parted.

He stared down at her. This thing he'd done so carelessly, this marriage he'd made without consideration, thinking only of his inheritance: it had become something momentous. This girl had given herself into his care, forever. She was his.

He bent and touched his mouth to hers, intending to make it brief, but her lips softened under his and she sighed and leant into him, and before he knew it he was kissing her deeply, his senses swimming with the taste, the scent and the feel of her.

"That's enough for now, lad." The minister's voice cut in dryly. "Save the rest for the honeymoon."

Cameron released her, dazed, still hungry. He stared at her in shock. She blinked up at him, blushing, a little dishevelled, her mouth soft and moist, her eyes dreamy.

His wife.

Afterwards, they returned to the minister's house for tea. "It's not much of a wedding breakfast, I'm afraid," Mrs Potts said, "but it's the best Morag and I can do at such short notice, and it'll keep you going until you get home."

"Your best is very fine thank you, Mrs Potts," Cameron assured her. There was shortbread and egg-and-bacon tart and Selkirk bannock and fresh-baked baps with butter and honey. And if Cameron and his cousins thought it a poor celebration to be washing such fine food down with tea instead of whisky, they knew better than to say so. Not in front of a minister.

Not that Cameron cared. He was watching his bride eat her way through every piece of food offered her with an expression of utter bliss.

Halfway through a slice of Selkirk bannock, she set it down with a huge, regretful sigh. "I'm sorry, but I canna eat a single mouthful more. It's the most delicious meal I've had in forever, Mrs Potts, Morag." She laughed. "Uncle Ewan thinks porridge is all a body needs."

He recalled what her uncle had said about her eating too much. She was as slender as a reed.

Cameron stood. "We'd best get along home now. Thank you for all you've done, Reverend Potts, Mrs Potts, Morag." He bowed to each. "You've turned this into a very special occasion."

At his words, Jeannie jumped up. "Oh, your dress," she said to Mrs Potts. "I should change back into—"

The older woman shook her head. "Keep the dress my dear, with my blessing. And here's a wee wedding present for you." She gave Jeannie a parcel wrapped in brown paper. "Open it tonight, before you go to bed."

For the sake of politeness Jeanie made a few half-hearted protests but she was glad to leave her old clothes – and her old life – behind. She hugged the motherly minister's wife and thanked her again.

Then it was time to mount up again, this time with Jeannie riding in front of Cameron, seated sideways across his saddle because the blue dress was too narrow-cut to allow for sitting astride – not without a scandalous amount of leg showing. Jeannie was made comfortable enough with a cushion borrowed from Mrs Potts and in a short time they were off and heading towards her new home.

With her new husband. The thought took her breath away. It was like a dream. His arms were wrapped around her holding her steady, warm and strong. Her husband.

Five

They breasted a hill and stopped to take in the view. A rocky promontory jutted deep into into the loch where a castle loomed, gloomy and forbidding. A village nestled at its foot, a scattering of neat cottages.

Jeannie eyed them eagerly. One of them would be hers. She couldn't wait. "Which house is yours?"

"The big one." He pointed.

Two cottages were larger than the others. One was on the outskirts of the village and the other was in the centre, facing the village square. "Is it the one in the town or the one next to the wee burn," she asked. She didn't mind which.

"The big one," he repeated.

"But—" She broke off. Did he mean? "You mean the castle?" Her voice came out in a squeak.

"Aye."

She twisted in the saddle to look him in the eye. "You're not some kind of a servant, are you?"

He grinned and shook his head.

Jeannie swallowed. "You mean to say you live in the—" She could see the answer in his eyes. He did. "But you said I'd be the woman of the house."

"You will."

"What job do you do in the castle?"

He just grinned. His cousins, who had recovered their high spirits once out of sight of the minister, guffawed. "He's the laird, lassie. From the moment you married him. You're the laird's wife."

"The laird's wife?" she echoed faintly. A hollow opened up in her. "You mean to say I'll be in charge of that, that enormous place?"

He smiled down, pleased at her amazement. "Aye."

They all beamed at her, as if it was some huge treat to be put in charge of a castle with no warning. Or training. Or even any clothes.

She thumped him on the shoulder, hard. "Why didn't you tell me?"

He gave her a bemused look and rubbed his shoulder. "Would it have made any difference?"

"Yes! No – I don't know. You should have warned me." Oh Lord, *the laird's wife*.

"What good would it have done?"

She thumped him again. "I could have prepared myself."

"Clothes, ye mean?" he asked cautiously.

"No, ye great thick-head! Where would I get clothes?" She tapped her forehead. "I mean up here. You told me I'd be mistress in my own home—"

"Well you will be—"

"—not the laird's wife—"

"It's the same thing."

She went to thump him again and he caught her fist, laughing.

"It's not the same thing," she said crossly. "A woman in her own cottage answers to nobody. A laird's wife answers to everyone. Everyone will have an opinion, from your uncle to the lowest scullery-maid. And if they don't think I'm up to the job – and they'll see at once I'm no fine high-born lady – they won't respect me, and they won't obey me – oh, they'll pretend to and be sweet as pie to the mistress's face but they'll resent me and the work will be done shoddily and—"

"For a shepherdess, you seem to know a lot about how a big house runs."

"I've only been a shepherdess for four years," she told him impatiently. "Before that my mother was housekeeper of a large house – she took the position after my father died and left us with no money. So believe me when I say—"

"Housekeeper?" he interrupted.

"Aye, she—"

"Then you'll know fine how to run a castle, won't ye?" he said, leaving her dumbfounded. He gave a pleased nod and, still holding her fist in one large hand, he urged his horse down the slope towards the castle.

Jeannie swallowed. She wanted to hit him for being so unreasonably blithe about the problems she faced, but somehow his confidence seeped slowly into her. She did know a little about running a grand house. From the wrong end of things, but still . . .

Besides, she had no choice. She was wed.

She could do this, she could. As long as nobody found out he'd fished his bride from a bog, she just might be able to pull it off.

Her confidence seeped away as the castle loomed closer. They trotted over a bridge and through an archway and came to a halt in a courtyard.

Ostlers ran out to take the reins of the horses. Cameron Fraser – she had to stop thinking of him by his full name, he was her husband now, not a stranger – *Cameron* dismounted and lifted Jeannie down. She stretched her cramped limbs in relief, shook her crumpled skirts out and tidied her hair.

"Ready?" Cameron asked her.

She wasn't, she wanted to run in the opposite direction but she nodded, and without warning he swept her into his arms and carried her up the steps to the great iron-studded oak door.

"What—?"

"Stop struggling. It's tradition. Carry the bride over the threshold," he said. His cousins ran ahead and banged loudly on the door, shouting that the laird had brought home a bride. As they reached it the door swung open. Cameron strode through it.

Jeannie clung to his neck, gazing around her, trying to look graceful. Her stomach was a battlefield of fluttering butterflies.

People came from everywhere, popping out of doorways and flowing down stairwells, staring at her, crowding in after Cameron, flocking to see the laird's bride, laughing and clapping and buzzing with surprised speculation.

"He married the first woman he found," Jimmie shouted exuberantly to the crowd. "Fished her out of a bog and married her!"

Jeannie's fingers curled into fists. "I'm going to kill your cousin," she muttered into Cameron's neck.

He laughed. "Best it's out from the beginning. You're my wife, nothing can change that."

"I'm still going to kill him."

Cameron carried her into a room they called the Great Hall. It was a big, barren-looking room with an ancient fireplace as big as a horse stall.

Cameron set her carefully on her feet, took her hand and raised it. "Meet your new mistress, Jeannie Macleay of the Isle of Lewis, now Mrs Cameron Fraser. And I am now running this estate."

There was a roar of approval and clapping. Jeannie was under no illusion that the approval was for her. It was Cameron they were cheering, and that he was, at last, the laird.

They came forward to be introduced, one by one, first relatives, of whom there were a surprising number. Jeannie tried to remember the names but they soon became a blur.

Of his newly deposed trustee uncle, there was no sign.

"And this is the housekeeper, Mrs Findlay," Cameron said.

Mrs Findlay was a tall, austere-looking, middle-aged woman. Dressed in crisply pressed shades of grey, she exuded efficiency.

Facing her, Jeannie felt tired and crumpled and inadequate, but everyone was watching and she would not be intimidated. She held out her hand pleasantly. "Mrs Findlay."

Instead of shaking Jeannie's hand the housekeeper handed her a large bunch of keys on a round metal circlet, saying stiffly, "The keys to the household, madam. As the laird's wife, they are yours by right."

The ring of keys weighed heavily in Jeannie's hand. Her mother had carried just such a collection on her belt. She took a deep breath, praying it was the right thing to do, and handed them back to the housekeeper, saying in a clear voice. "Thank you Mrs Findlay, but I'm sure you know what to do with these much better than I. I learned a little about the running of a great house from my mother, of course, but I'm a new bride and still have much to learn." She smiled and added, "I can see for myself the castle is beautifully run. I hope we'll work well together."

There was an almost audible sigh in the room as the housekeeper took the keys back. Thawing visibly, she said in a warmer tone, "I'm sure we will, madam. If it's convenient, I could show you the house and its workings tomorrow."

Jeannie nodded. "That would be very convenient, thank you."

As the housekeeper turned away, Cameron slipped Jeannie's hand in his and squeezed it briefly. "Perfect."

She felt a small glow of satisfaction, and as the rest of the household came up to be introduced, she addressed them with added confidence.

Suddenly a hush fell. The crowd parted and a tall, white haired courtier came slowly forwards. It was a wig, she saw as he came closer: Uncle Charles still affected the fashions of a bygone era.

Cameron introduced them stiffly, poised, Jeannie saw, to defend her from any insult his uncle might make her. The realization warmed her.

Uncle Charles, however was the perfect courtier. He bowed gracefully over Jeannie's hand and murmured everything that was correct, then shook his nephew's hand and congratulated him.

The watching household waited, but it soon became clear there would be no dramatic scene, and disappointed, people slowly drifted back to their duties.

Six

Dinner was almost ready. Jeannie was given time to wash and tidy herself, and a maidservant to assist her. While the maid did her best to neaten the crumpled, travel-stained dress, Jeannie washed her face and hands and brushed her hair and wound it into a neat coronet, but she had no fresh gown to change into and she felt very self-conscious when Cameron came to escort her to dinner. He was dressed formally in the kilt, though this time with no lace jabot. He still took her breath away.

"I'll need more clothes," she told him. "I have just this one dress to my name."

He nodded. "Wear this tonight." He dug into his sporran and pulled out a worn, flat box. She opened it to find a rope of lustrous, shimmering pearls. "My mother had a lot of jewels, but I'm told pearls are the most suitable for a bride."

He helped her twine them about her neck. They felt cool and heavy and magnificent against her skin, armour against the feelings of inadequacy that intensified as he led her down the staircase to the great hall, where they were to dine.

A piper sounded, piping the laird and his new bride in to dinner. The sound shivered down Jeannie's spine. She was now part of an ancient tradition.

Cameron's uncle sat at Jeannie's right hand and from the moment she was seated, began to engage her in light, polite conversation.

Bemused, Jeannie responded to his questions as best she could, but far from the personal interrogation she dreaded, she soon found he was entirely uninterested in herself and passionate about his plans for silk hangings for the great hall. He'd designed the hangings himself, was sorely disappointed with the cancellation of the order and clearly aimed to enlist her support in changing Cameron's mind.

"Such a barren and gloomy room, is it not? My nephew, lacking the refinement to appreciate such things, has already cancelled the order—"

On the other side of her, Cameron bristled.

"But I can see you're a lady of taste. Do you not think . . ."

"Mr Sinclair—"

He patted her hand. "Call me Uncle Charles, my dear. We're family now."

"Uncle Charles, then. I'm sorry but it's been a long day. Perhaps we could discuss this at a later date?" It wasn't a lie. She was exhausted. So much had happened. And there was still her wedding night ahead.

The older man acquiesced gracefully. She'd say this for him, he was a courtier to his beautifully manicured fingertips. Perhaps they could have the hangings locally woven out of wool, she thought. He was right, the hall could use some brightening, and it didn't have to be expensive. But she wasn't going to be drawn into a family quarrel in her first day.

"Are you ready?" Cameron asked her. He stood beside her chair, his hand out, ready to escort her upstairs.

Jeannie's heart beat a rapid tattoo. Her wedding night. She'd thought about it all afternoon, planned exactly what she was going to say . . .

The wine she'd been drinking at dinner tasted suddenly sour in her mouth. She'd find out now what kind of man she'd married.

At the door of her bedchamber – their bedchamber – he raised her hand and kissed it. "I'll leave you to get ready. I'll return in half an hour."

She nodded numbly, dread pooling in her stomach at the delay.

A maid waited inside. There was hot water in the jug and a fire blazed in the hearth. A wine decanter and two glasses stood on the table beside the bed. The very large bed. The sheets were turned down, the pillows plumped and waiting.

On the bed lay the brown paper parcel that the minister's wife had given her. She'd forgotten all about it. Someone must have found it in Cameron's saddlebags and brought it up.

She opened it and found a pretty nightgown, a soft white woollen shawl, a cake of the rose soap and a small china pot containing face cream. The nightgown was made of fine, soft lawn, narrowly pintucked and embroidered at the neck with tiny pink roses.

Jeannie hadn't worn anything so pretty to bed in her life. It would be a waste to wear it tonight but she couldn't resist.

The maid helped her off with her dress and brushed out her hair, then she sent the girl away. She washed with the rose soap, creamed her skin from the little china pot, then put on the dainty nightgown.

It slipped over her skin like feathers. So light. So insubstantial. Thank goodness for the fire.

She glanced at her reflection in the looking glass and her eyes widened. The nightdress was so fine it was practically transparent. She arranged the shawl around her, but though warm, it was fine and soft and clung lovingly to her shape. Too lovingly.

It would not do at all.

Through the doorway on the right of the room lay Cameron's dressing room. She hurried in and searched through it rapidly until she found the perfect thing, an old woollen fishing pullover, slightly unravelled at the neck. She pulled it on. It fell halfway to her knees. Perfect.

There was a knock on the door. He was here. She ran back into the bedchamber and took a flying leap on to the bed, landing just as the door opened.

Cameron took a deep breath and opened the door. He was about to take his bride and make a wife of her. He couldn't wait. Ever since he'd seen her walking down the aisle of the kirk, since he'd smelled the scent of her and tasted her mouth, his body had throbbed with the knowledge that this was his woman, and that tonight she'd be his.

He smiled. She sat cross-legged on the bed. Under his gaze she dragged the bedclothes up like a shield, covering her bare legs. And what the hell was she wearing his old pullover for? The room was perfectly warm – he'd ordered the fire himself.

Mind, he had no complaint; she looked very fetching in the shapeless old thing, one shoulder sliding out of the loose ravelled neck.

He couldn't wait to strip it off her.

She also looked pale and wary and a wee bit nervous. That was as it should be. Brides were nervous. Grooms were not.

Cameron shrugged off his coat. He wasn't the least bit nervous. He was, not to put too fine a point on it, well primed and raring for action. Well, his body was. But tonight, at least, his desires would have to take second place to hers.

He unbuttoned his waistcoat, placed it on top of his coat and loosened the ties at the neck of his shirt. Her eyes were on him, big and wide.

Cameron knew his way around a woman's body. He knew fine how to pleasure a woman. He'd gentle his bride and take her slow and easy, bringing her to the business with all the finesse at his fingertips – and that, he flattered himself, was considerable. She'd find pleasure in her marriage bed, he was determined on it. It would make her a more malleable, contented and obedient wife.

He pulled off his boots and in his stockinged feet walked towards the bed, smiling.

"Don't come any closer," she warned, her hands held up ready to ward him off.

Aye, she was nervous, all right. "Don't worry, lass, I'll be gentle—"

"I said stop!" she repeated. "There's something I need to say to you first."

Cameron shrugged and sat down on the end of the bed. "Go ahead."

She scooted back, about as far away from him as she could be and still be on the same bed. "I'm no' going to lie down with you tonight," she told him. "Not as a bride."

Bridal jitters. "Why not?" Cameron folded his arms and waited.

She nervously ran her tongue across her lips. His gaze followed the movement hungrily.

"I don't know you."

"Och, you do. I'm your husband," he said with a glimmer of amusement.

"I ken that fine," she flashed, "But we don't know each other and I won't – I can't lie down wi' a man I don't . . . I've only just . . . You don't know me at all."

"I know enough," he said, "and in the lying down together we will come to know each other."

She flushed, a wild rose colour that set his blood pounding. "What exactly do you know about me?"

Ah, so that was it. She had a past, some secret she was afeared he'd discover. "I don't care what you've done in the past, Jeannie. Our marriage starts fresh tonight." He slid along the bed towards her.

She shot off the bed. "Not tonight it doesn't. You will listen to me on this, Cameron Fraser!" She stood near the fire, her arms folded across the swell of her breasts, her blue eyes sparking. "I'm not ashamed of anything in my past if that's what you're implying – but you've proved my point. You know nothing about me. I'm not just some female body you pulled from a bog and wed to get your hands on an inheritance. I'm a person, with hopes and dreams and plans of my own. Aye, we're married, but it's not enough."

He frowned. What the devil was she on about? Of course she was a person. He could see that fine through the thin fabric of her nightdress,, her long, slender legs silhouetted by the firelight. The blood pooled in his groin.

But she was saying no, dammit. "I don't understand. I've given you my name, brought you to my home, introduced you to my family in all honour. What the hell else do you want?"

She narrowed her eyes. "Don't curse at me, Cameron Fraser." Her voice softened. "I know we're wed and I appreciate the honour you've done me, indeed I do. But if I'm to be a true wife to you, I want . . . I want . . ."

He flung himself off the bed and prowled slowly towards her, his temper on a knife edge. He'd got her measure now. He'd put a stop to this nonsense. "More jewels? Money? What?"

She swallowed. "I want the same as other brides."

"Clothes? A trousseau? I said I'd buy you—"

"I want to be courted."

He came to an abrupt halt. "Courted?" She wanted to be *courted*? By her *husband*?

She nodded. "Just for a wee while. Just until we know each other better. And then I'll feel more comfortable when we . . . you know." She glanced at the bed.

His anger slowly died. She was in earnest. And he had, after all, only known her for less than a day. He'd taken one look at her in the kirk and was ripe to tup her then and there, minister be damned.

But women were different, he knew.

"And what would this courtship entail?" He knew. Flowers, little gifts. Pretty speeches. And poetry, he thought gloomily. He hated poetry.

She bit her lip and considered it a moment. "Talking mainly," she said at last. "Getting to know each other. Perhaps a few walks."

It wasn't much to ask. "No poetry then?" he said, cheering up.

Her eyes lit. "Do you like poetry? My father was a poet."

"No," he said hastily. "I don't know any poems." Mainly dirty ones. "But I could teach you to ride."

"That would be lovely," she said in the kind of voice that told him she'd prefer he spouted poetry. And she waited, with that hopeful look in her eyes that unmanned him every damned time.

Capitulation loomed. "How long would this courting period last?" He didn't like the idea, didn't want to wait for what his body hungered for, but she was his wife and he owed her respect. And he couldn't withstand that damned appealing look.

"A week?"

He sighed. A week of waiting would probably kill him, especially if he had to look at those legs of hers much longer. But it wasn't an unreasonable request.

"All right, a week," he agreed. "On one condition."

"What's that?"

"We both sleep in the same bed – this bed. I give you my word I'll do nothing you don't want," he added before she could argue.

Courting couples did a great deal more than talking. Kissing, rolling around in the hay, all kinds of intimate exploration. He'd court her in bed with soft words and caresses. By the end of the week when they came to do the deed she'd be aching for him as he ached for her now.

She gave him a wary look, sensing a trap.

"I don't want people gossiping about our marriage," he explained, and that did the trick.

She nodded. "Very well, I agree."

"Right then." Cameron strode to the bed, flipped the covers back, pulled out his *sgian dhu* and cut his arm.

Seven

"What are you doing?" Jeannie gasped and flew across the room to him

He let a few drops of blood fall on the sheets before he allowed her to examine the cut.

"What on earth were you thinking of? Why would you do such a thing to yourself?" She grabbed a clean handkerchief and pressed it to the small cut. It was nothing, but he rather liked her fussing over him.

"I won't have the maids spreading rumours about your virginity. Or lack of it."

"I don't lack – oh." She broke off in blushing comprehension and stared at the stains on the sheet. "You cut yourself for me, for my honour," she whispered.

Cameron tried to look noble and brave. "It's noth—"

She flung her arms around him and kissed him, full on the mouth. He gathered her against him.

He'd cut himself for her, to protect her from gossip and

unkindness. What husband would do that for a bride who'd just refused him her bed?

Jeannie lifted her mouth to his and a kiss started in gratitude ended in passion. The taste of him entered her blood like hot strong whisky, wild and dark and thrilling, dissolving her doubts, her fears.

He grabbed the hem of the pullover and dragged it up. She hesitated. "It's scratchy," he murmured, and staring at his mouth, his beautiful, damp, wicked mouth, and his steady hazel eyes, she lifted her arms and let him drag the pullover over her head.

Even before he'd tossed it aside she was kissing him again. The taste of him was like wildfire in her blood.

Wanting poetry? Was she mad?

She didn't want poetry. She wanted Cameron. Her husband.

The salt-clean scent of his skin was so right, so familiar to her. Desperate to touch him she slipped her hands under his shirt, over his chest, caressing the smooth, hard planes, and all the time kissing, kissing . . .

He bent her back over the bed, half lying, grasping her by the hips and positioning her between his long brawny thighs, bare thighs, covered only by the kilt.

Her hands dropped to his waist. She could feel the buckles of his kilt.

Cameron eased her down on the bed, running his hands over her slender, lissome body, caressing her through the soft fine fabric of her nightdress. She pressed herself against him like a small eager cat, writhing in innocent eroticism, her limbs embracing him.

His kilt was riding up and as she moved she brushed against him. Cameron groaned. He was hard and throbbing and it was all he could do not to shove her nightgown up and take her.

But he'd given her his word.

She brushed against him again and he abruptly pulled away and swung his legs over the side of the bed. He sat there, panting, trying to lash into obedience the wild horses of his control.

"What's wrong?" She touched him tentatively on the shoulder.

He didn't reply. What the hell had happened? He was as out of control as a young boy with his first woman.

"Cameron?" She trailed her hand softly down his spine.

He shuddered and arched beneath her touch. "Don't do that!" There was a short, hurt silence and he added in a quieter voice, "Don't touch me."

"Don't you like it?"

"I like it fine."

"Then why?"

"Because it's stretching my control to its limits, that's why."

"Your control?" There was almost a purr to the way she said it.

"Aye, touch me again and I might not be able to keep my promise to you. And I don't break my word."

"I see."

The only sound in the room then was the crackling of the fire and Cameron's own heavy breathing. He tried to concentrate on pure thoughts, but the scent of her skin, of roses and warm, aroused woman teased his nostrils. Coals shifted in the fireplace and all he could think of was the way she would look clad in nothing but firelight. He gritted his teeth willing his rampant body to obedience.

"What if I want you to?"

His stomach lurched. Did she just say what he thought she'd said?

Her hands moved at his hips, there was the click of buckles and he felt his kilt begin to slide away. He turned around to face her. "What the hell?"

"I . . . I've changed my mind." In one movement she pulled her nightgown over her head and knelt there, naked, her heart in her eyes.

With a groan he pulled her to him. He lavished her with kisses, loving every inch of her skin with hands and mouth and body. She was warm satin, fragrant as petals and her hair flowed over her like the silky dark water of the peaty burn.

She shuddered and gasped and pressed herself against him, wrapping her long silky legs around him, plastering him with hot, slightly clumsy kisses that drove him purely wild.

He'd planned to wait, to take it slow and gentle but she was wild and eager and impatient and so greedy for him he couldn't hold himself back.

As he entered her she cried out, arching and shuddered, clutching him with hard little fingers, her thighs trembling and closing around him as her body accepted him deep inside. Welcoming him.

Ancient rhythms pounded through him and he shattered then, and at the spiralling edge of his awareness felt her shattering with him.

Eight

Cameron woke first in the morning. Usually after a night of lovemaking he sprang out of bed, raring to meet the day. Now he lay quietly, listening to the soft sound of her breathing, examining the unaccustomed feelings that lay heavy and full in his chest.

He was married. He had a wife. This was how he'd wake every morning for the rest of his life. He felt . . . He tasted the feelings floating inside him . . . Happy. Humbled. Awed.

Yesterday he'd sworn a mad, rash vow and performed the most reckless act of a somewhat reckless life. It could have been the biggest mistake of his life.

He glanced at the girl curled up against him, her silky chestnut hair spilling over her shoulder, half hiding her face.

Instead she was the biggest gift.

He lay there, breathing her in, the scent of her; roses and woman. His woman, his bride.

Her eyes fluttered open and she smiled sleepily. "Cameron," she breathed, and he couldn't help it, he had to kiss her, and then, well, he couldn't help himself again. He had no self-restraint, and apparently, neither had she.

Afterwards they lay entwined, their breathing slowing, skin to skin, gazing into each other's eyes.

After a while she gave a shivery sigh. "That was the loveliest way to wake up." She stretched and gave him a rueful smile. "I suppose this means the courtship is over."

And she looked at him with that damned look in her eyes that shattered him every time.

Cameron took a deep breath and began, "My love is like a red, red rose that's sweetly sprung in June, my love is like—" He broke off. She had tears in her eyes.

"What is it?" he said. "What's the matter?"

"Rabbie Burns," she whispered. "You're quoting Rabbie Burns to me on my wedding morning." Great crystal tears glittered on her lashes. What the hell had he done wrong?

"You said you liked poetry."

"You said you didn't."

"Aye, well, I promised you a courtship. And you do smell like a rose, and so I thought . . ." He swallowed. "They fit. The words I mean. They all fit. *All* the words." He scanned her face anxiously. Didn't she see what he was trying to tell her?

Her mouth quivered. "Cameron Fraser, I know we've only known each other for a day and a night, and you'll probably think it's foolish of me, and premature, but I think I'm falling in love with you."

She loved him. He wanted to shout it from the battlements. His chest felt full and heavy. He cupped her cheeks with his hands and kissed her. "It's neither foolish nor premature, Jeannie Macleay Fraser, but a proper thing in a bride."

"And you?" She gave him that look and waited. Och he was gone, he was truly gone.

"Perhaps I'll one day come to rue the day I plucked a wee bog sprite from the mud and married her, but I doubt it. Right now I think it's the cleverest thing I've done in all my life."

She tried to frown. "A bog sprite?"

Cameron grinned and kissed her. "Aye but this wee bog sprite smells like a rose." He kissed her again. "My bonnie lass." And again. "My red, red rose." And then because she might not have understood what the poem meant, "My love."

After the Gloaming

Leah Marie Brown

Oh! Samhain, that wicked and perilous season has once again come upon us, when the barrier between this world and the orbis alia *is dissolved and spirits roam free, wreaking chaos where once there was order; when the evil lurking in the shadowy chambers of men's hearts is exposed, leaving the innocent vulnerable.*
— Excerpt from Scottish journal

Scotland, October 31, 1513

Deidre Monreith clutched the edges of her hooded cloak to keep it from billowing in the wind gusting through the battlement of the crumbling tower and looked out over the vast, wooded domain that would one day belong to the man she loved.

To her right, the Solway Firth glimmered beneath the setting sun, reminding her of the angry, smouldering ashes that glowed many shades of orange in Potter Murray's oven.

And to her left, rising majestically from the centre of a triangular-shaped moat, was Caerlaverock Castle. Constructed of thick, amber-hued sandstone and boasting a double tower gatehouse, it was the most impressive castle in all of the lowlands.

Perhaps in all of Scotland.

For hundreds of years, the wretched, wily English had been crossing the border, pillaging the lowland villages and laying siege to Caerlaverock. Yet still she stood! Rampallions be damned!

Truth be known, the pride that swelled inside her when she looked upon Caerlaverock was a mere trickle when compared to the torrent she felt for the man destined to rule it.

Robert Maxwell, eldest son of John Maxwell, the fourth Lord Maxwell, would one day be master of Caerlaverock and all the Maxwell lands. Brave, handsome, charming and clever, Robert was to be the fifth Lord Maxwell, laird of the Clan Maxwell, commander of the mightiest garrison south of Edinburgh.

For a certainty, 'twas a challenge she knew he'd rise to with little effort. Had he not already proven himself a champion in the lists, effortlessly vanquishing many a battle-tried opponents?

And to his prodigious roll of admirable traits, she would one day add steadfast husband.

For Robert Maxwell loved her – Deirdre Monreith, the humble daughter of his father's bailiff.

Robert loved *her*! And soon he would climb the tower steps, take her in his arms, and whisper the sweet, wooing words that made her heart ache with gladness.

Ravaged by warfare and abandoned to nature, the derelict tower upon which she now stood was all that remained of the first Caerlaverock Castle. A forgotten place, nestled in the woods, it was where they met in secret, beyond the prying eyes of the hall.

The sound of a twig snapping somewhere beyond the tower walls drew her from her reverie and she suddenly realized the sun had set. She peered into the strange blue-black darkness that always followed the gloaming. Everything appeared to be as it should; and yet she could not dispel the pervasive sense of foreboding that had plagued her intermittently throughout the day. The ominous feeling had settled upon her, thick and heavy, like a mantle that could not be shirked.

Had something moved in the distance? Was that a light flickering near the water?

She leaned out over the battlement probing the thick, black forest and salt marshes. She searched for . . . something, anything that would disprove her ever-growing fears. But what could possibly be lurking in the darkness? She wasn't a child, after all. She no longer worried about *glaistigs*. She smirked now as she remembered how terrified she had once been by her da's tales of the nefarious spirit who rode under the cover of darkness, snatching unsuspecting souls from their beds, and carrying them away upon her headless steed.

Just as she was about to turn away, she noticed a dim, red light flickering in the distance.

"Beware the bean shìth, lass." She could almost hear her father's voice whispering in her ear. *"The female wraith with eyes of blazing red who leaves her otherly-world realm to keen on the doorstep of one about to die."*

"God's teeth! Deidre lass, have ye misplaced yer wits?"

She spun around and saw Robert standing near the top of the stairs, his ebony hair gleaming in the moonlight, his muscular arms crossed in front of his broad chest.

"Robert!"

"Come hither and move away from the wall before ye fall to yer death," he snapped, his tone unnaturally cold.

Something about his manner frightened her, increased her mounting sense of doom. She obeyed and quickly stepped away from the crumbling rock wall.

It was his wont to greet her with a pretty word or sonnet so why did he not remark on her beauty or take her in his arms? Something was amiss.

"I am to wed Janet Douglas," he confessed, confirming her suspicions in the worst manner imaginable.

The dagger-sharp pains assailing her heart, robbed her of breath.

"Nay!"

"Aye, 'tis true. We wed in six days time."

He turned, meaning to quit the tower, but she darted in front of him, blocking his path, desperate to retain that which she held so dear if only a moment longer.

"What shall I do?"

He frowned, as if truly perplexed by her query, and his brow knit together.

"Do?"

Tears clouded her vision.

"What shall I do . . . without ye?"

"Perchance, ye shall marry a cooper, flesher or swineherd and give him a hut full of squalling brats," he said in a tone devoid of warmth, a sardonic smile marring his handsome face.

"I pray ye stop," she cried, pressing her hands. "This cruel jest wounds me."

"I jest not. I mean to wed Janet Douglas."

"But I love ye!"

"Verily?" He shrugged. "Love is but a festering wound that heals when properly tended."

She stood in mute horror.

For a moment she feared an archer had fired a crossbow, for the pain assailing her heart was surely akin to that of an arrow to the chest. Who was this man standing before her, coldly sneering, as if they had never laughed and shared their dreams? As if he had never happened upon her in the bluebell woods nor secretly left those delicate blossoms upon her windowsill?

Something broke inside her, sending painful shards of light catapulting through her brain. Grief blinded her and muddled her wits. The grief abated, replaced by anger.

Fists clenched, she lunged forward. She meant to strike out at him, to inflict a fraction of the pain he had inflicted upon her, but he grabbed her wrists and shoved her violently from him.

Unprepared for the assault, she stumbled backwards until she felt the sharp edge of the top step beneath her feet. She seemed to hover a moment before falling into the yawning abyss.

She heard Robert cry out. She heard a sickening thud as her head struck the stone wall. She heard the rush of air roar in her ears as she made her spiralling descent and the curious crack her neck made just before she landed on the tower floor.

With blood filling her mouth and trickling down her face, she stared in stunned wonder at the shafts of silvery moonlight streaming in through the arrow slits.

And then, Deidre Monreith, daughter of Angus Monreith, bailiff to the great and mighty Lord Maxwell, heard no more.

Caerlaverock, Scotland, present day

Caden Maxwell sat in shades of darkness listening to the harsh, hacking coughs of the dying man and couldn't help but marvel at the capriciousness of Fate.

He had once vowed never to lift a finger to find his father and now here he was keeping vigil at the emaciated man's bedside.

Four months ago, Caden had been in his loft in downtown Seattle, enjoying the fruits of his labour as a successful day trader in the futures market. He had a tight-knit group of college buddies he met every Friday at Bad Albert's Tap and Grill for burgers, beer and blues. He played football every Saturday morning at Brighton Playfield, met his mother for brunch on Sundays, and volunteered at his local Boys and Girls Club.

His hectic, fulfilling life left little time for thinking about his biological father and the hole his absence had once created.

Then he received a letter from a man claiming to be his father. In concise, contrite terms James Steward Maxwell had explained that he had recently been diagnosed with lung cancer, was not expected to live more than a few months, and wanted to spend his final days getting to know the son he had neglected.

Caden's first impulse had been to crumple the letter and toss it into the waste bin, but years spent at a Catholic school, being taught the virtues of compassion and mercy by strict nuns, had instilled in him a disproportionate dose of guilt.

Cancer. Dying. Regrets. Final days.

He wrestled with his conscience for a few hours and then he remembered the words his mother often told him when he struggled with an important, moral decision.

"Listen to the voice in your heart, Caden, and do what you feel is right."

Early the next morning, he dialed the number embossed on the bottom of the expensive, crested stationery, just beneath James Maxwell's scrawling signature.

After a brief, awkward conversation with James Maxwell, he clicked on expedia.com and booked the next flight from Seattle to Edinburgh.

One 3,000-dollar Air France ticket, a thirteen-hour flight with a brief layover in Paris, an exhilarating two-hour drive down the A702 from Edinburgh to Dumfries later and he found himself at Blackstone House, James Maxwell's ancestral home situated on six acres of parkland near Caerlaverock Castle and the banks of the Solway Firth.

James drew a long, wheezy breath that roused Caden from his musings. He sat up, leaned forwards, and studied the sleeping man, waiting for his chest to rise again. A moment later, James awoke from his narcotics-induced slumber, his eyes widening in terror, as violent coughs racked his body.

"I'll get the nurse, but try to relax," he said, in a calm voice.

Caden pushed to his feet and had barely made it a step when the door opened and the home health care nurse hurried in, syringe in hand. She jabbed the needle into the IV line connected to James' hand and pushed the plunger.

"This will help relax the muscles and make it easier for you to breathe, Mister Maxwell."

She checked her patient's pulse and then turned to Caden.

"I'll sit here all night, why don't you get some sleep?"

"Thanks, but I'll stay."

Caden put his feet up on a stool, crossed his arms over his chest, and settled in for a long, uncomfortable night. Hades, James's mangy looking but lovable Scottish deerhound trotted into the room, walked to the bed and rested his head near his master's withered hand, then flopped down on the floor beside Caden's chair, emitting a pitiful sigh in the process.

Caden's eyes were just beginning to close when he heard strange, warbling as if someone were singing somewhere far in the distance. He assumed it was coming from the small, stone chapel located a few hundred yards from the manor and closed his eyes.

The warbling altered to an otherworldly keening; a deep and throaty moan that sounded like a woman grieving.

Hades ears perked up. He lifted his head, glared at the window and growled.

Caden stood and walked over to the window with Hades scrambling to follow. Pulling back the drapes, he peered into the darkness but saw only his reflection looking back at him. Then he saw something, a red light, flickering between the trees.

Hades growled deeper in his throat.

The light faded and a woman in an emerald gown with long platinum blond hair floating around her shoulders stepped out of the woods. She seemed to stare at him and as she moved closer, the light of the moon illuminated her features. Her moaning altered again, switching to a high-pitched screech.

Hades suddenly stopped growling. Reluctantly, Caden looked away from the woman to the frightened dog. Hades began to shake and a puddle of urine spread across the floor.

"It's okay boy," Caden said, patting his head.

When he looked out the window again, the woman had vanished.

The next evening found Caden resuming his bedside vigil. Outside, the wind howled through the naked trees surrounding Blackstone House, causing them to bend and sway like skeletons performing a macabre dance. Even the trees seemed to be portending James's death.

He was about to close his eyes, when something outside the window caught his attention. A movement, a whitish smudge on the velvety ebony night. Jumping to his feet, he crossed the room and peered into the inky darkness, but saw only leaves skittering over the neatly clipped lawn and the dark woods beyond.

He dropped his forehead to the cool windowpane and sighed. What was wrong with him? Was he losing his mind? Had he imagined the mournful singing and the woman in the green gown?

Hades began to growl low in his throat. His ears pulled back.

"What is it, boy?"

But Caden *knew*.

Someone lurked outside James Maxwell's bedroom window. The beautiful woman with the face of an angel and the voice of a demon had returned. Caden wondered if she was one of James's jilted lovers or perhaps a long lost daughter?

The warbling began again.

With Hades on his heels, he raced out of the sickroom and down the stairs, nearly colliding with Mrs Harriet in the dimly lit foyer. The elderly housekeeper clutched a heavy flashlight in her wrinkled hands.

"Do ye hear 'at unholy wailin' the wind is making?" She placed the flashlight on the hall table and switched off one of the lamps. "It sounds like a *bean shìth*."

Caden found it difficult to understand the woman's thick brogue but he thought she had said *bean sheath*.

What in hell is a bean sheath?

Before he could ask her what she had meant, Mrs Harriet shuffled out of the room, mumbling something about age turning her into a ridiculous daftie.

The warbling grew louder, stronger and Hades barked and lunged at the door. Caden looked out the window and saw the same red light he had noticed the night before, flickering in the woods beyond the front lawn.

He grabbed the flashlight before wrenching open the front door and plunging into the moonless night. It took a moment for his eyes to adjust but he could feel Hades by his side, hear his heavy panting.

The strange light suddenly disappeared and the woman in the green dress stepped out the woods, her long platinum hair floating about her shoulders.

Hades barked ferociously but the woman did not appear frightened. She stood between the skeletal trees and kept her gaze fixed on James Maxwell's bedroom window.

Hades took off running. The woman suddenly lifted her hand and the dog skidded to a stop. He spun in several circles, before stopping, bending his front leg, and pointing his nose in the direction of his master's window as if obeying some silent command.

Hades knows that woman.

Caden sprinted across the lawn. The closer he got to the woman, the more in-focus her features became. She had a beautiful face with almond-shaped eyes fringed by long lashes and pouty lips that reminded him of Angelina Jolie.

She looked at him then. Her eyes widened and she took a step back. Caden was almost to her when she took another step back and disappeared into the dark forest.

Caden clicked the flashlight on with his thumb and kept on running, weaving between trees and hurtling over logs. He could hear Hades barrelling through the underbrush behind him.

Finally, he saw her through the trees ahead of him.

She looked over her shoulder at him. Her mouth opened in a silent scream, her features changed from bewitching to hideous with wide, sunken black eyes, wrinkled skin that seemed to glow, and grizzled hair.

Caden suddenly felt feverish. His skin became slick with perspiration and his heart began to race. He had played competitive ball long enough to recognize the signs of a massive adrenaline dump.

I need to control my breathing!

He kept running but took slow, measured breaths.

Hades suddenly let out a terrifying yelp and forced Caden to abandon his pursuit.

He found the mangy beast only a few yards away, yelping and howling as if the hounds of hell were nipping at his heels. His collar had snagged on a lowlying branch and was choking him each time he moved. Caden quickly released the dog but by the time he had retraced his steps, the woman had vanished.

He considered abandoning the chase and returning to Blackstone House, but the adrenaline surging through his body propelled him on.

He walked through the woods, moving his flashlight in front of him in a wide, sweeping arc searching for signs of the woman.

Caden still believed the creature he pursued was merely a woman bent on revenge or mischief. A clever woman who was able to halt a charging deerhound with a single gesture, somehow alter her appearance, and slip over land littered with dry, crackly leaves without making a sound.

Doubt began to needle at him.

What if it wasn't a woman? What if it was one of the mythical creatures Mrs Harriet had prattled on about? If he had learned one thing since arriving at Blackstone House, it was that the Scots believed in the supernatural and revelled in telling stories about it. Ladies in white, headless horsemen, loch monsters, demons, fairies, phantoms. If he were to believe Mrs Harriet and the Guinness-fueled old men he'd spoken with at Gordon Pub, the hills and lochs were crawling with creatures.

His boots snapped twigs and crashed through the underbrush. The sound seemed amplified in the woods, making him feel unusually vulnerable. He didn't like feeling vulnerable.

The hairs rose on the back of his neck. Someone watched him.

He glanced over his shoulder, peering into the darkness. Only Hades followed, trotting several paces behind, his head hung low.

The sound of a twig snapping in the distance drew his attention. He swung his flashlight out before him, aiming it straight ahead. Nothing was there. The beam of light caught the spiralling descent of a brown leaf and Caden realized something was in the trees.

He raised the flashlight higher but nearly dropped it when he saw two glowing eyes staring back at him.

"Shit!"

Perched on a branch in a nearby tree sat a large grey owl, his obsidian gaze fixed on Caden. His head swivelled around, then he screeched, and Caden's heart stopped beating. The owl flapped his wings and flew off into the night sky.

Caden followed the owl's flight path until he came to the mudflats that led to the Solway Firth.

Hades growled.

Caden patted the dog's head, feeling the bristly fur on his palm. "Be quiet, boy."

Although the wind had died down, Caden shivered. The long sleeved T-shirt he wore beneath his rugby sweatshirt was damp with perspiration and clung to his arms and chest.

The clouds drifted apart and silvery moonlight reflected off the placid water. That's when Caden saw her. The woman in green knelt at the water's edge and was repeatedly plunging a garment into the sea. Her hair, once again platinum blond, hung like a curtain around her face.

Caden clicked off the flashlight, motioned for Hades to stay, and then moved slowly, stealthily towards the water's edge until he stood close enough to see the leather belt knotted around the waist of her medieval costume.

Costume? Of course!

He realized then that she was probably one of the people who reenacted medieval life at Clash of the Centuries, the medieval fair held each year at Caerlaverock. Though he thought Mrs Harriet had said it took place in the summer, not late October.

She plunged the stained garment into the water again and then dropped her chin to her chest. The sound of her soft weeping floated on the sea-stained breeze.

Caden suddenly felt guilty for chasing and spying on a woman who had done nothing more than trespass and disturb the peace of Blackstone with her strange, mournful tune.

He reached out to touch her shoulder but his hand passed through her.

"What the—?"

She looked up at him through her curtain of hair and gasped. Tears glittered like diamonds on her translucent cheeks. She was even more beautiful than he had first thought. He'd already noticed her kiss-worthy lips, but now he noticed her ample, round breasts which were almost disproportionately large on her petite, slender frame.

He tried to touch her shoulder again but his hand moved through her as if she were made of vapour.

She dashed the tears from her cheeks and stood, the top of her head coming to his chin.

"You can see me?"

"Yes."

"And hear me?"

"Obviously." Caden's thoughts spun around in his brain. He feebly grappled with the clues, trying to construct a logical explanation for the illogical situation before him. "Who are you? *What* are you?"

The ridiculousness of the situation struck him. He remembered the time he had been sick in bed with the flu and had channel surfed to an impossibly idiotic show called *Ghost Hunters* and how he'd snorted when the host had walked into an empty room of an old insane asylum and announced, "If there's anyone here, please make your presence known." Now here he was attempting to have a conversation with a transparent woman with banging curves and kissable lips.

"Five hundred years ago, I lived in a village near Caerlaverock. My name was Deidre Monreith."

Caden thought he detected a hysterical note in his chuckle. "Are you telling me you have travelled through time?"

She shook her head and the moonlight streamed off her hair like liquid silver.

"I am not a human from another time nor am I merely a ghost of what I once was. I am something far more tragic. I am a *bean shìth*."

"I don't understand," Caden grudgingly confessed. "What is a bean sheath?"

"A *bean shìth*," she corrected. "One who has been condemned to spend eternity as a messenger of death."

"Messenger of death?"

"Aye."

Her story was too outrageous and he began to wonder if he had unwittingly become a dupe in one of those television prank shows.

"So you're sort of like Santa Claus? You fly around at night but instead of bringing presents you bring death." Caden crossed his arms over his chest. "With six billion people on the planet, you must be awfully busy."

"You do not believe me, Caden Maxwell?"

Caden uncrossed his arms and motioned for Hades to come to him.

"Okay, who are you and how do you know my name?"

"I told you, I am a *bean shìth*."

Caden ignored her bizarre statement and repeated his second question. "How do you know my name?"

"I have known your name since it was given to you."

Hades trotted up and stood by Caden's side. The dog did not growl, shake or bark, but appeared strangely calm.

"You're a banshee?"

Deidre nodded.

"And you came to Blackstone House to let James Maxwell know that he is about to die?"

"Aye."

"You did that, so now what? Will you evaporate? Hop on a broom and fly over to France to scare the wits out of some other dying soul?"

Her eyes shimmered like the sea and for a moment she looked sad and weary.

"You do not understand."

"Enlighten me."

"I cannot leave this land." She looked at him in a raw, vulnerable way that made his heart ache. "Though it is not my wish, I am a *bean shìth* for the Maxwell Clan. Mine is a wretched existence, tied to the misery and sorrow of the descendants of a man who once caused me misery and sorrow."

He could not look away from her bewitching, green-eyed gaze. And the longer he looked in her eyes, the more he believed her story.

"You said you were once human. How did you become a banshee?"

Birds began chirping and weak, watery sunlight filtered through the black, silhouetted trees as dawn approached.

"I once loved a man named Robert Maxwell and I thought he loved me, too," she brushed past him and he thought he could almost feel the hem of her gown pass over his boots. "But I was mistaken. He was a wicked man."

He joined her and together they walked along the shore towards Caerlaverock Castle, towering over the trees in the distance. Hades followed.

"On the eve he was to ask my father for my hand, he told me that he intended to marry another. He was terribly cruel," her voice trembled.

Apparently, caught in a web of sticky memories, she fell silent. Caden did not press her. He waited patiently until she resumed her tale.

She told him about her quarrel with Robert Maxwell on the roof of the derelict tower, candidly describing his callousness and her heartbreak, and Caden found himself wondering if there was something written into the Maxwell DNA that caused them to treat women with cruel disregard.

He hoped not. He didn't think he would able to live with himself if he ever acted in such a way.

As she described her death at the hands of his ancestor, Caden felt a blend of emotions. Fortunately, the loathing he felt for Robert Maxwell – a man he'd never met, a man who had lived five hundred years before Caden's birth – was surpassed by his sympathy for Deirdre Monreith.

Without thinking, he reached for her hand and was shocked when he felt her warm, slender fingers intertwine with his.

They stopped walking and turned to look at each other. Deidre's form no longer shimmered. She was not a vapourous, amorphous shape but a solid, well-proportioned woman with real, smooth skin that glowed in the orange rays of dawn.

"I don't understand!" She blushed and pulled her hand away. "You touched me and I felt it! How can that be?"

Caden shrugged.

"Beats me. I am still trying to figure out how you became a banshee."

"I don't know, but I believe someone must have uttered a curse over my dying body. Ever since my death, I have spent my days and nights in an unearthly limbo, able to see and hear the world around me but unable to interact with the people in it. Until you, the only people who could see or hear me were the dying descendants of Robert Maxwell."

Deidre wrapped her arms around her waist and let out a sigh that nearly broke Caden's heart. There was a vulnerability about her that aroused primitive, protective instincts in him.

"I have spent five hundred years silently observing the Maxwells; a mute and reluctant witness to the lives of people Fate determined I should abhor." Deidre looked deep into his eyes in a way that both excited and unnerved him. "I've watched with anticipation the birth of each Maxwell heir, hoping he would be the one to unlock the secret of my curse, for there must be some reason I am tethered to this family by supernatural ties."

"Wait a minute!" Caden raked his fingers through his hair. "Are you saying you were present at my birth?"

"Aye . . . yes."

The breath left Caden's body in one violent exhalation, as if he had been tackled by a two-hundred and ninety pound defensive tackle. He took a seat on a boulder near the mudflats that joined the Solway Firth. Deidre joined him but did not press him to speak. He watched a gaggle of whooper swans gliding gracefully through the water while he tried to absorb her mind-blowing confession.

He had spent the last five years working as a day trader in the futures market, a challenging profession that required brains *and* balls. The most successful day traders possessed strong analytical skills, nerves of steel, and the ability to make a quick, shrewd decision despite shifting data. The most successful day traders were open-minded and unflappable. And he was definitely successful.

He believed he had made millions – for his clients and himself – because he possessed the ability to quickly process information. And yet, his mind reeled from all he had learned. He was trying to put it all in order, to find reason amid confusion, to alter long-held beliefs to adapt to the current trend. But accepting the downward movement of a particular stock was a lot easier than embracing the notion that a hot woman was really a banshee who had been haunting his father's family for generations.

He looked at Deidre.

"What did you see? The day I was born?"

Sadness altered her lovely features and she turned away.

"Sometimes it is better to leave the past buried lest you unearth more than you ever hoped to find."

"Really? Does that mean you don't want me to try to learn more about the circumstances surrounding your death and the curse that made you a banshee?"

She caught her lower lip between her pearly front teeth and nibbled on it.

"I will make you a bargain, Caden Maxwell. If you help me discover more about the curse, I will tell you what you wish to know about your birth."

Caden wanted to tell her that there was no need for her to bargain with him; he would have helped her anyway.

"It's a deal."

He held out his hand and she shook it.

"If you are bound to the Maxwells and a Maxwell caused your death, weren't you there to witness the charm?"

"Curse! It was a curse, not a charm."

"Right, curse."

"I do not remember the curse but I suspect Agnes is the one who cast it."

"Agnes?"

"Aye." She bent over and snatched a rock, rubbing the smooth, water-worn surface with her fingers. "Agnes Bowquat was a white witch who lived in a hut in the woods bordering Caerlaverock."

"White witch?"

His mind was spinning again. He thought white witches were villains who fed naughty boys Turkish Delight and turned fauns into statues, like in *The Chronicles of Narnia*.

"A white witch was someone who practised the ancient arts of healing and acted as a mediator between the earthly world and the spiritual worlds."

"I'm trying to wrap my head around all of this, but it's not easy."

Her eyes widened and she gasped.

"I'm sorry," he said, suddenly realizing his faux pas. "Poor choice of words. It's a saying – meaning I'm trying to comprehend everything you've told me."

Mollified, she finished telling him about the night of her death. She said she remembered lying on the cold stone, feeling the energy drain from her body and blood from her head ooze down her cheek. She remembered hearing Robert's footsteps echo in the stairwell and how good it had felt to close her eyes. The next thing she remembered was walking into Caerlaverock and realizing nobody could see or hear her.

"Five days after he killed me, Robert married Janet Douglas," she said, her voice thick with emotion.

"Jesus! What a bastard!"

He instantly felt guilty using such language in front of a lady, but Deidre did not seem to mind.

"Aye." Deidre flicked her wrist and sent the stone skipping across the glassine surface, then turned to look at him. "I am sorry to say most of Robert's descendants have been bastards. But you are different, I think."

"I hope so."

The weight of exhaustion pressed heavily upon him and he knew he should return to Blackstone House to rest and check on James, but he didn't want to leave Deidre. He stood and stretched his muscles.

When she saw him struggling to stifle a yawn, she smiled and said, "You are tired. You should go home and sleep."

"I can't leave you here alone," he said, holding out his hand to Deidre. "Come with me."

Deidre looked at Caden and her heart joyfully skipped a beat. How tempted she was to take his hand and let him lead her back to Blackstone House, but this was the first day in five hundred years that she was able to feel, physically and emotionally, and she did not know how long it would last. If this was her only day to be whole and human again, did she want to spend it in the home of a dying Maxwell? With the son of a dying Maxwell?

Caden smiled, a charming, lopsided grin that caused dimples to appear near the corners of his mouth and her heart to skip another beat. His dimpled grin and easy charm reminded her of Robert, but that's where the resemblance ended. Tall, tanned, ruggedly built, with dark blond hair and piercing blue eyes, Caden looked quite different from the Maxwells she had haunted.

She wondered what it would be like to be truly loved by a man as handsome and compassionate as Caden Maxwell.

She took his hand and together they walked through the woods to Blackstone House. He asked her many questions about her life before the curse and seemed particularly pleased when she confessed she had always wanted to learn how to blow glass.

"Seriously? That's cool," he said, holding a branch back so she could pass beneath it. "My mother teaches glassblowing at the Museum of Glass in Tacoma. It's just a hobby of hers but I know she would be happy to teach you if—"

He let his sentence fade away but his *if* lingered in the air. If the curse had finally been broken. If she remained human. If they were ever to see each other again. It amazed her that such a small word could contain so many hopes.

They were climbing the steps to Blackstone House when the front door suddenly swung open and a plump, elderly woman appeared, a worried frown tugging at the corners of her mouth.

"Thank God," she said, putting her hands on her hips. "Whar huv ye bin? Ah huv bin so worried aboot ye!"

"I am sorry I worried you, Mrs Harriet. I couldn't sleep so I went for a walk and must have lost track of time," Caden said, squeezing her hand gently and releasing it. "Is James all right?"

"Aye." Mrs Harriet's expression softened. "Yer da is resting."

Hades came loping up, his blue-grey fur flecked with dried mud and leaves, and would have trotted in the front door and across Mrs Harriet's freshly scrubbed floor had the housekeeper not grabbed him by the collar.

"Just whaur dae ye think ye gaun?"

With a docile and properly chastened Hades still firmly in her grasp, Mrs Harriet walked down the steps. "Ah left ye a plate o' neeps hash 'n' eggs 'n' thare ur fresh scones in th' basket on the table," she called over her shoulder before leading Hades around the house towards the stables.

Mrs Harriet passed through Deidre as if moving through thin air. Caden noticed the pain in Deidre's hazel eyes and the tears glistening on her long lashes and all he wanted to do was comfort her. Wrapping an arm around her shaking shoulders, he led her up the stairs to his room.

"She passed through me as if I weren't even there!" she sobbed, burying her face in her hands. "The curse has not been broken."

Nothing unsettled Caden more than a woman crying. It lacerated his heart like a shard of glass. It made him feel anxious and helpless.

Desperate to ease her suffering, Caden gathered Deidre up in his arms, carried her to the bed, and rocked her until her sobs subsided. He felt the warmth of her body through her thick gown, the curve of her shapely body on his thighs, the silky strands of her hair teasing his chin, and it took all of his self-control not to toss her on his bed, hike up her skirt, and bury himself between her thighs.

But Deidre was not like the other women he had known. He couldn't wine her, dine her, and nail her all in the same night. Even though she had spent the last five hundred years watching the world evolve, she was still from a different time, when women had gentle dispositions and delicate sensibilities.

When she looked up at him with tears still trembling on her lashes, the slender tether restraining his desire nearly snapped.

As a spirit of the netherworld, hovering near but never interacting with humans, Deidre had spent centuries watching people flirt and fall in love. Once, quite by accident, she had happened upon one of Robert's grandsons making love to a serving wench behind a boulder in the glen near Caerlaverock.

She'd often wondered what it would feel like to be kissed and caressed again, but had long since given up hope it would ever happen. Now, Caden Maxwell was pressing his lips to hers and pushing his tongue inside her mouth.

When she finally mustered the courage to reach up and run her fingers through his close-cropped, honey-hued hair, his passionate response chased away her fears and doubts. He moaned and deepened his kiss.

The stubble covering his cheeks abraded the tender skin around her mouth, but she did not mind. In fact, she liked the intriguing pleasure-pain sensations it aroused.

Agitation pricked at her, prodded her. She wanted something from him but did not know what.

Caden knew.

He lifted her gown, slid his broad hand up her thigh, and began teasing the apex of her womanhood with the tips of his fingers, brushing over it softly, again and again, until she felt as if she were dying a second time. Only this time there was no pain, only sweet ecstasy.

Caden woke four hours later with his arms still wrapped around Deidre. He pressed a kiss to her smooth forehead, before easing himself out of bed and heading to the kitchen for a bite to eat. When he had polished off two ham sandwiches, an apple, and a can of Coke, he made a similar feast for Deidre and carried it to his room. He found her fast asleep, so he left the plate of food on the nightstand beside his bed, and headed to the bathroom.

Caden ran his hands over the stubble covering his jaw and considered shaving, but decided he would rather take a quick shower.

Fifteen minutes later, he was dressed in his favourite pair of distressed jeans and an Abercrombie button down, and comfortably seated in James's library.

Caden had found a tattered, yellowing copy of his mother's book, *Lords of the Land: A Brief History of the Maxwell Clan*, in the library earlier in the week, haphazardly shelved between the leather-bound first editions of Sir Walter Scott's *Ivanhoe* and Jonathan Swift's *Gulliver's Travels*. Although he had grown up knowing that his mother, an esteemed historian and author and a woman he adored, had written a book about his father's clan, stubborn pride and resentment had prevented him from reading it.

A memory flashed in his brain. He was fourteen and had just spent the summer at football camp where he had practised hitting and spinning, defensive moves that helped running backs avoid getting tackled (a move he employed both on and off the field). For some reason, perhaps it had been seeing all of the proud fathers at the end of camp awards ceremony or the fact that he hadn't had a father to slap him on the back and tell him "good job, son" when he won the trophy for being the best running back in his age group, he'd returned home feeling curious about James Montague Maxwell, so when he thought his mom wasn't looking, he grabbed a copy of her book from the shelf in the living room. He'd just opened it when she walked in the room. Embarrassed, he closed the book and tossed it on the table, then grabbed the remote, turned the television on, and clicked to ESPN.

"Caden," she'd said, taking the remote from his hand and pushing the button to turn off the television. "There is nothing wrong with wanting to learn more about the man who helped create you."

"Why would I want to learn about anything about a man who had abandoned his wife and only son?"

His vehemence had surprise them both.

But he was no longer an angry boy.

He opened the book and began reading about the notorious Maxwells. Apparently, the third Lord Maxwell had been accused of killing two of his wives. The fourth Lord Maxwell, a notorious rake and daring soldier, had died at the Battle of Flodden Field, leaving behind a small army of bastards. The book described Robert Maxwell, the fifth Lord Maxwell and the man responsible for Deidre's death, as a slippery intriguer who conspired against his own countrymen with England's Henry VIII. Another Maxwell was found guilty of treason for his participation in the Jacobite rising of 1715 and was sentenced to death.

Disgusted, and even a little ashamed, Caden closed his mother's book and put it back on the shelf where he had found it. He moved round the library, scanning the titles of the many books, until a thick, red leather-bound book with the words *Witchcraft in Scotland: Tales and Trials* by Professor Alastair P. Wallace embossed in faded gold caught his attention.

He snatched the book from the shelf just as the door to the library opened.

A worried looking Deidre poked her head in, looked around, and then sighed in relief when she saw him.

"Look what I just found." He held the book out to her. "It's a book about the history of witchcraft in Scotland."

"Oh Caden," she said, stepping inside and closing the door behind. "Does it say anything about Agnes Bowquan? What about curses that turn a person into a *bean shìth*?"

"I don't know. I only just found it."

He walked over to the heavy oak table in the centre of the room and pulled out a chair for Deidre, then sat in the chair beside her. He opened the book and searched the table of contents for anything that might be related to Deidre.

"Look," she said, pointing at an entry halfway down the page. "There is a section on curses."

He flipped to page two hundred and sixty two and began reading aloud.

> "In the fifteenth century and early into the sixteenth century, the most powerful witches lived in the lowlands, where the ley lines intersect, and mystical energies flow as strong and mighty as the River Tweed. Arguably the most potent witch to live in that time was Agnes Bowquat (see also *witch hunt*) of Caerlaverock who was believed to be skilled in the art of healing."

Caden skimmed over an explanation of the art of healing and the difference between white and black witches until he came to the part he was looking for – there, mid-way down page two hundred and sixty four was a brief reference to Deidre.

> "At some point, Agnes Bowquat began practising black magic, casting her most powerful spell on a dying woman. The legend is that one night the son of a great lord found the woman he loved lying in a pool of blood after she had flung herself off the ramparts of his castle. Distraught, he took her body to Agnes. Instead of healing her, the black witch turned her into a *bean shìth*."

Caden stopped reading and looked at Deidre.

"Does it say how the curse is to be broken?"

He shook his head.

"It only says your soul is connected to the Maxwell Clan and therefore it will take a Maxwell to break the curse." Caden turned back to the book and read the last paragraph. "When a Maxwell proves himself worthy of her love, and gives his love in return, he will break the curse in four moons time."

Caden turned the page hoping to find more clues about Deidre's death and the curse placed upon her.

He was not disappointed. Reproduced on the next page were a newspaper article and a small black and white photo of a pile of bones in a heavy, scarred wooden box. The caption read: *Old bones found in a box during excavation of the old tower of Caerlaverock believed to be the remains of a woman who lived over four hundred years ago.*

"That's it! I think I know what will break the curse."

"You do?"

Caden nodded.

"Maybe you are still haunting the Maxwells because you were never given a proper burial. I'll find your bones and bury them."

"But how will you do that?"

Caden read the newspaper article again and saw the dateline was 5 August, 1956. He thought of Mrs Harriet. She had to be at least sixty-five years old. He wondered if she might know something about the bones.

He grabbed the book and headed for the door.

"Wait here!"

He searched in several rooms before he found Mrs Harriet asleep and snoring softly in a wingback chair in a cosy sitting room attached to one of the smaller downstairs bedrooms.

She jerked awake when he touched her shoulder.

"I'm sorry to disturb you, Mrs Harriet, but I was wondering if you might be able to help me with something."

"Ay coorse! Whit can ah dae fur ye?"

He showed her the article.

"Do you know anything about some old bones found at Caerlaverock?"

Mrs Harriet removed a pair of rectangular reading glasses from her sweater pocket, slid them on to her face, and squinted at the page. Her cloudy eyes moved slowly as she read the caption beneath the photo.

"Aye," she said, nodding her head. "Thaur was some excavatin' of th' auld castle an' moat years ago. Some of th' artifacts waur returned tae th' Maxwells."

"Where are they now? In a museum?"

She shook her head again and told him that she believed they were still stored in the old kitchen.

"Old kitchen?"

"Och aye, th' garage was once a scullery."

The garage? Deidre's bones were in his father's garage? Only in an old European house would one find priceless treasures haphazardly stored in an attic or garage.

"Thanks Mrs Harriet."

He pressed a kiss to the dear old woman's crumpled cheek before racing back up the stairs, anxious to share the information with Deidre, but when he got to the library, she wasn't there.

He crossed the hall to his room, but found it dark and empty, too. He grabbed his cashmere coat and scarf and was just about to go in search for her when James's hospice nurse rushed into the room.

"You might want to come," she said. "I think it is time."

James Montague Maxwell's time to die had finally arrived and there was nothing Caden, the hospice nurse, or the capable and unflappable Mrs Harriet could do to postpone it.

The emaciated man's chest rattled with each tortured breath and his blue eyes, yellow with jaundice, darted frantically back and forth as if terrified at the thought of dying alone.

"I'm here, " he said, taking his father's bony hand in his. "You're not alone."

James smiled weakly and then gestured with his free hand for Caden to move closer. When Caden knelt beside the bed, James sucked in a strangled breath and began speaking in a raspy whisper.

"I regret many things," he said, tears spilling down his cheeks. "But most of all, I am sorry I wasna the dad ye deserved."

Caden hugged his father and told him that he forgave him.

Just before James Montague Maxwell took his last breath, he turned his head towards the window and lifted his hand as if beckoning for someone.

Caden followed his father's gaze. Floating outside the window, her grizzled hair swirling about her slender shoulders, her eyes sunken into her face, was Deidre Monreith, banshee of the Maxwell Clan.

James took his last breath and Deidre began to wail.

Bleary-eyed and heavy-hearted, Caden found Deidre in the woods that separated Blackstone House from the mudflats and the sea. She was sitting on a stump, her head in her hands, sobbing.

Caden went to her and pulled her into his arms.

"Please don't cry," he whispered, kissing her forehead.

"I am sorry, Caden. So sorry."

He rubbed her back, inhaled the floral scent emanating from her hair, and sighed.

"You have no reason to apologise." He kissed her forehead again and stepped back, holding her at arm's length so she could look into his eyes. "You did not kill my father. You lamented his death."

He pulled her back into his arms and kissed her without restraint, searing her soul with his passion. When she pressed her body against his and moaned deep in her throat, Caden knew he had to possess her again, even if only for a moment.

After making love, Caden and Deidre spent several hours in the garage searching through dozens of old boxes and crates filled with mouldering clothes, yellowing photo albums and chipped porcelain.

"We don't have much time left," she said, looking nervously out through the arched doorway to the setting sun. "Once twilight has passed, I will become a *bean shìth* again."

"I'm sorry, sweetheart, but I don't think we're going to find the trunk before the sun sets."

"I don't think so, either," she said, sighing heavily. "Even so, there is something I would like to tell you before the light wanes completely and we cease to inhabit the same world."

Her grave manner captured Caden's attention. He set down the crowbar he had been using to pry open crates and took a seat on a wooden trunk filled with porcelain bric-a-brac.

"I want to tell you about your mother and father."

"What? Why now? We had a deal."

She perched on the edge of the crate opposite him.

"I know we had a deal, but I do not know how much longer you will be able to see me . . ."

He crossed his arms and leaned forwards until their noses nearly touched.

"Doubt who and what you will, Deidre Monreith, but *never* doubt me. I promise you, I will find your bones and break the curse."

The deep timbre of his voice, the earnestness of his avowal moved her nearly to tears. Why couldn't they have lived in the same time period? What cruel and dark force separated them?

"I believe you, Caden."

He kept his arms crossed but leaned back, apparently appeased so she continued.

"Your mother and father loved each other very much, but James Maxwell was immature. He wasn't ready to be a husband, let alone a father. One night, he went out with some friends, drank too much, and in a reckless, impulsive moment, did something he would spend the rest of his life regretting." Deidre sighed and shook her head. "He was unfaithful with your mother's best friend. When your mother found out, she was devastated. But she loved

James Maxwell so she stayed. He continued drinking heavily and one night he did not come home again."

"And she stayed with him, even after that?"

"Aye." Deidre winced at the pain palpable in Caden's voice. "Your mother waited until you were born and then she told James that he was not worthy of being the father to her child; that her child might inherit the Maxwell name, but he would not inherit their shame. She packed her bags and left and they never spoke again."

Caden sighed, dropped his chin to his chest, and shook his head. When he looked at her again, the signs of vulnerability had been erased from his face, replaced by the detached expression of one who had analysed and accepted a situation he recognized he could not alter.

"James Maxwell loved your mother and wanted to be your father, but his shame and stubborn pride kept him from ever reaching out. He repented, lived an honourable life and devoted a lot of his time to philanthropic pursuits."

"If he genuinely repented, why didn't he find me sooner?"

"Perhaps he felt unworthy of your love." Deidre shook her head. "It's so tragic. He loved you and your mother and he eventually became the man you both deserved, but it was too late . . ."

Caden continued to look for Deidre's bones, even after she silently slipped out of the garage and disappeared between the shadows of dusk.

He searched through a dozen boxes of knick-knacks, an armoire filled with dusty, moth-bitten riding apparel, and a steamer trunk of old tin toys. He found a tricorn hat, a startling number of empty whisky bottles, a jar of brass buttons, and a rusty bayonet, but no bones.

Using the crowbar, he pried the lid off the last of the crates and found Deidre's bones nestled in a bed of wood shavings. Caden plunged his hands in the curled bits of wood and lifted Deidre's yellowing skull from its resting place. The upper and lower teeth stood in neat rows but a rather large jigsaw puzzle shaped piece was missing from the left side of the heavy cranial bone.

Caden paced back and forth on the narrow strip of rocky shore where he'd first met Deidre, watching as the setting sun's blazing rays danced upon the sea. Soon the din of the day would fade away and all that would be left would be the splash of the undulating waves, the whisper of the breeze, the hoot of an owl. The vibrant world would be draped in muted shades of grey as the blanket of gloaming descended.

But what would happen after the gloaming?

Would Deidre come to him? Would she come to him again as a woman or a banshee? Had the curse been broken or would Caden be left standing alone on the water's edge?

The sun slipped lower beneath the horizon. Like a curtain closing at the theatre, the gloaming made an exit and darkness arrived.

Caden's heart thudded painfully in his chest. Minutes ticked by but Caden stubbornly refused to leave, refused to believe that Deidre was lost to him and his world.

Hades came bounding up, all gangly legs and ridiculous exuberance, splashing through the waves like a puppy. His tongue lolled out of his mouth and his tail wagged so violently it sent sprays of water all over Caden.

He looked at the silly beast and envied him in his ignorance. Dogs did not know what it meant to suffer heartbreak. Dogs did not know what it meant to love and lose.

Hades looked up at Caden. Despite the tail wagging and carefree bounding, the deerhound's big, brown eyes reflected sadness. Caden remembered the way the faithful beast had sat beside James's bed and the way he had howled after James's dead body had been carried out of Blackstone by two attendants from Henderson Funeral Home.

Caden squatted and wrapped his arm around the dog's neck.

"Maybe you're not so ignorant, after all. You know what it means to lose someone you love, don't you Hades?"

Hades thrust his nose forward and began to growl.

"What's wrong, boy?"

Caden followed the dog's gaze and saw Deidre standing at the edge of the woods. His heart swelled.

She ran to him. When they embraced, his arms did not pass through her.

"It's after the gloaming and you're still here, still human."

"I know!" She laughed and tipped her chin up to look at him. The light from the waxing moon shone on her face, turning her hazel eyes a lovely shade of emerald, and he thought he had never seen a more beautiful woman in his life. "You did it, Caden. You broke the curse. You made me human again. You've given me back my life."

"Yes," he said, kissing her lightly on the mouth. "Now the question I have for you Deidre Monreith is: would you consider spending that life with a Maxwell?"

Tears filled her eyes, but this time they were tears of joy.

"Aye," she said, laughing again. "I'll spend my life with you, Caden Maxwell."

Next Time

Donna Kauffman

One

This time, she'd definitely seen the ghost. Abby Ramsay stood at the window of her tower room and sipped her tea as she stared out across the castle inn courtyard. She felt preternaturally calm, considering what she'd observed, almost as if she was having an out of body experience. "I should be so lucky," she murmured, as she gently set the teacup and saucer on the small writing desk next to her. If only she could step out of her body, trade it in for a new one. Preferably one that wasn't going to give out on her so soon.

"But then, I wouldn't be here," she murmured, allowing a small smile as she returned her attention beyond the narrow, mullioned window. She'd been surprised and delighted when the handle at the bottom of the framed, heavy leaded glass had turned and she'd been able to swing the louvered window outwards, giving her a clear view across the courtyard, beyond the far corner tower, and onwards to the Black Cuillins beyond. In an earlier time of her life, she'd have been out there, climbing those dark, jagged peaks. But she'd made peace with her brief future and was simply happy to be here, in the midst of them, enjoying their grandeur.

At the moment, however, it wasn't the fog-shrouded, mystical mountains that held her attention. It was the tower across the courtyard. She watched, patiently, waiting for . . . something. It had all started with the flicker of light she'd seen through the turret window yesterday morning as she'd been out taking her stroll in the mists. Like most of the north side of the castle proper, the tower was falling to ruin. The turret at the top was crumbling, the windows long since empty of their glass, the ledges broken and fallen on to the stone piles below. According to the travel literature, it hadn't been habitable for more than a century.

So, it made no sense that she'd seen a light there, flickering, like candlelight or lamplight, which was why it had caught her attention in the first place. At first she thought it was one of the many adventurous hikers who came to stay at the Gillean Castle inn to take advantage of hiking Scotland's most jagged peaks. Maybe one of them had tried to climb up inside the tower.

But upon further inspection, as she'd got closer and slowly made her way around the tumble of stone at the tower base, she'd assured herself that what the travel guide and inn brochure had stated was true. Unless they could levitate, no one could be hanging around up inside what was left of that tower.

She'd told herself the flickering light could have been the sun glinting off something inside . . . but what? She'd managed to get close enough to peer inside and up. It was nothing more than a hollow shell of crumbling stone. Nothing glint-worthy to be found.

She'd toyed with the mystery for the remainder of the day, but the flickering light had never returned, and she hadn't come up with a workable explanation for what she'd seen. She'd amused herself as she'd drifted off to sleep the night before with the idea that perhaps she'd seen evidence of the infamous tower ghost. She wasn't certain what she believed about such things, but it had been a fanciful distraction and she'd fallen asleep more easily than she had in quite some time.

So, it had been quite the startling moment when she'd peered out of her own tower window in early dawn hours this morning, thinking about the flickering light . . . only to see the ghost himself standing in the open window of the tower ruin.

She remembered thinking that she'd been certain the local literature on the Gillean ghost had romanticized his appearance . . . but the reality out-distanced even the most avid imagination. The oil portrait rendering that hung in the castle hall proper didn't begin to do the man justice. He was quite tall, causing him to casually slouch in the open window frame, broad shoulder leaning against the stone. He wore a white shirt with billowing sleeves, the laces at the neck loose and open, like an old poet. Only when this poet had lifted his chin, shifting his gaze from whatever he was holding in his hand, to look across the courtyard, seemingly directly at her . . . he'd been anything but old. His was a face that could haunt dreams. That strong jaw, slash of brow and brooding mouth.

And that had been from across a misty courtyard. She couldn't imagine what kind of impact he'd have made up close and personal. Abby rubbed her arms, though the morning fog had long since lifted as the sun had edged well past the distant peaks by now.

She couldn't stop thinking about him, this ghost. And he had to be an apparition. Didn't he? The tower was gutted, she'd seen that with her own eyes. She continued to stare at it now, cold and dark, wind whistling through the crumbling window openings. No sign at all that anyone inhabited the place, much less with candlelight, billowing shirt, and perfect chin stubble.

The Gillean ghost was the stuff of legends. Although, through-out the centuries that had passed since the first sighting of him, no one had discovered his name, the story behind his being there, or a link to any of the clans who had inhabited the castle before. But he'd been seen many times over during that same time span. The description was always the same. The lore that had grown around him had launched many a tale or supposition. Most of them romantic folly, Abby had thought, but they'd made her smile nonetheless. For all anyone knew, he was a marauder with a black heart and a bloody sword who'd been cut down while looting and pillaging. Of course, that wasn't as romantic as the notion that he was a man in love, doomed to search the misty cliffs for his one and only. Or any of the other silly stories detailed in the local guides.

But now that she'd seen him herself . . . she wasn't sure what she believed. Or wanted to believe. The man she'd seen this morning surely hadn't looked like a looting marauder. Or, for that matter, an apparition.

She took a last sip of tea, replaced the cup again, then resolutely turned and plucked her jacket from the back of the chair. Her energy stores were at their best in the earlier part of the day. So, she was going to go explore the tower again, even more closely this time. Perhaps she could find a way to climb all the way inside. She wasn't even sure what she was looking for. Answers? Proof? The ghost himself?

It didn't matter, really. It was intriguing. And what else did she have to do with her time? Her strength would wane quickly, but it wasn't like she had to worry about whatever dangers might await. "What is it going to do?" she murmured. "Kill me?"

That was the one thing Abby no longer had to worry about. It was amazing how much more brave and courageous a person could feel when they knew they were going to die.

Two

She'd seen him. Not that she'd been the first. Not by a long shot. But he hadn't removed himself from sight upon discovery like he typically did. Instead, he'd welcomed her steady gaze. Had, in fact, looked back. Though he couldn't have said why. In all his visits to the tower, Calum had never once felt compelled to do that.

She hadn't even been that particularly striking. Soft brown hair, wide eyes and mouth, a narrow frame. And yet, he hadn't been able to look away.

And she hadn't looked at him like she was seeing a ghost.

He didn't get any enjoyment out of folks believing he was an afterworld wraith. Far from it. He'd much rather be left to his own devices, to enjoy the peace and solitude of Loch Sligachan and the towering presence of the Cuillins. That was why he came here when he needed to think, needed to get away. No' to play tricks on unsuspecting visitors. But, the castle inn, which had become more ruin than inn at this point in time, was remote enough, appealing mostly to outdoor adventurists, that it didn't happen all that often. So, when it did, it seemed a small price to pay for his haven.

He'd tried other places, other times in history but, for some time now, he'd come back to this place, this time. His tower had little left for comfort, but with his advanced abilities, he could work around that. The early twenty-first century had been a quiet one in the western Highlands. Still pure, despite its bloody history, with a sense of being largely untouched, reclaimed by Mother Nature. The endless green carpets of grass encroaching right up against the towering, jagged peaks that soared above them, soothed him. It looked much the same in his time. The mountains did, at any rate. The rest . . . well, that had changed. Changed with the needs of the people who had to sustain life from it. A life filled with challenges that those who lived during this time and in this place couldn't possibly fathom. And were fortunate in their ignorance.

In his time, people led a very different life from the one most likely lived by the woman who'd spied him this morning.

He'd looked into those wide, all-seeing eyes and, even across the stretch of the courtyard, he'd felt such a yearning. A yearning to go to her, talk with her, listen to tales of what life was like in these easier, calmer, more bountiful times. But why torture himself? He had to go back. There was too much to do. Only his weariness still lingered. More and more often, his slides through time didn't feel wide enough or long enough.

He stood at the edge of the cliffs now, beyond the castle yard proper, and looked down at the waves crashing against the shore below. He only had two more days but, weariness or no, this time he wished the window would come sooner. He was feeling far too on edge and that disconcerted him. He should be thinking of home, his home, in this very place, far into the distant future . . . and use his time here in the midst of peace and quiet, to figure out what his next step would be, how he could save what little was left.

A bit of something in his peripheral vision, a scarf, perhaps, caught up in a flap of wind, mercifully snatched his attention away from his chaotic thoughts. He turned to see a woman carefully picking her way in and around the fallen stones at the base of the tower. It was the woman from this morning.

Was she looking for him?

His heart raced, and it wasn't with trepidation. "Oh, aye, it's long past time, indeed, for ye to go," he murmured to himself.

Before Ailfrid had first successfully taught him how to use the windows, wormholes, and slivers to transverse back to any past time in history, Calum had entered into a pact with the aging, exiled physicist – and himself – to never encroach upon or impact the past in any way. Ailfrid had warned him that even the smallest action could have a ripple effect down through time that could alter the course of things far greater than he had the power to dabble in.

But, oh . . . aye, she made him want to dabble . . .

He watched as she paused when she got to the tower itself, bracing one hand on the rough stones. Then bent in half, quite suddenly, and seemed to convulse.

Calum didn't stop to think about the pact or the possible consequences of his response, but reacted purely on instinct. He was already at a dead run by the time she collapsed.

Three

There had been a knife of pain, followed by a gripping wave of overwhelming nausea . . . then the next thing Abby could remember feeling were strong arms lifting her up, cradling her. Maybe her time had come already, and this was what it felt like. After. Weightless and cradled and feeling forever safe. That wasn't so bad, she thought. In fact, as afterlives went, it was pretty damn good. Or maybe this was just transition. Whatever the case, she wasn't going to waste it debating how she felt about it. She was simply going to enjoy the sweet haven, the cocoon. She hadn't felt so . . . good, in a very long time.

"Are ye all right, then?"

She tensed at the sound of the deep, masculine voice, rich with that Scottish brogue that had always put a zip in her pulse. Which was, in large part, why the Highlands had been the final destination on her things-to-do-before-I-die list.

"Did ye hit your head when ye stumbled? No, don't move," he said, as she tried to pull away. "I have ye. You're safe."

Safe, yes. She felt that. Very much that. But where? And with whom?

She didn't open her eyes. She didn't want to. Not yet. "I – where am I?"

"Loch Sligachan," he said. "Gillean Castle."

Her eyelids fluttered open then. "I'm still here?"

"Aye," he said, lips quirking. "Where did ye think you'd be?"

She blinked and looked more clearly up at him. And froze. It was the ghost! So, she *was* dead after all. Maybe that was why he'd seemed so . . . lifelike to her. She had been destined to join him and hadn't known that was the plan. Was she going to haunt the castle as he did, then? Is that how it worked? Wherever you died was where you were doomed to linger? Was there some kind of plan for that, too?

Although, at the moment, as she thought about it, she couldn't really complain. If she had to stay somewhere for all eternity . . . this wasn't such a bad start.

He was even more arresting up close. Tanned skin, with lines feathering out from the corners of eyes so bright blue, they looked like crystals lit by the sun. He looked . . . otherworldly enough. She wondered if that was it, if that was why he seemed to all but glow.

"You feel so real," she said, only realizing she'd said it out loud when he looked surprised, then a little disconcerted.

"Allow me to help you back to the castle," he said, his face smoothing into a more impersonal expression. "Perhaps you should call a physitech to take a look. Make sure you haven't a concussion."

"Physitech?"

"Erm, doctor. Medical. Someone who tends to the ill and infirm," he clarified, and she could see the consternation, as if he was reaching for words that he wasn't familiar with. But he spoke beautiful English, albeit with a heavy brogue. Perhaps it was merely cultural. Skye was far to the north and west in the Highlands, and she knew that, in many places, Gaelic was still the native tongue and treasured amongst the long-timers.

But . . . what, exactly did that make him?

Then she realized what he was saying. Ghost or no, he was acting as if she'd just fallen and hit her head. Not like she'd crossed over. But how did that explain him being here and feeling so . . . solid? And warm, she noted. And strong. Not at all apparition-like, given she was apparently still mortal.

"I'm okay," she said, ignoring the whopper of a lie that was. For the purposes of needing him, she was fine. "You can let me go."

She started to move but, once again, he stilled her movement by tightening his arms around her. "Let's take this slowly, aye?"

"Aye," she echoed, closing her eyes against the return of the vicious pinch of a headache, knowing the worst of it would subside in a moment or two. Back to the dull, throbbing ache that was always there. She tried to hold on to the pleasure of what it had felt like to be pain free for those blissful first moments when she'd first felt his arms around her.

He waited until she opened her eyes again, and nodded, before very slowly pushing to a stand himself, taking her with him, but holding her pressed against his chest the entire time. "Tell me if the pain comes back."

"I'm – okay," she said, meaning it this time, though the assessment had nothing to do with her health concerns. He was tall. Much taller than her five-and-a-half feet. Her face was pressed against the soft, billowing linen she'd spied him wearing earlier that morning, and his arms felt incredibly good wrapped around her. The throb in her head seemed to diminish the more she breathed him in. "Who are you," she murmured, trying not to burrow her face in the warm heat of him, and failing rather spectacularly. She couldn't seem to make herself care enough to pull away, though. And he didn't seem to mind, so . . .

"Calum," he said, offering nothing more. "Come on then, let's get you out of this damp, chilly wind." But, instead of slowly supporting her to her feet, he scooped her up fully into his arms.

"Wait," she said, knowing she should, though, admittedly, her heart wasn't exactly in the protest.

"I dinnae think ye should be walking about quite yet." He didn't wait for a response, but merely turned and began carefully manoeuvring through the tumble of stone and rock.

"I—" She was forced to break off when her headache seized again.

"Let's get you inside," he said, frowning now, sounding very concerned.

She could have told him that he needn't worry. It wasn't like she was going to get better. Instead, she merely dipped her chin in a single nod, closed her eyes, and pressed her cheek once again against the soft linen as she instinctively sought solace. Even more surprising was that she found it in the steady rhythm of his heart.

She paid little attention to where he was going, though was vaguely surprised to feel them climbing so soon. Had he crossed the courtyard so quickly? She concentrated on getting a grip on the throb in her head and trusted him to do the rest. It was bad enough that she was playing the swooning maiden to his gallant rescuer. In a perfect world, she'd have been bold and daring, and it would have been her vivacious demeanour and infectious laughter that would have captured his attentions.

But her world was far from perfect. And she'd long since accepted that. So . . . she'd take what she could get and be happy with the serendipitous pleasure of it while it lasted.

She was thankful he appeared to be taking her to her room on the inn side of the castle without stopping to inform anyone of her little setback. Of course, he'd seen her at her window that morning, so he would know exactly where her room was. She had been torn over whether to tell the innkeeper about her . . . situation, not wanting to burden anyone unnecessarily if anything were to happen to her sooner than she'd anticipated. In the end, she'd chosen not to. She really didn't want to be the object of pity or concern, and if something happened . . . well, it happened.

She hadn't realized she was clinging to him, hand fisted in his

shirt, until he bent to put her down on the bed. Only . . . She
blinked her eyes open and looked around. This wasn't her room!
She squirmed, but he immediately tightened his hold.

"It's okay. We're in the tower, but ye have nothing to worry for.
I thought it best not to alarm anyone or create a scene. Unless of
course ye dinnae mind them all seeing ye being carted up to your
loft by a strange man."

He'd said it kindly, lightly, but he couldn't know the twinge it
plucked in her heart. It was the one thing on her list she hadn't
been able to manage: a passionate romance. You couldn't just
book those at the local travel agency. She'd wanted to know the
pleasure of having a meaningful, deep and abiding relationship
with someone. But, once her prognosis had been delivered . . .
how, in good conscience, could she do that to someone, knowing
what she was facing? Just say "yes, I want you, truly, madly,
deeply . . . and oh, by the way, I'll probably be dead before the
year is out."

She didn't think so.

Four

"I – I appreciate your thoughtfulness," Abby said, carefully, as he
set her gently down on the narrow bed tucked under the eave.
"Where are we?" She looked around. He'd said the tower, but
she'd looked up inside the tower – his tower – and none of this had
been there. Not the plank flooring, the feather-stuffed mattress, the
rough-hewn bedstand or the— "—Oil lamp."

He glanced at the brass fixture next to the bed. "Aye. Do you
want more light? Or heat? Are you cold?"

She looked towards the narrow window openings. There was no
glass and the sills along the bottom looked as crumbled and falling
to ruin as they did from the outside. The air swept in and swirled
about, cool and damp, as it would . . . inside a ruin. She looked
back to him. "How . . . how is this possible?"

He held her gaze for what felt like the longest time, but said
nothing. Instead, he stood and turned his back to her, crouching
down for a moment. An instant later, there was a blazing fire. In a
small fireplace. That she'd have sworn wasn't there – couldn't have
been there – just a second ago.

"It should warm up in a moment," was all he said, as he straightened and turned back to face her. His gaze was smooth, his

expression impenetrable. No hint of the roguish grin that had been hovering before.

She should be scrambling off the bed, trying to find her way out of this – dream? Hallucination? – she really had no idea. Maybe when she'd fallen she had struck her head and she was now on some kind of wild mind trip, still lying, unconscious, down on the rocks. Or maybe she really had passed over. Because none of this made any sense in the mortal, real world.

Whatever the case, whatever the explanation, she wasn't going anywhere until she found out. Because this was, by far, the most intriguing thing to have ever happened to her. Certainly the most fantastical. If she didn't count the fact that she'd come down with a systemic disorder so rare there wasn't even a name for it as yet. That was pretty fantastical, she supposed.

This, at least, had the potential to be fun. Besides, it wasn't like she had anything to lose by pursuing it.

"Will you answer me?" she asked, quite calmly, she thought.

He continued to regard her, then finally said, "What did you think, this morning, when you saw me here, inside this tower."

"That I'd finally seen the Gillean ghost," she responded easily. As if this were the most natural conversation to be having.

"Do ye believe in such things?"

She lifted one shoulder in a half shrug. "I've never really had cause to think about it. I've spent time lately, thinking about what happens after a person dies, but it never really extended to ghosts and haunting things."

She thought she spied a hint of amusement hovering around that oh-so-perfectly formed mouth.

"What's funny about that?" she asked, deciding she might as well go for broke. In fact, she couldn't recall ever feeling so . . . invigorated by her own potential. Not that he'd looked at her with desire in his beautiful blue eyes, or even male appreciation, really. But when he looked at her, as he was now, she felt like he was reaching down somewhere quite deep. She felt like no one and nothing existed inside that moment, except for her. It was quite heady stuff. Empowering, even. So . . . she went with that.

"You're . . . unexpected," he said.

"I think we can safely say we're both a little bit of that."

The amusement flickered into his eyes this time. "Aye."

"So, are you going to explain what – who – you really are?"

"Ye dinnae believe I'm a ghost then?"

"You seem pretty real to me."

"You're American," he said, instead. "What region? I'm no' familiar with the accent."

"I grew up just outside of D.C. across the river, in Virginia."

"D.C.?"

"Washington. Our capital city."

"Columbia," he said, nodding.

"The District of Columbia, yes."

His expression smoothed again, and she'd have sworn something flashed across his face. Something like sorrow. Or . . . pity.

"You don't think much of Washington? Or is it all of America that you disdain?"

He looked honestly surprised. "What makes you say that?"

"Your expression just then. It was less than . . . appreciative." She shifted her weight on the bed, turning to face him more directly. "That's okay. I understand global sentiment being what it is. We've had some relatively . . . uneven representation."

"It wasn't that."

She lifted a brow in question, but when he didn't elaborate, she said, "Then, what was it?"

He hesitated, then said, "What do you think about, when you think about your future?"

She grinned then, and watched as he blinked, and his throat even worked a little. *Hunh.* She wasn't sure what to make of that, but it made her feel good. "I think I'll miss finding out what happens next. I guess if I got to pick what happens after we die, my hope is that there is a heaven, and that I get to look down and watch. Or . . ." she added, trailing off for a moment, then deciding, what the heck. "Or . . . perhaps I'll be like you, haunting a particular place, and seeing what happens to it over time. Will you tell me? What it's like, I mean?"

"I was speaking of your future while here on earth."

"So was I," was all she said.

Abby wasn't sure why she thought he should know about her circumstances other than, she supposed, this felt to her like he was some kind of angel, or archangel even, sent to shepherd her from this realm to the next. It was as good an explanation as any. And seemed to have more going for it than the whole ghost thing. Except he'd been seen as one, on these very grounds, for so very long . . . how could he be anything else? Surely no angel needed to be sent to this desolate, remote place so often as to become some sort of folklore hero.

She sat upright and drew her knees in to her chest. A shield perhaps? She couldn't say. Or what she thought she needed shielding from. "I'll be discovering those answers soon enough," she told him. "So . . . naturally, I think about it."

"A rather morbid outlook for one as young as yourself."

She smiled again. "Hardly. Just pragmatic. By nature, I'm a sunny optimist. But nature, as it turns out, had something else in store for me."

"Meaning what, exactly?" He moved closer, but when she thought he might perch next to her on the bed, he instead pulled up a heretofore unseen footstool and crouched down on that instead.

It put his face closer to level with hers . . . and sent her heart rate doubling. It wasn't an entirely unwelcome response. "Meaning I may be young, but I don't have much time left," she said. "In fact, coming here is probably the last thing I'll get to do." Her lips curved. "That's why I was out there stumbling around the rocks. I wanted to figure out what you were, or who you were – or weren't – while I had the time and energy. I was – am – enjoying the mystery and playing detective."

His expression faltered, just briefly, and she was rather stunned by the flash of grief she saw on his face. He didn't even know her. Maybe he was just particularly sensitive to the plight of others.

"It's okay," she told him. "I'm at peace with it. I've had the time – plenty of time – to consider all of it. I'm focused on enjoying what time I do have, and not wasting it belabouring or whining about what I won't."

"You've quite a brave spirit," he said, still sounding quietly stunned.

"Hardly," she laughed. "Trust me, I wasn't okay at first, and not at all brave. But, at some point, you have to reconcile yourself with it. Or, at least, I did. And I have." She felt the overwhelming need to lean forwards, touch him, reassure him that she was truly at peace with herself, and her imminent, brief future. She had to curl her hands into her palms to keep from doing it. "Don't look so sad for me," she said, a thread of pleading in her voice. Though why it mattered what he thought, or felt, she hadn't a clue. It was just, in that moment . . . it felt vital that she reassure him somehow. That it mattered. That he mattered.

"I'm afraid I'm far more selfish than you," he said. "I am sad for you, as I would be for anyone in like circumstance. But I'm also sad for myself."

"I can go, if being around me—"

"No," he said, quite abruptly, even going so far as to reach out a hand to stop her, had she tried to make a move.

She hadn't, and his outburst should have alarmed her. But it just strengthened that need in her, to soothe his fears. "I don't want to go," she told him. Her lips curved. "I haven't solved the mystery of you, yet."

He opened his mouth, then shut it. "I don't even know your name."

"Abby. Ramsay."

His gaze flashed up at hers. "Ramsay."

She nodded. "My ancestors are from your bonny shores."

"You've been here before, then?"

She nodded. "Not here on Skye, to Sligachan. I wanted to see the Cuillins. I used to climb, and . . ." She shrugged again. "The pictures I saw of their dark peaks called to me. I know they're not the tallest or most challenging, but . . . they spoke to me. And when I saw this castle, found it had been turned into an inn . . . I don't know. I felt drawn here, compelled somehow."

"Is it what you'd hoped? Being here?"

She nodded, her smile spreading slowly. "More so all the time."

His lips twitched, but there was still such sadness in his eyes, and she hated that.

"Tell me," she said, "why you're sad for yourself."

He paused, looked down, then seemed to take stock as he looked at her again, always with that direct, steady gaze that reached so far past the surface. Or so it felt. She couldn't have said why, but there was no denying the connection she was feeling with him.

"I've been here many times," he began, then paused, but went on again before she could comment. "I've seen, and been seen, by any number of people." He leaned just a fraction closer, but it felt as if he'd somehow pushed deeply into her personal space, so probing was his gaze. "You were the first one I wanted to be seen by. The first one who made me look back."

His gaze was so intent, there was such . . . specificity in his tone, it made her breath catch and her throat tighten. "Why?" she managed. "Why me?" She knew herself to be nothing special, at least outwardly. She wasn't memorable in that striking way some people had. Her charisma was more subtle and quiet. Someone had to take the time to get to know her, to appreciate her. To

remember her. He'd had but an instant, the span of a gaze –
however heated it felt on her end – to look at her. And that was it.
How could she matter to him?

And, why did it matter so much to her?

"I dinnae rightly know," he said, which should have deflated her
hopes entirely. Only it didn't, because he went on to say, "I only
knew that I wanted to talk to you, listen to you, know you, somehow . . . It felt important, vital. Urgent, even. Like . . . I couldn't
miss the opportunity." He trailed off then, and glanced away. "Ye
must think me deranged. I'm talking like a mad man."

"I thought you were a ghost inhabiting a tower ruin, so there
isn't much you could do to unnerve me beyond that."

He glanced up then, a definite flash of a smile curving his lips. "I
suppose you have a point. Well, I can assure you I willnae keep ye
here beyond what you're willing to stay. And that my desires, while
not entirely under my control, are not mad in any way that presents
any danger to you."

"Pity," she said, shocking even herself with the clearly intoned
entendre.

His gaze caught hers squarely again and, in the moment that
immediately followed, there was a shift in the air between them.
And she felt like she went from being curious specimen to . . .
desirable woman. At least, that was how she was interpreting the
sudden flare in his eyes, the way his jaw tightened, and his body
leaned further forward, seemingly of its own volition. Wishful
thinking, perhaps, but . . .

She was leaning forwards, too, before she could give it any
thought, or save herself the embarrassment if she'd misread him.
But her heart was pounding so hard she couldn't focus her thoughts,
could only act. She'd think on it later.

He slid forward off the stool to his knees beside the low bed
frame. He took her hands into his, and they were broad, and strong,
and so warm. "I'm supposed to be the ghost, and yet it's you who're
haunting me."

"Calum, I—" She didn't know what to say. Her entire body
yearned to feel . . . something more. To feel . . . him.

He tugged her hands and she lowered her knees, let her feet slide
off the edge of the bed. He rose just enough to move in and, letting
go of her hands, slid his arm once again under her legs, bracing the
other at her back.

"What are you—?"

"Just . . . let me," he said, quietly. "Please." He shifted his weight to the bed, and settled her securely across his lap. "Abby, I don't know you," he said, as he tucked her in there, in his arms, against his chest, "and yet, the thought of losing you is – I canno' stand the thought of it." He cupped her cheek, drew her face up so he could look into her eyes. "How is that possible?"

She was living a dream now, surely she was. Once again the pain receded and she felt nothing but an infusion of warmth . . . even to the point of heat. Flaring in her belly, clenching the muscles between her thighs, making her nipples ache. Mercifully, for once, it had nothing to do with her weakened condition. In fact, it made her feel all too vital and alive, experiencing such an intensely female response.

She lifted a shaky hand to his face, her need for him spiking more sharply with the feel of his warm skin brushing her palm, the slight roughness of his cheek. "So real," she said. "But this can't be. Any of this," she said, making a short gesture to the room around her. "Can it?"

"Abby, I—"

"I'm dreaming this, aren't I?" she said, hoping to never wake up.

He turned his cheek, so his lips brushed across her palm. "I canno' explain this," he murmured against her skin, then shifted his face so their gazes met once again. "But . . . I can explain myself. How I'm here. Why I'm here."

She traced her fingertips along his jaw. "Not a ghost," she said, seeing the truth of it already in his eyes even before he shook his head. "Then . . . what?"

"A traveller," he said, then, after a long pause, added, "through time."

Five

Calum held her gaze, and tried not to think of the possible catastrophic events he could, right then, be putting into motion, by revealing the truth. By touching her, holding her, wanting her. The strength of it was beyond anything he should rightfully be feeling, and yet, that didn't change the fact that he was.

As was she, if the look in her eyes was anything to go by.

Was that what had drawn him here so many times, through so many years? Could there have been something to all the fanciful tales the locals had dreamt up, about a man haunting the cliffs, looking for his one and only? So ludicrous and simple-minded, he'd thought . . . and yet, looking into the lovely face of this total stranger, and feeling a pull so strong it was impossible to deny, a sadness so profound over the sense that he'd finally found her, only to so cruelly have her taken away from him forever . . . what else could explain such depth of emotion?

But what was he to do about it? What could he do?

As yet, he hadn't impacted anything, changed anything, had he? By her own admission, she wasn't long for this world, so whatever interaction he had with her, wouldn't change that outcome, or her, in any way.

Would it?

"Through . . . time?" she said, echoing his words, searching his face.

How was it he'd thought her plain or nondescript? Her eyes were such a soft grey, like the feathers of a dove, and he already knew they could be so serious, or probing, or sweet and smiling. Her mouth was wide, with lips a little plump and soft, and made her face so expressive, whether she was smiling or biting that bottom lip in pensive thought. He'd known her for the breadth of a mere moment in time, and yet he knew each and every one of those expressions would be indelibly etched in his mind, in his memory, forever.

"Aye," he said, trying to focus on what he wanted her to know, and how to explain himself. And not on how badly he wanted to spend whatever time they had together doing anything but talking. "We've learned, in future years, how to manipulate the time-space continuum."

"How far in the future did you—?" She had to stop and clear her throat, but he appreciated how hard she was working to keep calm, respond rationally, to what had to sound like the lunatic rantings of a man who'd gone raving bonkers.

"A few centuries. Five, actually, give or take."

Her eyes widened. "And you can just, what, pop in and out, like—"

"It's no' so simple as that, and no' everyone has the knowledge. It's a relatively new science to us and . . . very guarded. Very . . . controversial. No' everyone feels as I do – we do – about its use or potential."

"Why? Could anyone do it? If they knew how? I could see how

that would be chaotic. Can you control, precisely, when and where you . . . um, land?"

"It's relatively controlled, but no, no' everyone could do it. The science behind it must be understood, handled properly. We've learned how to destruct and reconstruct particles, so that . . ." Calum paused, shook his head. He shouldn't have done this. It was too much, and too risky. There were rules in place, boundaries never to be crossed, and they stood for a reason.

"Particle theory. Is that how you've manipulated these things into this space, into what is, otherwise, an empty tower?"

"Some of it is that, aye, some of it is time and space manipulation."

"So," she said, and he could see she was struggling to keep her wits about her. "The ghostly visits here. You've come here before, then. During different times."

He nodded. "I'm no' haunting the tower, no, but it was simpler to allow others to believe I was."

"But why come here at all? Is this where you're from in the future?" She closed her eyes briefly.

"Abby," he said, instantly alarmed. "Are you alright? Are you in pain? What can I—"

She blinked her eyes open. "No, it's not that, it's just . . . I can't believe I'm having this conversation, so calmly, like you just told me you were from Toledo and we're comparing itineraries or something. I can't believe we've only just met, and yet I'm here, and you're . . ." She trailed off then, and dipped her chin, withdrawing her hand from his cheek.

He tipped her face back to his. "Abby. Look at me, please."

She opened her eyes, and this time there was trepidation in those dove grey pools. From the woman who was facing death with such equanimity, it was lowering to think he'd done this to her.

"I'm sorry. I shouldn't have interfered. I shouldn't have come to you. Shouldn't have told you. There are strict rules and I believe in their purpose. We can't change the past, we can't affect anything that could create a ripple forwards, we canno'—"

"You haven't done anything, Calum, but told a dying woman who you really are. Nothing else has changed, nor will it."

He'd just gotten done telling himself the same thing, and yet the guilt and concern lingered. "Things in our time, they're no' good, Abby," he told her. "We're . . . struggling. Mightily. No' everyone believes in the application of such sciences, but there's a great fear that if the people found out they could move through time, they'd all rush to leave their challenging lives to find a more prosperous one in the past. Which could do untold damage to history and how the world is shaped—"

"Or untold good. If they brought knowledge with them that was helpful, perhaps wrongs would be righted before they happened. And the world, during your time, wouldn't be struggling."

"We can't know that, can't risk that. And we can't have a whole-sale abandonment of where we are now, or we'll have no hope of surviving beyond it."

"All the more reason, maybe, to rethink those rules. If it's going to end in chaos and destruction, or whatever it is that has levelled things so badly in your time . . . then what have you got to lose, really, my making use of the one potentially good tool you have at your disposal? Has anyone tried? Do you know, for certain, that catastrophic things will happen, and that the impact has to be negative?"

He shook his head. "It's a risk deemed too high to take."

"So . . . what would be the point of it then? This technology, or whatever you call it. What do you use it for if not to help yourselves in such dire times?"

"I—" He broke off then, and shook his head. "I don't know."

"Can you move forward, bring back technology that might help sooner rather than later?"

He shook his head. "No, we've no' figured that out as yet. We can only get back as far as our current time. It's a tricky thing . . . And, politically, there's a lot of controversy surrounding its use."

She nodded, a pensive look on her face. "I feel like there are a million and one questions I should be asking you," she said. "Like this is the chance of a lifetime to find out what happens next, well beyond anything I would ever have had the chance to know."

"You're quite . . . accepting, of all this."

She smiled then. "You know, that's just it. I don't have a lot of time to ponder and worry and consider. I'm just going with what feels right and true. I can't explain this, or you, anymore than I can explain why I'm the one who won't get a long life. In my situation, you learn to accept quickly and move on to dealing with things." Her smile widened. "Looks like you picked the exact right person to tell your mysterious secret to."

"Perhaps," he said, then his gaze drifted to her mouth, then back up to her eyes. Eyes that turned darker the longer he looked. "What if I were to tell you that I wanted to just go with what felt right and true? Right in this instant?"

"I—" She paused, cleared her throat. "I'd say I think that's a grand idea."

"Good," he said, and smiled as he lowered his mouth to hers.

Six

He brushed her lips with his, seeking, not tentative, but polite, gentlemanly, giving her the opportunity to pull away. Abby's heart was racing. If she was dreaming all of this, she congratulated herself for coming up with the best possible dream ever. She let herself feel him, taste him, and just teeter on that delicious brink of want and need, before relaxing and softening her lips under his, parting them a little . . . and inviting him in.

He didn't need to be asked twice.

He tipped her head back and kissed her fully, with absolute intent and not a moment's hesitation.

It was heady and intoxicating, being the recipient of such focused attention. Abby sunk her fingers into his hair and gave herself over fully to every sensation, to him.

The kiss quickly escalated and Abby encouraged every heart-pounding increase in intensity. When Calum shifted her from his lap, back on to the bed, and followed her down, the weight of his body resting alongside hers as he continued the sweet assault on her mouth, should have made her thankful and thrilled that she was experiencing all she'd wanted, and more than she'd ever thought to. So, she was unprepared for the sharp sting of tears that gathered at the corners of her eyes.

In a stunning testament to just how in tune with her he was, he almost immediately lifted his mouth from hers, and they were both breathing heavily when he said, "Are you okay? Am I hurting you? I shouldn't have—"

"No, no, that's not it," Abby said, curling her fingers into his shoulders and keeping him where he was, with the delicious weight of his body half on top of hers. "I'm not feeling any pain," she said, realizing, to her surprise, how true the statement was. "This is the very best I've felt in . . . forever. It's just . . ."

He turned her chin back to his when she would have looked away. All that concern in his beautiful blue eyes, and . . . all that sadness. It was more than she could bear.

"What is it?" he asked, gently stroking her face, as if she were fragile. She liked him better moments ago, when he was kissing her as if his very life depended on it.

She felt like, in that moment, hers most certainly did.

"I – this is—" She broke off, feeling foolish and silly. Which was somewhat ludicrous given that the events of the past few hours were anything but rational and smart. She took a breath, and even allowed herself the comfort of his steadily stroking, soothing fingers. Oh, to have had this all along, she thought, then immediately shut that down. She would not feel sorry for herself. That would never have gotten her here, and she was certainly not going to cave to that destructive way of thinking now.

But, when she looked at him, the definite pang in her heart told her she would fail this time in her mission to remain impervious to her limitations. "You're . . . what I wanted," she said, then watched his face.

There was no withdrawal, just that flash of instant arousal and awareness in his eyes, and the feeling of his hand, pausing, tensing, on the soft skin of her cheek.

"And now . . . this . . . it's perfect. It's . . . it could be, everything. But—"

"But we can take this, have this," Calum said. "I know there can't be anything beyond this. I have to travel back."

"And I have to travel on," she said, damning the little break in her voice. "I've been okay with that, at peace with it. But now . . ."

He closed his eyes, squeezed them shut, but not before she'd witnessed the pain and sadness there.

"This is surely insanity," she all but whispered. "It can't matter this much. We can't matter. Don't be sad for me. Be happy that you gave me this. I'll cherish it until my last breath. I don't want to go thinking that I've left you upset and wishing you'd never met me."

"Not that. Never that. But this feels like there is a greater purpose behind it. Maybe that's just rationale or wishful thinking, but I feel like I've waited forever for you, Abby. When I've been here, come back here, it was because I needed time to think, to sort things through, to figure out what to do next, how to help, to make things better. It's what I'm trained to do, motivated to do, focused on. My methods aren't widely accepted, and it's been a challenge to make any headway. But I have to, because what other choice is there?

"Only now it feels like I kept coming here because I was waiting for our paths to cross. And . . . and I can't believe that's all there is going to be to it. A brief crossing. I want more. I want to know more. For myself this time. So, you can't . . . this can't be all there is. Do you feel that?"

She nodded. "It's why I pulled back, it's why this hurt. I've been so thankful for everything I was able to do, to see, to experience. I should be thankful for this too, and I am. But . . . like you, I find I want more and now, for the first time since I've come to terms with the reality of my limited time, I'm feeling cheated. And it hurts, and . . . I'm scared. I don't want to die feeling like this, feeling like I'm not at peace, that I haven't done all I can, all I should."

His expression was stark. "I know." He leaned down and kissed her, deeply, with more emotion and passion than before and, terrified of feeling more, of sinking further into an abyss from which she wouldn't be able to climb back out of, she wanted to push him away, break the kiss, end the moment, and not invite in any more torturous wants or needs.

Only . . . she couldn't. Because did she want this – him – with everything that she had. So, she kissed him back, urged him to move more of his weight over her. When he hesitated, paused long enough to look into her eyes, she held his gaze squarely, evenly, and said, "Calum, if this is all we have, then . . . I want all there is to have. Do you understand?"

Both fierce desire and a maddening ache filled his now glittering eyes, and she feared, greatly, that he'd deny her this one request. She couldn't blame him, she supposed, but . . . to be this close, and not have the rest of what he promised . . . Was it wrong of her to reach, for this one final thing?

"Please," she said, her voice barely above a whisper.

His expression faltered and his fingers trembled against her skin. "Abby, I . . . I want, more than I should. I dinnae want to hurt you, you've been through so much—"

She cupped his cheek, and found a smile, which grew as she gave life to it. "Go gently with me, and you won't hurt me. I'm not so fragile as that. When you touch me, when you hold me, I feel only pleasure. Only you can give that rare gift to me. Will you, Calum?"

His eyes filled, but he nodded.

"So selfish of me," she said, but didn't keep him from lowering his mouth back to hers. "I don't want to hurt you, either."

"You won't," he said, "you canno'. This is . . . as you said, a gift. I am receiving one, too."

He kissed her softly this time, almost reverently. She wanted to sink her nails into his shoulders, and urge him to give himself over to his wants and needs, and take her as a man took a woman he fiercely desired. But she knew she didn't have the stamina for that, even to simply accept that, and so instead she accepted, gratefully, his care and concern for her, as he began making love to her with a simple, gentle sweetness that undid the rest of her defences entirely. In the end, it was a more thorough claiming than any heated union could have ever been.

He undressed her slowly, and she arched to meet him as his mouth covered one tightly budded nipple, then the other. She cried out as he carefully unbuttoned her pants and eased them down her hips, trailing kisses along the way, until he found her, warm, wet, and waiting for his touch, his tongue. He didn't disappoint, and Abby shoved aside any remaining shred of concern she had about what she was doing, and with whom, and simply gave herself completely over to him, and the wave upon wave of pleasure he was wringing, so perfectly, from her body. The same body that had only let her down . . . now felt like the perfect vessel, the one pathway she had to absolute bliss.

When he slipped out of his clothes and covered her body with his, opening herself to him was the most natural thing she'd ever done. And, instantly, the most rewarding, as he slowly, surely, and deeply filled her. She rose to meet him, but he kept her hips pinned to the bed, moving slowly inside of her, steadily, pushing her, taking her, until they both climbed towards a shattering climax. She went first, but her cries, and her hips lifting to his, pulling him in deeper, yanked him over the edge, too, in a deep, groaning release that was almost as fulfilling an experience as her own.

Afterwards, he slid his weight off of her, but rolled her to him and kept her close. "Are you okay?" he asked, his voice deeper, rougher, as he brushed her hair from her cheeks.

"I can honestly say that I've never, not for any moment in my life, been better."

He smiled then, and tucked her to his side, so her cheek was once again pressed against his chest. "Good," he said, stroking her back as their breathing steadied and his heart beat slowed beneath her cheek. "Aye, that is very, very good, indeed."

She smiled against his chest. "Indeed."

Seven

They must have fallen asleep, because when Calum woke, the sun had almost fully set. He acknowledged the weight of her, the warmth of her, pressed to his side, as instantly and naturally as if he always woke to find her there. His smile grew to a grin, and he wanted to pump his fist and roar to the skies, so primal did she make him feel. But that feeling was swiftly replaced by the remainder of the reality that was theirs, too.

The reality that she would be taken from him. Even if he chose to stay, he would lose her. Forever. He watched her sleep, happy to see that her face was composed and relaxed. He hoped she was sleeping soundly, free of any discomfort. He didn't know exactly what plagued her, but there were shadows under her eyes, and a wan paleness to her skin that indicated her less than optimum health. He knew she suffered from pain, and would have done anything to take it from her.

So sweet, so gentle, but fierce in her own way. The way she'd held his gaze as he'd taken her, proudly and boldly meeting him stroke for gentle stroke. Giving herself over to the pleasure he took even greater delight in bringing her, then matching him as they both went over the edge. He liked how she'd spoken her mind to him, challenging him, even though they'd just begun to know each other.

What if, he thought, what if he used the slivers and wormholes to keep coming back to her, in a time when she was still here. Still alive. In her tower room. Would he have to reintroduce himself every time? Or could he perfect it so that it was just after they'd met, so she'd welcome him each time. And they'd share a few blissful days. Over, and over. Would she remember that they had? Would he be able to withstand the knowledge of knowing they had if she didn't? Couldn't? What if she didn't accept him as she had this time, every time?

He closed his eyes, squeezed them shut. This is why it was wrong of him to be dabbling like this, so dangerously, with things not of his time. People not of his time. With her.

And then she came quietly and beautifully awake, and he thought, as her grey eyes flickered open, that if he could wake up every morning to that instant soft smile, the moment she looked at him, that there was nothing he couldn't conquer.

She reached up, stroked his face, his lips. "Calum," she said, and his heart raced, just hearing his name on her lips.

There was no way he could leave her. How could he never know this bliss ever again, not know more of her, always?

"Abby, I've been thinking—"

"So have I," she said.

He smiled. "You were asleep."

"Not the whole time, I wasn't. You're quite handsome, you know, even when you're sleeping."

He thought he might have felt a bit of heat in his face. "I'm glad you think so. I was just thinking that I would never tire of seeing you smile at me like that right after you wake up."

She held his gaze, but her smile grew almost tremulous.

"What's wrong, Abby? Are you feeling okay? Can I do anything?"

"I – maybe you can."

"Name it."

She paused, then took a steadying breath, and said, "What if you didn't have to? Never tire of this, I mean."

"I would give anything to find out."

"Would you?" She reached up, touched his face. "Would you take me back with you? Can you do that?"

"Abby, I told you—"

"Calum," she said, cutting him off, then pausing, before blurting out, "If could you take me back and . . . in your time, maybe they could—"

"—heal you," he finished, a look of awe on his face.

"I know you're not supposed to alter the past, but . . . in this case . . . and if you bring me right back . . . or even if I just stay there . . . then it wouldn't change anything here in my time. I'm going to be gone forever, soon enough. I could stay in the future. With you . . . or—"

He took her face in his hands, thunderstruck by the very idea. Why he hadn't thought of it, he didn't know . . . other than it was against all protocol and he simply hadn't imagined— "I – I don't know."

"Don't know if you could, or if you would?"

"I – I've never travelled in tandem."

"Has anyone?"

He nodded. "Ailfrid, the man who taught me. I don't know if I would be successful. And if I travelled back alone to learn, to perfect it, I don't know if I could time it precisely enough to come back here before . . ." He trailed off.

She nodded. "It's okay. I understand. It was horribly selfish of me to—"

"No, no, that's not it. You've made me think a lot more about the moratorium we've set on utilizing time travel. It's no' something that we'd be able to change, not widespread, in any rapid time, nor should we."

"But?"

"But . . . when I travel . . . only Ailfrid knows of it. It's . . . not exactly sanctioned."

She smiled, then. "Ah. A renegade."

"Only in this. And, perhaps, in some of my ideas for instigating change and progress. Abby, it's quite possible we could heal you. There are few ailments we haven't learned to conquer. Life expectancy is far longer than it is in your time. Centurians are so commonplace, it's an expected age to reach. But, as I said before . . . our time – my time – is otherwise not a good one. You could be healed, but you'd be living in a time of great strife and danger. No' much, if any, prosperity."

"Living longer would be prosperity enough. You wouldn't be responsible for me, Calum. I wouldn't expect—"

"I'd no' walk away from ye, Abby," he said, the almost instantaneous fierce response to thinking of her alone, without him, bringing out the stronger brogue of this day and time, than that of his own.

"Then . . . why don't you instil the changes you're thinking about. Utilize this gift you have, this skill you've learned. Move through time, figure out how to right things in the past, so you won't have to go through what you're all suffering in the future. You won't need permission, because it won't be happening."

He smiled then. "Save the world. As if it's so simple as all that."

"Individuals have made huge impacts in the dynamics of our world. You'll have something of an advantage. And even if you fail, Calum, you couldn't leave your people in worse shape. Yet you could be their great hope. I would be willing – wanting – to go with you. To help you. Would I stay healed?"

"You remain as ever you are when you leave. I age as I would in my time, regardless of the time I'm in. But then, I never stay that long. The windows are brief. Which is why I don't know how much impact I could have."

"Would you be willing to think about it? Even if you have to go back to do it. Would you try and come back to me – for me?"

"Abby . . ."

"I'm not begging you, Calum. Nor will I. You have to do what you think is best for all concerned, and that encompasses so many more than just me. I know this. I know what I'm asking. At least, I understand there are ramifications neither of us might comprehend now. But I keep thinking about the alternatives. For us both. I don't see where the risk isn't worth taking, no matter how you measure it. Obviously, I have nothing to lose here. But you have things you could gain. And my dedication to help you achieve them. Will you at least consider it? Think on it?"

He pulled her close again, felt her heart beating, felt the life pulsing inside of her . . . and though he had many misgivings, he already knew he had no choice. No choice at all.

The question before him wasn't if he could live with saving her. He could. He knew it was her only hope. And, selfishly, his own.

But could everyone else live with the choice that would be forced on them? By him?

Eight

Two mornings later, Abby was standing cliffside with Calum, still not quite believing how dramatically her life had changed in a mere forty-eight hours. And the most dramatic part hadn't even happened yet. Which was saying quite a lot.

"Are you certain of this?" she asked, for at least the dozenth time since Calum had told her he would take her with him.

He smiled at her, his hand steady in hers, as it had been for most of the past two days. They'd talked for most of it, sharing details of their lives, both broad and intensely intimate. They'd explored other things more intimately as well, but Calum was so concerned for her health that for the past day, he'd refused to do more than kiss her and stroke her face and hair. Admittedly, even that had been lovelier than she'd ever anticipated experiencing, especially now, so close to the end. So, she hadn't pushed. Calum wanted her to have all her strength for their planned transition.

He turned to her and framed her face. How was it that his own face had become so dear to her, so quickly? If she let herself think about it, she'd question all of it, most specifically her sanity. So . . . she didn't. She just stayed in the moment, and believed, with all that she had, that this was truly happening for her.

"Aye," he said, "as certain as I could ever be. You've convinced me that we're ignoring the one thing that could save us. It could be our only hope." He pulled her closer. "And you're mine." He tipped her chin up, then cupped her cheek. "So, first, I have to save you."

"I can't believe this is happening," she said, shakily, but smiling up into his twinkling blue eyes. "I know I asked – begged – you to consider it, but I still can't quite believe . . ."

He leaned down and kissed her. "Believe, Abby." Then he looked up at the sun, and turned back to the castle proper. "It's time." He lifted her into his arms. "Hold on tightly to me," he said, as she looped her arms around his neck. "I willnae know, precisely, where I will land. So, keep hold, until I tell you what to do next. Do ye ken, Abby? Ye must promise me to—"

"I promise. I won't do anything foolish, I swear." Then she laughed at the absurdity of that statement, and he joined her.

"Come here," he said, and kissed her.

And the world spun . . . and kept spinning.

She felt weightless, then squeezed more tightly than she could ever recall feeling. She would have squirmed, but Calum kept his lips on hers, and she felt as if his own life force was seeping into her body. She felt electric, alive, almost crackling with it, as if sparks would snap from the ends of her hair and her fingertips, were she only to open her eyes and cast a glance at them.

And then the spinning shifted, and became wonky and wobbly, and she felt her stomach pitch. She held on more tightly as panic began to creep in. *Trust, trust, trust.* She kept repeating the words in her mind, as it felt as if she were going to be ripped, bodily from him, and flung into some jagged, abrupt, and endless void. She held on, literally, for dear life.

And then suddenly, shudderingly, with a jolt that knocked the breath completely out of her, there was a thudding impact, as if the ground had suddenly rushed up to meet her.

There was pain, jarring pain, but then she was rolling, and strong arms were still around her, and before she could gather

her wits or her breath, she was pulled, bodily, hard up against him. Calum.

She forced her eyes open as she struggled to breathe before she passed out from asphyxiation.

Yes, Calum. Right there. Holding on to her.

Which meant . . .

She slowly turned her head . . . and saw the castle. Or the place where it would have stood. It was a pile of rubble now, with hardly more than two feet of wall left of the tower, and most of it overgrown with dried vegetation and scruffy, dead weeds.

"Cal—" She tried to speak, but all that came out was a guttural bark.

"Shh," he told her. "Wait, don't talk. We need to get—" He was whispering, though she hadn't seen anyone . . . or anything, for that matter. The mountains still framed the backdrop against the sky . . . which was a startling shade of orange. Not the orange of a sunset. It looked more . . . toxic.

"Hold on to me. We've got to get down below."

She didn't question him, but held on. Dear God, had she actually done it? Was she really in the twenty-sixth century?

She grunted as Calum picked up his pace, until he was jogging over the uneven ground. "Press your mouth to my shirt, don't breathe in more than you must."

"What about you?"

He didn't answer, but tucked her face against his chest and held it there with a firm hand.

And then there was a sliding, a groaning, like stones moving – giant stones, but she couldn't look, couldn't see . . .

An instant later it was cooler, the air less acrid. She looked up in time to indeed see a large stone wall shift and slide behind Calum, shutting out the orange sky and toxic air.

"Okay," he said, out of breath. "I'm going to let your feet slide to the ground, but I want you to hold on to me until we gather our—"

"Who have you there?"

They both turned at the sound of the deep, echoing voice, Abby stumbling and gripping on to Calum's shirt to keep herself upright.

The man was very short, and very old, leaning heavily on a rapier-like, shiny silver cane. He had a thin beard knotted in a single braid that reached almost to the ground, but it was his eyes that held Abby's attention. They were almost purely white.

"I'm Abby," she said, before Calum could speak for her. "Abby Ramsay. Don't be mad at him. I made him bring me."

"Ailfrid—" Calum began, but rather than look angry or upset, the old man's face split into a wide grin.

"The Ramsay. Ye've finally gone and done it, lad!"

"Ailfrid, I know what we agreed, but let me explain—"

"No need, my son. No need."

Abby looked between Ailfrid, who she knew from Calum was the man who'd taught him all about the physics and science of time travel, and Calum himself, who was looking as confused as she felt.

Ailfrid walked directly up to Abby and looked her up and down. His opaque eyes made it hard to look at him directly, but she didn't want to appear rude. Or weak. So she held his gaze and let him look his fill.

"Calum has told me much about you. It's an honour to meet you," she said, as he finished walking around her.

He stopped in front of her again. "You've come." He reached out a gnarled hand and cupped her forearm, then turned his hazed gaze directly to Calum. "You've saved us." He looked back at her. "She will save us. This I know."

Nine

And what Ailfrid said was true. Upon Calum's demands to know the truth, the wizened elf of a man had explained his visions, that he'd known there was a saviour coming, but that she'd have to choose to come to them of her own free will. Calum couldn't simply go find her and grab her, or coerce her to come. She had to find him, decide to come, choose to help. Calum was merely there to facilitate her journey. It was why Ailfrid had taught him, trained him, sent him back, time and again . . . to ready him for her, for the time she finally showed herself.

"And you brought her here on the very first crossing," he said, smiling almost beatifically now. "Come," he said, reaching for her hand. "We must heal you . . . so you can heal us."

She rested her hand on his arm, willing to go with him, appearing excited and eager to find out what happened next.

When Calum merely stood there as Ailfrid led her more deeply into their lab and home base, Ailfrid turned back. "You will guide her as she guides you. Are you up for this most important task?"

Calum didn't hesitate, but locked gazes with Abby, who was already smiling – beaming – at him and met her in a tight embrace as she ran to him.

"Aye," he said, holding on tightly, knowing he held everything in his arms. Everything. There would be no next time. Now was their time.

And it always would be.

Kidnapping the Laird

Terri Brisbin

One

"She'd make ye a fine wife."

Padruig Grant drank deeply from the cup he held and shook his head at his brother – his drunken brother.

"She is already my wife," he replied. They both watched Catriona MacDonnell as she sat talking to some of the other women at the gathering. Padruig glanced at his brother to see if the man was pissed and decided he must be. His marriage had been arranged to bring peace to the neighbouring and warring clans, so there was no doubt that he was married to the woman.

"Aye . . . nay . . . aye," his brother stuttered.

When he was in his cups, Padruig knew no one but their mother could successfully intervene and order Jamie Grant to his bed – and live to do it again. She was nowhere to be seen. Padruig caught the eye of his other younger brother who joined their small group sitting at table in the front of the hall.

"Dougal, I was just telling our brother that she would make him a fine wife," his brother slurred his words now – not a good sign at all. Slurring words usually sat one step before a brawl.

"Catriona *is* married to Padruig," Dougal took their brother's arm and slung it over his shoulders, guiding him to his feet and supporting him once he stood. "I'm hoping you can find a comely lass for me," his brother said to him as he eased Jamie away from the table. But, as most of this day had gone, this would go as well – not well that was. Jamie pulled away, straightened to his full height and glared at Padruig, wagging his finger to emphasize his words.

"Ye need bairns, Padruig. Wee'uns to carry our name and blood. And ye need them now," his brother declared. "Get rid of that harlot who shares yer bed and see to yer wife."

Padruig stood then, his blood beginning to boil with rage, and he crossed his arms, glaring right back at his brother. "She is the daughter of our enemy. Why are you so intent on our marriage being anything more than what you helped arrange it to be and when you know the circumstances?"

Jamie squinted and frowned. Why had Padruig tried to speak sensibly to him when he'd been celebrating and drinking since yesterday? "Aye, I arranged it between ye two. But, the MacDonnells are'na our enemies. I think of them as rivals."

Padruig could not help it then. He laughed aloud at his brother's declaration. "Rivals? Rivals, you say? The MacDonnells are nothing more than a band of thieving, cheating, criminals. Or have you forgotten already the cattle they stole from us? Or how they tried to push us from our lands here in Glenmoriston?" He shook his head, refusing to debate or argue when his brother was this drunk or to debate with anyone about *her*. Glancing up he noticed she was watching their exchange with some interest.

Damn it to hell! Why did she have to be a MacDonnell?

No one would argue that Catriona was a rare beauty with her heart-shaped face, clear blue eyes and wave upon glorious wave of gold-tinged auburn hair that reached to her hips when she unravelled it from the braid that usually confined it. And when she smiled, it was all he could do not to take her to her bed, peel off her garments, kiss her senseless and swive her until they could not move. His trews felt tight now as his cock surged in response to his thoughts about . . . his wife! Padruig could not be certain whether the lust in his blood for her showed on his face or not, but Catriona started and looked away, not meeting his gaze.

"Take him to his chambers, Dougal," Padruig ordered, now in a softer voice. His younger brother began to help their sibling from the hall when he paused and smiled at Padruig.

"Ye want her. She's yer wife," Dougal pointed out the obvious, but Padruig waited for the rest. "It may have begun as something else, but that doesna mean it canna be something more."

Padruig closed his eyes, hoping they would both be gone when he opened them. Thankfully, they were. But Catriona remained where she'd been for most of this evening – sitting with some of his younger cousins as far from him as she could be and yet still in the same room. She'd forged a friendship of sorts with his sister, who would leave in a few days to live with her husband's family in the western isles. What would Catriona do then? He heard footsteps approaching from his right and knew from Catriona's darkening gaze exactly who walked closer to him.

Seana's hand glided along his arm and across his shoulder, touching his hair and tangling in its length. She pressed her body against his back, allowing the fullness of her breasts to rest on him. Then she leaned over and whispered in his ear. He could imagine the smile that sat on her full lips as she spoke, confident in her position as his *leman*, his lover.

"Come now, Padruig. I am ready for bed," she said in that sultry voice that usually sent waves of lust through his blood. This time though, the expression on Catriona's face gave him pause.

If he did not know better, Padruig would have thought her bothered by Seana's presence or by her attentions to him. But he did know, the memory of their disastrous wedding night burned fresh within him even these four months later. And her words, filled with loathing and disgust as she demanded he stay away from her from that night on, yet echoed in his head. Padruig had not returned to her bed or even tried to since that night, seeking out comfort in Seana's warm embrace when he needed the softness of a woman.

But Padruig Grant was no fool and he knew better than anyone that he would seek out his wife if she gave but a sign that he would be welcomed. His pride and position as laird kept him from pursuing it and the current situation seemed to fulfil everyone's needs – his, his wife's, her clan's and even his leman's. Seana's caress was ill-timed though and a blatant attempt on her part to lay some claim on him before the clan. He turned back to shrug off her hand and, when he glanced back, Catriona stood.

Until now, she knew she'd kept her reactions under control, but being shamed before his entire family was more than even she could bear without a response of some kind. Catriona pulled her emotions back from the brink of complete exposure and looked away from the scene unfolding at the high table between her husband and his whore. If she stood too fast or if her hands shook a bit as she gathered her cloak, surely the women there understood.

As she walked out of the large hall where the Grants had gathered for the wedding feast of the laird's youngest sister, she was not certain which hurt more – being shown how little she mattered to her husband or the pity she saw in the eyes of those who watched.

Reaching the small chamber she now claimed as her own, Catriona added some peat to the smouldering pile in the small hearth there and waited for some heat to spread out from it before undressing. This room had been an addition to the stone keep, an additional cooking hearth and storage room used for large gatherings or when needed. Once things between her and Padruig had deteriorated the morning after their wedding, she'd moved her belongings into it and no one had questioned or bothered her. Gazing around the chamber, she shuddered. If her father ever learned of her treatment or that she'd been reduced to fleeing her husband's bed for the safety of an empty one, the fragile peace forced by this arranged marriage would be shattered.

And that was the only reason she even remained in this marriage, for her father had sworn that though she was the sacrificial lamb in this, she would not be led to slaughter. If she called on him and asked for his protection, Anghous MacDonnell would save his first-born from the Grants. And war would follow. Catriona would not, could not, allow her family to suffer for her pride. Undressing, she hurried to climb in under the layers of warm bedcovers. Hours later, she lay awake, her pride pricking her over the constant insults to it.

If she could only claim to hate him for the situation between them, it would be easier to accept. The truth of the matter was that she did not. He had accepted the terms of their marriage as she had – it was never meant to be a love match or more than a simple outward sign of the peace treaty between his family and hers. The only physical relationship demanded of them was to live in the same place and to consummate their vows at least once.

They did. They had.

When she demanded that he leave her alone and not seek to continue to do such things, he left her alone, allowing her to live unmolested and as she pleased in the keep. Other than keeping a leman, Padruig treated her respectfully and never raised a hand to her. And usually, she never drew his eye or his attention.

Until this night.

She supposed she was out of sorts because of witnessing her only friend in Glenmoriston getting married and knowing that Nairna would leave in but a few days. And from having to watch Nairna and her new husband look at each other with such love in their eyes. Nay, she knew it was because all evening and for days now, she'd watched her own husband, unable to ignore his masculine beauty or the strength in his body.

Catriona shifted in the small bed, pulling the bedcovers up higher to stay warm, hoping that warmth would draw her into sleep and away from these disturbing thoughts and feelings. After watching his treatment of his leman and his reaction to her many public caresses and even kisses, Catriona recognized lust when she saw it in his dark, green eyes. And tonight, as he met her gaze after arguing with his brother, lust shone there. And something deep within her told her he lusted – for her.

Another hour or two passed and the glimmer of an idea occurred to her about how to get past both her and Padruig's pride in the matter of their marriage. After he'd sworn in front of others that he would never ask to come to her bed, she understood he would not, even if she invited him. But something inside her heart wanted him to want her and wanted something more than this inconvenient, impersonal arranged marriage. Something deep in her soul wanted to have a husband like Nairna's who gazed on her with love in his eyes.

Damn her foolish heart but she wanted Padruig Grant to look at her that way.

Two

The moon rose above, shining enough light down for him to continue his journey home without waiting for dawn. The relentless spring rains had finally given way to drier days and pleasant nights. He was about two miles from the keep when they attacked. Padruig fought with all his strength, but they – four or five warriors – took him prisoner. A hood was tossed over his head, covering his eyes, and a gag tied around that. With his hands bound behind his head, he was trussed up like a roast in the cook's larder and tossed over the back of his own horse. Though Padruig tried to estimate their direction and distance, he lost track after only a few minutes of hanging upside down over a moving horse.

'Twas clear to him that whoever they were, they wanted him

alive, for once they got his sword away from him, they could have killed him. So, Padruig decided to wait before taking any action. Though laird of the clan, he had brothers to step into that chair if something happened to him, so he did not fear for the clan or its future. Even Catriona would be cared for. But why kidnap a laird? Only retribution and destruction could follow and who would gain?

They travelled for some time, up hills and down, near rushing water, until they drew to a halt and he was dragged from the horse. His legs shook and his head spun as they pulled him along a path, through a doorway that was too low for his height and into some kind of croft or cottage. His arms were untied and he was forced to sit on the dirt floor. Padruig grabbed the nearest kidnapper and pulled him down, too, but he was quickly subdued, this time chains replacing the ropes.

Padruig could not tell how many were present or who they were. They efficiently chained him to the wall, his arms separated and placed on either side of him. The chains were low enough and long enough only to let him sit or stand, but not to move more than a half-pace from the wall itself. Once he was secured, he heard his captors speaking, both inside and outside the building, but again in voices too low and too muffled to identify. The conversation continued for some minutes and he took advantage of their inattention to shift around and get some idea of how much movement he could accomplish in spite of the chains.

The door slammed, surprising him, and he heard hammers pounding nails into the frame around the door. He tried to yell against the gag, demanding answers, but between the noise of the hammering and the gag and hood, Padruig knew no one could hear him. Then, as quickly as this escapade had begun, he could hear them leaving – leaving him chained to a wall, and gagged. Padruig struggled then, pulling against the chains and trying to reach the knot in the gag to get free of it.

Who would do this? Who would take him prisoner and leave him so? Did they think to ransom him? Ha! The Grants could call many to their sides in a dispute or war, but they were not a wealthy clan. There would be no ransom for him. If he got free, he would beat the truth out of someone.

He twisted around and finally reached the knot behind his head and tugged it loose. Padruig loosened the canvas hood and drew it off. He expected not to be able to see anything in the dark, so the lamp burning on the table surprised him.

But the sight of Catriona standing there shocked him more.

Catriona swallowed against the fear and tried to meet his gaze. She had begun to reconsider this rash plan before she'd taken the first step, but now she knew it had been a mistake. He blinked and rubbed his eyes as though he did not believe what he was seeing and she recognized the moment when he accepted it was her before him.

Husband or not, Padruig Grant was a formidable man to have as an enemy. Even chained to a wall, the power in his arms was evident – his muscles rippled as he tested the resistance of the chains. A bruise darkened the edge of his jaw even now. Catriona fisted her hands and fought the urge to touch it. It must be the tension of this plot that made her notice such things now, when she'd rarely done so during the last four months.

"What is this, Catriona?" he asked her, his voice milder than she dreamed possible.

All of the words, all of the possible explanations she'd planned in the weeks while she laid her plans and none came to mind in this moment.

"Tell me!" he yelled louder than, his demand echoing around them both as his anger grew and the chains rattled against the stone wall behind him. Catriona trembled for a moment and then regained control over herself.

"Do you do your father's bidding? Who were your accomplices?" he asked again.

He pulled against the chains and she jumped back a step in reaction. Cat raised her hand and rubbed her forehead. Why had she ever thought this would work? Padruig somehow managed to climb to his feet. Now he used his height to intimidate her since his loud voice had not. Dougal had warned her of what to expect when Padruig lost his temper and so far, he knew his brother well. What had he advised? Oh, hold her ground. Let him yell. Then negotiate. She'd done that the morning after their wedding and it had worked, so Cat had every expectation that it would again . . . but this time with much different results.

Laughter bubbled inside her at this inappropriate time. From the anger in his eyes, the clenching of his jaws and the way he pulled against the chains, Cat understood there would be no negotiating with him for a while. She would be lucky to leave here alive, let alone with a husband. His brothers had not seemed worried over their safety, but that gave her no comfort – they were blood, she was a MacDonnell. She sighed and shook her head and, crossing her arms over her chest and standing as tall as possible, she spoke the words that entered her mind.

"I want a husband."

And then he responded as all Grants did – to her name, her family's history and based on the animosity that existed between their clans – with anger. If anyone remained behind after bringing him here and securing him, they would have heard his rants in spite of the boarded-up door and windows and in spite of the thick, stone walls of this house. He rained down curses on her and her clan. He fought against the chains until his wrists bled. Cat attempted to interrupt him several times to explain, but he did not stop . . .

Until he did.

Collapsing against the wall and sliding down to the floor, Padruig pulled in one ragged breath after another trying to regain his control. He'd always been lauded as the even-tempered of Micheil Grant's sons, but clearly he had inherited his father's ability to lose his self-control without warning. Though being attacked, beaten, kidnapped and threatened with death was more reason than most would expect. Now, he wiped across his face with his arm and tried to catch his breath.

"Another husband?" he asked in a voice hoarse from shouting. "There are far easier ways than this to get a new one." He jangled the chains for emphasis.

She did not say anything. Padruig could see that he'd frightened her out of saying anything now. Good. He could not ever remember displaying his anger like this, not even when faced with a wife who did not want him. That morning, he may have raised his voice, but that was more about the affront to his clan than to himself.

A pang of guilt touched him just then, reminding him of the way her words had indeed hurt him. And in a way that had nothing to do with his clan or hers, but in every way it was about him. His pride over his position in his clan had been offended. Worse, her words that morning had called his honour into question.

He watched as she silently walked around the chamber, gathering things he only now noticed and putting them on a wooden tray. She walked towards him and he stood, not wanting to miss the chance to get hold of her and force her to give over the key to the chains. It was then that he realized where they were, where she'd had him taken . . . and the implications of it.

Long ago his father had built a small house for his mother. Not one to live in, but one that sat on the stream that fed into the loch nearby. Her "lady's house" his father had called it and it became a place of refuge for his mother, a place of quiet and a place of privacy. From the far-away expression in their eyes whenever this place was mentioned, Padruig could only imagine, and did not want to, the time spent and the things done here. The sound of wood scraping along the floor drew his attention back and he saw Catriona pushing the tray nearer to him. She remained just far enough back so that he could not reach her, but close enough to manoeuvre the tray to sit within his reach.

A bowl of water. Some cloth scraps. A small jug. A piece of bread and another of cheese.

"You must be hungry," she said, walking across the room and sitting in the chair there. "You missed both the noon and evening meal."

He wanted to deny it, but his stomach chose that exact moment to rumble loudly, enough that he witnessed a fleeting smile pass over her mouth. Padruig slid back down and pulled the tray closer. She'd had him kidnapped but offered him food and water . . . and the small comforts to clean himself of the blood that now trickled down his arms and hands from his wrists. In the midst of planning such a radical thing, she'd taken time to notice he'd missed meals and had food ready for him.

Her eyelids began to flutter as she watched him eat. By the time he'd consumed the last crumb of food and drop of ale, she sat asleep in the chair, her head leaning to one side. Padruig would wait, not that he had any choice in the matter, and get his answers in the morn. Thinking on the implications of all of this, he realized something else.

She might want a new husband, but she did not wish him dead.

Or, at the least, not dead yet.

Three

Catriona woke with a start, forgetting where she was and why she was sleeping in a chair. Scant daylight entered through the one small window left uncovered near the doorway, revealing that morn had broken. She rubbed her neck as she straightened her head, easing the pain of sleeping with her head leaning to one side. Only as she did so did she remember . . . everything. "Good morn, Catriona," he said.

His tone was so pleasant she could have believed them meeting in the hall of the keep to break their fast. Glancing over at him, she gathered her loose hair back into its braid and stood, her arms and legs screaming in protest after hours spent in one position. He'd cleaned his wounds and wrapped some of the cloth rags around them to protect them from further injury. Cat stumbled as she stood and he moved against his chains. Had he tried to help her? She met his gaze and nodded at him.

"Padruig."

They lived separately, though under the same roof, so she had no experience with him in the mornings. Or the nights, though she knew, as did everyone in Clan Grant, how he spent those. Cat walked to the small hearth, stretching her arms and legs as she moved, and found the kindling there and started a fire.

Dougal and Jamie had been thorough in stocking this house for her use – the storage room below held weeks worth of food and supplies, a cistern fed fresh water through a pipe, and wood and peat stood waiting to be burned. She thought about the room above her head and felt her cheeks warm from a blush at the thought of the unusually large bed with its plush furs and bedcovers that sat waiting there. Cat turned back and found him watching her every move.

"I will have some porridge ready soon," she told him. This casual chatter would be difficult between them.

"So, you need me alive then?" he asked. His question was posed quietly, but it did not fool her – he was probing for information about her plans. Not that it surprised her.

Padruig had become laird a few years back and was accustomed to being in charge. He oversaw every aspect of the clan – its people, its farms, its lands and its future – and was considered, even by her father, to be one of the canniest men in Scotland. She tried to gather her thoughts and her arguments, but they remained scattered. Cat ignored him, or attempted to, and was successful in her attempts until he interrupted her again.

"I need to . . ."

He paused and so she was forced to face him. With a few gestures he indicated his need to take care of a personal task and Cat found herself with the heat rising in her cheeks at the thought of such a thing. She found a pot and slid it over to him, turning back to cooking, blushing even more when the sound of it reached her. Worse, he whistled throughout!

Cat focused on her task and soon the porridge bubbled in the cooking pot. She avoided looking over her shoulder at Padruig. Cat prepared the meal, scooping some into two bowls, adding a spoon in each, and then pouring some watered ale in cups. As the eldest sibling in a large group of them, cooking was something familiar to her. Though he probably knew it not, she'd been cooking meals at the keep for months, bringing with her the favourite recipes of her mother and her mother's mother and helping in ways that made her feel useful . . . especially since she was not fulfilling any wifely duties. She carried his bowl and cup over to him.

His grin was purely masculine, one that spoke of things left unspoken, one that dared her to meet his gaze, which she avoided while handling the rearrangement of the tray, the bowls and the cups. She removed the pot. Soon, he was eating and Cat sat in the chair doing the same. She understood that he would wait no longer for an explanation and that she had only the time it would take them to eat left to her.

Padruig could not help but grin. From fearing for his life to wondering what she would demand of him for his freedom, he'd thought on this situation all night. While she slept, he considered all or most of the possibilities and she had him puzzled. Her declaration the morning after they were wed, one that demanded he not trouble her again in that manner, set the pattern of their lives. If she had objected to his seeking a mistress, he would not have done so, but she showed no willingness for an intimate relationship between them. He shifted his position on the floor and waited for her to finish.

Catriona blushed then, under his gaze, and he wondered what had made her do so now. He'd watched it happen the night before, just before he lost his temper, when she'd glanced at the stairs leading to the loft above. Thinking on his own reaction to the purely decadent bed that lay waiting above them, he thought it must be that. Padruig finished his ale and put the cup and bowl back on the tray.

"So, now that I am fed and dry," he said, enjoying the way she coloured in reaction to his reference, "is it time to learn the truth of my fate?"

Catriona's expression changed in that instant from one of indecision. His wife had grown up in these last months under his constant watch. She did not know that he observed every move she made when they were together. She did not know that his family reported back to him about her activities, her health and even her unhappiness. Though circumspect in her words, he understood how she felt about her position within the clan and her reasons for remaining there.

Or at least he'd thought he knew until last night.

She glanced away and seemed to be struggling on the words to say, so he pushed a bit to get her started, realizing that they'd already spent more time alone together since his kidnapping than they had in the months since their wedding.

"You want a new husband."

"I did not say a *new* husband," she snapped back at him. "I said I wanted a husband."

"You have a husband," he replied. "Clearly you know who he is since you had him kidnapped." He pushed himself to his feet and tried to cross his arms until the short length of chain stopped him. "Speak plainly, Cat," he said. "Tell me why you did this and what will remove these chains."

She started at his words before speaking. Then he watched as she straightened her shoulders and stood, mirroring his own stance. But she could cross her arms.

"I find that our arrangement is not acceptable to me any longer, Padruig. I tire of being humiliated by your whore. I tire of being a wife, but not a wife," she said softly.

He let out his breath, stunned by her admission. Of all the things he thought he would hear, this was not any of them! He fought to keep the smile from his lips for her words could mean several things. To gain more insight, he asked, "When did you decide this?"

She shrugged and shook her head. He thought she would answer, but she did not, turning away for a moment. Dear God! She brushed tears from her eyes. Even on that disastrous morning she had not cried. "It matters not."

He recognized pride when he saw it and allowed her to keep hers. "So, you wish to end our marriage so that you can seek another?" He held out his hands with the chains. "Could you not simply have discussed this with me? Did you have to resort to violence?"

Padruig knew the moment he'd pushed her far enough, for the glimmer in her eyes was one he'd not seen before – pure anger. And he was much more adept at dealing with anger than with tears. "We both signed that marriage contract. We both are held to its clauses and both understand the cost of failure, Padruig. My father will not allow this marriage to be ended and neither will your clan – they, we, cannot afford the cost of it."

He understood in that moment what she sought – she'd brought him here to deal with this privately between them. To save both their pride. "Agreed. So remove these and we will discuss this." He held out his hands.

Padruig watched as she hesitated. "How do I know that . . ." she began to ask. He interrupted her.

"How do you know that I will carry out my end of whatever bargain we reach? I give you my word that I will abide by whatever agreement we make here, Cat. As laird and as your husband."

"Nay, that was not my meaning," she whispered. She sighed and then met his gaze. "I brought you here so that I could see if I could keep the bargain I offer, Padruig."

Confused now, but intrigued, he asked, "What are you offering? What do you seek from me if not an end to our marriage?"

"If you will rid yourself of that woman, I'll return to your bed."

There. She'd said it. Boldly. Clearly. Cat had not planned to expose her own doubt about her abilities to carry out this plan, never a good idea when trying to bargain, but the words had slipped out.

Would he laugh at her now? Would he threaten ungodly punishments for her actions? She knew that he might do that when she began making plans and so had taken pains not to allow anyone else near, so that she alone would bear his anger.

"Seana?" he asked, as though he had several women to choose from. That thought gave her pause, for mayhap he did have more than one.

"Aye," she answered. "Unless there are more who I do not know about?"

He did laugh then, but she did not feel that he was jesting at her expense. It gave her confidence to stand her ground. But his next question shattered that.

"How do you propose to replace her? You made it clear on our wedding night that my touch – how did you say it? – caused feelings of revulsion within you."

Damn but the man had committed her words to memory! He remembered nothing else she'd said but those? He was correct though, she'd said them and meant them, but being an innocent with no experience in the ways of passion, she had no idea of what to expect. The pain surprised her, as did many other things he did.

"I . . . I . . ." She could not find the words to explain. She shook her head. "This was a mistake. I knew it from the beginning," she said, pacing back and forth. "It will not work and I would have been better never having considered such a foolish thing."

Cat stood before the doorway – the nailed-shut-for-two-days doorway – and felt the weight of her misjudgments on her shoulders. If not for her pride, she would not be standing here, more humiliated before him than she'd ever been before her family. And worse, now she had to wait another two days before Dougal and Jamie would come back to free them from this place. She shivered realizing that he would be extremely angry when his brothers returned here and found him so.

"I accept."

The words echoed across the distance between them and, for a moment, Cat could not be certain she'd heard correctly. She turned to face him, surprised to find him observing her with a seriousness she'd not seen in his expression before.

"I accept your bargain, Cat." He nodded to emphasize his words. "If you prove you can bear my touch and will agree to return to my bed, I will send Seana back to her family."

It was everything she'd hoped for, but now what?

He must have read her thoughts for he held up his hands between them, rattling the chains and pointing out the first thing she must do. Her thoughts went blank when she tried to think of what she must do after that. Retrieving the key from where she'd hidden it, she began walking towards him. Padruig climbed to his feet waiting for her.

Panic was written in her eyes and in the frown that sat on her forehead. Padruig felt the need to ease her fears and allow her to keep her pride now that he understood more about what drove her to these daft actions. He'd allowed his pride to push her away and now he would have to bend to get her back. Though he was not usually the one to bend, he saw something in her eyes that promised such possibilities and such opportunities that he wanted to give her the chance.

"You have nothing to fear from me, Cat," he said softly.

She shook her head and he watched as the loosened tendrils of hair spun around her face, making her look softer than he'd seen. Her hands shook as she reached out with the key to remove the chains. When the chains fell away from his wrists, he stopped her from stepping away, taking her chin in his hand and guiding her mouth to his. Her mouth softened beneath his and he heard her breathing quicken.

More importantly, she did not pull away.

Her success at this was not hers to prove – it was his. He should have known better that first night. He should have taken her gently and not let his anger over the marriage contract interfere with that first experience. He should have introduced her to the pleasures of the marriage bed. But, he had failed her that night.

Padruig would not fail her this time.

Reaching around her head, he did the thing he'd thought of doing so many times – he tugged the leather tie free and let her hair unwind from its braid. Sliding his fingers through it, he tugged her towards him, holding her close as he deepened the kiss. He tilted his head and possessed her mouth as he'd recently fantasized about doing . . . and he did it over and over until they were both breathless. She watched him through each kiss and Padruig saw disbelief deep within her blue eyes as her body reacted even before she understood.

But he understood and his body did as well, his cock hardening and lengthening and readying itself for what was to happen between them. The blood thundered through his veins, lust heating it and pushing it faster and hotter through him. He took in and released several deep breaths, needing his control so that this time removed all the memories of the last from her mind. Padruig held her face near hers, kissing her more gently now, and sliding his other hand down along her neck and shoulder and skimming over the fullness of her breasts.

She gasped at the feel of such a caress.

Catriona waited for the inevitable as she enjoyed his kisses more than she had the first time. His tongue slipped into her mouth when she gasped and touched hers, sending shivers and chills throughout her body. As his hand moved away from her head and his fingers touched her breasts and then eased down over her belly, strange coils of tension began to twist deep within her. Just when she thought he would touch her *there,* he paused and kissed her more fiercely, before resting his hand on her hip.

Sensations unlike anything she'd felt raced through her blood and her heart and her body, urging her to move closer, to open to him and to this enticing heat that built from within her. When he stopped and lifted his head, she recognized merriment in his dark green eyes.

"Disgusted yet?" he asked in a deeper voice than usual. "Any revulsion or other loathing?"

He was jesting with her, but all she could think of was how different his touch was this time, how pleasant, nay, pleasurable it was compared to their first night. If she'd felt these kinds of sensations that night, the last four months would not have been wasted and empty.

"Nay," she said, shaking her head and laughing gently. "None yet."

The expression that filled his eyes then made her lose her breath, for it was hot and lustful. Could this truly work between them? Padruig dipped his head closer and kissed her again. She liked his kisses and allowed him to repeat that melding of their mouths again and again. Her body grew heated and wet between her legs and a strange and wondrous ache began to throb there, too. The urge to rub against him and the hardness of his strong body grew and she felt herself arch against him.

Before she knew what he was about, he'd scooped her up in his arms and began climbing the stairs to the loft. She wanted to ask him so many things but the feelings racing through her pushed all her questions and doubts aside as she allowed him to carry her towards that scandalous bed.

Daylight entered the chamber from the small windows all around the perimeter of the room. Not so large that anything could fit through them, but large enough to allow a good flow of light inside the loft, these windows made it possible to see him as he laid her on the bed and loosened his clothing. Tempted to look away, his command, or rather his demand, surprised her yet again.

"Look at me, Cat."

She did, watching as his strong hands unbuckled his belt and then dropped it at his feet. His tunic and trews followed, even his boots and hose, until he stood naked before her. She felt the heat rising in her cheeks as she watched his body react under her gaze. Cat followed the dark thatch of hair down his chest, past his belly and then to where his manhood rose from the curls, proving his readiness to join their bodies. She swallowed and then swallowed again, fighting the fear that tried to replace the heat in her.

"Trust me, Cat." This time his words were spoken softly, a plea more than an order and it warmed her. She nodded, though truly not certain she could.

Padruig knelt beside her, watching as her eyes widened and as her gaze flitted to touch on his cock and then away. She'd seemed to enjoy kissing so he eased her back and touched their mouths together. Tasting and teasing her lips and tongue, he waited until she panted before touching any other place on her body.

Though he wanted to touch her everywhere at once.

He almost forgot how innocent she was. He almost forgot the last four months. But when she reached out and boldly wrapped her hand around his hardened flesh, he forgot to breathe and forgot how to think at all. Trying to distract himself from the arousing caress, he began loosening the ties of her tunic and undergown and leaned down to suckle on her now-exposed breasts.

Had they always been this full? Had the nipples been this enticing rosy shade that night too? Their joining had been quick and accomplished in the dark, giving him no opportunity to savour her beauty or her lush womanly curves. This time it would be different for both of them. When she arched against his mouth as he took the tip of a breast into his mouth, he swirled his tongue around it until it pebbled tight and hard.

The gasps turned to moans, his and hers, as they teased each other with tempting kisses, arousing caresses and the need to join their bodies together. When he felt the readiness of her body and the heat and wetness between her legs, he eased on top of her, spreading her legs with his body and rubbed the centre of her arousal until he felt her body begin to tremble. Then, he pressed his hardness deep inside her, inch by inch, allowing her body to adjust as he filled her to her core.

The sounds she made drove him insane with the need to claim her, to bring her to completion now, one that he'd not accomplished that first night, and one that he could not fail to accomplish this time. Easing back out until only the tip of his cock remained within her flesh, he thrust deeper and deeper, feeling her flesh tighten around his, increasing his hardness and readying him to spill his seed there.

Cat could not believe the way her body felt in this moment. Not invaded or violated, but filled with his flesh until they were one. He urged her towards something with whispers and words and caresses and his body until hers responded in kind, rippling from where he thrust, sending waves and waves of indescribable pleasure through her, body and soul. Her muscles tightened, that tension building deep within sprang loose and she moaned out even as he spilled his seed. Her flesh responded, softening and opening, giving over to his complete possession. When she came back to herself, he lay on her, panting softly in her ear. Padruig eased off her, drawing her into his embrace and yet remaining within her at the same time.

She lay silent in his arms, listening to the steady beat of his heart and trying to understand all that had happened between them. He kissed her forehead as he eased out of her body and the place there ached with an emptiness she did not know she could feel. Had she pleased him enough to make him give up Seana though? She feared asking him anything that would mar the wondrous satisfaction that filled her in that moment. Still though, she wanted to know. But before she could ask him, he spoke.

"Did you prove it to yourself, Cat? Can you find pleasure in my bed?" He turned on his side and touched her cheek, drawing her gaze to his. "Will you return to my bed and be my wife in all ways?"

Catriona understood the cost of his question to his pride. He was admitting his part in the debacle that had sent them down this path of separation and unhappiness. Padruig was giving her a chance at fulfilment and happiness . . . and mayhap even love.

"Aye, if you'll have me, Padruig."

He smiled and her heart raced at the beauty of it – the masculine angles of his face eased at her words and his dark green eyes sparkled in reply. Still, there was one matter that needed to be clarified between them.

"And Seana?"

He laughed then, kissing her on the mouth quickly before nodding. "She left a sennight ago, Cat."

Catriona sat up, gathering her garments around her and shook her head. "You sent her away? Why?"

Padruig pushed up to sit next to her, quite at ease with his nakedness. "I had this foolish notion to ask my wife to return to my bed. I would have, but I was kidnapped before I could discuss it with her."

"You jest!" she said, unsure if she could or should believe his words. "You mean none of this was necessary?" She'd risked so much, not the least of which was his brothers' relationship with him as brother and as their laird if he discovered their involvement in her plot.

"Not necessary but, besides the ambush, quite enjoyable," he said, laughing. He grew serious then and stared at her intently. "Did it please you, Cat? Did I please you this time?" Had it not been obvious to him? She'd melted in his embrace, her body played by his touch and his hands and his mouth. As though she'd spoken the words aloud, he continued. "What happened between us that first night should never have happened. Will you be able to put it behind us and forgive me?"

Tears burned in her eyes but she dashed them away. She nodded, believing for the first time that they did have a chance at happiness together, something completely unthinkable just days before. He kissed her, pulling her close and holding her to him.

"When will Dougal and Jamie return to free us?"

Cat drew back, surprised at his words. Did he know or was he seeking out information? His mischievous smile told her that he did indeed know.

"In two days," she answered, watching his expression change into something dark and enticing and wicked.

"Time enough to begin . . ." he said, as he began kissing not just her mouth but her neck and then her shoulders and then . . . and then . . .

By the time his brothers arrived two days later, she could not move a muscle. His possession of her body complete and that of heart begun, she almost wished she'd told them to wait three days before returning.

Four

With the excuse of seeking out the good wine from the storage room below, Padruig pulled on his trews and climbed down the stairs to that chamber. Instead of heading for the barrel of wine, he sought the hidden door behind a storage trunk. Making his way through the tunnel and along the stream, he climbed up to the path and returned to the front of the house where his brothers waited.

Giving no warning, he grabbed and tossed Jamie to the ground and then managed to land a solid punch to Dougal's jaw before they realized he was there. The feel of it was satisfying, for he was certain that Dougal had been the one who sent him to his knees during the kidnapping.

"What the hell?" Dougal said, rubbing his face.

"That was for agreeing to carry out her foolish plan without telling me about it," Padruig said. Dougal shrugged as though kidnapping your brother and laird was a commonplace thing.

"Did it work?" he asked. "That's all I want to know." He crossed his arms over his chest and angled his head while waiting for Padruig to answer.

"Come back in two more days and I'll tell you," he answered. Those were all the words he was willing to say right now.

"I was right, Padruig. Just admit it," Dougal pushed.

Padruig did not answer. Instead he walked away, retracing his path back to the tunnel. He heard his brothers laugh as he did, but he cared not. The entire clan would know soon enough that he'd claimed his bride, even if it was four months late.

After entering the storage room and finding the wine, he climbed back up to the loft with it. Cat lay as he'd left her – replete and exhausted from his attentions. A purely male sense of satisfaction filled him now as well, knowing that he'd seen to her pleasure countless times already and would again now that they had two more days of privacy away from the world. As he climbed on to the wide surface of the bed, she stirred, reaching out and resting her hand on his stomach as he moved closer. He stirred, well his flesh did, and she welcomed him between her thighs with a delicious sigh he was coming to crave. When they could speak again, Cat reminded him that his brothers would arrive soon. Unwilling to confess that he could have escaped her at any time through the hidden door in the cellar, Padruig smiled and suggested that he remain kidnapped for two more days.

But it was four more days before the laird and lady returned to their keep.

Together.

Kissingate Magic

Annette Blair

The matchmaking fairy of Kissingate,
Every year capitulates
And brings a pair who hesitates,
A love meant to be.

She's the shape-shifting fairy of Kissingate
Nudging an intractable young prelate
Who lost what he could never see straight:
A love meant to be.

Kissingate, Scotland, 1846

One

Jacey Lockhart, hidden in the midnight shadows, fixed her hungry gaze on Gabriel Macgregor, the most formidable of the ghosts she had come home to face.

Gabriel the guarded – named for the bright angel, when he should have been named for the dark – lowered his head to avoid an old oak barn beam, the hint of a smile in his eyes . . . until he saw her.

The knave stepped back, stretched to his full towering height, and squared his shoulders to a stunning span – Lucifer, face carved in unforgiving angles.

Despite her resolve, Jacey wanted to catch the next train back to Essex, though she couldn't seem to move.

Here stood the father of her child, and firm between them, the lie she told denying it. In one stroke, she'd saved and destroyed him.

A horse shuffled in its stall, freeing hay musk into the air, breaking the silence, hazing the past, and allowing her to breathe.

As forbidding as her nemesis appeared in lantern light, dressed entirely in black, the tiny white lamb tucked into his frockcoat humanized him, the contrast bringing his cleric's collar into conspicuous relief. A rogue's heart, a vicar's trappings, and no one seemed to know, save her.

His face, lined and bronzed by age and parish responsibility, gave him a mature, patrician air. His hair, a tumble of sooty waves, thick and lush, showed grey at the temples. No ghost, but the bane of her existence in the flesh, more vitally masculine than ever.

He'd always been proud, even when they were children – he, a poor vicar's son, she, the heir to a fortune. But she'd reversed their roles. Now, a disinherited outcast, she stood, once again, before the boy who adored her, then hated her, with all his heart. "Gabriel," she said, wishing her voice didn't tremble and her body didn't remember.

Two

Gabriel wondered if the sum and substance of all his dreams, good and bad, could hear his stone cold heart knocking against his ribs. "Jace," he said, his rasp awkward.

He cleared his throat, but Suttie stepped up and kissed him on the cheek. Suttie, the ageless puppeteer whose gypsy wagon they'd once chased giggling down the High Street. "Welcome, both of you," Gabe said, his voice working, again, hope suddenly alive.

Suttie beamed. "I see you found the surprise I brought."

Found her? He thought. *He couldn't take his eyes off her.*

"Aye, Gabriel, I've come home. I'll stay in Suttie's wagon."

Gabe's chest ached for hiding his joy. "You'll both stay at Kirk Cottage. No argument, now."

Suttie beamed; Jacey looked terrified.

"Please, Lady Lockhart?" Gabe begged in the way Jace once commanded, for a piece of butterscotch pie, but the words evoked her fall from grace. "I apologise," he said. "That was thoughtless."

"Aye, it was." Jace turned to Suttie. "Can *I* stay in your gypsy wagon? I'll take the morning train back. I shouldn't have come."

Gabriel gave the lamb to Suttie, placed his hand against Jacey's back to propel her towards the vicarage, her body heat curling like a spiral around his icy heart.

Inside, she stepped from his touch. "I won't stay. I cannot."

If she left again, she'd never come back. The thought of losing her forever cut deep. Gabe turned to build up the fire in the hearth to chase away the damp, warm the lamb, and gather his wits.

Jacey, here, in his house, where he pictured her nearly every day. His Jacey. As beautiful as ever. More.

No, not his. Never again. That was past.

He was a vicar now, in control, unemotional, his passion a vice overcome. Long-buried. Dead. He turned to his guests. "Mackenzie's asleep, so I'll ready your rooms."

The lamb bleated. "She's hungry," Jace said.

"I planned to make a bottle." He felt big, clumsy beside Jace and remembered a time it didn't matter.

"Did her mother die?" she asked.

Gabriel took the lamb like a shield. "She's a twin and a runt." He stroked its neck and the mite closed its eyes in ecstasy.

Jacey watched transfixed, yearning in her emerald eyes. Seeing it, he might once have lowered her to the grass and—

The fire snapped. They stepped back, released by the sound.

"I'll fix a bottle—"

"I'll get you a bot—"

They spoke together, stopped together.

Gabe set the lamb on its wobbly legs and fetched the supplies Jace would need to feed it then he headed out to get their bags, Suttie beside him.

Three

Jacey watched him go and released her breath, a victim of the soul-deep longing that led to her downfall. Five years and she hadn't come to terms with it. Getting herself with child, without a husband, she'd disgraced her mother, a true Lady of the Manor.

After her babe's birth and death, she got a job at Briarhaven School, Essex, England, where she lived, taught needlework, and hid from the past.

Surprisingly, she came back to life, found her self-respect, and with the help of Suttie's letters, knew that before she could have a future, she must face her past.

Yesterday, Suttie had come for her. She'd set boldly forth to face the world she left behind, and ended trembling in a vicarage kitchen.

To calm herself, she warmed a pan of milk and rinsed a lambing bottle. She couldn't leave; she'd come for Gabriel's step-daughter, her motherless niece, who slept upstairs, the child she planned to take and raise. Only Gabriel stood between her and success.

Some things never changed.

Jacey sat by the hearth, coaxing the lamb into her lap by making use of its grip on the nipple.

First, she'd have to face a condemning village, Gabriel among them, a flock who considered him a saint and her a sinner. But he was human. Flawed. Jacey knew better than anyone.

Oddly enough, she'd forgiven him, but not herself.

Four

In the kitchen after bringing Suttie and her bags upstairs, Gabe stopped at the sight of Jace, while his old enemy, lust, returned for just looking at her.

He backed away and sat at the round old table, with its scarred slab top and legs big as tree trunks, not sure what to do with his hands.

"Where's Suttie?" Jace asked, her voice a wobbling croak.

"Fell asleep while I showed her the room. I threw a blanket over her. Is she getting old, our Suttie?"

"She certainly doesn't look it. More stubborn than anything, I think. We shouldn't have arrived so late, but Suttie insisted on driving through. I'm glad we didn't wake you."

Gabriel quit the table and dropped down beside Jace to stroke the drowsing lamb's lanolin-soft wool. Instantly, he saw his mistake. Too close, he thought. Oh, God, Jacey.

The mite roused at his attention and suckled as if it hadn't eaten in a week, until it pulled on air-bubbles, and Jace tried to wrest the empty bottle from its grip. When Jace won, his hand slipped and grazed her breast.

He froze at the contact, their gazes locked, a primitive energy rising hot and thick between them – an intangible yet undeniable force, savage in its intensity.

Jace bit her lip, drew blood. Did her body betray her as much as his? Gabriel lost his breath to lust, molten and heavy. He'd controlled passion for years, with his wife's staunch approval after their sorry wedding night. But a minute in Jace's company, and passion, like Lazarus, rose from the dead.

Trapped. By weakness. His strength lay in denying passion – a hard-won lesson. But around Jacey, desire overcame determination, and strength became a wisp of smoke where once burned a zealot's fire.

Jacey. Jace. Home. His Jace.

No, and again, no.

She'd made him call her Lady Lockhart when he wanted to call her Jace, like the rest of her friends did, except for the day he came home a new-minted vicar, when he finally called her *his*.

Once again, he felt like that runny-nosed boy with torn clothes and dirty nails. Why, when his clothes were new, his home comfortable and clean, elegant even? Why, when Jace's grey dress, mended and pressed to a pauper's shine, must once have been blue?

Trapped. By passion. By Jacey. Gabriel wanted to swear, to rage, to pull her into his arms and kiss her until she gave passion back, as Jacey surely could. If only he wasn't the *only* man who'd experienced her passion.

Gabriel crossed the kitchen to get as far from captivation as possible. He couldn't be near without taking her in his arms, any more than he could bear the reminder of her betrayal, and his foolishness.

"I'm looking forward to time with my niece," she said, her rush of words pulling him from pain but shivering him to his bones. He gazed at her, looking for no greater significance than her words betrayed. "You mean, *my daughter*," he said, foolishly desperate to stake his claim.

Jacey rose with the lamb in her arms. "Step-daughter," she corrected. "I hope she remembers her real father."

He'd face any and all demons, real or imagined, for Bridget. "Her father died before her birth. Her mother and I married before she turned two. I'm the only father she knows."

"I'm her aunt, kin by blood."

"Blood, *as we know*, does not always tell."

Jace stepped back under the weight of his verbal blow.

His barb, born of self-preservation, hurt him as much as it did her.

Ashamed of his callous words, he claimed the lamb, but couldn't calm. He wanted to take Jace into his arms, soothe her, and he wished to the devil he didn't bloody well care how Jacey Lockhart felt. "I'll show you to your room."

Preoccupied by his demons, Gabriel took the stairs first, realized he should have let a lady precede him, though this lady had been disowned, her title stripped, if only in word, by her own mother.

Then, again – as she had often reminded him – neither was he a gentleman.

He stopped to let her pass.

Five

Jacey leaned against the bedroom door. "No more tears," she whispered. "Look forward not back."

She squared her shoulders and saw a familiar silver dresser set, her sister Clara's hair things. Jacey covered her heart. Gabriel had given her his dead wife's room.

Jace traced the engraved initials on the hairbrush twice before she sought with her gaze the connecting door to Gabriel's bedroom.

Hope flared, but she squashed it. His choice of room meant nothing. This had been her sister's bedroom, after all.

Gabriel had been unbending and unforgiving, proof he didn't want her here. He acted the way he did the day she convinced him that her child . . . the day she lost him forever.

"Forever," she repeated, for her own sake. He'd also been Gabriel, more devilishly handsome than any man of the cloth – any man – had a right to be. He could never be hers, because to save him, she'd destroyed him.

Tired of regrets, Jacey sat on the edge of the old four-poster, stroked the faded coverlet on which Gabriel's mother had stitched primroses, when she was seven and wished the woman was her mother, too.

Only society could claim her own mother. For hugs, Jacey came to Kirk Cottage, more a home than Lockhart Keep, the ancient stone fortress on the hill. Gabriel had been the boy she made bow and scrape for fun. Back then, he did anything she asked.

Jacey wasn't sure when her disdain for the scabby-kneed peasant turned to something more. She remembered that after he'd come home a new-minted parson, life was bliss. Then it was hell.

She rose and worked her shoulders before putting on her nightdress. She'd aged, too, she saw in the mirror, but she'd not yet reached Gabriel's advanced age of thirty.

Life goes on, she thought. It can be good, or not, depending on what we make it. Tomorrow she'd meet her niece, and eventually she'd give the child a happy life, for Clara's sake.

Jacey took the note Suttie sent her from her bag, and read it, again:

Suttie, I need your help. My step-daughter is sullen and sad. Since her mother died, she rarely speaks, never laughs. A man like me, alone with a daughter to raise; it's killing me not knowing what to do for her. You made me smile when I was young and sad. You always knew how. Come with your puppets? A motherless four-year-old who never laughs; how can you resist? Come soon, my friend. Your Faithful Servant, Gabriel Macgregor.

He wanted Suttie but hadn't expected his past to come with her.

Jacey didn't want Bridget sad and unhappy. When she read the letter, she knew she had to come, lay old ghosts to rest, and get on with raising Bridget for Clara.

Behind the humble village cleric hid a stubborn, hard-headed and arrogant man, who would, in fact, be shocked to his black stockings to hear it. She imagined he could be difficult for a wee girl to live with.

In the note, Jace saw his plea, not only for the child, but the writer. He didn't know he'd asked for help, but Suttie did, and so did she.

Six

Thinking she should look in on Bridget, she threw on her old wrap, still tying it when she hit the hall, and headed towards the spare room, but stopped. Another door stood ajar, wide enough for her to see Gabriel bent over a wee figure settling her in for sleep. Jacey's heart cried out to see and meet her niece, but she'd wait for the child's sake.

Gabriel tucked Bridget in, whispered a word, kissed her wee head. When he straightened, Jacey read concern in an expression as clear and open as it had once been for her.

He saw her and tried to mask his emotions but failed. Rounding the bed, he came out into the hall, while Jacey stood rooted, knees weak. She had never been more aware of Gabriel as a man of the cloth as when his pastoral attire revealed so much of the flesh and blood man beneath.

He had discarded his black frockcoat, unbuttoned his waistcoat, the top buttons of his shirt, and tucked his snow-white cleric's collar into his pocket. His shirtsleeves, rolled to his elbows, left his muscular forearms bare. God strengthen her weak knees.

Bridget's door shut with a soft click, snapping her gaze to Gabriel.

Stepping before her, he raised a finger to trace a path down her cheek, his look penetrating. "Tear trails," he whispered, brows furrowed with regret. Jings, she should have wiped her face.

Isolation enveloped her, as if they were alone in the universe. She yearned to sleek her hands along his forearms – the hair soft as silk, her fingertips seemed to remember.

Gabriel grasped her lapels, stroked them up and down, while prickling waves of awareness reached the furthest depths of her being. Despite an inner caution, she allowed herself, for the first time since her return, to devour the flesh and blood vicar with her gaze.

His hair feathered away from his face, except for a curl on his brow. She swept the undisciplined strand aside.

His eyes closed, in ecstasy or pain, and she whisked her hand back, but he caught and placed it against his tripping heart.

His dark brows and deep-set eyes formed a perpetual scowl, a sternness denied by his heartbeat, though he didn't smile.

The rare times he did, the sun grew bright in the sky.

He kept her hand and moved close, his warmth and scent, tobacco and cloves, raised her to a place where memories lived, gold and good, and she welcomed him with all her heart.

"Jace," he breathed, his lips a whisper away.

She squeaked and found herself watching from the entry to her room.

He stood alone in the centre of the hall, wounded.

Jacey shut her door, having taken a painful step in exorcising her demons. So why did she feel like weeping?

Afraid she loved him still, that her body would react, even if her mind knew the danger, she should leave, but she and Bridget should get to know each other in a familiar setting.

No, she'd be strong where Gabriel was concerned. Soon enough, he'd remember he despised her and why. Better it should happen when she expected it.

She almost wished he expected the blow she'd deal him. But he'd said Bridget was unhappy in his letter. Who wouldn't be with a broody stepfather?

The child would be better off with an aunt who embraced joy. Oh, Gabe cared about her. It'd be easier to take Bridget, if he didn't. He begged help for his child and she came to claim that child.

There'd be no running. For Bridget, she'd have to stay, and if her instincts proved right, she'd go to the magistrate and claim her niece.

Regret and conviction battled in her mind until dawn.

Seven

Gabriel didn't sleep at all. He paced, brooded, and lusted for the woman on the other side of the connecting door.

"You're up early," Mackenzie said entering the kitchen, her grizzled hair at odd angles, as always of a morning. "Couldn't sleep?"

Gabriel shook his head, neither denying or confirming her supposition. The old meddler could interpret his response however she chose.

"Difficult sermon to write?"

God, he hated Mackenzie's prying. "I was up half the night delivering twin lambs to Lady Hamilton."

"That ewe's too old."

"Tell her that." Gabriel felt a smile forming, until he recalled the reason he'd paced. "Oh, and we have company, if you must know."

"Well, 'course, I must, so I can make more boxty and scotch eggs. Drop scones too, I'd warrant. How many and who?"

"Suttie Scotney and Jacey Lockhart."

The cast iron griddle hit the floor with a clatter. Mackenzie covered her cheeks, emotions marching across her features – fear, acceptance, then, oddly, relief. "'Bout time you two—"

Gabriel smacked the table with a hand. "No, by God!"

He startled the old bird into a screech.

"Mackenzie, forgive me." He took her arm, led her to a chair, and fetched a cup of water.

Her Scot scowl grew fierce. "Good thing Bridget's not up, or it'd take a month for her to look at you, again, after that outburst."

Why it mattered so much, Gabriel didn't know, but for the life of him, he'd get through to that wee bundle of bones with big eyes. "You're right."

"I'm always right," Mackenzie said, climbing the back stairs.

Gabriel sat at the table and scrubbed his face with his palms, the lamb butting his thigh. He leaned down to scratch its head, starved, like a beggar, for a hint of Jace's voice.

Jacey, getting dressed. Jace, in the hall in her night clothes, smoothing the hair from his brow. Jace with ruffles on her robe, pretty, like the first time he saw her in the Lockhart pew, in his father's Kirk. A three-year-old with dark ringlets, like Bridget looked today. The family resemblance was uncanny. Although, praise be, his wee one didn't resemble her aunt in temperament.

Back then, Jacey liked to work the vicar's scruffy son the way Suttie worked her puppets. But Gabriel adored Jace and followed her everywhere. He would have kissed the hem of her gown, surprised she never commanded it. Lord, she'd been a tyrant.

Then everything changed. He went to seminary. Rare visits home, he saw the changes in her. A woman grown, her raven hair formed a striking contrast to alabaster skin kissed by roses. Gull-winged brows hovered over bright emerald eyes and high, perfect cheekbones. Jace's smile could make poets weep.

Short conversations revealed the woman who replaced the brat to be beautiful inside and out. The day he came home, a scruff no more, he'd found her at their favourite haunt.

Perfection in a siren's body, lush, ripe, Jacey's smile illuminated her features, her arms opened to embrace him. And he was lost.

Drugged by her welcome, the opium of her skin, its taste and texture, he kissed her with a frightening passion.

Dark. Untamed. Forbidden.

The birds chattered, the heavens blessed them with sun, and in the ruins of Lockhart Keep, he gave his body, heart and soul, to the girl he'd loved his whole life.

Before three months passed, his love hardened his heart and sliced into his soul. His body wasn't so good, either, for some time after, as he hadn't cared to look after it.

Now she was back, tying him in knots, though she hadn't been back a day. Only one other person annoyed him as much – Nick Daventry, the father of her child.

Five years, and Gabe still wanted to beat Nick senseless.

"No more passion," he growled. It ruled him once and damned near finished him. He wouldn't let it rule him again.

Jacey would have to go.

Eight

Jacey opened her bedroom door, and her dear old nanny enveloped her in strong, welcoming arms.

"Mackenzie, he called you," Jacey said. "But I should have known. You, keeping house for the parson? You must want to beat his broody self ten times a day."

Nanny Mac chuckled and wiped her eyes. "Your mother sent me to your sister and I stayed to help with the bairn. Two years later, we came home, and Clara married himself. I promised on her deathbed, I'd stay and care for Bridget."

"How is Bridget, Mac? Will it be all right, do you think, to tell her who I am?"

Mac reared back, eyes wide.

"Too soon to mention I'm her mother's sister? I'll say I'm a friend, then."

Mac captured her hands. "Tell Bridget you're her aunt. Don't know what I was thinking. She needs you. Me, I play Granny, but Cricket doesn't know how to climb trees or run between raindrops. Those are your specialties."

Jacey grinned. "Gabriel won't like—"

"Himself likes nothing these days. But if anybody can snap him out of his sulks, it's you, if only to try his patience." Mac grinned. "Come sit with me while I make breakfast."

After a terse good-morning, Gabriel said nothing more.

Jace liked catching up with Mac, who raised her and her sister, though she hesitated to mention Clara around Gabriel. Less than two years married to Clara, and he's a widower. He must have loved her terribly, if his mood was any indication. Last night, she'd probably reminded him of Clara, and *that's* why he'd been so tender.

They made eye contact at the sound of small feet on the kitchen stairs. Jacey's heart nearly stopped at first sight of her niece.

Suttie dropped her fork.

The poppet on the stairs, watching her step, missed their surprise. Bridget's thick, black wavy hair paled her skin to milk. Not beautiful but striking, though she needed colour in her cheeks, bows in her hair. Sunshine. Laughter.

She needed her aunt. They needed each other.

Eyes glistening, Mac grasped Bridget's shoulders from behind and walked her over. "Look lovey, here is my Jacey, your mama's sister come to stay." Mac nodded above the child's head, as if to say she'd made the connection; no wonder her tears.

When Bridget looked up and their eyes met for the first time, Jacey's heart clenched, her soul mourned, and memory stirred. Shaken, but trying not to show it, she cupped Bridget's chin. She looked like Clara, Jace supposed, though darker than both her parents, more like *their* father, actually, hers and Clara's.

Bridget assessed her. "You look sad like me."

Gabriel caught the teapot he'd nearly upended. "Good morning Cricket." The soft smile he gave his step-daughter made him look younger.

Bridget turned her face into Mac's apron.

Gabriel's smile faded. Jacey reached out to him, but he turned a hostile look her way. He did not want to be consoled . . . by her.

Bridget tugged on her sleeve, reclaiming her attention.

"What is it, sweetheart?" Jacey asked.

"Your dress is old."

Despite her embarrassment, Jacey felt a rush of love so intense and unexpected, she ached. "I know."

Bridget stepped closer. She liked Myjacey. She talked soft and smelled of the flowers that grew in the water meadow, like Mama used to. Bridget liked that scent better than the petals in Mama's trunk, locked in the fusty old attic. They made her sad, and cross.

She leaned against Myjacey's soft body and shut her eyes to inhale the scent that almost made it seem as if . . .

"Mama," Bridget said.

Mac released a strangled sob, Gabriel paled, and pinpricks attacked Jacey's limbs.

Suttie brought the child over to kiss her head and raise her teacup. "To expected, and unexpected, ghosts."

Jacey took Bridget on her lap, and the child settled against her.

Jacey finger combed the hair from her appraising eyes, stifling a rush of emotion. "Are you hungry, sweetie?"

"Cricket," Bridget corrected.

"Cricket, then. What would you like for breakfast?"

"Boxty, please, with butter and sugar."

"Mmm. Your Mama and I used to . . ." Jacey hesitated, but Gabriel, Mac, and Bridget, waited. "We liked boxty best with strawberry jam."

Cricket looked towards Mac.

Hands on her hips, Mac harumphed. "I suppose you'll be wanting strawberry jam, now?"

Bridget nodded, eyes wide. "Aye, please."

To Jacey's pleasure, Bridget refused to leave her lap to eat, so Jace pulled the plate over, despite Gabriel's disapproval. She'd ached to hold a child since hers passed, and she wouldn't relinquish her niece for anyone.

Ignoring Gabriel's steely regard, Jacey kissed the top of her wee dark head.

Lack of appetite had naught to do with Bridget's size, and the wee thing had perfected the art of ignoring her stepfather. She reminded Jacey of herself as a girl, trying to work Gabriel like Suttie did her puppets. Did Gabriel realize Bridget manipulated him?

"I take it you like boxty with jam?" Jacey asked.

The lamb butted Bridget's leg, and she slid to the floor to pet the lamb. Ah, that's what she'd wanted to hear, Bridget's laugh.

Gabriel shot to his feet, and everyone looked up. He placed a kiss on his daughter's head. "Have a nice day, Cricket. Jace, walk me outside, will you?"

Jacey stood though Bridget caught her hand. "I'll be right back."

Gabriel's disapproval, more than anything, disturbed Jacey, as she walked him through the house and out the door. "Gabriel, I assure you, I did nothing. We just met."

"I'm aware of that," he said. "I saw your face."

"And I saw yours."

Gabriel shrugged. "She's fragile, our Bridget. I think, Jace, that she needs you." He took a deep, shuddering breath. "I don't know your plans, but—" He cleared his throat. "I'd appreciate it if you stayed for a while. Bridget's better already and, frankly, I'd do anything, anything, to see her happy again."

"Even keep me around?" She turned towards the house.

He caught her arm. "*I* wanted to be the one to breathe life back into her, damn it."

Nine

Gabe's words haunted Jacey as she took Bridget upstairs to look through Clara's things.

"I don't like the attic." Bridget pulled Jacey up short. "It smells fusty."

Jacey got her moving again. "You mean musty?"

"That too." Bridget sat in the middle of the stairs. "My legs hurt."

Jacey tugged her up. "You make me think of two wee girls I once knew, me and your mother."

"Did you whine, too?"

"Only when we didn't want to do something we didn't like."

"I don't like the attic. I don't want to go there."

Jacey grinned. "I figured that out."

Bridget gave a long-suffering sigh. "Why do we gotta go there?"

"Why do we *have* to go there?"

"That's what *I* want to know!"

"To sort through your mother's things." *You need to ken that she and I are two different people.*

"I have her special book." Bridget pulled Jacey in the opposite direction. "C'mon, it's in my room. You can have it."

"Not so fast, my wee beguiler. Attic now. I'll read your mama's book to you later. How's that?"

"It's not that kind of book." Bridget dragged her feet, catching the toes of her shoes on every step to slow them down.

Jacey bit her lip. She hadn't had such fun in years. "Your papa and I used to play here when we were young."

"I never saw my Papa. What did he look like?"

Jacey stopped. "I mean, your stepfather. What do you call him?"

Bridget shrugged. "Nothing."

No wonder the letter. Bridget barely talked to him.

The attic, a jaunty jumble of junk spoke of secrets and bygone days. Jacey stood Bridget on an old trunk at a round window. "See those turrets. That's Lockhart Towers, where your mama and I grew up. Oh, and there's your stepfather's carriage rattling down Parson's Hill." Jace turned to Bridget. "Why don't you call him Papa-Gabe. He wouldn't mind. He loves you, you know."

"I know." Bridget undid several of Jacey's buttons. "He calls me Cricket."

"That's how you know he loves you?"

Bridget nodded and touched Jacey's hair.

"Not by his hugs and kisses or the way he keeps your blankets tucked to your chin at night?"

Bridget finger-combed Jacey's hair, until her bun came out and hair fell over half her face. Bridget's eyes twinkled with mischief.

Jace caught her breath at the child's beauty. She hugged her, kissed her cheeks, lifted and twirled her. "I love you, I love you, I love you!" Jacey shouted.

Bridget sobbed, her arms around Jace's neck, her face pressed there.

Jace sat them on the trunk and sang:

> "Oh dear, what can this sadness mean?
> Jacey too fast with the flair?
> I promise to find you a basket of puppies,

A garland of lilies, a kitten and candy,
A dozen bright ribbons, all colours and dandy,
To tie up thy bonnie silk hair."

Bridget sat back and watched, transfixed. "Mama used to sing."

Jace guessed singing fixed everything, because Bridget scrambled off her lap and over to a trunk in a sunbeam, its dust motes like dancing fairies. "Do you want to see how tiny I was?" Bridget asked.

The first item, a soft, yellow bonnet, made Jace catch her breath.

She'd made a yellow embroidered nightgown and bonnet for *her* baby, which her mother buried the babe in. Jace knelt beside Bridget.

"I used to be *this* small!" Bridget tried it on, but it sat like a cone, and the ribbons didn't meet beneath her chin. She tossed it in Jacey's lap. "Wait till you see my favourite dress. It has pink roses and—"

Jacey crushed the bonnet made of the same yellow fabric. She remembered her mother saying she split the bolt and sent half to Clara in Wales. Clara was expecting Bridget at the time, a baby for her married daughter to show off. Not one to hide, like her unmarried daughter's.

"What's this, lovey, making a mess for me, are you?" Mac bustled in and repacked the baby clothes. "I thought you were looking for Clara's trunk," she said with a piercing look.

Mac carried the small trunk downstairs, claiming something without definition that Jacey wanted without reason.

Ten

Disappointed for no reason, Bridget's bonnet fell off her lap. Half expecting Nanny to grab it, Jace slipped it in her pocket.

Bridget stared into Clara's open trunk as if it held a nest of vipers. Jacey pulled her close and kissed her head. "Show me your favourite of Mama's dresses."

Bridget shook her head, swallowed and sniffed.

"Oh, Cricket, don't cry."

"What's this?" came a familiar voice. "Is somebody crying?" A puppet peeked around the doorjamb.

Bridget gasped and approached it, stopping a distance away. "I'm not crying. The smell inside my Mama's trunk itches my nose and makes my eyes . . . wet." She wiped her face with her sleeve. "What's your name?"

"I'm Harry the Handsome Hedgehog but I'm lonely. Can we talk?"

Bridget nodded, and Jace wondered if Suttie saw around corners. "What's your name?" Hedgehog asked.

"Bridget. My papa, but not; he calls me Cricket."

"You have a papa, but not?"

Bridget nodded again. "Papa Gabe."

Jacey worried about Gabriel's reaction to the name.

"Oh, *that* papa. Well, Cricket, I think something's bothering you. Maybe I can help."

Bridget sighed, raised her arms and dropped them in defeat. "I want to keep Myjacey and I'm afraid my Papa Gabe won't let me," she said in a rush.

"And who is Myjacey? A kitten, a puppy?"

Bridget took Jacey's hand and dragged her before Hedgehog. "She's my mama's sister and I want her to stay. Can you talk to my . . . to Papa Gabe for me?"

"Myjacey's your aunt, then?"

Bridget looked up at her. "Are you?"

Jace tweaked Bridget's nose and nodded. The lump in her throat made it impossible to speak.

"She *is* my aunt!" Which clearly pleased her.

Hedgehog bowed gallantly. "Hello Aunt Jacey."

"Nooo, it's Myjacey. Nanny Mac said so."

"Ach, sorry. Well, do you smell that?" Hedgehog's nose crinkled with a sniff. "I think luncheon is ready. Tattie drootle and tipsy custard, I'd say. Cricket, tell Papa Gabe how you feel about Myjacey. He cares very much about you, and Myjacey, and he wouldn't want either of you to worry. All right?"

Bridget sighed. "All right." She stepped into Jacey's arms after Hedgehog left. "Do we havta go through Mama's trunk?"

"No. Do you want to give me a tour of Kirk Farm after lunch?"

An hour later, hand in hand, Bridget explained every outbuilding from buttery to bower, dovecote to stable, as if Jace had never seen it before. When they passed her favourite climbing tree, she helped Bridget perch in the lowest, widest fork of its branches beside her. With a storybook tucked in her pocket, Jace opened to Snow White.

"I might have known," Gabriel said a short while later, hands on hips. "Tree climbing, first day."

Jacey gave one of his arms a playful shove with her foot. "Climb up," Jace said. "It's cosy."

Bridget scrambled into her lap, which clouded his expression, but the tempest cleared when Bridget said, "Shh," with a finger across her lips. "Pay 'tention."

He tapped Bridget's nose. "Quiet as a Kirk mouse."

He kept his promise, except for the "speaking" glances directed her way, while she became alive to details: her rasping voice and dry lips, the trembling hand she hid in the folds of Bridget's dress, her death-grip on the book, Gabe's thigh pressed to hers, him stroking the hair on the sleepy head against her breast.

Jace read slow, so the fairytale wouldn't end.

Eleven

That night, after she gave Bridget a bath, Jace took her down to say goodnight.

Gabriel raised a brow. "Bridget, you look lovely. Jace, you look like you lost a fight with a flapping duck."

Bridget cocked her head.

Had she never heard him say anything playful?

The task of putting her down for the night was Gabriel's. But after Bridget took his hand, she grabbed Jacey's and tugged her along.

A child between her and Gabriel, as should have been, but Nick offered to be her scapegoat, so she said he was the father. Gabe didn't lose his family parish. Her mother didn't get to throw him out, since the Lockharts owned the parish living.

In Bridget's room, Gabe shed his jacket and threw it over a chair. Bridget knelt on her bed to unbutton his waistcoat, undo his cuffs and roll his sleeves to his elbows.

He winked over Bridget's head, lurching Jace's heart. "Cricket likes buttons," he said.

Like a child, nose to the window, Jace gazed on a family scene she aspired to join.

Bridget freed Gabe's cleric's collar and tucked it into his breast pocket.

"Now, Myjacey." Bridget motioned her forward.

Jace got the bow at her bodice and her top three dress buttons undone, then she got a hug. Jacey masked her emotions and laid her cheek on Bridget's curls. "Thank you for a splendid day, sweetheart."

"I love you," Bridget whispered.

Gabriel went pale as chalk for the second time that day.

"I love you too, Cricket," Jace whispered, sad for him, elated for herself.

"Mama said you loved me," Bridget added, surprising them both.

Gabriel and Bridget knelt by her bed to say her prayers, but when Bridget started, Gabriel touched her arm, took Jacey's hand and pulled her down beside them. "Now you may begin, Cricket."

"Bless Mama and Papa in heaven," she said. "And make Papa Gabe let Myjacey stay. Amen."

After offering Gabe her rosebud lips, Bridget settled on her side. Gabriel tucked her blankets to her chin and kissed her brow. Jacey watched, until Bridget opened one eye. "Myjacey, you're s'posed to kiss me goodnight."

Jacey bent to her ear. "I didn't know I was allowed. See you for boxty and jam in the morning. Happy dreams."

A hand at her elbow, Gabriel guided her from the room.

"I'm sorry," she whispered the minute Bridget's door shut.

"What for?"

"Gabriel Macgregor, I know you better than you know yourself. You'd give your right arm to have her say she loves you, but I walk in and she says it to me."

Silent, he walked her to her bedroom door. "I fell in love with her, Jace, the first time Clara put her in my arms. You should have seen her. A wee tiny thing, even at two, with a thick crown of raven curls. She used to love it when I played with her, Clara egging us on. I'd pretend I was tired, but Bridget would laugh and beg for more."

"You're describing a different child."

"I know. Clara died and Bridget stopped laughing. Stopped looking at me. True, she said she loves you, but in the attic, she called me Papa Gabe, Suttie said, and frankly that's the best I've had from her in months." He ran a hand through his hair. "I think she blames me for her mother's death."

"Oh Gabriel, no." Jacey had never wanted to comfort him more, the urge so strong, and dangerous she stepped back. "She's confused. She'll be happy again soon."

"If you stay, maybe. One day with you and she's more herself." He turned away, ran a hand through his his hair, and turned back, as if he didn't know where to put himself. "It's good to discuss her

with you." He sighed. "I'm thanking you; this has been a good day
for me, too."

"Gabriel Macgregor, this is the most you've ever said to me."

He looked sheepish. "Wait till you hear one of my sermons. Stay,
Jace. For as long as you want."

"There'll be talk."

"To the devil with talk."

"It'll begin sooner than we think. Nick Daventry is home from
America."

Twelve

Nick Daventry. Even the cadence of the name dogged Gabriel. If
he lived to be a hundred, he'd never forget Jacey's words to him on
the day he'd gone to confess his paternity to her mother.

"It's not yours, Gabriel," Jacey said, waylaying him in the
parlour. "Nick Daventry is my baby's father."

In that first horrific moment, her words might have been an axe
blade in his back. From that day to this, Gabe wanted Nicholas
"bloody" Daventry to go straight to hell.

Now he was back. He should have stayed in America, but as
Jace's distant cousin, he'd come home to inherit Lockhart Keep,
after the death of his brother, who inherited in Jacey's place,
because her mother had disowned her.

He'd always suspected the woman would have ruined him, if
Jace's babe had been his. Give him sheep for company; they were
easier than his flock to deal with. He would be happy with a parish,
any parish, or simply a farm, and Bridget and Jacey.

To hell with everyone else. Well, Mackenzie. He guessed he'd
take her, too, the nosy old thing.

When he got home that afternoon, the best parlour looked like a
family of squirrels had danced the highland fling. In the doorway,
he stepped on something hard, the arm of an ugly French figurine
that belonged to his grandmother.

Mackenzie, sweeping up its remains by the hearth, didn't notice
him. Neither did anyone else.

Gabriel relaxed at the sight of Jacey's head tucked beneath the
camel-back settee, her gown, one of Clara's, had crinolines that
bobbed in the air, affording him a lovely view of her sweet backside.

Never before had lust, tenderness, and the urge to chuckle overcome him at one and the same time.

"Can you see it?" Jacey called.

"I can, almost, but it's wiggling a lot," Cricket said, from behind that piece of furniture.

"You have it, then?"

"Ouch. Not anymore."

"Where did it go?"

"Up. Inside."

Jacey's petticoats quivered, from shock or laughter, he didn't know. Before they finished their flutter, Jace backed out and sat on her knees, hands on hips. "Bridget Macgregor, are you saying your kitten disappeared into the sofa stuffing!"

What kitten?

Cricket came tottering into sight on high heels thrice her size, trailing a god-awful green dress and red boa, wearing a straw hat his mother once favoured. From its brim, dangled a clump of berries, and a moulting bluebird.

Gabriel cleared his throat.

Bridget and Jacey looked up, both with stunned surprise. Mackenzie grumbled louder, so Gabe confiscated her broom. "See to dinner," he said. "We'll clean up in here."

Gabriel turned back to the two people he loved most in the world. One would rather step around him as look at him. The other was bound to break him for good one of these days, especially if she discovered his lingering love. Still, there was no changing destiny.

He sat and crooked a finger to bring his comically adorable wee one over to him. And Cricket must actually have looked at him long enough to catch his summons, because she obeyed.

"Lovely dress," he said.

Her doe eyes came alive. "It's Mama's. Myjacey made it smell like the water meadow again." Bridget shoved her arm under his nose, so he sniffed it, nodded, and kissed her elbow. "Did you say, 'Myjacey?'" He looked at her and felt a rush of love he so strong, he had to clear his throat. "Haven't you noticed, Cricket, that everybody else calls her Jacey?"

Bridget nodded. "Mama called her that, but Nanny Mac called her Myjacey the day we met, and I like it *ever* so much better."

Jacey sent him a plea with her look, and a similar rush of love for her engulfed him. For a bold minute, he let it show, but Jace sat, as if enticed by it but ruling it a danger.

He knew exactly how she felt.

"Can I call you Myjacey?" Bridget asked, standing before Jace, undoing a bodice button or three, shyly waiting for her aunt's answer.

"Of course you can, sweetheart." Jace smiled at his daughter's plea, her cheeks like the rosebuds marching across the bit of chemise Cricket revealed. "Myjacey can be your special name for me, like Cricket is your papa's pet name for you."

Bridget gave him a nod, as if to say, "I told you", the way Jacey the brat had tended to do. Had Bridget learned it? Or was prideful stubbornness a Lockhart trait?

"Tell me about the kitten," Gabe said, to distract himself from Jace's open dress.

"Suttie gave it to me." Bridget sighed. "But it dist-appeared."

"No, it didn't," he said, not quite pleased to report. Gabe joined Jace on the settee and pointed to the padded back where the outline of two wee paws pushed on the fabric from inside.

"Oh, my, God," Jacey said. "We have to take the sofa apart."

Gabe sighed. "I knew you'd say that." He removed his jacket, waistcoat and collar, and rolled up his sleeves. Then he sat on the floor with his girls.

Two hours later, the sofa back flipped over the front, Bridget cuddled a wee white, blue-eyed kitten, trying to catch either bobbling hat berries or a bald bird.

Jacey massaged his back, because after sitting so long like a pretzel he couldn't straighten. "You're getting old," she said, working his spine.

He liked her hands so much, he wondered how to get a back kink tomorrow. "If I'm old, you're old."

"You'll always be older than me by three years."

Mackenzie stopped in the doorway and gasped. "You were going to clean up. It's thrice as messy."

"Er, have I come at a bad time?"

"Nick!" Jacey shot to her feet.

Gabe saw her skirt was stained with Eccles cake, her bodice splattered with jam, and he stopped her to re-button her dress.

Jace raised a brow. He'd known for hours that Bridget didn't button her up. "Your back got better fast." She turned to Nick. "I'm sorry I'm a mess."

Daventry smiled. "You never looked more beautiful."

Gabe placed a posessive hand on Jacey's shoulder.

"Is dinner still at eight?" Daventry asked.

"Oh, Lord," Jacey said. "I forgot I invited you."

Thirteen

Bridget's first dress-up tea party monologue made dinner less awkward.

"Bridget, you're eating too fast," Jacey said.

"I'm hungry. Lydia said our pig should not be Lady Cowper. We should call our cow that. Do you think so, Papa . . . Gabe?"

Jacey caught his pleasure at being directly addressed. "I think our pig is happy with her name. Though we could call them the Ladies Cowper and Pigger."

Cricket's eyes widened and Jace decided he and Bridget needed to play more.

"How can you be hungry," Mac asked. "After all those tea party sweets?"

Bridget dropped her fork.

"Bath time, lovey," Mac said. "Then bed. Wee lady's had a long day."

Gabe followed them up, and Jacey took Nick into the second-best parlour.

"Bridget's sick," Gabriel said from the doorway, a minute later, his look thunderous. "She's crying for you."

Jacey looked from one to the other, shrugged and left the room.

"I'll show you out," Gabriel said to Nick as she took the back stairs.

He caught up with her at the top.

"What did you do, shove him out the door?"

"I said goodbye."

Bridget raised her arms. "Myjacey, my tummy hurts."

"We've got her Nanny," Jacey said. "Go to bed."

"If this was a parlour needed cleaning," Nanny grumbled, "I wouldn't, but I expect you two can manage this one."

Bridget wasn't well enough to undo his buttons. Bad sign.

Gabe caught her watching him undo his cuffs. He quirked a brow, but she didn't turn away. He settled in the way she liked him best, collar in his pocket, sleeves rolled up.

Something about him, dressed, or undressed, in that "at home" way, made Jacey want to curl up in his arms before a fire and comb her fingers through the hair at his nape.

"Myjacey!" Bridget placed her hands on either side of Jacey's face.

"I'm sorry, sweet, what is it?"

Bridget was sick.

Jacey gave her a bath and Gabriel changed her bed.

Jacey stroked Bridget's fevered brow. "She's sound asleep. Go to bed. I'll stay with her."

Gabriel shook his head. "I'll wash and change, and when I get back, you change. We're, neither of us, sweet and fresh right now." He nodded. "Go on."

After washing, Jacey left her hair loose down her back.

This time, she tied the ribbons beneath her breasts on the buttercup silk robe a bit tighter, and pinched her cheeks, before she left her room.

When she returned, approval leapt in Gabe's eyes as he went out to change.

Jacey checked Bridget's brow, pulled up her covers and opened the window.

She wondered where to go from here when Gabe came back in. He wore a black brocade dressing gown, and if she thought he looked good in shirtsleeves . . .

He gathered her in his arms and came for her mouth with the same greedy hunger he'd shown the day he came home from the seminary.

Jacey embraced the perfection of his kiss. His big hands explored, as if he didn't have enough time to learn her, again.

Jacey's head swam, her body ached. Her kiss was meant to drive him wild.

He sought closer contact and revealed his arousal, caressing the sides of her breasts, nearing the place she ached.

Her soul rejoiced; her body wept for more.

"Papa? Myjacey?" Bridget's voice penetrated the sensual fog, and they jumped apart so fast, Jacey hit her head on the window.

"Cricket," Gabriel said, clearing his throat.

"How do you feel, sweetheart?" Jacey asked.

"I'm thirsty. Hungry too."

"I've heard this song before," Gabe said.

Jacey put Bridget's slippers on her. "Her stomach is empty. Perhaps a piece of toast to nibble on?"

"As long as I get more of what I was nibbling on."

Fourteen

Jacey brought Bridget down for toast, but she fell asleep, half a slice in her hand.

Gabriel rose to take his daughter from her arms, his proximity sending skittering spirals of need to every nerve in her body. "Stay," he said.

Jacey wrapped her arms around herself, chilled, bereft, glad Bridget had woken when she did. This was too fast, and between them: questions, lies, doubt, uncertainty, pain – hers, his.

"We need to talk," Gabriel said from the bottom of the stairs, hands buried in his dressing gown pockets. He never looked so much like that fallen angel, but now she wished he'd spread his wings and take her in.

"What should we talk about?" she asked.

"Everything."

Ah. There it was. "You're right." She placed a chunk of cheese and a knife beside the bread on the table and put on a pot of tea. "Where do you want to begin?"

He cut off a chunk of cheese and broke it in half.

She accepted the half he held out to her. As she took it, she knew, wherever life took her, she'd never be more "home" or more complete than at this moment, with him. "Your choice."

"Why is Nick back from America at the same time you've come home?"

"Coincidence?"

"I won't have him under my roof again." Gabe stood. "I'm sorry. That wasn't necessary, but you broke me, Jace."

She watched him climb the stairs, tired and beaten.

Aye, she broke him. She knew it when she did. Otherwise, she would have snuffed the dignity and self-respect he craved, before he got it.

Besides, after losing him, then losing her daughter – damn it, she'd been broken, too. In her room, the connecting door might have been painted with the word "temptation".

Telling him the truth played on her mind, but why? To prove herself a liar? So he'd confess and lose his flock's respect?

If he believed her, he'd know he was the only man she loved, but nothing mattered now, except Bridget.

Jacey placed her hand against the connecting door. He'd paced for some time, but all seemed quiet now. She turned the knob.

A lamp beside his bed bathed the room in a soft glow. Gabriel sat up, naked to his waist, baring a solid wall of flesh and muscle. Aye, she'd once run her fingers through the mat of dark silk, but she hadn't seen it.

He looked so anguished, Jacey turned to go.

"Jace." A plea she couldn't deny. Then she was in his arms, in his bed, and he was ravishing her mouth.

Her clothes fell away under his seeking hands.

Not yet, her rational mind warned, not with things unsaid. But her body carried a demand of its own, and Jacey couldn't speak or think; she could only feel.

The hair on his chest abraded and caressed, as did his day's growth of beard against her face and breasts, inciting new heat to build on the rest. He kissed and suckled, ravenous, greedy and ready, fulfilling four years of lonely dreams.

Fifteen

He knew his strength lay in denying passion, but Jacey filled his senses, her taste, her scent, her feel. She arched against him, whispered his name. Hearing it on her lips made him hard. Jacey, softer than silk, warmer than sunshine, his other half.

He cupped her bottom, and gazed into passion-bright eyes. She was his, only his . . . and Nicholas Daventry's.

Like a winter flood, the thought washed over him. He groaned and fell against his pillows.

Jacey whimpered, bereft, and he pulled her tight against him, to console them both. If he didn't get hold of himself, he'd weep with her.

"Passion," he said, voice rusty, "almost killed me the last time, Jace." He held her away from him, to see her face and for needed distance. "After you left – once I wanted to live again – I learned to control it."

"No, Gabe. Not that."

"When I thought the babe was mine – hell, getting you and a child was like a reward. Who cared if I lost my living, I would have you. But when you said it wasn't mine . . ." He cleared his throat. "Learning to control my passion was difficult. Until today, I thought I succeeded. I hate its wild unpredictability. Yet when you're around, my passion has power. You have power."

"Gabriel, you act as if it was *all* your fault. There were two of us in Lockhart Keep. I experienced a love bright and beautiful, as might have happened tonight."

He laughed, bitterly. "*You* might not frighten easily, Jace, but it frightened your sister."

"Clara?"

"I frightened her so much, she wept on our wedding night."

"Clara was afraid of everything."

"Don't talk ill of the dead. She loved you. When she was sick, she—"

Jacey stilled. "Clara did what?"

"She said she'd never forgive me if I didn't fetch you after she was gone."

"But you didn't."

"One year. I had three months to go. I was counting days, but I didn't know if I would." He stroked her cheek. He'd never felt like this about Clara. "We'll never know. You came to me."

"I came for Bridget, to take her away and raise her myself."

He sat up, his back straight, hair in disarray. "I wouldn't let you."

"You're her stepfather, Gabriel, no relation at all."

He rounded on her. "I swear, Jace, if I were her real father, I'd disappear with her so you'd never find her."

Jace tugged the sheet around her unable to hide her panic. "You're a good and decent man, Gabriel. You'll do what's best for her, as will I. We simply have to figure out which of us is best."

"She's mine. I know what's best for her," he shouted.

"You don't. She plays you like one of Suttie's puppets, like I used to do, which makes you sick with worry. She couldn't control losing her mother, so she tries to . . . buttonhole you. Losing her mother must have given her the sense she couldn't keep anyone where she wanted them. When I was a child, I counted on two people. One of them was you at my heels, or *wherever I wanted you.*

"Bridget is holding you by an invisible tether – call it love – pulling you this way and that. Just watch her. You can practically see her consider in which direction she'll tug. You've had her two years, but you haven't figured her out yet."

"Don't pretend to know my daughter." Gabriel donned his dressing gown, tying it with a vicious yank.

He looked at her and his ire vanished on the instant. "Jace, I cannot stay angry with you in my bed, a sheet between my mouth and your body, your hair a veil I want wrapped around me."

Sixteen

Jacey responded physically to his words. Aware of her power, she raised her hands above her head to stretch like a cat. "I like your passion." She didn't want him to deny passion.

He waivered in his resolve. "My passion becomes wild, almost savage, but only with you."

"You said you were passionate with Clara." Not for the first time, jealousy of her sister beat in her breast.

Gabriel went to gaze out on the night. "I wanted with Clara what I'd had with you. It was impossible; she wasn't you. It never happened again."

Jacey sat straighter. "So you'll never be with a woman, again, never share your body?" *With me*, she wanted to add.

She held the sheet around her and went to the connecting door. "Jace, who else did you count on as a child, besides me?"

She looked straight at him. "Nick," she said pointedly. "To get me out of trouble." But Gabriel didn't get it.

She'd destroyed their love. In her own bed, she wept. Telling him Nick got her out of trouble was as close as she dared get to telling Gabe the truth.

Her decision to lie about her child's father hardened him, not his passion, and she felt powerless against fixing it. She saved him when he didn't want saving. If he knew, she felt he would never forgive her. The rift between them couldn't be repaired.

An hour before Sunday service, Jacey took Bridget to visit her baby's grave. "Baby Girl Lockhart," the stone said, the date of birth and death the same. They left bouquets of heather and thistle.

Bridget traced the chiselled numbers with her fingers. "I know these numbers. Mama wrote them in her special book."

She hugged Bridget and swallowed. "It was nice of your Mama to record it. My Mama didn't."

In the front pew, Mac leaned towards her. "Pray hard, young lady," she whispered. "I found your missing slipper."

Jacey frowned. "So?"

"Found it changing *his* bed." She pointed to Gabriel at the pulpit.

His sermon, eloquent and magnetic, like him, bore a lesson. He even looked devilishly handsome in a cassock.

She loved him as much as ever, adored him, wanted a future with him, please God. She'd confess, if only he'd forgive

On the kirk steps, Prout pushed Olivia at him. "I told Livvy I'd pay for the new kirk as soon as the vicarage is *cleaned out* so Liv can decorate. After all, everything's set, except for the ring on her finger."

Jacey gasped and Mac hurried Bridget away.

"Given the company you keep," Prout warned, "donations may dry up."

Gabe frowned. "My Lady, may I remind you that charity is a virtue."

Prout gave her a highbrow snub. "I don't know why you persist in keeping such company, when *you* insisted, for decency's sake, that she leave in the first place."

Jace walked

"Jacey, Jace," Gabriel called, right behind her.

She ran from her port in a storm, because *he* her sent her away.

The gypsy wagon sat near the stables, horses hitched, Suttie beside them. "Suttie, please take me away."

"Ah, Jace." Suttie lifted her chin. "If you went, what would we tell the wee one with her nose pressed to the window?"

Gabriel grasped her shoulders. "Jace, look at me."

She focused on his cassock and wondered what he wore beneath it.

His sigh, heavy with regret, made her look up. "I wanted you gone, Jace, because of ignorant, callous fools who judge. You lost your child; you didn't need to be flogged with words."

"You wanted me gone, Gabriel Macgregor," she snapped. "Because *you* didn't want anyone to know your truth."

Suttie blew them each a kiss. "Take the wagon."

Jace heard the lock click open.

Seventeen

Panic and Passion seemed to meld inside Gabriel, as if he were fighting for his life. "Jace, please," he begged. "There's too much between us to be torn apart by spiteful words."

"*Your* spiteful words, evidently."

She fought him, so he swept her up, set her in Suttie's wagon, and locked the door. Ignoring her threat of castration, he climbed on the box and flicked the reins.

The window behind him opened before they cleared the drive. "You'll go to hell for this, vicar."

"Without ballocks, I take it." He laughed, and passed the kirk, and inside, he saw Jace at the side window waving at the slack-jawed Prouts.

Gabe urged the horses faster while the clouds spilled over.

The rain sliding down his neck made him reconsider. Turn back? Keep going? In other words: "Give up and die?" or "Fight for his life?"

He'd never got Jace out of his blood. She lived in every drop that pumped his heart. Forget the past, he needed her as much as his next breath. He loved her more than life, God help him.

Jacey failed to break the lock. Rain poured from troughs not buckets. The idiot must be soaked.

For the second time, she threw open the window behind him. "Blast it, Gabriel, stop and get out of the rain."

He didn't turn his head, but . . . "How can you laugh? So help me, when I get my hands on you, I'm going to *beat* you."

"I'll hold you to that."

She shut the window as hard as she dared.

Who knew Gabe was so impulsive he'd steal a sinner before his flock?

Jace stopped. Gabriel Macgregor had never been impulsive in his life, except the day he came home from the seminary.

She curled up in Suttie's bed.

Their favourite haunt, hers and Gabriel's, had been the ruins of Lockhart Keep, where their daughter was conceived.

After her mother sent her away, she dreamed he'd come for her, sweep her off her feet and take her home. Could this be the day?

When pigs flew above the rainclouds.

Gabe should have known she'd give him up before she caused him to give up his dream to repair his father's failures and breathe new life into his home and parish.

Look at him, posture rigid, no hat or coat, defying the elements to get his way. Stubborn. Dear. Travelling a road as turbulent and deep as the man mocking it.

"Gabriel," she called, and he looked back, surprised, to see her.

"Self-punishment won't help. Take me home."

The horses faltered on the flooded road, and when Jacey thought he had them under control, lightning struck nearby.

They bolted, tearing the reins from Gabe's hands as they raced towards the trees.

Gabriel fought to keep his seat and shouted for her to get back.

She did, and watched him climb over the seat and through the window. He'd barely cleared the window when Jace saw the horses choose opposite sides of an ancient oak.

The wagon hit, a limb pushing through the window, shattering glass, splintering wood.

Gabriel swore and landed on top of her.

Books flew from a railed shelf, hitting him, head and shoulders.

The wagon teetered once, twice, three shuddering times, then it settled, with a huge creaking groan, nearly upright, impaled by a tree.

Eighteen

Gabe's heart and breathing slowed, and though freezing wet, he appreciated his mattress, and enjoyed it for one delectable beat before raising his aching head and staring into her wide, emerald eyes.

Shafts of white-hot current shot between them, as if each were the opposite poles of the same lightening bolt.

She must feel his physical reaction, and given her lowered lids, she answered its call. "You're . . . wet," she said, licking rain from her lips.

"As are you." The timbre of his voice surprised him. Afraid to crush her, Gabriel rolled to her side, his erection prodding her thigh as he kissed the rain from her lips.

A salty kiss. Tears, not rain.

He sat up. "Are you hurt?" He ran his hands over her, feeling for breaks.

Jacey shot to her feet with no escape. The entire wagon would fit in the vicarage entry, but it was homey, warm and dry, unlike them, except where the impaling branch dripped rain.

She stood as far from him as she could.

Only one thing to do. He peeled away his cold, soaking vestments.

"What are you doing? You're a vicar for God's sake."

"But a man for my own sake, the way you first knew me."

"A boy. I knew you as a boy first."

"An urchin, you mean. I despised that boy."

"Because he wasn't perfect, but humanity is allowed."

"Right." He unbuttoned his shirt.

She backed into the branch and it sprinkled them with rain. "Look what you've brought us to," she snapped. "You can't make me believe you cast me out other than to save your sorry self from being exposed as having been . . . ensnared . . . in my wanton web. You—"

"Jace, you're babbling."

"I wanted you gone for *your* own good! Prout would have had you stoned in all but fact if you stayed."

"Don't be disrespectful of your mother-in-law." Jace lit a candle against the drear.

"There'll be a frost fair in hell before I marry the harpy's whelp." Gabriel discarded his wet shirt. "We both know I'm *as* human, and a damned sight more imperfect than you. Nobody's humanity calls to mine more than yours, Jacey Lockhart, soon to be Macgregor, after this day's work."

"Nothing happened to—"

"That won't matter." He unbuttoned his trousers.

She found no place to run, so he advanced, giving her less. "If we removed your crinolines, we'd have more room."

She thought about that, exhilarated as Gabriel knelt and lifted the hem of her gown. He undid the tapes at her waist, his arms warm and soaking through at her belly. Her crinoline fell over his head.

Jacey pulled it up, allowing him to continue, her face warm.

He looked at her, eyes dancing, hair askew, and her heart fluttered while her underskirts fell, forming smaller and smaller circles.

Gabriel stroked the front of her cotton drawers, rushing warmth to her core, rested his cheek there before he turned, opened his mouth against her, and whispered her name like a prayer.

She gasped, combed her hands through his hair, and held him there.

He slid his cool hands along the backs of her thighs, up beneath her drawers, to cup her bare bottom, then he splayed them to stroke and tease where she ached for him.

Jacey released a shuddering sigh, and Gabriel stood and opened his mouth over hers. Ravenous, he swallowed her sighs, and became as much a part of her as the night she conceived their child.

He lightly stroked her as he undid the buttons at her bodice, freed her arms from her sleeves, and she had no strength to resist.

"That's my sweet Jace," he whispered as he slid her dress down, palms skimming skin, until he cleared her hips and that garment joined the rest.

He took her hand and she stepped over her clothes, to face her lover. Her camisole came up and over her head.

In corset, chemisette and stockings, Jacey wished they were silk and lace, not serviceable cotton, yet Gabriel regarded her with hunger.

She'd dreamed of this for years, because she loved this dignified, handsome, stubborn, broody man more than her life.

She wouldn't change this time together, despite the inevitable pain.

Nineteen

Gabriel unlaced her corset and slipped his hands inside from the back to cup her breasts.

Jacey leaned against him as he rubbed her nipples, whispered his adoration, his breath and lips warm along her neck and shoulders.

Potent points of pleasure coursed through her. Her happiness soared, her womanhood flowered.

Gabe did away with the corset, and lifted a breast to suckle through her chemisette while he reacquainted himself with the heat of her beneath her drawers. Then, they, too, were gone, and Jacey stood naked before the man she loved.

She disposed of his trousers in a thrumming beat and found a new item of male attire. Underbreeches. She circled him, to get a good look.

Sliding her hand across the front, loving her ability to make his eager member pulsate, she found a slit in the garment, enough to accommodate her hand.

He gasped when she found him, rigid and thick, then she did away with the underbreeches and cupped his ballocks while she worked him.

She made him groan, and beg, and buck, and plead for her to stop, but more, and hurry and, "Wait!"

He set her on the bed and ravaged her mouth. Hard to her soft, cool to her hot, he dipped where she curved, arched where she plunged, fitting deliciously and perfectly well.

"Gabriel. You feel so good, this is good; it's right and—"

"Just kisses," he said. "Kisses and touches enough for pleasure. Nothing that causes babies."

"You're mistaken if you think only *dark* passion causes babies."

"Shut up, Jace, and kiss me."

Just touching brought wild pleasure when touching just so, in just the right places, and with the right person and rhythm. Tongues touching, dancing, mating. Hands, legs, mouths everywhere.

She learned a new form of pleasure without mating. Yet something seemed missing, something sad and poignant, disappointing, like sliding down a snow-slick hill, not quite fast enough. Despite that, pleasure grew, burst and set them free.

Like two spoons in the wee bed, they slept, until Jace woke and examined his man parts in the soft light of dawn, along and around, up and down, rolling her finger around his moist tip.

When she dared kiss that tip, he woke with a surge and a groan, and she was on her back, him deep inside her.

He brought her higher in three deep strokes than he had all night.

So blessedly good, his weight atop her. She'd take him any way she could, but this glorious, ordained way, this was perfect.

They climbed and soared, then like water cascading down a mountain – pure, bubbling, wild and free – they floated as one, peaceful, at rest.

After a time, he reversed their positions and settled her atop him in lazy contentment.

"Gabriel, we're at peace now, right? We've formed a truce?"

"As your mattress, I say, aye, peace."

"Was her service beautiful?"

"What service, pet?"

"My baby's funeral. Did you make it wonderful? Tell me."

"Ach, Jace, your Mother wanted no service. The babe was stillborn."

"No, I heard her cry. Mama said she didn't, but I remember."

"She had no service, sweet." Gabe wiped her cheeks with the corner of a blanket. "We'll ask the gravedigger, and if there was nothing graveside, I'll do a service."

"Who'd come?"

"You, me, Bridget, Mackenzie . . . and Nick."

"You'd do that for me? With Nick?"

He settled her head on his chest. "Aye, love, I'd do anything for you. Even give you to Nick, though I'd rather keep you for myself."

Twenty

He'd always wanted her. Now he wanted everything. And for the first time, he admitted it, and she fell asleep.

She stirred in his arms, snuggled her face deeper into his neck, moved and moaned. Parts of her must be tender. He'd kiss her better.

First he'd settle the matter of their marriage, then perhaps he'd let her out of bed.

He guessed he had no choice. She should be dressed if anyone spotted the wagon.

Jacey shifted and rubbed her nose back and forth, hard, against the hair on his chest.

He chuckled. "Itchy nose means you're coming into money."

She smiled lazily and stretched in that rod-hardening feline way, her limbs sliding sinuously along his own. "Don't need money. I have you."

"Not yet, but you will."

She regarded him soberly. "I will what?"

"Have me."

"In the biblical sense?"

"Well, aye. You'll have me that way, often."

Jace took her luscious bottom lip between her teeth, making him want to bite it, but her silence made him nervous. "You ken that after last night, we must marry."

"Must we?" She rose quickly, placing his favourite parts in perilous danger. "We'll speak no more about it."

Distracted by her pert breasts and fine bottom, he let the subject drop, for now. She rummaged and blushed, until a nearly see-through shirt covered her to her thighs.

He raised his knee to hide his reaction, or she'd find something else to wear. She was acting that contrary.

"Jace, listen. Bridget needs a mother, and if you marry me, you can save me from a mother-in-law who carries a pitchfork."

That brought thunderclouds to her brow.

"I know," he said, looking for food, "I might lose my Kirk over this, but—" He caught her ludicrous expression. "What?" he asked.

She pointed to his raging manhood with annoyed amazement.

"Sorry. I forgot."

"You can forget something that big? It's in your way for pity's sake."

"I'm hungry."

"For food, even?"

"That too, aye." He looked into a tin. "Sodabread." He bit into it and offered her the tin. "Needs jam."

Jacey took a jar off the floor. "I saw it rolling around before, before . . ."

Gabriel raised a brow. "Before we hit the tree? Stripped? Laid hands on each other? Burned each other alive?"

She about strangled him, her cheeks strawberry-bright. "Before any of it, blast you. Will you put on some clothes?"

"They're wet."

"Suttie must have something you can wear." Jace rummaged. "Here put this on." She handed him another old shirt.

It didn't meet in the front to button or cover . . . anything.

He chuckled at the sight, her: half dressed, half appalled.

"At least it keeps my back warm. Come closer and warm my . . . front."

That set her spine. "I will not marry you, Gabriel Macgregor. Not to save you from the Prouts. Damn you for suggesting it."

He hung her clothes over the branch, to hide his disappointment.

"Hello the wagon? Anybody inside?"

"Hello," Jacey shouted. "The door's jammed. Can you get us out?" Her voice wobbled, as if she might cry as she stepped into her wet crinolines.

Twenty-one

More than a day after they left, they returned to Kirk Cottage.

From the hall, they saw Bridget, on her stomach, on the settee, chin in hands, speaking to Hedgehog, peeking over the arm of the settee.

Hedgehog stroked her hair. "Tell me what you remember about your mother."

"She used to sing, but not as often as Myjacey. Once, Papa looked sad, and Mama said she knew he missed Myjacey when she sang."

"Hedgehog, this makes me sad to remember."

"You'll feel better, if you tell me what's bothering you."

Bridget sighed. "Mama said she wouldn't rest in heaven if Papa didn't go get Myjacey. He held her and said he was sorry. He and

Mama cried. Me too." Bridget swallowed. "They didn't know I saw."

She wiped her eyes. "I know Papa likes me, but I wish he liked Mama enough to keep her and *not* send her to heaven."

Jacey took Gabriel's arm, in support and comfort, and it was a measure of his shock that he let her.

"Yesterday Papa took Myjacey, and they didn't come home, and I'm afraid he sent her to heaven."

"Your Mama was very sick," Hedgehog said.

"God would have let Papa keep Mama, if he asked. Mama said God listens to Papa, 'cause he talks Sundays and everybody hardly falls asleep. Why didn't Papa like Mama enough to keep her?"

"Cricket, Mama stopped hurting when God took her home."

"After Mama went away for hours, Papa said God took her to heaven. Now Myjacey's been gone that long, and I'm afraid *she's* with God. If she is, I'll never forgive Papa, Hedgehog!"

"Cricket," Jacey said.

Bridget launched herself into Jacey's arms.

Gabriel looked rooted in horror, because in his daughter's eyes, he'd failed at the single most important task of his life. He'd failed to rescue her mother from the clutches of death.

"You're wrong, sweetheart," Jacey said. "Papa prayed hard to keep her. Your Mama wrote and told me so."

Like Gabriel, Bridget looked at her. "She did?"

Jacey nodded. "That's why Papa cried holding Mama, because he knew God said no, and your mama was going to heaven. That's why he was sorry."

"Did you, Papa, pray hard to keep Mama?" Bridget asked.

"So hard," Gabriel said, hugging Bridget.

A few hours after the reunion, and after she and Gabe had bathed and eaten, they all met the gravedigger at her daughter's grave. "Angus," Jacey said. "When you buried my baby, were graveside prayers said over her wee casket?"

"I din bury no baby, m'Lady. I put the stone here, like your Ma said, which she paid me not to say." He shrugged. "I don't s'pose it matters now she's dead."

Jacey covered her mouth with a hand. Mac wept into her apron. Bridget traced the numbers on the gravestone.

"Dig her up," Jace said, and Mac wailed. "Don't, thank you, Angus." She turned towards the house. "Bridget, get your Mama's book. Mac, I'll have that trunk of baby clothes, please."

Mac shook her head.

"Mackenzie," Gabriel said.

Clara's bible noted Baby Lockhart's date of birth and death. A week later, Bridget Lockhart Spencer's birth was recorded.

Jace stared until the words blurred. She opened the trunk. "This is probably a waste of time. When I heard there was no funeral, I thought . . ."

She found the yellow embroidered sacque to match the bonnet and held it up, her heart racing. "Clara in Scotland, me here, and we make the same gown?" She trembled with hope as she snipped the stitches at the back hem.

When she opened it, she sobbed.

"Jace, you're upsetting Bridget. Mackenzie," Gabriel added. "Take Bridget to the kitchen."

Twenty-two

Gabe carried Jace to the settee. She laughed while she cried.

"Are we going a wee bit daft, love?"

"Gabriel, my baby didn't die. Mother lied. She sent her to Clara. Probably to legitimize her."

"You don't mean . . . Bridget is *yours*?"

"Dearest, you may never forgive me, but she's more than *my* daughter—"

Gabe groaned. "Right; she's Nick's."

"Remember how I counted on Nick to get me out of trouble. Think about it."

"I don't understand."

Jace kissed him with all her love, and though he was confused, he put love into his kiss.

"Gabriel," Jace said, "Bridget is more than my daughter, she's *our* daughter." She showed him the sacque. "I embroidered *'Baby Macgregor'* inside. I wanted the truth *somewhere*."

He stroked the embroidery: "I fathered your child? Not Nick?"

"My mother couldn't make his life hell in America, so I waited for him to leave, then I named him, with his permission."

"Jace. That about killed me. If I wasn't so happy, I'd . . ."

"I didn't want you defrocked. You'd just taken holy orders. Your father's parish was yours, you had your family name to mend. How could I destroy your dreams?"

"I wanted our babe," he said. "And you, you were more my dream than anything. Didn't you know?"

The resultant kiss lasted longer, meant more, because they'd added honesty and forgiveness. "I love you Gabriel."

"I love you, Jace, and our daughter. Bridget is ours. Jace, you bore my child and the stigma of sin to protect *me*. " He cupped her face. "Marry me, please. I'll try to be worthy."

Jace kissed his palm. "With our passion; we'll have six more."

"At least," he said, hearing a whispered "shush". "Hear that, Mackenzie?" he called. "You'll have a job here forever."

"We hear," Bridget said, throwing open the door and climbing into their laps. "Nanny Mac says you're my *real* Mama and Papa. *She* brought me to my first mama to keep me till 'you two came to your senses'."

"Did she now?" Gabe eyed Mackenzie.

"I have to go tell Suttie and Hedgehog," Bridget said.

"Suttie's gone," Mac said, "though I didn't hear the wagon. She left a note: 'My work is done. Fairy kisses and long happy lives. Suttie.'"

"We'll do just fine right here, won't we, darling? You're right about Papa. Lots of growl but no bite."

Her MacKinnon

Sandy Blair

The Legend

I came into being on Beltane morn' on the shores of Skye in the year of our Lord 1490.

In my veins runs the blood of Alpin, king of the Picts and father of Cinaed mac Ailpin king of Scots, of Bebe, king of Norway and that of the first abbots of Iona.

Brought down by treachery before my time, my immortal soul does not rest. My essence remains with the gold signet ring – bearing the hand clutching the cross – that I and all those who came before me wore.

I am the MacKinnon, then and now.

Board's Head Pub, Isle of Skye, present day

One

"Come on, man, just one half and a half."

Since the last thing A.J. MacKinnon needed was another dram and a half-pint of ale, Mickey shook his head. "You've had quite enough for one day, A.J. Go home to that pretty wife of yours before she worries herself sick."

A.J. made a sound at the back of his throat. "The bitch is already dead to the world . . . or pretendin' to be."

No. More likely Maggie was pacing, her eyes brimming with tears and silent accusations. Why his cousin stayed with this sorry excuse for a man no one in the family could figure out.

Sure, Alistair Jerome MacKinnon stood an easy six feet four inches, had a head full of auburn hair and blue eyes that could stop a clock – even had an aura about him that initially drew you in – but soon enough you discovered he was all hot air and pretention. Cold sober, the man couldn't keep a job to save his soul. Drunk, he got mean. Real mean. And this evening, he'd arrived drunk as a lord after being fired from yet another job. This time it was from one Mickey had found for him.

Having heard enough, Mickey leaned forwards, hands fisted on his centuries-old oak bar. "Do not be talking like that about Maggie. She's a good woman, better than you deserve and well you know it."

Bleary-eyed and sullen, A.J. muttered, "Oh ya? Well, I've news for you. She's a blubbering nag." He thumped his fist on the bar again. "Come on, just one more for the road."

Mickey was fed up and needed to close, so he came around the bar and grabbed A.J. by the scuff; no mean task given the man stood a full head taller than he and outweighed him by an easy three stones. "Let's go. Your pockets are bare and I'll not be extending credit."

Maggie was working two jobs as it was.

A.J., cursing and boxing the air, stumbled forwards. In the parking lot, Mickey gave A.J. a shove. "Go home."

A.J. staggered to his beat-up Ford Focus and got behind the wheel. When the engine finally sputtered to life, Mickey slammed the pub door closed and shut off the lights.

Had his last customer been anyone other than A.J., he'd have taken the car keys and seen the man home, but A.J. and Maggie lived only a quarter mile up the road. Being well past midnight, there wouldn't be another soul on the road till dawn so he'd be safe enough.

Maggie pushed aside the lace curtain and peered into the night. "Where the hell can he be at this hour?"

A.J. had promised he'd only stop by the Boar's Head to thank Mickey for finding him the job at the Portree restaurant, then come straight home for a celebration dinner, which should have been hours ago.

Worried A.J. might be passed out in the pub's parking lot, she reached for the telephone to call Mickey, only to remember her service had been cut off weeks ago. Cursing, tears springing to her eyes, she continued pacing.

This was *not* the life she'd envisioned when she's fallen in love and married A.J. MacKinnon, who claimed to be the legitimate heir to the MacKinnon legacy. According to A.J., the MacKinnon ring he wore, given to him by his grandfather, had been passed down to the rightful heir for centuries. The Mackinnon title was by all rights his, not some distant cousin's. Only A.J. had no way of proving it – other than his having the ring, which was no proof at all according to their high-priced solicitor. The court needed birth and marriage records dating back to the beginning of time, but the crucial evidence of his lineage had been lost to war and a kirk fire.

Peering out the window, Maggie cursed A.J.'s grandfather yet again for filling his head with grandiose nonsense. This crazy obsession – of his having the blood of kings running in his veins – was eating A.J. alive, and had turned him from the charming and ambitious lover she'd fallen for during their whirlwind courtship five years ago into a bitter man she barely recognized. Worse, when he drank he blamed everyone but himself for his every failing. Bosses were out to get him. The small cottage she'd inherited was a joke. The meals she prepared weren't fit for dogs. Worse, whenever she lashed back, he called her a shrew. How she'd managed to escape his fists when he went on one of his drunken rampages was still a mystery. Thank God, he was prone to stumbling and falling whenever he swung a fist.

But then would come morning – or more often afternoon – and he'd stumble out of the bedroom, beg her forgiveness, saying it had only been the whisky talking, making him a bloody ass. He'd profess his love and swear never to do it again. And because she'd once loved him beyond reason, had pledged to love and honour him in good times and bad, she hung on, desperate to believe, putting *her* dreams on hold. And all because A.J. couldn't pass a pub if he had a penny in his pocket.

She hated admitting it but Mickey had been right when he'd repeatedly warned her that if she married in haste she'd repent in leisure.

The mantel clock struck two and she dashed the tears from her cheeks. All this pacing and fretting was getting her nowhere.

Hoping Mickey had at least seen A.J., she pulled her cardigan from the wall-mounted coat rack by the door. Outside, she hunched against the wind coming off Inner Sound, its choppy water reflecting moonlight like a fractured mirror, bathing both the empty two-lane carriageway before her and the mountains at her back in a cool white glow.

Only minutes down the road she caught the pungent scent of fire on the wind. Alarmed, she looked back at her home, then at her immediate neighbours, then towards the village. A hundred yards ahead she saw ghostly columns rising from beneath the bridge that spanned a burn.

"Please dear God, no."

Heart hammering, she broke into a run.

Racing on to the bridge, the stench of petrol made her stomach heave. She leaned over the railing and peered into the darkness below. Oh dear God, is that a car? The wind shifted, brushing the smoke aside. In the rubble below lay a listing undercarriage and four wheels.

"*A.J.!*"

The annoying beeps and thumps drew Alex out of his turbulent dreams only a moment before cool fingers pried open his right eye. Piercing light, as hot as steel in a smithy's forge, stabbed his brain.

Good God almighty!

He swung an arm to bat the offender away.

"Ah, he's finally waking up," said a man on his left.

A feminine voice – *her* voice, said, "A.J., can you hear me? Sweetheart, open your eyes."

Not on your life, woman. Not after what just happened. Head aching unmercifully, still in a haze, Alex tried to roll away from his tormentors only to come to a groaning stop.

Saint Columba, have mercy! Every damn bone in his body ached as if he'd been hurled from a catapult and into a curtain wall. Worse, something hard and dry clotted his throat. Fearing he'd choke to death, he reached up to pull the obstruction out and the man grasped his wrist.

"Leave it alone."

Like hell, he would. Alex wrenched free of the man's grip and before anyone could naysay him, jerked the obstruction free and gasped. Searing pain tore at his throat. Behind him, an ear-shattering whistle sounded.

The man cursed and the wailing ceased. Alex, his throat on fire, cautiously peered through his lashes.

Who were these people leaning over him? The woman, dark circles under beautiful green eyes, he must know – the sight of her summoned feelings of warmth and protection – but not so the grey-haired man dressed in the odd blue garments holding his wrists.

Alex wrenched his arms free. "Leave me . . . be!"

Good God, his throat hurt. Hell, everything hurt.

The woman – Maggie, aye, that was her name – stroked his cheek. "Shhh, it's alright, A.J. You had an accident and you're in hospital."

Hospital? He was neither poor nor infirm so why . . . ?

And why did she keep addressing him as A-jay?

He looked about the strange green room. Not liking or under-standing any of it, his heart hammered and the beeping became a frantic rhythm.

Humph! The *what* and *why* of all this insanity mattered not. He would eventually sort it all out . . . after he made good his escape.

He bolted upright only to feel wires and snaking tubes pull at his bruised and torn flesh. Head swimming, he jerked against his restraints and swung his legs over the bedside.

Maggie held up her hands as if to stop him, just as the man shouted, "Mr MacKinnon, stop! You need to lie down."

Grasping Maggie's shoulder for balance, Alex ripped the wires from his chest and jerked out the tube embedded in his arm, send-ing blood and water flying. Over a new screeching, he croaked, "Leaving."

Head hanging and seeing a yellow tube dangling betwixt his legs, he jerked on it and nearly passed out. *Holy Saint Columba!*

The sheep buggers had even invaded his manhood!

Maggie grasped his chin as he fought for breath. "Listen to me. Doctor MacDonald will take it out if you'll just *lie down*."

Behind him, the doctor said, "Listen to your wife, Mr MacKinnon. I'll take the catheter out if you'll just lie back down."

Panting, Alex shook his head. Wife? Nay, Maggie was not his wife but the drunkard's. Aye, that much he did know, although how he knew he could not recall. "Ye'll take the bloody thing out whilst I sit." If he dared lie back down the bastards would, in all likelihood, tie him to the bed.

The doctor huffed. A moment later a disembodied female voice said, "May I help you?"

At his back, the doctor said, "I need a ten cc syringe in 114."

The voice responded, "I'll be right there."

Augh! Another heathen was coming.

A moment later a thin lass of about twenty years, her garments much like the doctors, came in. The doctor pulled the tip from a clear tube she'd handed him, exposing a long needle. When the doctor reached betwixt his legs, Alex clamped a hand over the man's arm, growling, "And what do ye think yer doing?"

"I have to take the fluid out of the ball that's holding the tube inside you. It won't hurt."

"Upon my honour should it, you're a dead man." Glaring, Alex reluctantly released the doctor's arm.

To his great relief the man was as good as his word. The nasty tube only smarted as it came clear of his body.

With Maggie's help, Alex – alarmed more by the softness of his body than by any of its many injuries – dressed then found himself staring at a mountain of documents he could make neither head nor tail of.

"Just sign here and here," the woman in blue said, marking the pages with an "x" then handing him her odd writing implement.

After scribing "A. J. MacFhionghuin" where she'd indicated and noting the date, which came as a shock, he shoved the pages towards her. "Am I now free to leave?"

"Yes."

"Humph!" He stood and held out his arm expecting Maggie to place her hand on his wrist. Instead, she threaded her arm through his and he caught her scent, of strawberries and lavender, which summoned a strange mix of lust and great yearning – then one of blind fury. He shook his head to clear it, took two steps and found himself before a mirror.

The reflected countenance was not the one he well remembered. Close, but definitely not the same. Thinking it a trick, he stuck out his tongue.

Dear God above, 'tis no illusion.

He leaned towards the glass. He truly was alive. Once again flesh and blood! In A.J. MacKinnon's body.

His legs, no sturdier than sea kelp, began to buckle. By sheer force of will, he locked his knees and took another step towards the door and freedom.

Outside, he cleared his lungs of the building's stench and allowed Maggie to guide him to a waiting conveyance, whereupon she opened a door and bid he sit inside. He did. Having no idea what was happening, where he was or where they were going, he still knew any place had to be better than the one he'd just escaped.

Getting in beside him, she asked, "Are you alright?"

"Aye." A lie if ever there was one, but then he'd yet to fathom what had befallen him.

Brow furrowed, her full lips compressed into a hard line, she put the conveyance in motion. "You scared the shit out of me, A.J. If I hadn't found you when I did you would have died at the bottom of that ravine."

He nodded, recalling the roar of steel fracturing on rock, of falling, the stench of fire . . . and pain. Aye, he remembered A.J.'s pain and then gasping in agony as A.J.'s pain became his. "I did not intend such."

"No? Then what the hell did you expect driving blind drunk?" She heaved a sigh. "The car's a total loss."

"I'm sorry."

When she shot him a scathing glance, he decided the less he said at this juncture the better and turned his attention to his surroundings.

The Cuillin Mountains straddling Skye were just as he'd left them. As were the small isles nestled betwixt the mainland and his home. Aye, he knew precisely where he was but . . .

He looked at Maggie. "Who does this . . ." the word escaped him, "belong to, if not ye?"

She frowned. "You don't remember?"

He shook his head as he pointed to the road. "Ye'd best pay heed, m'lady."

Their conveyance jerked and the oncoming vehicle issued a strident bleep as it whizzed past. "The car belongs to Mickey." She then muttered, "I knew I shouldn't have let you sign yourself out." After a minute she asked. "Do you know where you are?"

"On the eastern shore of Skye." So much looked familiar – particularly she – but then too much was foreign. His very self included.

"As soon as we get home, you're going to bed."

Nay, he most certainly was *not* going to bed. He'd had quite enough of bed and so apparently had A.J., if this soft body was any indication.

The road twisted, Portree and its harbour disappeared behind them, and he turned his attention to A.J.'s pretty wife as she, frowning, kept her focus on the carriage road. Studying the glorious chestnut hair curling about her heart-shaped face and the lovely manner in which her neck arched, the memory of her smiling up at him bloomed. Hearing her whisper, "I love you," his heart tripped and he found himself smiling. But then another memory took shape, of Maggie cowering, and the rush of unbridled fury swelled deep within his chest.

Thankful finally to be home, Maggie turned into the drive fronting the small cottage she'd inherited from her parents, the home her husband took so little pride in.

A. J., normally talkative when trying to placate her, hadn't said a word since apologising for the wreck. But more troubling than even his uncharacteristic silence was his stilted speech on those few times when he had spoken.

The doctors had assured her they had no reason to believe he'd suffered any permanent brain damage, but what if they were wrong? He'd been in a coma for twenty-four hours.

Her unease grew when they went inside and A.J. looked about their parlour as if trying to orient himself. He then strode into the kitchen and looked out the window. Shaking his head, he told her, "Yer garden needs tending."

"I'll get right to it after I finish cooking, cleaning and slinging fish and chips all day then doing the MacMillan's mending."

He looked at her, his face an expressionless mask. "'Twas simply an observation."

"If you say so." Too tired to argue, she tossed her sweater over the back of the nearest chair and opened the refrigerator. "There's only leftovers for lunch." And they were lucky to have that.

"Whatever ye lust."

There it was again. That accent.

She barely touched her food while A. J. dived in with both hands. After wolfing down a sandwich and sopping up the last of his potato soup with half a loaf of bread, he leaned back in his chair and patted his middle. "'Twas very good. Thank ye."

She blinked. A.J. hadn't said thank you, much less complimented her cooking, in . . . she couldn't remember how long. "You suffered one hell of a concussion, didn't you?"

Without waiting for an answer, she stood and cleared the table. "I need to find a present for Mickey and Bridget's wedding this weekend, change my shifts at the restaurant – since I'm now going to have to ride a bus to work – then return Mickey's car."

She'd had her eye on a lovely pair of silver challises for her cousin's wedding, but now couldn't afford them. She'd need every penny she could scrape together for a down payment on a new car. Worse, she'd be earning a lot less working days instead of evenings at the King's Arms.

She snatched up the keys. "You rest. I'll be back as soon as I can." Cursing the day she ever set eyes on A. J. MacKinnon, she walked out the door.

"Maggie."

She turned to find A.J. had followed her out. He came around the car and pulled her gently to his chest, then hooked a finger under her chin. "Look at me, lass."

She did. A mistake. His vivid blue gaze bore into hers as it had in their earlier and better days, causing warmth and longing to spread through her chest.

Knowing that particular look could turn her legs to jelly, she tried to turn away, but his left hand slipped beneath her hair and before she could react he captured her mouth with his. His kiss, initially tentative, grew slowly more possessive. God! He hadn't kissed her like this . . .

Too soon he raised his head and smiled at her. "Take care, lass."

Watching Maggie take her leave, Alex shook his head. "I do believe she hates me . . . or wants to."

Knowing there was little he could do about it until he cleared his head and got his new limbs moving as they ought, he walked through the croft and out the back door, his goal the red granite ridges that he'd prowled seven centuries past. Mayhap his beloved mountains could bring some understanding of how his soul had changed places with that of A.J. MacKinnon's.

A good hour later, huffing and heart all but flailing through his ribs, Alex collapsed on an outcrop overlooking the sea and hung his head. Good God almighty, how on earth had the man functioned like this?

Had an enemy come up behind him, he'd be dead. He hadn't the strength to wield a wee *sgian duhb*, much less his broad sword.

"This will not do."

He wiped the sweat from his eyes and looked at the broad acreage that had once been the collection point for thousands of MacKinnon cattle destined for the fairs at Crieth, then at the place Maggie and A.J. called home. The croft was a shambles. Shutters were listing, the roof missing slate . . . and the kale yard! The plot was naught but bramble and tumbling stone. Alex shook his head, not understanding how a man could allow such to happen.

And what had Maggie meant by changing shifts? Did she labour because her sorry sot of a husband wouldn't?

Having no answers, he rose and made his way towards the jagged ruins that had once been *his* home at the tip of the peninsular. As he drew ever closer, an invisible band tightened about his chest and tears burned at the back of his throat. When had this happened? How?

Standing before what had once been a formidable curtain wall he picked a stone from the rubble, dusted it off and carefully placed it where it belonged. Directly above and to the right had once been the chamber in which his wife had given her life to see Ian born.

His son, his bonnie son, was gone now along with everyone else he'd known and loved – followed by generations of clansmen. All had gone to their final reward but not him . . . thanks to his brother's villainy.

Why couldn't the bastard have accepted his lot, of being the second son and destined for religious life? But nay, Angus had to covet what had been Alex's by right of birth.

Through blurring tears, Alex studied the signet ring he'd worn then – and now again wore. His uncle Collin had taken it from Alex's hand before burial against Angus's furious protests.

"'Tis now rightfully the lad's," his uncle had snarled. He'd then secured the ring around his own neck, saying that when Ian came of age, he would wear it. The next day his uncle had clasped Alex's infant to his chest and escaped with him to the protection of Mull.

When his son came of age his uncle kept his pledge. Ian, seeped in the legend, put on the ring and then went to war but to no avail. The king and political expediency were against him. And still he fought on.

Upon Ian's death, the ring and the tale passed to his son. And so it went for centuries.

With his essence tied to the ring, Alex often experienced the emotions of the wearer – some better men than others, but all of them his bloodline. Time passed. Kings came and went, as did heirs and fortunes. And then it passed to A.J.

It saddened him that his glimpses into A.J.'s life more often involved the ring than they did the beautiful Maggie.

"Hmmm." Aye, that made perfect sense. He'd become flesh and blood again because A.J. had died without an heir.

Just the thought of Maggie's bonny green eyes, pert breasts and curls did send his blood racing. But he'd not be bedding her any time soon. Leastwise not in her current frame of mind.

"Humph! So, now that I've solved the mystery, what can I do about it?"

Watching the courting oystercatchers and lapwings whirl over the surf, he laughed, recalling a heady exhilaration as A.J. courted and won fair Maggie. But the man had never taken to hearth and home, the deplorable condition of the croft being certain proof.

Mayhap . . .

He stood and, grinning, headed home.

Two

A horn blasted. Maggie jerked awake and, blinking, looked out the bus window. Oh good, she was almost home.

Elsa, more than willing to trade shifts with her, had taken a week to arrange after-school care for her wee ones, leaving Maggie with no choice but to work her shift *and* part of Elsa's. She did appreciate the extra pay but hadn't seen the sun all week. Thank God the long shifts were over and she'd been able to leave the restaurant on time today.

She yawned, wondering what, if anything, A.J. was doing. Nothing, most likely.

The bus came to a stop and she stumbled out. Lifting her face to the glorious sun, she closed her eyes and, smiling, waited for the bus to pull away and the oncoming lorries to pass. When they did, she opened her eyes and stared at the charming house before her. Unlike her home, this croft gleamed with a new coat of whitewash, its shutters were straight and glossy black and the window boxes, sporting bright yellow flowers, were painted red.

"Damn it!" She'd got off at the wrong place.

Praying the bus driver would look in his rearview mirror, she started waving and shouting, running after the bus, only to watch it disappeared around the bend.

"Great. Just great."

On the verge of tears, feet aching, she looked about, trying to orient herself – praying she hadn't in her exhaustion taken the wrong bus altogether.

"Uhmm . . ." There's the bridge and, beyond it, she could see what she was sure was the Boar Head's slate roof. She looked over her shoulder at the rocky shoreline. This *was* the right place. She looked at the croft. What wasn't right was the sight before her.

Was she dreaming?

Halfway up the front path she came to a halt as the front door opened and Daisy MacDonald came out.

"Oh! Hello, Maggie. I was just leaving."

Maggie studied the pretty young woman, wondering what on earth she was doing in her home . . . if this was, in fact, her home. "Good day."

"I hope you don't mind but while I was at it I put a loaf in the oven. Should be ready in about a half hour." Coming abreast of Maggie, she whispered, "I don't know what you've been feeding him, love, but whatever it is, I want some for my man."

Maggie, slack-jawed, nodded. What in bloody hell is going on?

Determined to find out, she waited until Daisy left then stomped up the path only to come to a stop upon seeing that the yellow flowers adorning the window boxes were dandelions. "Why would anyone . . . ?"

She opened the front door and her knees buckled. The furniture, under an inch of dust and clutter when she left this morning, now gleamed. As did the floor. The laundry she'd dumped on the sofa to be folded tonight had vanished as well. And just as shocking . . . the telly was off.

"A.J.? Where are you?"

She walked into the kitchen and gaped, finding every surface spotless and a pot of peeled potatoes sitting on the stove ready to be cooked. Sniffing, smelling meatloaf and lemon disinfectant, she muttered, "I'm definitely dreaming."

She checked the bathroom, found it immaculate and then, half-dreading she'd discover A.J. in a rumpled bed, peered into their bedroom and was stunned to find everything within set to rights as well. "I just don't believe this."

A god-awful crash sounded at the rear. Not knowing what to expect next, she raced through the house and out the back door, only to have her breath catch at the sight of her husband standing in her garden, wearing nothing but a pair of shorts riding low on his hips, his body and face a ruddy, glistening bronze.

Oh my.

"Ah, there ye be, Maggie." He tossed a boulder as if it were a pebble into their rusty wheel barrel and waved towards her garden. "What think ye?"

"Uhmm . . ." With effort she tore her gaze from the bronze god to look around the yard. Two of the garden's stone walls had been repaired and the third, the worst by far, had been knocked down and was in the process of being rebuilt. The weeds that once choked the plot were now piled in a shoulder high mound in the centre of the garden ready for a match. "You did all this?"

"Aye, but I cannot take credit for whatever went on inside. That's all Daisy's doing . . . and a mean negotiator, she is, too."

"You paid her?" With what?

He scowled as if she were daft. "Of course not. I noticed a ewe escaping from her pasture and I feared more would follow and be killed on yon carriageway, so I scooped up the beastie and knocked on her door. Learning her husband was abed with a lame back, and thinking this could prove fortuitous, I asked if she'd be willing to work a trade; in return for me mending her fence would she be willing to do a bit of cleaning? She said she would . . . if I'd also take down the weeds about her place. Well, what choice did I have?"

"None?" He'd lost his mind.

Grinning, A.J. nodded. "So after I had her flock contained, I knocked on her door again and asked where I might find her scythe. I knew we had naught for I'd already checked," he jabbed a thumb over his shoulder, "yon shed."

"Oh my God, you whitewashed that as well."

He shrugged. "I was already coated in the nasty stuff so thought why not. Anyway, ye will not believe what the woman handed me. Not a scythe but a contraption on wheels with revolving blades. Ye just shove and *whaaaack* . . . off goes the grass neat as ye please. Truly amazing."

Oh. Dear. God. "Sweetie . . ."

"Aye?"

Maggie forced a smile. "Why don't we go inside now? I think you've had quite enough sun for one day." And as soon as he turned on the telly to watch Taggart – he never missed the crime show – she'd be running to the Boar's Head and calling the doctor.

He examined his arms and his chest for sunburn, both of which looked, to Maggie, far more muscled than she could ever recall them being in the five years she'd known him.

"Hmm, I am a wee bit singed. Alright then. The rest can wait for the morrow." As he came abreast of her, he bent and kissed her nose. "I'm starving. What's for supper?"

Shaken, she mumbled, "Food."

Inside, she lit the burner under the potatoes then pushed him towards the bathroom. "Go take a shower."

He cocked an arm and sniffed. "Augh, I am a bit ripe."

"That you are. Now away with you and don't use all the shampoo."

The moment he disappeared into the bathroom, Maggie collapsed on to the nearest chair. Although she much preferred this new and greatly improved A.J. over the old one, she couldn't ignore the fact that something was drastically wrong with him.

People who sustained head injuries often suffered amnesia, which might explain A.J.'s confusion about lawnmowers, but certainly didn't explain all the frenetic labour. And it certainly didn't explain his stilted English. But then again, hadn't she recently read about a woman in London who, after a week-long coma, began speaking with a Russian accent? And not one of the London specialists she'd seen could explain it.

"*Mag-gie!*"

Oh Lord, now what? "I'm coming!"

Oh. My. Word.

A.J. stood naked before the bathroom mirror, his ass as white and firm as dual moons, the rest of his bronzed body flexing. "'Tis stuck," he said.

Feeling a bit breathless, she reluctantly slid her gaze from his glorious backside to his reflection. "Huh?"

"The brush, lass. 'Tis stuck as fast as burr on a dog's arse."

She blinked, saw he was grinning at her in the mirror and finally looked to where he pointed – to find the handle of her hairbrush sticking out from beneath the tangled mess of his wet hair. "How on earth . . . ?"

She pointed to the edge of the tub. "Sit. I can't untangle it with you standing."

He dutifully turned towards the tub and her mouth went dry. He was well on his way to being fully engorged – something she hadn't seen in well over a year. Her heart did the old *thubbidy-thub*.

"Uhmm . . . face the wall." She opened the window, hoping some cold air would knock some sense into her heart.

"Did you find the present, lass?"

"Huh?" Lord, he smelled good.

"The present, lass. Did you find one?"

"Oh, yes, I did." She carefully rotated the brush, pulling free only two and three stands at a time. "Thank you for all the work you've done about the house, the garden."

"Yer most welcome." After a moment, he asked. "What am I to wear to this eve?"

"Your blue suit." Her hands stilled. "A.J., please promise me something."

He craned his neck to look at her. "Aye?"

"Promise me you won't get drunk tonight." The whisky and ale would be flowing like water at the wedding reception. And she really did want to enjoy herself.

He reached over his shoulder and took her left hand in his. Running a finger over her wedding band, he said, "Upon my honour, I will not embarrass ye."

Right.

She'd given him the perfect opportunity to say he'd learned his lesson and wouldn't drink and he couldn't say it.

She jerked the brush free and stomped out of the room.

Two hours later, she found him standing before the parluor window looking like a man on the way to the gallows. The suit he'd worn on their wedding day was now too tight at the shoulders and too loose at the waist. The shirt he'd left open to mid-chest. "Come here."

He did, his eyes raking over her from her hair to her shoes. "Ye look most lovely. Pale green is most becoming on ye."

"Thank you." She did feel pretty in the bridesmaid gown she'd made and prayed Bridget felt the same in her wedding gown.

She tried to button his shirt and, failing, pointed towards the bedroom. "Go on. We need to find something else for you to wear."

She pulled the cream-coloured sweater she'd knitted during their first year of marriage from the wardrobe. "Try this."

He was out of his jacket and shirt and into the sweater before she could blink. Running his hands over the intricate nubs and cables, he smiled. "'Tis perfect."

So why had he never worn it?

Inside the kirk, Alex smiled at those who greeted them, assuming A.J. had known them. At the third pew, Maggie stopped and handed him her purse. "Take a seat. I'll meet you after the ceremony."

He slid into the pew and nodded to the strangers sitting next to him.

"We heard about the accident," the grey-haired woman to his left all but shouted, "How are you feeling?"

"Verra well, thank ye. 'Tis a glorious day, aye?"

Her snow-white eyebrows tented over dull blue eyes. "That's good, dear."

When she said no more Alex shrugged and turned his attention to his stark surroundings. Had Rome grown so poor or his clansmen so slack that they no longer bothered with artisans and gold leaf? Humph! His chapel, only half this size, had at least been properly adorned.

The piper and fiddler changed tune and the people around him looked over their shoulders. Following suit, his heart swelled.

There she was, his Maggie, a wreath of flowers decorating her glorious curls, a bouquet of white roses in her hands. Lovely, but not any more so than when she'd come into the bathroom and had flushed to a heart-catching pink. Aye, she might be angry with him but beneath her breast beat a heart not yet dead to him, and happy he was to learn it.

But next time he might think twice before doing something as rash as purposely tangling a brush in his hair. She'd damn near scalped him wrenching it out.

The music changed and the congregation rose. The bride glowed as she walked down the aisle in a pretty white gown and took her place next to the groom, who stood proud and smiling, flushed with happiness.

Feeling an unaccountable stab of jealousy, he looked at Maggie, wondering if she felt as he did. He found her eyes glistening with unshed tears. Without being told, he knew them to be not those of joy, but of loss and longing. Wanting nothing more than to bolt from the pew and take her into his arms, he forced himself to remain rooted. He had, after all, promised not to embarrass her.

After the ceremony, they gathered at the Boar's Head Pub, a place Alex could only recall in unpleasant flashes, but this time music and laughter greeted them. Maggie took one look at the crowd, most of which already had ale in hand and caught her lower lip betwixt her teeth. Hoping to distract her from her worry, he leaned down and pointed to the table set up on the opposite wall. "Look at yon cake."

"Lovely, isn't it?" Maggie then pointed to another couple. "There's Marilyn and John."

Stomach rumbling, he guided her through the throng to the couple. Maggie greeted them as old friends and Alex followed suit, although he didn't recognize either of them, they apparently having had little impact on A.J.'s turbulent life – likely a good thing.

"We really like what you've done about your place," the man said. "Almost didn't recognize it as we passed."

Maggie grinned. "I didn't either the first time I saw it. And you should see what he's doing with the garden."

The conversation turned to cultivation and Alex eyed the lasses setting up a buffet in the adjoining room. Humph. If he didn't put something in his stomach soon, he'd be keeling over. None too soon the bride and groom entered. During the cheering, a lass appeared at his elbow with a tray of stemmed goblets. He took two and handed one to Maggie. The man he presumed to be the bride's father proposed a toast. The moment the bubbly liquid hit his tongue Alex grimaced. More toasts ensued. When Maggie emptied her glass, he handed her his full one. "I mean no offense to our host," he whispered in her ear, "but are ye sure they're not trying to kill us, lass?"

"Since when do you turn down champagne?"

He shrugged.

Another serving lass came by, this time with wider goblets filled with more pale wine. "Some chardonnay?" she asked.

Since it looked suspiciously like the last, he shook his head. What he would have appreciated was whisky. What he *needed* was food.

Finally a third serving lass came by and offered them bits of salmon on bread. He would have kissed her had he promised not to embarrass Maggie.

While Maggie chatted, he stood behind her right shoulder, eating everything the serving lasses had to offer until they disappeared, and the bride and groom, having greeted everyone, began their first dance.

Moved by the way the pair looked at each other, he slipped his arms about Maggie's waist. She, relaxed, rested her head on his chest as she watched the couple and he couldn't help but wonder how A.J. could have let something so precious as her fond regard slip through his fingers.

Thank God he'd been able to assert his will on A.J. whenever the ass had taken it into his head to raise his fist to her and had been able to throw the friggin' idiot off balance.

At least she no longer had that to fear.

He watched as others began dancing. Their steps were far different from those he'd been taught but then no two couples appeared to be doing the same thing. The music changed again and Maggie swayed with the rhythm. Grinning, he leaned forward and whispered in her ear, "May I have this dance?"

She craned her neck to look up at him. "But you don't dance."

"Who said?"

She grinned. "You."

"Then I lied."

With a hand at the small of her back, he guided her to the centre of the group. Preferring the way some men wrapped their arms about their woman, he followed suit and Maggie slipped her arms about his neck. Looking up at him, she said, "You're full of surprises these days, Mr MacKinnon."

"Ye know not the half of it, m'lady." But hopefully, she'd come to learn more. He'd grown bone weary of her putting her back to him every night. In hopes of rectifying the situation, he whispered, "Yon bride is fair but ye, my love, are lovelier."

She cocked her head, a small smile playing at the corner of her full lips. "You think so?"

"Aye, I truly do." He'd thought so from the first moment he caught sight of her. "Do you recall our meeting?"

"Of course. You were showing off for your friends at the Broadford Fair, had just won a teddy bear. You turned around . . ."

"And our eyes met. My heart stopped, never having seen anything so lovely." He smiled at the memory. Aye, he'd wanted her with every fibre of his being upon first sight.

Dear God above, *he* had . . . not A.J.

"What's wrong?"

He shook his head. "Naught, but that I've royally tupped up what should have been – could have been."

Her eyes grew glassy and she threaded her fingers through the hair at his nape. "Time has a way of mending wounds . . . if we really care."

"I do care, Mary Magdalene MacKinnon, more than ye shall ever know."

He kissed her then, trying to impart all that he felt, the joy of feeling her in his arms and his regret for all the heartache his need had caused her.

Feeling a tap on his arm, he pulled out of the luxurious haze

Maggie had induced and found Mickey grinning up at him. "Time to eat, Romeo."

He looked about and found everyone, including the musicians, had moved into the adjacent room before the buffet. He then looked at Maggie and found her blushing. "Shall we?"

She shook her head. "I'll eat in a bit. I want to speak with Bridget."

"As ye lust."

Mouth watering, he stood in line and studied the awesome sight spread before him. Some foods he recognized, others were foreign but he would try it all. And look, lobster! He loaded his plate and returned to their table to find Maggie in animated chatter with a new couple. He devoured the beef and ham then dug into the lobster, having saved the best for last. He'd only taken two bites out of the succulent tail when Maggie yelped and knocked the fork from his hand. "You know you can't eat that! You're allergic to shellfish."

"I am? What means allergic?"

"Oh God." She looked about in panic then grabbed his arm. "Come on, we have to get you to the hospital. Oh, shit! We don't have a car. Stay, don't move." She ran across the room and grabbed Mickey by the arm. A moment later, she returned with Mickey and another man. Taking his arm, her panic obvious in her lovely countenance, she shouted, "Come on!"

He looked longingly at the lobster but didn't argue only because his mouth did feel most strange. By the time he slid into the back bench of the conveyance with *Police* stenciled on its door, he could feel his face swelling. What the hell was happening now?

One look at Maggie's countenance told him whatever it was had her most alarmed. "I ha na meth to—"

God, his tongue felt like a fleece pelt.

She held tight to his hand. "Sshhh, you'll be fine . . . as soon as we get you a shot." To the driver she shouted, "Please hurry!"

By the time she ushered him into the hospital and spoke with the woman behind the glass, spots were dancing before his eyes. A doctor stuck a needle in his arm then tried to place a mask on his face. He knocked it away, having enough trouble breathing as it was.

Maggie stroked his back. "A.J., the oxygen will help."

Leaning on his arms, his lungs sucking for all they were worth, he shook his head. All he needed was air. To be let be . . . so he could focus on breathing.

Maggie, tears streaming, murmured something to the doctor. Alex breathed and they waited. And waited. Finally, the tightness in his throat eased and he could draw a breath without sounding like an ill-made whistle. Shoulders hunched, he looked at Maggie. "My apologies for embarrassing ye yet again, love."

"You didn't. What you did was scared me near to death."

He blew through his teeth. Scared himself near to death as well. He straightened and slid off the bed.

"No, we can't leave just yet."

"But we must. The wedding—"

She pressed a finger to his lips. "You aren't going anywhere until the doctor says you can and certainly not before I get a prescription for an epinephrine kit."

He had no idea what she was going on about but the look in her eyes told him she'd make his life a living hell if he thought to naysay her so, huffing, he sat. And thought.

By the time the doctor said they could leave, he had no doubt that his continued ignorance would be the death of him. That if he planned to live long enough to make love again – much less make and raise a son, he had to enlist Maggie's help. And the only way he could do that was to tell her the truth.

But to ensure her belief he still had a good bit of work to do.

Three

At dawn the next morn, Alex stood on the stoop and smiled as if he hadn't a care in the world, waved as the bus bearing Maggie to Portree pulled away. The moment it disappeared, he ran to the shed.

Whilst looking for the scythe, he'd spied a carefully covered stash covered in clear sheeting. Given the care with which he'd found the objects and boxes wrapped, he knew it had to be Maggie's handiwork, A.J. being a sloth.

Uncovering only roll upon roll of fabric, he frowned. He opened the first box and uncovered hundreds of colourful spools. In another, he found all manner of sewing sundries from needles and measures to buttons. In another, skeins of finely-spun wool in a rainbow of colours.

Humph! This store made no sense. Maggie, the least vain woman he'd ever met, rarely wore anything but her tight blue trews and that God-awful serving wench livery. Spying the edge of a large battered trunk, he worked his way through broken furniture hoping it held the answer.

The lock proved no obstacle. "Let us see what yer hiding, Maggie my love."

He lifted the lid and pulled out several books from the chest. Hmmm, clothing styles dating back centuries. He opened the next, finding only descriptions of textiles and their manufacture. He dug deeper and pulled out a large, green leather-bound and gilt edged volume. "Ah, this is more like it."

He opened the cover expecting to find a ledger or diary but instead found page after page of beautiful drawings, some in charcoal while others were coloured in lovely vivid hues. And all with the initials M.M.M. penned at the bottom.

So this was her dream, to be a *modess*. He sighed. This he could not make happen. Disappointed, he started putting all of it back as he found it, bumping his shoulder against a teetering pile of fractured furniture. A tube of yellowed paper fell at his feet. He opened it and found architectural renderings labelled Sky High Designs, Maggie MacKinnon Proprietor.

He studied each of the pages then grinned.

Moments later he pushed through the Boar's Head door. "Mickey, a word if ye please."

Looking none to pleased to see him, Mickey nodded. "What can I do for you A.J.?"

He smiled. Mickey loathed A.J., which meant he respected and cared deeply for Maggie.

"Take yer ease, Mickey. I've not come to drink ye dry. I need yer opinion on these."

He spread the curled pages on the counter and Mickey smirked. "I haven't seen these in ages. Thought she'd lost them."

Alex pointed to a circle. "Do you know their meaning?"

"They're lighting fixtures." He flipped a page. "This is the electrical schematic for the entire shop she'd planned." He flipped another and grinned. "Ah, the façade she envisioned. Too bad she never had the money." He rolled up the papers.

"Do ye know a man who might be available to do such lights?"

An hour later, Alex had all the information he needed and bid Mickey adieu. To his surprise, Mickey followed him out. "A.J., wait."

"Aye?"

"I should have driven you home that night. I'm sorry."

Ah. "Believe it or not, I'm most glad that ye had not."

Mickey thought on that then said, "Where are you off to?"

"Portree."

"If you can wait a few minutes, I'll give you a lift into town. I have to pick up some supplies."

"Thank you."

Entering the outskirts of the town, Alex was again taken by how much had changed since his time. "May I ask a *boon*?"

Mickey grinned. "A boon, huh? What is it?"

"I need yer help in keeping Maggie occupied in a few days whilst I get a few things accomplished about the place. Might ye be able to help with that?"

"I'm sure it can be arranged. Just tell me when."

"Thank ye."

A few days turned into a fortnight but finally Alex was ready. When Maggie went to work, he walked to the Boar's Head and rang the bell.

Mickey, one eye open and his wiry hair askew, opened the door. "Do you not have a clock, MacKinnon?"

"Aye, ye lazy sloth, I do. Now to why I'm here. Today is the day! I need ye to get and hold Maggie 'til I come fetch her. I've much yet to do and don't wanther coming home and finding me half done." Just thinking about what he'd yet to do made him weary.

"Alright. I'll pick her up from work and Bridget will keep her occupied." He started to close the door, then peered out again. "Did John finish with the electrical?"

"Aye and then some." To Alex's amazement the auld man had brought in and installed a most bonnie hanging lamp of wrought iron. A gift for Maggie, he'd said. A good man, John.

Alex ran back to the house where he pulled out the drill Mickey had taught him to use. Off came the storage shed's old door and on went the new. Off came the weatherworn shutters that had been masking the new windows and on went the new. He worked as if possessed until he was satisfied all was in order. He could only pray 'twould be enough.

He found Maggie in the pub chatting with Bridget. Seeing him, she smiled. "I was beginning to wonder if you'd forgotten me."

He gave her a quick kiss and took her hand. "Never. Come, I've something to show ye."

Seeing that Mickey and Bridget, grinning like idiots, had followed them out, she asked, "What do they know that I don't?"

His middle in knots, he smiled down at her. "Ye'll see soon enough."

As their home came into view, Maggie looked up at him then back at the croft. "Oh! Oh my God."

She broke into a run only to come to a halt before the shop door. A hand pressed to her lips, she pointed to the sign he'd spent hours ever so carefully painting. "I never thought . . ."

"Go inside."

Bouncing in place on the red granite stoop, she drew a deep breath and opened the door. He reached past her and flipped on the lights only to hear her gasp as she took in the interior. Knowing it was smaller than her plans, he quickly assured her, "Once ye've a few patrons, we can knock an arch in yon wall and build the new room so all will appear just as it does in yer renderings."

He'd been alarmed learning how expensive construction was in this time. Had he not been able to barter brawn for those services he had no talent for . . .

"I love it."

"Are ye sure, lass?" Tears were streaming down her cheeks at a hellish rate as she walked about the room, her hand sliding over the fabrics, her work counter and then the colourful spools Bridget had insisted he mount on walls pegs. She stopped before her desk.

"You bought a computer?"

"Aye, Mickey said ye would need such and Bridget said we should get the silver," He shrugged. "The man said ye need go back to his shop and get yer special drawing . . . uhmm?"

"Programming?"

"Aye, that's what he said, and in the drawer ye'll find something else." He forgot what Mickey had called it.

She opened the drawer. "Oh! A cellphone."

He nodded. "And all is working here and in the croft." He'd been disgusted to learn A.J. had been slack about paying his debts but all had been set to rights thanks in great part to Bridget getting testy with those involved.

Shaking her head, Maggie whispered, "I just can't believe you did all this . . . for me."

"I did have a bit of help and auld John gifted ye with the splendid lamp."

She wrapped her arms about his neck. "I don't know how to

thank you for making this dream come true. I love it, but how could you afford it?"

Greatly relieved she appeared most pleased despite the shop falling short of her designs, he stroked her back. "That will take some time to explain."

Taking her by the hand, he didn't stop walking until they came to the old castle ruins where he led her to a grass knoll. "Please sit."

Shaking, as much from anxiety as from the shock of his gift, she sat. He settled behind her, his legs and arms wrapping about her. Taking her hands in his, he whispered, "I love ye beyond reason, woman, have for a long time, so please keep that in mind as I tell ye what ye'll doubtless find alarming."

Oh dear God, he's had an affair. Had guilt been the driving force behind him building the shop? Or has he got us so far in debt that he's now scared?

She held her breath, readied for the blow as he said, "Ye may have noticed that on occasion I have little or no knowledge of things I should . . . such as why I should not eat lobster."

Tell me about it. "I have noticed."

"There is a good reason. You see . . . I am not Alistair Jerome – A.J. as you call him – but am Alexander James MacKinnon, born on Beltane morn' in the year of our Lord 1490, in this very place. For reasons I have yet to fathom, my soul has remained with the MacKinnon ring until that night A.J. drove off the bridge. As his soul took flight my soul entered his lifeless form."

"*What?*" She tried to rise but he held her fast.

"Shhh, lass. Just hear me out and then I shall let ye go."

Oh God, he has lost his mind.

"I know not why. I just know that it did and I am now again alive and breathing." He heaved a sigh. "Did you know the keep at our backs was once four storeys tall? Aye, and 'twas on its upper most level, in the solar, that my son was born and my wife died."

"You were married."

"Aye, to the MacDonalds' youngest daughter, Mhairie Elizabeth. Ours was naught but a marriage to ensure the peace betwixt our clans but she proved a brave lass. As she lay dying, the childbed fever all but setting her flesh afire, she said her only regret," his voice cracked, "was that she would not see our bonny son grow."

Maggie craned her neck and found shimmering tears trapped behind his thick black lashes. My God, he believes every word he's saying. And only Mhairie's death had been recorded. Not how she died.

He smiled down at her. "My son was christened Ian John MacKinnon after his grandfathers. I was so proud. He was so perfect. Not long after, however, I was killed—"

"I know. I've heard this story a dozen times."

"Hmm, I imagine you have, but none know what I'm about to tell ye. I felt no pain – only surprise – when the blade ran through me. I did, though, feel the boot on my ass as my assailant pulled his sword free, and that, I assure you, I did feel.

"As I tumbled to the earth, my life's blood spilling on yon mountain, I twisted and saw not my enemy as I fully expected, but the satisfied countenance of my younger brother. Angus."

"Your *brother*?" The records said that Alexander had died in a battle with the Campbells, and that Angus then became the liege lord. They said nothing about murder.

"Aye. Such hate, such loathing filled me . . ."

She listened, half mesmerized, half mute with horror.

"So centuries came and went and slowly my fury ebbed but what did remain of *me* still sensed and felt, celebrated and wept – albeit erratically – until I awoke in A.J."

His arms had relaxed their hold on her and she was able to rotate and, kneeling, face him. "A.J.—"

"Alex. Please call me Alex."

"Alright." She had to placate him until she could get him help. "Alex . . ." God, that sounded strange, "I know you believe this, but I'm having a little difficulty doing so."

He nodded. "I have no doubt that ye do. Worse, I fear 'twas I – and not A.J. – that wooed and won ye. There, at the foot of those mountains, I saw ye through his eyes and became enchanted. Had I not done so, he – obsessed as he was with the legacy – might not have thought to pursue ye, and ye, my love, would not have suffered his wrath. Ye would have . . . should have had a better life."

"That's not tr—"

He pressed a finger to her lips. "Nay, ye feared him and well ye should have." He brushed a lock from her eyes. "I was there, lass. I saw. I heard. But all I could do to cease his madness was unbalance him, make him fall." He cleared his throat. "And because I could sense *only* his exaltations and rages, I know naught of what else went on betwixt ye." He leaned forwards and kissed her brow. "What other dreams do ye harbour, lass?"

The tears she'd been fighting fell. How strange. He had to go insane before even thinking to ask. How sad is that? But since he did ask, she said, "I had dreams of some day having a family."

"Gentle and loving as ye are, I think ye should." He held out his hands. "Look, lass."

The ring. Oh. My. God. "You're not wearing the ring." He never took it off. Ever. Wouldn't wear a wedding band because the *ring* held that place of honour.

He nodded and pulled her to his chest. Resting his chin on top of her head, he silently stared across the Inner Sound as she, listening to the steady thud of his heart, tried desperately to sort out all he had said.

"Some day I would verra much like to hear another son call me Da, Maggie. But I will not suffer that child going through what others of my line have. Some day I will die again and dare not trust that history won't repeat itself. I sold the ring, Maggie. Went to Portree thinking to have it melted down for money to build yer shop, but the goldsmith took one look and took me across to Oban, where he introduced me to a man who studied what he called Mid-evil history." He made a derisive sound at the back of his throat. "A more suitable name I cannot imagine.

"He bought the ring, Maggie, and paid handsomely for it. So 'tis safely gone."

She looked up, not knowing what expression she might find on his face, and found him smiling at her in that intense and special way he had when they'd first courted. Her heart nearly broke.

And she knew. Every word he had spoken was true.

The man she'd fallen in love with and who now held her was . . . the MacKinnon.

Four

"Come on, Da, just one more!"

Maggie glanced at the kitchen clock and shook her head. Her sons had their father wrapped about their little fingers. Knowing he would acquiesce, she tiptoed to their room, peeked in and found the lads piled like puppies on Alex.

As she grinned, he murmured, "Alright, but only *one* more else Mama will have my hide." He picked up another storybook and the children put up a howl.

"Not that one, Da," Robbie, four years, and the spitting image of his father, whined. "We want to hear the story of the MacKinnon."

"Yes, tell us again about the MacKinnon," chimed five-year-old Collin, "and this time don't forget the part about the dragon."

Her husband, fighting a grin, heaved a huge sigh. "As ye lust."

Giggling, the lads scrambled and settled to either side of him. As Alex wrapped an arm about each, they looked up with such adoration, her heart nearly burst.

"Once upon a time," Alex began, "there lived a great liege lord named—"

"The MacKinnon!" they both chorused.

"Aye, and in his veins ran the blood of—"

"Alpin, king of the Picts," Collin cried.

Alex nodded, "And father of—"

"Cinead mac Alipin, king of Scotland!" Robbie added, not to be outdone by his precocious sibling.

"Right and let's not forget Bebe—"

"King of Norway," they shouted in unison.

"Aye, and his best friend was—"

"King Arthur!"

Alex looked from one to the other. "Who's telling this story, ye or me?" He huffed in proper dragon fashion sending the lads into giggling fits. "As I was saying, the MacKinnon and King Arthur loved the same fair lass, who was known to control the fiercest dragons in the land. Her name was Mary Magdalene."

"That's Mama!" giggled Collin. "They loved Lady Guinevere, Da."

"Oh, that's right, 'twas Lady Guinevere. So, both finding the lady most fair and fulsome and both wanting control over her fire-breathing dragons for their own purposes, they decided the best way to choose who should wed her was to fight to the *death*."

Maggie rolled her eyes. It was easy to see how Alex had become the most popular tour guide at the Tourist Centre. That he looked divine in a kilt while armed to the teeth probably didn't hurt either.

"With their broadswords," said Robbie, swinging his imaginary sword in a broad arc.

"Aye, but Lady Guinevere, being much wiser, said to the battling kings, 'Nay, the man who can ride my favourite and most fierce dragon shall have my hand and no other.' And so . . ."

Grinning, Maggie tiptoed back to the kitchen.

The Mackinnon's handsome heirs would learn more of their clan's history through silly tales and lore as they grew but, true to his word, Alex would hold secret their legacy.

And she now had a secret of her own to share once the lads were asleep. In this morning's post she'd found a letter she'd only dreamed of receiving. One from London, bearing the royal crest. Skye High Designs was now the proud – oh so proud – holder of a Royal Warrant of Appointment.

Long live the man who had made her dreams come true.

Long live . . . Her MacKinnon.

The Reiver

Jackie Barbosa

Lochmorton Castle, West March, 1595

Duncan Maxwell grabbed one of the pitch torches from its sconce
on the dungeon wall, and ducked to avoid hitting his head on the
lintel, as he entered the small, dark cell. The reiver his men had
captured in the wee hours of the morning huddled in the far corner.
The figure neither looked up to see who had entered nor flinched
at the sound of the heavy wooden door thudding shut. Duncan
knew that his presence had been registered, however, for the young-
ster's spine stiffened and his respiration increased.

"Well, reiver, what have you to say for yourself?"

The boy didn't move.

Duncan sighed. So that was the way it was going to be. He didn't
relish the notion of threatening a child, but he would do what he
must to find out who was responsible for the recent raids on his
territory resulting in the loss of a dozen cattle and twice that many
sheep. His men were getting restless and angry and would soon
begin to take out their frustrations in raids of their own.

He strode over to the lad and grabbed him by the collar, pulling
him up with one hand until the boy's feet dangled several inches
from the floor. It was far easier than it ought to have been, even for
a man of Duncan's unusual height and strength. He grimaced,
wondering when the child had last eaten, for he weighed little more
than a wet cat.

Notwithstanding his sympathy for the boy's plight, Duncan gave
him a none-too-gentle shake. "Answer me, lad, or you ken I'll have
no choice but to hang you on the morrow."

Still, the boy ignored him. Duncan had to give him credit – he was brave and loyal, if not bright.

"Come on, boy, you can't be more than fourteen. Do you want to die before you've even swived your first wench?"

That brought the boy's head up. In the light of the torch, his eyes glittered black with malice. He drew back his head and spat in Duncan's face.

Under any other circumstances, such an action would have brought a swift and violent reaction. But, at the precise moment the spittle hit his chin, Duncan realized his mistake. His gaunt-faced, dirty-cheeked prisoner was no lad, but a girl.

He was so startled by the revelation that he nearly dropped her. Christ in heaven, what manner of raiding party would permit a *girl* to ride with them? Bad enough to think they'd impress a child, but a female? The very idea bespoke an unthinkable brand of madness and desperation.

Filled with remorse at having treated her so roughly, he set her gently on her feet, half-fearing she'd crumple back to the floor in a heap. To his relief, she held her ground, staring up at him defiantly with wide, thick-lashed eyes that might be either dark brown or deep blue. Although her cheek and jaw bones were far too prominent, no doubt a consequence of poor nutrition, her heart-shaped face and bowed lips were unmistakably feminine. His men must have been blind to mistake her for a boy.

But then, to be fair, they had come upon the raiders at night and had brought her directly back to the dungeon, which was hardly well-lit. The possibility that their captive might be female would never have crossed their minds, as it hadn't his until he'd got a good look at her face. If she had kept her head down, he might not have recognized the truth, either. Christ, he might have kept her in the dungeon for weeks on end without ever realizing what a treasure he had been handed.

For however mad and desperate her clan must be to bring her along on a raid, they would be ever madder and more desperate to ransom her back. And he would gladly stretch the necks of the men responsible for reiving his livestock in payment for her safe return.

"Let's begin again, shall we? I am Duncan Maxwell, laird of Lochmorton Castle, and you are . . .?"

Silence.

He tried another tack. "I'm sure your family is very concerned for your safety. Would you not like to get word to them that you're well and in no danger?"

More silence. She had the fortitude of a stone, he had to give her that.

But then something happened which betrayed her. A long, low gurgle issued from the region of her belly.

"Your first name, then, in exchange for your breakfast."

At that, he could almost see her salivate. She was terribly hungry, almost starved. Duncan wished he didn't have to use her privation against her, but this was no time for an attack of conscience. Especially when *she* was the thief, and he was not responsible for her condition.

She raised her head and thrust her chin out. "You already have my name, Duncan Maxwell, laird of Lochmorton Castle."

His brow furrowed. He most surely did not know her name.

"You said it when you first came in," she clarified.

Duncan thought back. What had he said when he'd entered the cell? *Well, reiver, what have you to say for yourself?* Cheeky, that's what she was.

"Reiver is not your name, and we both know it."

"Aye, well, it's the only one you're going to get," she said with a shrug. The gesture drew attention to the thin, pitiful shoulders beneath the oversized linen shirt she wore. He found his gaze drawn lower, involuntarily seeking the outline of her breasts. She must have bound them, he decided. Either that or she was exceptionally small-bosomed.

For some peculiar reason, the image of breasts so tiny he could encompass their entirety in his mouth flashed through his brain, bringing with it an immediate flare of lust.

Duncan shook himself, puzzled by his response. Small breasts did not appeal to him. He preferred his women full and curvaceous . . . not to mention welcoming. Odd that his body didn't seem to agree with this assessment. Even filthy and scrawny as she was, he couldn't dismiss his awareness that she was young and female and utterly in his power.

If he chose to take her to his bed, no one would say him nay. No one but her, and her only defences – an excess of bravado and a sharp tongue – would be easy enough to overcome. Duncan wasn't a vain man, but he was well aware of his effect on females of the species, and he doubted this slip of a woman would be any exception. And once she'd sweetened up under his assault, she'd likely tell him not only her name, but anything and everything else he wanted to know.

The scheme built itself before he was even fully aware he had conceived it. She was cold, hungry, and alone. Her clansmen had turned tail and deserted her, undoubtedly believing she would swing by morning for their collective crime. Any person subjected to the kind of privation she'd obviously suffered would likely be more easily seduced by kindness than by cruelty. You caught more fish by baiting hooks than throwing rocks, after all.

He smiled, benign and beneficent in his newfound, if devious, magnanimity. "Very well, Reiver, you've admitted what you are if not whom. For now, I think that's sufficient for breakfast and an improvement in your accommodation."

True to her brothers' descriptions, the Maxwell of Lochmorton was huge and forbidding, a veritable beast in a tartan. Although for a beast, she had to admit he had remarkably comely features, despite the telltale scar – the Lockerbie lick – that slashed across one cheek. The warm glow of the torch flickered across the rugged terrain of his face, dominated by a prominent brow ridge and a long, hawkish nose that had obviously been broken more than once. But when he smiled . . . it was as if the clouds had parted to admit the sun, flooding the hard landscape in bright, beautiful light.

Surely it was only hunger that made her sway precariously towards him. She hadn't eaten a proper meal in three days.

He probably thought she was weak because she was female. That if he plied her with food and drink and a warm, soft bed, she would betray her family. He could not be more wrong.

Even so, she would bide her time and play his game, pretending to be the noble hostage. But there would be no ransom. A rescue was equally out of the question. Eventually, he would realize the truth and hang her for a thief. No Scottish border laird could afford to allow a reiver to go unpunished, even a female one.

In the meantime, however, it would be good to be well-fed, dry and comfortable, especially at the laird of Lochmorton's expense.

But she would give him nothing. He was a Maxwell. Her mortal enemy. And that she would never forget. Or forgive.

Duncan always knew when Reva – as he had taken to calling her – entered the room he was in. In the two months since she'd become his "honoured guest", he had come no closer to determining her real first name or her identity, but his nerves had become intimately acquainted with every nuance of her bearing. He recognized instantly the weight and rhythm of her footfalls, the cadence of her breath, the citrusy scent that was uniquely hers.

Despite the low, buzzing din in the castle's main hall, each and every harbinger of her arrival registered on him in ripples of aware-ness, like pebbles cast into a still, blue lake. It came as no surprise to him at all, therefore, when she set her trencher of blood sausage and bread in the centre of the long table and sat down to eat. As always, she studiously ignored his presence, bending her head over her food so that her auburn curls partially shielded her face from his view. Fortunately, her hair, which had been cropped in defer-ence to her masquerade as a boy, was still too short to hide much, and so Duncan could still make out the elegant slope of her nose and the stubborn point of her chin.

As he watched her tear off a hunk of the bread and wrap it around the sausage, he pondered what name to give her today.

It was a game he had devised since her second day at Lochmorton. At each meal, he greeted her with a different name, hoping she might betray by some small reaction her true first name. She had, of course, never so much as flinched as he worked his way through all of the more common women's names, both Scottish and English, and a few much more uncommon ones as well. At this point, he was fairly well out of likely options, but he wasn't about to give up the game.

When she opened her small, bow-shaped mouth wide to encom-pass the makeshift sausage roll, which bore an undeniable resemblance to a phallus, Duncan went soft and hard all in the same moment. Of course, she immediately spoiled the effect by sinking her teeth into the sausage and tearing a large bite from it, but the sheer bliss that suffused her features as she chewed was equally, if not more, erotic. Christ, he wanted to see that look on her face when she was naked and spread out beneath him. He wanted that look to be for *him*.

His body's response was an absolute puzzle to him. In any other circumstance, he would likely not have given her a second glance. Although six weeks of proper meals had eliminated the emaciated, hunted look she'd had that first morning and filled out some of her curves, she had *not* been binding her breasts as he had suspected. The dark green gown she wore – a cast-off from his sister, Alys – fit well enough from top to bottom and across the shoulders, but gaped at the chest despite obvious attempts at alteration.

Duncan found himself trying to catch a peek down the bodice as she bent over her trencher. He cursed himself. Even when he couldn't think of a single reason to be attracted to her, he couldn't stop thinking about bedding her. It was perverse. She was nothing he thought he wanted in a woman . . . and everything he desired.

And that gave him this morning's name.

"Good morrow, Venus."

He expected the same response he always got, which was, of course, none. So he was surprised when she raised her chin with a jerk and fixed him with a blistering stare. A casual observer might have called her eyes brown or perhaps hazel but, to Duncan, her eyes were the colour of the moors – a dark, mossy green flecked with rich brown and bright gold – and like the moors, they could appear at one moment soft and inviting, at another fierce and forbidding.

At the moment, their mood was definitely the latter. "It is one thing to attempt to make me betray myself, but quite another to openly mock me, sir."

Duncan's eyebrows went up. "Whatever makes you think I'm mocking you?"

"I have looked in a mirror on more than one occasion," she said with a snort, "and I am well aware I am no man's ideal of feminine beauty."

"Perhaps you have spent your life in the company of the wrong men."

"And if you think you will trick me into revealing who those men are with such a transparent attempt at flattery, you are bound for disappointment."

Duncan blinked. Of course, he hadn't been thinking that at all, but he *should* have been. After two months of good food and a warm bed, she ought to be softening by now. Any other woman would have cracked, he was sure. Yet, if anything, his reiver seemed to be digging her heels in even more. It was almost as if she *wanted* him to execute her.

Christ, what sort of a monster did she take him for?

The sort who plans to execute her loved ones if she reveals their identity, his conscience pointed out.

But that was the way of the border. Reivers must be brought to account. She knew it as well as he did, which was no doubt why she guarded her secrets the way a vestal virgin guarded her virtue.

She didn't trust him, and she shouldn't. But he wished, with a heavy ache in his chest, that it were otherwise.

There was no denying it: Lochmorton Castle was a happy place. Everyone had enough to eat, warm clothes, and a solid roof over their heads. Children frolicked in the courtyard when the weather was good and in the hall when it was not. The clansfolk went about their daily tasks with great cheer, unconcerned about what the morrow would bring.

And it was all because of *him*. The Maxwell.

They could do nothing but sing his praises. Since he had become chieftain two years ago upon his father's untimely death at Dryfe Sands, the clan's fortunes had been utterly transformed. The livestock were plentiful, the crops meticulously tended, the larders well-stocked. His people felt safe and secure. No one dared to threaten Duncan Maxwell openly, and though the occasional raid could not be prevented – *begging your pardon for mentioning it, miss* – they had never in memory been so prosperous or content.

The worst part of it was that their contentment was contagious. She had expected to be treated with disdain, or even contempt. Instead, she had received nothing but kindness. When the women had discovered that she could not sew, and so could not alter the gowns they thoughtfully provided her, they did not deride her, but rather offered to teach her if she was willing to learn.

After a lifetime of being told that the Maxwells were the root of all evil, it was disorienting, and she had slowly found herself admiring Duncan Maxwell in spite of herself. He was everything a clan chieftain should be – wise, strong, dependable and honest. In short, everything her uncle was not.

As her hatred had seeped out of her over the course of the past few weeks, it was replaced with something even more difficult to bear: the hopeless, soul-deep longing that he could be hers.

Which was why, when he had called her Venus this morning at breakfast, she had reacted so sharply and uncharacteristically. She wanted more than anything for him to find her beautiful and desirable, but she knew such a wish was as foolish as it was impossible. Yet, when he'd looked at her with his sharp blue eyes and told her she must have spent her life in the company of the wrong men, her throat had thickened with the realization that it was true. Her family was nothing *but* wrong men, although perhaps not in precisely the way Duncan Maxwell implied.

Still, she could not betray them. They were her flesh and blood.

One thing was clear, however. If she stayed here at Lochmorton much longer, the Maxwell clan would become more of a family to her than her flesh and blood had ever been and pleasing Duncan Maxwell more important to her than a lifetime of loyalties.

She had to do something drastic. And soon.

When Reva didn't appear at mealtime for the third morning in a row, Duncan went looking for her. Although she'd lost her gaunt, emaciated appearance, she was still too thin to stop eating. If she was fasting in the hopes he'd feel guilty and release her, she needed to be disabused of that notion immediately. And if she was ill – God forbid – he would see to her care.

He did not find her in her chamber, which came as something of a relief, for if she could exercise her freedom to roam the castle at will, she could not be sick – or at least not terribly so. After fruitless searches of several common rooms, he located her at last on the upper floor of the tower.

She stood in front of a tall, narrow window to the left of the stairs, her forehead pressed against the glass as she surveyed the harsh landscape that spread out below. The sky was overcast, and so the light filtering in through the wavy glass illuminated her profile in a cool, silvery glow.

"I do hope you are not planning to jump," he said, hoping to inject a bit of levity.

At the sound of his voice, she turned to look at him. Her expression was so bleak, Duncan's heart wrenched as if it were trying to twist its way out of his chest. For a few seconds, he was terrified that she really would go so far as to throw herself to her death just to escape him. Was he really that horrible a beast for doing what any other sensible landowner would do in his position?

A wry smile flitted across her lips. "I suppose if I did, it would rather severely damage my value as a hostage."

Her words cut him to the quick.

"Do you really believe that is the only reason your death would pain me?"

She shrugged. "What other reason could there be?"

He shouldn't have been surprised. He shouldn't have been insulted. But he was. Umbrage collided with pent-up lust and frustration. With three strides, he devoured the broad expanse of floor separating them, grabbed her upper arms, and yanked her against his chest.

"What other reason? How about this?" he growled before crushing his mouth to hers in a fierce, hungry kiss.

To his surprise, she didn't try to pull away or resist, but instead parted her lips to accept the demanding thrust of his tongue. And then she went further, answering his strokes with small feints and parries of her own. He groaned and framed her face with his hands, angling her head to ensure the best possible access to the buttersweet territory of her mouth. She wound her arms around his neck in response, answering him measure for measure. And he found himself grinding his rising erection against the slight swell of her belly.

She nestled against him like a tiny, delicate bird. The difference in their size and strength should have alarmed him. He had the power to crush her without even trying, and yet, he didn't for a second fear the possibility, for like the heather she might appear small and lovely and fragile, but she was strong and enduring and utterly suited to this world, a product of its harsh, unforgiving landscape.

And this kiss – this dark, needful, ardent kiss – felt like the first truly honest interaction they'd ever had. For once, she wasn't ignoring or evading or resisting his questions, but telling him, with her lips and her tongue and her ragged breathing, exactly what she was thinking and feeling. Things like *please* and *don't stop* and most of all – *more*. And damned if he wasn't thinking and feeling the same things. He might well have borne her to the cold, hard stone floor and taken her right then and there had not the flavour of salt interrupted his enjoyment of the moment.

He paused. It tasted like . . . tears.

She was weeping. Silently, even as she continued to kiss him without reservation, tears streamed from her eyes and mingled with the sweet, tangy taste of her mouth.

He broke the kiss and raised his head. Her eyes were glazed – both with passion and with misery. Christ, what was he doing to her? Perhaps he was capable of crushing her, after all. "Please do not cry. I do not want to hurt you."

"Then let me go," she whispered.

"You know I cannot do that." Although now he wasn't sure why he couldn't. Was it because he had to punish the raiders for challenging his authority and stealing his clan's property? Or just because he wanted to keep her for his own selfish and impure reasons? He wasn't even sure which notion he hated the least. But he knew one thing for certain: releasing her was not an option.

She turned her head and gazed out the window again. "Perhaps I should have jumped."

Panic gripped his chest. "Do not say that. You would not."

"Nay, you're right. I would not. I'm far too great a coward." She swiped at her eyes and gave him a watery smile. "And perhaps a wee bit melodramatic. I'm no' accustomed to being cooped up indoors for such long periods of time, you see."

"You've spent a great deal of time outside, then?" he asked, hoping not to sound as if he was prying, although of course he was. The more he knew about her, the greater the likelihood he could find out who she really was. His men had canvassed the countryside in search of anyone who might know of a young woman who'd gone missing, but so far, they'd had no luck. Perhaps they'd just been looking in the wrong places.

And if they look in the right places and find her family, what will you do then? Are you sure you want to know?

He shook off the unpleasant questions.

"Oh, nearly all of my life," she was saying, her face animating with pleasant memories. "We didn't have much of a place to be inside, you ken. Certainly nothing so grand as this."

So, they'd been poor, living, most likely, in a small, sod-roofed cottage on some godforsaken corner of some wealthy laird's estate. They'd had the resources for good, strong horses and decent firearms, of course, but those were the tools of the trade, every bit as much a necessity for a reiver as a plough and seed for a farmer.

And if they'd had horses . . .

"Would you like to go for a ride?"

She gave him a shocked look, and he thought perhaps she'd recognized the double entendre, which was perfectly understandable given that he'd been on the verge of riding her good and hard just moments ago. He jerked his head in the direction of the window. "Out there," he clarified. "On horseback."

Her eyes widened and there was no mistaking the joy that sparkled in their moor-coloured depths. "Really? You would give me a horse and allow me to ride? Aren't you afraid I will try to escape?"

"Aye, that is a problem," he admitted, as much to himself as to her. But if she did try to escape, she wouldn't get far. He would determine which of his horses she rode, and he would choose the sorriest, slowest nag in his stable to ensure she'd not outrun him. Not that he had any horse that could outrun his Curaidh. But still, he would prefer she made him a promise. "Will you give me your word that you will not try to escape? In exchange for a few hours outside these walls."

Her teeth worried her lower lip for a minute, but then she nodded. "Aye, I give you my word I will not try to escape."

"Then I am not worried. Be ready tomorrow an hour after breakfast." He started for the stairwell, then checked his step and looked over his shoulder at her. She looked soft and thoroughly kissed and he ached to return and finish what he'd started, but now that he had a plan for ferreting out the truth, he must execute it. "And Reva?"

"Aye?"

"You will come down to breakfast tomorrow morning. If you do not eat, I cannot in good conscience allow you to ride."

She bowed her head, the very picture of meek subservience. "Aye, sir."

He should have known right then that he was in trouble.

Duncan had never seen a man, let alone a woman, who appeared more at home on a horse than Reva.

True to his plan, he had instructed his stablehand to saddle the oldest, tiredest nag in his stable. This didn't mean the roan mare was a poor or useless mount, of course; no one in the West March could afford to keep horses that weren't up to the demands of border life. Still, Ruadh was a bit past her prime and, having foaled several months ago, should have been nowhere near capable of matching Curaidh for speed or stamina.

And yet, with Reva on her back, Ruadh showed no signs of flagging spirits or energy. If anything, the horse seemed as enthusiastic and joyful at the opportunity to be out on the moors as her rider. Together, they moved effortlessly over the rough, uneven terrain, horse and rider flowing together as one.

"Race you to that outcropping," Reva challenged, pointing to a rock formation several hundred yards distant.

Her face was so full of life, so different from the bleak, hopeless expression of yesterday, that Duncan couldn't resist. What harm could come of it? If it made her happy, if it endeared him to her even a little, it could only help his cause. Perhaps he'd even let her win.

He grinned at her. "You're on!"

Reva, being Reva, didn't wait for a starter's mark. She kneed Ruadh's flanks and leaned over the mare's neck. The animal surged forward without so much as a half-second's hesitation. By the time Duncan spurred Curaidh into action, Reva held a lead of almost a hundred yards.

There would be no question of *letting* her win now. He would be fortunate if she didn't beat him outright, at least over this short distance.

He bent low and murmured Gaelic encouragements in his mount's ear. The musket he'd slung over his shoulder in the event of an attack slapped hard against his back with each thundering beat of Curaidh's hooves.

They were making up ground, but not quickly enough to overtake her before the finish line. She reached the outcropping just strides before he did, her laughter ringing out like chimes as she pulled the mare to a halt.

"I win," she said, her features glowing with triumph.

"You cheated," he pointed out, referring to the head start she'd taken. Curaidh's flanks heaved beneath him. By contrast, her horse barely looked winded.

"Aye, but you kenned I don't play fair already."

"Fair enough." He shook his head as he gave his horse a soothing pat. "How on earth did my men catch you when you can ride like that? I'm sure the horse you had that night was in much better condition than Ruadh here."

She shrugged. "They were supposed to catch me," she said.

"What do you mean, they were supposed to catch you?" His mind raced with possibilities. Was she a spy? An assassin? Neither seemed remotely likely, and yet . . .

"If we were ever interrupted during a raid, it was my job to create a distraction and allow the rest to escape, even if it meant my capture. The assumption was that since I was female, no one would actually execute me for the raid and I'd soon be set free." She smiled winningly at him, as if to give him the opportunity to remedy his failure to behave according to expectation.

"You mean you'd done this before?" He was horrified. Damn it, she could have been killed any number of times before she'd crossed his path. He might even have hanged her himself without realizing . . . His stomach turned.

"Ride with my family on raids? Oh aye, all the time."

"Christ, Reva . . ." He closed his eyes. "But then . . . why didn't you tell me straight away that night that you were a woman?"

Her mouth drew into a straight, tight line. "I wanted you to execute me."

"What! In the name of God, why?"

"You're a Maxwell. I knew you wouldn't let me go. I knew you'd try to get me to betray my family. I thought death would be easier to bear than that." She drew a ragged breath. "Than this."

"Than what?" She looked up at him, her eyes filling with tears.

"Falling in love with you."

He couldn't think of a single thing she could have said in that moment that would have surprised – or thrilled – him more. His heart threatened to burst through his rib cage.

She loved him. As God was his witness, nothing mattered but that. He didn't care who she was, where she had come from, or what she had done. As long as she loved him, everything could be made right.

"Loving me is not so terrible as all that, is it?"

She shook her head. "Perhaps not. But I did not want to. And now that I do . . . I do not know what to do."

Duncan smiled gently. "Then you've no choice but to follow my lead."

She nodded, her smile watery in return. "Aye."

"Come with me," he said, turning Curaidh away from the outcropping. "I know exactly what to do."

He led her to one of the many small cottages that dotted Lochmorton's landscape. Most would be occupied come planting time, but now it was after the harvest and most of his people had moved inside the castle walls in preparation for winter.

After helping her dismount, he brought her inside. She looked uncertainly around the small, sparsely furnished room. There was a fireplace, a few wooden chairs, and a bed.

"Why did you bring me here?"

Duncan caressed her cheek with one thumb. "To make you my wife."

"Surely you cannot mean to marry me," she gasped.

"I can and I do. I love you in return, Reva, and I shall settle for nothing less than making an honest woman of you."

"'Tis a little late now," she teased. She eyed the room even more dubiously than before. "But surely you should have brought me to a priest if that was your intent."

He chuckled. "And so I shall . . . but I have been more priestly myself than I would like these past months. With your permission, I would like to remedy that now."

"You mean . . . ?" She glanced to the bed and back to him.

"Aye," he said, drawing her into his embrace, "I wish to make love to you. If you will permit me, of course." His voice was rougher – and more pleading – than he would have liked.

"That doesna sound like the proper way to make either an honest woman or a wife of me," she observed, but the barest hint of a smile teased the corners of her lips as she said it.

He pressed his lips against her forehead. "No, but it is the only way to make a sane man of me. Knowing you love me, I cannot bear another minute of this torture."

"Torture?"

"Aye, lass, you've had me tied in knots since that moment in my dungeon that I realized you were no lad. If you will not have me now, I do not know if I will make it whole to the wedding." He moved his mouth to her temple and was pleased by her shiver of response.

She pulled away slightly and tilted her head to one side, her eyes sparkling with mischief. "My brothers always told me not to listen to a man when he claimed he'd sustain an injury if he did not have me in his bed. They say 'twas a ploy, that no harm ever came of waiting."

He laughed and slid his hands from where they rested at the small of her back to cup her buttocks. She had worn breeches for their ride, and being treated to the sight of the rounded curve of her backside had been tempting him all day. "I never said my harm would be physical. 'Twill be entirely mental."

She made thoughtful, scrunched-up faces as though considering this claim while he kneaded the firm muscles with his hands. Perhaps he wasn't as fond of large breasts as he'd once believed. A generous set of hindquarters more than made up for any lack.

"Ah, well," she sighed at last, "I suppose a mad Maxwell will do me no good as a husband. Very well, Duncan Maxwell of Lochmorton. You may make love to me."

With a groan of relief, he lifted her in his arms and carried her to the bed. It was unmade and a bit lumpy, but he hoped she wouldn't notice either discomfort. He knew he wouldn't.

He first removed his plaid, which he had worn over shirt and breeches in deference to the autumn chill, and spread it out atop the bare mattress. When he was finished, he set about undressing her. She blushed when he removed her shirt and covered her breasts with her hands, but he pushed them away with a gentle shake of his head.

"Do not be ashamed, *runag*. They are just as I imagined. Small and firm and the perfect size to fit in my mouth."

"In your mouth?" she asked, her eyes wide with puzzlement.

Her innocence was adorable. After such a difficult life, that she should come to him so obviously untouched seemed something of a miracle. That she had come to him at all was miracle enough.

He bent his head and encompassed the entire, lovely rosebud of one breast in his mouth. The salty tang of her skin was in perfect harmony with the lemony scent that clung to her.

"Oh," she sighed in wonderment as he flicked his tongue across the hardening nipple.

"You see. Perfect, just as I said."

The remainder of her garb came off with greater ease and less resistance. As each inch of her was revealed, he found more beauty to explore with his hands and mouth – the velvet-skinned expanse of her belly, the swirl of dark red-tinged curls at the apex of her thighs, the unexpected length of her slender yet muscular thighs and calves.

His own clothes he removed with even greater alacrity, nearly frantic in his need to lie with her, naked skin to naked skin. When he knelt between her thighs and eased his way inside her, he shook with the effort to maintain his control, fearful both of hurting her and of reaching his pleasure before he found hers.

He needn't have worried. She wrapped her arms and legs around him the way she'd wrapped herself around his heart and urged him on. They rocked together as though they had made love like this hundreds of times before, each attuned to the other's rhythms and sensations as both climbed towards the precipice and then tipped over it, in unison, into rapture.

The only thing that marred his pleasure was that, when she cried out his name, he could not call out hers in return.

★   ★   ★

"You shall have to give your name for the wedding ceremony, you know," he observed some time later.

She lifted her head from its cradle in his shoulder and looked down at him, her expression guarded and a little sad. "You know I cannot," she whispered.

"What if I promised not to seek revenge upon your family for the raid?"

Her eyebrows flew up her forehead. "You would do that? For me?"

He stroked her hair. "Aye, lass, I would. In fact, perhaps I should be thanking them."

"Why?"

"Because if they had not tried to reive my cattle that night, I would never have met you."

He pulled her head down towards his and gave her what he meant to be a sweet and reassuring kiss, but the instant their mouths touched, his intent was entirely forgotten. Her lips parted, ardent and inviting, and her tongue darted daringly into his mouth. He groaned as a fresh wave of desire spiralled down through his loins. With no small effort, he broke the kiss and forced his raging need back under control. While he could make love to her a half dozen more times without consequence, the same could not be said for her. She would be sore enough on the ride back to Lochmorton as it was.

As he drew away, she reached up and traced her thumb across the scar that marred his left cheek. "Did it hurt terribly?" she asked.

He recognized that she was changing the subject, but decided to go along with it. "Aye. Like fire."

The memory of that day was as crisp as if it had happened yesterday, and yet as confused and chaotic as the events themselves. His father had insisted that they join their cousin, John, Lord Maxwell, in his campaign against Sir James Johnstone. With decades of enmity between the Maxwells and the Johnstones, there'd been no doubt that the battle would be bloody and ugly.

What both his father and Lord Maxwell had failed to anticipate was the formidable advantage the Johnstones' familiarity with the terrain of Dryfe Sands would give them despite their smaller numbers. Lord John had died in the ambush mere seconds after crossing the river. Duncan's father, along with a sizable portion of the Maxwell, Armstrong, and Douglas clan had followed him to the grave minutes later. Duncan himself had managed to escape with the routed army, but not before receiving the sharp tip of a

Johnstone sword to the cheek. He had sworn on that day never again to enter a battle on territory he didn't know as well as his own newly-altered face. And never to forgive the Johnstones for their perfidy.

But he did not want the hostility those old memories inspired to interrupt the peaceful contentment of the moment, and so he placed his hand over hers and held it against his cheek. "But at least I know now never to trust a Johnstone."

"Aye, that you do," she said softly, resting her head back on the curve of his shoulder. For the time being, he decided to let the issue of her name rest. After a few moments of silence, she stirred in his arms.

"What is the trouble now, *runag*?"

"I need to . . . that is . . ." she stuttered, her cheeks pinkening. "I must go outside and relieve myself," she finished in an embarrassed rush.

Being a gentleman, of course he allowed her to get up and put on her shirt and breeches before heading out into the windy chill of the afternoon. And after what had just passed between them, it didn't occur to him to follow her outside to keep an eye on her. After all, he trusted her.

It was only when he heard the sound of horse's hooves that he realized the truth.

She hadn't needed to relieve herself at all. All along, she had planned to escape.

The border between Maxwell and Johnstone land was in sight. Jamie Johnstone, great-niece of Sir James Johnstone and one of his many namesakes – albeit, as far as she knew, the only female one – was nearly home.

Duncan Maxwell's big black stallion bore her over the rough, rocky terrain with breathtaking speed and ease. Saddled now with the roan mare he'd given her to ride, the laird of Lochmorton would never overtake them before she reached safety. Likely, he would not even try.

Free. She was almost free.

Why, then, did she feel as though her heart was being torn to shreds and pounded into the ground with every beat of the horse's hooves? Her throat was raw and her eyes burned, but still she rode towards the border.

This was for the best. If Duncan discovered the truth of who she was, he would hate her. He had said himself he had learned never to trust a Johnstone. Until that moment, she had held out the smallest sliver of hope that they could be happy, that perhaps he did not share in his family's ingrained hatred towards hers. But that had always been a slim and dangerous hope, for she had known from the beginning that he had been at Dryfe Sands, that he had lost his father there. The Lockerbie lick on his cheek told the tale of his participation in the battle, even if his tongue did not. And how could a man fail to despise the people who had killed his own father?

Her people.

She slowed the horse to a walk after the crossing the border. There was no indication that she was being followed, and although the animal showed no signs of tiring, even a horse as magnificent as Curaidh could not maintain such a breakneck pace indefinitely. It would be difficult to convince her brothers to return a horse as fine as he to the Maxwell stable, but she could not in good conscience keep him.

That alone told her a lot had changed. Once upon a time, she'd had no conscience at all.

Jamie Johnstone's days as a reiver were over.

Squinting in the darkness, Jamie closed the stall door behind Curaidh, wincing at the loud creak of the hinges. She paused for a moment, listening for any hint of a human presence, but heard only the annoyed snorts and curious whickers of horses whose nightly rest had been disturbed.

She took a deep, cleansing breath. It was ridiculous for her to be so on edge. No one would anticipate a reiver breaking into his stables to *return* a horse. A smile tickled her lips as she thought about Duncan's reaction on the morrow, when he discovered his prized steed had been returned – though her brothers, ever the opportunists, had seen to it that the stallion had left a few "deposits" with several of the Johnstone mares in the months before they'd brought him back.

Of course, James and Robbie still thought this entire plan was mad and dangerous. And yet, perhaps because they felt some latent sense of guilt for her months of imprisonment in Maxwell territory – a fate they considered several orders of magnitude worse than death – they had acquiesced to her decision. And now, she was but a few steps from meeting them outside.

Not so mad or dangerous this . . .

"Oof!" Just feet from the door, she came to an abrupt halt against an immovable object that felt remarkably warm and strangely malleable. Rather like a human chest. And a damnably familiar one at that.

Damn and blast!

"So, reiver, we meet again." Duncan's voice was low and gravelly and terribly arousing. He grabbed her wrists and yanked her flush against his body. Her eyes widened. It seemed she wasn't the only one who was aroused. "What did you come to steal this time?"

"You know as well as I that I have not stolen anything from you," she retorted. *Please, let James and Robert have got away.* As long as they were safe, she could bear any indignity at Duncan Maxwell's hands. She reckoned she deserved every one he could dish out after what she'd done.

"On the contrary," he murmured against the top her head, "you've stolen my heart. I was hoping you came to return it."

The raw, unconcealed pain in his voice took her aback.

"I – I—" she stammered. Her heart hammered like a black-smith's mallet against her breastbone. "I came to return Curaidh."

"I know," he said softly, grazing her ear with his lips as he spoke.

Gooseflesh rose on her skin, racing down her arm. She didn't know what to make of this strange situation. It seemed rather more like seduction than detention.

"What do you want?"

"I should think that would be obvious. I want you, Jamie Johnstone."

She gasped, incredulous. "You know my name!"

"Aye, lass."

"But – but how?"

"You did not think I just *let* you escape, did you?"

She stared up at him blankly, a rather fruitless enterprise in light of the darkness. "What choice did you have? You had a slow horse and no clothes on."

"True, and I could not have prevented you from getting away . . . not without shooting you, and though I'll admit I was sorely tempted, I might have missed and shot Curaidh instead. But in any event, 'twas simple enough to track where you'd gone, *runag*. And once I realized you were a Johnstone, it was only a matter of making inquiries of the right people to discover the rest."

Jamie's mind whirled. All these months, he had known who she was, who her family was, and yet he'd made no effort to exact justice for the raid. He could have petitioned the Warden for redress, or even the king, but obviously he had not.

"Since then, I've been waiting for you," he added, brushing her cheek with the back of his hand. "Not entirely patiently."

"What? But – what on earth could have made you believe I would come back?"

He shrugged. "I know you, and I knew you would not steal from me. Not after what we shared."

"But I ran away—"

He pressed his finger to her lips to shush her. "I did not give you much choice, did I? Telling you I'd never trust a Johnstone. That was why you asked about the scar, wasn't it?"

"Aye," she admitted. "I wanted to know if you still hated my family for what happened at Dryfe Sands."

"And I did. Then, and for some time afterwards. And I was furious with you for breaking your promise."

"I didn't promise I would not escape. I promised not to *try* to," she pointed out.

He chuckled. "Aye, I recall now you were very specific when you made the promise. Notwithstanding, I was very angry – and hurt. I considered coming after you, going to the Warden, demanding satisfaction from the king. But in the end, I realized this is the only thing that would ever bring me true satisfaction." His mouth swooped down and captured hers.

Aye, aye, he was right. This was the only thing she wanted, the only thing that truly mattered. She would never want anything else in life if only she could have this – the pepper-sweet taste of his mouth, the warm, solid breadth of his body, and the truths they could only seem to communicate this way.

He lifted his head. "I am ready to declare an end to this branch of the Maxwell-Johnstone feud. What do you say we start a new alliance in its place?"

"I would love that, but what about my brothers? I am not so sure they'll go along."

"My brother, Ewan, is out there right now, negotiating a bride price for you. I think 'tis safe to say they'll find the terms favourable." His voice dropped an octave. "I'd even give them Curaidh in exchange for you."

Joy blazed in her heart. "I love you, Duncan Maxwell."

"As I love you, Reiver of my heart."

Forever Mine

Donna Grant

One

The silence hung heavy and thick in the air. Just like the mist that swirled eerily, almost unnaturally, around the group of men lying in wait for their deadly enemy.

Braden MacAlister knew the time was right. He would attack and kill Niall MacDougall once and for all. Order would be restored to the land again.

And maybe then Braden could plan more than ambushes.

A horse snorted in the distance, the sound carrying in the stillness of the predawn hour. His foe was right on schedule. Braden had waited for this day for two years. He had planned and plotted and planned some more. All had to go perfectly.

His men, all marked outlaws like himself, were fierce Highlanders and vicious, brutal opponents in battle. They would be the ones to set things right. They would be the ones to end the malevolence.

The pass where Niall had to travel was narrow, confining him and his men between two mountains. Most would have gone around but Niall was a man who liked to prove he couldn't be taken.

A slow smile spread Braden's lips. Today, things were going to change.

The soft, four-toned whistle sliced through the early morning air. It was the signal from Keith that Niall neared.

Braden had seen this moment many times in his mind. He'd thought out every possibility. Every move. Every countermove. He was as prepared as he could ever be.

He released a long breath when he caught sight of the first horse as it came around the bend. Behind the guard, Braden spotted Niall's dark head, his hair tied in a neat queue at his neck. And with Niall was his company of twenty men.

Niall never travelled alone. He knew how much he was despised throughout Scotland. Everyone said it was just a matter of time before he was killed.

Another whistle, softer, but in the two-tone that meant trouble. Braden narrowed his gaze on his opponent. What was Niall up to?

And then Braden saw the wagon. The metal bars on the small upper windows told him all he needed to know about the occupants.

Prisoners.

Braden glanced across the road to his men. He waited for their nod of agreement to continue with their mission before he looked to the men beside and behind him.

Niall had taken from all of them in one form or another. Each warrior wanted his revenge, needed retribution for the atrocities. Each man wanted to be the one to strike the killing blow.

Braden tightened his grip on his sword and on the dagger he held in the other hand. The smirk on Niall's all-too-perfect face was too much to bear. But before this day ended, Braden would see that smile erased.

For ever.

Niall jerked his horse to a halt almost directly across from Braden. Niall was tall and blessed with exceptional looks that made women do all sorts of things to gain his attention.

But he had a heart as evil as the devil.

Braden knew Niall couldn't see him in the thick grass and plentiful boulders. Yet, the way Niall's eyes searched the mountainsides, it seemed he was looking for something.

"Come out, come out wherever you are, Braden MacAlister," Niall taunted.

Braden stiffened. There was no way Niall could have discovered his plans. Braden trusted his men explicably. None of them would have betrayed him.

Braden didn't move. His men stayed as motionless as he. Braden didn't have long to wait before Niall lifted a hand to one of the guards near the wagon.

The door at the back of the wagon opened, the squeak was loud but soon drowned out by a startled cry.

"They have women," Rory whispered as he leaned next to Braden.

Braden couldn't see who was taken from the wagon as the guard pushed the prisoner through the throng of horses and men. With a shove, the prisoner stumbled and fell to her knees in a whirl of lavender skirt, her hair as black as midnight.

Niall jumped from his mount and grabbed the woman by the hair. Her hands instantly went to his to try and lessen the pain. She hurried to climb to her feet.

"I would see you now, Braden. Show yourself or I kill the wench," Niall bellowed.

The mist had moved away from Niall and his men, as if it knew the black depths of their hearts and wanted no part of it.

Braden had no choice but to help the woman. Too many innocents had already died. He wouldn't have her death on his soul, wouldn't add the weight of another blameless life to his already considerable burden.

"Be ready," Braden murmured to Rory.

Braden sheathed his sword, but kept his dagger ready in his left hand, the blade tucked against his forearm. He leapt atop the boulder he'd been hiding behind and glared down at the man who dared to call himself a Scot, much less a Highlander.

Jean was on the tip of her toes, trying to keep her hair from being yanked from her scalp. She had known no good would come from Niall MacDougall's visit to her clan. What she hadn't foreseen was him taking women and children as prisoners to force her clansmen to his service.

Niall had at first managed to lure a number of women to his side with his easy smile and handsomeness. But those women had learned quickly enough that a face and body as eye-catching as Niall's couldn't hide his evil for long.

Jean's gaze searched the mountainside as Niall called for Braden MacAlister. Braden's name had been whispered about the land for over a year now. Each time his name was repeated, each time he struck out to kill Niall, belief in him grew. Swelled. Expanded.

Braden was their last hope.

Many called him a ghost because of the way he moved from one place to the next with nary a sound, leaving no trace. Jean had hoped she might get to see the mighty Highlander. But she would have preferred it not to be while the tip of a sword was pressed into the small of her back.

"He will come for you," Niall whispered in her ear. "It's not in him to let an innocent die."

"Unlike you."

It was out of her mouth before she could think better of it. Then again, she had no illusions. Niall planned to kill her no matter what Braden did or didn't do.

He chuckled. "Aye. Not like me."

Jean jerked against his grasp, but his fingers wouldn't loosen their hold of her hair. Tears stung her eyes from the pain, and she bit her tongue to keep from crying out.

Blood filled her mouth, the metallic taste making her gag. She was about to kick Niall when a man suddenly appeared atop a boulder to her left.

He stood like an ancient god of old with mist swirling around him, clinging to his bare chest and legs corded with sinew. Coiled violence emanated from him.

Braden MacAlister wore no shirt, only his kilt of red, green and blue. She drank in the sight of bronze skin over sculpted muscles. His shoulders were wide and thick. His arms hung casually at his side. He stood with his legs apart, his feet encased in boots up to his knees.

But it was the blue paint on his face, neck and chest that robbed her of breath.

He had marked himself, just as the ancient Celts had done so many years ago. Seeing Braden, with his eyes fixed on Niall and his dark, wavy locks falling about his face, proved that he was the ghost whispered about over the tables of Scotland.

"Ah, Braden," Niall said. "I told the wench you wouldna let her die."

Jean knew she needed to get away. It didn't take a warrior to see that a battle was brewing. And she had no desire to be caught in the middle of it.

"Let the woman go."

Braden's demand was softly spoken, but his words were laced with steel.

Niall merely laughed. "For a price."

"Name it."

"Your head."

Jean sucked in a breath. Her life meant nothing, but the freedom of their people meant everything. "Nay," she said.

Braden's gaze shifted to her. Their eyes locked, and she shook her head, praying he didn't give himself over to Niall and his men.

The blade at her back pierced her skin. It was so unexpected that she couldn't hold back her cry.

"Say more, you stupid bitch, and I'll see you skewered on my blade," Niall spat.

A war cry tore from Braden's lips and he launched himself at Niall. Men poured from the mountain, their faces covered in the same blue paint as Braden.

Chaos erupted. Swords were drawn and war cries deafened her ears.

Niall jerked her against him, using her body as a shield. Two of his guards moved to protect him, swords and shields at the ready.

Jean couldn't take her gaze off Braden. It was as if time slowed as he sailed through the air. His deep-set eyes were locked on the guards who blocked him from Niall.

Braden's left arm came up and around. She saw the blade the instant the guard on her right did. The man tried to duck, but Braden was too quick. With lightning speed he sliced the guard's neck.

When Braden landed, he spun and unsheathed his sword in one fluid movement. His weapon was up in time to block the second guard's attack.

The clang of swords, cries of pain – and of death – surrounded Jean. She knew she couldn't sit back and wait to be saved. If she wanted to get away from Niall, she'd have to do it herself.

The fact he had her body pulled against his as a sort of cowardly shield only made her despise him more. The blade poking into her back didn't help things either.

But her father had always said she was resourceful.

Jean made a fist and swung it down and back as hard as she could. She knew she connected with Niall's groin by the way air wheezed from his lungs and the dagger dropped from his hand.

She tried to run, but he still had a handful of her hair though he was bent double now, his face red as spittle fell from his lips. He glared at her, fury and the promise of death in his blue eyes.

"Let go," Jean demanded and she clawed at his handsome face.

The malice she saw in Niall's stare almost gave her pause. Almost. Jean's fingers found his eyes and she felt her nails bend backwards sickeningly. She sank her other fingers into his skin, felt the thick texture of blood as it fell from the cuts she dug.

Niall bellowed and released her to cover his eyes. His nostrils flared with anger, deadly intent in his gaze. Jean prepared herself for death.

"You, bitch! How dare you mark my face," he bellowed.

Just when Niall would have stepped towards her, a horse reared, kicking him with its hooves and sending him spinning backwards. The other horses began to dance around, the scent of blood and shouts from the men spooking them.

Jean backed away, careful not to run into any of the men locked in combat. When she looked to where Niall had fallen, she couldn't find him.

She searched everywhere to no avail. He was gone.

Suddenly, a large hand wrapped around her arm. Jean raised her fist, prepared to strike whoever dared to touch her, only to find herself staring into startling blue eyes framed by thick black lashes.

She looked her fill at Braden's square jaw and high forehead, his aquiline nose, and his wide lips. She liked how his lower lip was fuller than the top. She found herself staring at his mouth as she forgot everything but the man holding her.

"Are you hurt?" Braden asked.

Jean shook her head slowly, struck anew at the presence of Braden MacAlister. Blood coated him, but she didn't know if it was his or that of his opponents.

Braden glanced around. "Where is MacDougall?"

"I . . . I struck him. The horses reared and kicked him, and then he was gone."

"*Shite*. He cannot have gone far."

Jean watched and Braden motioned some of his men to follow as he scouted for Niall's trail. Niall's guards, those who had dared to stand against the great Braden MacAlister, had all been killed, their bodies lying still upon the ground.

She swallowed the bile in her throat and lifted her skirts running towards the wagon and the other prisoners. Jean jerked at the lock, hoping to find it open. Unfortunately, the guards hadn't been as stupid as she'd hoped.

"Damn," she murmured and slammed her hand against the wood.

"Is there a problem?"

Jean whirled around at the deep voice to find one of Braden's men, all meaty shoulders and barrel chest. "I cannot unlock the wagon."

The man smiled, showing even white teeth and a twinkle in his dark brown gaze. "Allow me, lass."

Jean stepped aside. As soon as she was out of the way, the man slammed the hilt of his sword against the lock. It busted open spectacularly and the chain fell away.

Braden's man opened the door for the captives, but no one moved. They were petrified with fear. Jean stood beside the Highlander and smiled, calling into the wagon to the terrified women and children.

"It's all right," she told them and she held out her hand. "You can come out now."

In moments, she was surrounded by the rest of Braden's men, helping her encourage the rest of the women and children out of the wagon. Jean found water skins and hurried to pass those around.

One warrior moved to her side. "Why did MacDougall take all of you?"

"To ensure that my clansmen did as he wanted."

"Foul bastard," the man said with a curl of his lip. "What clan, lass?"

"MacKay. I'm Jean MacKay."

"Well, Jean, lass," he said with a friendly smile. "I'm Keith MacAlister, at your service. I'm thinking Braden will want to escort you and the others back to your clan."

Jean let out a sigh of relief, but before she could thank him, a shout drew their attention. She followed Keith to a circle of men who gathered around one of their fallen brothers on the ground. It took only one look at the gaping wound for Jean to nudge the men aside and decide on a course of action.

"Let me tend him," she said as she knelt beside the warrior. The cut on his leg went clean to the bone. Jean licked her lips and glanced over her shoulder at Keith. "I'm going to need water and bandages. And needle and thread."

Keith let out a deep breath, his eyes troubled. "We have no needle and thread here."

"The wound is too deep. I must stop the bleeding."

"Bind Colin's leg for now," said a deep voice to her right. "We must get moving."

Jean jerked her head around to find Braden watching her. Something was stuffed in her hand. Jean had no choice but to turn her attention back to the wounded man. With Keith's help she was able to bind the wound as tightly as she could. It would staunch the blood, but not for long.

She rose as the others lifted Colin into the wagon. Jean looked at the women and children gathered in a tight circle, then to Braden. Someone needed to go along to tend Colin's wound and she knew she could help.

Jean squared her shoulders and walked to Braden. He paused in his conversation with Keith and another man when he caught sight of her.

She waited until the other two warriors walked away before she spoke to Braden.

"I can help Colin. He's going to need to be stitched."

One side of Braden's lips tilted in a small smile. "We've learned to mend each other's wounds."

"I've no doubt, but Colin's wound is to the bone. A fever will most likely set in. You will need someone to watch him."

"Why would you want to help?"

She understood his suspicion, even if she didn't like it. "You and your men are trying to help all of us. You need every man you have for your continued attacks on Niall. You've already got Colin down and several others wounded. Would you leave yet another fighter behind to watch Colin?"

For long, heart-racing moments Braden stared at her, his striking blue eyes made only brighter by the paint still visible on his face. "If, for even a moment, I think you are spying on us . . ."

"I'm not," she said before he could finish. "I only want to help."

"So be it, Jean MacKay."

Two

Jean wiped her brow with the back of her hand. Her lower back ached from leaning over Colin's prone form and wiping his fevered skin. The dwelling they were in was nothing more than tartans strung together around thick poles. A tent, but a roomy enough one.

She had no idea how long she had been in Braden's camp. He'd covered her eyes to prevent her from seeing the direction they rode. She would never have told anyone where the camp was located, but he hadn't believed her.

Not that she blamed him.

Jean leaned back and arched her spine, her hands at her lower back. She blew out a breath, concern knotting her stomach. Colin hadn't improved since they had arrived.

She'd cleaned and stitched his wound, but the fever had set in much too quickly for her liking. All she could do now was pray he was strong enough to overcome the fever.

"You need to rest."

Jean whirled around at the sound of the voice. She licked her lips and watched the tall, thickly-built Highlander move into the tent and stand beside her.

Keith and Braden were rarely separated – it was obvious Keith was Braden's right hand, the man Braden most depended on.

"You concern should be with your friend," Jean said.

Keith grunted and placed his large hand on Colin's forehead. "It is my concern for him that gives voice to the obvious. You are exhausted. You will do Colin no good if you collapse."

"I would never." Jean rose to her feet and clenched her hands. "I gave my word that I would look after him."

The slow smile that pulled at Keith's lips only increased her irritation. "You've got a temper. Good. It'll keep Braden on his toes."

Jean blinked, unsure she heard him correctly. "What did you say?"

"There's food awaiting, lass. Get some before it's gone. I'll stay with Colin for a wee bit."

Keith quickly occupied the stool beside the cot. Jean took a step back, stunned, before she turned and exited the tent. Once outside, she paused and surveyed the camp. She had known Braden had many followers, but she hadn't realized just how many fought with him.

The number was staggering. The sheer quantity of tents that dotted that hilltop and surrounding valley left her in awe. It would only be a matter of time now before Niall MacDougall was gone forever.

Her stomach growled, and she wasted no time in getting food. She sighed as the last bite slid down her throat. The meal would fortify her. She hadn't realized how weary she had been until that moment.

Jean rose and started back to Colin when she caught sight of a large dwelling near the centre of camp. As someone exited the tent, she spotted Braden within.

Before she knew it, she was standing before his tent. Jean hesitated only a moment before she lifted the tartan and ducked inside.

She let the material fall silently closed behind her as her gaze roamed over the inside of the dwelling.

To the right were two chairs facing each other. Off to the back was the MacAlister tartan spread on the ground for Braden's bed. To the right was a chest. In the middle of the tent was a table where a map was spread out with Braden leaning over it, absorbed in his thoughts.

Gone was the blue paint that had covered his upper body and face and made him appear wild and untamed. Braden now wore a saffron shirt with his kilt. The sleeves were rolled up to his elbows, showing thick black hair on his forearms.

He appeared as any other Highlander, but Jean knew differently. She had seen the warrior he could become, had seen his unquenchable need for vengeance, both for himself and for his people.

She would keep the image of him jumping from the boulder to save her forever in her memory. She had been prepared to die, but Braden hadn't let her.

Suddenly, he lifted his head and looked at her.

Jean folded her hands and tried to calm the heart that now raced inside her chest. Being so near Braden affected her thoughts and her body in a way that had never happened to her before.

It wasn't just the power he wielded. It was more than his determination to right the wrongs done to their people.

It was him – the bold, passionate, handsome man with the long, dark hair and the bright blue eyes – that stole her breath.

She wanted to be near him, not because he had rescued her, but because she wanted to know this man who risked everything for his clan.

"I was about to come see you and Colin. Is he well?"

His voice, smooth and deep, made her skin tingle with awareness. She found herself wondering what it would be like to be his woman, to know the warmth of his lips and his tender touch. To hold him, touch him.

Feel him.

"For the moment," she answered. "A fever has set in."

Braden's jaw clenched as he glanced away. "Are there any herbs I can get for you? Anything that could help him?"

"Only time and prayers can help him right now. I've cleaned the wound, used herbs to speed the healing, and stitched him. There is nothing more."

"Colin is a good man. I wouldna see him die."

Jean gave a small nod of her head. "Then I will leave you to your duties and return to mine. Sorry to have disturbed you."

She had turned and reached for the cloth to exit when his words halted her.

"Thank you."

Jean looked back at Braden and lost herself in his blue eyes. There was something about him, something in the way he held himself, and spoke, and treated others, that made him a natural leader. He was young, but even the older, more experienced Highlanders followed him because they knew this young man was the answer to their prayers.

"It is I should thank you. You've taken a stand against Niall when others wouldn't dare."

Braden had known Jean would disrupt his life the moment he had set eyes on her. She was beautiful, headstrong, and unyielding.

She was exactly the type of woman he would want for himself. If he had time for a woman.

Her long light-brown hair was thick and straight, held away from her oval face in a braid that fell over her shoulder and came to rest beside her breast. She had skin the colour of cream and it was unblemished except for a small mole on the right side of her wide, full lips. Dark brows curved gently over large, expressive tawny eyes. Though she was of average height, she had the bountiful curves he had coveted at first sight. There was no doubt Jean MacKay had snatched his attention from the instant he saw her.

She was a distraction he could ill afford. But one he couldn't do without.

In two strides, Braden was before her. He let the pads of his fingers stroke the barest of touches down her smooth cheek before he dropped his hand.

How long had it been since he'd held a woman? Since he had felt warm flesh, touched silky skin, or kissed soft lips? How long had it been since he'd sunk between a woman's thighs into her hot, wet heat?

The aching need clawing his belly for Jean was enough to warn him to steer clear of the beauty. Though his mind told him to leave, his body – and his heart – urged him to stay.

He was powerless to do anything but. Jean was like a bright ray of light in his dark, dreary world of death and vengeance.

The hope he saw in her tawny eyes restored the fire inside him. He burned not just for a victory over Niall, but he burned *for her*.

His hands itched to pull her against him. He wanted her body pressed tightly to his own. The need was so strong, so potent, that Braden found himself leaning towards her.

He bit back a groan when he saw her eyes widen and her lips part. God help him but he was going to get his first taste of the stunning Jean MacKay.

Their bodies were just breaths apart. The pulse at her neck was erratic and rapid, as if she too longed for the kiss. That knowledge made Braden's hunger swell and intensify.

Her hand brushed his as she leaned towards him. Braden slid his fingers between hers until their hands were clasped. He could feel the heat of her skin, hear the breath pass through her lips.

Her gaze was fastened on his mouth, and it was all Braden could do not to crush her against him. The ache in his cock and the yearning, the longing, was too much to bear.

He would have his kiss.

He would have Jean.

"Braden!"

He bit back a curse. Jean turned away from him as Rory entered the tent. Braden glared at his friend.

Rory looked from Braden to Jean and back again before he sent Braden an apologetic grimace.

"What is it?" Braden asked.

"The women and children of clan MacKay are once more with their families. They want to know when Jean will be returned."

"When I know Colin will survive," she answered before Braden could.

Braden looked at her before turning back to Rory. "Thank you for seeing them to their clan. You did tell them Jean was safe?"

"Aye," Rory said with a firm nod of his red head. "Her father, Laird MacKay, wasna pleased to hear she is here."

Braden felt as if he'd been punched in the stomach. How many times had he spoken with Laird MacKay? How many times had he been to their clan, sat inside the castle? But not once had he ever known the laird to have a daughter.

He could only assume the laird had made sure Jean was nowhere near when Braden visited.

Braden turned to Jean. "You're Laird MacKay's daughter?"

She gave a small shrug and crossed her arms over her chest. "My father raised me to follow my heart and make the right choices. He knows I'm here because I want to be."

"Aye," Rory said. "The old laird said much the same thing. He did give me a warning to pass to ye, Braden."

Braden sighed, knowing what was coming. "What might that be?"

"He said that if one hair on her head is harmed, he'll be coming for you."

MacKay was one man Braden wanted kept as a supporter. He did not need him as an adversary. But Braden's hunger for Jean was going to be difficult to control.

As if knowing his thoughts were on her, Jean said, "I need to return to Colin."

Braden watched the sway of her hips as she walked from his tent. His blood was on fire as need rode him hard, begged him to take the woman into his arms.

"I'm no' sure you should be dallying with MacKay's daughter," Rory said.

Braden faced his friend. "Aye. The lass isna for me."

"Good. Now, do you want the news on Niall?"

Three

Jean couldn't stop herself from touching the spot on her cheek that Braden's fingers had brushed. The contact had been so fleeting, so soft, that it was almost as if it hadn't happened.

But she had felt the stroke of his fingers, had felt the heat of his skin.

It had left her shaken, dazed. His bright blue eyes had darkened with desire, and the not-so-firm grip Jean had on her control had vanished.

All she had wanted was Braden's kiss. She had yearned to know the taste of him, to feel the width and breath of his shoulders beneath her hands.

Jean exhaled loudly and walked into the tent to see Keith still sitting beside Colin.

"Lass, are you all right?" Keith asked, a frown marring his tanned face.

Jean nodded. She feared she wouldn't be able to speak, so she didn't even try.

"Nothing has changed. I had hoped he would shake off the fever by now."

Jean put her hand on Keith's shoulder and squeezed. "One never knows with a fever. Colin is strong. He will be able to rid himself of the infection."

"I pray you're correct," Keith said as he rose to his feet. He looked at her a moment with shrewd, knowing eyes. "You've seen Braden."

"Aye. He was curious as to Colin's recovery."

Keith grunted in response. "I'll be near. Just let me know if you need anything."

Jean resumed her seat next to Colin and wrung out the cloth to dab along his heated skin. She had a feeling it was going to be a very long night.

Braden rubbed his eyes with his thumb and forefinger. He'd been poring over the maps with Keith and Rory, hoping to discern where Niall had disappeared.

"We almost had him," Rory said.

Braden slammed his hand on the table. "Almost isna good enough. He's gone."

"We'll find him," Keith stated in his usual calm voice. "There aren't many places he could have gone."

Braden began to chuckle. He realized there was only one place Niall could be. "He's at MacAlister Castle."

"We have spies there," Rory said. "They would have seen him."

Braden's frustration grew with each day that passed that Niall still lived, so he understood the irritation that filled Rory's words. "He went through unseen just as he did when he came into my home before and murdered my father, my uncle and my sister."

"He's not human," Keith muttered.

Braden had long believed that Niall had sold his soul to the devil. He hated even admitting the bastard was related to him, but there was no denying Niall was his cousin.

Few knew that small detail, but the ones who did understood why Braden was so determined to stop the bastard.

"You know the castle better than anyone, Braden," Keith said. "I've told you before, we can get inside and take him. Your people are still loyal to you."

Braden's mind raced with possibilities. "It may come to taking the castle. We'll need more men."

"MacKay said you could count on him. There are other lairds who would join you as well," Rory said.

Braden looked from Rory to Keith before he nodded. "Get everyone to send some men. We're going to need all the Highlanders we can get."

He turned on his heel and started towards the entrance when Keith's voice stopped him.

"Where are you going? Doona you want to begin to plan?"

Braden couldn't think of anything but tawny eyes and full, ripe lips begging to be kissed. "I need to check on Colin. I'll return shortly."

As he exited Braden could have sworn he heard Keith snort. He didn't care that Keith knew the real reason that he wanted to check on Colin was to see Jean.

Braden cared about his men. All of them. They risked their lives every time they went into battle against Niall. But, this time, it wasn't Colin that kept intruding on his thoughts.

He ducked inside Colin's tent to see Jean slumped over, her head on her arms as she slept. Braden watched her for a moment, content to take in the sight of her at his leisure.

There had been many women who had caught his eye, but none had made him burn as Jean did. What was it about her? She was head-turning with her midnight locks, ochre eyes, and body made for sin. But it was the fire inside her, so like the untamed spirit he himself possessed, that called to him.

Braden had kept himself detached from anyone other than his men for fear that Niall might use them against him. Braden was already testing fate merely by keeping Jean in his camp. If Niall ever discovered how much Braden wanted Jean, her life would be over.

Despite the warnings in his mind, Braden couldn't keep away from her. He crossed the distance between them on silent feet.

An onyx lock had come free of her braid and fell over her cheek. Braden lifted the shiny strand, amazed at its cool, soft texture. He held it a moment longer before he tucked it behind her ear.

He had to fist his hand to keep from touching her, and turned on his heel. He grabbed a blanket and spread it on the ground at the back of the tent. Then he slowly, carefully lifted Jean in his arms and laid her on the blanket.

He had lowered her to the tartan, but he was not yet ready to release her. She exhaled softly and turned on to her side away from him. Braden couldn't help the grin that pulled at his lips.

Nor could he halt the overwhelming temptation to reach for her.

He caressed her cheek down to her jaw with the back of his fingers. No skin had ever felt so smooth, ever looked so velvety.

A long, ragged breath left his body. He ached to touch more of her. He yearned to know every enchanting inch of her body. To drown in her heat, succumb to her charms. Surrender to the driving need to have her.

Braden rose, his control slipping through his fingers with every moment. He sat on the stool Jean had been sitting on as she tended to Colin.

He didn't know how long he sat wiping Colin's fevered brow before Keith came in. His friend furrowed his brow as he saw Braden.

"What are you doing here?"

"Allowing her to rest," Braden answered. He motioned to Jean on the blanket.

Keith grumbled as he saw Jean there. "You should have called me."

"I've been thinking about gaining access to the castle."

"Aye, I knew you would be."

Braden licked his lips and dropped the cloth in the bowl of water. MacAlister castle had been his home from the moment he was brought into the world. He knew every crack and crevice there was. The problem was – so did Niall.

"If we're going to succeed, there is only one way to get inside."

Keith's hazel eyes narrowed. "The secret passages?"

"Nay. Niall knows of them."

"Through the postern door of the castle wall?"

Braden shook his head. "Niall will keep that well guarded."

"I'm no' going to like your idea am I?" Keith asked as he crossed his arms over his barrel chest and flattened his lips.

"Nay, you aren't. We are going to walk through the gates."

Keith's mouth gaped open as his arms fell limply to his sides. "Did you get hit in the head during the battle, Braden? It's the only thing I can think of as to why you would come up with such a daft plan."

"I've no' been hit," Braden said as he tried to hide his smile. "If you listen to my plan, you'll see how it'll work."

"What I see is that you'll be taken. Everyone at the castle knows your face."

Braden lifted a shoulder as he shrugged. "No. By the time I get done they willna."

"You know I'd follow you into Hell itself."

"Unfortunately, my friend, that's exactly where we'll be heading."

Keith nodded. "When do you want to execute this plan of yours?"

"I'd prefer to go tonight, but I need to wait and hear from the lairds to see how many men we can count on."

"What do you need me to do?"

Braden grinned. "Care to visit the village?"

Jean rolled onto her back and stretched. There was a crick in her neck that was going to bother her for days. She frowned and tried to think what could have caused it. Then, she remembered.

Colin.

Her eyes flew open. The sound of muffled voices drifted to her. She concentrated, trying to determine each word. She could hear Braden's voice, his timbre comforting her in ways she wasn't ready to understand. He was speaking of plans to invade MacAlister castle.

And then Braden walked into the tent towards her. Jean sat up, her gaze clashing with his own.

"How long have I been asleep?" she asked.

"Not long enough."

Jean climbed to her feet and moved to Colin. She put her hand on his forehead and blinked. "When did his fever break?"

"A few hours ago," Braden said. "I didna wish to wake you."

She didn't remember falling asleep, much less lying down. Jean was glad that Colin's fever had broken, but that meant there was no need for her in the camp now. Braden would send her home.

Unless she could find a reason to stay.

"I canna thank you enough for tending to Colin," Braden said. He rubbed his hand along his whiskered jaw and looked away. "I suppose I need to send you back to your father."

"I'd rather stay."

The words were out of Jean's mouth before she could be ashamed at what she was saying.

"Every moment you stay here puts your life in danger."

"It doesn't matter where I am. If Niall wishes to do me harm, he will."

"Your father can protect you."

Jean took a deep breath and folded her hands at her waist. "Niall used a ruse to draw my father and his best men from our keep – he slaughtered dozens of our sheep and left the tartan of our neighbour as blame. Once my father and his men had left to question the neighbour, Niall attacked. The men left on guard were powerless when Niall to threatened to kill a child in order to get inside the keep."

Braden cursed and put his hands on his hips. He shook his head.

"Whatever you are planning to do to Niall, I want to help. I'm not a warrior and I have little skill with a blade, but there are other things I can do. I can tend to wounds, cook meals, or anything else you would ask of me."

Braden stared at her for several long moments. "Why? Why would you risk your life?"

"Why would you risk yours? This is my land as well. He has come to my clan, harmed my people. Let me help."

"I shouldna allow it."

Jean smiled and silently rejoiced. "But you will."

"If anything happens to you, your father will never forgive me."

"Nothing will happen to me," she promised.

Four

Braden knew he was a fool. He told himself he could keep Jean safer than her father could, but he knew it for the lie it was. He just couldn't let her go.

He'd been wracking his mind for a reason to keep her in his camp. Braden had never expected Jean to come up with a solution herself. But that's what she'd done.

"I've already received a missive from your father," Braden said. "He is gathering his men and riding to the camp on the morrow."

"Did you doubt he would aid you?" Jean asked.

"Nay. He's an honourable man. He told me I could count on him."

"Will you tell me the plan?"

Braden hesitated, not because he didn't trust her, but because it was imperative all were surprised.

Before he could answer, Colin groaned. Braden and Jean bent

over him. Colin's eyes cracked open as he swallowed several times.

"Braden?"

"Easy, my friend." Braden said. "You've been very ill."

Jean held a cup in front of Colin. "You need to drink."

Braden helped Colin to lift his head as Jean slowly tilted the cup to his lips. Once Colin had drunk his full Braden lowered his head.

"Are you in pain?" Jean asked him.

Colin's lips were pinched, but he shook his fair head. "Nothing I canna handle."

"We all know how brave you are," Braden said. "But if Jean can give you something to help, allow her to do it. I'm going to need you."

Colin grinned as Braden knew he would. Braden then lifted his gaze to Jean and gave her a small nod before he walked out of the tent.

He paused once outside and looked around his camp. Several years ago it had been just him, Keith, and a handful of the men that left the castle with him. He hadn't known quite what to do when other men began showing up at his camp wanting to fight alongside him.

After Niall's betrayal, Braden hadn't known who to trust. Yet, in the end, he had to accept anyone willing to fight against his traitorous cousin.

As Niall's power grew across the land, so did Braden's army. Niall, though, was always one step ahead. Always just out of reach.

Braden walked mindlessly around the camp. Their homes didn't do much to keep them warm in the harsh Highland winters, but the men had always made do.

It was after a few women and children, made homeless by Niall's rampage, came to Braden looking for shelter that he knew more drastic measures had to be taken. His camp was one of men ready and waiting for battle. It wasn't fit for any other inhabitants.

He had found places for those in need with other clans – clans large enough and powerful enough to keep these women and children hidden and safe. But that couldn't last forever.

Braden scrubbed a hand down his face. His latest plan could well get him killed. He should already be dead. How he survived the night his father, uncle and sister died was a mystery to him.

He had been late returning to the castle after a night carousing with some friends. Braden never expected to walk into the castle to such silence.

Or to find his younger sister on the stairs with blood staining the front of her gown from a wound to her chest, and her blue eyes open and empty.

It hadn't taken Braden long to discover his father and uncle as well. Rage unlike anything he had ever experienced filled him.

He had his sword drawn and ready to slay the murderer of his family when Keith had found him. Keith told him about Niall, how he had snuck into the castle, and how he was now on the hunt for Braden.

It went against everything Braden believed in to leave the castle, but he had to live if he was to see his family avenged. Fate had spared him, and in doing so allowed Braden to be a thorn in Niall's side.

A thorn that hadn't done as much damage yet as it would have liked.

Braden let his eyes wander over the camp. Men were set in small groups near their tents, talking, planning. Others were on patrol. Still others were training on foot and horseback.

He had been destined to be laird of his people, to protect his lands and clan at all costs. Braden had never thought he would be fighting to regain his lands and protect all of Scotland.

It all rested on his shoulders now. Come what may, he would not – could not – fail.

Jean let Rory usher her out of Colin's tent. She should still be tending him, but Rory had wanted some time alone with her patient.

She bit her lip as she walked among the many tents. Besides herself, she saw only three other women. Two were bent with age, their white hair pulled away from their faces. They sat together readying food for the next meal.

The other woman was older than Jean, but still young enough to catch the eyes of the men. Mary, her name was. Clearly, Mary was there for their enjoyment.

Jean wondered if the woman had visited Braden. Then she immediately questioned why she should even care.

She watched everyone finishing their morning meal. Her stomach rumbled, but there was more on her mind than food. She didn't know how long she would be in Braden's camp. Somehow she had convinced him to allow her to stay, but that could be cut short at any time.

Despite the danger she was in, she wanted to remain there. She wanted to help Braden in his fight to topple Niall.

Jean came to a halt as her gaze fell upon Braden. His saffron shirt was thrown over his shoulder and water dripped from the ends of his hair after a bath in the nearby stream.

His striking sapphire eyes held her transfixed. Riveted. Spellbound.

The camp fell away, leaving only the two of them. Her heart pounded like a drum in her chest. Her blood heated and rushed though her body.

When he took a step to her, Jean's stomach dropped to her feet.

Someone called Braden's name, breaking the trance that had held them. He turned away from her. Was that regret she saw in his face? Jean squeezed her eyes shut and tried not to dwell on her disappointment.

She knew that whatever drew her and Braden together was special, a bond that couldn't be ignored. If only they could have the time to explore it further.

It was just another reason for her to despise Niall. If he hadn't come, there would be no need for Braden to lead an army.

And you might never have known him at all.

There was no getting around that fact. Jean took a deep breath and walked to the stream at the back of the camp to prepare for the day.

She had just knelt by the water's edge and splashed the cold liquid on her face when she heard her name. Jean looked over her shoulder to see one of Braden's men.

"Braden would like to see you."

Jean nodded and stood. When she reached Braden's tent, two more men stood outside. One leaned down and lifted the flap for her to enter.

She ducked inside. Braden stood facing her, his hands behind his back. "You wished to see me?"

"You offered your services to help," Braden said.

"I did."

Braden glanced at Keith. "How are you with a needle?"

Jean blinked. She had imagined being asked many different things in order to help Braden but sewing hadn't been one of them. "You wish me to sew?"

"I do. I need cloaks and other garments made as quickly as you can. You will have help. Doona worry about the quality. The items need to appear poorly done."

Jean took the material dumped into her arms by Keith and looked at the coarse material. "I gather you willna be wearing your kilts."

"The less you know the better, lass," Keith said softly.

Jean raised her gaze to Braden, but he was bent over documents, his hands braced on the table. "How many cloaks and garments do I need to make?"

"As many as you can by nightfall," Keith answered.

"Nightfall?" she repeated, not hiding her shock.

"Whatever you can do will be enough."

Jean nodded and left the tent. If she was going to be of any help, she needed to get busy.

Braden let out a breath once Jean was gone. He knew she wanted to know the details of his strategy. And he wanted to tell her.

Yet he couldn't.

Somehow, Niall had learned of Braden's plan yesterday. This could only mean there was a spy in the camp. Braden had no way of knowing who it could be. His remedy was to confide only in those that he trusted completely – Rory and Keith.

The others would only know what they were to do, not how it all connected. Unfortunately, Jean also had to be kept in the dark.

Braden knew in his gut he could trust her. He had seen the fear in her eyes when she was Niall's captive. That kind of terror couldn't be faked.

Even her father, and the other lairds coming to aid Braden, wouldn't be told everything. Braden would send them to the location where they would wait for his signal to attack. They wouldn't know anything about Braden infiltrating the castle or anything about his intentions for Niall.

This was Braden's last chance to end Niall's evil reign. If he couldn't, if he failed . . .

He didn't even want to think along those lines. Too many lives were at stake, too much at risk. He had to win tomorrow. For his father, his sister, his uncle and the other innocents that had got in Niall's way for his bid for power.

Braden wanted Niall dead, but he knew that to get the justice everyone needed, the murdering tyrant had to be brought before the king – along with the "trophies" he liked to collect from his victims.

Niall's strange behaviour had been well known throughout the family. But no one had thought he would switch his cruelty from animals to people.

"Jean is a curious one," Keith said, breaking into Braden's thoughts. "She will want to know why she is garbing us in such clothing."

Braden exhaled long and slow. "Doona worry. I will tell her nothing."

"You may not have to. She's a smart one, she is. She is likely to figure it all out."

Braden hadn't considered that. "Even if she does, it makes no difference. She willna be with us."

Keith crossed his arms over his chest and grimaced. "I've followed you wherever you've led me, Braden, but I want you to know this plan of yours is daft."

"And likely to get us all killed. Aye, my friend, I ken."

Keith left the tent to carry out his orders. Braden returned his attention the map of the castle and the surrounding area. He knew the land better than anyone. There were places where those loyal to him could gain a great advantage, and places where he knew he could ambush Niall's men.

So many things had to go right for the plan to work. The most important was getting into the castle.

When he finally raised his head it was to see two trenchers on the table in front of him. One of cheese, bread and cold meat from the noon meal, and the second still steaming with haggis.

Braden's stomach demanded food. He sat and devoured both trenchers before reaching for the bottle of ale. He needed to stretch his legs and back, needed to see the faces of those who trusted him to defeat Niall.

He set aside the empty bottle of ale and rose to exit his tent. The sun was all but set in the horizon, casting vivid pinks and purples over half the sky, while the blanket of night was pulled over the other half.

Several fires dotted the camp, casting faces in orange glows. Many sharpened their swords and dirks as they spoke in low tones. Others checked their horses.

The night before a battle was one of quiet conversations as each man prepared for what could be the last hours of his life.

Braden made a loop of the camp, stopping to speak to his men along the way. He wanted to find Jean. He might not be able to hold her or kiss her as his own, but he could watch over her.

His gaze sought out her dark locks and beautiful figure. When he found her folding one of her newly sewn cloaks, an unusual calm settled over him. Her mere presence in his camp had given him the tranquillity he had sought since he had lost everything to Niall.

It wasn't just her beauty, but her strength that drew him.

She set the cloak atop a pile of others and straightened. Her eyes lifted to the sky, and then she turned her head to him.

Braden knew he should walk away, knew he needed to leave her. But he couldn't. He wanted Jean with a need that both alarmed him and gave him courage.

He strode to her, ignoring those who called his name. He didn't stop until he stood in front of her. No words were spoken as their eyes sought each other.

Desire, hot and powerful, pulsed between them. It was too intense to ignore, too potent to withstand. And too vibrant to walk away from.

His fingers slid over her arm to her hand before he led her to his tent.

Five

Jean willingly followed Braden to his tent. Once inside, he halted and turned to her. He reached for her arms and pulled her towards him.

She lost herself in the longing, the hunger she saw in his smouldering blue eyes.

Her hands rose and settled on his abdomen. She could feel the ripple of muscle beneath her hand through his saffron shirt. They were so close the heat from his body wrapped around her, cocooning her.

Beckoning her.

He shifted closer so their bodies touched, melded. Jean moved her hands up Braden's chest to his shoulders until her fingers threaded with the cool strands of his brown hair.

Braden lowered his head, his gaze dropping to her mouth. Jean's breath locked inside her. Her stomach fluttered as she eagerly awaited his kiss.

The first brush of his lips stole her breath.

She melted against him as his kiss became more insistent. A moan, deep and hungry, rose from Braden when she returned the kiss.

His tongue licked her lips before sweeping between them and teasing her own tongue. He plundered her lips, besieged her mind.

Jean's fingers dug into his shoulders as she fought to keep her legs beneath her. His mouth slanted over hers, kissing her deeply. And thoroughly.

Passion flared hot and true inside her, filling her veins, and settled in the pit of her stomach. Each stroke of his tongue wound her desire tighter, heavier.

Braden kissed Jean with all the passion, all the longing he possessed. It began as a gentle kiss, one to coax and entice. But a single taste of her and he forgot everything but raw, unabashed hunger.

It was a kiss to lay his claim.

His arms tightened about her, bringing her closer, locking her shapely body firmly along his length. He felt her soft touch as her fingers plunged into his hair.

Braden's mind told him to be cautious, to not allow himself to be pulled under by the overwhelming need for her. But the temptation was too great.

He fell headlong into the desire. He plunged in and forgot all reason.

Nothing mattered but Jean. And the flare of pleasure that pounded in his veins.

Braden tasted her unleashed passion and craved more. He wanted all of her, everything she had to offer.

Another satisfied moan tore from him as Jean pressed against him, as if she too sought to get closer. Whatever control Braden had thought to hold on to vanished in that moment.

She was his.

With one arm holding her, he reached between them and cupped her breast. Her fingers tightened at his neck, a heartbeat before she arched into his hand.

Jean forgot to breathe as Braden's hand seduced her with every caress, every stroke. Her breasts swelled and ached, her nipples hardened seeking more of his touch.

Braden's tongue trust against hers as his fingers found her sensitive peak through her gown and teased her.

Passion grew, tightened within her. She knew there was no turning away from such wondrous desire. Turning away never even entered her mind.

She wanted to touch his skin, to feel the heat of his flesh against her. As soon as she tugged on his shirt, Braden reached for her skirts.

The kiss ended as, one by one, items of clothing were removed hastily. Desire escalated with the removal of each garment. Until they stood naked together.

Jean sucked in a ragged, broken breath as Braden dragged her against him. His body was hot and so very hard. She had little time to look her fill before Braden claimed her mouth once more. His hands were urgent, needy, as they roamed.

She sighed into his kiss and let her hands travel over the muscled expanse of his chest at her leisure, learning him – until Braden's lips travelled down her neck and his mouth closed over her nipple. She cried out, seeking more, wanting more. Always more.

They tumbled to the ground, skin to skin. Their limbs tangled as their hands learned and discovered. Seeking, seizing. Urgent and commanding. With each touch, each sigh, the desire that bound them grew tighter, stronger. Undeniable.

Jean moaned when he moved on top her, nudging her legs apart with his knees. She arched her back, his name upon her lips, when his fingers found her and stroked between her thighs.

Her body burned with need and pleasure that mixed and balled in her stomach. She lifted her hips, seeking more of the heady bliss. Her desire spiked and coalesced as he teased her body until she was mindless with need.

She tugged at him, needing him on her so she could feel his weight. She wanted to be closer to him.

Braden lay over her, his thighs set between hers. He held still for one heartbeat, two . . . and he stared down at her. His bright blue gaze held her mesmerized with his dark intensity.

Then he kissed her. Their lips locked, tongue meeting tongue. He set his hips, and with one powerful thrust, slid inside her. Jean stilled as the shaft of pain sliced through her. It ate away at the pleasure, threatened to consume her. All the while Braden kissed her. Hot and urgent. Needy. Hungrily. He withdrew and plunged again. Deeper. Harder.

Her entire being centred on Braden and the desire that wound tighter and tighter, higher and higher within her. They burned, the pleasure burning them in a tide neither could restrain.

Braden didn't try to deny the longing in his heart, didn't try to reject the all-consuming impulse to take Jean and be damned of the consequences.

No amount of rationalizing had been able to turn him away from the hunger for Jean that clawed at him. It was a craving sunk deep, all the way to his soul.

He rejoiced as he pinned her beneath him, her lush curves cushioning him. Every moan and cry of pleasure that fell from her lips pushed him to take her higher.

She shifted, her legs rising to wrap around his waist. He sank deeper into her, her hot sheath holding him tight.

Jean rocked beneath him as he plunged faster, harder. Their ragged breaths filled the tent as sweat beaded their skin. Her body began to tense as her eyes grew heavy.

Braden felt the tension in her rise. Her fingers gripped his arms, her nails digging into his skin. She was close, so very close.

He needed to see her climax, to see her surrender to the desire that had taken both of them. It pushed him, roared in his blood. Demanded that she succumb.

She gave a soft cry as she shattered.

Braden gloried in the joy etched over her face and his name on her lips. Still convulsing around him, Braden couldn't hold back his own orgasm. He thrust once, twice and then gave into the pleasure with a roar.

The climax was intense, heady as it swept him along. He had never felt anything so primitive, so mind-melting. He collapsed on top of her. Her arms encircled him, holding him in an embrace of contentment, of peace.

After a moment, he used his elbows to lift himself a little so he could look down at her. She smiled and smoothed a lock of hair that fell over his forehead.

He cupped the side of her head with each hand and lost himself in her amber eyes. "I fear I willna ever let you go now."

"Good. I'm right where I want to be."

Her words made his chest constrict. For the first time in two years he wanted to think about his future. With Jean by his side.

"You are mine now," he vowed, just before his lips descended upon hers.

Six

Jean wrapped her arms around herself as she stood outside Braden's tent and watched everyone readying for the coming battle.

Sometime during the night a horse and small cart had been brought to the camp. Braden, Keith, Rory and Colin all stood around it, deep in conversation.

Braden suddenly lifted his head. Their gazes collided. They had spent the few remaining hours of the night talking and making love.

She feared for Braden and his plan. He had told her very little, but it hadn't taken her long to deduce he feared there was a spy in his camp. The only one who knew the entire plan was Braden. Everyone else just knew their parts.

Jean watched as Mary settled one of the cloaks around her shoulders. Jean had told Braden she wanted to help, but he had refused, telling her in no uncertain terms that she was to stay in the camp.

She swallowed past the lump of dread that filled her throat. Mary said something to Keith before walking away with hurried steps. A fearful glance over her shoulder told Jean all she needed to know.

Jean didn't hesitate as she lifted her skirts and moved between two tents so Braden wouldn't see her. She found Mary standing behind one of the other tents, tears coursing down her face.

"I canna do it," Mary said when she saw Jean. "I'm scared."

Jean looked around to make sure no one was near. "Give me the cloak and gown."

Mary blinked. "Milady?"

"Hurry," Jean said as she began to pull off her own clothing.

She had little time to get the crude gown and cloak in place and return to the cart before Braden and the others grew suspicious.

Once the coarse brown gown was in place and the cloak around her shoulders, Jean lifted the hood over her head. "Take my gown and return to Braden's tent," she told Mary. "If they find you before everyone has left, they'll bring you."

Mary nodded and grabbed Jean's gown before rushing away. Jean released a deep breath and squared her shoulders. She made her way to the cart.

"Did you get what you needed?" Keith asked.

Jean nodded her head.

"Good," Braden said. "Let's get going."

Keith helped Jean into the cart as Braden lifted a panel in the floor and slipped inside to lay flat across the length of the cart. Colin covered Braden once he was stretched out on his back.

"I'm sorry you couldna find Jean to say farewell once more," Colin said.

Braden grimaced. "Just make sure you doona tear the stitches of your wound lest she have your head."

Colin laughed and settled his back against the seat where Jean was. "You've made yourself clear, Braden. No fighting for me. I'm just here to make sure this ruse works."

Jean shuddered, a shadow of foreboding racing down her spine.

Keith climbed up next to her and slapped the reigns for the horse to go. "Doona worry, Mary. Just remember. Once we reach the castle, stay out of the way."

"I still say we shouldna bring her," Colin said.

"It's part of the ruse," Braden's voice said from below the floor of the cart. "Niall willna believe two men, one wounded, and the other with a woman, will attempt to breech his walls for an attack."

Keith snorted. "Proves what a fool he is."

Jean kept her face forward. They were still close enough to the camp that they could stop and send her back. Not only did she want to help Braden, but she wouldn't allow Mary to put everyone's life in danger because she was scared.

"You haven't said much," Keith whispered as he leaned towards her.

Jean shrugged her shoulders.

"I ken you're scared, lass, but you will be safe. Braden, and the rest of us, have sworn to it."

Jean covered her mouth with her hand and coughed. "I know," she squeaked out.

There was a moment of silence where she could feel Keith's gaze. Her heart pounded so loudly she was sure he would hear it.

Strong fingers grabbed her chin and forced her head around. Jean put her finger to her lips and shook her head in the hope Keith would keep silent.

"Shite," he murmured as he dropped his arm. "Braden is going to skin me alive."

Jean scooted closer so they wouldn't be overheard. "Nay. Mary couldn't do it, and I wouldn't have her endangering any of you."

"Braden was clear," Keith grumbled. "You werena to be involved."

"He need never know. As soon as we're inside the castle gates I will hide."

A muscle in Keith's jaw ticked. "This isna a good idea."

"It's the only way."

Jean met Keith's challenging gaze until he let out a long breath and scrunched his face.

She sat back, relieved that she had won. It would be well after midday before they reached MacAlister Castle, and the further away from the camp they travelled, the more Jean couldn't shake her uneasy feeling.

For better or worse she was now part of Braden's attack.

Another bead of sweat travelled down Braden's brow and into his hair. He didn't especially like small spaces, and being confined below the cart's floor left little room to manoeuvre.

Or to breathe.

Braden couldn't even lift his arm to wipe the sweat that dripped into his eyes. He blinked rapidly to stop the stinging, but it did no good.

For all his discomfort, he wouldn't complain if his plan worked. If Niall was stopped then a few hours of suffering would be well worth it.

He bit back a grunt as one of the cart's wheel fell into a deep rut, jarring him. His mind needed to be on the upcoming battle, but all he could think about was Jean.

And their night together.

It had been . . . soul-stirring. Moving. Exciting. Glorious.

The dawn had come all too soon. It had taken everything Braden had to leave her behind. At least at the camp she would be safe from Niall and any danger.

"Not much longer," Colin said to him as he leaned towards the cart floor.

Braden didn't bother to answer. There had been little to no conversation since their departure from the camp. It was just as well though.

He inhaled deeply and focused his mind on his plan. Everything hinged on whether they got through the castle gates. From there, once Braden was out of the cart and inside the castle, Colin would send the signal for the other men.

Braden smiled, expectation and exhilaration taking hold of him. His fingers wrapped around the hilt of his sword at his side. He itched to feel the familiar weight of the blade as it sliced through the air, as it embedded in Niall's body.

He closed his eyes, his elaborate plan floating through his mind. His father would tell him he was overreaching, and he would be correct. His father had always been right.

But in this instance, Braden had no choice.

He'd been fighting Niall for two years. Two long, brutal years of innocent deaths and violence that never stopped.

Now he had Jean. She'd already been in Niall's hands once. Braden knew she wouldn't survive a second time. If somehow Braden failed and Niall discovered what Jean meant to him . . . Braden couldn't even finish the thought.

The cart began to slow, and then stopped when someone shouted for them to halt.

Braden held his breath.

"State your business," a loud voice demanded.

Braden paid no attention to Keith's explanation as more guards came around the back of the cart and began to question Colin.

There was a grunt as one of the guards grabbed Colin's wounded leg and tore at the bindings to ensure that Colin was indeed injured.

A few words later and Keith clucked to the horse.

Braden closed his eyes and sent up a prayer of thanks as they rolled beneath the large gatehouse and into the bailey of the castle.

He didn't need to see to know there were two guards at each tower of the gatehouse and more patrolled the battlements atop the castle wall.

He didn't need to see to know the blacksmith's shop was behind him and to the right, that the chapel was two shops to the left of the blacksmith and connected to the castle, or that the stable was to his left.

He didn't need to see to know there were exactly ten steps from the bailey up to the castle doors.

Because he had counted those steps every day of his life since he could walk.

This was his home, a home that had been stolen from him. A home that had once held happy memories, but was now filled with the ghosts of his father, uncle and sister.

The cart circled the bailey and came to rest next to the stable just as Braden had instructed. He waited until Keith, Mary and Colin were out of the cart and well away before he gave a hard shove against the wood at his side.

The board popped off at the bottom. Braden grasped the board and scooted from his hiding spot, hidden beside the stable wall, before he dropped to the ground.

Carefully, silently, he replaced the board. After a look around to make sure no one was watching, he slipped into the stable.

As he was in the MacAlister plaid, no one paid him any heed. His people still wore their clan tartan with pride. But it was his face he worried about. He pulled the hood of his cloak over his head so that his face was in shadow.

Braden glanced at his favorite horse who nickered when he neared. As much as Braden wanted to stop and stroke the sleek grey coat, he couldn't.

He exited the back of the stable and turned to the left to walk behind the buildings to the chapel. As he neared the chapel, his heart quickened.

Already he had progressed farther into his plot than he had expected he would. Even if Niall somehow caught him, the other clans would come. They would surround the castle. And a battle that would be spoken about for centuries would ensue.

Niall's reign would come to an end no matter what.

Braden peered around the chapel to see Colin standing at the gate talking to the guards. It was the sign that his other men should begin to infiltrate the castle.

As much as Braden wanted to kill Niall, he couldn't. Niall needed to be brought before the king and tried for his unspeakable crimes. The king would decide what sort of death Niall deserved.

Braden pushed against the stone that unlocked the door to the back of the chapel. There a soft thud before the wooden door opened a crack.

He urged the door open just enough so that he could slip inside. Braden pulled the door closed behind him before ducking into the shadows.

Despite his need to move, he stayed still for a moment. He had to be prudent.

When he was sure that no one else was in the chapel, Braden hurried behind the altar in a crouch. His fingers gripped at the wooden floorboards at the base of the altar and he worked on lifting them. For a moment nothing happened, and then the boards gave way.

Braden glanced at the single section of five boards in his hands. They fit so snugly together that no one had ever seen the seam and realized it was a trap door.

He set the boards aside and sat on the outside of the hole so that his legs dangled into the darkness beneath him. No light was needed. Though Braden had never had to use this tunnel from the chapel before, his father had made him travel all the underground tunnels so often that Braden knew them as well as he knew the castle.

He jumped into the tunnel and landed with his knees bent. After a moment, he straightened, reached for the boards and settled them back into place over the tunnel entrance.

Then he started running. To the castle. To Niall and the end of all he had wrought.

Seven

Jean clutched her cloak so tightly her fingers began to ache. Keith had deposited her between two shops while he and Colin played their parts.

She saw Colin talking to the guards at the gate. Was this some sort of sign for the others? Jean was turning away when she spotted Braden. He walked with strong, purposeful steps on his way to the chapel. She wanted to go to him, to help him. To hold him.

But instead she held her ground.

It wouldn't be long now before her father and the other clans surrounded the castle. She had promised Keith she would make her way out of the castle before the battle began. As much as she wanted to be around to aid them, she knew she would only be a hindrance.

Jean didn't walk through the middle of the bailey. She kept close to the shops, mingling with the occupants. She was constantly on the lookout for Niall.

She was almost to the gate when someone rammed a shoulder into her, spinning her around. Jean was ready to bolt until she saw Keith's ashen face.

He weaved on his feet, his breathing laboured. Jean saw the blood dripping from the fingers of his left hand.

"Keith?"

He tried to smile but only tilted towards her.

Jean quickly grabbed his hulking form and backed him into an alley between the shops. "Keith, what happened?"

"The guard I took down got lucky," he rasped. "I didn't get out of the way . . . in time."

Jean lifted his cloak and grimaced when she saw the wound in his
side. If she could tend to it he would live. "I need to get you out of
here."

"Nay," he growled. "I'm to be inside the castle for Braden."

"In this condition you would only get yourself and Braden
killed."

"Bind the wound," he ordered, his eyes hard. "I willna let Braden
down."

Jean inwardly cursed as she lifted her gown and tore off a piece
of her shift. She wound it around Keith. "This won't be enough to
stop the bleeding, but it should slow it."

"It'll have to do, lass."

"Nay," she said and grabbed his shoulder. "Tell me what needs
to be done and I'll do it."

He shook his head sadly, as he struggled to keep upright. "You
canna."

"I can do it better than you can in your condition. Tell me,
Keith."

"Braden will kill me."

"I won't get caught."

Keith's gaze stabbed her. "You better no'."

"Tell me. Then get to Colin."

Jean listened to every word, memorizing every detail. She swallowed and looked at the dark grey stone of the castle.

"Can you do it?" Keith asked.

"Aye. For Braden I can."

Keith's meaty hand clamped on her shoulder. "Good luck, lass.
You're going to need it."

Braden paused in the tunnel as he reached what could be the last
door that stood between him and Niall. He withdrew his weapon
and put an ear to the door, listening for any sounds.

Braden had taken the tunnel that lead to the master chamber.
The chamber Niall had taken for himself, of course.

He slowly opened the hidden door and stepped into the room.
One glance showed that Niall was nowhere to be found. The chamber however was in complete disarray.

Braden made his way silently into the corridor. Niall knew that
one day Braden would come to try to take back his castle so Niall
had guards set up everywhere.

It didn't deter Braden, however.

He crept up behind the first guard and knocked him on the back of the head with the hilt of his sword, then dragged him into the nearest chamber. He tore the linens and bound and gagged the guard.

Braden didn't tarry and moved down the hallway looking out for the next guard. There were a few of the guards that were more troublesome than the others but Braden wouldn't be stopped. Not now. Not now that he was in his home.

Jean pushed open the castle doors and stepped inside the great hall. A few servants walked briskly to and from the kitchen. Three guards were locked in conversation.

So far no one had noticed her. And Jean wanted it kept that way.

She quietly shut the doors behind her. Head down, she made for the stairs. She was just steps away from reaching them when the hood of her cloak was ripped from her head.

"Well, well, well," said a male voice laced with humour.

Jean spun around and jerked her shoulder to wrench the cloak from the man's grasp.

"What do you think you're doing?" he demanded.

"It's none of your business."

His gaze narrowed as he took a step towards her. "Everything that involves Lord Niall is my business."

Jean's blood ran cold as she stared into eyes black as pitch. This must be the commander of Niall's guards. He had the look of a man accustomed to being having his every word followed.

A man you didn't say no to.

She couldn't fail before she had even begun. "Then you'll have to tell Lord Niall why you have detained his . . . guest."

The two guards behind the commander cackled with laughter. But the man before her merely looked her up and down. "You're pretty enough, but not like the other women my lord prefers."

Jean shrugged and tried to look as nonchalant as she could. "I'm just a woman. What do I know of the minds of men?"

The man smiled as he leered at her. "Maybe when Lord Niall is through with you I'll have a sample."

"Maybe. If Lord Niall is occupied, maybe we could take a little time to ourselves. I may not be Lord Niall's usual type, but you are certainly mine." Jean ended with a wink.

The man regarded her a moment, though she saw the interest

that brightened his black eyes. "Call me Simon. Lord Niall would kill me if he knew."

"I certainly wouldn't tell him, Simon."

The commander held out his arm for her before he looked back at the other two guards. "I'm going to escort Lord Niall's guest into his chamber."

Jean swallowed past the lump of anxiety that had wedged in her throat. Her fingers itched to grasp the pommel of the dagger Keith had slid into her palm. She needed to stay calm and focused.

It would take a perfect plunge with the dagger, and in just the right place, to kill Simon. Jean knew how to do neither. Keith would have simply killed him and taken the key.

She had to come up with another way to get into the room and get rid of the commander.

Jean allowed him to lead her into a small bedroom. He leaned against the door as he slid the bolt into place and smiled. She looked around the room to take in her surroundings. The bed loomed large to her left. It was made even more pronounced when the commander walked to it and held out his hand.

The key to Niall's chamber was around his neck, hanging on the outside of his shirt and tunic. It was just a matter of getting to it.

"I hope you aren't going to keep me waiting," Simon said.

Jean grinned and gave her hips a pronounced sway as she walked to him. "I wouldn't dream of doing such a thing to a fine man like yourself."

"Just what I wanted to hear." He lifted his kilt and stroked his arousal. "Come. I want it inside you."

Jean glanced at the small table beside the bed and spied a goblet and a small chest. Those were the only two things within her reach, besides her dagger, with which to inflict enough harm to knock Simon unconscious.

She put herself between him and the table. Her fingers deftly caught the goblet behind her and tucked it into the folds at the back of her cloak as she put her other hand on his chest.

"You want me badly, don't you?" she asked.

"Desperately," he panted. "Doona make me wait another moment."

Jean pulled him away from the bed until she could walk around him. "I'd like to look a wee bit more over such an impressive warrior."

He didn't stop her as she walked behind him. Jean took a deep breath and brought the goblet down on the back of his head.

There was a loud grunt before he staggered and turned to face her. He blinked as he looked at first her and then the goblet. "What have you done, wench?"

Jean was trying to figure out what to do next when he crumpled to the floor. She tossed aside the goblet and grasped the pommel of the dagger.

She found the thin leather cord around his neck where the small gold key dangled. Jean cut the leather and took the key. With one last look at the commander, she rose and raced to the door.

Keith had told her she would find Braden on the second floor near the stairs leading down to the great hall. Jean didn't know how much time she had before Simon awoke and set off the alarm.

She reached the landing to the great hall and leaned against the wall. She found it most odd that there were no guards in the corridors, just the two sitting below in the great hall.

It had to be Braden's doing, but where was he? He needed the key. Without it, he would have no proof of Niall's deeds. Jean waited several more moments, her anxiety rising with each beat of her heart.

Could something have happened to detain him? Maybe she needed to get the evidence herself?

Keith had explained that the master chamber, which he was sure Niall would have claimed for his own, was on the third level. Jean prayed she remembered Keith's instructions about how to reach the master chamber. If not . . .

She refused to think along those lines.

Every step inside the castle added to her foreboding. It grew until it clung to her, weighing her down and making her doubt her every move.

Several corridors, numerous turns, and two stairways later, Jean stood in front of Niall's chamber.

No guards had stood in her way, there had been no guards at all. She had been relieved since she hadn't thought she could have overpowered them with her dagger. Now there was just a door between her and Niall's defeat.

And whatever was behind that door.

Eight

Jean cracked open the door to Niall's chambers and peered around it. Her gaze swept the large room and, thankfully, found it empty.

She squeezed inside and went straight to the wall where a large square chest was imbedded. Jean slipped the key into the chest's lock and turned.

With a click the door popped open. Jean stared at the small box inside, a box that could change everything. She began to reach for it when the sound of laughter halted her.

"I expected Braden, not you, Jean. However, it's just like my cousin to send someone to do the things he doesna have the courage to do himself."

A sizzle of fear crept over her skin as she turned to face Niall. "You think you know so much. But you don't."

"On the contrary, my lady, I know a great deal." He motioned with his hand and Mary stepped into view.

All the breath left Jean as she realized Mary was the traitor in Braden's camp. "Why?" she asked Mary.

Mary shrugged slim shoulders and smiled at Niall. "Because he asked it of me."

Jean couldn't believe everything was going to fall apart. "Mary, you do realize Niall doesn't care about you."

"He said he'll marry me," Mary murmured, her devoted eyes on Niall.

Niall laughed and jerked his head to the door. "I'll find you later, Mary. Right now, I've other things to tend to."

Jean seethed, but she held her tongue until she learned just what he had planned.

He ran a hand across the red mark that had scarred him from his eye to his cheek. A mark she had given him. "You've scarred me."

"I wish I'd done more."

"I think maybe I should give you a scar of your own."

Jean lifted her chin and raised her brow.

Niall chuckled. "I've known that one day Braden would try to take the castle from me. He will learn soon enough it isn't possible. This castle should have been mine. I've made sure of that now."

"Your time here is through."

Niall smiled, evil pouring off him. "Do you know what's in the box you've worked so diligently to acquire?"

Jean kept silent. She didn't know. Whatever it was, it was evidence that would seal Niall's fate.

"Ah, so Braden didna tell you. I like to keep trophies of my kills. I would have a trophy of Braden as well had he been caught that night as he was supposed to be. Unfortunately, for the past two years he's managed to evade every attempt I've made to end his life."

Jean's knees threatened to buckle as Niall's words sunk into her brain. "You're insane."

"I think it's time we find Braden. I know he's somewhere in the castle."

"He's not," Jean lied. "I was to get the box and deliver it to him."

Niall chuckled and shook his head. "Doona play me for a fool. Braden wouldna send you alone."

Jean was going to continue arguing but Niall lifted his sword pointed the blade at her heart.

"It's time I killed my cousin. And you, my lady, are going to help me do it."

Braden cursed as he paused to look out a window into the bailey. He spotted several of his men who had managed to hinder – or kill – guards and take their positions. Niall had so many men that the infiltration had been easy.

But where was Keith?

Braden had waited near the stairs leading to the great hall far longer than he had liked, yet Keith had never shown. There was only one thing that would have kept Keith from getting to Braden. Death.

He would have to find the commander and get the key himself.

Braden knew something was wrong when the servants around the castle began to leave. And no new guards came to check on the others.

And there was no sign of Keith or Niall.

Braden leaned his head against the stone wall and sighed. He had hoped he would come out of this attack alive. He thought of Jean, of the peace and contentment her mere presence gave him.

He wanted to spend the rest of his life with her in his arms. He wanted to grow old with her, to see her belly swell with their children, and watch those children grow.

But, somehow, he had always known he would never have such a future. Niall had made sure of that.

The thump of boot heels on the stones drew his attention. He pressed against the wall, his sword held in front of him. To his right was a corner where two corridors intersected. Those foot falls were coming right towards him.

Braden waited patiently. He knew it was Niall, knew the time had come for them to battle each other. No escape for either of them this time.

One would die.

And one would live.

The sounds came closer, reached the corner. Braden twisted his blade and swung it to his right, the edge of his sword at the throat of the intruder.

His eyes widened as he heard a small, feminine gasp. It was as if a dagger had plunged into his heart when he recognized Jean.

"What are you doing here?" he whispered.

Her face crumpled as a tear fell onto her cheek. "I'm sorry."

Braden frowned.

Someone shoved Jean from behind. She stumbled, but quickly righted herself as the tip of a sword was pressed into her back.

Niall came into view.

"I knew I was going to enjoy the last expression on your face," Nail said. "It's almost been worth all the trouble you've caused me these past years."

Rage burned and simmered through Braden. The mere fact Niall had hold of Jean made Braden want to run him through. "Trouble? You've not seen what I have in store for you."

There were shouts from outside the castle and the sound of something rumbling. Braden smiled. The clans had gathered.

Niall's nostrils flared as he glared at Braden. He grabbed Jean's arm and shoved her into a nearby chamber so he could look out the window.

Braden followed them and watched Niall's building fury. "You didna really think you could get away with your murders forever, did you? Whether you kill me or not, there are others that know of the box of your trophies."

"So I'll destroy it," Niall said as he whirled around, spittle flying from his lips.

Braden didn't like how close Niall was to Jean. "There will be enough testimonies by the lairds to convince the king of your trespasses even without the box. Your reign ends today."

"I doona believe so, cousin," Nail said through clenched teeth.

"I see the way you watch Jean, the way you try so hard not to alert me to her presence. You care for her. You've allowed her to meddle in our affairs. And for that, you get to watch me kill her."

Red flooded Braden's vision. He knew he needed to end all this. He bellowed and raised his sword over his head. Niall had no choice but to release Jean or be impaled.

Niall jumped out of the way, shoving Jean into the wall as he did. Out of the corner of his eye, Braden noticed that Jean was completely still after she hit the floor.

He wanted to go to her, to see if she was all right. But first he had to kill Niall.

Braden rotated his wrist, sending his sword slicing around him. "I've been waiting a long time for this moment."

Niall swung his sword at Braden's head. Braden blocked the attack and spun, aiming his blade at Niall's throat. Niall leaned backwards, but not quick enough.

Braden smiled when he saw the blood bead on his cousin's throat. "I'll take you piece by piece if I must."

Niall touched his neck and looked at the blood on his fingers. "I hope you enjoyed that, cousin, because that's all you're going to get from me."

There were no more words and they clashed once more. Again and again Niall attacked, and each time Braden effortlessly blocked him. Niall's anger was making him careless, sloppy.

With his left hand, Braden grabbed at the hand in which Niall held his sword. He elbowed Niall twice in the face before he swung back his fist and connected with his jaw. Blood gushed from Niall's broken nose. His scream of fury was music to Braden's ears.

Jean split open her eyes. Pain thudded through her head. She lifted a hand to her brow and came away with something thick and sticky on her fingers.

Blood.

She heard a horrible, angry scream and turned her head in time to see Braden's triumphant smile. With blood pouring down Niall's face, she found herself smiling as well.

Jean watched in fascination as Braden's sword moved with such speed and grace. Niall was no match for Braden's skill.

The sound of swords clanging ended in a rush. Braden knocked Niall's steel out of his hands. There wasn't a moment's hesitation as Braden plunged his blade into Niall's abdomen.

Niall clawed at Braden's arms and his knees buckled and he crumpled to the floor.

Braden withdrew his sword. "It's over. Finally." Niall had breathed his last.

"Aye," Jean whispered.

Braden's head whipped around. He was at her side in the next instant, his hands gentle as they cupped her face. "Are you hurt?"

"Just my head. I'll be fine."

"I've never been so scared in my life as I was when I saw he had you yet again."

Jean smiled up at the man who had captured her heart. "I'm sorry."

Braden pulled her into his arms. She closed her eyes and listened to the steady beat of his heart. This is where she always wanted to be. In Braden's arms.

Braden helped her to her feet, and they made their way to the battlements. As soon as Braden's men saw him they let up a cheer that was echoed by the clans who surrounded the castle.

"It worked," Braden mumbled as he looked out over the sea of warriors.

Jean smiled and threaded her fingers with his. "Of course it did."

"There's just one thing missing now that I have my home returned." He turned his head until his bright blue eyes met hers. "You."

Jean's heart thumped wildly in her chest. "What is it that you want, Braden MacAlister?"

"You. With me always. I'm asking you to be my wife."

She smiled through the tears that flooded her eyes. "I want nothing more."

His mouth descended on hers for a kiss filled with passion and promise, of longing . . . and love.

"God's blood," he whispered into her neck as he held her tightly. "I love you, Jean MacKay."

"And I love you."

"Good," said a deep, booming voice behind Braden. A voice Jean recognized all too well.

Braden stepped away from her and faced her father. "Laird MacKay."

"Laird MacAlister," her father replied.

"Thank you for coming," Braden said.

"I gave my word."

Braden looked at Jean and smiled. "I would ask one more thing, Laird MacKay."

"What might that be?"

"I would like to wed Jean."

Her father's hazel gaze turned to her. "And you Jean? What do you want?"

"I want to marry Braden."

Her father's lips pressed together as he stared at them a moment before he heaved a great sigh. "Than I suppose we ought to plan a wedding."

Deafening cheers erupted around them. But Jean heard nothing. She was lost in Braden's eyes and the pleasure of his kiss.

The Laird's French Bride

Connie Brockway

The castle buzzed with activity. Floors were mopped, privies limed, larders stocked, bedding laundered. Carpets were beaten, faces washed and new tapers set in place of the old, even if the old were not yet burnt out. All of this was being done because Rob Macalduie, the young Laird of Barras's would-be bride was on her way to inspect his holdings, buildings and his people to see they were worthy of her. In addition, she was coming to look over the young the laird himself with much the same purpose in mind. If she liked what she saw, they would be wed three days hence. If not, she would leave.

For as well as being a very rich girl raised in the French courts and fostered by the powerful Duke of Gordon, Jeanne Forbes and was one of the king's favourites. As such, even though a marriage between her and Rob would unify their two Highland clans – clans that had been fighting for generations – the duke had given her the unprecedented prerogative to deny Rob's suit if she didn't find favour with him. It was not a pronouncement that anyone in either clan – their wealth and manpower depleted by years of contention – liked.

What if this Jeanne with her *frenchified* notions took a dislike to a tapestry in the Great Hall? Or what if they served her mutton and she preferred beef? What if she favoured slender men dressed in black velvet and lace? Well, she'd certainly not find his likes in the tall, broad-shouldered and heavy muscled figure of Rob Macalduie who'd spent most of his twenty-two years swinging a claymore.

How *could* the king have agreed to leave the fates of his brave liegemen to the whim of a seventeen-year-old girl?

But he had and there was nothing for it but to hope that Jeanne Forbes understood her duty. At least, everyone agreed, Rob understood what was at stake. Which is why he'd been driving his servants and kinsmen this past fortnight, exhorting them to scrape lower, bend a deeper knee, and above all to be careful of what they said and in what tone they said it.

None of which sat well with his cousin, Alex Graham, who thought it all well below the dignity of a laird of Barras to humble himself for a girl. But then Alex also thought he would have made the better laird than young Rob and – in spite of the old man naming Rob his chosen heir with his dying breath – should have been named such with the old laird's passing four years ago. It was a claim that Rob had never bothered nor needed to refute. He'd let his record on the battlefield and the prosperity his people enjoyed speak for his ability to lead. Now, he wanted to guide them on to a new path – one of peace. Truth be told, at twenty-two Rob Macalduie of Barras was sick unto death of death.

Indeed, Rob was so sick of killing and raiding, ambushes and slaughter, and so set on the notion of peace, that he'd taken pen to paper to court Jeanne Forbes from afar. He'd begun his suit nearly a year ago when the subject of an arranged marriage between them had first been broached by the king himself. His first letter still had the power to embarrass him in recollection.

Young girls, his aunts had counselled him, love pretty words, particularly words they could wrap in ribbons and tuck beneath their pillows at night. If securing her hand entailed having to spout sweet-sounding inanities then, by all that was holy, inanities he'd spout. He would have done far more to secure welfare for his clan.

He'd been surprised when in her returning letter she'd bade him dispense with such fudge and went on to advise him not to bother writing again in an ill-fated attempt to convince her that he was the sort of man he imagined she must want. Thenceforth he'd dispensed with the inanities and written her, if not eloquently, honestly.

In return for his efforts, he found himself discovering his bride's nature. Her letters revealed Jeanne Forbes to be practical and willful, comically pleased with her own cunning – though Rob suspected she wasn't nearly so sly as she imagined herself to be – generous, quick-witted and engaging.

The only thing he didn't know about his bride was what she looked like.

At the start of their correspondence she had made the stipulation that they should not tell each other anything of their physical appearance, as appearances can change in a heartbeat – a point she graphically illustrated in a tale about an uncle who rode down to a pub one night a bonny, braw man and returned two days later sans nose, one eye and an ear, lost in a brawl in the tavern's yard. She thought they should instead focus on that which mattered more – their characters, their values, their temperaments.

Which was all very fine and high-minded, but when everything was said and done, though mature far beyond his years, at his core Rob was still a young man and could not help but want what every young man wants, which was a bonny armful in his bed. But, he couldn't insist. She had him, in all ways, at *point nonplus*. He needed to win her, not the other way round.

Which is why he stood now surrounded by his closest kin in the small gatehouse annexed to his small castle's outer curtain wall, awaiting the arrival of his would-be bride, about whose looks the only thing he knew was that she had red hair like all the Forbes. His men would have laughed themselves sick if they'd known how apprehensive he was. He'd stood unarmed and afoot and, without a tremor, faced down the mounted charge of his enemy; he'd dived into an ice-choked loch with nary a second thought to drag an unconscious kinsman from its frigid clasp; he'd felt a broadsword plunge into his shoulder but fought on without check until the battle was over. Yet at the thought of meeting this lass, this Jeanne Forbes, his belly clenched and his heart stuttered in his throat.

What if despite her lofty-minded intentions, despite the communion they'd found in their letters, despite what he wanted, what their people *needed*, she would not accept him as her husband?

He had never doubted himself before. He had never been allowed that luxury. A laird must be purposeful and certain, show no doubt or indecisiveness. And he hadn't. But that was as laird. As suitor . . . what did he know of his strengths – if he had any – or weaknesses? Even if she was a squat, sour dumpling with a pockmarked face or a bony, unsmiling crone, Jeanne Forbes was a prize and a plum one at that.

He, on the other hand, was but a minor lord. Not pretty. Uneducated. Without court manners. She bent to his suit and he knew it well. Barras was a lesser estate, his clan negligible in the Highland hierarchy. His castle might be well-made and snug in winter, cool in summer, but there was no gainsaying it was small. He had no money for velvet gowns and jewels, no troubadour to

sing her to sleep at night, no imported spices to tempt her palate –
nor even a cook who'd know how to use them – all things her letters
had revealed she was accustomed to. She improved his prospects;
he did not improve hers.

What if she took one look at Barras castle and decided to
return to the French court where she'd been raised? And the
worst of it was that not all he feared had a political foundation.
Whatever the girl looked like, whether or not she was a beauty,
her words had found their way into his imagination, his mind . . .
his heart.

For the third time in as many minutes he glanced out the small,
narrow window at the road leading to the castle gates. Though still
some miles off, her party could be seen making its slow, stately
approach. A dozen men-at-arms and half again as many courtiers
pranced about a pair of large, richly painted wagons. Outriders in
hunting garb rode the fields on either side of the road, their falcons
sweeping the sky above, their coloured jesses streaming like banners
against the blue summer sky.

"She'll be pox-faced, have no doubt of it," Colin Frasier, his
uncle, warned him for tenth time. "Why else would she be so old
and not yet wed?"

"At seventeen, she's hardly a hag."

"She'll be pretty enough," allowed his foster brother, Francis
Macalvoy. "But as cold as the Shetlands in January. French women
are all cold."

"Ach. I say tumble her on her arse and spread her legs wide."
Alex, arms crossed over his chest, sneered. "She'll say 'aye' soon
enough she's with child."

"I might warn you, anyone raping the lady is far more like to find
themselves beheaded then bedded."

At the sound of the female voice the men swung toward the
doorway. A slender young woman stood silhouetted in the doorframe. The afternoon sun set a nimbus glowing around rich,
red-gold coloured curls that fell in long ringlets over her shoulders
and flirted with creamy bosom displayed above her gown's low
décolletage. Her eyes were dark and tip-tilted at the outer corners,
lending her a faintly exotic air. Her brows were equally dark and
elegantly arched. A lovely, breathtaking lass.

She wore a mantua of rich blue linen, the front skirt pulled back
and fastened into a train that revealed the front of the embroidered
petticoat beneath. The bodice was simple, the décolletage low and

square cut, but the exposed corset beneath was studded with pearls and tooled in silver threads, laced tightly up the front and ending in a pronounced V at the waist. Around her shoulders hung a soft, primrose-coloured cloak. A fashion not seen in the Highlands, the effect was lush and rich and provocative.

But it was not her dress that struck silence into the four men, nor her amused tone, nor even the sight of her rampant red-gold tresses or dark, flashing eyes. It was the white bitch standing silently at her side, the girl's hand resting lightly atop its wide, anvil shaped skull.

She wasn't a particularly large dog, but from her thick neck and powerful shoulders to the heavy, rounded haunches and deep chest everything about her bespoke immense power. Dark, intelligent eyes stared unblinkingly at them from above a jaw bulging with massive muscles. A dark teardrop-shaped mark rode beneath one eye.

Rob had seen this sort of dog before. Called an Alaunt, it was used on the battlefield, terrifying the enemy with its tenacity and ferocity. Of late, however, he'd seen it being used in baiting, a "sport" for which Rob, as one who'd been on both sides of similarly savage and unfair matches, had no love.

Why this slip of a girl was companioned by so fierce a creature interested him. And who the bloody hell was she – aside from the obvious answer that she was kin of Jeanne's, a fact attested to by the red hair. But as such, why would Jeanne Forbes send her lady's maid unescorted to his castle?

"I have heard the Scots were a reticent lot, but hadn't realized they were mutes," the girl declared as their surprised silence dragged on. "Of course, being overheard plotting the rape of one of the king's favourites might rob the hubris from even the most arrogant Highlander."

Her gaze was flickering between the faces of the men silently regarding her, finally coming to rest on Francis Macalvoy's lavishly clad figure.

Ah, Rob thought, *she has been sent beforehand to report back to her mistress her impressions of Jeanne's future husband and has decided that Francis must be the laird.*

Certainly he looked the part more than Rob. Francis liked well the nicer things of life and dressed in finery and frippery whenever the opportunity arose. 'Twas a crime that even though he wore his dun-coloured hair cut to his shoulders and scented, his face would never win a lady's heart. Beneath a thick beetling brow, a battleaxe had skewed an already over-sized lantern jaw permanently out of alignment and the pox had added their deep marks to his gentle, homely visage.

But whatever beauty he'd never claim about his face, Francis seemed determined to make his own in his dress. To greet Jeanne Forbes, he'd donned a grey doublet, slashed and pinked as were his trunk hose. His trews were a deep burgundy and the cloak suspended from his shoulder was deep green velvet lined in gold.

In contrast, Rob doubtless looked his subordinate. He wore but a simple *leine* and leather waistcoat under a short coat of dark green wool and, of course, his plaid, belted at the waist. Except for his stockings and shoes, his legs were bare. He'd caught his hair back from his face and bound it, not bothering to let it flow to his shoulders like Francis in the style his foster brother assured him was most admired at court. Well, they weren't at court, and best this girl reported back to her mistress that the laird of Barras was no popinjay.

"Some of us speak, lady," Alex said, a curl on his lip. "Though we prefer action to words. Perhaps you'd care for a demonstration?" He leered at her as he stepped forward and Rob was about to intervene when a great, deep rumble issued from the chest of the white dog. Alex stopped, uneasily regarding the tensed bitch who'd stood up now, her hackles raised.

"Who are you, lass? What are you doing here, unescorted and unprotected?" his uncle, Colin Frasier asked.

The girl touched the dog's head and at once the bitch dropped to a sit. She smiled, steel as well as humour in her gaze. "I'm hardly unprotected, as you see. And as to who I am, I'm Joan, maid of milady's chamber. And as to why I'm here, I come bringing the Laird of Barras a gift from the Lady Forbes."

Once more her gaze flickered towards Francis who, Rob was amused to suspect, seemed to have been struck mute by the sight of a real French lady. At least French-raised. That hair was born in the Highlands and no doubt of it.

"And what would that be, Joan?" Rob asked, coming forward from where he'd stood in the back.

The girl's gaze swept over him, widening a bit in an expression Rob could not read before a faint blush spread over her cheeks, confounding and beguiling him all at once, for he had said nothing to give rise to that sweet blush and yet once he'd seen it, it lodged in his heart, enchanting him. Caught offguard, he shook off the sudden, intense attraction. 'Twould never do to go lusting after his bride's companion. He was not that sort of man and he had no intentions of becoming one.

"Well?"

In answer, the girl reached beneath her cloak and withdrew from some inner pocket a small, wriggling white creature, a pup but a few weeks old, Rob guessed.

"He's an Alaunt," the girl said proudly, petting the broad head of the beast beside her. "Paula here's only whelp. Both Paula and the sire's ancestors came from the Holy Lands, brought back with the crusaders from my . . . my lady's family. I," the girl's eyes fell, suddenly shy, "I trained her."

"Paula?" Alex burst out, laughing. "Ye named the bitch Paula?"

"Aye," she said. "For the saint."

"What sort of name is that for a baiting dog?" Alex jeered.

Joan swung towards him, her eyes flashing. "She's no baiting dog and never will be. She's a companion and a guardian should there be cause. But she'll not *ever* spill her blood for the obscene pleasure of a bunch of drunken *boys*." Her eyes flashed with contempt and disgust.

At this, Alex surged forward in fury, only to meet the immovable bulk of Rob's massive arm. "Stay, Alex," he murmured through clenched teeth.

His cousin needed no further instruction. Alex was a loyal man, if not a temperate one. He spun away from Rob, stalking to the door and shoving the girl aside as he passed, spitting down at her, "I'd keep the bitch close if I were you," and Rob, already angry at Alex's treatment of Jeanne Forbe's liege woman, felt a black rage seize him.

Before he realized his own intent, he'd snatched Alex back and spun him around, gripping him around the neck and slamming him to his knees.

"By God, Alex, you go too far," he rumbled. "If you—"

"Stay!"

Rob felt another's hand on his shoulder.

"Leave off!"

Again he heard Francis's urgent voice and looked up to meet his foster brother's worried gaze over Alex's head.

"Let him go or Joan will be forced to report to her mistress that having no foreigners to fight we fall upon each other like the very pit dogs she decries," Francis said in a low voice. "Leave off, I say."

Thank god for Francis's reasoned calm, a calm for which Rob himself was usually known. But some instinct had snapped to life at Alex's threat and he knew that he would never allow any man to lay rough hands on the gallant girl. With a bare nod of acquiescence, he released his hold on Alex's throat, leaving his cousin sputtering and groping his way out the door with the aid of his amazed father.

He looked up at Joan. Her hand was clenched at her bosom, her eyes wide and frightened. Her gown's sleeve had pulled up revealing a crescent-shaped red welt on her forearm. Rob froze.

He knew the story of that scar: a brazier filled with roasting nuts, a greedy toddler and inattentive nurse. He knew because in one of her first letters to him Jeanne Forbes had written him about her "battle scars".

Jeanne, not Joan.

But then, Joan was simply the Scottish version of Jeanne. She had come, Rob realized, to learn about him covertly. If she had arrived as herself, his behaviour would be at its best and his kin and servants would keep their tongues well guarded. But if she arrived as a simple companion, she would be more likely to learn what his servants and kinsmen thought of him.

It was, he acknowledged, a practical ploy. And a cunning game.

One that two people could play . . .

The dark-haired young giant moved with lethal quickness for one so large and broad-shouldered. One moment the sneering, fair-haired Scot was growling his threat and the next he was on his knees clawing uselessly at the vise-like grip around his throat. And then the man Jeanne took to be her intended husband – for who else but he would be wearing such princely garb? – proved further proof of this supposition by staying the giant's hand and sending the other two men from the room.

He was a judicious man then, neither passionate like the young giant nor violent like the other. A worthy man, then. A man who understood prudence and politics. She should be happy. Delighted. For political reasons had brought her here to this small castle to accept its laird as her husband.

She shouldn't be surprised by his actions. In his letters, Rob Macalduie's commitment to a lasting peace amongst the feuding Highlanders had been framed in careful, weighted words. His thoughtful and circumspect letters had demonstrated the statecraft that would be necessary to ensure it. Aye, he was a statesmen in the making, was Rob Macalduie.

And it was for just that reason she had ventured on this impersonation. For Rob Macalduie's words had been *too* carefully select, too self-conscious, had sometimes made her feel that she'd revealed too much of herself in her own effusive ramblings while discovering too little about him. She wanted to know, to *really* know, what sort of man she'd agreed to wed. It was a small enough thing to insist upon.

She studied her fiancé now as he stood in deep and tense conversation with the young Scot whose broad back all but obliterated her view of the laird. She'd been told that Rob Macalduie had been in more battles than she had years and it stood to reason that he'd carry physical reminders of them. She knew that physical beauty was a vanity and an illusion but . . . she had hoped that he'd be not unpleasant to look at.

But alas, he was. His brow overhung deep-set eyes like a rock shelf over small pebbles, and his heavy brow stretched across that great land bridge like a brown weasel. His huge jaw hung at an oblique angle, caved in at one side. But he did have kind eyes – worried eyes, but kind – and his hair was pretty, thick as a lass's, long and scented. And he was well-shaped. Though not so well-shaped as the large young warrior who had turned towards her.

Now, *he* was handsome. His eyes were a clear green, fringed by thick short black lashes, his brow high and clear, his nose was bold and straight. His jaw was clean-shaven, his shoulders and the breadth of his chest beneath the leather waistcoat strong and hard, and the size of his hands and the length of his muscular legs and –

Oh my. She pulled her gaze away, feeling her face growing hot. His wide, well-shaped mouth quirked in a smile. The brigand! The great lout! He obviously thought she'd blushed because of him. Well, aye. She had. But he was no gentleman to make note of it.

And 'twould not do, besides! He would be her kinsman in but a few days.

"Lady," the laird was saying and, even though it was hard to pay him the heed he merited when the younger man was watching her so intently, she forced herself to do so.

"Aye, sir?"

"When will your lady be arriving?"

Lady? Oh. Oh! He meant *her*! She must stop paying heed to the grinning Highlander.

"If I may make a request, sir. She bids your indulgence in letting me be her eyes and ears here for a single day."

"Why so?" asked the giant.

She essayed a prim smile. "So that when I return to her tomorrow I might teach her better how best to please."

"Ach!" At this the young giant broke into laughter, winning a sharp look from his laird. "Those are pretty words, lassie. Skilful. Are they yours . . . or hers?" His smile was vulpine.

Damn the man. He would make his laird doubt her. "Sir?" she managed to say with a guileless smile.

"Faith, yer a beauty," he murmured, his gaze roving over her person so openly she felt another blush rise. Why didn't the laird *do* something? But then, why should he? If his man indulged in a flirtation with his intended's companion, what matter was it to him?

Well, it would presumably be a great matter when she revealed who she was. She should do so now, before this got out of hand and the black-haired giant found himself exiled when the laird recalled his brazenness towards her. But . . . she hadn't learned anything of the laird yet and very soon it would be too late. She would be married to him. This would be her most promising opportunity to see him as his people saw him. Perhaps her only opportunity.

She would be careful. Starting now. She turned away from the dark-haired Highlander towards the laird, ignoring the giant.

But he refused to be ignored.

"But, won't your lady be uncomfortable, sleeping in a wagon on a narrow cot with a lumpy mattress?" he murmured from close behind her. "Why subject her to that when here her bed would be strong. And broad. And firm."

He wasn't talking about beds. Fire flashed up her throat and into her face as she heard the laird make some sort of constrictive sound in his throat. She could feel the giant coming closer, caught a faint scent of pine and heather and a rich sort of earthiness. She glanced down at Paula. The white bitch was looking at the man, wagging her tail, her tongue lolling happily. The tart!

She looked up, meeting the laird's sympathetic gaze, silently praying he would agree to her request and take her away from this man's proximity.

"Sir?" she asked.

"Faith, lady, do what you must," the laird said, unhappily it seemed to her. "Since your mistress is not to arrive today, there're other matters to which I must attend."

"Of course," she said. "I would not be in the way. If you could send one of the women to—"

"There's no need to take some poor woman from her duties, or her leisure, when I am already here and more than willing to act as your guide . . ." the young warrior said. "Joan."

No. No! "But," she sputtered, "don't you have things to do, too?" She cast a desperate look at the laird. "Doesn't he have things to do?"

"Like what?" asked the giant.

"Like . . . hacking things? Sharpening your claymore?"

"Though kindly meant I am certain, you may lay aside your concern regarding both my prowess and my sword. I promise you that my prowess is at its zenith and my claymore is . . . well-shaped."

"Oh!" She gasped.

"He's right, lady," the laird said. "You'll not find a better guide nor a more knowledgeable one and so I will leave you in his care."

"But, what of Paula? And what of her pup?"

"They'd best stay with you until . . . They'd best stay with you for now." And with that, the laird sketched a quick bow and left.

Slowly, Jeanne turned around to regard her guide. He was standing with his fists on his hips, his bare legs braced wide beneath his belted kilt. She'd never seen so large, so intimidating, so virile a young man.

"Well, Joan," he said, his teeth flashing white and strong in his dark, handsome face, "what would you like to see first?"

She blushed, her cheeks turning as bright as autumn apples and ducked her head. Rob was utterly captivated. Her letters had revealed her intelligence and character, but not her youth or femininity. Hers was a girl's blush, shy and unknowingly seductive and Rob felt his body react to its sweet temptation.

To disguise his discomfort, he hunkered down on his heels and held out his hand to Paula, palm down, fingers curled under. At once, the white bitch came forwards, tail-wagging, ears notched back in pleasure at the invitation. She sniffed his hand and he scratched her silky neck. Needing no further encouragement, she bowled into him, knocking him flat on his arse, and proceeded to bathe his face with her great pink tongue. He laughed and this only encouraged her further, for she squirmed in delight, planting her great boulder head in his lap and rolling over so that her four paws waved in the air.

"Ye great hussy!"

Rob looked up to find Jeanne smiling down at them. He grinned back. "I like a lass who's a bit of a tart."

"*Bit* of a tart?" She laughed and the sound was lovely, infectious, but then recalling herself, her smile faded and the blush deepened. She raised her chin to a haughty angle – because even though for all she knew "Joan" could be his equal or even his subordinate, Jeanne Forbes was definitely his superior – and demanded, "What is your name?"

It must have dawned on her then that she had not been introduced to anyone for her brows knit together. "What is anyone's name? Who *were* those men?"

He rose, dumping poor Paula at his feet and sketched a bow. "Forgive our poor manners. 'Tisn't everyday Barras is treated to the company of someone so elegant and exotic as yer fair self."

She eyed him closely but since his words were no less than the truth, she could find no deceit nor mockery in his face or tone and so blushed again, making him smile even broader.

"My name is Rob, my lady," he said then, catching the slight widening of her eyes, added, "Aye. 'Tis a name as common as bracken in the Highlands, I'm afraid. As to who the others might be," he continued, not giving her time to ask his surname, "the older man is Colin Frasier, the laird's uncle and the graceless cur he hauled out of here is his son, Alex." He left off naming Francis, but then she assumed she already knew his identity.

"Now, where would you like to go?" he said, offering her his arm. After a second, she took it. "What would you like to know?"

He smiled down into her tip-tilted eyes. Her lashes were so long they brushed the delicate flesh beneath her arched brows. This close he saw her eyes were the colour of wild honey, a rich glowing amber. Eyes a man could get lost in. "What would you like to see? How can my laird win your . . . mistress's heart? What would impress her most? What least? Let's connive between the two of us, Joan, to see this union come to pass. And then," he covered her delicate hand with his and felt the fingers flutter like a captive bird beneath, "we'll have time to devote to getting to know one another."

"Oh!" A gasp escaped her lips and she turned her head away. "No! No. Never."

"Never?" he asked, cocking his head, pleased. Despite their mutual attraction, she understood honour and duty, the meaning of sacred vows and political necessity. Once sworn to Rob

Macalduie she would be his and no other's – no matter how much she might want to. And she did.

He could tell from the agitation that lifted the delicate lace kerchief covering the soft swells of her bosom, by the colour staining her throat and the warmth of the hand beneath his, the glow in her eyes, the catch of her breath . . .

"Well, there's a sadness then," he said, trying not to sound too cheerful about it. He gave a gusty sigh. "But if that's the way it is, far be it from me to try and foist my attentions on an unwilling maiden. So then, where is it you wanted to go?"

Her head swung up, her gaze sharp with disappointment and, aye, exasperation. He almost laughed. He'd apparently given up too easily and her pride did not like it much.

"The stables," she said frostily.

He was surprised. He would have thought she would want to inspect the Great Hall, the solars or the stores, the buttery or the chapel, places where the wealth of a lord could be gauged. But he nodded and led her with the white pup in her hand from the gatehouse annexe across the bailey, Paula trotting behind. No one looked surprised by their passage or took particular note of him, though Jeanne in her finery and the great, muscled dog at her side drew many an interested glance.

His people were used to seeing him hither and yon about the castle. He'd been born and raised within these walls and, while treating him with deference, everyone accepted that theirs was a laird who must know everything about those things and people for whom he was responsible. There was no room he had not been in, no roof he had not climbed over, no floor he hadn't trod, no person with whom he hadn't shared a word and a drink.

They entered the stables at the far end of the bailey, Paula hard on their heels. The light inside was soft and diffused, the horses in their stalls whickering softly at the sight of the strange dog.

"Who goes?" a young man's voice croaked from overhead. A second later a gangly lad of fifteen or sixteen years jumped down from the loft where he'd been napping or – a giggle from above caught Rob's wry attention – indulging in another more pleasurable pastime. One look at his laird and the boy dissolved into abashed silence for which Rob thankfully offered up a prayer.

"I'm showing the lady the stables, Davie. I won't need your help so you can go to the kitchen and have Maura fetch you a cold glass of buttermilk." He glanced up. "And one for yer friend, too. If she's a mind to come . . . *No.* Not word from you now. Yer secret's safe with me."

"Thank—"

"I said, *not a word,*" Rob repeated. "I meant it."

The wide-eyed lad bobbed his head and, with a backward glance at Jeanne, made a *tching* sound at which a pretty young face, round-cheeked and dusky-skinned, appeared above them. Without a second's hesitation the girl swung her legs over the edge and dropped lightly to the ground. Then with a giggle and blush, she grabbed hold of Davie's hand, hastily pulling him through the stable door, leaving him and Jeanne alone. At last.

"You know the stable lad's name."

"Aye."

"Does the laird?"

"Aye. Of course."

"No. Not 'of course'. I've been in many a castle where the lord wouldn't know the name of his cook, let alone the stable boy."

"Well," said Rob comfortably, "this isn't such a grand castle as those."

"Oh, I don't know," she murmured, releasing his arm and walking down the aisle separating the stalls. The ground underneath was even and freshly spread with sweet hay. The scent of warm horse, grain and dust filled the air. His gaze followed her, the gentle sway of her hips, the straight spine and shiny red-gold hair.

She stopped outside his stallion's stall and looked back over her shoulder at him. "An Arabian steed?" she asked.

"Half," he answered. "The other half is Highland mare. In other words, no particular lineage."

"Hm," she said, reaching in and rubbing her hand down the great steed's velvety face. Rob was unconcerned. He didn't tolerate vicious animals in his stables.

"Why did you ask to see the stables first?" he asked curiously.

She gave a little shrug. "A lord would make sure his chapel's cross was shined and his larder well-stocked to impress a woman he hoped to marry. The solars would be fitted anew with linens and draperies, the halls swept, tapestries borrowed, beaten and hung. It's an easy enough thing to make a place look wealthy and well-tended. It's not so easy to make a hungry horse look fat. And a mucked-out stall tells more about a lord's husbandry than a clean dining hall."

Young and girlish and innocent she might be, but Jeanne Forbes was also smart and canny. They'd make an imposing team. He nodded.

"And do the stables tell you anything else about the laird of Barras?"

"Aye," she said. "The temperament of his horse tells me he would rather persuade than conquer. Am I right?"

He hesitated, uncertain if her words were meant as a compliment or a criticism. Many men – and women – considered intimidation the only way to see things done. "Force doesn't make a thing love you, only fear you, and it's the nature of things to try to destroy those they fear. You can only hold a thing to you through trust."

She regarded him silently. Her expression was impossible to read. "Are those your sentiments, Rob? Or the laird's?"

"We share like views," he said.

"Hm." The pup she carried had begun mewling, causing Paula to dance lightly before her mistress. With a chuckle, Jeanne pushed opened the door to an empty stall and carefully laid the pup on a bed of straw in the corner. At once, Paula flopped down and the pup began nursing.

Jeanne rose, dusting the hay from her skirts, and came back to him. The light filtering in from the open doors glazed her hair with a fiery sheen and the air in stables dusted her skin with a fine golden talc. He wanted very much to take her in his arms and lick the fine powder from her brow, her cheeks, and her lips . . . She tipped her head back, eyeing him seriously and he realized she didn't have the slightest notion of the effect she had on him, or where his errant thoughts were taking him. Them.

"What sort of man is the laird, Rob?"

He started, unprepared for the question. He'd expected her to ask him about Barras's power, land, loyalties, even his faults but not something so all encompassing, so intimate.

"I am uncertain as to your meaning, lady," he said slowly.

"Is he a good man?"

"Well, now, paining me though it does to say, he's not much for church-going."

"No, no," she said impatiently, shaking her head. "Let me ask this . . . what does he value?"

That was easier. "Honesty. Hard work. Peace."

His answer didn't appear to satisfy her. "But what of the *man*?" she insisted. Then an inspiration seemed to come to her. "What will he do with the pup?"

"He'll value him as a gift from his lady."

"He'll not have him fight? Or will he?" She was standing very close now, her expression worried. He could see the ruby sheen in the shadows of her red-gold hair, a sprinkling of gingery freckles across the bridge of her nose.

"No. That I can promise. He's no love of violence for its own sake." She smelled like sun and soap and she was regarding him so earnestly, so seriously and he wanted . . . He wanted . . .

He reached across the space separating them and tipped her chin up. Her lips parted in surprise and before she could react he'd bent down and brushed a kiss over her mouth. He heard her breath catch and he shifted closer, this time letting his lips cling. Her own were soft and plush and warm and sweet. So sweet. She swayed and he caught her wrists together, bracing her hands against his chest as his kiss deepened, his tongue sliding between her lips to taste—

She shoved against him, hard, and he stumbled back, amused and aroused and pleased, because he wanted her and she wanted him. He had never imagined, never had the hubris to hope, that their union could be more than an expedience for both of them. But now . . . he nearly laughed with the joy of it, the wonder and fortune of it. She would be his mistress as well as wife, and he would be her lover in addition to husband. Although she didn't know this yet. Indeed, at the moment she looked decidedly put out.

"Why did you do that?" she shouted.

"Well, Joan," he said in his most reasonable tone, "yer a lass and I'm a man and the stables are as private a place as a solar, and you looked willing and lord knows I am, so . . . why not?"

Half of him hoped she would choose now to dispense with her masquerade so they might go forth in honesty. But the other half of him, that half that was still a boy, reacted to the girlishness of her blushes and stutters. *That* half liked not being cautious, politic, and wise beyond his years, and liked that for these moments she wasn't Jeanne Forbes, who held the future of his portion of the Highlands in her hands, but "Joan", a pretty, hot-headed, passionate girl.

Apparently, "Joan" didn't appreciate his answer. She gasped. "How dare you? I am not some tart to be tumbled in a *stall*!"

He gave her a lop-sided grin. "How about in a loft?"

Her eyes grew round and he decided to take her momentary silence as consent. Besides, he was in a lather to taste her again, to feel her hands on him. He scooped her up while she was still floundering for a reply. She was light and finely made but well curved and womanly.

He'd one foot on the ladder leading up before she managed to sputter, "Put me down, you great ox! I'm not some doxy! I'm . . . I'm . . ."

He didn't put her down, but neither did he start up the ladder, instead he waited, interested to see what she'd say, how far she'd take her masquerade.

"I'm . . . I'm *betrothed*!" she blurted out.

"Aye?" he said, feigning surprise. He bounced her higher up in his arms and in response she flung her arms around his neck, clinging. He liked the feel of her arms around him and he bent his head down, nuzzling her neck. Her skin was velvety and smooth, like sun-warmed chamois. The pulse at the base of her throat trip-hammered beneath his lips.

Delicately, he nipped the tender skin and heard her draw in a startled breath. Her arms tightened. "Didn't you hear me?" she asked in a high and unnatural voice. "I'm to be wed!"

"No matter, lass. So am I."

And as quickly as he said the words, he found himself with a hellcat in his arms. With a strangled sound of fury, she pummelled at his chest, kicking her feet and flaying about so violently that he almost dropped her. Startled, at the last second she clutched hold of his leine, trying to keep herself from falling, but tearing his shirt open at the chest in the process. Taking advantage of her momentary stillness, he repositioned her in his arms, grinning wickedly down into her upturned face.

"Have a care, lass," he said. "I'm eager, too, but not so wealthy that I can afford to have one of my best shirts ripped."

He waited for her to start struggling again but instead she simply stared at him, her exotic eyes widening and then, before he understood what was happening, her arms wrapped tight around his neck and she was drawing herself fully against him, the soft roundness of her breasts crushed to his naked chest.

"Take me, then. Take me *now*!" she whispered huskily a second before her mouth found his.

"*What*?"

If she wasn't so furious at him, she would have laughed at the dumbstruck expression on Rob's face. *Rob Macalduie's face*. But she *was* furious, whether at him for leading her on or at herself for being so roused by his kisses that, for a moment there, before she'd tumbled to his true identity, she had actually decided to let him have a few more kisses. Because she'd never been kissed like that before, never had the tingling in her lips stretch in a taut wire of need to the very pit of her belly. And deeper.

Not that she would have ever sanctioned anything *more* and she would *never* have let him kiss her in the first place had she known what he'd been about, but once he had, oh, aye! It was amazing, stirring, and as potent as the brandy from the king's own cellar.

Even as she'd been anticipating another kiss, she'd been promising herself that she would not betray her husband once the marriage vows were spoken. She had also been telling herself that there was no betrayal in sharing a simple kiss with a would-be suitor before she'd even properly met her intended groom. It was a mere kiss. A simple thing to remember when she closed her eyes three nights hence on her wedding night and accept the laird's attentions. She wondered briefly who he was, the man she'd mistaken for her future husband.

"I said," she repeated patiently, "take me now."

"But . . ."

Clearly, this wasn't going the way Rob had anticipated. Somehow, she managed to keep from laughing and feigned a confused expression.

"Don't you want me? Have you changed your mind?" she asked sweetly, arching her back, just a little, so that her bosom swelled against his hot flesh.

"God, no!" he whispered hoarsely.

She almost took pity on him. After all, she'd begun this game and she supposed she deserved his goading. How far would he go, she wondered? He assumed she didn't know who he was yet. Was he using this encounter as a test of her virtue? She thought not, mostly because he'd no more control of the desire raking his body than she.

His great chest rose and fell in a heavy rhythm, his breathing harsh and ragged. A strand of hair curled against his damp throat and his eyes were dark with hunger.

"Then . . ." Her fingertips played in the crisp dark hair covering his chest and he shuddered, "are you going to take me up to the hayloft?"

Her gaze flashed to the ladder and his arms tightened about her.

"Lady, perhaps you are right," he said, sounding desperate, "perhaps we should consider the ramifications of our acts."

She pouted, plucking the glass token hanging on his chest and giving it a rough tug. It was the token that had given him away, a small glass vial containing a glint of red-gold, a strand of her own hair that she'd sent to him last year. He'd obviously forgotten he wore it.

Of course, she now realized he knew who she was, too, and had been playing with her, punishing her for her deception by pretending to seduce her. Only now it had become real. She knew this because she knew he would never try to seduce one of Jeanne Forbe's own companions on the virtual eve of his marriage. Not because she mistook him for a saint. No, the reason she knew he must realize her identity was because he had politicked and manoeuvred and argued for their marriage and he wouldn't risk that for a tumble in the hay even had she been the Medici witch, Helen of Troy and Cleopatra all rolled into one. If she knew nothing else about Rob Macalduie it was this: he wasn't stupid.

"If you've suddenly lost your . . . will, so be it," she said. "But in that case there's no need for us to stand about hoping it returns. I should like next to see the chap—"

"I have not *lost my will*!" he thundered. "I have *will* aplenty, lady, and am half a mind to—"

"What I want takes no mind at all," she cut in, reaching up and pushing the dark hair from his handsome face. "Simply . . . *will*."

He threw back his head, groaning. She smiled. He was too honourable to take her under these circumstances. The question was, was she?

She turned in his arms, letting imagination lead where experience failed her. She pressed her lips against the heavy plane of his chest and then, quite deliberately, touched the tip of her tongue to the salty skin and trailed a long, searing line to the base of his throat. He drew in a long, shaking breath in response and she laced her fingers around the back of his wide neck, pulling his face down to hers. Their mouth met in a heated kiss, open and hungering, locked into a fever of yearning, their tongues dancing together. The fervour of their actions caused her gown to pucker and pull, her breast escaping above the décolletage and rubbing erotically against him. Its touch galvanized him.

With a low sound of anger, he dipped down, setting her on her feet. She swayed, suddenly being ripped from his embrace, dizzy, suffused with unfulfilled longing. She put a hand up to steady herself and he backed away from her. His chest was working like a bellows; his gaze was predatory and keen, frantic and raw.

"Mother of Mercy, how to tell you who I am?" he breathed in a low voice not meant for her ears. "How do I right this?"

But she did hear and was pleased beyond measure by his words, his honour, his self-restraint. Rob Macalduie was a man she could love. May already be in love with, truth be told, and had been falling in love with at the arrival of each new letter, circumspect, reasoned, but flavoured with hints of wry humour and self-deprecation.

"I know who you are," she said breathlessly. "You are Rob."

"Aye, but—"

"Rob Macalduie, Laird of Barras, betrothed to Jeanne Forbes who you well know is . . . me."

For a moment he simply stared at him and for an instance, Jeanne feared she might have read into his character things that were not there, and hoped she was not wrong, but then his handsome face lit with a huge grin. "You knew!"

"Aye, but for a far shorter time than you did."

"Faith, lass, we'll make a fearsome pair, I warrant," he said, still smiling, handsome great devil of a Highlander that he was.

"I warrant," she agreed, suddenly shy beneath the hungry, roving, possessive glint in his eyes.

"So, now that we've been revealed to one another, what next?" he asked, still looking greatly amused, oddly proud and decidedly boyish.

She thought of all the things her uncle and the king had told her to explore, all the questions a prudent woman would ask a prospective groom, all the things she ought to insist she see, the people she must ask to interview. But then her gaze caught on a piece of hay drifting lazily down from above.

"I've always wanted a proper tour of a hayloft," she said.

And soon enough, she had one.

Author Biographies

Marta Acosta
Author of the award-winning Casa Dracula series, she is a *Romantic Times* award nominee. Her first young-adult gothic novel, *The Shadow Girl of Birch Grove*, will be published in 2012. She also writes romantic comedies as Grace Coopersmith (*Nancy's Theory of Style*).
www.martaacosta.com

Jackie Barbosa
Jackie knew she wanted to be a writer by the time she was seven years old. After detours into academia – she holds a Master's degree in Classics from the University of Chicago – and the software industry, she is at last achieving her lifelong dream of writing romantic fiction, and is published by Kensington Books and Harlequin.
www.jackiebarbosa.com

Annette Blair
Award-winning author who owes her paranormal roots to Salem, Massachusetts, where she stumbled into the serendipitous role of Accidental Witch Writer, her bewitching romantic comedies became her first national bestsellers (magick or destiny?). Her thirty-plus titles include her popular Works Like Magick novels and Vintage Magic Mysteries.
www.annetteblair.com

Sandy Blair
Winner of a National Readers Choice Award and RITA nominee, she continues to make the Barnes and Noble and Amazon national bestseller lists with her light-hearted Highlander novels.
www.sandyblair.net

Terri Brisbin

When not being an award-winning author of compelling, emotional and sexy historical romances set in medieval Scotland and England, Terri Brisbin is a married mom of three and dental hygienist to hundreds in southern New Jersey.
www.terribrisbin.com

Connie Brockway

New York Times and *USA Today* bestselling author and two-time winner of the RITA, with starred reviews from *Publishers Weekly* and *Library Journal*, when not writing historical romance and irreverent women's fiction, Brockway makes her home in the Minnesota tundra where she plans to stay until they plant her. *If* they can dig through the perma frost.
www.conniebrockway.com

Leah Marie Brown

Leah Marie Brown has worked as a newspaper reporter and television journalist. Her freelance articles have appeared in magazines including *Writer's Digest*, *Parenting*, and *Seventeen*. She has written six historical romance novels set in her beloved France and maintains an award-winning website dedicated to Marie Antoinette.
www.leahmariebrown.com

Jacquie D'Alessandro

Jacquie is the *New York Times* and *USA Today* bestselling author of more than thirty historical and contemporary romances. She grew up in New York where she dreamed of being swept away by a dashing rogue riding a spirited stallion. When her hero finally showed up, he was dressed in jeans and drove a Volkswagen, but she recognized him anyway. They married after both graduating from Hofstra University and are living their happily-ever-afters in Atlanta.
www.jacquied.com

Anne Gracie

Anne Gracie was born and raised mostly in Australia, but lived in Scotland as a child and is deeply, foolishly romantic about it – even knowing about the miserable weather and the midges! She's an award-winning, bestselling author published by Berkley books for whom she writes Regency historicals. She regularly blogs with the word wenches at *http://wordwenches.typepad.com/*.
www.annegracie.com

Donna Grant
Bestselling, award-winning author of dark, sexy, historical paranormals, she's written more than twenty-five novels and a wide variety of romance from Scottish medieval to dark fantasy to time travel, from paranormal to erotic. She lives in Texas with her husband, two children, a dog and three cats.
www.donnagrant.com

Patricia Grasso
Author of eighteen historical romance novels comprising the Devereux series, the Dukes and Douglas trilogies, the Russian Princes series, and her Flambeau sisters series. Her books have been translated into fifteen languages.
www.patriciagrasso.com

Lois Greiman
Born on a cattle ranch in central North Dakota, she learned to ride and spit with the best of them. Since selling her first novel in 1992, she has gone on to publish over thirty romantic comedies, historical romances, stories for children, as well as the fun-loving Random House-published mysteries under the pen name Christina McMullen. A two-time RITA finalist, she has won such prestigious honours as the *Romantic Times* Storyteller Of The Year and the LaVyrle Spencer Award. She currently lives on the Minnesota tundra with her family, some of whom are human.
www.loisgreiman.com

Jackie Ivie
Jackie Ivie lives with her family in Alaska, where she combines being a wife, mother, retired USPS manager and electronics apprentice with a massive love of writing lovable Alpha Male heroes in Scottish historical settings. She's the award-winning author of eight historical romances, all featuring strong heroines and a "knight" fated to be hers.
www.jackieivie.com

Elle Jasper
Elle Jasper is a full-time writer and lives amongst the moss and shadows of Savannah, Georgia.
www.ellejasper.com

Donna Kauffman
USA Today bestselling author of contemporary Scottish fiction, she is a former RITA finalist who has been featured in *Cosmopolitan*

magazine, and reviewed everywhere from *Kirkus*, to *Library Journal*, to *Entertainment Weekly*.
www.donnakauffman.com

Kimberly Killion

Award-winning author of sexy Scottish medievals, she was nominated for a RITA for *Her One Desire*, her debut novel. Her next book, *Highland Dragon*, won *Romantic Times* magazine's Historical KISS Award.
www.kimberlykillion.com

Julianne MacLean

Three-time RITA finalist and *USA Today* bestselling author of fifteen historical romances. The first book in her new Highlander trilogy, *Captured By The Highlander*, is released in 2011.
www.juliannemaclean.com

Debbie Mazzuca

Author of Scottish-set paranormal historicals, her debut *Lord of the Isles*, the first book in the MacLeods series, was published in 2010.
www.debbiemazzuca.com

Heather McCollum

A 2009 Golden Heart Finalist, her books *Prophecy* and *Magick*, the first two titles in her historical paranormal romance series The Dragonfly Chronicles, were published in 2010.
www.heathermccollum.com

Susan Sizemore

New York Times bestselling author of numerous works of romance, fantasy and science fiction. She resides in the American Midwest.
www.susansizemore.com